ANN VICTORIA ROBERTS

LIAM'S STORY

ARNWOOD
PRESS

Published by Arnwood Press 2014

First published in the United Kingdom in 1991
by Chatto & Windus Limited

Electronic edition published in 2012 by Arnwood Press
Print edition published in 2014 by Arnwood Press

Arnwood Press
98 Hamble Lane, Southampton SO31 4HU

A CIP catalogue record for this book is available from the British Library.

ISBN 978-0-9929584-1-1

Drawings are by the author and are © Ann Victoria Roberts.
The map is © Ned Hoste.
Typeset by Ned Hoste
Printed in by CPI Group (UK)

About the Author

Ann Victoria Roberts travelled widely with her Master Mariner husband when her children were young, and began her writing career while he was away at sea. Trained as an artist, she prefers painting pictures with words and regards good historical fiction as a pleasurable way to discover the past.

Her first two novels, *Louisa Elliott* and *Liam's Story* (published as *Morning's Gate* in the US) were inspired by a family diary written in 1916, and created headlines when they were sold for a record sum by a debut author. The books were translated into several languages, becoming bestsellers around the world. They are now available as ebooks.

Ann went on to write the chilling ghost story, *Dagger Lane* – set in countryside just north of York – in which a modern historian and his writer wife are haunted by events from the past. In *Moon Rising*, 1880s Whitby forms the backdrop to a gripping tale of passion and possession. Amidst storms and shipwrecks, legends and folk tales, the genesis of Bram Stoker's Dracula – and its aftermath – is gradually revealed. Currently out of print, these two novels are due to appear as ebooks in the near future.

Ann's experiences at sea – and a chance encounter – led to the writing of her fifth novel, *The Master's Tale* (2011) based on the life of Captain EJ Smith of the Titanic. In the novel, the Captain tells his story from beyond the grave, remembering lost loves and past achievements – and seeking his mistakes…

You can follow Ann on
Facebook: https://www.facebook.com/AnnVictoriaRoberts
Or Twitter: https://twitter.com/Ann_V_Roberts

For more information about Ann's books, interests and travels, go to her website: http://annvictoriaroberts.co.uk

Author's Note

Liam's Story was inspired by a diary written in 1916 by a young soldier serving with the Australian Imperial Force. In the novel, all that relates to WWI is based upon that diary and extensive research undertaken to verify it. The rest of the novel is fiction and, except with regard to public figures, the characters are not intended to resemble real people, either living or dead.

Like its predecessor, *Louisa Elliott*, I felt this edition needed a fresh look for a new readership. It is not markedly different from the original, and I hope old fans will forgive me for small changes undertaken for the sake of clarity.

A note for new readers: the 'modern' part of the tale is set in the mid-1980s, and so has become a period piece in itself. The origins of the war in the Persian Gulf have largely been forgotten, but I wrote this account in homage to seafarers both past and present, the unsung heroes who do a difficult and dangerous job on a daily basis.

I remain indebted to all those who assisted with the original research. Of the many books consulted, four were invaluable: *The Official History of Australia in the War of 1914–1918* by C.E.W. Bean (University of Queensland Press); *The Anzacs* by Patsy Adam-Smith (Nelson); *The Broken Years* by Bill Gammage (Penguin) and *Pozières*, by Peter Charlton (Leo Cooper).

Ann Victoria Roberts

For Peter Scott Roberts with all my love

Breathless, we flung us on the windy hill,
Laughed in the sun, and kissed the lovely grass.
You said, 'Through glory and ecstasy we pass;
Wind, sun, and earth remain, the birds sing still,
When we are old, are old...'
'And when we die
All's over that is ours; and life burns on
Through other lovers, other lips,' said I...

From *The Hill* by Rupert Brooke

WORLD WAR I
MAP OF FRANCE AND BELGIUM

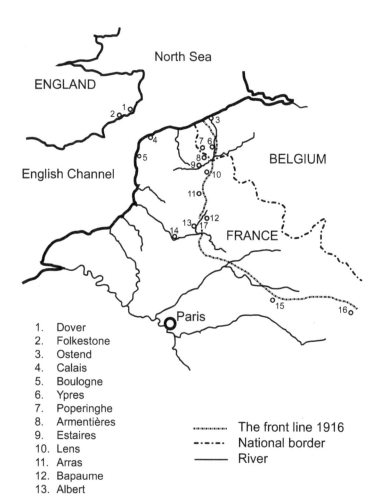

1. Dover
2. Folkestone
3. Ostend
4. Calais
5. Boulogne
6. Ypres
7. Poperinghe
8. Armentières
9. Estaires
10. Lens
11. Arras
12. Bapaume
13. Albert
14. Amiens
15. Rheims
16. Verdun

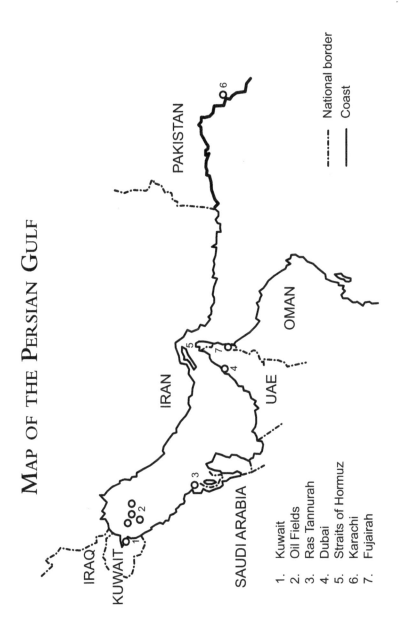

MAP OF THE PERSIAN GULF

IRAQ

KUWAIT

IRAN

PAKISTAN

OMAN

UAE

SAUDI ARABIA

1. Kuwait
2. Oil Fields
3. Ras Tannurah
4. Dubai
5. Straits of Hormuz
6. Karachi
7. Fujairah

–·–·– National border

——— Coast

ONE

All over England the year was dying in a blaze of glory. The shortening days were blessed at noon by cobalt skies and brilliant sun, by a warmth which belied early morning frosts and chilling mists at twilight. Tempted by the weather, groups of late tourists ventured forth to enjoy some lingering views before winter quickened everyone's step and made the cosiness of tea-shops more attractive.

In York, Americans with cameras exclaimed before the Minster, backing into the road for better shots of the famous twin towers, while a party of Japanese, with the stoic expressions of dedicated tourists on a tight schedule, brushed past as they left by the west door. Clutching her guide-book, Zoe Clifford paused, debating whether or not to go inside. It was not yet twelve and she had the rest of the afternoon, but four or five hours might not be enough to do what she had planned, and the Minster deserved an hour or more to itself, an hour which might be regretted later in the day.

Reluctantly she stepped back, joining those transatlantic cousins on the pavement's edge, staring up, with them, at fine stone tracery and those soaring white pinnacles, two hundred feet above the ground. In full sunlight and against a cloudless blue sky, the effect was dazzling. And magnetic: she did not want to leave. Half-regretting her decision, she contented herself with a walk around the outside, astonished by the cathedral's length and size, the way it dwarfed everything nearby.

With the massive east window at her back, Zoe stood for a moment in a clear triangle of space, contemplating the long, half-timbered building of St William's College, the line of trees that faced it, and a medieval archway that led into the street beyond. What seemed a dolls'-house scale of chimney stacks and irregular rooflines marked that narrow thoroughfare, and she thought how satisfying it must be to gaze up at the Minster every day from one of those tiny windows. As she turned, a huge bell began to toll the dozen strokes of noon, the deep, sonorous note reverberating against her breast-bone. Its solemn grandeur was like a knell for the dying year, underscoring the glorious, golden day, and the fact that she was alone.

For a moment she stood quite still, eyes closed; as the last stroke died away, she wondered why it was that beauty perceived alone should be so poignant, and why it made loneliness so much harder to bear.

On a deep breath she turned away and completed her circuit of the Minster. By the south transept she cut across the road to enter a paved walkway which led into the city's maze of medieval streets. A cup of coffee and a sandwich went some way towards restoring her emotional balance, and, with her mind set on more immediate matters, she consulted her guide again.

Gillygate, the street she wanted, ran, according to the map, just beyond and parallel to the city wall, not far from the Minster. She checked the number of the house against her notes, and mentally prepared herself for disappointment. For all she knew, Gillygate might well have been a slum, razed to the ground decades ago, or crushingly redeveloped in the brave new world of the 1960s. Anything could have happened; the chances of finding her great-grandmother's birthplace intact were very slim, but looking for that house was one of her reasons for being in York.

According to a birth certificate obtained some weeks ago, Zoe's great-grandmother had been born in the late summer of 1897, the year of Queen Victoria's Diamond Jubilee. She was named Letitia Mary Duncannon Elliott, which was something of a surprise, as no one in the family could ever recall Letitia using the name *Duncannon*. It did not even appear on her marriage lines, although one Robert Devereux Duncannon had been a witness at her wedding. Was there a mystery there, Zoe wondered, stuffing notes and guide back into her capacious shoulder-bag, or was it simply that the Elliotts had wanted to impress wealthy relatives at the birth of their only daughter?

Zoe inclined towards the latter theory, although her mother

always maintained that Letitia – who was never called *Grandmother* – had been a walking mystery until the day she died.

Mysterious perhaps; aggressively independent and more than a little eccentric she certainly was. As a child, and contrary to the rest of her immediate family, Zoe had always liked her: probably because the old lady had never given a damn for anyone's opinion and frequently said so. She had possessed an amazing ability to confound people, Zoe's mother particularly, reducing that strong-willed but intensely conventional woman to tears of abject frustration. And as a child, subject to her mother's arbitrary decisions, Zoe had admired that quality. Even now, when time and the beginnings of maturity enabled her to understand something of Marian's problems, there was still a strong bias towards Letitia.

She was, after all, the only member of her family with whom Zoe felt any affinity. Mother, father, a couple of aunts and a few cousins on her father's side, shared little in common with Zoe. She liked her father, and had it not been for the divorce, might have been closer to him; but it could hardly be said that they understood each other. And Marian would never be any different, Zoe thought, regretting, not for the first time, that she could not like her mother more.

For a few brief weeks, the ten-year-old child and the woman of seventy-three had been like allies resisting a common foe. Those weeks stood out in Zoe's memory as being the happiest of her childhood. Her biggest regret was that Letitia had not lived long enough to share the secrets of her past. Some deep-seated instinct – or was it mere wishful thinking? – pressed Zoe into the conviction that the roots of her identity lay here, in York, amongst the long-dead members of Letitia Elliott's family, rather than with her father's line of Surrey stockbrokers and businessmen. She needed to discover that identity, needed to know why she was the odd one out, the wilful, creative, unconventional child of such conservative parents. Perhaps, understanding herself, she might then learn to understand other people.

Passing beneath the great square mass of Bootham Bar, Zoe made her way around the corner and into Gillygate. Unconsciously slowing her step, she was aware of a smile touching her lips as it dawned on her that structurally at least, the street could have changed little in the past hundred years. But if shop fronts had been restored, their original purpose had changed: less butchers and bakers, more cafes and gift shops with a variety of bijou goods on display. She quickened her step, counting numbers as best she could. Most were missing, which was frustrating; but then she saw the house she was looking for, its number clearly displayed on the door. Three stories high, broad-fronted, windows and doorway compatible with the 1850s – Letitia's birthplace was still there.

Not merely intact, but a guest-house, clean and bright and apparently newly-furbished, with pretty curtains at upper windows and draped lace at street level. Zoe could scarcely believe such good fortune. For maybe half a minute she hesitated, staring up at rusty-pink brick, gleaming paintwork and a bright brass knocker on the dark blue door. The temptation to be inside that house was too much. She had cheque-book and credit cards, and her return rail ticket would be just as valid tomorrow as it was today. On a surge of anticipation she rang the bell.

A middle-aged woman answered, inviting her into a narrow hall. The reception desk was no more than a half-moon table with a vase of chrysanthemums and a visitors' book, but after a cursory glance at her booking plan, the woman said yes, she could offer a single room. It was small and on the second floor, but, she added with a smile, it had the advantage of quietness and an excellent view of the Minster.

The stairway ran across the house, dividing front from rear, and doubled back on itself at a half-landing. On the first floor the corridor was broad, with a modern glass fire-door leading to a second staircase. On the upper floor the landing was smaller, with three doors opening off.

'Here we are. You'll be nice and quiet, there's nobody to trouble you next door, which is a family room, and children can be a bit noisy. Bathroom across the way, here – and all to yourself.' The landlady, who had introduced herself as Mrs Bilton, opened the door of a single room and went across to a low-silled window, bending her head to look out. 'There, you can see the Minster, now the leaves are falling. Trouble is, in summer the trees form too thick a screen – people complain. I keep telling my husband we should have them cut down.'

Zoe was horrified by the idea. 'Oh, no, you mustn't do that! Just tell people to come in the winter, instead.'

'Well, perhaps we should have them thinned out – then everybody's happy!'

Warming to Mrs Bilton's amusement, Zoe was almost tempted to reveal the significance of her visit, but to start talking now would waste too much time. Confidences, with perhaps a tour of the whole house, would be better left until later. While the sun lasted, she wanted to be out, seeing as much of the city as possible. Above those grassy, wooded ramparts, the white city wall divided Gillygate's back yards from the Minster precincts. It was hard to believe that she was just a few hundred yards from where she had stood at noon.

'Can you walk on those walls?' she asked, noticing for the first time the heads bobbing between the crenellations.

'Yes, of course – but I should hurry if you want to do it this afternoon, dear. They close the walls at dusk.'

Zoe was given the times of breakfast and a front door key, and, with a cheerful wave, set forth down Gillygate. Returning to Bootham Bar she could barely contain her elation as she climbed the steps. Inside the great room above the archway, she touched ancient limestone blocks, ran her fingers over the wooden portcullis and pictured it being lowered to bar the road beneath. She looked down on medieval Petergate, a huddle of projecting gables and tiny windows against the backdrop of the Minster's great west front.

The people walking below made her think of Letitia, who must have passed beneath the Bar innumerable times. No doubt with her parents – and her brothers. Zoe tried to imagine them in this room, wondering if, as children, they had enjoyed pretending to be soldiers defending the city...

A sudden shiver reminded her that the afternoon was slipping away. So easy to be side-tracked, she thought, making her way out into the open air. At street level, the picture was a close and detailed one, but from the height of the city walls she saw at once that it was the broad sweep of the canvas which took the eye. Above a sea of roofs and chimney-pots, the Minster rose like an enormous ship in full sail, catching the falling light of late afternoon, and shadowing the narrow streets around it.

Couples passed her, and a large party, complete with guide, politely excused themselves as she lingered, entranced by the views. There was fascination on every side, from the undisguised age of the backs of houses on Gillygate, to the elegant expanse of the seventeenth-century Treasurer's House within the walls, its tree-shaded grounds carpeted in bronze and gold. Autumn was a season for nostalgia, she always felt, the scent of dying leaves so evocative of the past. As the shadows lengthened she thought again of Letitia, leaving this place for London and her tragically brief marriage; could not help wondering why she had settled for Sussex and a house her parents-in-law had ensured she would never own, when York in all its beauty was here, waiting. Her family, too. The parents she never talked about, the brothers she had mentioned but once. Why did she leave, Zoe wondered; and why did she never come back? And what had happened to those brothers of hers, two handsome young men in a photograph sent from France in the summer of 1916?

In a cloudless sky, the sun was setting, no more than a fiery rim of gold low down in the south-west. There was a damp chill in the air, and above the chimney-stacks and pantiled roofs, an orange haze was deepening to red.

As she came to Monk Bar, a uniformed attendant was waiting, looking out for stragglers on the walls before he locked up for the night. With a sigh of resignation he held the heavy oak door, and as she stepped inside the stairwell, closed it behind her. It was very dark, and the limestone walls within the Bar were smooth and cold, like those of a dungeon. The attendant's feet, in heavy boots, echoed behind her. With no light but that of the tiny doorway below, Zoe felt her way gingerly down those well-worn steps, and with some relief emerged into the everyday bustle of the street.

Goodramgate was busy, home-going shoppers edging carefully along narrow pavements, avoiding traffic which passed alarmingly close along that ancient and idiosyncratic thoroughfare. Across the way a pharmacist's brightly-lit window reminded her that she had brought no luggage. Pausing to buy some essentials, she crammed the parcels into an already bulging bag, tucking it beneath her arm for safety as she wove her way between traffic and passers-by.

In the darkening sky, a vestige of natural light remained. Above the jettied buildings of that winding city street, it had deepened to an astonishing colour, like the French blue in renaissance paintings of the nativity. Gazing up as she walked, Zoe stopped as she reached a junction, arrested by an unexpected view of the Minster, the whole of its east end floodlit against the dark blue sky. White and perfect as ivory, it stood in mighty gothic splendour, dwarfing all that stood before it.

With some surprise, Zoe realized that she was facing the spot where she had stood at noon, and across the street was the little archway leading into Minster Yard.

Standing beneath its shelter, she simply stood and stared, knowing this to be a rare and perfect moment, and wanting to preserve it in her memory. The traffic had eased and the flow of pedestrians dwindled to a few hardy strollers who paused to look for a moment before passing on. It was numbingly cold, but Zoe hardly noticed. Her keen artist's eye was absorbing colour and light, the vastness of the picture and its tiniest details. Intent upon the whole, she suddenly noticed a strange phenomenon. What appeared to be thick white smoke was billowing from the Minster roof and curling round pinnacles and piers.

Alarmed, thinking it was caused by fire, she darted forward across the cobbles. Before St William's College she stopped short. There was no smell of burning, no sign of flames, but like smoke from some bloody but silent battlefield, the moving cloud drifted slowly towards her.

Roofs and chimneys which had stood in stark silhouette were rapidly obscured. The carved relief of gothic masonry faded, insubstantial as a dream in that swirling mist. Images of death replaced it, so real she could almost hear the boom of the guns, smell the cordite. Men advanced and fell before her eyes, their silent cries an obscenity. She cringed, screwing her eyes tight shut against it, but when she dared to look again they were gone. White light dazzled her, and all over her body, her skin was tingling with tiny shocks. Surrounded by that drifting mist, the whole of the east end seemed to be moving, advancing and receding, pulsing with some great inner power. In the silence time was irrelevant, past and present were one, divided only by the pitiful awareness of five human senses. And it seemed those limitations were melting...

For a moment, drawn forward, Zoe was convinced that if she walked into that mist, she would simply be absorbed by it, that she would cease to exist. On the verge of acquiescence she hesitated; she shivered, and the moment was gone.

The touch of the mist was like a cold, damp shroud; trembling violently she turned away, fighting weakness and an urge to sink to her knees. Her eyes were stinging and her steps uncertain as she retreated towards the reassuring bustle of the everyday world.

A tall man, wearing a light raincoat, gave her a searching glance as she hesitated beside him at the kerb; meeting his eyes, Zoe lifted her chin and glared, every muscle tensed against inner trembling and a ridiculous desire to flee.

With another quick glance to the right, Stephen Elliott took in the line of high cheekbones and dark, tumbling curls, and despite the fierce look she had just bestowed, thought she was the prettiest young woman he had seen in a long time. The road cleared and she stepped across before him, a determined set to her shoulders, and aggression in her stride.

Watching her round the opposite corner, he was intrigued. He had seen her standing there, watching the mist curl across the Minster roof, as fascinated by the evening's freak weather conditions as he was himself. Others had paused briefly and then walked on, but she had been watching for several minutes, unnerved, he thought, by those curling fingers of mist. Drifting and sinking on cold currents of air, they looked like an army of ghosts advancing across the cobbles...

Amused by his own fancies, Stephen crossed the street and headed for home. A moment later he was climbing the stairs to his own flat in Bedern. Glancing at the time, he stacked his purchases on the kitchen table, knowing he would have to hurry to finish his packing and meet that appointment for dinner with friends at Strensall.

He picked up the telephone, calling first an old acquaintance with whom he usually left his car when going away, and with the arrangements made for its collection, called his sister's number in Harrogate.

Assuring Pamela that he was all packed and ready, he repeated his destination, told her the ship's name, and said no, he was not at all sure where he would be over the festive season.

'It might well be West Africa, since the ship's been on that run for a while, but it's impossible to say for sure. From Philadelphia we really could go anywhere – it all depends on the charterers and the price of oil...'

Suppressing a sigh, Stephen listened while his sister indulged in the usual exhortations regarding correspondence – which with her was infrequent – and healthy eating, in his opinion a contradiction in terms when applied to most of what came out of a ship's galley. But to point out what she already knew was a waste of time. Pamela was a teacher, and could not get out of the habit of lecturing people, himself particularly. He was holding onto his patience until she launched into the subject of sexually-transmitted diseases.

'For God's sake, Pam,' he interrupted sharply, 'I'm thirty-six, not sixteen! I do listen to the world news, I have heard of AIDS, and believe it or not, I do know what condoms are for!'

His blunt response prompted outrage at the other end of the line. When her voice had settled to a bearable level, he said, 'Look, Pam, I'm going away in the morning. I might not be back for another six months. Let's part friends, shall we?'

Reluctantly, she gave her assent. At last, having soothed her ruffled feathers, he was able to end the conversation and rescue his underwear from the tumble drier. Adding those final items to his suitcase, Stephen ironed a couple of shirts before going to shower and shave. Twenty minutes later he was backing his Jaguar from its garage and wondering how soon he could decently say his farewells and return for a good night's sleep. By six in the morning he must be on his way to Philadelphia, and by this time tomorrow be taking over command of the 120,000 tonne tanker, MV *Nordic*.

Two

Lying awake at the top of the house on Gillygate, Zoe's thoughts kept returning to the Minster, to the deep blue sky above, and the fog billowing around it like smoke. In the intervening hours, after a hearty meal and two glasses of good red wine, she had regained both nerve and logic. Natural phenomena, she told herself firmly, had created that rolling mist, and floodlights an illusion of light and movement. Better than any theatrical effect, although that vision of death could have had no bearing on weather conditions, freak or otherwise. As for that tingling sensation, warming her blood like a caress...

She shied away from it, not wanting to examine her own reactions too closely. With something of an effort, Zoe pushed it to the back of her mind, concentrating instead on the pretty little bedroom with its daisy-patterned wallpaper and matching curtains. She wondered what it had looked like ninety years ago. Considerably more austere, she decided. On the top floor and without benefit of a fireplace, it had probably been part of the servants' quarters, and in a house this size, servants would have been essential.

Mrs Bilton, sadly, knew little of its history, but her interest had been aroused by Zoe's questions, and she had obligingly shown her guest all the unoccupied rooms. She explained that extensive alterations had been made to the kitchens some ten years before, when the range had been ripped out, together with massive shelves and deep, floor-to-ceiling cupboards. The last owners, however, had seen the novelty of retaining the open fireplaces elsewhere, and Mrs Bilton was particularly pleased about that.

Admiring the polished mahogany mantelpiece in the front sitting room, and imagining Letitia's family gathered before a blazing coal fire, Zoe had asked, only half jokingly, whether the house was possessed of any ghosts.

Her reply was in the negative, but Mrs Bilton had gone on to mention ghosts she did know about, from the well-documented Roman soldiers in the cellars of the Treasurer's House, to other, less publicity-conscious apparitions. There was a story about ghostly children playing in Bedern, and at the rear of a shop down Gillygate, assistants sometimes saw a little old lady dressed in black – 'as solid-looking as you and me, they say' – crossing the yard...

With her own strange experience still fresh in her mind, Zoe had shivered a little at that, but made no comment. Brought up between divorced parents and the hearty, no-nonsense tenets of an Anglican girls' school, she tended to be wary of revealing too much to strangers, especially on this particular subject. Although in the past she had never seen anything untoward, she was always aware of place and atmosphere, sometimes acutely so. She tended to think that places absorbed events, in the manner of a sponge, and that strong emotions leaked back into the atmosphere, slowly, over hundreds of years. But it was no more than a feeling, which put into words sounded silly; although no more so than the idea of ghosts clinging to one place, perpetually re-enacting one moment from long and human lives which must have contained far more dramatic events than crossing the yard to bring in the washing.

But York was old, with almost two thousand years of history behind it. Perhaps, as Mrs Bilton claimed, the city was a place where the past had no means of escape. If ghostly figures were indeed as commonplace as she maintained, then possibly that experience by the Minster was less strange than she imagined. Part of the city, part of the place itself.

Except that the last pitched battle York had witnessed was during the Civil War, some three hundred years ago; and the images Zoe had seen were not those of Roundheads and Royalists, but of men more modern than that, in uniforms of the Great War...

Three weeks later, after several hours closeted within the charity-sale atmosphere of St Catherine's House, Zoe fought her way home through the misery of a wet London rush-hour. There was fine, drizzly rain in the wind blowing off Kensington Gardens, but she lifted her face to it in gratitude as she stepped off the bus. Despite the chilliness of early December, for her it had been a hot, crowded, frustrating day, in which she had learned more about sharp elbows, territorial rights, and the extent of human obsessiveness, than she had so far learned about the Elliotts.

Scorning her umbrella, she slowly walked the few hundred yards down Queen's Gate. The policeman on duty at the Middle-Eastern embassy was one she knew. He said good evening as she passed, and touched his cap. Zoe continued smiling as she climbed the steps to her own door, knowing that she should not flirt so obviously yet with no intention of discontinuing the habit. Such old-fashioned manners seemed to match the dignity of these elegant, stuccoed terraces. She loved Queen's Gate, loved the broad pavements, the porticoed houses, the tall plane trees, and the sheer, Victorian grandeur of it all. It was such a pity, she often thought, that the air of ease and confidence it exuded was no more than a lingering breath from another age. Family houses, with servants by the dozen, had mostly been split into apartments decades ago; and since then had come hotels and offices, and most recent of all, the embassies. Diplomats from oil-rich Middle-Eastern countries now occupied the former homes of men who had ruled an empire. Zoe found a certain irony in that.

Four flights of broad, shallow stairs led to her flat, and it was a matter of pride to run all the way up, even though she usually fell through the door, gasping. This evening was no exception. As usual, she filled the kettle, switched it on, then collapsed on the sofa to recover while it boiled.

Considering her scribbled notes over a pot of scalding coffee, it became apparent that the day had yielded little in the way of fresh information. The Reference Library in York had proved a gold-mine, while St Catherine's House seemed full of dross where the Elliotts were concerned. Expensive dross, too. The birth certificates she had ordered were several pounds each, and she had only ordered those in pique at being unable to find the two she had set her heart upon.

'So where were you born?' she demanded of the sepia photograph on the bookcase; but two half-smiles returned her frown, and two pairs of eyes regarded her with silent amusement, as though they shared a private joke.

The two young men in the photograph were Letitia's brothers.

Zoe knew because Letitia had said so, once, a long time ago, but without that information she might never have guessed. To begin with, they were not very much alike; and secondly, they were wearing the uniforms of different countries. In what seemed to be standard British infantry issue, one was seated in an armchair, a peaked cap resting against his knee, while the other, dressed in the uniform of the Australian forces, leaned against the arm. By comparison, he looked crumpled and scruffy, leather gaiters and boots appearing white and dull, as though covered in mud. His distinctive bush hat, caught up at one side, was pushed back, lending a slightly rakish air and revealing hair and brows which were much lighter in tone than his brother's. He might even have been blond, whereas the other was dark, his hair close-cropped above a slender, handsome face.

Nevertheless, despite that youthful perfection, Zoe found the Australian more attractive. Less obviously handsome, his features were broader, stronger, the mouth more full. It was the kind of mouth she would have liked to see drawn back in a hearty laugh. She had the impression that his smile in the photograph was a shade quirky, suppressing amusement which longed to burst forth over that studiously casual pose. As though the two of them had had a great day together, rounded off by a few drinks and a decision to have their pictures taken for the folks back home.

She did not have to remove the frame to know what was written on the back of that cheap postcard sent from a small French town in the summer of 1916, it had been committed to memory years before. *'Found each other at last! Congratulations on the wedding, Tish – wish we could have been there – Yours, Robin and Liam.'*

But which was which? And had either of them survived the war? Letitia never said, and Zoe had no way of knowing. Having possessed that photograph for more than half her life, until recently she had not given it much practical consideration. Hidden away for years amongst old sketchbooks and the reading matter of her youth, it had been resurrected during an attempt to dispense with rubbish and create more space.

Strange, she thought, what a turn of the heart it had given her; like some forgotten memento of an old love-affair.

She smiled, but at an age when the other girls at school were screaming over pop stars and busy joining fan clubs, Zoe had been sighing over this very photograph and reading Rupert Brooke. A strange passion for a young girl, some might have said; although in terms of accessibility, the two were about equal, and the war poets were as young and blighted as any chart-topping rock group. In those days the brothers had been her secret fantasy, part of a necessary insulation against the very public, overwhelming and lonely life of boarding school. They had fulfilled the roles of lovers and guardians, coming to her in the quiet times before sleep, listening to her thoughts and comforting her tears. To Zoe at that time, their presence had been unquestionable; only now, remembering, did she find that faintly disturbing. To appease herself, she put it down to adolescence and a peculiarly vivid imagination, which she had thankfully managed to harness to better use.

It was odd, however, that her rediscovery of the old photograph and its companion – one of Letitia when she was in her twenties – should have set her wondering about the Elliotts as a family. Questions never before considered had leapt to mind and taken hold, becoming more insistent as the answers continued to elude her.

Marian apparently knew nothing, and the more Zoe pressed, the more annoyed her mother became. She could not understand why Zoe wanted to know these things. The Elliotts were as remote to her as aboriginal tribesmen, and what they did, whether they were the landed gentry Letitia had once been known to claim, or paupers dying in the local workhouse, Marian neither knew nor cared. They were dead and gone, so what did it matter? What possible use could knowing about them be to people living now? Zoe should concentrate upon improving her social life, which was non-existent as far as Marian could see, and let the dead rest in peace.

That pious sentiment cut no ice with her daughter. Marian did not wish peace upon the woman who had reared her after her parents' untimely deaths; indeed, Zoe suspected that her mother would have liked to think of Letitia suffering in purgatory for her sins. And that irritation at being questioned only served to make

Zoe more determined to unearth the answers. Family history was a popular hobby, apparently: there were books on the subject, offering guidelines to research amongst archives both accessible and remote.

She would have the answers eventually. If frustrations were frequent, the satisfaction of discovery was equal to that of solving a complex detective story, with the added pleasure of knowing that the story would surely expand.

Back-tracking from Letitia's marriage lines, it had been easy to establish her birth, but her brothers were proving something of a problem. If not born in England – and Zoe was almost certain they were not – then it was possible that their parents had been living in either Scotland or Ireland at the time. Or even, she thought wryly, Australia. Nevertheless, wherever their travels had taken them, the family had been living in York by 1897, the year of their daughter's birth.

Pondering the possibilities, Zoe reached for the notebook in which she had written up all the information gleaned so far. At the top were listed details taken from Letitia's birth certificate: father Edward Elliott, Bookbinder; mother Louisa Elliott, formerly Elliott. Zoe had added a note that Edward and Louisa were possibly cousins, a supposition borne out later by information gathered in York.

Before leaving the city, she had made a visit to the Reference Library, and, with the aid of a keen young assistant, managed to establish the tenancy of the house on Gillygate. Not all the street directories had survived, but of the half-dozen extant between the years 1880 and 1898, one Mary Elliott was listed as the householder. Having expected to see a man's name, Zoe had been surprised; even more so to find that the house was described as a commercial hotel. Not a private residence at all, which rather deflated her illusion that the Elliotts had been living there in some style.

She was struck, too, by the coincidence of the house having been a hotel then, as it was now. Only for the past ten years, but still...

By 1902, however, 'Elliott's Commercial Hotel' was in the possession of a Mrs Eliza Greenwood, who offered lodgings. Zoe could only assume that the Elliotts had left for larger premises.

Intrigued by the identity of this Mary Elliott, Zoe had then bearded the young assistant afresh, and been delighted to discover that a look at the local census returns might throw light on the matter. The hundred-year block on those ten-yearly returns was something of an annoyance, and meant that the year 1881 was the latest available. She waited for the relevant microfilm to be found, and watched in fascination as it was set up for viewing. Finding Gillygate for herself was a time-consuming task, but eventually the street came to light, and at last she found what she was seeking.

There, for one night in April, 1881, were all its residents. Not only their names and ages, but their occupations, relationships and places of birth. They were all there: Mary Elliott, head of household and a widow; her three daughters, her nephew Edward, one servant and four guests. It was so exciting, she wanted to jump up and shout the news aloud; but repressed by the silence in the library, she simply left the screen and found her helper. 'I've found them,' she had whispered, grinning delightedly from ear to ear, and the girl had smiled with genuine pleasure.

She had written down, exactly, all that the census divulged. Mary Elliott had been born in Lincolnshire, while her three daughters, of whom Louisa at fourteen had been the eldest, were all born in York. Edward's birthplace was Darlington in North Yorkshire, and he was twenty-six in 1881, and a bookbinder. As a family, Zoe reflected, they had certainly moved around, which destroyed assumptions that only in recent times had people become truly mobile.

So, they had travelled, and to have been in business presupposed a certain intelligence. In that day and age, widowed, with three young children to bring up and no social security as a safety net, Mary Elliott must have been both capable and astute. Also determined and strong. Zoe admired that. Recalling Letitia's second name, *Mary*, she wondered whether her great-grandmother had favoured the old woman, and an image came to mind of a smart, plump, grey-haired woman with shrewd blue eyes and a slightly cynical smile. For all her eccentricities, Letitia had been nobody's fool, and Zoe rather suspected Mary Elliott of being a similarly tough character.

What really intrigued her, however, was the relationship

between Mary's eldest daughter, Louisa, and her nephew Edward Elliott. First cousins, with a gap of twelve years between them; she a young girl, ripe for romance, and he a man. Living in the same house, or just visiting? It was impossible to say, but Zoe could not help wondering whether he had taken advantage of close proximity, perhaps made Louisa pregnant, and then had to marry her. There may have been a family row, occasioned by disapproval of the situation and their close blood relationship – they could even have moved away from York, then for some reason been forced to return and eat humble pie at Mary Elliott's table.

It was a tempting theory, but no more than supposition. With such slender facts to hand, a dozen different interpretations were possible.

Sighing, Zoe wished that her great-grandmother had not been so close-mouthed, wished she could have been the average elderly woman, delighted to talk about her own and her family's past. That she had not, made Zoe wonder whether she was ashamed of those comparatively humble origins. Her claim to be descended from landed gentry seemed to bear that out; but Zoe was determined not to reveal Letitia as either liar or romancer until the full story was known. And for that, what she needed were some other Elliott descendants, people who had known Letitia, Liam and Robin, and understood something of their background.

It was a tall order, she realized that. The carnage of the First World War could have wiped out one or both of those young men, and it was quite possible that Zoe was the only descendant of that family left alive.

But no, she would not allow herself to believe that, nor admit defeat before every avenue of research was exhausted. Besides, something deep inside kept urging her on, something more vital than just the thrill of the chase.

Hunger impinged upon those considerations, together with the realization that in less than an hour, Philip was coming to collect her, and they were meeting Clare and David at yet another little bistro that David had discovered.

Her glow of pleasure was not entirely unalloyed. She liked Philip, but had always found his friend David rather overbearing. The thought of another evening in his company – the third in short succession – was not one she relished. It was a shame on more than one account since he had recently become engaged to Clare, one of Zoe's oldest friends. Not the closest by any means, but the two women had somehow retained their connection since schooldays, while most of the others had fallen by the wayside.

Naturally, they had seen much less of each other once the romance with David became serious, and a small kernel of cynicism in Zoe was aware that these recent invitations were prompted largely by David's desire to set up his old friend Philip with a girlfriend. He had been working in Brussels for the past two years, and was rather out of touch. But it was also to Zoe's advantage, and for that she was grateful. In recent months she had become something of a hermit, too taken up with a sudden rush of commissions and her own desire to consolidate her reputation as an illustrator, to pay much attention to a social life.

So it had been a pleasant surprise to meet Philip, and to feel the pull of mutual attraction. He was really very good-looking, if a little unsure of himself, which Zoe found charming. And with the shyness in abeyance, he could be amusing, full of fascinating anecdotes about life in the European Community. Away from his friend David's shadow, Zoe felt that he might be more interesting still.

Musing happily on the possibilities, she showered and changed into a flowing calf-length skirt and silk blouse, its dark emerald lending a touch of green to her clear grey eyes. For once, her hair was behaving, with little tendrils of curls framing her face. Surveying her reflection, she had just decided, as Philip arrived, that her ensemble needed something else...

Spotting the shawl she wanted as he waited in the lobby, Zoe whipped it off the sofa back, shook its silk folds vigorously, and arranged it around her shoulders. Her companion looked on in some surprise.

'Isn't that part of the decor?'

It was her turn to be surprised. 'Well, yes...' She gave him a consciously winning smile. 'But it goes rather well with what I'm wearing, don't you think?'

He smiled and nodded, but she had the feeling that he did not quite approve. She sighed. Perhaps his mother was a woman whose possessions were static rather than fluid; or he was afraid that the shawl was dusty after weeks on a sofa-back. Well, maybe it was, but to Zoe that mattered less than the fact that it completed her outfit.

For a moment she hesitated, wondering whether she should give in to his sense of propriety and discard the prettily-patterned shawl in favour of something more respectable; but no, that would be like shedding part of her personality, and Philip must learn to accept her as she was, warts, shawls, dust and all.

At the last moment, as they left the flat, he managed to save her mood and the evening by telling her that David had gone down with laryngitis. As the rising young barrister was due in court on Monday morning, he had felt he must stay at home and save his voice.

It was excellent news.

Waking alone next morning, she surveyed the disappointment of the night before and wondered what was wrong. Was she really so unattractive? Had she tried too hard to seduce him? Perhaps he was turned-off by pushy women.

Whatever the reason, it was a frustrating end to a wonderful evening. It had begun so well: dinner, then a nightclub, some great music, dancing. And he was a good dancer – she'd been seduced by his pleasure in the music into thinking they were really in tune. Coffee back here at the flat – closeness on the sofa, some passionate kisses, a bit of fondling – yes, it was all going well. Even then, she'd hardly been trying. But suddenly, just as she thought he was going to whisk her into the bedroom, he'd looked at his watch and said he had an early start in the morning. Regretful, apologetic, but he really did have to go.

He'd said he would call her, but she didn't imagine he would. Something had turned him off, but she didn't know what.

An hour later, Polly, her friend from the flat above, dispelled such ideas with an airy wave of the hand. 'Listen, darling, you didn't do anything wrong. Maybe he lives with his mother and she was waiting up...'

'He never mentioned his mother.'

Polly dissolved into laughter. 'Well, you never know – he's just back from Europe, maybe he's still flat-hunting and didn't like to say he's lodging with a dragon. Don't beat your breast over it. He'll call you, I'm sure.'

'You're right, Polly,' Zoe agreed with a sigh, 'but I thought...' She shook her head, not entirely reassured. 'Anyway, thanks for the coffee and the sympathy. I should go and do some cleaning – Mother is threatening a visit!'

Through tall windows the searching rays of low winter sun revealed layers of dust in places she had barely noticed for months. A dull grey film deadened the marble fireplace and softened the edge of black bookshelves in the alcove. Cobwebs hung like hammocks from the room's high corners. Zoe groaned at the thought of dragging the stepladders out, but a blitz on the cleaning was probably just the thing to rid herself of gloom.

What the flat needed, Zoe decided, was redecorating, but it would have to wait until the spring. Four years since its last fresh coat of paint, and the memory of weeks of back-breaking work was enough to make the idea of starting again feel like masochism. But the place had been filthy before she moved in, the victim of years of neglect, requiring more physical effort than anything she had undertaken, before or since. Then, it had been the kind of challenge she needed, an effective cure for post-examination blues, and a broken love-affair.

But in spite of the dirt and mustiness, as soon as she saw the flat Zoe had been aware of its beautiful proportions, and a sense of welcome. That first impression never changed. It still gave her pleasure to return after even a short absence, and in this room she worked better and more consistently than anywhere else.

By lunchtime she had a pile of dirty dusters, but both she and the room were showing signs of improvement. By the time she returned to her work-table, her memory of the night before was ready to be pushed to the back of her mind. The quick flush of excitement as she glanced through a series of sketches was enough to banish Philip from her thoughts.

She was aware of a strong sense of satisfaction. It was good, after years of study, struggle, and a few professional blind-alleys, to be doing what she had always wanted to do, and to be doing it with a certain amount of success. The illustrations before her were at different stages of completion, for a new, expensive edition of Hans Christian Andersen's Fairy Tales. It was her most lucrative commission so far, and the kind of work at which she excelled, exotic, detailed, subtly coloured, reminiscent of another age.

Amongst her favourite books as a child had been some first editions illustrated by Arthur Rackham; and as a student she had been influenced by the sure, bold lines of Beardsley and Eric Gill. Her style as an illustrator reflected that early partiality, and a resurgence of interest in art nouveau had recently put Zoe's work in some demand.

It was immensely gratifying. At last she could think of paying her father a more realistic rent, although true to form, James Clifford said she owed him nothing, that her success was enough and she should enjoy it. Zoe could not forget that he owned the roof over her head, and while he might be a wealthy man with several more profitable leases in his possession, it was no excuse to take his generosity for granted. To counter her protests, he often said that he might be thinking of selling the place now that it was so desirable, but she knew he had no intention of doing so. Since her abortive affair at college, with Kit, James Clifford had been delighted to see his only daughter progress, emotionally and materially, into independent adulthood. Other than her friendship, he wanted nothing more.

Thoughts of Kit made her smile, particularly when she compared him with Philip Dent. It was like standing a scruffy mongrel beside a well-trained pedigree gun-dog. But while the gun-dog was well-mannered – possibly too well-mannered, on reflection – the mongrel had been more fun to play with. For a while, at least.

THREE

In the Gulf of Guinea, just south of the Equator, the sun was making its rapid descent into the sea. The heat on deck was phenomenal, every steel plate throwing back what it had absorbed during the course of the day. In crisp white shirt and shorts, Stephen Elliott was taking one of his apparently casual strolls along the raised cat-walk, sharp eyes taking note of maintenance done and yet to do, assessing the progress made by his Chinese crew and balancing it against overtime claimed.

He climbed up to the fo'c'sle, noting patches of rust which demanded attention, and cast his eye over winches and mooring equipment checked that afternoon. He peered into the anchor housing and leaned over the bow, visually assuring himself that all was secure; and then he relaxed, enjoying the breeze which gave an illusion of coolness, the silence which soothed his ears. The bridge, his cabin, all the after-end accommodation, suffered constant noise, incessant vibration from generators and engines, twenty-four hours a day; these few minutes, while the crew were below and most of his officers in the bar enjoying a drink before dinner, were Stephen Elliott's moments of luxury.

The sun's lower edge touched the horizon; within a moment or two it was gone, leaving night-clouds streaked with red and gold below a purple sky. The high drama of a tropical sunset never failed to please him, expanding his mind beyond the mundane, beyond ship and cargo and the weight of his responsibility for twenty-six lives. For a few minutes he could forget who he was and what he was, and stand outside himself, at one with the sea and the sky.

A precious moment of freedom, all too brief. Behind him stood the mass of his everyday life, and before his eyes the light was fading.

Sighing, he made his way back down the shadowy deck, his mind returning to practical matters. In a little over twelve hours they would be arriving at the port of Cabinda; or, more precisely, mooring alongside a single buoy, fifteen miles off the coast. And a day later, having loaded 80,000 tonnes of oil, the *Nordic* would sail on to Muanda, at the mouth of the Congo, and load some more. With a full cargo, worth something like 30 million dollars, the ship would make its return journey to Philadelphia, eighteen days away across the Atlantic.

In the way of light relief, the round trip did not have much to recommend it. Six weeks, without mail or shore-leave, of absolute and utter boredom punctuated at three-week intervals by the madness of pilots and port officials, essential repairs, ship-chandlers, agents, surveyors, bills of lading, notes of protest, all designed to keep every last man on his toes from dawn through till dawn, and maybe the dawn after that. The personal test, Stephen always felt, was whether he could stay awake for thirty or forty hours, keep his good temper, forget nothing and no one, and still get his ship safely to sea at the end of it. So far he had never failed, but with every voyage the demands were increasing, the ships getting older, the personnel fewer; what had once been a challenge was becoming, for him, an endurance test.

As ever, almost halfway through the trip, he found himself wondering what it was that kept him at sea, what streak of masochism drove him back, time after time, when all the fun had long since gone. Habit, he supposed. Money, certainly. And perhaps a residue of hope that the next ship would be better. The present charter was as boring as a bus trip up and down the same stretch of road; except that this particular bus was old and cantankerous and liable to stall at the least convenient moment. And it was no good, he reflected, saying that the engine was somebody else's responsibility; when you were doing the driving, you were the one held responsible.

On a deep breath before he went inside, Stephen tried to stop worrying, looked for something, anything, to lighten the boredom which was always his chief enemy. Philadelphia might, just might prove interesting next time round. He smiled, remembering the attractive divorcee who was acting as water clerk for the agent. If he could only steal a few hours away from the ship, he might take her out to dinner, and then...

But a month later, when the ship arrived back in the States, Stephen's intentions seemed doomed to remain fantasies. The pretty redhead flirted discreetly, stayed to lunch on board, and accepted his invitation to dinner in town. His hopes rose. But there was a discrepancy with the cargo figures, arguments with marine surveyors and representatives of the receiving company which went on half the night. He phoned her at eight, and then again at half-past ten; she agreed, very gracefully, that there was no point in waiting for him. Disappointed and frustrated, Stephen returned to his office sharp-tongued and prepared to give no quarter on those cargo figures. His temper was not eased by knowing that he was right and the receiving company wrong.

She arrived the next morning before they sailed, looking fresh and maddeningly sexy in a crisp white shirt and thigh-hugging black trousers. Despite his lack of sleep and the presence of her superior, all it needed was one regretful, conspiratorial glance, and Stephen was well aware of all that he had missed the night before.

'I'll be taking a vacation next time,' she whispered as her boss stood talking to the Chief, 'but give me a call anyway – maybe we can fix something?'

'I'd like that,' he murmured, wondering whether the ship would allow more than an hour's respite. Only after she had gone did Stephen realize that next time round in Philly, he was due to go home. It was a measure of the effect she had on him that he had forgotten. In the course of the next six weeks, however, the MV *Nordic* managed to erase all such considerations from his mind.

After dark off the coast of Angola, the engines suddenly failed. With the ringing of the automatic alarms, Stephen cast his book aside and headed for the bridge.

He took the steps two at a time. On the bridge, he addressed the 3rd Mate. 'Have you switched the NUC lights on?'

'Yes, sir.'

It took a moment for his eyes to adjust to the darkness. As the alarms ceased their ringing, the young officer addressed him, his voice squeaky with nerves. 'Ship on the starboard beam, Captain – taking no evasive action.'

'Have you called him up?' Stephen asked, glancing at the radar plot and picking up the binoculars. The other ship was indeed right on the beam, and in these circumstances, a little too close for comfort.

As he reached for the VHF radio, the Mate arrived, curious as ever, clad in flapping sandals and a pair of shorts. 'What the hell's he playing at?' he muttered, gazing out over the bridge wing. 'Is he blind or what?'

'Probably gone to sleep.' The engine room telephone began to ring. 'Answer that, will you, Johnny? Should be the Chief.'

Ignoring what was going on around him, Stephen started to transmit on Channel 16, the hailing frequency, anxiety controlled beneath a thin veneer of calm.

'This is the Liberian ship *Nordic*, in position five degrees, three minutes south, and nine degrees, fifty-two minutes east, bound in a south-easterly direction, calling the northbound ship on my starboard side.'

Releasing the transmit button, he waited for a reply. For perhaps half a minute he sweated as the distance closed between them. Had the other watch-keeper abandoned his bridge altogether?

On his second call, a thickly-accented voice replied, sounding irritated. '*Nordic*, this is the Greek ship *Lemnos*. I receive you.'

With fury edging his voice, Stephen called again. '*Lemnos*, this is *Nordic* – Channel 8, please.'

'O.K. *Nordic*, with me that is fine. Channel 8, going down.'

Changing channels, requesting confirmation that he could be heard, Stephen declared with cutting emphasis: 'My vessel is not under command. I have engine failure and request a wide berth – do you understand?'

English was the language of the sea, but sometimes understanding was limited, and this was no time to be wondering whether the message was clear.

'O.K. *Nordic*, I understand fine. I alter my course to port.'

'Sensible, sensible,' the Mate whispered.

'*Lemnos*, this is *Nordic*. Thank you. Have a pleasant voyage. Out.'

On another wordy response, the transmission was over. Returning the VHF to Channel 16, Stephen let out a long, pent-up breath. 'Seems we woke him up.'

'Not before time, silly bugger.'

'Just make sure he does turn to port.'

As the *Lemnos* visibly changed course, Johnny called into the darkness, 'That's it, mate – you can do it. Left hand down a bit and you'll be clear!'

Stephen gave a dry smile as he watched the other ship come around their stern. He wondered why its name should seem familiar. Eventually it came to him. 'Lemnos – that's in the Aegean, isn't it?'

'No idea – the only Greek island I know is Crete. The girlfriend dragged me there last leave. In August – she got sunburn.'

For a moment the name tugged at the back of Stephen's mind. Dismissing it, he turned his attention to the breakdown. 'So what did the Chief have to say?'

'Main generator's packed in – number two failed to start for some god-forsaken reason, and number three is lying around the engine room in bits. They've been working on it all day, he says.'

'Wonderful. And what's the prognosis?'

'Didn't want to commit himself at this stage.'

'Well, he's going to have to.' Stephen pictured the engineers slaving below in intense heat and humidity, trying to root out the cause of this too-frequent occurrence. He glanced at his watch. Almost eight, and the pilot booked for first light off Cabinda, about half-past five. With time in hand, he had planned to slow down for the next few hours; but could the repairs be done in that small margin? If not, it meant cancelling the pilot, cancelling their slot in the queue of ships waiting to load. Cancellations cost money. A lot of money. He would not be popular with his managers sitting tight in their London office. Nor with the charterers in Hong Kong.

On the ledge below the bridge windows were matches and a packet of Marlboro. 'Thought you were giving up?' he remarked to the 3rd Mate, and at the young man's sheepish grin, took a cigarette and handed the packet back to him. Then he telephoned the engine room.

'We've got about an hour and a half. Two will be pushing it. After that we'll need fifteen knots out of her to get us there in time. Can you do it?'

The reply was brief, the other phone slammed down. Raising

an eyebrow, Stephen replaced his receiver with exaggerated care. With no generators to power the air-conditioning, it was becoming hot and sticky even in the wheelhouse. In his cabin, it would be worse. He dreaded to think what it was like below, in the engine room.

He pushed his cigarette into the sand box and went outside. 'Johnny, get one of the stewards to take down a couple of cases of soft drinks, will you? Charge to the company account.'

Unbuttoning his shirt, he breathed deeply, watching the lights of the *Lemnos* receding safely into the distance. Out on the bridge wing, scarcely a breeze touched his skin.

'Well,' he remarked softly as the Mate joined him, 'thank God it's a calm night.'

Two weeks later they were battling a storm off Cape Hatteras when the Radio Officer arrived on the bridge with a telex from Portishead. Normally a cheery individual, today he was frowning.

Suspecting bad news, Stephen was just about to ask what the office had dreamed up now, when Sparks said quietly, 'It's personal, Captain – you might want to read it in private.'

Opening the envelope, Stephen retired to the chart room. The message was from his aunt in York. 'SORRY TO LET YOU KNOW LIKE THIS STEPHEN BUT SARAH PASSED AWAY LAST NIGHT IN HER SLEEP. VERY PEACEFUL. LOVE JOAN.'

The words shocked him, and yet he had been expecting it.

Joan's last news, received some weeks ago, had been that his grandmother Sarah was in hospital, recovering from a bout of pneumonia. He had thought then that it could be the beginning of the end. For a moment the words blurred. Poor Joan. Truly alone, now. He bowed his head, forming a silent prayer for her, and for the repose of his grandmother's soul.

Sarah Elliott had been a stiff, reserved woman, and yet she and Stephen had been on good terms, somehow closer since his father's death. He'd wondered as he came away – as he had for years on similar occasions – whether he would see her again. As family grew older, the partings became more poignant.

Sparks was waiting, watching mountains of spray leaping over the fo'c'sle. Huge green seas were rolling down the deck.

'My grandmother,' Stephen explained, drawing a deep breath. 'She had her ninetieth birthday just days before I came away. Not quite a party,' he added with a wry smile, 'but she seemed to enjoy it.'

'A good innings, then?'

'Well, she had a long life – and a hard one, mostly.' He stared at the turbulent waves, thinking of her, thinking of the sadness. 'She lived through two world wars. She lost her husband while she was still young – and then her son, ten years ago. My father was only in his fifties.'

'I'm sorry to hear that.'

'Yes, not an easy life.' After a moment, Stephen shook his head. 'Ah well, I'd better compose a reply to this. I'll bring it down later.'

'Right you are, sir.'

In the end he sent a message to his aunt saying that he would phone her. He was due to leave the ship in Philadelphia, and, having given Joan the expected date of his return, she agreed to delay the funeral by a day or so until he could be sure of being in York.

Another twenty-four hours, he told her, and they should be picking up the Delaware pilot. A day to hand over the job to the new Master, and then he'd be home the day after that. Joan sounded grateful. There would be few enough relatives as it was. Stephen's presence, she said, would be a comfort.

With a sigh, later, he remembered the pretty water-clerk, the one he had hoped to spend some time with before leaving the States. Finding her telephone number, he made his apologies, explained the reason for his change of plan, and said – as he had said at other times, to other women – that he hoped they would meet again someday.

It was possible, but he prayed his next return to Philadelphia would be aboard some other ship. Stephen blamed *Nordic's* problems on long-term neglect by other owners, but after a worrying series of minor accidents and near-disasters, the Mate claimed she was jinxed. Even the Chief, frustrated beyond reason, had started calling the old tanker a bitch, and saying she was out to get him. It was becoming personal.

With Cape May on the starboard hand as they came into Delaware Bay, there was shipping everywhere. On the bridge, feeling the grip of apprehension, Stephen prayed for a smooth passage into Philadelphia. Please God, no more heart-stopping incidents: just let him get safely alongside, to the airport and home.

Coming up the Delaware River on half speed, with the pilot safely aboard and the tug made fast, all seemed to be going well. On the pilot's advice Stephen ordered Slow Ahead to facilitate the next manoeuvre, when the pilot ordered, 'Stop Engines,' to take off more way as they turned to approach the berth.

'Stop Engines,' the 2nd Mate echoed.

Out on the bridge wing, Stephen heard the ring of the telegraph. Beside him, the pilot was judging distances.

'Slow Astern,' he shouted.

Hard on the heels of that order came an asthmatic cough from the engines.

From the wheelhouse, the 2nd Mate shouted: 'Engine not running Astern, Captain!'

Stephen raced in to look at the rev counter: down to zero. The engines had stopped with the previous order, failed to re-start. The silence was horrifying.

He took the telegraph, jerked the levers to Stop and then again to Slow Astern. Again the jangling of bells as the message went through to the automated control system. A flicker of the rev counter, another cough, and then silence.

He reached for the phone to call the engine control room. The phone was dead.

Grabbing the emergency phone he cranked the handle. Seconds ticked by. The Chief picked up. 'We've no revs,' Stephen barked, 'and we're heading for the berth. What's happening?'

'Electrical failure. We're onto it – starting her up on manual.'

For several terrible, palpitating minutes Stephen could do nothing. Clenching the telegraph with whitening knuckles, he watched his ship heading under her own momentum for the berth and the airport's main runway beyond. He visualized catastrophe: ripped and twisted bows embedded in concrete, a full cargo of oil spilling out into the river, fire-hoses, foam detergents, and a courtroom full of Federal lawyers baying for his blood.

'What's that tug doing, Mr Pilot?'

'Full astern and pulling on the starboard shoulder, Captain.' His voice was tense. 'I doubt she can do it alone.'

'It's not enough,' Stephen muttered.

He prayed for a miracle. Just one response to Full Astern, just a minute or two of power to assist that tug...

The airport lights were getting closer. Booms and hoses strung out along the berth were nightmare puppets: a monster waiting to devour them whole.

Rigid beside him, the pilot held his breath.

Suddenly, at the last possible moment, the engines jerked into life with a resounding thud and cough of thick black smoke. On a jangling of bells Stephen slammed the telegraph to Full Astern, handed over to the 2nd Mate and raced outside. The tug was hard astern against the quarter, the bow rope stretched taut. Please God the combined force would bring her round and stop her in time...

It was a desperately close-run thing, but suddenly, miraculously, they were in position for the berth. With a shiver but no time for relief, Stephen took over, the pilot ordered Half Astern, Slow Astern, and moments later they were coming alongside. As they touched the berth lightly, ropes went out and shoreside workers began tying up. Out on the main deck, like actors called from the wings, seamen were rolling out the gangway.

Gasping with relief, Stephen mopped his face and neck. 'Thanks be to God,' he murmured. His shirt was wet through.

'You know, Mr Pilot,' he confessed later as his heart rate began to slow, 'for a while there, I thought I wouldn't need a taxi for the airport!'

The Chief, staggering up to the bridge in an oily, sweat-soaked boilersuit, spluttered with appreciative laughter. But the Delaware pilot seemed to find such levity in bad taste. He left with a very curt goodnight.

As Customs and Immigration officers went through the ship's papers in his office, Stephen closed the cabin door and tossed down a very large whisky. With no accidents, no catastrophes, and with his Master's Certificate still intact, he told himself he was a lucky man. Unable to believe the truth of it, he was still sweating and trembling an hour later.

By the time the relieving Master arrived, Stephen had calmed himself sufficiently to begin his handover. Fortunately his replacement was a man he knew well, and Stephen's cautionary tale of the *Nordic*'s tendency to perform circus tricks was taken seriously.

As the big American jet lifted off from the tarmac, Stephen could see the *Nordic* alongside the berth, just yards from Philadelphia's main runway. With the spring sunshine winking back from the waters of the Delaware, he craned his head to take a last look. Those final minutes, replaying like a badly-staged melodrama in his mind's eye, made his heart pound afresh. But if nothing else, that last trick had guaranteed an immediate trip to a lay-by berth and some major repairs. The Chief, for one, was a happier man.

Leaving Kennedy just after six in the evening, he arrived at Heathrow in plenty of time to catch one of the mid-morning flights to Leeds-Bradford. His long limbs were aching and cramped with confinement, his eyes stinging from too little sleep, but as soon as he stepped onto the tarmac at Yeadon, a bracing blast of March air whipped exhaustion away.

The sun was shining from a china blue sky, fleecy clouds scudding across that high, unprotected plateau; and way below, in the Wharfe valley, it would be a mild, slightly breezy morning. He knew, because he had lived there once. Just three miles from the airport, and convenient for a commuter, which was how he often described himself.

Five years, he thought as the taxi sped down Pool Bank, taking those steep, snaking corners with contempt. Five years since his divorce from Ruth, but a journey like this, so familiar, so unchanging, could make it seem like yesterday.

He wished it were otherwise, because in a strange way it still hurt, even after all this time. Was she happy, he wondered, with her new life and her safe, reliable husband? Secure in the conviction that he would come home each evening for his dinner, be there every weekend to dig the garden and put up shelves? Whenever he thought of her, Stephen always wondered that. No children though, and that continued to surprise him. She had wanted children. It was one of the reasons she gave for wanting to end their marriage.

With children, she claimed, her life would have been that of a single-parent family, and that was not good enough. It was a hypothetical argument and, from Stephen's point of view, unfair. She had known what he did for a living before she married him; known also that he had no plans to give it up. Known, but not believed it. Ruth had imagined that love and marriage would change him; that she, with all the power at her command, could persuade him that her ideas were best. And her ideas, being the most conventional, had to be right.

Ruth hated being alone, and it seemed wrong to her that he should go away and leave her for months at a time. Stephen had countered that by saying she could give up teaching and travel with him. Other wives did. Sadly, her first voyage, undertaken during an extended summer break, had proved such a failure she refused to repeat it. Bored by endless days at sea, Ruth missed friends, family, shopping; she even missed her own cooking. Admittedly, the food that trip had been poor, and the long journey across the Pacific notable only for its sunbathing hours. But she had not tried to enjoy it. Unlike Stephen, she read very little for pleasure, while he could sit for hours with any kind of book, and frequently did. It was such relaxation, such a perfect escape. But Ruth had even accused him of escaping from her.

At the time he had convinced himself, out of love for her, that it was not her fault. Looking back he knew he had secretly resented her attitude. Now he wished he had tackled it, brought it out into the open. Wished too, with the clarity of hindsight, that he had been less enthralled by physical need; but that had always been his vulnerable point. Now that he was older, he could admit it, even laugh at the antics of his youth.

What he could not laugh about was his wife's betrayal. Stephen had remained faithful throughout the period of their marriage, wearing his virtue like a hair shirt and expecting a loving reward for his pains, yet that last couple of years had provided few rewards, loving or otherwise.

When Ruth told him she had met someone else, he was stunned. When she admitted to a long-standing affair and said she wanted a divorce, his rage was uncontrollable. He had had to leave the house; had gone to his sister's, which was a mistake. Pamela's lack of real sympathy had made things worse; she could see the situation only through her best friend's eyes, and for that Stephen had never really forgiven her. Even now he was careful in conversation with his sister. In the old days she and Ruth had told each other everything, and he had no reason to suppose their habits had changed.

At that time, he remembered, he had sorely missed his parents, both of whom had died while he was away at sea. His mother from cancer, his father of a sudden heart-attack a few years later. As far as Stephen was aware they had enjoyed a good and happy relationship. With a sudden flash of insight, he realized that he had rather naively expected all marriages to be like that.

For him, marriage had obviously been a mistake, yet he still missed his wife. Like every other awareness, it was so much more acute when he was returning home.

While ever he remained at sea, Stephen knew he would not marry again. It was too hazardous a course to attempt twice in one lifetime. Nor, on the other hand, would he consider giving up his career simply for the sake of marriage. If he ever did give it up – and the idea pressed him more and more with every voyage – it would have to be for something better, something he really wanted to do. And as yet he had not found it. He wondered whether he ever would.

There was no answer to that. Banishing the question, he shook his head. The day was too new, too brilliant, to waste on impossibilities. Instead, he gave himself up to the pleasure of the journey: winter wheat, fresh and green, the dark richness of ploughed fields and pink blossom in gardens along the way. All a delight to eyes starved of such beauty for five long months.

With the Minster towers in sight against the horizon, Stephen found himself thinking again of his grandmother and the forthcoming funeral. But not even that sadness could dent his joy as the taxi bore him into the city. All the familiar landmarks were there to greet him: Micklegate Bar, proud as ever, then left past the station and over the river. And suddenly there it was, up close and gleaming in the midday sun: the great west front of the Minster.

He smiled. It was good to be home.

Joan had recently called at the flat. Beside the mail stacked neatly at one end of the breakfast bar, was a note, telling him that electricity and water were turned on, fridge and freezer stocked with basic essentials. His heart warmed to her. Despite her grief, despite all other necessary arrangements, she had somehow found time to do what she always did, making his homecoming as smooth as possible.

Stephen made himself some coffee, smoked a cigarette and spent a good five minutes deciding whether to defrost something in the microwave, or eat out. Ultimately, the thought of having to make conversation with anyone, even his favourite lunchtime barmaid, was too much. Instead he reached for the frying pan and cooked himself a satisfying English breakfast. Within an hour he was in bed, sleeping the sleep of the utterly exhausted.

When the alarm rang at six, he was drowsily tempted to ignore it. The rest he had had was not enough, but would suffice for the time being. With mind still numbed and body sluggish, he forced himself out of bed and into the shower.

Pulling on an old pair of jeans, Stephen went through into the sitting room, a towel still draped around his naked shoulders. He slipped a tape into the stereo, smiling as the music of Dire Straits, almost Spanish in its passionate cadences, swelled to fill the room. Beyond the window, Goodramgate's black, uneven rooflines stood dramatically against the floodlit Minster. Its purity touched his soul as always, while the music stirred longings not entirely spiritual. He found himself remembering his last night at home, the strange light and sudden, swirling mist; and a girl, silhouetted against it. The memory was as clear as yesterday, but all that was long gone. The daffodils were in bloom again beneath the city walls, and it was time for him to pick up the threads of his other life.

Pouring himself a drink, he sat down to flick through the collection of mail, immediately consigning a whole bundle of circulars to the waste-paper bin. Bank and fuel statements were pushed to one side for later perusal, leaving a few letters, mainly from friends abroad, which had arrived too late to be sent on to the ship. There was a note from the shipping company, querying his report on an injured seaman, which raised a muttered oath; and another, addressed in a neat, italic hand, which made him frown.

The postmark was London, dated just after Christmas; and for a moment Stephen wondered why his aunt had neglected to forward it. Then he saw her message, scribbled in pencil on the back: 'We had one of these, so no point in sending it on – Joan.'

Intrigued, he extracted a single sheet of typescript from the already unsealed envelope. The message, from a London address, was photocopied:

'As there are 52 Elliotts in the York phone book, and no gender indicated, I hope you will forgive the impersonal nature of this letter, and understand that it is prompted simply by my desire to know something about the family to whom I am related.

'I am the great-grand-daughter of Letitia Mary Elliott, who was born in York in 1897, and died in Sussex in 1972. I understand that Letitia, whose nickname was Tisha, had two brothers, Robin and Liam, both of whom served in the First World War. I would like to make contact with anyone who might be descended from them.

'Obviously this is very much a shot in the dark – not all the Elliotts in York will be related. But I sincerely hope that someone is – and that one of you will reply.'

The signature was bold and clear – Zoe Clifford.

Bemused, Stephen read it through again, and then a third time. Letitia Mary Elliott was a name that meant nothing to him, but his grandfather, Robert Elliott – known as Robin – had certainly served during the First World War. As had his brother, William Elliott. Known as Liam. Had to be the same family, Stephen decided, those names were not common.

At first it struck him as very odd. Then he recalled a friend who was researching her family history, and realized this young woman was probably doing the same thing. Privately, he thought Zoe Clifford was wasting her time; apart from Liam, who had emigrated to Australia, the Elliotts had done nothing remarkable that he was aware of. No royal bastards, no fortunes in chancery, not even a poacher sentenced to be hanged.

Turning the envelope over, scanning Joan's message again, Stephen picked up the telephone. For perhaps half an hour they talked about his grandmother, about the long weeks in hospital and her peaceful end. Joan had been with her, and although she did not break down in the telling, Stephen could hear the rough emotion in her voice.

Stephen offered to come over once he had eaten, but Joan put him off.

'No, love, come tomorrow, have some lunch with me. We can talk then. The funeral's eleven o'clock on Thursday – I did say, didn't I? Pamela's coming, of course, but there won't be many others.' Joan sighed. 'A few friends of mine, that's all.'

The service at All Saints Goodramgate was short, followed by an interment at the old cemetery, much overgrown since his visits as a child. Stephen had never known his grandfather, but he knew Robin Elliott's grave. As the new coffin was lowered, he was thinking of his parents, grieving more for them than for his grandmother; and so, it seemed was Pamela, for she was suddenly clinging to his arm.

'Awful, isn't it?' she whispered, wiping away a tear. 'I'm glad Mum and Dad were cremated.'

He sighed, not sure he agreed. 'Well, at least their ashes are here.'

Dry-eyed, Joan scattered some earth and then turned to Stephen. 'They're together again,' she said sadly. 'It was what she always wanted.'

Back at the house, Joan had prepared sandwiches and a plain cake. There were more guests than Stephen had expected – three ladies, friends of Joan, and two men of similar age. Old soldiers, from their conversation. They made small-talk at first and then relaxed under the influence of sherry and whisky into reminiscence. The war, the thirties, the fifties – he caught Pamela's polite smile and realized she was keen to be off. She nodded to her husband, and Stephen saw him glance at his watch.

'Chris has to get back to work, I'm afraid – and I must be home for the children…'

They made their apologies to Joan, who frowned and said she was sorry they had to go. Stephen heard her say that there were things she'd been hoping to discuss with them; but Pamela promised to come again soon.

'One Saturday, Aunt Joan, we'll bring the children over. But why don't you come to us?' she added brightly. 'It will be a change for you…'

And maybe Joan would go, Stephen thought, but not without a definite arrangement.

An hour later, the other guests were also leaving, and it seemed to Stephen that his aunt was glad to see them away. He was about to fetch his coat when she stayed him with a gesture.

'Let's have a cup of tea,' she said. 'I'm exhausted.'

Stephen made the tea, and they settled down before the fire.

'I was hoping Pam would stay a while. But as soon as I saw Christopher, I knew they'd have to dash off. It was good of him to come, but I wish…' She shook her head. 'I wanted to talk to you both.'

'What is it?' he prompted.

'Well, I've been thinking about this for a long time, so don't say I'm rushing things. If I don't do it now, I never will.' She took a deep breath and leaned towards him. 'I've decided to buy a flat, Stephen. Never could abide this place, and now Mother's gone, I can't wait to get out. The sooner the better.'

He was taken aback. 'Are you sure? It's very sudden. Shouldn't you wait a while?'

'I've waited for years, love. Tried to persuade your Gran, but she wouldn't have it. This was her home, she said, she'd lived here since she was married, and she intended to die here. Well,' Joan added, 'she didn't quite get her wish, but near enough.' Again, a deep sigh and that regretful shake of the head. 'I knew, once she went into hospital, she wouldn't come home…'

He saw the glint of tears and was very much afraid that this decision was too soon. She dismissed his protests with a wave of the hand.

'I want something small and easy to clean – and above all, Stephen – warm. My arthritis isn't getting any better, you know, and so much wants doing here. Quite frankly, love, I can't afford the maintenance, not on one pension. So I've taken advice and I'm selling. Buying a nice little one-bedroomed affair off Walmgate.'

'*Walmgate?*'

'Oh, don't sound so snobbish,' she said, suddenly brisk. 'Those new flats are lovely – central heating, double-glazing, fitted kitchen, the lot. Nearly as smart as yours,' she added archly.

Stephen laughed. 'Listen, you don't have to sell it to me. You're the one who's always been so disparaging about Walmgate.'

'Well,' she conceded, 'it was dreadful before the war. But it's come up in the world since then, you know – and with the price of property the way it is, beggars can't be choosers.'

Suspecting his aunt was in a far from beggarly situation, he smiled. 'Well, this house should fetch a decent price. I know it needs a lot of work doing, but even so...'

It was a pleasant late-Victorian house, with deep bay windows on a quiet street just outside the city walls. Apart from a first-floor bathroom installed during the early 1950s, and a kitchen of roughly the same era, the house had barely changed from the day it was built. Fireplaces and picture-rails were all intact, together with door knobs, cast-iron coat pegs in the hall, fancy floor tiles and stained glass in the porch door. For someone with sympathy and plenty of money to spend on re-wiring and a damp-proof course, the place would be a delight. If he could bear to give up his view of the Minster, Stephen thought, he might be half-tempted himself...

'It won't happen overnight, I know, but I shall have to prepare. So if there's anything you or Pamela would like, I want you to say so. I'll keep my favourite items, but most of the furniture's going to the salerooms – I want something new and bright to cheer me up.'

'And you deserve it,' he said, squeezing her hand. Never married, his aunt had devoted her life to caring for other people. Perhaps it did seem sudden, this desire for change, but he felt Joan Elliott was entitled to it. 'Whatever you decide – or should I say, whenever – I'll try to help. I've got a couple of months' leave, so if you move house while I'm at home, then all the better. In the meantime,' he added as tears sprang to her eyes again, 'if there's anything you need a hand with, just let me know.'

She said there was, and there was more she needed to discuss, but she was tired. Stephen knew it was time to go, but he felt guilty leaving her alone. With assurances that she would be fine – TV and an early bed tonight – he promised to call the next morning.

Ten minutes later he was climbing the stairs to his flat.

It was only as he was preparing his evening meal that he remembered the letter. He picked up the envelope, re-read the contents, and stuffed it into his coat pocket. Tomorrow he must remember to ask Joan about that.

She was in the kitchen when he arrived, preparing pastry for a meat and potato pie.

'But I was supposed to be taking you out for lunch,' Stephen protested, kissing her warm and rosy cheek. 'Anyway, I've brought these for you.' He whipped a bunch of daffodils from behind his back, delighted by her surprise. The flowers were plunged into a cut glass vase and set upon the dining table.

His third visit in as many days, and yet, as he looked at his grandmother's empty fireside chair, it seemed odd not to see her there. She had been for him – as he was sure he was for her – a link with his father. For a moment he bitterly regretted his career. It had taken him away from so much.

The family was shrinking. His sister had children, but the Elliott name would soon be gone – from this family at least. The thought made him sadder than ever.

Thoughts of family reminded him of the letter in his coat pocket, but Joan's thoughts were on more immediate matters. Over the next hour, as the pie released its tantalizing aromas, she explained the problem of the attic.

'I really need some help with this. You see, there's trunks and things up there I can't possibly take with me, but I can't just send them to the tip. Not without going through everything – and to be honest, love, I just can't face it. I've already spoken to Pamela – she hasn't got room, and anyway, I doubt she'd have the patience.' She gazed at Stephen, her eyes full of appeal. 'So I wondered – would you? You've got time on your hands while you're on leave – and a spare bedroom…'

Bemused, Stephen mentally assessed the contents of his 'spare' room. 'Well, Joan – I don't know – how much stuff is there?'

Clearly, that was the cue she was waiting for. 'Come and look.'

Having checked the progress of the pie, she led the way to the attic, climbing steep wooden steps with little grunts of effort. With her hand on the narrow, half-glazed door, she paused to catch her breath. 'It's all up here – including Dad's photographic equipment. But that's going to the museum, so don't panic.'

'Thank heavens for that.' He smiled, but in the midst of curiosity came an involuntary thrill which transported him back to childhood. On rare occasions he had been allowed to come up here; not to play, but to look at the giant camera and huge glass negatives which had been part of his grandfather's life. Robin Elliott had trained as a photographer before the First World War, and afterwards had run his own business on Monkgate. Hundreds of photographs, not all of them mounted, lay in boxes and drawers beneath the eaves.

But he had forgotten the trunks. As soon as Joan pointed to them memory came flooding back. The big black metal one, with its brass studs and clasps, had books in it, he was sure. Tomes from the last century: bound copies of illustrated journals, old bibles and history books. And photographs – albums of them – which he and Pamela had sometimes been allowed to look at when they were young. For a moment he was a child again, hushed and expectant, wondering at the treasure hidden within. And then he smiled, recalling disappointment: books and photographs seemed dull stuff indeed when his imagination had painted gold coins and strings of pearls.

The other box, smaller, leather-bound, with its oversized padlock, had always remained closed. Whenever they asked, Gran said the key was missing.

To his surprise, after a very short search, Joan produced a key from the top drawer of a painted chest.

Before he could stop himself, Stephen said: 'I thought that was lost?'

His aunt gave him a sidelong look. 'She always said that.' After some persuasion the key turned, but the catch refused to give until Stephen wrenched at it. The hinges were stiff, too, squeaking in protest as he lifted the lid.

'Good grief,' he murmured, thinking of his own lightweight luggage, 'to think people travelled with these things. No wonder they needed porters!'

There was a layer of old newspapers covering the contents, and beneath, a sectioned drawer with several small boxes and three tiny pairs of children's shoes. The leather was stiff with age.

'And who did they belong to, I wonder?'

'My father,' his aunt replied softly, 'and his brother and sister.' After a moment, clearing her throat, she said: 'Granny was so sentimental – Louisa, her name was – she couldn't bear to part with anything, especially letters. Just take out that drawer...'

He hesitated. The sight of those little shoes, Stephen felt, was ridiculously disturbing. They were such an intimate part of someone else's past, he did not want to touch them; nor, suddenly, did he want to see the rest. Time was telescoped alarmingly, the gap of a hundred years no longer existed; it was here, beneath his hand, and it made him shiver.

As he crouched before the trunk, Joan released the catches and tugged at the wooden drawer. Reluctantly, Stephen helped her to lift it out. Beneath, tied with ribbon, were bundles of letters. Dozens of them. The uppermost ones, with envelopes yellowed and brittle, were directed to a Mrs L. Elliott. One, Stephen noticed, was clearly postmarked Dublin, the year 1922.

'Did you know these were here?' he asked. 'But of course, you must have done. Have you ever been through them?'

Joan shook her head. 'No. I couldn't, somehow. I remember her very well, you see. She was my favourite person when I was a little girl – the sort of person you could tell your troubles to.' Joan smiled, a regretful, affectionate smile; and then she sighed. 'She died in 1944, just before D-Day.' There was a pause, in which Stephen recalled the significance of that date to Joan. On one of the French beaches, her fiancé had been killed.

'Was she very old?'

'She was seventy-seven – a good age, then.' She paused again. 'Poor Granny.'

'Why do you say that?' he asked gently.

'Well, she outlived most of her own family – apart from that daughter of hers, who never bothered – and she seemed so sad and confused towards the end, talking to people who weren't there. It got on Mother's nerves, I'm afraid.'

'But she kept her things?'

'Well, they were precious to Granny, and I don't think Mother liked to dispose of them.' Lifting one packet of envelopes, she spotted another with familiar handwriting. 'Just a minute – I think some of these are my Dad's letters. Yes,' she said slowly, scanning the addresses, 'they are. His letters to Mother. She must have put them here for safe-keeping.' For a moment, overcome, she held them against her breast. 'I'll have to keep these – you don't mind, do you?'

'No, of course not,' Stephen said, surprised. In truth he wanted none of them, but was afraid to say so. He supposed he would have to store the two trunks, but could not imagine wading through the contents.

'So you will take them?'

With a wry smile, he agreed, hoisting the smaller trunk to take it downstairs. It was surprisingly heavy. The other, containing books, would have to be emptied first.

Back in the kitchen, his aunt ticked off the problem of the attic on a lengthy list. If she had been exhausted the day before – and with good reason, Stephen thought – as they sat down to eat he noticed she was brighter. Solving a few problems seemed to have put grief to one side and restored her energy.

'Now then, about that letter you didn't send on. You said you'd had one too?'

The tale she told over their meal was strangely inconclusive. Zoe Clifford's missive had arrived in January, and Joan had written back saying yes, they were related through Letitia's brother, Robin.

'But as I said, Letitia left York such a long time ago, I didn't think we could be much help. Then we had a phone call a few days later, and she sounded so grateful that I'd written back to her, I felt sorry we couldn't tell her more.

'I could explain the relationship, of course – I'd have been first cousin to Letitia's daughter who was killed in 1942. But Zoe wanted to know something about Robin and Liam, when and where they were born, and where their parents had been married. I thought my Dad was born in York, but Zoe said she'd checked, and he wasn't. When I asked Mother, later, she said he was born in Dublin.'

'*Dublin*? I never knew that.'

'Nor did I! He'd come to York as a baby, apparently. But he never spoke of it, and Mother didn't know any more than that.'

'A bit of a mystery, then?'

'Certainly is. Anyway, on the phone Zoe said she had to be in York for another appointment in a few days' time, and could she call to see us? Well, I fancied to meet her – she'd got me intrigued. And I thought Mother would like to meet a long-lost relative who wanted to talk about the past – it might buck her up a bit.'

Across the table, Joan smiled ruefully and set down her fork. 'It never occurred to me there might be anything wrong, or that Mother wouldn't want to see this young woman – but she was furious. To be honest,' she sighed, 'we had quite a row about it. Of course, by then, I couldn't very well put Zoe off.'

Stephen frowned. 'So what was wrong?'

'Well, it was Tisha, you see – Letitia Mary, if you please, was *my* father's sister. A no-good baggage if ever there was one, according to Mother. She'd known her as a girl – but I never met her, so I can't comment.'

'Bad memories?' Stephen asked, finishing the last of a delicious meal.

'Seems so. Apparently Zoe had a look of Tisha, that was the problem. When she arrived, Mother took one glance and simply clammed up. Wouldn't tell her anything, bar the barest essentials. And I didn't want to upset the applecart by mentioning the boxes in the attic – I'd never have heard the last of it.'

'But you liked her?' Stephen said, knowing his aunt to be a good judge of character.

'Yes, I did,' she replied emphatically. 'She was a nice, cheerful, honest sort of girl. Very well spoken. I got the impression there was plenty of money somewhere in the background – she certainly wasn't after sponging from us.

'No,' Joan added as she cleared their plates away, 'all she wanted was what we could tell her. And in the end, it wasn't much. Mother gave her a few names and places and birthdays she could remember – very grudgingly, might I add – and that was that.

What she wouldn't tell her – and she could have done, I'm sure of it – was why Tisha left York and never came back.'

Helping himself to a piece of cake, Stephen smiled. In the manner of the worldly-wise, he said: 'The old, old story, I suppose. Got pregnant and ran away.'

His aunt shook her head. 'No, I don't think so. That's too simple. And Mother would have said – to me, at least – if it'd been that. When I tackled her about it afterwards, she just kept on about what a dreadful little snob Tisha was, how cruel she'd been to her mother, and how it served her right that she died alone, and without friends.'

Shocked by that vindictiveness, Stephen said: 'That doesn't sound like Gran.'

'No. But she obviously detested Tisha – and I'd love to know why.'

'She asked the girl plenty of questions, I imagine?'

'Oh, yes. Mother got Tisha's life-story, practically. And she lapped it up, I'm sorry to say. Like an old cat with a bowl of cream.'

With an eye for the passing afternoon, Stephen asked whether she had been in touch with Zoe Clifford since, but his aunt said no, she had been too busy hospital visiting. There had been so much to attend to, letters were the last thing she could think about. But now Stephen was home, she hoped he might get in touch with her.

'But what can I tell her?' he demanded. 'Anyway, we've never met.'

'She's very nice,' his aunt insisted, 'and very pretty, too. I think you'd like her,' she added with a smile.

'I'm too old for young girls,' he told her, laughing. 'She'll think I've got one foot in the grave. And what's the point, anyway? I can't tell her any more than you can.'

'But I've given you the boxes, haven't I? Bound to be something in there.'

Four

Clinging to the top of a stepladder, Zoe arched her back and swept the paint-roller back and forth, struggling to reach the corner and leave no faint patches. The ceiling and two walls were done and looking good, and already she was feeling better, working the aggression from her system, making a clean sweep in more ways than one.

What a waste of time, she kept thinking: she had been a fool to think it could ever have worked between her and Philip. He just wasn't her type at all. Well, it was over; she had told him so, and the sooner he accepted it, the better.

The telephone rang, a muffled, pathetic chirping that brought forth curses as she struggled to regain her balance. 'If that's him *again*,' she muttered furiously, 'I'll kill him.' For a moment she considered not answering; but it might just be a business call, and she could not afford to ignore those. Hurriedly, she climbed down, peeling back dust-sheets and cushions to reach the buried telephone.

Suspicion edged her voice. 'Hello?'

A man's voice bade Zoe good afternoon and asked for her by name. Not Philip, obviously: this voice was deeper, with northern undertones. Even as she wondered, he gave his name as Stephen Elliott, mentioning his aunt and York in explanation for the call. A little shaft of surprise cut through her; she had not expected to hear from the Elliotts again.

Sinking down onto the sofa, she listened while he briefly outlined the situation. At news of his grandmother's death, she expressed the proper condolences, but could not keep the excitement out of her voice when he mentioned the contents of boxes which were now in his possession.

'But that's wonderful. Have you been through them?'

'Only a cursory search,' he said. 'There hasn't been time for more. There are a lot of photographs – some identified – which might be of interest to you, and what looks like hundreds of letters.' With a chuckle he admitted that he hadn't yet tackled those. 'But what you will find interesting, I'm sure, are the birth and marriage certificates.' He paused at that point, and she wondered why. Old Mrs Elliott, Robin's widow, had reluctantly told her that the brothers were born in Ireland, which was a severe disappointment. Zoe had read enough books on genealogy to know that few if any state records had survived the Irish Civil War, and felt that her research had come to an abrupt and frustrating end.

But perhaps she was wrong.

'You've found the original certificates?'

'Yes.'

Taking a deep breath, she said, 'I'd love to see them.'

There was another pause. 'Well, if you'd like to come up to York, just say when. I'm available most days for the next few weeks, so we can make it to your convenience...'

Determined to grab the opportunity before he could change his mind, she plunged in firmly. 'That's very kind of you, Mr Elliott. I'd like to make it soon, if I may – how about next week?' Ignoring the chaos around her, she added impulsively: 'Would Monday suit?'

A little surprised, he said that it would, and the requisite arrangements were made. Zoe would catch the train which arrived closest to midday, while he and his aunt would meet her at the station.

Her excitement refused to be quenched, even by the task she had set herself. If she was planning to be in York on Monday, the decorating would have to be finished by then, even if it meant working every hour over the weekend. But it was a challenge and worth it. After weeks in which the Elliotts had had to take a back seat, she could hardly wait to see those letters and take up the chase again.

With a fresh surge of energy, she climbed the ladder and resumed her painting.

By the following evening – Friday – the walls were a deep shade of cream, so much warmer than the stark white she had employed as a reaction to dirt and grime when she first moved in. She was busily undercoating the bookshelves when she heard the buzz of the doorbell.

At the sound of Philip's voice over the intercom, her heart sank. No matter that she was decorating and covered in paint, that the flat was a mess with nowhere to sit – he had to talk to her. Wearily, she pressed the door-release button and let him in. But she was determined not to be held up; leaving the lobby door open, Zoe returned, somewhat grimly, to her task.

She heard him come in but did not turn. For at least a minute he stood and watched her, his eyes boring into her back. When she could stand it no longer, she wiped her brush and stood it in a jar. Immaculate as ever, he looked so incongruous against the dust-sheets and rolled-up rugs, Zoe wanted to laugh. But the situation was far from funny. His misery communicated itself to her, promoting guilt, resentment, and ultimately, anger.

'Philip, why are you doing this? We've said all there is to say – and I'm not going to change my mind.'

'No, you had your say,' he reminded her tersely, 'but I was too angry the other night. I've telephoned, and you wouldn't agree to meet me, so I thought I'd better call in person.'

That put Zoe in the wrong, and made her angrier still. 'I can't think why – I've nothing more to say.'

'Well I have. Won't you listen to me? Please?'

With bad grace, she dragged dust-sheets aside and made a space for him on one sofa, brought a couple of cans of lager from the kitchen – no glasses, just to irritate him further – and sat herself down on the other. They were at odd angles to one another, and he had to twist himself awkwardly to look at her. He toyed with the can, but did not open it.

'I'm sorry I lost my temper,' he said with an effort at contrition. 'I shouldn't have said all those things. I didn't mean them, Zoe, honestly.'

'Oh, but you did, Philip, and that's a fact. What you said was unpleasant and hurtful, but it only serves to underline what I was trying to say to you – that we really don't have anything in common.'

'I don't agree. We like similar things – theatres, concerts, galleries – we've had some wonderful times together...'

'You only like them because you think you should – because it sounds good to say you went to see a Chekhov play, or the latest exhibition at the Tate. You haven't the first clue what they're about – and neither has your wonderful friend *David*.' Zoe took a long pull at the lager and watched him wince.

'Oh, yes – that's what it's all about, isn't it? David. You're screwed up with jealousy!'

His childishness did not amuse her. As ever when she was really angry, Zoe's voice dropped and took on a cutting edge. 'That's not true. I'm not jealous of David – I just don't like him. I'm sure he must be brilliant in court, but I do wish he wouldn't practise on his friends. He isn't kind, Philip – can't you see that? He belittles you, and you let him. He does the same to Clare, and it hurts me just as much.

'That girl used to have a mind of her own – but not anymore. He says *jump*, and she asks *how high*? I don't like it. Nor do I enjoy seeing him do the same to you. If you were a match for him, fair enough – but you're not. You're far too nice to be a friend of his.'

He flushed, with embarrassment or anger, she was not sure. Eventually, he said: 'Look, if that's what you really think, why end it between us? Can't we try again? We've been honest with each other, we know the problems, why can't we settle them?'

'I've told you why.'

'But Zoe – you mean so much to me. I can't bear it – this week's been hell...'

For a moment she felt sorry, remembering. Guilty, too. But sympathy would only make it worse. 'You'll get over it, Philip – people do. I'm sorry – I'm not unfeeling, just trying to be practical. Things just weren't right between us.' With an urge to be specific, she bit it back, and finished lamely, 'You know that as well as I do.'

'Forget David and Clare – we don't have to see them – '

'No.' His simplicity was infuriating. Once it had charmed her. Dear God! Did he not realize how impossible he was? 'You'd never forgive me,' she said grimly, 'for coming between you and your oldest friend.'

After a while, he said: 'I suppose you feel like that about Clare?

You blame David for coming between you?'

It was not true: she blamed Clare for being such a fool. 'Yes,' she lied, 'I suppose I do.'

Frustrated, guilty, wishing he would go, she stood up, only to have her pacing intercepted. After a small hesitation, he kissed her, clumsily. She did not protest, but wondered how his lips could ever have been exciting. For the sake of all that had been between them – and on her part it had never been enough – she kissed him gently on the cheek. 'Philip, to be happy, you have to be able to be yourself – not what you think the world expects you to be...'

But he was not prepared to accept that, and stayed on, trying to talk her round to his point of view, becoming more depressed as he perceived the futility of it. In the end Zoe lost patience and even her pity evaporated. She told him he would have to go; she had work to do, work that must be finished before Monday, as she was going to York for a couple of days.

'I see. York. I suppose that means you're still chasing a lot of ghosts. Well, between them and your art, I hope you're happy. Real life's obviously a bit much for you.' He paused in the lobby, his hand on the open door. 'Goodbye, Zoe.'

Once he had gone, needing to let off steam she went upstairs to see her friend Polly, but Polly was out. Hardly surprising on a Friday evening, but Zoe was disappointed. Returning to her own flat, she poured herself a large brandy and grabbed brushes and paint with grim determination. At half past midnight, when her friend came back, she was still busy.

Polly had seen the lights from outside and called in with a friend, fortunately a tactful sort who soon saw that he was not required, and left. When he had gone, Zoe poured her heart out, and then had a good cry because she was angry and tired.

'I wouldn't care, but he didn't even offer to help me!' she protested, wiping her eyes. 'Just sat there and moaned on – making it impossible for me to get on with the job!'

'Obviously not the practical kind,' Polly observed. She put away the paintbrushes and the brandy bottle, made some coffee, and with a few succinct comments on life, love, and the nature of men, ushered Zoe off to bed.

Clare rang at lunchtime. It was not a pleasant conversation. Clare, it seemed, was appalled by Zoe's behaviour, accusing her of using Philip and – what was worse – trying to destroy his long-standing friendship with David.

Zoe was in no mood to take those accusations calmly. If it was a matter of using people, she said, David had done his fair share.

'You don't like David,' Clare said furiously, and Zoe agreed with her. Clare slammed down the phone and that was that.

Cursing roundly, unsure which of the three deserved most odium, she slipped a tape into the stereo. For the rest of the afternoon the flat vibrated to the sounds of a heavy metal band. By the time she was ready to fall into bed that night, most of the painting was done.

Next morning, viewing her handiwork, Zoe was pleased to see that the overall effect was that of a gentle, spacious, elegant room, reflecting none of the anger that had gone into its transformation. Finishing off, she began to appreciate it, her mood lightening in response to Polly's enthusiasm and her offer to help clear up.

It was too soon to replace the books, but with rugs unrolled, sofas pushed back and Zoe's worktable standing in its proper place before the windows, the room was acquiring an old familiarity. Pictures were re-hung, a couple of examples of her own work, some Beardsley prints, a copy of a portrait by Gwen John, and one small, original abstract, souvenir of her first love-affair. There were other small mementoes dotted about the flat, but Philip had given her nothing more lasting than a stiff bouquet of flowers.

Pouring out the final episode of the saga, Zoe admitted she was more distressed by the end of an old friendship than by the loss of a lover. But as Polly observed, men tended to come and go, while friends were usually more long-term.

'It's not surprising you feel sad about Clare.'

'You're right,' Zoe admitted with a sigh. 'We met at boarding school – both new girls, feeling scared and very raw. Of course we clung together for a while. I remember telling her about Letitia and how amazing she was – I even showed her these old photographs.' Rescuing the framed likenesses of Letitia and her brothers, Zoe knew her sadness had just as much to do with them.

'Clare knew how important they were to me. I thought she'd understand my need to find the missing pieces of the jigsaw.'

'And did she?'

'No, I don't think so. Like David – like my mother, in fact – she felt it was all in the past and therefore irrelevant.' Smiling ruefully, Zoe shook her head. 'Is it me? Am I really such an idiot? '

'No, it's important to you.' She leaned over Zoe's shoulder to look at the sepia images. 'What is it about old photos? I mean, look at them – she's stunning, and there they are, two young, dishy blokes in their twenties, captured forever by the click of a camera. All those years ago. You just long to know about them.' She gave a throaty chuckle. 'Lord, even I want to know what happened after that, and they're nothing to do with me!'

Zoe laughed, suddenly feeling better. 'Well, that's the point – I'm hoping to find out!'

When her friend had gone, Zoe lingered for a while, looking at the brothers. Her last trip to York had managed to establish, at long last, the Australian soldier's name. 'Liam,' she softly whispered, and as always, it gave her an absurd rush of pleasure to speak his name.

Two hours after leaving King's Cross, the Intercity 125 was pulling into York. It had been a gloomy morning in London, steadily improving as the train swished northward. York was sunny, with blue skies and cotton-wool clouds, and a strong breeze which caught Zoe's skirts as she stepped down onto the platform.

The exit was on the far side, and from the overhead bridge which spanned the tracks she immediately spotted Joan Elliott's generous form. Beside her was a tall man with light brown hair. Striking rather than handsome, he stood with hands thrust deep into the pockets of a Burberry raincoat.

They were clearly together, so he must be the man she had spoken to on the telephone. Stephen Elliott, old Sarah Elliott's grandson. Descending the steps, she saw he was much younger than she had expected. Somehow, with a generation between them, she had imagined him more her mother's age. Noting the deep tan as she came down the steps, Zoe suddenly remembered that he had said something about working abroad. Perhaps the tan was genuine.

For a moment she was enveloped in Joan Elliott's warm embrace, then he stepped forward, smiling, his handshake dry and firm.

He said he was delighted, while his eyes seemed intent upon registering everything about her. Almost before she knew it, he had relieved her of the overnight bag and was steering both women through the concourse. Had she not been so intent upon his aunt's conversation, Zoe felt that she might have been annoyed.

But all irritation fled as they came out of the station. Directly facing them across a broad and busy thoroughfare, the city walls seemed to be smiling above ramparts covered in daffodils. The sight was so unexpected, and so welcoming, it brought smiles and an involuntary halt. Zoe thought that she had never seen anything so uplifting as that waving mass of cheerful yellow flowers.

'Aren't they *beautiful?*'

'They certainly are,' he agreed. 'Almost worth being away to come back to this.'

Zoe glanced up in surprise. 'Yes, I can imagine. You said you'd been abroad, Mr Elliott,' she reminded him brightly. 'Was it anywhere interesting?'

He chuckled as they moved on. 'Not really. And by the way, the name's Stephen.'

Not a man for conversational gambits, Zoe thought with dismay.

Taking her arm, Joan Elliott told her not to be foiled. 'He does it all the time, you know – lets people think he's a travelling salesman, or some such nonsense, just because it amuses him. He's not,' she declared, shaking a finger at his mischievous grin. 'He's a Master Mariner, and I'm very proud of him.'

'There now, Joan, you've done it again – just spoiled my best line...'

Zoe could not help laughing. 'And what's that?'

'I usually say, in answer to the next question, that I travel in oil and steel – it sounds so much more impressive.'

'Oh, come now, *Captain* Elliott – I'm impressed already!'

Across the gleaming, dark-green bonnet of a Jaguar XJ-S, he smiled at her, a curiously intimate, knowing smile. 'Now it's my turn to be impressed, Miss Clifford – most people have no idea what a Master Mariner does.'

Zoe had once known a girl whose father was at sea, but she did not intend to reveal the source of her information. Let him wonder, she thought, as she sank back against soft leather upholstery. While Joan pointed out various places of interest, Zoe was mentally assessing the man in the driving seat: probably unmarried, an eye for the ladies, and judging by the car, as image-conscious as Philip Dent. But was he? She stole another look at Stephen Elliott, noticed that while the sweater looked new, his old Burberry wore a comfortable patina of age. His hair, she decided, would have benefited from trip to the barber's. She smiled and almost forgave him the car.

He dropped Zoe and his aunt outside the hotel on Gillygate, with an arrangement to meet them by his flat in Bedern.

'He can park his car there,' Joan explained as he drove off. 'It's impossible anywhere else in town, so many streets are blocked to traffic now. I'm glad I don't drive.'

Zoe said she did, but doubted whether her disreputable old car would cope with the journey north, which was why she travelled any distance by train.

She checked in and Mrs Bilton was glad to see her, handing Zoe the usual two keys, and smiling at Joan Elliott's unabashed curiosity.

'So was Granny Louisa born here?' Joan asked Zoe as they went upstairs.

'No, but she and Edward were living here at the time of Letitia's birth. She was the youngest, so I imagine the boys were here too. Robin was your father, wasn't he? Liam was the one who went to Australia?'

'Yes, that's right.' Joan paused, peering out at a network of twigs and branches, and the Minster towers beyond. 'Fancy my father living here, and I never knew. It's strange, Granny Louisa often talked about her cottage at Clementhorpe, but she never mentioned Gillygate...'

There was wistfulness in her eyes and voice, and Zoe thought she was about to say more. But with a glance at her watch, she was suddenly brisk, reminding Zoe that Stephen was waiting to take them to lunch.

Conversation over their meal, Zoe thought later, was rather like a business meeting. With the salient points covered – Stephen's profession, Zoe's work as an illustrator, and Joan's decision to move house – they were beginning to see where each of them stood in relation to each other and the Elliott family.

Over coffee, Stephen introduced the main topic: the birth certificates he had found in that box full of letters. Zoe was at first surprised, and then embarrassed as she read Joan's reaction.

'There was a marriage certificate too,' Stephen said dryly.'They should have matched. A marriage followed by three children, roughly a couple of years apart, that's what you'd expect. But it wasn't like that.They didn't marry until years later…'

'I'd no idea,' Joan confessed to Zoe. Coming so soon after her mother's death, these facts had clearly been a shock to her. It seemed that lies had been told and deceits continued, but by whom and for what reason, she had no idea.

Zoe could see she was upset, and did not know what to say.

Refusing a second cup of coffee, the older woman said that she would leave them. She had the estate agent to see and some shopping to do; and she had no real wish to be present while they probed the mystery of Louisa Elliott's life.

'It's not that I mind you doing that,' she explained gently to Zoe, 'but I couldn't. I'd like to know what was going on – and if I can answer any questions at all, I'll be happy to do so. But I don't want to go through those papers myself. Besides,' she added with a sad smile, 'you seem to know what you're doing – I wouldn't know where to start.'

Watching her retreating back, Zoe was seized with guilt, seeing herself as the harbinger of pain, and wondering what Pandora's box had been opened by those first, innocent enquiries of hers. About to say something fatuous to the man beside her, such as his grandmother Sarah had been right, and she should never have come, she was silenced by the pressure of his hand on her arm.

'Don't say it,' he softly advised, 'and stop feeling guilty – I can see it in your face. I did ask Joan, a day or so before I phoned you, whether she wanted me to go ahead with this.' He paused, seemed suddenly aware that he was touching her, and removed his hand. 'She was so shattered, I didn't think she'd want anyone to know about it – least of all a comparative stranger. But,' he smiled,'in her own way,Joan's as curious now as you are.And she's accepted you as family, which, I may say, is quite a compliment.'

Zoe glanced away, feeling a rush of pleasure and embarrassment warm her cheeks. 'It is indeed, but…'

'But sooner or later, one of us would have gone through that box, and we would have discovered the anomalies anyway. You can't just throw out the remains of someone's life without examining it first. That was Joan's point in giving the paperwork to me. But it's a responsibility,' he added with a sigh, 'and probably why Sarah didn't throw anything away. She can't have gone through those letters – they've been undisturbed, I'm sure, since Louisa put them there.'

On an indrawn breath, Zoe said: 'I just wish I hadn't been the one to force the issue.'

His blue eyes caught the light and creased into a warm smile. 'Don't worry about it.'

He rose to pay the bill, and she studied him unobserved. There was something familiar about his features, but she could not decide what it was. He turned and she glanced away, not wanting to be caught staring.

By comparison with the crush of pedestrians in the heart of town, St Andrewgate was almost deserted, peopled largely by workmen engaged in the process of renovating old property and building new. Zoe's eyes were everywhere, noting the details of windows and brickwork; Stephen had to touch her arm to direct her through a narrow footpath between the houses. It opened into a pretty courtyard, and with some surprise she realized they were back in Bedern, and that he was searching for the keys to his flat.

'It's a strange name, *Bedern* – what does it mean?'

'Oh, there's a plaque over there, by the entrance. *House of Prayer*, I think – from the Anglo-Saxon.'

For the first time she noticed an ancient limestone wall, punctuated by lancet windows. Stephen said it had once been part of the college of the Vicars Choral, laymen attached to the Minster. The rest of the buildings – no more than a collection of medieval houses like those in the Shambles – had disappeared long ago.

'It was handy for the Minster, just across the street, but they were turned out at the Reformation. From what I can gather,' he added with a grin, 'they were no great loss. More a bunch of medieval lager louts – drinking, brawling in the street, upsetting local residents. It seems nothing much changes!'

Warming to him, she chuckled at the image he created, but it was hard to imagine such things within the precincts of this modern development.

'And then there was a ragged school here in the last century.' He paused, looking at the sunlit walls, the pretty little gardens full of spring flowers. 'But it seems the children are still here,' he said whimsically. 'They say you can hear them sometimes, laughing and playing...'

Zoe glanced in surprise. 'Have you heard them?'

With a wry smile he nodded. 'Possibly, just once, coming home late one night. I'd never heard the story, and honestly thought a bunch of kids were messing about – but I walked right round the place and couldn't find them. When I asked the neighbours, I found other people had heard it too – right here, in this courtyard.'

'How strange. York seems to be full of ghosts...'

'So they say. I used to scoff at things like that, now I'm not so sure...'

Beyond the limestone wall with its lancet windows, was a deep archway. When Stephen said the street beyond was Goodramgate, a sudden, sharp memory drew her towards it. She paused in shadow, seeing the other arch leading into Minster Yard. The east end of the cathedral was perhaps a hundred yards distant. She shivered, remembering the mist and those strange images conjured against a shifting wall of light.

As Stephen joined her, she glanced at him, and for a second he seemed taken aback. For a long moment neither of them spoke. As Zoe looked away, he asked her, gently, whether she had been in York the previous autumn, one evening about six, when mist was billowing around the Minster.

It was as though he read her mind. Startled, Zoe nodded. With a smile Stephen explained that he had been watching those freak weather conditions when he noticed her.

'You know, ever since you stepped off that train, I've been trying to think where I'd seen you before. I remember noticing someone standing by the old College. And then you came towards me, and glared at me before you crossed the road…'

'Did I? What an extraordinary memory you must have!'

With a rueful chuckle, he denied it. 'Not at all. It's just that it was my last night at home – I remember the mist, it was a very odd occurrence – and I remember seeing you too. The only extraordinary thing about it is that I have these gaps in my life. I go off to sea – and a few months later I come back. But to me, it's as though those months have never been.' He paused. 'It's an odd sensation.'

She thought it must be, and said so. Grateful for such a prosaic explanation, Zoe felt it answered that nagging feeling she had, that she should know him, too. Obviously, they had seen each other that night, but she retained no conscious memory of it.

They went back to the courtyard. Unlocking his door, Stephen invited her in. At the top of a flight of stairs, several doors opened off the windowed landing. She caught a glimpse of a tidy kitchen before following him into the sitting room; but then, with no more than an impression of books and pictures and modern furniture, Zoe's attention was caught by the view. Tall chimney stacks, pitched roofs of slate and weathered pantiles, mellow bricks and tiny windows, the whole formed a foreground for the magic of the Minster itself. The picture was framed by the window, and she knew without doubt why Stephen Elliott lived here, and she both admired and envied him.

He was watching her face, her reactions. She made no attempt to disguise her pleasure, because he deserved to know that she appreciated it too. Laughing, she said: 'You're a lucky man.'

He chuckled in agreement, telling her to sit down and enjoy the view while he made some coffee. A little while later, sharing the window-seat with the tray between them, Zoe was suddenly aware of feeling relaxed and happy. Stephen Elliott, she decided, was very easy to be with. His questions never seemed to probe, and yet almost without realizing it, she found that they had moved from neutral topics to more personal ones, that she was revealing more of herself than usual, certainly on so short an acquaintance.

Conversation flowed back and forth between them, as though they had known each other for years. He spoke, briefly, about his marriage and divorce. While he did not dwell upon the reasons for its ending, she understood that he must have felt betrayed. It was probably why he had not remarried, despite his evident liking for women. He spoke affectionately of his aunt, and of the wives of close friends, and Zoe could see that his social life was not limited to a few drinking cronies, but encompassed a broad, if scattered field. He was often away for weekends, visiting old friends on leave, and that was why he enjoyed his car. It was an extravagance, he said, but it transported him about the country in comfort, and was such a pleasure to drive. Besides, he admitted with a disarming grin, the Jaguar was something he had always wanted.

What a change from Philip, she thought, glancing around the room as Stephen went to make another drink. Philip's flat was smart to the point of sterility, with a few coffee-table tomes, one enormous picture, three large ornaments, and furniture which was designed for utility rather than comfort. She would be hard-pressed, tomorrow, to recount Stephen's bits and pieces. Books almost filled one wall, a collection of unusual pictures and ornaments was displayed haphazardly, while things like letters, calculator and keys were dotted on various surfaces about the room.

The ashtray, she noticed, was almost full. He smoked too much, but she could understand it; after a year without cigarettes herself, passing cravings could still catch her unawares.

He came back with the coffee in two steaming mugs, all pretensions at gentility, with cups and cream and sugar bowls, had disappeared, for which she was thankful. It was good to know that he felt as relaxed as she did. Outside the light was falling, and between them lay the softness of dusk.

Only as he moved to light one of the lamps did either of them notice the time and then Stephen was all concern at having wasted it, enquiring as to her plans for the evening.

'Well,' she said easily, 'apart from having to be back at the hotel sometime to sleep, I don't have any plans. And after that excellent lunch, I'm not even hungry. Perhaps we could have a look at those papers this evening? That is, if you don't mind?'

'Not a problem,' he assured her. 'There's salad and things in the fridge – if you like, we could share something later?'

On that agreement he went to fetch a thick, decorated album from an open shelf on the bookcase. It was old, the ties and tassels faded, its embossed and gilded cover shabby with use.

'Before we take a look at those certificates, I thought you might like to see a few photographs. Just to show who we're talking about.'

Flicking through the first few pages, he came to a pair of portraits, the first of a young woman with cropped, curly hair, and a rather challenging set to her chin. She had a lovely face, intelligent eyes and a well-shaped, generous mouth. Stephen said that her smile fascinated him. Like the Mona Lisa's, he could not decide whether it was amused, disdainful, uncertain, or downright sexy; although as a man, he preferred to think the latter.

Zoe laughed and shook her head. 'Wishful thinking. She looks proud, to me – and just a shade disdainful. But she does remind me of someone...' Zoe gazed intently for a moment, shading the lower half of the face. 'It's her eyes and the shape of her forehead...'

His mouth twitched with amusement. He glanced quickly at Zoe, and then back at the album. 'Forget what I said about her smile, and ignore the hairstyle – who does she remind you of?'

'I'm not sure – I think it's Letitia...'

'She's like *you*. Oh, not feature for feature,' he amended hastily, 'I don't mean that. But you do have a look of her – at least, I think you do...'

For the first time, Zoe was lost for words. He seemed to regret that impulsive statement and was about to pass on to the next portrait, but she stayed his hand. 'Who is she?'

'Louisa Elliott. My great-grandmother.'

'And my great-great-grandmother,' Zoe mused, trying to sound calm and reflective, to dispel the sudden tension that was between them. 'Well, she was Letitia's mother, and I was supposed to favour her in looks, so maybe that explains it.' She smiled. 'I can't see it, myself, but as you say, resemblance isn't always a matter of matching features.

'But I'm surprised,' Zoe added. 'She looks as though she knew her own mind – she's not a bit the simpering victim I imagined.'

Amused by her use of the word, he said: 'Why *victim*?'

'Well, it was just my interpretation of the facts – or what seemed to be the facts. Although it seems I was wrong on both counts.' Indicating the other portrait, that of a youngish, bearded man in a frock coat, she enquired who he was.

'That's Edward Elliott, Louisa's husband. It seems he was also her cousin, and I'd say it was taken some years before they married. By my calculations she was thirty-two when they tied the knot, and he must have been forty-four.'

'*As old as that*? But – '

'Yes I know. The reason you couldn't find any record of their marriage, is that you didn't look far enough. That's the certificate I was telling you about earlier – they didn't marry until 1899.'

'But what about the children?'

'Good question,' he observed dryly. 'Hang on to it for a minute, will you, and take a look at these.'

Stephen produced two more photographs, ones he had found inserted, loose, between the pages. One was an informal group photograph, taken in a garden; the other, which he now laid before Zoe, was a seated portrait of a man in military dress uniform. By its style and insignia, he was an officer, possibly in his thirties. He was well-built, and long legs gave an impression of height; he had a moustache, crisp black hair and a strong-featured face. On the back of the stiff card mount, was the photographer's name and Dublin address. Turning it over again, looking at that slightly arrogant smile, Zoe experienced an irrational feeling of disquiet.

'And who, pray, is he?'

Stephen pursed his lips. 'Well, I can't prove it, but I'm almost sure his name was Robert Duncannon.'

Zoe bit her lip. 'Witness at Letitia's wedding.'

'The writer of many letters.'

'A rich, close relative?' She looked to Stephen for the answer. 'Or something else?'

He raised a single, quizzical eyebrow. 'You tell me.'

FIVE

Music was playing softly, and the dining table was covered with papers and photographs. Stephen leaned back and stretched, aware of tender amusement as he surveyed Zoe's bent head, the intent expression on her face. Her skin made him think of Ireland and misty mornings, and it was impossible not to smile as he imagined its softness against his lips.

They had been working together for hours, and he was beginning to wonder whether she would go on all night, following every little item like clues in a treasure hunt. The handful of letters they had looked at raised more questions than they answered, generating curiosity and enthusiasm, provoking reactions that had already revealed more of their true selves than weeks of normal acquaintance might have done.

He liked her. Tremendously. No edge, no affectations, no artifice. Despite the perfect vowels and privileged background, she was no spoiled brat. And she was sharp and funny and oddly vulnerable, and – oh, be honest, Elliott, his practical self said, you want to go to bed with her, you know you do, you fancied her from the minute you first laid eyes on her...

She looked up, clear grey eyes wide and questioning, as though his thoughts had somehow reached her, changed the atmosphere between them. As perhaps they had. He did not look away and nor did she; he saw her expression change with a quick rush of blood to her cheeks. Awareness crackled between them like a sustained electric charge.

The letter she held trembled. She bowed her head and a fall of dark curls hid that sudden warmth, but did not obscure the sharp rise and fall of her breasts.

Breathless, tense with desire, Stephen forced himself to his feet. 'I'll make some coffee,' he said, but could not resist touching her, very lightly, as he passed.

Leaning forwards against the sink, he took a long, deep breath and released it very slowly. Within moments he was once more in control, although his blood was still running hot, eager, after months of enforced abstinence, to grab at this prime opportunity. Which would not only be a mistake, he told his reflection in the glass, but a breach of good manners. Calm down, he ordered silently, take her back to the hotel, give her time; even if she leaves York tomorrow, she'll be back, you know she will...

And anyway, he told himself as he returned with the coffee, it was always possible to suggest a meeting in London.

Before she could remark on the time, he said easily: 'It's late, Zoe – and you must be tired. Why don't we have this coffee and call it a day? I'll walk you back to Gillygate, and we can begin again tomorrow.'

She was instantly contrite. 'Oh, I'm sorry, I've kept you – I wasn't thinking.'

'Not at all.' With what he hoped was a disarming smile, Stephen took her hand and briefly squeezed it. 'I'm a night owl – always have been. It's you I'm thinking of – all that decorating you were telling me about. It's a wonder you're not on your knees.'

There was gratitude in her response and something of understanding. With confidence restored, it was easier, a few minutes later, to fetch her coat and make arrangements for the following day.

His hands lingered for a moment beneath her hair; then, as she turned to face him, traced the line of her jaw. She thought, for one breathtaking moment, that he was about to kiss her.

But all he said was, 'I'm so glad we've met,' before opening the door.

It was no more than a few steps to the place of that first, brief sighting. Through Bedern, beneath its dark archway, across Goodramgate, to the arch which led into Minster Yard. Sheltered from a searching night wind, they paused beneath the upper storey of a quaint half-house. Once, as Stephen said, it had been part of a long row, but since the demolition of its neighbours to one side, it stood somewhat redundant, with a new, wide access beside it.

There was an old photograph of that part of Goodramgate, framed, on Stephen's sitting-room wall; even so, Zoe found it hard to reconcile image and reality. She turned her eyes to the Minster, its floodlit tracery framed by the night and the trees and the long, low building of St William's College. There was no mist, nothing was moving, and apart from the faint sounds of revelry coming from a nearby public house, all was silent.

Sharing her memory of that night, he said again that he remembered seeing her as she hurried towards the mist; then she had halted, standing so still, so entranced, that he had been intrigued. 'Then you turned suddenly, and came towards me. I didn't want to be caught, like some sinister peeping Tom, so I moved out of the shadows here, and pretended to be waiting to cross the road.'

She chuckled, squeezing his hand. 'I didn't see you...'

'No, you didn't. Your mind was on something else. Tell me,' he added, searching her face intently, 'what was it that unnerved you?'

Startled by his perception, Zoe shook her head, looked away. 'I'm not sure.' For a moment she hesitated. 'It's hard to explain. Something – I don't know what it was – in the mist. Like your children in Bedern, except I didn't hear anything, it was more...' Her voice tailed away. The more she sought for words to describe it, the more they eluded her. And although she wanted him to understand, she was afraid he would think her mad. 'I can't explain,' she said finally, glancing up with mute appeal. 'Perhaps I might try, when I know you a little better...'

'I hope so,' he whispered; and in that least expected moment, Stephen bent his head and kissed her. It was very tender, very brief, but in that moment she felt she needed his strength, his solidity. Involuntarily, she clung to him, burying her face against the lapels of his coat. For a little while he held her very close, sheltering her between himself and the old oak timbers of the little arch. When his lips met hers again they were warm and sensual, seeking her response but not demanding it, until the touch of his tongue set her senses aflame, obliterating everything in a dizzying surge of emotion. Passion flared then, and she was aware of his hunger and her own desire to satisfy it. It was like a physical shock when he detached himself, standing back to grip her hands with painful force.

'I'm sorry,' he whispered, 'this won't do, will it?'

Still breathing raggedly, he cupped her face between trembling fingers and kissed her forehead. With grim determination he led her on through Minster Yard.

She had difficulty keeping up with his long, rapid strides, but he swept on, regardless. In a state of shock, Zoe hardly knew what to make of him, still less so when he stopped before the south transept, and said tersely: 'If you decide to stay another night, will you stay with me?'

She faltered at his abruptness, and could not immediately reply. Images of the recent past – fleeting but clear – flashed through her mind. Philip and his inexperience, the innate prudery which had left her wondering, ultimately, whether he really liked or approved of women. By contrast, Stephen's masculinity was reassuring. Almost without thinking, she nodded gravely. 'Yes, Stephen, I will.'

A smile twitched the corner of his mouth. 'Good,' he murmured, slipping an arm around her shoulders. 'On a promise like that, I might just get some sleep tonight...'

But he did not sleep well. The stimulation of mind and body left him restless, his thoughts a jumble of Zoe the desirable woman, and Zoe his blood relation, descendant, as he was, of all those other Elliotts. Leaving her at the door of that house on Gillygate had given him the oddest feeling, as though he knew the place, and all this had happened before.

Déjà vu, of course, as common as it was inexplicable, yet disturbing enough to set his mind running over the evening's facts and suppositions, and the mass of detail still contained in that little trunk. As much as Zoe, he wanted now to discover the truth behind those birth certificates.

Waking early, with chores done and those old letters gathered together in their original order, he went to call for her just before ten. As Zoe paid her bill, he glanced into the guests' sitting room with interest, an interest which prompted Mrs Bilton to ask whether he would like to look at the rest of the house, as his cousin had already done.

Agreeing, Stephen found it an extraordinary experience. His

own people had lived here for more than twenty years, and, climbing the stairs to those elegant rooms on the first floor, he felt as he had when opening those boxes for the very first time: that here the past was a little too close, touching strange emotions and responses. Having thought of himself as a modern man, shaped by circumstance and environment into solitary independence, it was hard to come to terms with this new awareness, this feeling that he might be no more than a link in a very long chain.

And that chain had unexpectedly coiled back on itself, bringing him face to face with earlier Elliotts, people who shared the same name and the same genes, whose lives had been shaped in this house, this city; whose eyes had looked out on streets not immeasurably different from the ones he saw today. More personal, more immediate, was the awareness that at the crossing of the chain stood Zoe Clifford, a woman as much a part of the Elliotts as he was himself. The progression of that thought was daunting. So much so that he was glad to abandon it, sighing with relief as they said their goodbyes to Mrs Bilton and stepped out into the brisk morning.

'What did you think?' Zoe demanded as they rounded the corner into Lord Mayor's Walk. All along the moat, beneath the high walls, daffodils were dancing in the stiff breeze, echoing her own lively spirits.

'It was certainly interesting,' he said cautiously. 'Before you told me, I'd no idea they were in the hotel business.'

'But how did you *feel*,' she pressed, 'being there?'

On a short laugh, Stephen squeezed her hand. 'Later,' he said, 'when I know you better.'

Her eager smile turned into a grimace. 'Oh, dear – bad as that?'

'No, not bad, more – disturbing, I think. Difficult to explain.'

With a sideways glance, Zoe sought to reassure him. 'It's all right – I understand.'

Back at the flat, he was all practicality, setting bundles of letters on the table, together with notepads and pens. The albums were set out too, each with a sheet of paper inside the flyleaf, giving the approximate dates. Although the letters had been grouped by Louisa Elliott into years and correspondents, it was important,

Stephen said, to be organized themselves, otherwise vital points could easily be overlooked. And surely, now that they had a fair idea of the family's circumstances while they were living in Gillygate, it might be as well to turn to the earlier letters first, instead of reading haphazardly as bundles came to hand.

Listening, agreeing with every word, it struck Zoe that for a man who only yesterday had confessed his reluctance to invade someone else's past, Stephen Elliott was being very efficient. Aware of her limited time in York, did his desire to help conflict with other, more personal needs? Remembering last night, she thought it must, but he was making such a concerted effort to give her a firm base for further enquiry, she had not the heart to distract him.

Nevertheless, with Stephen working in the other room, it was hard to concentrate. As it had last night, she found her mind going back over that intense moment of physical awareness. Warmth and liking had blossomed almost from the first, and had it been no more than that, Zoe would have been immensely grateful for this meeting with someone who shared not just her ancestry, but humour, outlook, and even certain reservations. He said he knew nothing about art, but he was interested in photography, so understood more than he claimed; and he was extremely well-read. What touched her most of all was his unprompted confession, that he too had always felt an odd one out.

To his immediate family, Stephen's boyhood passion for ships and the sea had seemed an aberration; and his desire to travel the world for a living was viewed with a mixture of indulgence and mild disapproval. 'My sister,' he had said, 'still treats me like an elderly Jim Hawkins – as though she's constantly wondering when I'm going to get a proper job and settle down.' Although he seemed to be amused, Zoe had sensed an underlying resentment. She knew it well, having experienced much the same with regard to her own chosen career. And not just from Marian.

But the sexual attraction had been something of a shock. She was glad the moment had not been pursued, that he had tried to give her time. Even so, recognizing his impatience, feeling its echo in herself, Zoe was still faintly aghast at her own reactions. In the past, such things had been very much a matter of time, and never, ever, had she fallen into bed with a man on the very first date; yet last night she had been more than willing. That kiss had shaken her, both physically and emotionally, exciting her in ways she could not recall since – well, since Kit. She had been in love with Kit, but never since. Fond of one or two, certainly – but not head over heels in love.

It was a little daunting to feel that it was happening again. But it was too late to back out, and besides, she wanted him. With an effort, Zoe forced her mind away from Stephen, and back to Louisa Elliott's letters.

Deciphering the idiosyncrasies of other people's handwriting was slow work, but after an hour of establishing names and dates, Zoe had deduced that in the move from Gillygate in the late 1890s, Louisa must have destroyed much previous correspondence. It was frustrating, because by that time the children were already born, and there seemed to be no reference to their parentage. The earliest letters were postmarked Dublin in the spring of 1899, all from someone called Letty, who seemed to be a friend of some standing. From her correspondence, which was full of gardening advice, Zoe deduced that the two women had shared a common passion, and that Louisa was at that time setting up her kitchen garden. Letty had apparently visited them, with a child called Georgina, because later missives referred to Louisa's cottage and its delightful setting by the riverside.

Could that cottage have been the one in that group photograph? Zoe wondered. Needing Stephen's opinion, she crossed the landing to the sunny room where he was sorting books from the larger trunk. Intent upon something, unaware of her presence, he was crouched with his back to her, sweater discarded, shirtsleeves rolled back over tanned and muscular forearms. Shadow made a deep indentation of his spine, a long, pleasing curve from shoulders to haunches, which the artist longed to record and the woman to touch. Something, perhaps the intensity of her gaze, made him turn.

Poised there, regarding her steadily, for a long moment Stephen did not move. When he did it was slowly, in one smooth movement, the little book which had taken his attention still in his hand. She felt its cover cold against her neck as he kissed her, and the kiss was quick and hard with suppressed desire, his breath coming short as he crushed her against him.

Lying in bed with him afterwards, warm with love and satisfaction, Zoe was beyond speech. They had come together so quickly, it made her heart race to think of it. Wanting to recapture something of that first touch, she ran a hand over his chest and the flatness of his stomach, seeing, through half-closed lids, the perfect lines of his body. After years spent working under a southern sun, he was lean and hard and bronzed, and beside him she felt soft and deliciously fragile.

Unprepared for the depth and range of her own responses, Zoe was also astonished by his. She had wondered, last night, whether a man so absolutely in control of himself would make love as though painting by numbers. That he had not only relinquished that iron control, but made love with such unselfconscious abandon, was something that brought a smile to her lips. And when he felt that little curve of happiness and drew back to look at her, she saw the same delight in his eyes. Wonderment, too. He looked at her for some time before he spoke.

'I do believe,' he sighed, 'that for the first time in my entire life, I've been granted a reward for good behaviour.' Enveloping her in a warm bear-hug, he chuckled softly and kissed her. 'And at the risk of sounding like a philanderer, I have to tell you that this is the point where I'm usually apologizing and promising to do better next time!

'But on this occasion,' he whispered against her mouth, 'I really do have the feeling that there's no need to apologize at all...'

A little bubble of laughter escaped her, but as she gave herself up to his embrace, Zoe was thankful that he had not enquired as to her period of abstinence. But that had been a depressing encounter, and she would not think of it now...

It was some time later that he felt for his shirt and the cigarettes which lived in his breast pocket. He smoked in silence, caressing her gently as he might have done a child. Zoe felt oddly separated then, as though his thoughts had abandoned her. Hesitantly, she ventured to ask what he was thinking, and was not entirely reassured by the wry smile her question prompted.

'A great many things,' Stephen said softly, 'mostly concerned with you.'

'What things?'

'I should have thought it was obvious. In twenty-four hours, this little research project of yours has developed along lines neither of us could have envisaged.' There was a long pause, and then he said: 'But tomorrow, you're going back to London.'

The statement hung between them ominously, a cloud heralding responsibility and separation, which should perhaps have been taken into account; yet all had fled before that urgent physical need, and Zoe could not regret its satisfaction. Tracing the line of her cheek, he ran a finger beneath her chin, making her look at him. The conflict she felt was mirrored in his eyes.

'I don't want you to go.'

'But I shall have to. Sooner or later, if not tomorrow. My work's there.' For the first time she half regretted it. The work she had loved and striven to do, which had been all in all until a moment ago, was suddenly something she wanted to lay aside, if only temporarily. There had to be a way of resolving the problem; but it would take time and thought and planning.

'Don't ask me to think about it now,' she begged, laying her lips against his shoulder, his cheek, his mouth. 'I'll try to work something out, even if I have to go back to London to do it.'

'But you'll come back?'

'Of course,' she promised with a suddenly wicked grin. 'I haven't got through those letters yet!' She gave a little yelp as Stephen pinched her, rolled over and saw the time in red digital numbers on his bedside alarm. It was nearly one o'clock. 'What time did you say your aunt was coming over?'

'After lunch.'

'Then I think we'd better get dressed…'

With a muttered exclamation, he agreed with her. 'Joan's a broad-minded lady, but I don't think she'd appreciate finding us like this!'

Fully clothed, with her hair brushed and fresh make-up enhancing eyes that were perhaps too revealing, Zoe returned to the bedroom to pick up her watch. On the bedside chest was the little book Stephen had been holding before they undressed.

Bound in scuffed black leather, it had the initials W.E. embossed in gold on the front cover. Curious, Zoe picked it up. It was a diary, dated 1916, each page closely written in tiny, copperplate script. The owner, she saw at last, had been one William Elliott, serving with a machine-gun company of the Australian Imperial Force...

William Elliott – Liam. *Liam*! His name ran through her like a shock, bringing startling flashes of memory: his face on a dozen photographs, that strange vision in the fog...

Stephen's voice called to her as she sank weakly onto the bed. A moment later he appeared in the doorway, smiling, saying they had better eat before Joan arrived, and what would she like for lunch?

She looked up, seeing him as though for the very first time, knowing that smile, those eyes, recognizing the familiarity which had hovered on the edge of memory for the past twenty-four hours. In eyes, mouth, and shape of face, Stephen was so very like Liam Elliott. A modern man, older in years than the young soldier had been, but with two generations between them, the resemblance was still there. Was that what had attracted her to him? The possibility passed over her like an icy wave.

Alarmed by her expression and that sudden, violent shiver, Stephen went to her immediately, touching her cold face, kissing it, chaffing her hands. She was like someone in a trance. Then, abruptly, she pulled away from him.

He saw the diary and picked it up. As she rose and moved away, he said hesitantly: 'I found this in the bottom of the small trunk...' Stephen broke off, wondering how to describe that odd sensation. He supposed excitement must have caused that physical tingling, like a series of small shocks spreading up from his fingertips.

And then he had turned and seen Zoe.

Just remembering that moment, the look on her face, the feel of her as they embraced, was enough to make him want her again. Releasing a long, pent-up breath, he went to her and made her face him.

'Did I do something wrong? Did I hurt you?' She shook her head, but kept her eyes averted. Stephen held her close, nuzzling her hair, stroking the silky curls, touching his lips to her temple. 'Then tell me what it is.'

She stiffened for a moment, then relaxed, burying her face in his neck in a negative, bemused sort of way. 'I don't know – I think I'm going mad.'

It was so ridiculous, he almost laughed. 'Don't be silly, why should you think that?'

'The queerest things keep happening – I don't know how to explain them, or even where to start. Just now, I suppose it was that diary, realizing whose it was – it gave me a shock. And then, seeing you…' Her voice faltered, became even more muffled, so that he had to strain to hear the rest, something about the Minster and that evening in the fog…

The doorbell rang shrilly. On a low expletive Stephen gripped her shoulders, asked whether he should make some excuse, put off Joan's visit until later.

'No – no, I'm all right,' Zoe said, straightening her shoulders and pushing back her hair. 'We'll talk later.'

'We *must*,' he insisted.

Joan's visit prompted discussion of births and deaths, intricate family relationships and house moves, past and present. She was in better spirits, having come to terms with the job they were doing, and although none of their suspicions could yet be confirmed, her attitude was one of rueful acceptance. Having had time to mull over the anomaly of her father's birth certificate, various other things had apparently sprung to mind, like odd bits of jigsaw which suddenly slipped into place with ease. Those revelations prompted more questions, until the afternoon slipped away, and Zoe's moment of disturbance seemed very much a thing of the past.

Fascinated by the older woman, at ease with her, Zoe was amused by the conspiratorial smile she gave Stephen as she was leaving.

'I told you you'd like her, didn't I?' was uttered in a stage whisper, which left both Zoe and Stephen laughing and slightly embarrassed.

Afterwards, when she had gone, Zoe said: 'I feel as though I've been adopted – as though I really am family, instead of a total stranger…'

'But you are family, and she likes you,' Stephen said simply. 'So do I.'

But as though his aunt's warmth reminded him by contrast of other, less generous family members, he went on to warn her about his sister. 'If you ever meet Pam – and you may, she has a habit of dropping in when she's in town – you must expect a very thorough going-over. She'll disapprove on principle, I'm afraid, whether she likes you or not. My ex-wife was – and is – her best friend. It doesn't seem to matter that I was the injured party – according to Pamela, it was all my fault in the first place for not buckling under, staying at home and taking a shore job...' He sighed. 'For all she's my sister, we have very little in common.'

'Have you never considered working ashore? Seriously, I mean?'

'I didn't in those days. Now, I think of it more and more. But,' he shrugged, 'I'm faced with the eternal problem of what does Jolly Jack *do*, once he swallows the anchor? Short of marine surveying, which would bore me to tears, I can't think of a thing.'

'You could always write your memoirs,' she said wickedly, 'I'm sure they'd be fascinating!' Warming to the idea as he laughed and shook his head, she added: 'And what about Joseph Conrad? He wrote some wonderful novels, didn't he?'

'Be careful, my love – you're treading on my heart!' And with that he fetched her coat and told her they were going out.

He took her to a small restaurant down one of York's quainter back streets. Over drinks, Stephen's avoidance of the subject begun before Joan Elliott's arrival was, she felt, deliberate. As he regaled her with stories of his early life at sea, characters he had known, places he had visited, she forgot that unnerving moment in laughter; and the likeness which had seemed so uncanny, receded. He was himself, no other. Warm, vital, alive, and with eyes that told her she was beautiful and very much desired. Face to face, looking into those eyes, so blue against the gold of his skin, Zoe knew that it was Stephen she wanted, would have wanted, whatever his name, whatever his ancestry. The rest was just coincidence. In that context she felt she could deal with it and, when the time came, talk about it with some degree of detachment.

It was dark when they left, but not very late, the city quiet and left to itself in mid-week solitude. York was a different place at night,

Zoe sensed it immediately, as though unrestricted by the crush of visitors, the city was breathing in satisfied calm. Old streetlamps cast gentle light on older buildings, which in their age and lack of vanity were immensely reassuring. Like old eyes, the windows dozed, having seen everything before. This city, she felt, could be neither shocked nor surprised, and current interest in all things past was simply another phase in a long and ongoing history.

Traversing a series of ancient alleys on their walk through town towards the riverside, Zoe was aware of feet which had trodden these paths before. She found herself wondering, at every turn, whether those other Elliotts had walked this way, seen that beautifully-turned corner, noticed a church's perfect tower. And the river itself, reflecting lights, bridges, staiths: it was a view that could have changed little in the intervening years.

Saying nothing, Stephen simply drew her closer. She knew he felt as she did; knew too, that even without their shared ancestry, he would have understood her growing affinity for this place. With some reluctance and on a promise to return, they moved away.

Walking back up Stonegate, with the great central tower of the Minster illuminated above the chimney-stacks, Stephen pointed to a ship's figurehead supporting a jutting upper storey; and a little further, paused to show her Coffee Yard, where Edward Elliott had once been in business as a bookbinder. Innocently said, it was a reminder of the return address in Liam's diary; the quietness of separate thoughts descended in that short journey home to Stephen's flat.

Stephen poured a drink for them both and lit the fire; found the tape of an old and very English film-score by Richard Rodney Bennett and slipped that into the stereo. For a moment he stood watching Zoe, framed against the window. The haunting, plaintive melody echoed something inside him, a tenderness for her that was impossible to put into words. Almost hesitantly, he placed his hands on her shoulders, laid his cheek against her hair; beyond them both, standing dramatically against the night sky, was the floodlit Minster.

With Liam still on his mind, Stephen wondered what she was thinking, and whether she really wanted to tell him what the connection was between the diary and that night in the mist. Her very quietness seemed a prelude, as though she was trying to marshal thoughts and words for something evanescent. Then, as though it was vital to explain all that had happened to her that evening, she began by describing her walk and the sky's intense, remarkable blue. Her voice was low and clear, a lyrical counterpoint to the music. But as the melody strengthened, building up to a storm, her words became shorter, sharper, describing that battlefield in the mist with staccato clarity.

He almost wished she had not told him. The strangeness of it chilled him. He remembered the shock of touching the cover, reading random pages of Liam's meticulous script, written amidst the mud and horror of the Western Front. And he recalled with acute intensity that sense he had had, of holding someone else's life in his hands.

He drew Zoe closer, breathing in the scent of her hair and skin; and then, so strongly that he almost uttered the words, he wanted to tell her that he loved her. Overcome by the unexpected power of those words, he struggled for mastery, telling himself that love was the last thing he wanted to feel. Love meant involvement on a total scale, the pain of parting, the dread of betrayal; love meant anguish, jealousy, and the heart-chilling certainty that it was a word of variable meaning.

It passed. The words left him. Shaken, he buried his face against her hair, looked out at the floodlit pinnacles above the silhouette of Goodramgate, and told himself not to be a fool. He wanted her companionship, yes; and the pleasure her body offered was enticing; but the rest he was willing to forgo.

She turned, clinging for a moment before drawing back to search his eyes; he did not look away, but on a slow release of breath, said: 'Come to bed now – I need you.'

With that first, feverish disrobing in both their minds, they undressed each other slowly. Lingering over the fragrance of her skin, his hands tenderly explored every curve and hollow, lips teasing, reaching down to the fullness of her breasts and the soft, rounded curve of her abdomen. He wanted to appreciate her, to take his time, despite urgent need, to please them both to the full. And she knew his intent, he could see it in her eyes, in the parting of a smile; feel it in her touch. Desire and acquiescence, and a constant, flickering excitement which found its echo in himself.

They embraced and held apart, touched lightly and gripped with passion; explored each other fully until it was impossible to hold back. With urgent satisfaction they came together; and thrusting deep into the soft moist heart of her, he rolled, bringing her over until she was astride him, and he could feast his eyes on the sight of her. Winter-pale skin, almost translucent in the lamp's glow, and rosy-pink buds of breasts shadowed in a dark fall of curls as she shook her head. He touched her gently, reverently, entranced by the different textures of hair and skin, by his own bronzed hands against her breasts; and then she smiled and began to move against him, and all else was forgotten in that deep, seductive, obliterating rhythm.

It was as astonishing as the first time. Better, he decided; and finding unexpected reserves in himself, Stephen took her again, this time pushing every response to the limit. Only afterwards, as she lay exhausted against him, did he wonder why. What was he trying to prove? That she was bloody good in bed, or that he was better than all the other men she must have slept with? Or was it simply that he was trying to eradicate, with sex, the powerful emotions she aroused?

If any of that was true, he thought painfully, then it would appear to be something of a pointless exercise. Caressing the smoothness of her back, listening to the gentle sighs of her breathing, it seemed to Stephen that each encounter drew them closer together. She was exciting and beautiful and generous, and he wanted all that she could give. A moment later he found himself considering what the cost might be to her.

It was probably as well, he reflected sadly, that she would soon be on her way back to her life in London. Once she had gone, perhaps it might be better not to encourage too speedy a return.

It was one thing to reach that decision in the dark hours of the night, quite another to implement it. Although Zoe stayed another day, when it came to the point, Stephen could hardly bear to see her go. At the very last moment, with laughter and kisses and the knowledge that they were both acting crazily, he stuffed a few things in an overnight bag while she grabbed bundles of letters and photographs, and they set off for London in the Jaguar.

An atmosphere of truancy pervaded that journey; they laughed a lot and played rock music very loud, arriving at Zoe's flat just as dusk was falling. The air, as she opened the door, was pungent with new paint, and, apologizing for it, she rushed across to raise the tall sash windows and disperse the smell. Books were stacked all over the floor, ornaments and photographs on a long white table, while a draughtsman's drawing board rose at an angle beside it. Obsessed by the chaos, for a few minutes she dashed about, beginning one task and then another. Stephen caught hold of her, told her to pour them both a drink, and then he would help her to straighten things out.

But with the drink only half consumed, she remembered Polly. 'I must go and tell her I'm back – she's been keeping an eye on things for me, and she must be wondering why I was away so long...'

She dashed off, leaving Stephen bemused. Where she had begun to replace books on shelves, he thought he would continue, trusting that the stacks corresponded with certain places. If he was wrong, he reflected, then Zoe would have to re-organize them; but in the meantime, they would be off the floor. Intrigued by her taste in literature, and enjoying the task, he was startled by the asthmatic buzzing of the doorbell. For a moment he wondered what it was. Having established its source, he was then faced with operating the ancient intercom.

'Yes?'

A woman's voice answered. 'Philip? Is that you?'

'No. This is Zoe Clifford's flat.'

'Well, yes, I know it is.' There was an anxious pause. 'Is she there?'

It seemed odd to Stephen to be conducting a conversation like this, so he explained Zoe's momentary absence and invited the woman in. Wondering who Philip might be, he pressed what he hoped was the door-release button, left the door to the flat open, and returned to the books.

He felt rather than heard Zoe's visitor enter, and turned to see a young woman whose bold, fashionable appearance sat oddly with the look of uncertainty in her eyes.

'Why don't you sit down? She shouldn't be long. I'm Stephen

Elliott, by the way – Zoe's cousin.'

'Oh. Thank you.' Her glance flickered over him and away before wandering nervously back again. 'I'm Clare,' she said, 'an old friend of Zoe's.' There was another pause in which Stephen read suspicion, thought processes casting back for any mention of male cousins.

Sensing the unspoken demand as to why he was there, he continued placing books on shelves.

'I've been trying to get hold of her for days.' It was almost an accusation.

'She's been in York.'

'Oh. York... ?'

'Chasing up some family history. I've been helping her.'

'Oh, I see...' And with a quick glance, Stephen saw that she did, that the topic suddenly answered many questions and opened a slot into which he might fit. Suspicion was replaced by hostility.

Seconds later, he heard Zoe's voice, light with laughter as she called her thanks to Polly. He wanted to warn her, although he could not have said why. Seeing her change of expression as she came in, he wished he had been able to.

Greetings between the two women were cool, despite Clare's explanations and the halting apology for some row they had evidently had over the telephone. Embarrassed, Stephen asked whether he should disappear for an hour.

'No – no, Stephen, there's no need for that.' But Zoe was embarrassed too, torn between different loyalties.

'In that case, perhaps I should make us all a cup of coffee?' And with that he escaped to the kitchen, leaving the women to settle their differences alone. Although he closed the door firmly, it connected with the sitting room, and he could still hear what was being said. He ran the cold tap, clattered a few items of crockery, turned the gas up full, and lit a cigarette, but in his mind's eye he could see Zoe's face, closed and still, feel her restraint in the pauses. Whatever the other woman had done, it had managed to upset Zoe mightily, and she was not ready to forgive, that much was clear. It seemed to him that she was accepting the apologies in order to get rid of Clare.

But Clare was bent upon confession, admitting to certain problems with someone called David and begging Zoe's understanding. Zoe seemed ready to go along with that, even to the extent of suggesting another meeting so that she and Clare could talk things over. That was agreed, and the voices faded a little as they moved into the lobby; then he heard Clare say something about Philip. Clare felt sorry for him, she said, and still felt Zoe had behaved badly; she supposed it was because of this new man, and thought she might at least have been a little more honest, instead of blaming David for everything...

Zoe's voice faded to a murmur, as though they had stepped out onto the landing. It was frustrating: he would have liked to hear her reply to that. If the demise of this man Philip was as recent as it seemed, he wondered whether Zoe would feel able to admit that she and Stephen had only just met.

Initially, he was not unduly concerned, although as the minutes ticked by he did begin to wonder why she had omitted to mention it. Had it been some months past, he could have understood, but something so recent?

He shrugged, told himself that he preferred not to know. He had told her, briefly, about Ruth, and she had told him, with equal brevity, about the married man she had met at college, some mad artist with a passion for women and booze. A fiasco, apparently, but it had been important. And with a similar time-span between those relationships, they were relegated to their proper place. It struck him that just as he would never think of giving her a list of his previous affairs, so he would not want a list of hers. But still...

Who the hell was this Philip, anyway?

Zoe came running up the stairs, upset and apologetic. Waiting for her to calm down, he handed her a cup of cooling coffee and lit another cigarette.

'I suppose you heard most of that?'

'I did, yes. Hard not to.'

'And I suppose,' she went on heavily, 'you must be wondering what on earth it was all about?'

With a dry smile, he nodded. 'But only if you want to tell me – don't feel you have to.'

That she did feel he merited an explanation was something of a mixed blessing. Stephen discovered far more about her relationship with Clare – and by association, her fiance, David – than he did about Philip. From what she did say, he thought the man sounded spineless, but he refused to comment. Or to probe. She was young yet, and women were often attracted to the oddest of men. Whether she had slept with Philip, whether there had been emotional involvement, was something he preferred not to know. She told him it had been over even before he spoke to her on the telephone. And he believed her. Nevertheless, it bothered him.

In truth, Zoe was ashamed. She would have given almost anything for Stephen not to have witnessed the scene between herself and Clare. It was so hard to explain old ties, harder still when any sympathy she might have felt had disappeared in the face of Clare's blatant tactlessness. In retrospect, of course, she did feel sorry for Clare, and was more convinced than ever that her engagement to David was a mistake. But it was impossible to say so. The most she could do was to stay in touch occasionally, and hope against hope that Clare saw the pitfalls for herself.

But because of the connection with Philip, Zoe did not feel able to explain her suspicions to Stephen. To say, yes, I slept with Philip, but he was pretty hopeless in bed, and to be honest, I think the person he really fancies is David, except he's not aware of it, was too crass. What would he think of her? She thought pretty badly of herself. Could not imagine how blind she had been, not to see what appeared so obvious now. But if her suspicions were correct – and there was no way of proving them – then he was more to be pitied than judged. What a situation! For long enough, Zoe had thought it was simply lack of confidence. She had tried to wean him away from the abominable David. But that, it would seem, was the last thing he wanted.

She was appalled by her own arrogance. And her mother would never understand: Marian had liked Philip, knew his family in Sussex. But Stephen was a different matter altogether. Zoe felt that she had behaved both badly and stupidly, and somehow damaged her standing in Stephen's eyes. Oh, if only Clare had stayed away, or telephoned, then they could have met privately, and saved all this fuss.

Awake in the small hours, with Stephen asleep beside her, she castigated herself more severely than ever he would have thought to do. She prayed with anxious fervency that this incident would cast no further shadows. Her mood this evening had been abstracted enough to concern him, and while he asked no questions, she knew he was wondering.

Zoe's answer to anxiety had always been work. Needing a similar distraction now, she slipped out of bed and lit the lamps in the sitting room. With a hot drink and a bundle of Louisa Elliott's letters, she settled down to read. As ever, more questions were raised than were answered, but she jotted them down in a notebook, occasionally breaking to look at photographs, particularly those of Liam. Having now seen pictures of Stephen as a young man, she was more than ever struck by the likeness between them; but her studiously casual comment the other day had caused no apparent surprise. Almost nonchalantly, he said his grandmother, Sarah, who had known Liam as a boy, had often remarked on it. But Zoe thought that light response as careful as her own. Stephen's interest in Liam's diary was now as great as her obsession with the letters.

Amongst Louisa's photographs was a head and shoulders portrait of a young nurse, probably taken during the First World War. Although her hair was mostly covered by a winged white headdress, Zoe was convinced she was the young woman who also appeared in the group photograph, taken perhaps a year or so earlier. From the later correspondence, Zoe had deduced that she must be Georgina, Robert Duncannon's daughter.

And Robert Duncannon was now identified positively as the young officer photographed in Dublin before the turn of the century; almost certainly he was also the man at the centre of that much later family group. In a dark civilian suit he was older, greyer, heavier, but the strong lines of nose and brow and jaw were unmistakable. Relaxing on a garden seat, smiling at the camera, he dominated the picture as he had probably dominated the people in his life.

To one side of him sat Louisa, her expression sweeter, softened by life and experience into kindliness; and on her other side was Edward, less relaxed, frowning against the light. He had been more difficult to identify, having abandoned the beard of earlier portraits. For all the passing years, he was still remarkably handsome, his features fine, the mouth gentle. In his younger days, Joan had said, Edward was something of a poet; an image which suited him better, Zoe felt, than that of a bookbinder with a business of his own.

Before them on the grass was a girl in white, a girl with rounded cheeks and slanting, dark-fringed eyes. Zoe's own photograph of Letitia showed a sophisticated young woman in her twenties, but there was no mistaking those eyes, nor the thick, unruly hair that Zoe herself had inherited.

On Robert Duncannon's right, sat the young woman now identified as his daughter, Georgina. She sat straight-backed, hands folded neatly into her lap, smooth blonde hair swept back from a delicately-boned face. The posture, the simple, dark dress, made Zoe think of a nun. A very beautiful nun. No wonder Liam gazed at her so attentively. She would turn heads, Zoe decided, wherever she went.

Yes, they were all there, with the exception of Robin, and as Stephen said, he was probably the one taking the photograph. The Elliotts and their wealthy relatives from Dublin, the Duncannons. A happy family group, captured in the garden of a pretty cottage on a summer's afternoon. But Zoe wished she could establish the exact relationship between them.

It really was too bad that the Irish records were lost.

Six

Mellow pantiles, uneven in places, roofed an elderly cottage of rusty-pink brick. The projecting scullery was not quite central, and the windows, half-hidden beneath encroaching ivy, were set with even less regard for balance. Yet overall the effect was charming, the impression that of a place which was loved, despite its idiosyncrasies. To the north, a high wall flanked by Lombardy poplars gave shelter to fruit trees and an abundance of vegetables, while a screen of roses divided the kitchen garden from a broad strip of lawn.

With his back to that mass of pale pink roses, Robin Elliott peered through the lens of his borrowed camera, and wished his brother would try to look as though he belonged to the group, instead of standing so tall and uncompromising behind them. Frowning, too. He was bored and eager to be off, but Robin was determined to have one more picture, and to make it a good one.

Calling out to Liam to bend, kneel, or otherwise shrink into place, he waited while Georgina organized him. Liam leaned forward, resting his elbows on the seat back, his face turned towards her, smiling; she turned to the camera, folded her hands, and Robin pressed the shutter release.

Immediately, they all began to move. 'Oh, don't rush away,' Robin pleaded. 'Let's have just one more.'

'But you've taken half a dozen already,' his mother pointed out. 'And we can't sit here all afternoon, posing – I've got tea to make, if nothing else. Come on, Tisha,' she added, taking her daughter's arm before she could disappear, 'we've got things to do.'

There was an audible groan from the girl, and a reluctant droop to her shoulders as she headed for the kitchen. Turning to their hostess, Georgina Duncannon asked whether she needed more help.

'No, dear – you sit and talk to your father. I know you don't see him very often.'

But Robert Duncannon was apparently more interested in examining the photographic equipment, demanding to know how it worked, and what the time exposures needed to be. Flattered, Robin was only too keen to share his knowledge, to talk about the career upon which he had so recently embarked. He was even more impressed by Colonel Duncannon's interest in his other activities, particularly his part-time membership of the local volunteer force.

'If you should ever change your mind, and decide to make the army your profession,' Liam overheard him say, 'do get in touch with me first. I have a little influence at the War Office, and might be able to do something for you.'

Watching them with their heads together, just for a moment the two struck Liam as being very much alike. And the resemblance was more profound than that of shared height and colouring. Very briefly, he was disturbed by it; and then his brother moved, and the similarity was gone.

It seemed, glancing round, that there was something dour in his father's steady observation of the pair. Liam wondered why. Was it Robin's obsession with photographing anything and everything in sight? Or could it be that their father was less than pleased to be entertaining this wealthy, distant relative with his fine clothes and expansive manner? Their mother, certainly, had been quite overcome by that unexpected note which arrived as they were sitting down to Saturday dinner, thrown as close to panic as he had ever seen her. And since the Colonel's arrival with Georgina an hour ago, she had been smiling and chattering like a young girl. That, too, was unusual. Perhaps his father was jealous?

The thought crossed his mind fleetingly, and was as quickly dismissed. After all, he reasoned, married couples with grown children had no cause to be racked by emotions like that.

On the seat before him, Georgina was also alert to that conversation between her father and Robin. He could see tension in her spine and the set of her smooth blonde head, and thinking she was hurt by her father's careless neglect, Liam was ready to condemn the man forever. As he moved, however, she glanced round at Liam, and the eyes which met his softened into a smile.

'What a pity,' she remarked lightly, 'that photographs can't show colour. Those roses are so beautiful.'

Although he knew it was not the roses which had claimed her attention, Liam went along with the fiction, suggesting she should return to paint them one afternoon. At that she laughed, saying her expertise was too limited, she could never do them justice. He denied it, having seen some of her botanical drawings, and the painting she had done for his mother, which now had pride of place in the parlour. They argued, amicably, and as she stood up he straightened, ready to fall in with whatever she wanted to do, wherever she wanted to go. He liked her immensely. She was so easy to be with, quiet and self-effacing, so gently humorous that sometimes it was a while before her wit was appreciated. There was such an attractive lilt to her voice, with a little bubble of laughter in it, he could have listened to her for hours. She often teased him for his seriousness, but from her he did not mind. Unlike his sister's barbed wit, Georgina Duncannon's held no hint of mockery.

For the last three months, since arriving in York to nurse at the Retreat, she had been visiting regularly, spending most of her days off at the cottage, helping his mother in the kitchen or garden, and joining the family for their evening meal. Georgina's affection for his mother often surprised him; he tended to forget that they were distantly related, and Georgina had known them all for years. That she remembered him as a small child, far more clearly than he remembered her, was sometimes embarrassing. It also underlined the gulf between them, the great divide of age and class. She could, he knew, have spent her life in Dublin considering nothing more strenuous than her social obligations, but she had chosen, instead, to become a nurse. With one course of training behind her, she had recently embarked upon another, at the Quaker hospital for the mentally ill.

Georgina worked harder than he did, and his heart ached at the sight of her ungloved hands, often red and chapped from the zealous use of carbolic. In that respect at least, Liam could understand the Colonel's anger at his daughter's choice of vocation. She tended to laugh about it, but to defy her father's authority must have required a matching strength of will. Looking at her now, it was hard to believe. Touching pretty shrubs, pausing to lean close to a full-blown rose, she seemed no less fragile than they.

Newly-painted railings guarded the front garden like a row of bright-green spears, and recalling recent hours spent chipping at rust, Liam flushed with pleasure at her praise. He was particularly proud of having cured the gate's long-lasting squeak, despite his father's claim that it would not be cured for long. For now, however, the gate was opening easily, and at Georgina's suggestion that they should walk a little way along the riverbank, Liam readily agreed.

In one direction, the sandy, tree-shaded path led past allotment gardens and a boat-building yard, and ultimately into town. To the right, it meandered past woods and open meadows where he and his brother and sister had played as children. Liam always thought how well-placed they were, within a few minutes' walk of the city, yet having miles of open countryside to hand. He had learned to swim in the river, learned to row, too; and now, when he needed to escape, he had his bicycle, handy for riding to work, but handier still for exploring outlying villages on his own. Unlike Robin, his interests were solitary ones, and except when Georgina was around, Liam much preferred his own company.

As he closed the gate, the sound of cat-calls and whistles reached them from the far bank. Beneath the trees on New Walk, Liam caught sight of some girls in colourful finery, hurrying along before a group of soldiers from the nearby barracks. In some embarrassment, he remarked that the girls should know better: New Walk was notorious in that respect. But Georgina smiled impishly, saying she thought the girls were heading towards the fairground on St George's Field, and were determined to have some handsome escorts.

For a moment they stood and watched the progress of that unsubtle courtship, and sure enough, the girls slowed down, introductions were made, and the group moved on together, towards the fair. They could hear, distantly, the sound of deep base notes from a Gavioli organ, overlaid by snatches of a popular melody.

They looked at each other, and looked away. After a short

pause, Georgina said she had never been to a fair. Liam, who had been to several over the years, was surprised. His sense of decorum, however, made him point out that fairs could be rough and rowdy, hardly fit for a lady. Looking crestfallen, Georgina said yes, her Aunt Letty would agree; but a moment later she declared that she would love to go.

'I know I shouldn't,' she said with a quick, upward glance, 'and particularly today... But they'll be gone by my next day off, and I might never get another chance...'

Her appeal found its mark. Liam looked up-river towards Skeldergate Bridge, assessing the time it would take to walk round to St George's Field. Then he glanced back at the house, thinking of her father, and his mother making the tea. Suddenly he remembered the old rowing boat which was often moored by the slipway, and stepped down the bank to see if it was there.

'Wait a minute, I haven't got my hat!'

He grinned. 'If you go back for that, they'll want to know where you're going.'

'You're right,' she agreed, feeling reckless, infected by a desire to be young and silly and happy, instead of the serious, dedicated woman she had become. She felt guilty, too, remembering the reason for her father's visit. The guilt, however, merely spurred her on.

They hurried towards the slipway. Liam handed her down the bank and into the boat, and in one neat movement took his place by the oars. With long, smooth strokes he soon had them across the river. As they passed beneath Blue Bridge and into the stream of the Foss, he explained his intention. He would moor in the Foss Basin, where the boat would be safer, and the facility of steps made alighting easier. From there it was but a few yards to the fairground.

Georgina admired his capability, was touched by the over-protective, very formal way he escorted her. At home amongst his family he was usually relaxed, saying little, but happy to be in her company. It was easy to treat him like a younger brother, and he made no objection to that. For the first time, however, they were out together in a public place, and that seemed to have set every sense on the alert, made a young man of the boy she usually teased. Watching Liam as they pushed through the noisy, laughing crowd, it suddenly came to her that he was behaving as he might have done with a girl he was courting. Silly though it was, the idea was so touching it brought a lump to her throat. Very quickly she looked away, exclaiming at the stalls and sideshows, the music and the crowds.

There was an enormously fat, bearded lady, who looked stronger, Liam said, than the so-called strong man in his tights and leopard skin; and a shooting gallery doing excellent business amongst the young soldiers present. At one of the stalls he bought her a bag of pink and white coconut ice, presenting it shyly and refusing to take any for himself. Then, among the gaily-coloured stalls and that dazzle of noise and movement, they found the source of the music, the biggest crowd.

There was a huge roundabout with pairs of painted wooden horses rising and falling, and here and there a carriage for two turning to the music of the great Gavioli fair organ. It was such a delightful sight, Georgina clapped her hands like a child, saying they must have a ride, she could not possibly leave without trying it. In the end they had two turns, once in a carriage and next on the horses, going round and round until she was dizzy. It was like dancing, she said; only much, much better, more like flying, and she loved it. Her delight was infectious, and as he helped her down, Liam was laughing too, eyes sparkling, teeth white against the smooth summer gold of his skin. She was so happy and he was so beautiful, she wanted to hug him. But as his hand lingered on hers she drew it away, pushing on through the crush before he should notice her silliness getting out of hand.

'It's time we went,' Georgina reminded him, and as they stood to assess their bearings, she noticed a tight knot of men behind one of the tents. There was a scuffling within the ring, and at first she thought it no more than rivalries that had developed into a fight. Then a dog yelped and another squealed, and she saw a sheen of lustful eagerness on faces that were turned towards her, money changing hands.

'Whatever's happening over there?'

Liam's smile faded. 'Dog-baiting. But they won't be at it long,' he added gruffly, 'here's the constable.' Even as he spoke, the warning was given and the ring broke, men scattering in all directions. Slavering and bleeding, the dogs were dragged apart and leashed, their keepers feigning outrage and aggression in an attempt to cover their guilt. Georgina was struck by a horrible similarity between them: evil, predatory eyes and snarling mouths. The men, she thought, were more repulsive than their dogs.

She was glad to be led away. They walked back in silence to where they had left the boat, saying little as they re-crossed the river. That sickening scene had taken the edge off the afternoon, reminding Liam of a reality which could never match up to his dreams, and Georgina of unpleasantness waiting in the wings.

Tying up, walking the few yards back to the cottage, she would have preferred to stop, to sit for a while on the riverbank, and tell him why her father had come to York today. But it was a long, sad, complicated story; and once begun, she was afraid she would cry. That would never do. 'People don't want to know your sadness,' Aunt Letty always said. 'If asked, you're very well, thank you, and you must never complain.'

Aunt Letty was good and she was kind, and Georgina loved her dearly, but oh, she often longed to be honest, to tell someone how she really felt. Especially now, with her mother dead only two days, and the funeral to face, and the past welling up like a tidal wave. Stoic to the last, Aunt Letty would never understand, and her father, Georgina knew, was simply glad to be free of that poor mad woman who had haunted his life for twenty-five years. Impossible to be honest with him, when so much of her sadness was tied up with his abrupt comings and goings, and lengthy, interminable absences.

Louisa was the only one who would understand; yet how could she talk to her, now? It would have to wait until after the funeral, when she came back from Dublin. But her next day off could be a fortnight away.

Georgina had been well-trained. She was a little quieter than usual when she and Liam returned, but amongst the constant buzz of conversation it went unnoticed. They were just in time for tea, and some instinct kept them both from admitting where they had been. It would be their secret, she thought, catching

Liam's eye as he sat down, and no one could be shocked at that unsuitable entertainment when she should have been grieving.

In the parlour, the table was out to its fullest extent and set as though for a banquet, with white damask and silver cutlery, china plates and a centre-piece of midsummer flowers. Three varieties of pie graced the setting, with salads and cold meats and eggs in mayonnaise; and on the dresser stood a crystal dish of ripe crimson strawberries, with a matching jug full of cream.

Georgina was amazed at the speed with which this unexpected visit had been catered for. In the kitchen, Louisa admitted she had baked a larger amount than usual that morning; the rest was quickly put together, and the strawberries and salad were fresh from the garden. With a smile, she handed over a tray, turning to the range to rescue a boiling kettle.

'Did my father say why he'd come to York today?'

'Well, no,' the older woman admitted, looking slightly puzzled. 'I imagined he'd come to visit you for a few days. Was there something else?' she asked keenly.

'It's not important now – I'll tell you later.'

Louisa shot her a look of enquiry, then with a sympathetic smile patted her arm. 'Make it soon.'

With another ridiculous lump in her throat, Georgina went through into the parlour and took her place next to Liam. Her father faced her, with Tisha and Robin on either side, and Edward at the head of the table. As Louisa took her place at the foot, Georgina thought how little she had changed. More matronly, of course, and with fine lines around her eyes and mouth, but the beauty of her smile had not diminished. At that sparkle of amusement in Louisa's eyes, her father responded with even more gallantry than usual.

She had watched him in recent years with various women, and knew him well enough to detect the slightest insincerity. And she was old enough to know what he wanted and from whom. Once she had been appalled, but nursing had taught Georgina the simplest facts of life, and experience with the mentally deranged had inured her to shock. Now, she accepted that her father had physical desires, and in the absence of a wife must seek satisfaction where he could. Not that it seemed to have been difficult: Robert

Duncannon could be both generous and affectionate, and even at fifty, was still an attractive man.

Watching him, remembering the years between – nine or ten, surely, since his last brief visit here – Georgina was astonished to realize that her father's inclinations towards Louisa were still unchanged. Despite Edward, despite the gathered family in this haven of domestic peace, he could still want Louisa, and be careless enough to let it show. Darting an anxious glance around the table, she noted Edward's studiously blank expression and burned for him. Robin and Tisha were arguing amicably, noticing nothing, but Liam, beside her, was tense with all the alertness of a young male in the presence of a threat.

Beset by a furious sense of panic, she wished her father would simply go, get on the next train to London and not come back. As soon as they were alone she would tell him so. It was unfair that he should come here, after all this time, charming Louisa, making her remember things which were surely best forgotten.

With sharp frustration she moved, accidentally scattering cutlery from her plate. The knife shot across Liam's lap, depositing blobs of mayonnaise as it landed by his feet. Exclaiming, apologizing, Georgina seized the distraction. Grabbing Liam's arm, she almost dragged him into the kitchen, handing him cloths and instructions, hurrying back to deal with the other damage. But she saw that she had broken her father's spell. While Louisa bent to wipe the mess from the carpet, Robert Duncannon remembered his manners and turned his attention to Edward.

In the kitchen, Liam was ruefully surveying the state of his best suit. Regretting the action which had caused the damage, hoping it was not irrevocable, Georgina apologized again. He glanced up from beneath a lock of thick fair hair, his mouth twisting into a wry grin.

'It's all right,' he murmured, 'there's no need to fuss.'

Straightening, he held her gaze, seeming suddenly much older. In the depth and shrewdness of his glance, for the first time she saw a likeness to her father. It unnerved her, and she did not know why.

Dismissing the idea, she told herself that Liam was nothing like Robert Duncannon. In looks he was his mother's son, in character he was Edward's. Sensitive, something of a dreamer, he was a boy still trying to find his feet. A boy who turned to her for advice, because to voice his uncertainties to either of his parents would have hurt them. A sharp memory of that stolen hour at the fair, however, his protectiveness and a hand which might have lingered on hers, caused a sudden apprehension. Sternly, she told herself that he regarded her as a sister, there was nothing more to it than that.

Although she repeated the litany several times in the course of the next hour, Georgina found herself taking surreptitious glances for confirmation. With similar looks, Liam seemed to be keeping an eye on her father, who was now behaving himself admirably, engaging the younger members of the family in conversation. If anything, Tisha was the one who was flirting. Just sixteen and working as a clerk at the new confectionery works outside town, she was full of her own achievements. Conscious, too, of a pretty face and blossoming figure, she angled unashamedly for compliments. And laughing, Robert Duncannon indulged her, just as Edward did.

She was that kind of girl, Georgina thought without envy, one who would always have men on her side. The pity of it was that Tisha had so little compassion in her heart. Self-centred and acquisitive, it seemed all she wanted were the trappings of wealth. One day, no doubt, she would find a man to provide them. In the meantime it galled her that the Elliotts continued to live in this humble riverside cottage, when their means should have run to a town-house with at least one live-in servant. That her mother enjoyed gardening, selling excess produce to neighbours and passers-by, was another source of embarrassment. In Tisha's eyes, Edward Elliott was a man of some substance, respected both socially and professionally: his wife should not demean herself by selling fruit and vegetables like any common market trader.

In short, the girl was a snob. Robin might ignore it, find excuses for it, sometimes even be on her side, but Liam never would. Idealistic and uncompromising, he found it hard to forgive his sister for the dissensions she caused, and most particularly, for the pain she inflicted on his mother.

He must learn to bend, Georgina thought anxiously, learn to give a little, before life dealt blows which could break him. His brother Robin resembled her father, sharing a certain resilience of spirit which marked them out as survivors. But Liam was different. Liam worried her, because in that very upright stance he was vulnerable, and as things stood at the moment, danger walked too close to him.

The sun was setting as they said their goodbyes at the gate, farewells which were a little too prolonged for Georgina's taste; and Edward's too, she thought, reading his expression. Impatient, keen to put some distance between him and her father, she hurried along the sandy path, slowing only as her feet touched cobblestones before the bridge. Here, the jolly fairground music was louder, and with her mind on what had driven her there that afternoon, rather than the joy of it, she spoke more sharply than intended.

'You know, Daddy, you could have written. There was no need to travel all this way.'

Robert paused, a little out of breath at her youthful haste, and a little hurt that she should address him so. 'I haven't seen you,' he reminded her, 'for several months. Is it unnatural that I should want to see for myself how you are?'

His daughter's profile, beneath that uncompromisingly plain hat, reminded him of his sister's in one of her more intransigent moods. Indeed, as Georgina grew older, he could see the likeness more and more. Fair where Letty was dark, nevertheless his daughter had the same fine bone-structure, inherited from Robert's Irish mother. And Letty too had been beautiful in her youth. For a moment, he was tempted to be cruel, to tell his blonde and willowy daughter that if she was not careful, she would end up a prickly, angular old maid like her aunt.

But he was fond of Letty, and was it entirely her fault that she had never married? Letty could have had any one of a dozen suitors, even in her thirties. Instead, she had taken on the care of a new-born baby, and turned her back on society. Despite Robert's pangs of guilt, she had never reproached him on that score; indeed, when pressed, always said Georgina had given her the chance of knowing something of motherhood, without having to suffer the inconvenience of a husband. That always reassured him, always made him laugh.

He was not laughing now, however. Letty had managed to instil too many of her own unconventional views into this child of his, denied her too many frivolities. With talents both musical and artistic, and looks remarkable enough to set any red-blooded young man after her hand in marriage, Georgina evinced no interest in anything but nursing. She cared not a whit for clothes, jewellery social diversions; instead, she had demanded, persuaded, cajoled and virtually blackmailed him into agreeing to this further nonsense. As if nursing the physically sick were not enough, Georgina must now insist on caring for those poor mad souls at the Retreat. With her background, he would have supposed such a place to be abhorrent to her, but her letters were full of compassion for her patients, and praise for the Quaker staff. Looking at Georgina now as she strode so disapprovingly beside him, Robert could imagine her marrying some dour Quaker doctor, and producing serious Quaker children. The thought depressed him.

But at least, he told himself, apart from her delicate colouring, she was nothing like Charlotte, and that was something to be eternally thankful for. Once, he had been horribly afraid that Georgina would turn out like her mother, but there seemed little fear of that now. Unconventional she might be, and even obsessive when it came to her vocation, but his daughter was also warm and affectionate, which was something Charlotte had never been.

Now her mother was dead, Robert had ensured that she would inherit most of Charlotte's wealth. That is, most of what was left. It never failed to astonish him how much had gone in medical bills and nursing home fees, how much had been swallowed by structural repairs to the family home in Waterford, and the house in Dublin. Then, a few years ago, there had been some ill-advised investments, reducing the income, making huge inroads on the capital, so that the remains were pitiful. Although he regretted it, Robert could say with hand on heart that little had been diverted to his own personal use. Never forgetting how cleverly he had been trapped into that farce of a marriage, to him Charlotte's fortune had always seemed like blood money.

Sighing, he remarked: 'I thought the news I had to impart was better *said*. However, I'm glad to see it hasn't been too distressing for you.'

It was not said unkindly, but he could see the observation hurt her. Saying nothing, she looked away, and he wondered what she was thinking, whether in fact she was more distressed by her mother's death than he imagined. But it was a difficult topic. Instead he chose what he considered a safer one, telling her she was working too hard, that he had spoken to the Superintendent of the hospital and arranged a week's leave of absence for her. He felt Georgina's displeasure at that, the defensiveness which came into being whenever her independence was threatened.

As they climbed the hill towards the hospital, he discovered something of her thoughts, and they were at such a tangent to what might have been expected that Robert was taken aback.

'You won't go back to the cottage, will you?'

'What? Tonight? No, of course not.'

'Tonight, tomorrow, *anytime*,' she said tersely. 'Don't go back, please.'

Astonished by her temerity, Robert stopped. 'Why ever not?'

'You know why. It's not fair – to any of them. Not after all these years.'

'Georgina,' he said heavily, 'it's *my* business, not yours, and I'll thank you not to interfere. You have no right...'

'I have *every* right!' she declared with force. 'They mean as much to me as they do to you. Probably more, if truth be known. I was *curling* with embarrassment for Edward this afternoon – and while you may not have noticed, Liam was watching you like a hawk!'

'Was he, by God? I didn't realize...'

'No,' came the quick reply, 'you were too taken up with Louisa. *You* might be free, Daddy, but she's not!'

Guilty colour flooded his face. Aware of it, Robert took refuge in anger. 'Watch your tongue, miss!'

Georgina shook her head. 'I'm sorry. But if I don't remind you, Daddy, who will?'

That unexpected maturity startled him, as did the power of her observation. Momentarily humbled by it, he squeezed her hand. 'Do I need such reminders?'

'Not usually,' she conceded, 'but this time it's important.'

'In that case, I'll try to remember it.'

A porter opened the gate for them, and Robert walked with his daughter up the drive. It was a fine house, he thought, with a mellow, comfortable air to it, more like a gentleman's country residence than a hospital. Surprising, since the place had been built specifically to house the mentally ill, and was less than half a mile from the edge of town. From the outside it was not unlike that other place in Ireland where Charlotte had been confined for the past fifteen years, but its interior was different. Here there were no nuns in rustling black robes, no coloured plaster saints, and the fine paintings which graced the Retreat's walls would not have been out of place in Robert's Dublin home. The staff were approachable too; pleasant, ordinary people, with no great air of piety.

Robert's chief difficulty was distinguishing one from another, for as Georgina explained, rank, both social and authoritative, went unstressed and unadvertised. Faced with an array of doors without name or number, it was a mystery to him how people found their way about. Used to the clear-cut structure of army life, he wondered also how order was kept so effectively. The principle of mutual respect, as explained by his daughter, sounded a fine aim, but in his experience human failings generally made mincemeat of such ideals.

That it worked here, however, had been obvious to Robert that morning as the Superintendent showed him round. And in reading the words of its founder, that the Retreat should be a place *in which the unhappy might obtain refuge*, he was reminded of similar words spoken by the Mother Superior of that obscure little order of nursing nuns in Ireland. Only after remarking on that to his daughter, did Robert learn that the Irish doctor in charge had spent a considerable amount of time at the Quaker hospital. Influenced by its success, he had gone on to spread those principles elsewhere.

How strange, he thought, as he saw Georgina to her door, that so many things came full circle, and that the line should so often begin and end with York. Leaving her, he stood for a moment outside, on the crest of the hill on which the hospital was built, gazing out over the darkening grounds. On one side he could see the Minster's towers, catching the last residue of light from the west, while below him, beyond grounds and grassy strays, he could just make out the Barracks. A few lights were twinkling there, reminding him with sudden, but not unwelcome nostalgia, of his own tour of duty there.

Savouring the memory and its banishment of the twenty years between, for a moment he was thirty again, impulsive and hot-blooded, and with Charlotte on his mind, just a little crazy, too. Living too hard, drinking too much, searching for a panacea which always eluded him. And then, unexpectedly, at that little hotel on Gillygate, he had met Louisa, and she had changed everything.

Not materially, of course. That travesty of a marriage did not go away, nor did it cease to plague him, but Louisa had banished its morbid fascination. Once free of that, Robert's life had regained its balance, become bearable, even enjoyable at times. He supposed, looking back, that it should have gone no further, yet even under the closest examination, he could not see where he had forced the issue. He had put his situation honestly before her, and she had rejected him; and taking the honourable path, he had stayed away.

Fate, however, seemed to have had other plans in store. Never, if he lived to be ninety, would he forget that summer's evening – so like this one! – when Louisa had made that unexpected visit to his lodgings at Fulford. That, for him, was where it had really begun, the point where honour and pain and loneliness assumed the aspect of unwanted baggage on life's hard road. Having abandoned them, he had set out, quite deliberately, to take her.

With all he knew now, and all that had happened between, Robert would not have changed those two years, even if he could. Like a many-faceted jewel, that time stood out, its dark depths and shafts of light still glowing in his memory. Nothing, since, had matched it.

It was all very well, he thought, for Georgina to tell him what he must and must not do. She knew too little, and her perspective was different. Seeing Louisa again was a revelation for which he had been unprepared. After all these years, he had expected her to seem older, unattractive against the picture he held in his heart. He should have known better. The warmth of her smile did not change, nor the light in her eyes, and she had matured with grace.

Yes, he thought, smiling into the darkness, Louisa Elliott was still a lovely woman, natural and artless as ever; but that had always been her attraction.

Wanting to see her again, he knew he would return. Next time, however, he would not make the mistake of calling when the family were gathered. Next time, he would ensure that he saw her alone.

SEVEN

In the house there was nowhere to talk. Nowhere, that is, with sufficient privacy. Tisha was helping in the kitchen and would soon be going to bed. There, the upper walls were too thin to allow much more than a hushed whisper. By the window's fading light Robin was writing a log of photographs taken that afternoon, and, slumped on the sofa with an oil-lamp already lit, Liam was absorbed by a book. He looked set to stay up all night. Irritated by that calm family scene and unable to find distraction, Edward waited with gnawing impatience for Louisa to finish clearing away.

Able to stand his thoughts no longer, he went outside to pace the length of the garden until she should join him. Against a low band of pink, the trees seemed no more than black paper cut-outs, with a random pattern of holes here and there. A pretty illusion, he thought, life imitating art, masking its three-dimensional reality. He looked back at the cottage, all quaint angles and lack of symmetry, and knew it rested on insecure foundations; yet in the last rosy glow from the west, it presented a delightful picture of rural peace. He wondered whether the years of happiness beneath its roof had been a similar illusion, resting on equally insecure foundations, maintained with ease only while Robert Duncannon stayed away.

It was a bitter thought, and an alarming one. Loving Louisa as he did, for him the years of their marriage had been the happiest of his life. Not usually given to jealousy, where Robert Duncannon was concerned, Edward found it difficult to be rational.

She came at last, pausing to remove her apron and reaching up to hang it on a peg behind the door. He stood beneath the trees in the orchard, watching her maddeningly slow progress along the path, loving her beyond everything. The pauses she made, her comments on the vegetables and burgeoning raspberry canes – quite audible in the stillness – illustrated her reluctance to air the subject which tormented him.

And she was aware of his torment. Brightly determined at first, her smile became uncertain as she discerned his face, then faded altogether. Choked by the sheer volume of words which begged for release, for a moment Edward could say nothing. In the silence she stiffened, turning her back before uttering the briefest apology.

'And so you *should* be sorry,' he muttered fiercely, taking her arm. 'Come on – we can't talk here – every word will carry back to the house.'

Not until they were a good hundred yards down the towpath did he speak again, and in his anger and apprehension the words were staccato, his phrases short and disjointed. Not trusting Robert Duncannon, Edward's accusations came out badly, making his wife the guilty party, the one to blame for that brazen flirtation in front of the children, the one who encouraged a man who stood to ruin them all. In her turn, Louisa was furious, accusing him of irrational and unreasonable jealousy.

'It's not every day we have visitors,' she declared hotly. 'Would you have me sit like a spectre at the feast, ignoring him?'

It was an unfortunate analogy, one which prompted bitter sarcasm. Edward had been informed of Charlotte Duncannon's death only as their guests were leaving.

'*Spectre at the feast*,' he repeated with a harsh laugh, 'is a curiously apt phrase. The spectre should have been his *wife*, don't you think? She's the one so recently dead! Not that anyone would have suspected it – he was giving an impression of an extremely happy man!'

'Given those circumstances, Edward,' she retorted, 'I should think he is. I doubt you'd be heartbroken, either!'

'I'd at least try to observe the decencies!'

Biting back a cutting reply, Louisa turned away, gazing through the purple shades of evening towards the river's far bank. In the distance street-lights twinkled, and beyond the houses flanking Fulford Road stood the Barracks. Even after all these years the place drew her eyes like a magnet. And yet she had been happy with Edward, content and peaceful. Only in the last year or so had they argued at all, and that was mainly over Tisha. Usually Louisa was the one who was hurt and accusatory; it was painful to be on the receiving end of Edward's resentment.

Wanting to placate him, she said with forced calm: 'Robert said nothing at all about Charlotte until after we'd eaten – and he explained then that he hadn't wanted to spoil our day with news of her death.'

But Edward's anger was not to be diffused so easily. 'How very thoughtful of him! A pity he didn't consider how his visit might spoil the rest of our lives.'

'Oh, Edward,' she sighed, 'don't exaggerate.'

On a deep breath he paused, taking his wife's arm, making her turn to face him. With an effort he calmed his temper, put stays on the fear and jealousy which threatened more destruction than even Robert Duncannon could accomplish.

'Louisa, I'm not exaggerating. He hasn't been near us for years, and suddenly he turns up, out of the blue, all charm and good humour. And you welcomed him like the prodigal returned,' he said, pausing to let the accusation sink in. 'What worries me more, is the effect on the children.'

'He's Georgina's father, for goodness' sake. She visits us – why shouldn't he?'

Her attempt at a nonchalant shrug irritated Edward further. 'And she's another one!' he exclaimed. 'Oh, I know she's a delightful girl, and you're very fond of her – but in her own way, Louisa, she's as dangerous as he is. Can't you see that?'

'What?' she demanded. 'See what?'

'She's young and beautiful and exceptionally charming – to all of us. We're all very fond of her, wouldn't you say?'

'Yes, but...'

'But one of us is more than just *fond* of the girl. One of us is quite besotted by Robert's daughter, *or hadn't you noticed?*'

Louisa's breath caught in her throat. For several seconds she absorbed the grimness of her husband's expression, the angry glitter of his eyes in the half-light. 'Who?'

With chilling abruptness he turned, seemed about to leave her standing there, but then he paused, and on a sharp release

110

of breath shook his head. Suddenly, all that uncharacteristic fury was gone, and in its place was sadness and perplexity, and a deep, loving compassion which in that moment was as unwelcome as his jealousy.

'So you haven't noticed,' he said softly, 'I didn't think you had. I've been trying to tell you for weeks, trying to find the right words.'

'Which of them?' But there was no real need to ask. With his wide range of interests and string of friends, Robin hardly had time to eat these days, much less to fall in love. Anyway, she thought, he was far too young. But so was Liam. Perhaps he did admire Georgina – she was, after all, an admirable young woman – but it was no more than that. Could not be more than that.

'I suppose you mean Liam?' she said derisively.

'I do indeed.' Before she could interrupt, he went on quickly, 'Calf-love it may be, I don't dispute that. I'm not suggesting Georgina's encouraged him, but she is drawn to him, Louisa – and he's flattered by that. What young man wouldn't be? So, he imagines himself in love. Spends his time daydreaming about her, instead of getting on with his work. He never was the most diligent apprentice,' Edward added with bitter humour, 'but recently his concentration has been nonexistent.'

A tight band seemed to be squeezing Louisa's heart. Liam, in love at eighteen? The idea was ludicrous. And with *Robert's daughter*? It was unthinkable. 'What nonsense!' she exclaimed. 'I've never heard anything so silly in my life.'

'There's nothing silly about it. Tragic, yes – especially if he should try to show how he feels.'

That was too much. 'He *wouldn't*!'

'But he's young, Louisa – he *might*.'

'She wouldn't – '

'No, I'm sure she wouldn't. But,' he added heavily, 'the situation mustn't be allowed to get that far.'

In the gathering darkness Louisa paced up and down, six paces along the path, six paces back, arms folded and hugged into her body as though holding a grievous hurt. 'You're making something out of nothing,' she accused, her voice harsh with pain, 'finding reasons to stop Georgina from seeing us. Liam isn't in love with her at all – he's just unhappy in the business. He's not cut out for that kind of work – have you considered that?'

'He was happy enough in the beginning,' Edward said defensively. 'I gave him every opportunity to choose what he would do.'

'He didn't know what he wanted to do – you talked him into it.'

Desperately hurt by that, Edward was nevertheless aware that she was steering him away from the heart of the problem. Having comfortably avoided the subject for years, now, when danger threatened, she was ill-prepared to face it. In many ways, Edward reflected, he was just as much to blame; but with Robert Duncannon apparently content to leave them be, it had been difficult to press Louisa into action. The time had never seemed right. Now, however, some kind of action was essential. And if she could not be persuaded that truth was the only armour, then he would have to defend his family with the only weapons at his disposal.

'I think you must explain to Georgina that her frequent visits are not desirable. And you must tell her why. She knows the situation – she wouldn't wish to hurt us further.'

'Edward, I can't!'

'And as for her *father*,' he stated grimly, 'I'll not have him over my doorstep. You're *my* wife, Louisa, and the cottage is *my* home – I won't countenance his presence again.'

Burning beneath that implied mistrust, she asked scathingly: 'After all these years, do you trust me so little?'

Angrily, he turned on her. 'I don't trust *him*. But even if I did, I still wouldn't want him in my house. Not now – not after all this time. His presence gives rise to too much speculation – and people have long memories. Do you want the gossip to start again?'

She did not reply to that, but he could see resentment in her stance, in the outward thrust of her chin. She did not want to believe him, did not want to accept that what he said might be true. Searching for something to convince her, he recalled a painful moment from the turmoil of impressions which had attacked that afternoon. Watching young Robin with Robert Duncannon, their heads together over that borrowed camera,

Edward had been stricken by a marked similarity of height and posture and colouring, and the almost mirror image of their profiles. Georgina, he was sure, had also noticed the resemblance. How long before someone else remarked on it?

Louisa's anger and frustration burned for most of the following day, taking her through a vicious attack on the kitchen range and an assault on weeds in the vegetable plot. By late afternoon her fury was spent, and although she wept a few tears over an old photograph kept with her private things, she was sensible enough to admit that Edward was right. Washed and changed into a clean cotton dress, she felt better, more able to think. Seeing the dangers clearly, it seemed sensible to point them out to Robert; and she must do it, not Edward. That was the easiest part. She had learned to live without Robert long ago, and despite the excitement of seeing him yesterday, she was well aware of the trouble another visit could cause.

Having made that decision, and forgiven Edward for his jealousy, her doubts and heart-searchings were largely reserved for his other suspicions. She could not believe that Liam entertained anything more than a brotherly affection for Georgina; and until she was convinced of it, would do nothing to hurt the girl. That she would be hurt by such action as Edward proposed, Louisa had no doubt. In seeking to protect his own, Edward's loyalties were clearly marked, while hers were often confused, particularly with regard to Robert and his family. Guilt came into it as well as love.

The three years she had spent in Dublin before her marriage cast long shadows. She had loved Robert's daughter from the first, and could not forget the pain of parting. That Robert had also abandoned her shortly afterwards was hard to forgive: with his regiment safe in Ireland, there had been no need for him to volunteer for the Sudan. Even now, she could not view that war as anything more than an excuse for his leaving.

Although she had seen the girl rarely over the succeeding years, Louisa felt she knew Georgina better than her father did. She treasured this new, adult friendship, finding a sympathy and understanding which was sadly lacking in her relationship with Tisha. Her own daughter, Louisa reflected unhappily, was a chip off another block, reminding her of her sister Blanche, and her mother's sister, Elizabeth. How odd it was, she thought, that Edward should love Tisha so blindly, seeing few of the shortcomings which in those other women had grieved him so much.

That bias never failed to be baffling. Georgina's choice of vocation, however, was not. Unlike Letty and Robert, she understood why the girl had decided to become a nurse, and why she had chosen the most difficult aspect, the nursing of the mentally ill. That passionate concern for life's unfortunates had been instilled by Letty, and from there it was no more than a step to Charlotte Duncannon, who had been strange when Robert married her, and beyond redemption after Georgina's birth. The girl was no stranger to madness, nor its various treatments. It seemed logical to Louisa that being the person she was, Georgina Duncannon should feel the need to care for those who shared her mother's afflictions.

Nor did it surprise her that the daughter of a woman so irredeemably insane, should have made a vow never to marry. That had come out during one long and very serious conversation, and she had asked Louisa not to repeat it. She was, she said, afraid of developing the same brand of insanity: too little was known about heredity, and she would not wish to pass a similar affliction onto her children. Although Louisa admired the sentiments involved, she did wonder whether that decision would hold if Georgina ever fell in love. From her own experience, Louisa knew how hard it was to stick to principle where passion was involved.

If the girl had gone to Dublin for the funeral, they would not see her again for a while. In the meantime she would drop a few questions and watch Liam's reaction. The real test, however, would be to see them together. Armed with those warnings of Edward's, then she would know the truth of the situation.

With the heightened perception of those who hold a secret passion, Liam was alerted by his mother's enquiries, to the extent that he dare phrase no direct questions with regard to Georgina's continued absence. It also seemed to him that the tension at home was connected to his father's tetchiness at work, and from pure instinct attributed it to his unsuitable and unrequited love for Colonel Duncannon's daughter.

Unhappy, missing Georgina to distraction, Liam did try to submerge his anxieties in the work at hand, but his heart and mind were elsewhere. His forgetfulness brought constant recriminations. At the end of ten days, convinced that something was wrong, he took to cycling past the Retreat each evening in the hopes of seeing her. By the third occasion, desperation had fuelled enough courage for him to write a note in which he said he must see her, would wait for an hour in case she might be free, and again the following evening.

It was one thing to write the note, quite another to persuade the porter to pass it on. It was more than his job was worth, the man said, to pass *billy-doos* to the nurses. Liam's offer of a tip would persuade him only to leave the note on the board by the nurses' quarters, where Miss Duncannon might find it in the morning; he would do no more.

Liam had to be content with that. Disconsolate, he went home, but when he returned just before seven the following evening, Georgina was already watching from a high point overlooking the road. He caught the movement of something white beneath the overhanging trees, looked up and realized Georgina was signalling to him. A moment later she came out of the drive on a bicycle, and with barely a glance in his direction, started pedalling away towards the village of Heslington. Bemused for a moment, he simply stood with his bike by the roadside, but as she disappeared beyond the crest of the hill, he re-mounted and went after her through golden light and lengthening shadows. Not too quickly, however. He had sense enough to keep some distance between them until they were clear of the village.

She cycled with confidence, quickly gaining speed, so he had no difficulty in following at what was, for him, a natural pace. With the last house behind him, he pressed a little harder, intending to overtake; but as the gap between them shortened, Liam found himself fascinated by the shape of her back, her narrow waist and flaring, womanly hips. In a simple straw hat and white blouse, she sat forward in the saddle, navy skirt pulled tight under a neat, provocative bottom, while her thighs moved rhythmically with the pedals. He was unable to tear his eyes away.

A moment later, his thoughts were shaming him; with an effort he forced himself to overtake. It was none too soon. Rounding the next bend she slowed, stopping as he drew level. Flushed with exercise and agitation, he thought she looked more beautiful than ever; but her words were sharp and concise.

'Liam, this won't do! You must not pester the porter with notes – you'll get me into serious trouble!'

Crushed by the tone of that reproof, stunned by its unexpectedness, for a moment Liam stared in disbelief. Sharply, he turned his bicycle. He would have ridden off but she grasped his arm.

'I'm sorry – you didn't know. It must be something vital, of course it must, but we're not supposed to meet young men outside the hospital gates.'

Ashamed of his thoughtlessness, Liam hung his head. She tugged gently at his sleeve. 'Come on – we'll park the bikes out of sight and walk a little way. I've got an hour or so before I go on duty.'

There was a dry, rutted cart-track just a few yards up the road, leading between fields of ripening wheat. Dog-rose and honeysuckle threaded the hedge, while tall spikes of fox-glove pierced the shadows beneath. Along the border of the field a few early poppies reared silken scarlet heads. The air was full of mingling scents of earth and grass and flowers, and in the low evening sunlight all was somnolent and still. As they walked, Liam's tension began to ease, but his first words to her came out badly.

'Where have you been? It's been so long since your last visit, I thought there must be something wrong.'

It was clear she was surprised by his vehemence. 'Didn't your mother tell you I was going to Dublin? She knew, I'm sure she did.'

'Nobody tells me anything,' he said bitterly. 'But why Dublin? I think you might have said, since you knew you were going!' Georgina stopped at that, her frown deepening, and Liam realized the mistake in showing his anguish. 'I thought we were friends,' he finished lamely.

'We are friends,' she said quietly. 'And I'm sorry I didn't say. I thought it would have been explained later, after we'd gone.'

For a while they walked on in silence. When she began to speak, in short, wrung-out sentences, he was at first incredulous, and then ashamed. He could only imagine her loss in terms of losing his own mother, and that she should have set aside her grief to the extent she had, was astounding. That he had taken her to the fair that day, with no idea of the news her father had come to impart, was also rather hurtful. He wished she could have confided in him, and said so.

On an indrawn breath, she said, 'I would have, but to be truthful, Liam, I heard the music and just longed to do something silly. It was my suggestion, so don't blame yourself. And afterwards – well, there wasn't time.'

It was hard to understand, but he was touched by her confession. Six years his senior, Georgina had always seemed mature and somehow invulnerable. He had talked to her, trusted her with his difficulties and listened to her advice, but for the first time he was seeing her as a suffering human being with problems far greater than his own. Forced to place himself in the role of comforter, it was new to him and awkward.

Imagining his own mother incarcerated for fifteen years in a mental hospital, Liam winced. That Georgina had never known Charlotte Duncannon as a mother in the true sense was harder to grasp, yet he felt the tragedy of never knowing warmth and comfort as a child. He declared, with some feeling, that it must have been worse than being an orphan.

'Yes,' she said thoughtfully, 'I suppose it was. Of course, we visited, my aunt and I, over the years... but I doubt she knew me.'

'But that's terrible...'

'It certainly wasn't easy.' Locked into her own thoughts, memories of a past which did not include him, Georgina stared unseeing over the still, golden fields; while he ached for her, wishing he could know her feelings, experience her emotions. The gap of inches which separated them as they walked, might well have been miles. Liam was painfully conscious of all that divided them: age and gender, circumstance and experience. He had long been convinced that to kiss her would be to transform everything, that joined in a passionate yet tender embrace, he would absorb all that she was, just as she would know him, feel as he felt, love as he loved.

The sheer impossibility of it made him sigh.

Georgina turned to him and smiled, and with a touch that was all too brief, pressed his hand. 'Oh, Liam! I didn't mean to make you sad, too. Let's change this awful subject, and talk about you instead. What have you been doing while I've been away?'

With a short laugh, Liam shook his head. 'Nothing much. In more trouble than ever with my father, I'm afraid.'

'I'm sorry to hear that. What's wrong this time?'

'Hard to say. It's just how he is.' Trying to be dismissive, he laughed again. 'I can't seem to do anything right, and yet when I try to tackle him about the accounts and keeping them up to date – which he's terrible at, he leaves things outstanding for *months* – he tells me not to be clever, and to mind my own business!'

'Oh, dear.'

'I don't know why, Georgina, but I can't talk to him anymore. We used to get on so well, but now all he does is *bite*. To hear him talk, I'm no good at the job, I'm mean to Tisha, I don't help in the garden, and I go out too much. But if I stay in,' Liam added bitterly, 'he accuses me of reading too much and going to bed too late. But Robin comes and goes as he pleases, and never a word to him. And as for Tisha – well, she might not get away with much when Mother's there, but she winds Dad round her little finger. She can do no wrong, while I can do no right!'

'And it's not fair,' Georgina chided with gentle humour.

He grimaced at that. 'No, it *isn't*, and it makes me mad. I don't know what to do. Maybe I'm not as good at the job as I should be – but I find it tedious. I didn't think I would, but I do. And I must admit I hate being inside all the time. That's why I go out in the evenings – I need the fresh air.'

'Have you tried talking to him – outside work, I mean?'

'No, but I don't think I could at the moment.'

She suggested enlisting Louisa's help, but he explained that his mother had also been strange with him recently and the atmosphere at home was taut in the extreme. 'I mean, she didn't even see fit to tell me that your mother had died!'

After that, they were both silent for a while, each considering possible motives. A grassy bank by a gap in the hedge looked too inviting to ignore. Liam flopped down dejectedly, chewing on a piece of grass, while Georgina stood looking down at him, deep in contemplation. Youth was so terribly painful, she thought, remembering her own; and harder still when things were never explained, when you had to struggle alone in the dark.

A wave of love and compassion swept over her, and she wished he was still a little boy to be fussed and petted and coaxed back to smiles. Instead he was tall and broad-shouldered and self-consciously tragic, sprawled there on the grass: handsome enough to break a young girl's heart. How easy he would be to fall in love with, she thought, envying the girls he might choose. With his straightness and honesty, he would never betray, never abandon the ones he loved.

Thinking of the honesty he deserved, she longed to tell him why things were as they were at home, but the secret was not hers to divulge, and the pain of keeping silent was bitter indeed.

'So,' she said firmly, sitting down beside him, 'what *would* you do, given a totally free rein?'

He glanced up, startled by the abrupt change of subject. A smile began to play at the corner of his mouth. After a moment, discarding that chewed piece of grass, he said: 'A totally free rein? No ties, no apprenticeship?'

'No ties,' she stressed, wondering why it was so important, and why she should wait with bated breath for his reply.

'If I had money, I'd travel the world,' he said softly, aware that with this confession he was trusting her with his most cherished dreams. 'Travel until I got tired and found a place to settle. And then I'd write about it.' He glanced at her again, half afraid she might be laughing; but she was gazing intently into his face, willing him to go on. Suddenly, smiling, he said: 'But if I hadn't any money – which I haven't – I'd simply go abroad to work. Canada, Australia, America – somewhere new and untouched. Farming probably, but it wouldn't really matter.'

'And then you'd write?'

'Eventually. When I'd lived a little, had something to write about.'

Stunned by the simplicity of it, by its very obviousness, Georgina wondered why no one had thought to ask him before. He was a young man who loved the outdoors, not the sort to welcome being cooped up in a small, airless space, making books for other people to read, ledgers for other people to enter columns of tiny figures. Writing books, yes, she could see that, eventually. Writing about adventures and foreign lands he might have had a hand in conquering.

With all the undercurrents at home, especially now her father was taking such belated interest, Liam would be better away from it. 'Why don't you?' she asked with breathless intensity, but even as the words left her lips, she thought how much she would miss him.

'How can I?' Liam whispered, aware that he could never leave without knowing her fully, never say goodbye until she knew him too.

'But you can!'

He looked away. 'I have my apprenticeship to finish,' he said abruptly, gathering himself together. 'Perhaps after that...'

He stood up. Georgina saw at once that she had failed him somehow, but did not know what to say. With a sudden shiver, she realized it was time for her to go. Pursued by night clouds, the sun had dipped below the horizon: the golden light was gone, the land a uniform shade of grey.

Eight

Since he had to be in Ireland for his wife's funeral, Robert's superior at the War Office had asked whether he would mind staying on to attend to some official business. Aware that it would save another journey immediately afterwards, Robert agreed, but not without some degree of concern for his daughter, forced to make the long journey back to York alone.

The War Office business kept him in Dublin for several days. Days in which he was forced to listen to his sister Letty's catalogue of anxieties regarding her niece, also her admonitions on his role as her father. With his conscience suitably nagged into life, on his return he wrote to Georgina, but her reply was not reassuring. The letter seemed flat and depressed – understandable, perhaps, in the circumstances, but leaving much apparently unsaid. With a couple of days at his disposal, Robert decided to pay her another visit. The decision cheered him, especially when it came to him that if he timed it carefully, he might also spend an hour or so with Louisa.

A telephone call to the Retreat's superintendent established his daughter's free time and a suitable appointment. The following morning he took a cab to King's Cross and caught the express for York. Depositing his bags at the Royal Station Hotel, Robert found himself thinking of the summer of '99, when Kruger's antics in the Transvaal had kept everyone in suspense. Knowing war was coming, seeing too clearly the impossibility of family life, Robert had finally relinquished his ties with Louisa. It was what she had wanted, but it had taken a war to make him see the sense of it.

As he approached the riverside with its unchanging vistas, the flourishing trees and soft, sandy path, he remembered all the old passions, and the jealousy which had made it so hard to accept her marriage. Even now he found it difficult to believe that Louisa had really preferred a quiet life with Edward to the heady passion she had shared with him. Their relationship had been passionate, perhaps too much so, heaven and hell at times; but recalling the sparks that had flashed between them so recently, Robert knew the magic was still alive, stirring the embers of that old affair.

There had never been anyone to match her. Desire remained, despite the other women, the years abroad, the stupid things he had said and done. She was a loving and lovable woman, and he still wanted her, that was the hell of it.

With the cottage in sight, a frisson of nervous anticipation made him pause. Screened by trees and the lie of the land, it stood no more than a few hundred yards from busy riverside wharves and the spread of new housing off Bishopthorpe Road. In the nearby meadows cows munched contentedly, giving an illusion of deepest countryside. On the river a couple of barges were idling their way downstream, and in Louisa's front garden the subdued buzz of bees foraging amongst the flowers was almost the only sound.

Outside the gate, in dappled shade, Robert noticed a wooden board, listing fruits and vegetables – *all fresh from the garden* – and their respective prices. Envisaging possible interruptions, his euphoria evaporated. With a sigh he pushed open the newly-painted gate, hoping his walk would merit at least a cool drink and a shady seat. A light tap on the front door produced no answer. At the back of the house the kitchen door stood open, but she was not inside, and even the garden seemed deserted.

A moment later, with her sleeves pushed back and wearing a sunbonnet, Louisa emerged from behind the screen of glorious pink roses, bearing a gardening trug full of lettuce and soft fruits.

He felt his breath catch. Seeing her like that, he was instantly transported back twenty years, to an afternoon when they had walked across broad meadows, she in a pretty cotton dress and flapping sunbonnet, he minus jacket and tie, to that wood outside Blankney. And there, under an oak wreathed about with mistletoe, they had made love for the very first time...

The memory was so clear, it was almost painful. She was as graceful as ever. And just as desirable. Meeting his gaze she paused, pushing back a few stray tendrils of hair which had escaped the loose chignon beneath her bonnet. As a young woman, she had worn her hair cropped short like a boy's, a mark of independence that in those days had suited her very well. Now she was older, he preferred the softer image.

Seeing him, Louisa's expression hovered between pleasure and dismay, and settled, ultimately, into a wry smile. Her step was resolute as she approached, as though she had decided to make the best of things. It was not an encouraging start; and as he kissed her cheek it seemed to Robert that her eyes weighed him rather too well.

'You shouldn't be here,' she said, laying a hand against his heart. 'Although, having said that, I have to admit I'm pleased to see you.'

'You don't sound it,' he said with light reproof.

'Perhaps *pleased* is the wrong word,' she observed cryptically. '*Thankful* would be nearer the mark.'

He made to follow her inside, but she stopped him. 'Edward said – after your last visit – that he wouldn't have you across his doorstep again. And you can't blame him. So don't make me tell a lie. Stay there,' she added, 'and I'll fetch you something to drink.'

She came out a few minutes later with a tray of glasses and a jug of lemonade, setting it down on a stool before the long garden seat. 'I said I'd write to you and explain the situation,' Louisa began, 'but since then something else has been worrying me. Something you should know about, since it concerns Georgina.'

Sighing heavily, she glanced at him, and he saw anxiety and apprehension lurking there. Then, quite unexpectedly, she slipped a brown, work-roughened hand into his. Robert was far from sure whether she was seeking comfort, or giving it.

'I should have written,' she murmured huskily, 'but I've been putting it off, simply because it would have been so hard to express in a letter. So I'm glad to see you, even though Edward will be furious if he knows you've been here again.' Her eyes met his and pleaded with him. 'We have to talk – and very seriously – about our children.'

At the age of fourteen, Edward had begun his working life in Fossgate, apprenticed to a firm of printers and bookbinders. He had stayed with the same firm for twenty-five years before opening his own business in the maze of courts and alleys which in those days constituted Piccadilly. Eight years later, in 1901, he had moved on. His old premises had recently disappeared under a new, broad thoroughfare; now, walking down the new Piccadilly, Edward could no longer distinguish the place where his old business had been. It seemed very strange.

York was changing and growing, but although change was needed he found it hard to accept and even harder to like what he saw. It was, he suspected, a symptom of age. He was growing old and becoming entrenched, finding safety in familiar things, resenting the turmoil brought about by progress. Only in the unchanging heart of the city could he close his eyes to it.

The area of Minster Gates, Stonegate and its adjacent alleyway, Coffee Yard, was the traditional home of York publishing, and although his premises were ancient and even less practical than the old ones in Piccadilly, it gave Edward a sense of satisfaction to know that writers, printers and bookbinders had occupied the place for centuries before him.

Coffee Yard was, in reality, no more than a paved short-cut leading between tall medieval buildings. It ran past a walled courtyard and beneath the upper floors of two half-timbered houses, emerging eventually into Grape Lane. Narrow on the ground floor, Edward's premises opened out to more spacious rooms above. The huge oak beams and steep staircases, odd angles and unsquare walls, had made the moving of equipment something of a nightmare; now, with offices below and workrooms on the middle and upper floors, they were well-settled. For light and size Edward's favourite was in the middle, where two massive Georgian windows had been installed at the beginning of the previous century. It had drawbacks, however: freezing cold in winter, it needed a good fire in the hearth, while summer sun often made the heat unbearable.

Sighing as he returned from lunch and a visit to the bank, Edward stood for a moment in the cool alleyway, relishing the breeze and the shade. As his bank manager had suggested, it was probably an afternoon for contemplating the accounts, a job that Liam had been badgering him about for weeks.

In that respect the lad was methodical, but Edward wished he was a better bookbinder. As apprentices went, Liam was not a bad one; but if only, Edward thought, he would stop making such foolish mistakes! It was lack of application that afflicted him, not lack of ability, and his carelessness was increasing. Attributable, Edward was sure, to calf-love and the uneasy proximity of Georgina Duncannon. The sooner Louisa saw that and took steps to rectify it, the better.

In an irritable humour, Edward went inside. Amongst the clutter on his desk, was the lunchtime post.

In the rear ground-floor room, Liam was using the guillotine, cutting boards for a set of twelve books. Remembering an earlier mistake, when he had cut a complete set fractionally short, he checked every one against a template. As the outside door banged and Edward went into his office, Liam marked the time with some resentment. An hour and a half for lunch, he thought bitterly, knowing anything over his own half-hour would be an occasion for criticism. Wearing no more than a thick apron over his shirt and trousers, he was still sweating, his shirt damp with it, despite its open neck and rolled back sleeves. Wiping his forehead, Liam gathered the boards together and went back up the winding staircase to the next floor.

Heat, and the pungent, sickly smell of horse-glue hit him as he entered the workroom. Angrily, he reached across a wide bench to force up the sash another two inches. With that sharp movement the cord snapped, bringing the lower window crashing down. He swore roundly, not caring whether his father heard him, and a moment later Edward's foot was on the stair.

Liam ground out an apology between gritted teeth. 'It's so bloody hot in here, I was only trying to get a bit more air into the place! It's broken – I'm sorry.'

But Edward's attention was not confined to the window. In his hand was an opened parcel. In an overly dramatic gesture, he peeled off the paper and flung it aside.

'What do you call this?' he demanded, holding out a large tome, expensively bound in leather.

Recognizing it as one of a set he had been allowed to help with, Liam took it resentfully, wondering what minor blemish had been found. While Edward looked on, he turned it over and over, examining spine and engraving, the smooth gold edges of the paper.

'I can't see anything wrong with it.'

'Open it!'

Liam did so, and his heart sank. He had bound the book upside down.

The ensuing row was explosive, fuelled by the heat and a score of festering resentments. For Edward, the book was the last straw in a pack of other stupid mistakes; while Liam, who had rarely answered back before, countered the charges of incompetence with a few of his own. He brought up the subject of the neglected accounts, telling his father that if he did not pay more attention to outstanding bills, bankruptcy would be the next step. Grossly insulted, Edward grabbed a heavy bookbinding manual and flung it into the boy's outstretched arms.

'And if you paid less attention to young women beyond your age and station,' he snapped, 'and more to your work, you might have a job to look forward to in ten years' time!'

Liam's heart seemed to halt in his breast.

So I was right, he thought: they do know what I feel for Georgina. Hurt more by that one shot than anything else, Liam placed the manual carefully on the bench. Without a word he removed his glue-spotted apron and reached for his jacket and tie. Edward watched him, his expression sardonic.

'And where do you think you're going?'

'Does it matter?' Liam asked, fixing his collar.

'The work matters.'

'Not to me. Not anymore.' With that he clattered down the stairs and into the yard for his bike.

Short of a dignified answer, Edward could only bite his tongue and watch him go.

Smarting from the argument, yet curiously elated by his bravery in walking out, Liam cycled through town in the early afternoon heat, convinced he had done the right thing. If nothing else, it would show his father that he was not prepared to tolerate such constant, belittling criticism. He hated that sharpness of manner which took no account of his efforts or abilities. The book was a stupid mistake, he could admit that, but it had been done at the end of a long, hot day, and the thing was rectifiable.

No, it was more than his carelessness, more than the other silly things he had done and forgotten to do, the whole list of which had been itemized for his benefit. It was all a matter of his affection for Georgina, that friendship which for him, at least, had grown into love. She was so far beyond his reach, he knew it could never come to anything, despite all his dreams and fantasies. He simply loved to be with her: was that so very wrong? His parents' disapproval was hurtful and incomprehensible. It seemed to Liam that since they liked and admired Georgina, any fault must lie with him. He knew he was not good enough for her, but it might have been expected that his parents would think otherwise.

He decided to go home and have it out with his mother. She could usually be counted upon to see his point of view, and she was generally more forthright than his father. Whatever the outcome, Liam knew that the argument had brought something to a head. With regard to his immediate future, at least. Perhaps he should go abroad, as Georgina suggested; it would be hard to leave, but in the leaving she might realize she loved him too, and follow, eventually...

Still in the realms of fantasy, Liam cycled along the riverbank, glad of the shade provided by the trees. He dismounted at the gate, pushing it open fully, careful not to chip the new paint. In his eagerness to solve a problem, he abandoned his bike by the side wall and walked round on the grass. Within a couple of paces the sound of voices halted him.

At first he thought his mother must be talking to a neighbour, someone buying fruit or flowers from the garden; then he heard his name mentioned, and a responding male voice which set every hackle bristling.

Not again! He pictured Georgina's father flirting with his mother over tea on the lawn. The very idea made him want to rush round the corner and put a stop to it. But words penetrated, freezing anger and action simultaneously, making him listen almost without breathing.

Entirely unaware of a listener only yards away, Robert and Louisa were speaking heatedly, possessed as much by old passions and grievances, as by the immediate problem.

'I'll say it again, Louisa – this situation should never have been allowed to arise. She's their sister, for God's sake, and they should all have been told years ago.'

'Half-sister,' Louisa repeated through gritted teeth, 'and I'll thank you not to tell me what *I should* have done. The responsibility of bringing them up was left to me, while you gallivanted round the world, playing soldiers!'

'You left *me*, remember? To marry another man! I would never have abandoned you, Louisa, and you know it.'

With a catch in her voice, Louisa said: 'Why do you always go back to that? I married Edward because I loved him, because he needed me and we understood each other in ways you and I never did. It's been a good marriage, and he's been a good father to your children – far better than you ever were or will be!'

'This is getting us nowhere,' Robert declared bitterly. 'His virtues don't interest me. The point is it's time you stopped sticking your head in the sand, Louisa. Tell Liam the truth, for God's sake. Tell him straight – that he's my son, and Georgina's his sister. She's always known – she doesn't need warning off!'

Stunned and disbelieving, shocked to the point where he thought he was going to be physically sick, for a moment Liam hunched himself against the wall. He was Robert Duncannon's son? Georgina, his sister? No, it couldn't be!

With his head spinning, he stumbled away. Grabbing his bike for support, he crashed it through the gateway, mounted on leaden limbs and rode off down-river. Wobbling dangerously for the first few hundred yards, he fell off twice, eventually regained his balance, and pedalled furiously the three or four miles to Bishopthorpe, as though speed could outdistance the pain. Just before the village, too violently distressed to face other human beings, Liam flung the bike aside, stripped off his clothes and made a perfect dive into the river. He swam almost a mile up-stream before exhaustion overtook him, and floated back, staring up at the wide blue sky, at trees dark in their midsummer leaf, and the larks singing joyously above.

The physical world seemed possessed of a burning clarity, illogical and unreasonable against the appalling destruction of his life. The sun warmed his face while his body, like his mind, was numb. For a while he imagined drowning, but knew he could not by act of will. It would have to be cramp, or weeds dragging him under, and either were possible with the river so low and the water so cold. He passed the spot where he had left his clothes, and on the next curve there was the Archbishop's Palace, its graceful walls rising from the river, the mullioned windows glinting like eyes as he floated past.

The current was strong there, and swimming back against it took tremendous effort. When he reached the place where he had dived in, it was all he could do to scramble out. Wet and shivering uncontrollably, he pulled on pants and trousers, lying back like a dead man in the hot afternoon sun.

Grievously wounded but feeling no pain, Liam examined the shreds that were left. Strangely, in that moment, he doubted nothing of what he had heard. It all fitted too well. That extraordinary likeness between Robin and Robert Duncannon: even the names. His mother's reluctance to mention Mrs Duncannon. Short tempers, jealousy, tension: he almost laughed when he thought of his own innocent, pathetic interpretation. He even felt a queer, detached pity for the man who had been his father. But Edward Elliott was his father no more; and it seemed his adored mother was no better than the women who flaunted themselves after dark on New Walk. No wonder she could flirt so brazenly with the Colonel, Liam thought bitterly: he was her lover, the father of her children. The man who sat at the head of her table was simply someone she had married to cover her sin.

And Georgina Duncannon, the woman he had loved and dreamed of making his own, was as forbidden a fruit as ever came out of the Garden of Eden. She was his sister. Her father was his father, and Liam hated him.

After a little while he fell asleep, waking hours later to find that some kindly passer-by had spread his shirt over his chest to protect him from the sun. Nevertheless, he was confused and shivering and his skin felt hot and tight. Dressing clumsily, his first thought was to get home for something to eat and drink, particularly to drink, since he had a raging thirst. Then he remembered and was violently sick.

What he had been able to contemplate with such icy calm after his swim, was suddenly impossible to face without cursing and weeping. For several minutes he did just that, then fatigue claimed him again, and he dropped by the river's edge. He felt alone, bereft, as though his entire family had been wiped out by some freak accident; and, like someone so tragically bereaved, could not believe it.

Amidst the shock and pain, the thing to which he kept returning was Robert Duncannon's claim that Georgina was his sister and had always known it. If that was truth, then it turned his love for her into something abhorrent; perverted the time and attention she had bestowed into sadistic amusement; made him demand with silent, bitter repetition, why she could not have told him. Her knowledge, her silence, had made of him an ignorant, gullible fool. Had she pitied him, Liam wondered, or simply laughed at his obvious adoration? Either way it was insupportable, unforgivable, and he knew he would never be able to face her again.

But it could not be true, Liam thought, could not be true. If it was, then his whole life was a lie, without the smallest foundation. His parents had always insisted on honesty: how could people like that have built their lives on deceit? Perhaps he should go home and ask them. Perhaps he would find that it had all been a terrible nightmare: Robert Duncannon had never been to the cottage, his mother had never said those things, and all would be as it was before. But a low, evil voice in his mind kept reminding him that he had heard that angry exchange, and because of it, nothing would ever be the same again.

Time passed, dusk became darkness and still he sat there. Rinsing his face in the cool water, Liam's mind grasped at straws: perhaps they knew he was there and wanted only to shock him, to stop him loving Georgina. Perhaps they were rehearsing lines from a play...

But names were mentioned, the voice replied, his name, her name, his father's name. No, not his father. His real father was Colonel Duncannon, the arrogant bastard, the charmer, ladies' man, the cavalry officer who thought himself so much better than Edward Elliott...

'The *bastard*,' Liam whispered, repeating the word like an incantation as he dragged his bike out of the long grass. He used it all the way home. It was the only protection he had against the wall of pain which was crashing around him.

Louisa glanced yet again at the clock. It was almost eleven and Liam had been gone since two. Where on earth could he be at this time? Robin had been to the drill hall, and on his way home had questioned most of his acquaintances, but nobody had seen him, and Louisa's anxiety was turning to panic. At his desk, Edward was working, an excuse, she knew, for waiting up for Liam, even though he seemed convinced the boy was worrying them deliberately.

'He's paying me back,' Edward had said several times that evening, 'for telling him off this afternoon.'

Arriving home just after six, he had been irritated to find Liam still missing, and with justifiable anger had repeated the tale of what had passed between them in the workshop. 'It won't do,' he kept saying, 'the boy must understand that he cannot simply walk out on an employer, even though I am his father. He wouldn't get away with it anywhere else, and he must realize he can't get away with it now. I'm afraid there'll have to be some plain speaking when he does come home.'

But while Edward went over the situation several times for her benefit, Louisa began to wonder whether Liam had already come home that afternoon. And if he had, what had he overheard? There had been a noise, enough to penetrate Robert's consciousness, enough to stop him in mid-flow and make him look round the corner. They had gone together into the front garden, even glanced along the towpath, but apart from the gate standing open, there was no sign of anyone. At the time it had been disturbing, but inexplicable. Shortly afterwards, hardly on better terms, Robert had said he must go.

With awful dread that their mysterious visitor may have been Liam, Louisa had tried to find a way of telling Edward, but she had been reluctant to provoke harsh words over Robert's illicit visit while her other son was in the house. At last Robin went out, but then Tisha arrived home with a girlfriend, and they had clung maddeningly to the garden, discussing the latest fashions and people at work in girlish, affected voices.

Wishing them far enough, Louisa was astonished to hear her garden being praised by the friend, and Tisha saying airily that yes, it was wonderful to have this touch of rural peace, so much pleasanter than living in town. Ordinarily, Louisa would have smothered a laugh at such affected nonsense, but in that moment she could have smacked Tisha for her insincerity and that desire to impress. Usually, she was inordinately keen to keep her friends on *their* home ground, rather than her own.

The friend eventually went home just as Robin returned. Touchingly concerned about his brother, he had offered to go out again, but Liam could have gone in any direction, and Louisa was far from convinced that he would return at all. Keeping her voice light, she had sent her younger son to bed half an hour ago, but still had not broached the subject to Edward.

At her sigh, Edward turned. 'Don't worry,' he said gently, 'he will be back. And even if he decides to stay out all night, he can't come to much harm. It's hardly the middle of winter.'

Twisting a handkerchief between her fingers, Louisa shook her head. 'It's not that.' She took a deep breath. 'Something else is worrying me. I think he might have come back this afternoon, when...'

The sound of footsteps on the path halted her in mid-sentence; she dashed into the kitchen while Edward slowly pushed back his chair.

She stood like someone frozen to the spot. As he strode quickly to her side, Edward immediately saw why. In shadows cast by the oil-lamp, Liam stood against the closed door, his eyes glittering feverishly, his face suffused. At first Edward thought he was drunk, but then he moved, and in the light his brows and thick, tumbled hair gleamed in contrast to his sunburned skin.

Without uttering a word the boy went to the sink, turned on the tap and cupped his hands beneath it, drinking like someone dying of thirst, splashing the rest over face and neck. As though a spell had been broken, Louisa grabbed a pint pot from the shelf, and as she handed it to him, touched his head and neck. Her gentle fingers might have been those of a torturer: as he flinched away, Liam told her harshly to leave him alone.

'I won't hurt you,' his mother protested, reaching out again, 'I only want to feel if you have a temperature...'

'What if I have? It's no business of yours. Get away – don't touch me.'

Gingerly dabbing his face with a towel, he backed out of reach. But he need not have bothered, Edward thought; holding the sink for support, Louisa was staring as though Liam had struck her physically. For a second, Edward wanted to hit him, wanted to grab him by the collar and kick him up the stairs to bed. But the boy was obviously ill, his behaviour so completely out of character that Edward knew he must be calmed, not provoked.

'If you're not feeling well, Liam,' he said quietly, drawing out a couple of chairs, 'why don't you sit down and tell us where you've been?' Ignoring him for the moment, he turned to Louisa and gently persuaded her into a chair. Drawing out another, Edward seated himself and repeated his suggestion.

'Obviously,' he went on, 'you've been in the sun all afternoon – not very wise, as I'm sure you'll agree. But that's the penalty you're paying for going off half-cocked. Next time, perhaps you'll remember it.'

Dropping the towel, Liam started to laugh. It was a harsh, mirthless sound which seemed to hurt him even more than it hurt them to hear it. 'Oh, I'm not likely to forget this afternoon,' he said with bitter irony. 'Rest assured, Father, I'll remember it to my dying day!'

'What do you mean?' Edward whispered, his heart plummeting in sudden fear. He glanced at Louisa, ashen-faced with shock, and knew, instantly, that something had occurred which had nothing to do with the argument in Coffee Yard. 'What does he mean?' he demanded of her, but with eyes only for Liam, she merely shook her head.

'Didn't you tell him?' Liam demanded. 'Didn't you tell him who was here this afternoon and what you were discussing? Didn't you say you were talking about me and Georgina – and that he told you it was time you told the truth?'

By the ghastliness of their faces, Liam knew he had managed to stun them both, knew he had the upper hand for once, and the knowledge gave him a sense of tremendous power. Outside, the child which remained in him had quaked at the temerity of a frontal attack, but a lover's pain and a man's anger had smothered its mewling voice; that sense of power killed it outright. He wanted to hurt them, as much as he had been hurt, and was prepared to give no quarter.

'Tell me,' he asked conversationally of his mother, 'has the Colonel always been your lover, or did you give him up on your wedding day?'

'That's *enough*,' Edward hissed, thrusting himself between the two and forcing Liam back. 'This is your *mother*, for heaven's sake! Have you no respect?'

There were no denials, Liam noted. Something else in him died. Less than a foot from the man who had been his father, Liam drew himself up to his full height. He had the advantage of four or five inches. Looking down into Edward's face, noting its greyness, its anger and distress, Liam felt no pity at all.

'I have no respect,' he declared implacably, 'for either of you.'

The older man seemed to shrink before his eyes. Sagging backwards against the table, he slowly shook his head.

'Oh, my God,' he murmured under his breath, 'what have we done?' Like someone in a dream, he turned to his wife. 'Robert was here, then? Today? Why didn't you tell me?'

She answered faintly: 'I don't know. I should have – I tried to...' With a great effort she rose to her feet, taking a step towards Liam, her hand extended like a beggar. 'I'm sorry,' she cried as he jerked away. 'Liam, love, I'm sorry! It wasn't intended – we didn't know you were there – I don't know what you heard, but – '

'Spare me your excuses! Try the *truth* for a change. *Why* didn't you tell me before? Why did you let me go on believing something that wasn't true?' His mother winced and he enjoyed it, letting his voice gather power as the words rushed out in a torrent. 'Everything I believed in is lies – everything. There's nothing left – my life is destroyed. You've taken it all away and made a fool of me. I *loved* you – I loved my father, but he's not my father at all. I loved Georgina, too – stupidly, ridiculously, hopelessly, but still I *loved* her.

'But I didn't know,' he whispered, 'I didn't know she was my sister...' There was a hard pain in his chest and in his throat, a pain which might have found ease in tears, but he forced it down, determined not to give way.

'She should never have come here,' Edward murmured distractedly.

'So your lies could have gone unchallenged?'

'No – so your pain could have been avoided! That was all your mother ever wanted – to spare you and Robin and Tisha the agony of knowing you were the children of a man she could never marry!'

'Oh, yes, I forgot,' Liam said with something akin to a sneer, 'he was married, Mother, wasn't he? So you added the sin of adultery to that of fornication – and then married your cousin in an attempt to cover it up!' Hating her for being so much less than perfect, for destroying his image of her as a mother and as a woman, Liam never noticed the hand Edward raised against him. The fist which crashed into his jaw sent him staggering sideways, and as he flung out an arm to save himself, brought down a shelf full of crockery.

There was a second crash as Robin burst into the kitchen, sending the door juddering against its hinges, then a moment's horrified silence. As Liam gathered himself together, ready to strike back, Robin leapt forward, pinioning his arms, urging him to come away, not to make things worse. Sparing barely a glance for his anguished mother, or his father massaging painful knuckles, the younger boy dragged Liam out of the room.

Tisha was sitting halfway up the stairs, knees tucked beneath her chin, eyes huge in a pale, shocked face. She seemed to be staring at nothing, made no response to her brother's request, and even as Robin brushed past, pulling Liam with him, she did not move.

Gruffly, from the top of the stairs, he told her to go to bed; but for the moment he was more concerned with his brother, who, on the point of collapse, was bleeding profusely from a cut lip. In their shared bedroom Robin poured water into a basin and silently bathed his brother's face. With no assistance he stripped off Liam's clothes and made him lie down in the big bed they had shared since childhood. Although it was many years since they had wrapped their arms around each other in sleep, when Robin climbed in he curled around his older brother.

Tisha did not stir. She listened to her mother's sobs and her father's pleas, his bitter, anguished recriminations, which were directed as much against himself as anyone else. It was frightening to hear her calm, assured, beloved father so distressed, and awful to realize his vulnerability. She heard her mother crying over Liam, repeating his name like a litany; a chair scraped on the stone floor below, there was a scuffle of feet, a cry from her mother and more muffled sobs. Tisha's heart hardened. Liam was her mother's favourite and always had been. She would grieve for him and less for Robin, but not at all for her daughter.

Robert Duncannon's name was repeated several times, and it slowly dawned on Tisha that the witty, handsome army officer she so admired was, in fact, her father. She realized too that Edward hated him. For the moment, however, that was less important than her need to be comforted. The secure world she so enjoyed kicking against was suddenly no more: she was suspended in a yawning, echoing void and nobody seemed aware of it. Obsessed with their own misery, her parents cared nothing for Tisha's, while Robin and Liam had each other, and would not welcome her.

She heard Edward telling her mother to come to bed. With a cold hand round her heart, Tisha crept silently away.

Overtaken by exhaustion, neither Edward nor Louisa had the heart to face their children then. 'Tomorrow,' Edward said as he helped her to undress, 'we must sort it out tomorrow. Things will seem different in the morning.'

'Do you hate me?' she asked as they lay together between the linen sheets.

'How could I hate you,' he whispered into the darkness, 'when I've loved you from the moment you were born?' He drew her, unresisting, into his arms, wiping away the tears with gentle, loving hands. He kissed her forehead as she nestled against him, knowing, in spite of everything, that Louisa needed him and always would. His bitterness and resentment were reserved for Robert Duncannon, not through jealousy, but because he had always known his capacity for destruction. And now those fears were fact.

Seeking words which would comfort her, Edward looked back over the years. Linked by the closeness of their blood relationship, the two lives seemed one. It was ironic, Edward thought, that those close links should have made his feelings for her seem so incestuous, to the extent that he had not declared himself, and subsequently lost her to Robert Duncannon. That was his biggest regret. And now the appalling irony was that Liam should fall in love with Robert's daughter, not knowing the incestuous nature of his feelings for her.

Feeling the boy's pain, regretting the fury which had prompted him to strike out, nevertheless Edward had to admit to a certain sense of relief. Horrible though that scene had been, now at least things were out in the open. He would not have wished it so, and his regrets were legion when he thought of the past's lost opportunities, but always he had been bound by Louisa's desire for secrecy. Edward knew he should have overridden her, that things should never have been allowed to come to this pass; but they were, after all, Louisa's children, and he their father in name only. However, he had loved them as though they were his own, and in retrospect was able to understand the tension which had made him so short-tempered in recent months: a need to speak to Liam, to tell him the truth, conflicting with his loyalty to Louisa.

He did not blame her for the afternoon's sequence of events, or if he did, he blamed himself in equal measure. Knowing the depth of her love for her eldest child, and understanding, too, her propensity for guilt, he was more deeply concerned for her than he was for the children. He felt for them, for Liam particularly. But they were young and had always been loved, and he was sure their hearts would mend. Where his wife was concerned, he was not so sure. In the old days, before they were married, she had suffered greatly. Edward did not want her to suffer like that again.

Tomorrow, he thought, when the sun was up, would be the time to gather themselves and talk honestly and openly about the past – his own as well as Louisa's – and then, hopefully, they could begin to discuss the future.

Liam awoke with a shaft of sunlight in his eyes, just after half-past four. His head was throbbing and his mouth was sore, proving, if proof were needed, that yesterday's events were real. Wincing with pain and unbidden memory, he turned away from the light.

On the pillow beside him, innocent in sleep, Robin's face was curiously unmarked by the grief which had broken in the hours of darkness.

Although they were different, and might not have chosen each other as friends, Liam was never more aware of the bonds which existed between them. But that was another pain he did not want to feel. For a moment he acknowledged the debt he owed to his brother. Without his intervention, Liam knew he might have done unforgivable, irretrievable damage. The grief they had shared afterwards, the tortured questions he had answered, Liam thrust aside. He would not dwell on that, just as he would not think of yesterday.

With sleep, thank God, the torture had subsided, leaving him cold and empty and capable of thought. Now was the time to go, before claims were made upon him, before apologies and explanations and other people's pain could screw him down with guilt. Liam knew, as surely as the sun had risen and would duly set, that to be forced into Georgina's presence after this, would be the most unbearable agony a man could imagine. He saw her eyes smiling at him, imagined her hair loose and tumbling about her face; thought of that supple, slender figure, and knew he would always want her. No matter who she was or what she was, however misplaced his heart, he would always, always love her. But he could not face her pity.

Trying not to wake his brother, Liam rolled out of bed and stifled a groan. He was hurting all over, muscles aching, skin tender, head throbbing. Dried blood had caked his lips together and left his mouth tasting foul. He felt physically and mentally soiled, and surveyed yesterday's stained and crumpled clothes with distaste. Opening a drawer with great care, he found two sets of clean linen, and taking his suit and a spare pair of trousers from the wardrobe, crept downstairs to wash in the kitchen.

Stuffing the spare clothing into a knapsack, together with his razor and a cake of soap, he added half a loaf of bread and some cheese, and slipped his post office savings book into an inner pocket. That, together with this week's unspent allowance, might pay for meals and a few days' cheap lodgings. He must trust to fortune for the rest. Knotting his tie, he slipped on his jacket and glanced in the mirror to give his hair a final brush. It was wet, but several shades lighter than his skin. Although his lower lip was bruised and swollen, the cut was much less noticeable. All in all, he thought dispassionately, he looked better than he felt, which as far as a prospective employer was concerned, was all that mattered. He hoped his journey would pass without incident.

With his hand on the door, Liam remembered something; for a moment he wavered, but need won. He went to Robin's neat stack of photographs on the sideboard, flicked through them and found a set of portraits, postcard-sized, of members of the family. They had been isolated and enlarged from the group photographs, and there were several of each: just one, surely, would not be missed.

Guiltily, hearing a movement above, Liam pushed that portrait of Georgina between the leaves of his savings-book and rearranged the others into neatness. He hurried into the hall just as Robin came down the stairs. He was fully dressed.

Liam stood for a moment, saying nothing, then jerked his head. 'If you want to talk,' he murmured, 'you'd better come outside.'

They walked around the house on the grass, and opening the gate, Liam blessed the fact that he had cured its tortured squeak; it did not occur to him that had he left it alone, his mother and Robert Duncannon might have been warned of his approach, and thus not blighted his hopes so abruptly.

Liam led the way to where he had left his bike the night before. Some instinct had made him hide it in the hedge rather than run the risk of having it taken from him and locked away. As he pulled it free of twigs and branches, Robin asked what his plans were.

'I'm leaving York, looking for another job, something entirely different. I'm not going to say what and where, because if you know, as I said last night, they'll worm it out of you, and probably come looking. I don't want that. Not yet, anyway,' he amended, seeing his brother's crestfallen glance. 'Once I get a place, I'll be in touch.'

'Why can't we go together?'

Liam looked up, taking in Robin's unruly dark hair, the thin, pale face. He was tougher than he looked, but still Liam knew his intention would not suit the younger boy. He might well regret it, probably for the rest of his life. 'Don't be stupid. You've got a good job, you'll do well at it. I don't think you'd care for what I intend to do.'

'And what's that?'

'Ask no questions, and you'll be told no lies.'

Standing four-square across the sandy path, Robin gave a snort of disgust. 'Then you're as bad as they are.'

'Shut up!' Liam hissed. 'Do you want to wake the whole house?' He grasped the handlebars of his bike with a purpose, and told his brother to move. 'Let me go, before somebody comes out and tries to stop me.'

'I shall leave anyway,' Robin announced stubbornly. 'I was thinking about it last night. I'm going to join up.'

'Well, that's a bloody stupid thing to do. You'll get nowhere in the army.'

'It'll get me away from here.'

'Please yourself then,' Liam muttered harshly. 'Make your own mistakes, but you're not coming with me.'

Pressing forward on the pedals, he edged his brother out of the way. 'Say goodbye to Tisha for me.' He turned again and paused. 'Tell her – tell her I'm sorry, won't you?'

'What for?'

'I don't know. Everything, I suppose.'

'What if I see Georgie?'

'Nothing,' Liam whispered, turning away. 'Nothing at all.'

Out there on the towpath, neither of them noticed the face at the window of their bedroom. A pair of blue eyes, fringed with dark lashes, watched their goodbyes with a mixture of envy and pain. Tisha had lain awake all night, listening to whispered words and the creaks of the old house. She had waited in vain for someone to come and comfort her. Nobody came, not even her father, whose favourite she had always been. But he was not her father anymore, so maybe that explained it. She saw her younger brother watching as Liam rode away, and was relieved that he was not going too. As Robin came into the house she went back to her own room, determined to pretend to be asleep. Pride would not let her admit to anyone that she had suffered from their neglect.

In warm, early morning sun, Liam rode past empty cattle pens outside the Walmgate walls, and by the massive barbican turned right onto the broad highroad which led across the East Riding and ultimately to the busy port of Kingston-upon-Hull. By the side of the road, a scuffed and worn mounting block announced a distance of 37 miles. A long way, but if he was lucky, Liam thought, pushing his hat firmly onto his head, he would reach the port before the sun touched the meridian. A sudden sense of his momentous decision made him turn and look back. The old walled city was beginning to stir to yet another day: it did not seem the slightest bit dismayed by his defection.

White limestone defences gleamed in the sun, and the Minster's towers soared into the blue; below stood Coffee Yard, and strangely, at the thought of it, Liam could have wept for all that he was leaving behind.

But York was part of the past, and for him the past must be a closed book. It was time to press on towards the rest of his life. There would be a berth, no doubt, on some tramp steamer, shipping out of Hull; he could work his passage to somewhere. Destinations, at the moment, were irrelevant.

NINE

The daffodils were almost gone, and what remained of them was being whipped and flattened by the wind. As they left the station Stephen grabbed Zoe to prevent her being blown into the road. Large drops of rain hit the backs of her legs with the force of pennies. She was glad Stephen had brought the car.

The telephone was ringing as they entered the flat. Dropping Zoe's case at the top of the stairs, he hurried to answer it. At a more leisurely pace she followed, tactfully going into the kitchen to make coffee for them both. It was impossible, however, not to catch something of the conversation, and she wondered who on earth it could be on the other end of the line. Stephen's replies were curt, his voice so deep with disapproval, she was afraid it must be his ex-wife.

'Well, it's bloody short notice,' he said at last, 'but I'll see what I can do... Yes, I'll make it somehow, but give me an hour to sort things out... You'll phone me back? Good.' The sharp release of his breath as he replaced the receiver was eloquent; the single expletive which followed, more so.

At sight of his face, Zoe braced herself; but before she could ask, he took her into his arms, holding her tight and very close. When he released her, there was a difference in him. He reminded her of the Stephen she had known that first day: holding himself back, setting deliberate distance between them.

'I'm sorry, love. It seems you've had a wasted journey.'

'Nonsense,' she said bravely, aware of hollowness inside. 'I'm here and I'm with you – that's not wasted.' He lit a cigarette, lost in thought; she was forced to ask for an explanation.

With an abrupt gesture, he apologized. 'Sorry – thought you'd gathered. That was the company. They want me back, tonight preferably. Teesport – Middlesbrough. It's a bugger of a place to get to – it'll have to be a taxi.'

'Tonight?' She was astonished and highly indignant. 'But surely they can't do this? Your leave's not up for – how long did you say, another two weeks?'

Stephen stood back, regarding her steadily, one eyebrow raised in that familiar, slightly ironic way he had. 'Believe me, Zoe, it's all part of the job. Shipping companies can do what they like. They're a law unto themselves.'

'But why the short notice? Surely they knew the ship was coming in?'

'They did, but the Old Man's not due off for another month. He was thrown across the wheelhouse last night and broke his leg. Heavy weather, and the ship's in ballast – no cargo. She was rolling like a pig, apparently.'

'Oh.'

'Yes.' Stephen leaned across to look out of the window. Trees by the Minster were still tossing like candy floss. Musing on that, he looked worried. 'If it continues like this, they'll never get her in tonight. I'll have to keep in touch with the agent...'

While Stephen telephoned for a taxi to pick him up at midnight, Zoe inspected fridge and freezer for something with which to make a meal. He had planned to take her out to their favourite restaurant, but with so much to do, there would not be time. She defrosted a couple of thick chops, and by the time his next call was over, had jacket potatoes in the microwave, and was preparing a salad. Not very original, she thought, but quick and nourishing; and with six hours to go, some instinct told her it was better to eat now, before anguish took hold and appetites disappeared completely. Hers, if not Stephen's. He was used to this, while she was not.

'There is one bonus to all this,' he announced, stealing a stick of celery. 'I don't know if you recall him saying, when we were up there last weekend, but Mac's joining as Chief.'

'Is he?' she asked with genuine pleasure, having an instant picture of the burly Chief Engineer, with his big red beard and beaming smile. MacDonald Petersen's mother had been a Scot, his father a Norwegian seaman. Mac had been brought up in Newcastle; now, he and his wife lived in the small market town of

Alnwick, in the heart of Northumberland.

She and Stephen had spent a weekend with Mac and Irene; it had been sunny and warm and full of laughter. Smiling, remembering, Zoe reached up to kiss Stephen's cheek. Bravely, she said, 'Well then, it should be a good trip for you.'

'Better than the last one, anyway. And this ship is relatively new, so we shouldn't have too many problems.'

They both had cause, later, to remember those words.

'I expect Irene will be driving Mac to Teesport,' she said casually, clearing their plates away. Nodding as he lit a cigarette, Stephen was poring over a list of essentials. 'Do you think,' she ventured, slowly, 'that I might come along, too?'

His head came up sharply, eyes narrowing through a haze of blue smoke. 'To the ship? I'd rather you didn't.'

It was curtly said, and Zoe turned abruptly for the kitchen. To cover her distress she turned on the radio, and as fate would have it, the voice of Phil Collins filled the air, singing apt and emotive lyrics from *Against All Odds*.

A cry from the heart of a man who had watched his wife walk away; after all she'd been to him, after all they had shared, he was left with nothing more than memories. The singer's impassioned pleading for her to turn around, to see him as he really was, so echoed Zoe's feelings for Stephen that she could have cried out. Sloshing water into the sink she let emotion flow with it, hoping those words, that music, were saying as much to Stephen as to herself.

She whispered fiercely, echoing the lyrics as she clattered dishes on to the draining board, feeling the truth of every phrase. There was much she wanted to say, and a dozen reasons why he would do anything but listen; his going would indeed leave an empty space, and as for the odds against him coming back to her...

Stephen snapped the radio off. The silence, for a second, was tangible.

'That,' he said roughly, 'is why I've always said I won't have a woman standing on a godforsaken quayside, waving goodbye to me!'

He turned on his heel, slamming a door after him. But she

could hear him in the bedroom, banging about as he threw things into his suitcase. Her own, she noticed, was still standing in the hall where it had been abandoned earlier. For a moment, she considered picking it up and heading straight back to London. After all, what was the point in staying? He was going away, and Zoe had a stomach-churning suspicion that half a year's absence was going to be crippling, and with no guarantee at the end of it that she would see him again.

If he had said nothing at all, she could have hoped, but Stephen had made it abundantly plain that he did not expect her to wait for him. She was young, he said, and had a lot of living to do; there was really no point in making commitments she was bound to regret later. It did not seem to matter that she was ready to make such a commitment; he did not want it, and that knowledge stopped the words on her tongue. He seemed to read her mind, and whenever sentiment threatened, managed to turn it aside, as though he was determined, at all costs, to divert her.

It negated everything that had passed between them, left her doubting every instinct that said he did care, that these few weeks had been as important to him as they were to her.

Working at home in London, while Stephen had been helping his aunt move into her new flat, Zoe had been thinking things over. It seemed to her that there had been a subtle change in him, dating back to the first night of their arrival in London, to that scene with Clare, and the mention of Philip Dent. After that, things were never as spontaneous again. It was as though the seed of doubt had crept in, perhaps reminding him of other hurts and the transitory nature of past relationships.

Whether or not he trusted Zoe was immaterial, the barriers were up and likely to remain so.

She had steeled herself to raise the matter this weekend, to override all his objections and say what was on her mind; and, if necessary, to explain Philip Dent once and for all. She had been determined to tell Stephen to stop treating her like an inexperienced girl, as though his extra decade and one failed marriage made him an expert on life and love. Perhaps she did have a lot to learn, but as the child of divorced parents she had gained a certain wisdom; and she was not entirely green where men were concerned. She knew what she felt for Stephen, and his magnanimous gift of freedom was not one to treasure.

Surely she had meant something to him, something more than just a pleasant interlude between voyages? Did she not deserve more than just a note of thanks and a quick farewell?

But while she planned fine speeches, time had been running out. If only she had known. She could have put the work on hold and spent these last few days with Stephen. Plagued by such thoughts, when he reappeared, looking contrite, she could do no more than raise an abandoned glass of wine in mock salute.

'Cheers,' she said, unable to curb the edge to her voice. 'Would you rather I left now, or do you want to kiss me goodbye, first?'

'I don't want to kiss you goodbye at all,' he muttered grimly, 'because I don't want to bloody well go. They've cut two weeks off my leave – two weeks I was hoping to spend with you.'

Anger melted at that, bringing a lump to her throat as he took her into his arms.

'I'm sorry, love,' he whispered, 'it's the leaving.' He gave a rueful grin as he released her. 'Like going to prison for six months – except you don't get time off for good behaviour!'

Despite the gallows humour, she could feel the tension and the conflict. It seemed to Zoe that he could not make up his mind whether he wanted her there, or wished her far away. Wanting him to know how she felt, she kissed him passionately; but even as he responded they were interrupted by the telephone.

Swearing, he went to answer it. This time Zoe listened unashamedly. It was obviously some hard-pressed worker from the company's London office, having to stay late that Friday night to clear things up. Stephen's replies were all in the affirmative this time, although he did express anxiety about the weather. As he listened he jotted down details and instructions. Repeating the agent's name, address and telephone number, he assured his interrogator that he would meet the ship as soon as she came alongside.

When he came off the phone, he stood for a moment, lost in thought. Then, abruptly, he turned to Zoe. 'Do you really want to come up to Teesport? I warn you, it could mean hanging around all night...'

She struggled for nonchalance. 'Well, I did think it might be interesting,' she remarked. 'My previous experience of ships has been limited to cross-Channel ferries.'

For the first time that evening, he laughed. 'I think you'll find a hundred-thousand tonne tanker somewhat different!' He picked up the telephone. 'I'll get onto the agent, then, and arrange a dock-pass for you.' Briefly, he grinned at her. 'Can't have you being mistaken for a lady of the night, can we?'

There were other calls to make: one to Joan, who was obviously being kind and refusing to hold him up. She had a message for Zoe, telling her to get in touch, soon. Then a call to his sister, who was less understanding, and seemed to want to talk for hours. Zoe began to think he would never be finished, and the hands of the clock seemed to be spinning round. The wind, however, was lessening. With a final call to the agent in Middlesbrough, who said conditions on the coast were looking hopeful, Stephen cleared the line and left the receiver off the hook.

With a sigh of immense weariness, he pulled Zoe to his side. 'Let's go to bed.'

He loved her tenderly, with a long, slow gentleness that made her sad. Although she swore she would not give in to entreaties, the effort required was almost beyond her.

She saved her tears for the shower, afterwards, but he knew she was crying. He held her closer while the water washed over them both.

Carefully applied make-up and a fluffy pink sweater gave an impression of cheerfulness. Waiting for Stephen to finish packing, she made sandwiches and a flask of coffee, which would be welcome, he said, if they had a long wait on an exposed quayside.

He joined her in the sitting room, looking business-like in a pale grey suit and tie. With his Burberry and a thick scarf over his arm, he peered down into Bedern, looking for the taxi. Zoe's eyes were on the Minster, hazy in the driving rain. Even in that weather, the chimneypots of Goodramgate stood out like a theatrical silhouette.

'Well,' Stephen said, glancing at his watch, 'it's midnight – I hope he's not going to be late.'

Almost before his words were out, a pair of headlights lit up the courtyard below. Simultaneously, other lights were extinguished, and the Minster disappeared like the good fairy in a pantomime. A nightly occurrence, Stephen said, but Zoe had never witnessed it before; it seemed ominous and she shivered.

Her spirits revived once they were on the road. The A19 was practically deserted, their driver silent in his desire to do his job and get back home again.

Speeding through a sleeping village, her hand enclosed in Stephen's, Zoe suddenly thought of Liam. In the next moment, Stephen mentioned the diary, which at the last moment he had slipped into his pocket. He said he would give it some attention while he was away, produce a typed-up version, which he could photocopy and send on to Zoe.

'It will give me something to do between ports,' he said dryly. 'Several weeks at sea without a break can be mind-bending.'

'Any idea where you'll be going?'

'Mediterranean, I think. But from there it could be anywhere.'

About to ask him for his address, Zoe bit the question back. He would probably give it to her of his own volition; if not, she would get it from Joan. Inhibited by the driver's presence, she thought it better to stick to impersonal matters.

'How did Liam get to Australia? Is it mentioned in the diary?'

'Only the anniversary of his arrival date. January 1914. Poor sod – he didn't have long there, did he? Eight months in Australia – then the war broke out and he was on his way back again.'

'Would he have emigrated, do you think?'

'He might have done,' Stephen said doubtfully, 'but for that he'd have had to get parental permission. And I get the impression he left rather abruptly. No, I think he probably worked his passage.'

'Could he do that?'

'Plenty did. In my time, too. Signed on as deckhand, looking for a bit of adventure, wanting to see the world, that sort of thing, and found it was a bloody sight tougher than they expected. Or they met a girl in one of the ports, or saw Australia as the land of opportunity – which it was. Back then, it was the easiest thing in the world to jump ship out there. If you kept your nose clean for a couple of years, you were all right, Blue, you could stay!'

He chuckled, telling her something of his early days aboard

refrigerated cargo ships on the Australian coast. Ships then had spent weeks in every port. To Zoe it sounded like an endless round of parties and fishing trips, and races back to the ship after being ashore all night.

'But the work was hard – long trips and not much home leave – and all for the princely sum of a few pounds a week!'

He laughed, but then went on more wistfully, 'When I was a lad, you'd see red ensigns by the score in every port of the world. But all that's finished now, the Merchant Navy's finished. It's been dying, quietly, for all sorts of reasons. Greed, selfishness, government inaction – you name it. And if it's not dead already, it's on its last gasp. Just pray there's never another Falklands, Zoe – because if there is, the government will be hard-pressed to find a fishing boat to supply the Fleet!'

Resenting the fact that he had to go back to a job that was no longer what it had been, Stephen seemed to feel the need to talk it out of his system. Pressing his hand, Zoe let him carry on. She had heard the good side: now, when he was feeling low, she might hear the less attractive aspects, and know him better.

She heard tales of redundancies and enforced retirements, junior officers who were forced ashore in search of whatever other employment they could find. Old-established shipping companies giving up general cargo in favour of container fleets, road haulage, even travel companies selling holidays in the sun. She heard of takeovers by foreign entrepreneurs, British crews ousted by cheaper crews from the Far East. And a few die-hard British companies who ceased to be ship-owners in favour of being ship-managers, managing for foreign-flag consortia registered in the world's tax havens.

'They're no more than box-numbers in places like the Bahamas and Hong Kong. They run ships registered in Liberia and Panama. And they employ people like me. I'm a mercenary these days,' he added with a touch of defensive arrogance, 'working for whoever pays best. And it's a buyer's market out there, Zoe, which is why I don't argue too strongly when I get phone calls like the one I had tonight.

'If I'd refused to go, they might have said okay, and gone on to the next name on the list. They might have given me another call in a couple of months' time – but there again, they might not. I can't take that risk – not if I want to go on working for them.'

'Is it so bad,' she asked, 'that you wouldn't get a job elsewhere?'

'Oh, no – I'd find another job with another company, all right. But I doubt the pay would be as good. And from what I hear, the conditions could well be a bloody sight worse. At least I know this bunch. They might be tough, but they're not likely to go under.'

There was tension in him, and an ambivalence Zoe found difficult to understand. She wanted to say: 'If you hate it so much, why do it? Why not give up, and find something else?' He had no dependants, and apart from his car, Stephen's tastes were not extravagant, his lifestyle modest without being miserly. She would not have said that money was particularly important to him, yet with regard to his job, it obviously was. A flash of insight made her suspect that it was part of the hate: if I have to do it, he might have said, I'll get the best rate there is.

But did he have to do it? She was back to her original question. Perhaps, beneath the resentment, love still existed, desire still burned, as in a failing marriage. The sea had been his first love, and more than that, his refuge; it must be hard to admit that the relationship was over. Stephen Elliott, Zoe began to realize, was a man who liked to succeed, and that might be a clue to his relationship with her. With one broken marriage behind him, he was not about to place himself in a position to lose again.

The road would not have been easy, she reflected, stealing a glance at that uncompromising profile, even if Stephen's career had kept him in York, but to have him regularly away, and for five or six months at a time, made it hard indeed. Surveying the boulders of his fixed ideas, the chasms of widely differing experience, for a moment Zoe was swamped by gloom. But then she comforted herself with the thought that she had always enjoyed a challenge, and her success so far had not been won without taking chances. To let him go without a fight would be foolish, but to prove him wrong would be no easy task. Suddenly, however, Zoe wanted to do just that.

The broad acres of North Yorkshire became Cleveland, and from a raised section of motorway Zoe saw Teesport spread out before her like a glittering, spangled carpet. Black night, black sea, and as they drew closer, the man-made mystery of piers and refineries; shadows and shining steel, massive storage tanks bearing the legends of half a dozen oil companies; ships alongside, funnels lit up, decks that were pools of light. There was excitement here and an air of romance which defied the cold commercial heart of it. Merchant ships, by their very definition, Stephen might have said, were always commercial, yet Zoe could not have been more thoroughly besotted had those prosaic, unlovely vessels been a group of clipper ships or four-masted schooners.

Where are they going? What oceans will they cross? What sights will they see? The questions, unuttered, filled her head. This was Stephen's world, and with that first glance she both envied and pitied him, beginning to understand the feelings that drew him back to sea, time after time. Like a lover to a fickle mistress, she thought, pressing his hand.

He slipped an arm around her shoulders, leaning across to peer out of the window, trying to get his bearings. There was a light in his eyes which spoke of a challenge accepted, a firmness of speech as he addressed the driver, which held nothing of regret.

From its funnel Stephen was able to identify the ship coming in, but it took their driver some time to find the entrance to the oil terminal. It was almost half-past one when they arrived, with no sign of Mac and Irene. No sign, either, of the agent. The guard on the gate seemed to have little information, and restricted access meant that they could not go through to the berth without an official pass.

Ten minutes later the agent arrived, full of apologies, explaining that the ship was only just alongside, but his information was that they were having problems with the gangway, damaged in heavy weather the night before. With the right documentation and the taxi dismissed, the young man took them through the terminal in his car.

It was so huge, Zoe did not at first recognize it as a ship. It appeared, between two towering gantries, as a sheer black wall of steel some fifty or sixty feet in height. Straight-sided, when she had thought ships' hulls were curved, bridge and accommodation rising like a floodlit tower-block at the after-end, while the name, *Damaris*, and port of registry were emblazoned in huge white letters across a squared-off stern.

Men were milling about on deck and quay, and it transpired that a temporary gangway would have to be rigged. While they were waiting for that, another car arrived, this time with Mac and Irene. They exchanged hugs and greetings, and after a rapid assessment of the situation, broke out the coffee and sandwiches. It was like a party, Zoe thought, in the dead of night, in the teeth of a chilling wind, with the biggest ship she had ever seen looming over them. It was so bizarre, she could not help laughing, and her laughter infected Irene, until in the end even the men were dryly amused, shaking their heads and muttering that the performance was about par for the course.

'And anyway, whoever joined a ship during office hours?' Mac wanted to know.

But by a quarter to three the gangway was rigged, Customs and Excise officers boarding with the agent. Stephen hoisted his baggage, Mac did likewise, preparing to carry it up that steep and narrow wooden gangway. Zoe eyed the angle and the ropes with horror. It looked like a plank set against the north face of the Eiger. Fortunately, one of the Filipino crew descended halfway to take the luggage, and the two men returned to escort Zoe and Irene to the top.

'Just think,' Irene gasped as she struggled to regain her breath, 'we've got to go down that, before long.'

'I prefer not to think about it,' Zoe replied with feeling. 'I might be tempted to stow away, instead!'

'Don't,' Stephen warned, 'else I'll clap you in irons, and feed you on bread and water!'

All jokes ended as they met the Mate. Zoe hung back while he and Stephen discussed the Captain; glancing down onto the quay, she saw an ambulance drawing in between the gantries. Inside the accommodation, they climbed several flights of stairs to reach the Master's cabin. She waited in the office with the agent and a Customs officer as the Mate took Stephen into a bedroom. Through two open doors, she could just see the foot of a double bed and a man's legs, one of which was bound into a heavy splint.

'Bad business,' the agent commented. 'He was on the bridge, apparently, and a sudden bad roll sent him flying across the wheel-house. Smashed his leg against the radar.'

Zoe winced. She noticed, suddenly, an object on the floor which looked like an instrument of medieval torture. The agent told her it was a stretcher, the type which enclosed a body from neck to foot. The Captain, he said, would be manhandled off the ship in that. Thinking of that perilous gangway, Zoe did not envy him, at the mercy of whoever was carrying him down.

Two uniformed ambulancemen arrived at the door. They were shown through into the bedroom; two very slight crew members stood out in the alleyway, looking nervous. As well they might, Zoe thought, wondering whether they were the ones designated for the job of carrying the stretcher. Stephen appeared, carrying a sheaf of papers. He had a word with the Customs officer and then turned to Zoe.

'I think you should make yourself scarce while they get him out of here. I'll take you to Mac's cabin – you can have a natter with Irene. I'll give you a shout when we're all clear.'

Mac and the Chief Engineer were busy in the office, but the retiring Chief greeted Zoe cheerfully, showing her through into his dayroom where Irene was flicking through a magazine. He told her to help herself to a drink.

Irene was sipping a glass of cola. 'I'm driving,' she explained, 'but there's spirits by the bottle there. You have what you want.'

Gratefully, Zoe helped herself to a generous tot of brandy. Despite her padded jacket, cold had seeped into her bones, and there seemed to be no heating on the ship. The warming liquid stilled her shivering and dispelled the tiredness, but her conversation with Irene was interrupted by sounds of activity from the other end of the alleyway. At a sudden shout, both Mac and the Chief responded instantly. Hesitantly, the two women went to see what was wrong.

'We need a bit more muscle,' Stephen was saying. The two ambulancemen were kneeling by the stretcher, obviously unhappy with the situation. Mac was strong enough to oblige, and as though from nowhere another burly figure materialised, oil-streaked and boiler-suited, with forearms like an Olympic weight-lifter. Between them they began the journey down those endless flights of steps, past at least half a dozen fire-doors, and onto the deck.

Kneeling on the couch beneath a large, square window, Irene watched their progress with bated breath. Beside her, Zoe could hardly bear to look. As the stretcher was lifted from deck to gangway, and over the side, she pictured that tremendous drop and felt sick. The little group slowly disappeared from sight and Irene turned away, her face blanched of colour.

'I think I will have that drink, after all,' she said shakily.

Stephen was standing at the top of the gangway, tension in every muscle. Eventually, he relaxed, turned with a smile to the Mate standing by, and Zoe knew that they had handled the man on the stretcher without mishap.

'It's all right,' she said, and the two women clasped hands in mutual relief.

Despite the chill of the night, Mac was sweating when he returned, his red beard glistening. Dismissing his wife's concern as so much fuss, he poured himself a beer, and returned to the office and that mound of paperwork.

Zoe's remark that there seemed an awful lot to do was greeted by laughter from Irene. 'There always is. It's like having a new head of department every five or six months – and only half a day for the handover. After that, they're on their own.'

Zoe shook her head. 'I couldn't cope – it would drive me crazy.'

'Me too, but they seem to thrive on it...'

When Stephen reappeared he had changed into smart black trousers and a navy-blue, military-style sweater. As though emphasizing his air of authority, the four gold stripes of his epaulettes glinted in the light, and Zoe suddenly found herself thinking of Robert Duncannon, wedded far more securely to the army, it seemed, than he had been to any woman. The uniform might be different, she thought, but its effect was the same, completing the change in Stephen which had begun, she realized now, with that telephone call in York. He was colder, harder, behind some invisible wall that she sensed but could not break. He was responding to people and situations with his usual good humour, but that ready smile – so genuine before – never quite reached his eyes.

She followed him back to the cabin with the word Captain over the door; a cabin which was now his. He closed the door between office and dayroom, and for a moment leaned against it.

'And so it begins,' he said laconically. 'But I thought you might like to see what I'll be calling home for the next few months...'

There was an awkwardness between them, and both were aware of it. Zoe played her part, looked round, obligingly poked her head into the bedroom. It was beautifully fitted out, finished in teak like the dayroom, with cupboards everywhere and tasteful though unimaginative pictures on the walls. The dayroom even had potted plants growing in a window-box.

'Like Captain Bligh,' she said in a feeble attempt at a joke.

'Well, let's hope the Mate is no Mr Christian.'

In the ensuing silence, he looked out of the window. 'It'll be getting light, soon. Irene will want to be going. She said she'd give you a lift to the station.'

He reached for her, held her in his arms, but Zoe could not respond. She felt sick and cold inside, and was wishing she had not been so eager to come. It would have been better, surely, to have said goodbye in York; in this environment, of which he was so obviously a part, he was a stranger. When he had said, once, that she did not know him, Zoe had thought him callous, the words an excuse for setting distance between them. Now she saw the truth of the claim, and wanted only to escape. The vow she had made in the car was folly in the extreme.

Turning away, Stephen wrote something quickly on a piece of card. It was the ship's name and the company's London address. As he handed it to her, he said tersely: 'This will always find me. Let me know how you get on with the letters.'

'Yes, I will.' Any pleasure she might have felt was neutralized by that request. He had given her permission to hold all those letters for as long as was necessary, but Zoe wondered whether she really wanted to know what they contained. A catalogue of tragedy, caused by at least one unresolved love-affair, was how they were beginning to strike her. Did she really need them to underline her own particular misery?

155

Ten

The film Stephen had had developed and printed in La Coruna had produced two passable photographs of Zoe and one that was excellent. It had been taken beneath the archway where they had first kissed, on a bright day with light reflecting into her face. Her hair was loose and soft, like a dark cloud about her head, pale skin and clear grey eyes luminous in the surrounding shadows. About her mouth hovered a gentle half-smile which made her more tantalizing than ever. Sometime, Stephen promised himself, he would have the print enlarged and framed, but for the moment it was mounted on a hand-made card beside his bed.

It had been another hot, breathless Mediterranean day, their third spent drifting off Greece, awaiting orders. Showering after an afternoon swim in the ship's tiny pool, Stephen changed into fresh white shorts and shirt and sat down to fasten a pair of sandals. As always his eyes went to the photograph, and yet again he remembered his last sight of her, the brief wave before she stepped into Irene's car, the bright little smile that was so obviously forced. That determined bravery had touched him more deeply than tears ever could. By comparison he thought of Ruth, who had wept copiously every time he went away, wringing guilt out of him like blood. Just one of his reasons for not wanting Zoe to accompany him to Teesport.

Dread, however, had been outweighed by the need to keep her with him to the last possible moment, that and a desire to show off a little, to let her see something of what the job entailed. And in the seeing, perhaps she might understand for herself the impossibility of anything lasting. Nevertheless, Stephen could not help lacerating himself with memory, could no more consign her photograph to the watery deep than he could cast himself overboard. He needed Zoe Clifford, and in itself that knowledge was a crippling thing.

He had wanted, so often, to put his feelings into words. The first time it had come unbidden, and with such force that even now he could recall the effort to contain it. He had been aware, even then, that the affair was more than just physical.

As ever, he told himself that it was unfair to impose a lifetime of separations upon a woman he loved, that promises which could not be kept should neither be made nor exacted; that he was being cruel to be ultimately kind. Somehow, though, those fine principles had an empty ring about them when he thought of Zoe, and he seemed to be thinking of her all the time, remembering things she had said and done, her sympathy and tenderness, and the ease he felt, just being with her.

Stephen had known he was going to miss her, but it was worse than that: he wanted her so much that he ached with it. The job was usually an antidote to such feelings, sufficiently demanding in the first month to erase most memories of home; but this was a ship that behaved itself, the crew competent and good-humoured, his officers professional. Within days Stephen had come to grips with the paperwork, and things were ticking over with all the ease of a well-oiled machine. He hated himself for wishing problems, but he could have done with a few to take his mind off Zoe.

The nights were the worst. Although he had never been one for spending much time in the officers' bar, he found himself dropping in after dinner, ostensibly with the intention of getting to know them all, but really to postpone the moment when his cabin door was closed and he would be alone. Mac seemed to know what was on his mind, but sensibly, forbore to comment. Even if he had, Stephen knew he could not have discussed the heart of the problem, the tormenting fear that Zoe would meet someone else while he was away, someone younger and more interesting, someone who was around for 365 days of the year.

During the day, he told himself not to be paranoid, that if she loved him she would be there, waiting, when he returned. And if she truly loved him she would always be there. He told himself that it was for her sake that he had refused to impose the burden of his feelings, steering her away from making a commitment to him in return.

She was young and beautiful and extremely talented; and with such a solitary occupation, she needed a social life. He could not imagine her being alone for very long. He wished, however, that he could be more genuinely sanguine about that. She would never know how much it had cost him to pretend.

But in the dark hours of the night, he knew it all went back to that old boyfriend of hers, a relationship that had ended only a matter of days before he and Zoe met, and had never really been explained. *Off with the old, and on with the new* – was that how she operated? While the sun was up, he did not think so, but shut in his cabin, with only books and music for company, he thought of his ex-wife, whom he had trusted completely, and he was no longer so sure of Zoe.

It was hard to admit, but the progress of Zoe's life had become more important to him than the questions which brought them together. Almost his only consolation was the fact that she was keen to go on with her research into those letters, and had promised to keep him up to date. On his side, Stephen had the diary, parts of which they had read together; but the writing was so tiny, and on such thin paper, it was hard to grasp the sense of it immediately. They both agreed that a transcript would make things easier.

Not that he had managed more than a few pages since leaving Teesport. So far his communication with Zoe consisted of a postcard from Spain, which should have been a letter, except that he was hurting too much to pen more than a few innocuous lines. Since then he had wasted innumerable sheets of paper, on which he had expressed, far too eloquently, his love and need of her. He thought the trick might be to forget himself – and Zoe too – by concentrating instead upon that point of mutual interest, the Elliotts. Then he could be as eloquent as he wanted to be, without expressing personal feelings at all.

But even that had its problems. Halfway through his letter, Stephen found himself thinking of their separate reactions to those cold, brief certificates. The truth, still unproved, seemed more and more obvious: that the father of Louisa's children was Robert Duncannon, not Edward Elliott. Liam and Robin had been born in Dublin, and, like Tisha, both bore *Duncannon* as a middle name. At that time, Robert's regiment had been stationed in Dublin after a two-year sojourn in York. Edward, meanwhile, according to fresh examination of the street directories, was still conducting his business in York. All the pointers were there, even to the fact of Tisha's subsequent birth at the house on Gillygate. When she was born, Robert was serving in the Sudan; he had even been awarded a medal for bravery at the Battle of Omdurman in 1898. It was not until late the following year that Louisa had married Edward.

Zoe's sympathies were all with those two. She had Robert down for a careless seducer, ready to abandon his mistress for some convenient foreign war as soon as he grew tired of her. 'After all,' she had said pointedly, 'they didn't know much about birth control in those days, did they?'

Rather guiltily, Stephen had felt obliged to leap to Robert Duncannon's defence. It struck him that Zoe was making an oblique reference to their own relationship, its parallels deviating only in one respect. As Stephen said, the man was an army officer, and he had his job to do; to which Zoe had countered with the information gleaned from the Public Records Office: that Robert had gone to the Sudan on secondment to the Egyptian Cavalry. His own regiment had stayed in Dublin, and he had rejoined them with the rank of major just in time to earn more medals in South Africa. Presumably, after Louisa was safely married to Edward.

'We don't know that,' Stephen had said, and he had gone on to point out that Zoe was virtually accusing Louisa of using her cousin as a ticket to security and respectability.

'And if she did,' came the sharp response, 'who could blame her? In her circumstances, and with three children under five years old, I might have been tempted to do the same!'

That heated exchange, in retrospect, was revealing of both their characters. Nevertheless, he sympathized with Robert Duncannon. Feeling as he did about Zoe, recalling the power of that initial attraction, Stephen could understand only too well what the man must have felt for Louisa Elliott. And then there was the other side of the coin, ambition. He knew a lot about that, too, about the love of the job and the drive to succeed. Perhaps Robert Duncannon had suffered a similar duality, unable to give up his army career no matter the depth of his love for Louisa.

He shook his head, slightly bemused by the power of those long-dead forebears. It seemed incredible that they should have, from the distance of the grave, the ability to intrude to such an extent. As though, once thought of, they began to live again, using the cognizance of their descendants to settle old scores. Or, he thought with startling insight, to resolve problems which had been outstanding for more than seventy years.

That idea, unwelcome and unnerving, sent a chill up his spine. 'Come on, Elliott,' he muttered to himself, 'don't be ridiculous.'

Abandoning the letter, he went to have a beer with Mac.

The ship's rare, three-day pause was the chief topic of conversation over dinner in the saloon. In the hot, dry weather much maintenance had been done, to the imbalance of the overtime chart for the month. Hours of sleep and sunbathing had been indulged in; but it was unsettling not knowing where they were bound and for what cargo. It could, quite literally, have been anywhere in the world. Disliking idleness, Stephen was keen to get on with the job; keen also to arrive at a port where mail might be delivered. Already he was wondering whether Zoe would have written, and if so, what.

An impromptu darts contest enlivened the evening, but with the approach of midnight Stephen left the bar to do his usual rounds before bed. In the dimly-lit chartroom the third Mate was writing up the log-book, while out on the bridge-wing, a watchman was looking for his relief at twelve. It was quiet and calm, the ship hardly moving at all. Satisfied that things were as they should be, Stephen left the darkened wheelhouse for the soft night outside.

It was warmer in the open air, and with the main engine shut down, very quiet. On an impulse, he climbed a ladder to the topmost deck above the bridge, breathing deeply, looking up at that dazzling array of stars, like a gem-studded net surrounding the earth. In those latitudes, with no other lights to distract the eye, even the tiniest pin-pricks were visible, from the fine dust of the distant nebulas to the glittering beauty of the nearer stars, like diamonds on black velvet. He picked out the constellation of Orion, the hunter, with Sirius, the dog-star, close at his heels.

Cassiopeia's Chair, and the Plough, far to the north. In England it would be nine o'clock, on a clear night just dark enough to see the stars in open countryside; but with the lights of London to contend with...

He sighed. Did city-dwellers ever notice what was above them?

On thoughts of Zoe his mind drifted for a while, again, not happily. Below him the watch changed, and all became silent once more. He felt terribly alone, not a new sensation by any means, but it was suddenly acute. Not for the first time, he envied Mac and Irene their twenty years of married life, the trust which was palpable between them. He was aware that the failure of trust lay in himself, and he wished it could be otherwise. From this distance it seemed a trivial thing, especially compared with his daily responsibilities at sea. If he were alone at home, here he was even more so, where the burden of all decisions lay ultimately with him. Master under God, was how one Old Man had signed himself in Stephen's youth, and the ancient term, valid since the days of the first Elizabeth, had remained forever with him. Never more true than on a night like this, when a man could believe himself the only soul left alive on earth. The stars pressed closer, and it was like looking at the face of eternity.

Once, he had named half a dozen for Zoe, straight off, and she had been impressed by the knowledge which enabled him to guide a ship across the faceless oceans of the world. But what were half a dozen stars amongst the thousands he could see, the innumerable millions beyond the reach of even the strongest telescope? Infinity, eternity: without some kind of faith a man could go mad just trying to comprehend it. Yet the stars formed their unchanging patterns, the planets moved on their appointed courses, all ordained by a maker whose purpose would always be the profoundest mystery. The only way to retain sanity was to believe in that purpose, even while the ultimate aim remained forever out of sight.

Was there really such a thing as free will, he wondered; or was everything planned to the last detail? Was he destined to go on like this till death reached out and claimed him; or had he just been given his last remaining chance of happiness, and stupidly, ridiculously, turned it down?

If so, it was too late for regrets. With one last, long look at that dazzling array of stars, Stephen told himself that the course was set, the voyage, wherever it led, must be made.

Just before noon the next day a telex message arrived. The ship was to proceed with all speed to the Soviet port of Odessa, for fuel oils. Immediately, Stephen collared the Second Mate, who was just about to go on watch, to ask what charts they had for the Aegean Sea. Particularly for the Dardanelles, that narrow entrance into the Black Sea which had caused such problems for Churchill in the First World War.

On the bridge they checked the charts together. All the necessary ones were present, but had not been corrected for some time. With a grin at the inches-high stack of Admiralty Notices to Mariners, Stephen remarked that the young man would have his work cut out over the next few days. Reaching for the first of them, the Second Mate agreed.

'I wouldn't care, sir,' he added with a sigh, 'but I've just corrected all the ones for North Africa. The Mate was laying me odds that we'd be heading there.'

'Never can tell, in this business.'

He left him to it, but once the ship was again under way, Stephen returned to discuss courses and distances. He needed to work out an estimated time of arrival for transmitting to the company's London office and the charterers in Hong Kong. Poring over various charts, noting the position of several islands with familiar names, Stephen suddenly spotted the island of Lemnos. Way to the north, not far from the Dardanelles.

And there it was, Gelibolu – Gallipoli – the peninsula where the Australians had fought such terrible battles in 1915, and where Liam Elliott had received his first baptism of fire. Stephen felt chill and grim looking at that long neck of land. Every one of those young men must have wondered what on earth they were doing there, when they had joined up to prevent the Kaiser's forces from overrunning Europe, and ultimately, their own mother country.

How the hell did you get involved, he silently asked of Liam, feeling with uncanny surety that soldiering was not that young man's aim and never had been. Had he been caught up in a kind of war fever? Or simply swept along with the rest, a victim of the times in which he found himself? Robin, fully trained by August 1914, would no doubt, in his ignorance, have been excited by the thought of seeing some real action, as many were; while Robert Duncannon must have viewed it all with the caution of a seasoned campaigner. But Liam? Stephen shook his head.

After dinner that evening he refused Mac's offer of a drink in the bar, taking himself back to his cabin instead. With only a few days between here and Istanbul, where mail could be posted, it was time to add something to the transcript he had promised Zoe. But first, he thought, he would read a bit more of the diary. Although the year of writing was 1916, Liam had inserted details of important dates in the previous two years. Some were tersely revealing.

January 13th, for instance. In that little black-bound book, Liam had recorded his arrival at Port Melbourne in 1914. Two days later he stated: '*Left the ship, walked inland.*'

Eleven

With no specific plan or destination, Liam worked odd days here and there, listening as he went, following suggestions, weighed down by nothing heavier than the pack on his back and the need to eat at reasonable intervals.

Taken up as he was with each day's survival, the journey was too full of interest and incident for him to dwell much upon what had been left behind, and that meandering, six-month voyage across the oceans of the world had set mental as well as physical distance between the unhappy boy and the rapidly maturing young man. Work he did in exchange for a few shillings or a meal, finding the food another pleasure, wholesome and plentiful, unlike the weevil-infested victuals aboard ship, or the strange dishes he had encountered in Greece and Lebanon and the Far East. At the height of the Australian summer it was hot and dry, but the outdoor life was clean and stars made a canopy for his bed. Preferable by far to the cramped and stinking quarters allocated to him in the ship's fo'c'sle.

In the tropics water had been rationed, while in foul weather everything was wet. The bosun had been a tyrant, the old hands adept at passing all the worst jobs to the least-experienced deckie, while his peers had found him uncongenial and subsequently left him alone. Liam found himself thankful for quick wits and fingers which had learned to be deft in Edward's workshop. Ignorant to begin with, he had quickly learned the right ways of coiling a rope, holy-stoning a wooden deck and chipping at rust. Physically, the most difficult task had been learning to handle the ship's wheel in heavy seas, to keep her on the right course; but he had managed that too, and had a steering certificate to prove it.

There were no certificates to illustrate the rest of his education. Lessons which taught him to obey orders instantly, without

164

question or complaint and in the worst of conditions; and most important of all, how to stand his ground with men older and more experienced than himself. It was a hard school and there was no escape: a man was confined between ports like a prisoner, forced to tolerate his companions and even form some kind of relationship with them. On occasion, lives might depend on it.

He had been tempted to jump ship many times between Hull and Hong Kong, and only the whisper of Australia, like a ripple of excitement throughout the ship, stayed him. Even then, Liam did not leave at the first opportunity. Having learned the wisdom of consideration, he ignored Fremantle and Adelaide in favour of Melbourne. Escaping into a well-established city would make him less noticeable as a newcomer, and the State of Victoria was apparently richer, the climate more congenial.

He spent more than a month on the road, travelling first towards the north-west and Bendigo. In the thickly-forested hills, however, work other than timber-clearing was scarce. He moved east after that, labouring at the odd logging camp as he went, picking his way along tracks through magnificent forests of tall, straight eucalypts, their peculiar fragrance a source of constant pleasure. Shady glens full of tall tree ferns, small, whispering streams, and here and there a log cabin or weather-boarded bungalow with wide verandahs would occasionally surprise him. The inhabitants were usually friendly and unafraid, finding small jobs for him to do or offering food and drink as a gesture of kindness. Although the people considered themselves British and spoke a rough approximation of his mother tongue, Liam was pleased to discover few other parallels. Like the untamed continent they inhabited, there seemed nothing small about the people he encountered. They had open faces and a relaxed way of moving, a confidence which was almost tangible. And in a land of immigrants strangers were accepted and questions not asked beyond casual enquiries as to where he was headed. Who he was, where he came from, what he had done before, seemed unimportant. No one asked and he never said. In all his time on the road, only the present and immediate future had any importance. The past was irrelevant.

Out near Yarra Glen, he discovered that he had come in a wide circle around Melbourne, and that if he wanted work of any permanent nature it would have to be on the plains. Unwilling to move closer to the city, he headed south, found work for a few days on a large farm near Lilydale, then crossed a smaller range of hills, where the forests were just as beautiful but surprisingly more populated.

Before, he had often walked for a full day without seeing another living soul; in these hills and gullies there were cabins and clearings every few miles. There was even a village with a railway station, a pretty little place hemmed in by flowering trees and giant ferns, but after the solitude of the forests, even Fern Tree Gully was too busy. He soon discovered why. From there it was almost possible to see Melbourne, some twenty miles away, and the Dandenong Ranges were the coolest place within easy reach of the city. In a broad arc between, well-watered by creeks which rose in those hills, lay some of the richest farmland in Australia. He heard it was as good for garden produce as it was for grazing; and the railway link between Melbourne and the market town of Dandenong, some ten miles to the south, meant a quick and easy transfer of goods. Everyone he spoke to mentioned Dandenong, and although he was uncertain, a desire to settle for a while, plus a pressing need for money to replace boots and worn-out clothing, made Liam decide to try his luck there. It was big enough to ensure work for a while, and if what he wanted proved elusive, he could always move on.

The town was well-established, formed mainly around the crossing of the routes between Melbourne and the south-east, and from the hills in the north to the coast. The former became a broad main street, shaded from the intense heat of mid-afternoon by immense red-barked gums. At the crossroads stood a grand town hall, faced by shops and hotels clearly designed to impress by their size and two-storied grandeur. To one who knew the age and permanence of cities back home, Dandenong was no more than a small, brash child; but it was confident despite its rawness, and in his weary, shabby state, Liam was not sure he was equal to its demands.

It had been a dry, ten-mile hike from the hills, and he was in need of a drink and a wash. Resting on his haunches with his back against a tree trunk, Liam spent a good while watching the comings and goings from various hostelries, and eventually chose not the smallest, but the one whose customers were least concerned with their attire.

His decision was confirmed by the approach of a labourer from the blacksmith's shop. In dusty moleskins and an open-necked shirt, the man had overseen the shoeing of two sturdy horses before casually taking his leave and crossing the road to the hotel. As he passed, he glanced at the figure beneath the tree and gave him a nod in greeting. A few minutes later, Liam slowly gathered his things together and followed. The man was at the bar, ordering a beer. Liam went through to the washroom, so thankful for the sight of water running from a tap that he dipped his head to drink even before sluicing hands and face. In the cracked, fly-blown mirror his reflection was something of a surprise, the face much leaner and harder than he remembered, cheekbones pared of the flesh, jaw revealed as having a grim, determined set to it. His skin, now that it was free of dust, was a rich, golden brown, hardly the look of a recent arrival. The image pleased him; even the dark gold stubble glinting along his jaw marked him out as a man, not a boy.

Feeling suddenly more confident, he raked the remains of a comb through thick, dusty hair, tucked in his shirt and slapped a hand over corduroys that were tattered and frayed; his boots were beyond hope. A moment later he was in the bar, ordering a large beer with what remained of his last day's pay. With luck, he reflected as the cool, bitter liquid slaked his throat, there would be enough to order a meal; if not, he must go hungry. Thirst, however, was not something he could ignore.

The man he had followed into the hotel was still leaning against the counter, having little to do, apparently, but take account of the small company gathered in the dark, bare room. Without bothering to disguise his curiosity, he watched Liam drink, smiling as he set the glass down.

'Looks as though you needed that.'

'Been on the road,' Liam admitted ruefully. 'It's a dry walk from the hills.'

'Thought I hadn't seen you around.' He fished a squashed packet of cigarettes from his breast pocket and offered it to Liam. 'Smoke?'

Trying to disguise the depth of his gratitude, Liam accepted; he had been without tobacco for days, and the beer had released afresh all his longings for a cigarette. Less openly than his companion, he indulged in a little observation himself. Close to, the man was younger than he had thought, late twenties, perhaps, shorter and stockier than Liam, with the walnut tan that goes with near-black hair and dark brown eyes. There was intelligence and good humour in the lines of his face, although Liam noted that the nose had been broken at some time and a deep scar bisected one eyebrow, lending his companion an eternally quizzical look. His expression seemed to be asking questions even when nothing was said, so that Liam found himself talking, about his situation, his most recent travels, and the need for work.

For a moment the other man narrowed his eyes, and the glance that ran over Liam was surprisingly hard and shrewd.

'Well,' he announced, 'I won't pretend you're in clover here, no matter what they told you up north. There's been a bit of a drought, as you must've noticed, and bosses are laying men off, not setting 'em on.' He pursed his lips for a moment. 'Still, it's not bothered us too much where we are, and we're a bit short-handed with the harvest coming on. The boss might be willing to set you on, but there again, he might not. Depends. Can't promise anything, but if you want to come out with me, it's worth a try.'

'What's he like?'

'All right, if you're straight. He's a Welshman, came out here about thirty years back, with not much more than the clothes he stood up in. He's done pretty good though. His name's Maddox.' The young man grinned. 'And mine's Hanley. Ned Hanley. The old folks – my Dad's folks, that is – came out from Tyneside, way back. Where're you from?'

'Yorkshire.'

'Good cricket team, that. You'll be right,' he said with an encouraging grin. As though the matter had been decided, he ordered two more beers.

He assumed Liam could ride, but Liam had no experience with horses. In the end they both walked, leading the freshly-shod mares along the dusty road, the distance a little over five miles.

It was beautiful country, gently rolling grassland interspersed with woody pockets, the meandering lines of eucalypts following various watercourses down from the northern hills. On the horizon they curved away, deep blue in the falling light.

Every so often there were stands of ghost gums, trunks and branches white against dark foliage, bent and twisted shapes reaching out like wraiths across the fields. There was something beseeching about them, a strange, other-worldly beauty that Liam felt he would have painted, if only he knew how. And then he thought of Georgina, how well she could have portrayed them, and how she would have exclaimed over this strange land. A family of kangaroos, disturbed by their approach, went leaping and bounding away. As Liam stopped to admire them, Ned cursed his lack of a gun; they were pests, he said, breaking fences, ruining crops, a nightmare for every farmer in these parts.

Their presence underlined the difference of this landscape, and yet with its lines of trees and well-defined fields, cattle grazing here and there and crops ripening into late-summer gold, it was not entirely strange. It was a land being tamed by Europeans, and to Liam's eyes it bore a familiar stamp. This was a place where he could settle, where he could learn to love the land; he was suddenly anxious to be accepted by Ned Hanley's boss.

A broad, five-barred gate bearing the name MADDOX, marked the entrance to the Welshman's land. It was a spread of almost a thousand acres, Ned said, with various crops and a few acres of vegetables, but the main interest was beef cattle. Behind good fences which lined the red dirt drive, Liam saw some of the herd munching contentedly beneath the trees. In a paddock close to the house horses grazed, no thoroughbreds to be sure, but good, sturdy cobs suitable for hard work.

Behind a colourful, fenced-off garden sat the house itself, long and low with deep verandahs and a corrugated roof. It was hardly a colonial mansion but it spoke of permanence and solid assets. Maddox was not a man struggling in the wilderness, he was well-organized and here to stay. Liam admired that, knowing, as he weighed all before him, that he wanted the same for himself. One day.

But every man has to start somewhere. Waiting for Ned to find the farmer and explain his presence, Liam sensed this was the first rung on his particular ladder. Anxiety gnawed at him. He wanted, with an urgency which astonished him, to be accepted here.

Ewan Maddox was short and heavily built, with thick, iron-grey hair and black eyes which missed nothing. He was also a man of few words, his questions limited to essentials. In return, Liam was as honest as he needed to be, saying he knew little of farming but was keen to learn; and without false modesty claimed to be a good worker. That much he was sure of. He gave his name, as he had done since leaving home, as Bill Elliott. The short, hard, masculine name appealed to him in his new persona, far preferable to the soft diminutive which he had accepted but never understood until that last day. Liam was the name by which his family knew him; Liam represented the Irishness which came from Robert Duncannon, a man he would never acknowledge as his father. No one else, he swore, would ever use that name again.

Knowing nothing of the young man's background, Ewan Maddox weighed him with shrewd eyes, assessing height and bones and the whipcord slenderness produced by too little of the right food. Gauging what he might become, the older man asked him to give a hand at shifting some sacks of grain in the barn. Liam performed the task with ease. Maddox told him he was hired, on trial, for a month.

Delighted, Liam stammered his thanks, but Maddox had turned away, while Ned simply winked his approval and told him to come across to the bunk house and settle in.

The men's quarters faced the back of the house, opposite kitchens and storehouses and the quarters where the female servants lived. Usually, Ned said, there were two, but one had recently run off with one of the hands, so if Liam wanted to stay, he advised him not to make eyes at the other girl.

'Mrs Maddox has had enough of it,' he grinned, 'so we're all on a promise to keep ourselves to ourselves!' He went on to give a potted history of the family, explaining that the eldest son and daughter were both married and living elsewhere, the son managing his in-law's farm for them. Another daughter, Mary, was a nurse at the big hospital in Melbourne, so they didn't see her too often, but she was a decent sort, not stand-offish at all. Then there was a son at university, supposed to be studying agriculture, Ned said dryly, although when he was at home he spent most of his time out in the bush, looking at trees and collecting flowers.

'Never make a farmer, won't Lewis, no matter how hard the old man pushes him. He'd rather be a whatchamacallit – he did tell me, but I forget – somebody who studies plants, he said.'

Liam grinned. 'Botanist – was that it?'

'Yeah, that's the word.' There was a spark of mockery in the other man's sudden amusement. 'Don't tell me you had an education?'

'Not really – I just read a lot.'

'Well, you won't find many books here, mate – the most we get to see is the weekly paper.'

'Never mind – I'll get by.' Liam dumped his pack by the wooden bunk indicated. Like the walls it was constructed of solid baulks of timber, roughly planed and pegged together. Unlike most of the others it had no bedding, but Ned Hanley explained that Mrs Maddox kept that sort of thing in the house. In a lean-to outside was a pump with an overhead shower, a stone sink with a tap, and a couple of cubicles. Mrs Maddox saw to the laundry, but she expected the men to wash and shave regularly.

'If you pass muster, you eat in the kitchen, like family – if you don't, you eat on your own, out here!'

It sounded fair enough to Liam. After weeks of living rough, he could hardly wait to get under that shower.

It was good to be rid of dust and grime which had accumulated despite his frequent resort to mountain creeks; better still to don the clean if ill-fitting clothes Mrs Maddox lent him while his own were laundered. Refreshed, Liam's only problem after that was an empty, grumbling stomach. Shortly after seven, that too was taken care of. In the cool of evening the farmer's wife doled out massive plates of stew and dumplings, followed by hearty portions of fruit pie and cream. Liam ate till he thought he would burst, grateful for every delicious mouthful.

Mrs Maddox, he decided, was sharp but kind, as voluble as her husband was silent, and still with the sing-song accents of her native Wales. With her prematurely white hair and long pointed nose, she reminded him of a little Jack Russell, lots of bark and a few nips to the ankles, but basically affectionate. He thought he would like her.

Until they had the measure of him, the other hands treated the newcomer warily, but in his months at sea Liam had learned something of diplomacy and the value of a smile. He said little, kept his past to himself and worked hard.

Arriving just as the harvest was about to begin, Liam was plunged immediately into an exhausting regime, up at dawn to follow the reaping machine, stacking the stooks into neat pyramids, while the stubble stabbed at every exposed bit of skin. It was hot, dusty, back-breaking work, yet he enjoyed it, falling into bed just after dark to sleep the sleep of the just.

Mrs Maddox and Ella, the general help, milked the handful of dairy cows and worked the kitchen garden, releasing Mr Maddox and all six hands to what was essential in the fields. After the reaping came threshing and winnowing, gathering oats and barley into sacks and the straw into barns for winter bedding. Hay, gathered well before Christmas, already stood in stacks beyond the yard.

For weeks there was little time for anything but work and sleep, but as soon as it began to slacken off, Ned grabbed Liam one morning and ushered him into one of the nearby paddocks for his first riding lesson. Daunted though he was, Liam was secretly elated. It had crossed his mind more than once that Ewan Maddox might have taken him on purely for the harvest, and be thinking of some reason to dismiss him. But if Ned had been told to teach him to ride, the farmer must be thinking of keeping him on.

Smiling as he hitched himself up onto the rails of the fence, Liam watched Ned saddle up. Having tightened the girths, he casually ran his hands down from withers to fetlocks, examining legs and hooves with an expert eye. Memory jerked then, like a sickening physical jolt, and Liam was suddenly a child again, small and suspicious and confused, watching another dark-haired man in boots and breeches perform a similar action.

Words rose from the past: 'You don't know what to call me, do you, Liam?' and his mind clamped shut on the question, leaving him white-faced and trembling.

Mistaking the reason, Ned Hanley suddenly laughed, assuring

the green newcomer that old Daisy was the dullest, quietest mare ever bred, guaranteed not to shy or rear, even in a thunderstorm. With an effort, Liam thrust aside that picture from childhood and managed to concentrate on the lesson. Each day before work the lessons continued, and within a fortnight he was pronounced capable of riding out alone.

To his surprise, Liam found something immensely satisfying about being able to control an animal so much larger and stronger than himself. He discovered, after a while, that he had something of a way with horses and, as he graduated to more spirited mounts than Daisy, that he rode well. That his affinity may have been inherited from Robert Duncannon, the cavalry officer who had lived and worked with horses all his life, was something Liam refused to consider. Nevertheless, that early, unconnected memory returned to plague him at odd moments. He felt like an amnesiac in possession of one solitary clue to his identity, except it was an identity he did not want.

Several times he dreamed of a large house with long windows which dwarfed him, and an intricate fanlight above a massive front door. He had a strong feeling that the house was real, but he could not remember where it was. Sometimes a little girl with blonde ringlets appeared; at other times, his mother, weeping and wringing her hands. Each time he woke in distress, to find sleep impossible afterwards.

To smother the memories, he drove himself hard.

March was the season for ploughing, and while he was learning to handle horses in the shafts, he begged to be taught how to drive a plough. Little Nobby, who was the expert, tired of the game long before Liam; he wanted to lie on his bunk after a long day, he said, and teaching somebody was twice as hard as doing it yourself. So Liam practised on his own with old Daisy, learning to laugh back at the audience watching from the rails.

He ate well and mostly slept well, putting on weight and muscle despite the regime he set himself. When Mrs Maddox remonstrated with him, he said he liked to keep busy, whereas in reality he was afraid to relax. He needed something with which to divert his mind when he did stop for the day, but having read every newspaper and farming journal in the bunk room, what he really longed for was a book.

Ned was good company and Liam counted him a friend, but the other man's weak point was a lack of education. His tendency to mock it made enquiries about books difficult. Liam had never seen Ewan Maddox with anything other than a newspaper or a treatise on cattle, and his wife had no time to read, merely listening to what her husband saw fit to relate. But at Easter, when their son Lewis returned for his vacation, Liam spied an opportunity.

A dark, heavily-built young man, Lewis might have been Ewan Maddox thirty years previously. He was far from the airy, bookish youth that Liam had been led to expect. A keen horseman, he rode out every day, and it was on a joint excursion that Liam found courage to speak up.

'What sort of books?'

'Well, anything, really – I just like to read.'

Lewis Maddox considered. 'The Mechanics Institute has a library – it's in the Town Hall. Open most evenings, if you can manage to get down. But I've got all sorts in my room at home – if you're not particular, I'll pass a few your way. And my sister has plenty of novels – a few classics among the romance, I'm sure,' he added with a short laugh. 'Mary won't mind.'

Liam was uncertain about that, but meeting Mary Maddox a few days later, he thought her brother might be right. She was a plain, practical young woman, sure of herself but by no means overbearing. She talked as easily to her father's hired hands as she did to the maid, Ella, seeming to regard all of them as a kind of extended family. Liam imagined that to her, that was what they were. Old Murphy had been with them since before she was born, while Arnie and Ella, who were brother and sister, had virtually been adopted by Mrs Maddox after being orphaned by a bush fire some ten years back. Bert and Ned were more recent, and Ned, although he had all the qualities of leadership required by a foreman, had only been at the Maddox place just over a year. Watching him keeping a covert eye on the daughter of the house, Liam wondered whether Ned's ambitions to own his own land someday, did not centre upon the sturdy, capable figure of Mary Maddox. But nothing was said, and Liam did not ask.

Easter Day dawned bright and clear, and under Mrs Maddox's persuasion, they all set off in the open wagon for morning service at the Methodist church in Dandenong. It was a long time since Liam had been in any church, and although the service was strange to him with its lengthy prayers and unfamiliar hymns, he thought he preferred it to the set ritual of the Prayer Book. It seemed more sincere. Sitting there with his head bowed, pretending to add his own silent petitions to the words of the preacher, he found himself thinking about God, and wondering about his own faith. He had believed, once upon a time; although since leaving home he had not spared the Almighty much more than a passing curse. Admittedly, that had been when things seemed at their lowest, but even so, he felt ashamed. Did he believe? He was not sure. If there was a God, why did He allow such things to happen? He had been happy, and then…

On the trembling edge of pain, his mind winced away. It was better not to think, and he was happy enough now, so why bother about the past? Nothing could change it. Live for today, he thought, and if you can, work towards a better future. But where God came into that philosophy was something of a mystery.

It was on the way back that Mary Maddox brought up the matter of the books. 'Lew says you could do with something to read. I'll sort out a few novels for you and let you have them before I go back to Melbourne.'

Her directness threw him a little, forcing a stammer to his thanks.

'It's all right,' she smiled, 'I'm a keen reader myself.'

He caught Ned's louring glance and for a moment regretted mentioning the subject to anyone. If Mary noticed it, she pretended not to, and a moment later was talking about organizing a picnic in the hills for the following day. It was a public holiday and likely to be one of the last fine days of autumn, and she was determined they should all make the best of it. Her father shook his head; he did not want to go trailing miles into the hills, to be faced by crowds of city-dwellers. His wife nodded her agreement, but thought it a good idea for the younger ones.

'I'll fix some food, if you want to get yourselves off.'

Liam glanced at Ned, who was being unusually reticent. Lewis chided him, saying that all he ever did was go into town to drink in bars. A day in the hills would be good for him. Ned's scowl deepened.

Lewis turned to the others. 'Billy will come, I know – what about Arnie, and you, Bert?'

Arnie was keen, but Murphy and Bert and little Nobby all had things to do, apparently. As though he was bestowing a favour, instead of the other way around, Ned eventually allowed himself to be persuaded. Mary teased him unmercifully, and for a while Liam thought he would back out, but on Monday morning, he was ready and waiting in his smartest coat and breeches.

In boots and divided skirt, Mary looked good, Liam thought; and so it seemed did Ned, who contrived to keep his horse close to hers most of the way. Liam's mount did not take kindly to being kept at the back, but he had no intention of spoiling Ned's pitch: the matter of the books was bad enough.

As ever when he left the farm, Lewis was in his element, and with an interested listener was keen to identify the various species of shrubs and trees along the way. All along the gullies, edging every meandering creek, were the tree ferns, their delicate fronds filtering the sunlight, making dappled patterns across the tracks. It was green and fresh, alive with the fluttering of bright cockatoos and tinkling bell-birds, and the sudden sharp patter of rain-showers on shimmering leaves. And when the rain stopped, as it did within minutes, the aromatic scent of the gums permeated the air, delicate and invigorating, like new green wine.

Liam started to talk about his first weeks in Australia, the journey, the logging camps, how he had come to the Maddox farm. Lewis was keen to hear what Liam had seen and done, but it transpired that logging was an activity he deplored. The native Australian species, he declared with conviction, would soon be extinct unless it was stopped.

'And all that will be left,' he added derisively, 'will be the precious exotics imported by gardeners for their wealthy and ignorant clients!'

Casting his eyes over the dense woodland which surrounded them, Liam doubted it. Knowing from experience how many thousands of acres there must be in this small part of Victoria, he guessed it would take an army a lifetime to clear the Dandenong ranges. But he kept the thought to himself.

Meanwhile, despite objections from Lewis, Mary set out their picnic in a clearing near Belgrave. The severed trunks, her brother declared, looked like amputated elephant's feet, and he would not eat his food amongst such carnage. They all laughed, but he took his share back into the forest, joining them only as the little party pressed on towards the settlement.

Beside tracks and roads which ran off into the trees, Liam spied campers in tents, and slab-sided huts with bark roofs. By contrast, there were imposing mansions too, but the little town was constructed mainly of weatherboard and corrugated iron. To his amazement, there was also a narrow-gauge railway running to Emerald and Gembrook.

With the eagerness of a child, Arnie leapt at Mary's suggestion of taking a trip on the train. The horses were tethered in the shade, their fares paid, and they clambered aboard. Tiny carriages, open to the elements, rattled behind a miniature locomotive which chugged and skidded up seemingly impossible gradients and around tight, snaking bends. City folk, out to enjoy a fine holiday weekend, exclaimed over unspoiled beauty, while Liam was intrigued by the feats of engineering necessary to drive the line through.

Conscious of the shortening afternoon, they travelled only as far as Emerald, returning by the next train. Even so, the sun was well down in the sky by the time they unhitched the horses. Abandoning the scenic route on Ned's advice, they took the longer but safer road home, arriving just after dark. Mrs Maddox was anxious enough to give them a scolding, but her daughter was unrepentant. She had had a wonderful day, she said, and in that, Liam knew, she spoke for them all.

Liam got his books, Mary's selection first, because she was returning to the hospital in Melbourne. With her departure and the evidence of her gift on his shelf, Ned's comments became more than usually caustic. Liam ignored him, burying his head in a fat, well-read edition of Dickens' *Bleak House*. Before he had finished that, Lewis came over to the bunkhouse with a dozen or so others, covering a wide range of subjects from the flora and fauna of Australia to biographies of eminent explorers and empire-builders.

In a few weeks Liam had gone through the life of Captain James Cook, a Yorkshireman like himself, and a fairly recent assessment of the wool trade, with its opposite pole in Bradford. He remembered that his mother's father had been a wool merchant, and that set off a stream of unwelcome associations. After that, glancing at the novels, he skipped *Wuthering Heights* and its companion volume, *Jane Eyre*, and settled for something less emotional.

What he could not avoid, however, were his own memories. As the fine weather began to break, they became increasingly more insistent. Watching bronze and yellow beech leaves scatter across Mrs Maddox's garden, it came to him that in England it would be spring, and instead of fading marigolds and fuschias, his mother's garden would be dancing with daffodils. He thought of that mass of golden flowers along the ramparts, and the Minster's towers gleaming against a bright blue sky, and felt an unexpected lump come to his throat. In that moment he would have given almost anything to see York again, to be able to walk beside its broad, slow-moving river and watch the barges unloading along the staiths. Not that he wanted to leave Australia, Liam told himself, simply that he would have liked to reassure himself that York was still there, unchanged. From where he stood, it might well have disappeared forever.

Moved by a sense of guilt, a few days later he sat down to write to his brother, fulfilling a promise made so long ago that it had been forgotten for months. The letter said little about his journey out, concentrating instead upon his present good fortune, and the excellence of his employers.

'I seem to have been accepted here,' he added in closing, 'and intend to stay for as long as they'll have me. I'm saving hard, though, because I want a place of my own one day.'

That was true. Except to the library, Liam did not often go into town, preferring to busy himself in the tack room, polishing saddles or repairing broken bits of harness. On one particularly cold, wet Saturday, however, when the others had gone off on their usual jaunt, he settled down on his bunk to read. Crossing the yard, Mrs Maddox looked in with some surprise. It was far too cold, she said, to be sitting there; if he wanted to, he could come inside.

In the warm kitchen, surrounded by the comforting smell of cakes and new baked bread, the murmur of women's voices lulled him into reverie. Staring into the fire, he was soon drifting pleasantly, at home in the cottage on a winter's afternoon, his mother rolling out pastry, her wedding ring clicking rhythmically against a hollow earthenware rolling-pin.

Comfort and an awareness of affection enveloped him, he was warm and happy and there would be scones and home-made jam for tea. As his mother brushed past to check the oven, she ruffled his hair and told him to move, his long legs were in the way...

'Billy, will you move – I want to get to the fire.'

Laughter brought him back with a start. Ella, the buxom girl who helped in the house, was nudging his feet; Mrs Maddox was chuckling as she rolled fresh pastry. Panic-stricken for a moment, Liam stared from one to the other, feeling like a child amongst strangers, whose mother has suddenly abandoned him. Like a child he wanted to cry, was horribly afraid that he might, and with his chest hard and tight with disappointment, left them abruptly.

He heard Ella's sudden: 'Well!' followed by a nervous giggle, and footsteps which halted as he slammed the door. Drenched by rain as he crossed the yard, Liam gave vent to tears he could not control, all the more violent because they had been restrained for so long. But before he had reached the shelter of the bunkroom, grief had turned again to fury, to that same impotent rage which had so consumed him a year ago.

Regardless of wet clothes, he lay on his bed, staring at nothing, while the rain drummed with steady monotony on the corrugated roof. It grew dark, but no sense of urgency possessed him; Ned and the others would not be back much before midnight. He was startled when the door opened and a solitary figure entered, shrouded by a cape. A woman's voice uttered a muffled exclamation, set something down with a clatter and proceeded to light a lamp.

'Here,' Mrs Maddox announced. 'It's some dinner I've brought you. Get it eaten now before Ewan catches me. I've tried to keep it warm, thinking you was coming in for it – '

He took the tray, for a moment too astonished even to thank her. She stood at the foot of his bunk in the long room, regarding him with tense concern. Liam could not meet that gaze. Mumbling his thanks, he began to eat, amazed at his own hunger.

'Homesick, are you? Only natural – I was myself for a long time. But it catches you unexpected...' When he did not reply, she sighed with a touch of exasperation, just as his own mother did sometimes. With a sharp click of her tongue, Mrs Maddox added: 'Don't say much, do you? Might do some good if you did. Ah well, you know where I am if you want to talk – and it will go no further.'

Liam believed her, but did not know what to say. 'Thank you,' was all he could manage. Ridiculously moved by her kindness, nevertheless he wished she would leave him alone. As though sensing it, she turned to go.

'Don't forget now.'

He did not forget, but gratitude at that time seemed no more than an additional burden he could do without. A small part of him wanted to be mothered and comforted, but his own image of manhood mocked it. There was, too, the deeper fear of what he might say once he began to talk. Embarrassment made him gruff with Mrs Maddox for a while after that, but she did not seem to notice and treated him no differently. He was, however, glad of the drier weather which kept all of them busy.

The *Dandenong Journal* came to them once a week, and Melbourne newspapers were brought whenever Lewis or his sister Mary came home. Towards the end of July, the rumours of impending war in Europe grew stronger, setting the whole area agog with excitement. It was all anyone talked about, and the eagerness to get into town to find out more, was suddenly stronger than the allure of bars and female company. If Europe erupted, the consensus of opinion was that Britain would not stay out of it, and if Britain stepped in, then so would Australia. Older, and with two sons of fighting age, Ewan Maddox tried to quash the jingoism at his table. His wife was openly anxious, but the men were obsessed by the topic and would not leave it alone.

Liam was surprised by the evidence of conflicting passions amongst men he thought he knew well. Old Murphy, whom he had imagined to be as Australian as the outback, gave vent to such invective against England that Liam was almost convinced his list of injustices were personal instead of two generations old. Ned, on the other hand, who could claim a similar inheritance through his Tyneside Irish grandparents, thought Murphy was a silly old fool and said so. Nursing his own secret connections with both England and her other island, Liam simply listened while the argument threatened to come to blows. Enraged by the three who were against him, Murphy suddenly forgot his age and would have taken them all on. He danced like a wizened old gnome while Arnie, whose strength was greater than his intellect, held him back.

It seemed that only Arnie and Liam were neutral, the former because he did not understand what it was all about, and the latter because his own future was more important to him than somebody else's past.

There were plenty like him, but on his trips into town it seemed there was always a fight going on somewhere, and it was not always a matter of national prejudice. The Irish, who were numerous and loved a good argument anyway, were the most noticeable; but there were also well-settled Englishmen who professed no love for the mother country which had either kicked them out or provided so little they'd felt obliged to leave. For them, Australia should stay out of the coming conflict. Their opinions were not popular with the overtly patriotic youngsters who had been brought up on a scholastic diet of Empire and militarism and absolute allegiance to the monarchy.

Liam tried very hard to stay out of it. If a direct opinion was demanded, all he would say was that it would never come to war, and they were all being premature. That did not endear him, and more often than not provoked a bit of sniping from Ned, who accused him of being 'bloody clever'. When they were on their own, however, he pressed Liam for an answer.

'So what if it does come to it, Billy, what will you do?'

'Look, leave me alone, will you?' Liam snapped back, exasperated beyond endurance. 'I've just bloody well got here, for heaven's sake, I've no intentions of dashing back at the first trumpet-call!'

Ned was aghast, 'Well, of all the...' He broke off, letting whatever insult had sprung to mind die before it reached his lips. 'You want to be careful who you say that to, mate – them as don't know you might get the wrong idea.'

Liam dropped the harness he was working on and stood up, his fists clenched. 'All right, spit it out! You think because I'm not waving a flag and backing you up, I'm some sort of coward!'

'No! No, honest, I don't. But you being English and that, I can't figure you out. I'd've thought you'd be dead keen!'

'Well, I'm not. For a start, I like it here. I came here to settle, to make something of myself by my own efforts. I'm not rushing to throw all that away. And another thing – I've got a lot of respect for Ewan Maddox. He didn't have to take me on, but he did, and he kept his word. How's he going to manage if everybody takes off together? Have you thought of that?'

'Same as everybody else, I suppose.'

'And what about your grand ideas?'

'They'll just have to wait,' came the quick reply. 'Do you think I could sit here, stashing my pay every week, while other blokes go off to do the fighting? Not me, mate! Not me.'

That stirred uncomfortable considerations. Lighting a cigarette, Liam went outside. He handed the packet to Ned, who lit up with a certain grim satisfaction.

'I won't pretend I don't know what you mean,' Liam said slowly. 'I've got a young brother at home, who said he was going to join up...'

That night, remembering the last words they had exchanged on the towpath, he wondered where Robin was now, and what he was doing. He thought of Georgina, too, resurrecting the photograph his brother had taken before that precious world fell apart. She was happy and smiling then: did she smile like that now? He loved her still, knew with absolute certainty that he always would. With a whole year and thirteen thousand miles between them, his feelings for her had not altered one whit; he recalled little things she said, the times they had spent alone together. And it still hurt to look at her captured image.

Ned had no need to be jealous over Mary Maddox. Liam just wished he could tell him so.

A few days later, as he returned chilled and hungry from mending fences on the far border of the property, Mrs Maddox called out from the kitchen that he had a letter waiting. Having had Georgina on his mind for days, he hoped it might be from her, that she might have been given his address from Robin's letter and written something, anything, to suggest that she understood what had driven him away, missed him, might once have loved him too...

But the letter was from his brother, written from a town with a French name on the island of Jersey. Robin had indeed done as he had threatened that day, and having joined the 2nd Battalion the Green Howards, was now quartered in the Channel Islands. And having a wonderful time, Liam thought as he read the first page, wondering also how much longer the holiday would last. According to Robin, army life was just the ticket; and he seemed as excited at the prospect of war as most of the youth in Dandenong. Liam shook his head.

But just as Liam had glossed over the agonies of his trip out to Australia, so did his brother skip the immediate aftermath of Liam's departure, except to say that everyone had been upset, their mother especially. He went on to say that Edward had resisted the idea of Robin joining up, right to the moment he went, although his mother had reluctantly given her assent, and that was all he needed.

The next few paragraphs aroused fury. Robin had apparently had an interview with Robert Duncannon in York, and although he had proudly resisted the Colonel's offer of help, it seemed he had in some way fallen under his spell. As he rapidly scanned the following pages, Liam cursed his brother for a trusting, gullible child. Incredulous at first, he read to the end, then read it again, slowly, anger mounting with every sentence.

'... He's not nearly so bad as you make him out, and was most concerned about you. We talked, man to man, which I thought very decent, considering his position. He told me quite frankly that he had wanted to marry Mother more than anything in the world, but he couldn't, because he was married already. Georgina's mother was ill when he married her, a sort of mental illness that was not so bad to start with but got worse, only nobody told him about it. Her family knew, but they just wanted to get rid of her. Then he came to York and met Mother, and later on she went to live with him and his sister in Dublin. Georgina was very little then, and Mother helped to look after her, which is why she thinks such a lot of Mother, and I must say she was very good to her after you went away. We were all so worried and nobody knew what to do for the best. It took her a few weeks to get over it, but I dare say she will be happy now that she knows where you are and that you are safe. Dad, too.

'I expect the Colonel will be relieved as well, because he blames himself for everything. But he didn't blame Dad for marrying her, and his main regret was that he couldn't have married her himself. He said he was still very fond of her, and had never met a finer woman...'

I'll bet! Liam thought with bitter derision. As simple as that. Nothing about the lies and the grief, the sheer destruction that ill-begotten affair had brought about. And in the next breath Robin was preaching forgiveness. Never, Liam thought. Never, if he lived to be ninety, would he forgive them for what they had done.

He lit a cigarette and smoked furiously for a minute. Slightly calmer, he read on to the end. There was a line or two about Tisha, who wrote to Robin sometimes, and then Georgina was mentioned again. Her name seemed to leap off the page, and he was so starved for news of her that he read the sentence several times, trying to extract every possible meaning from its casual brevity.

'... her letter arrived by the same post as yours. She is still at the Retreat and working hard, so too busy to write often, but I know she will be as relieved as everyone else when she gets my letter to say you are safe and well...'

So, she had been worried about him. But so, it seemed, had everyone else. And he had managed to upset his mother for several weeks. He suffered unexpected pangs of guilt at that, guilt that he managed to smother in a fresh surge of anger against Robin. The ease with which he had been seduced into sympathy with their mother and Robert Duncannon infuriated him, and it was some time before he could consider that apparent defection with any degree of objectivity.

When he did, it came to him that Robin had always been the one to sympathize – with everybody. There was nothing treacherous about it, it was simply that he could generally be relied upon to see both sides of every problem. Generous, even-tempered and with affection to spare, Robin was usually the peacemaker, the one who would always look for the best in people. It was unfortunate, Liam decided, that because of his goodness he could also be manipulated, especially by those without scruples. Tisha was a past master at that; and so, it seemed, was Robert Duncannon.

Forgiving his brother, trying not to be unduly harsh in his reply, Liam was also consumed by concern. Several weeks had passed since that letter was written, and war seemed more inevitable by the day. With Robin on his mind, Liam was suddenly just as eager as his companions to know the latest news. And that need to know had become a passion which fired everyone he met.

During the last few days, with Austria declaring war on the Balkan state of Serbia, and Russia heaving itself into a threatening position on behalf of its tiny neighbour, it looked as though all the major powers in Europe were on the brink of mobilization. The news took time to arrive, however. On 3rd August they read that Germany had sided with Austria-Hungary and declared war on Russia; and two days later, on France. The Germans' unreasonable demand for free passage through Belgium, in order to attack an innocent neighbour, aroused British passions worldwide. The declaration of war upon Germany was a foregone conclusion.

That declaration, made on 4th August, did not reach Australia until the 6th. Liam had been detailed to go into town that day, and the atmosphere of tension and excitement struck him instantly. There was a great crowd outside the post office on Lonsdale Street, and another by the offices of the *Journal,* where single sheets were being pasted up before they were dry. Shortly after one, the news they were all waiting for came through from Sydney. Britain was at war, and Australia would back her to the hilt. '*To the last man and the last shilling,*' as one politician declared.

Grabbing one of those single, printed sheets as they were handed out, Liam fought his way through the crowd and paused on a street corner to read it. Within seconds half a dozen people were at his elbow, almost tearing the paper from his hands. Their reactions varied from unbounded elation to grim disgust, but most agreed that it was right. Germany should not be allowed to run rough-shod over Europe. With her worldwide interests in conflict with those of the British Empire, where would the aggression stop?

There was a report of a German merchant ship scuttling out of Port Melbourne, shots – '*the first of the War*' – fired across her bows, and a piece about two German warships, *Scharnhorst* and *Gneisenau*, at large in the Pacific. Suddenly, that war in Europe was no longer half a world away. Seized by emotions both violent and unexpected, Liam did not wait for further news. Mounting his horse he rode some distance out along the Stud Road, then stopped to consider his feelings afresh. He would enlist, he could do no other. He could not stand by while others fought to defend his right to live in this earthly paradise; and if in defending Australia he was also helping to defend England, then so he should. It should not be left to boys like Robin. Besides, Liam reasoned, justifying that abrupt change of heart, his self-respect would shrivel to think that his young brother was in the thick of it, while he, Liam, was sitting safe out here.

He thought of Georgina, and wondered whether he would see her again; perhaps he would, if he returned to England.

Sighing, he carefully folded the paper and tucked it into his pocket. Time to return: all at the Maddox farm would be waiting on the news he brought.

Despite their wholehearted eagerness to support the old country, when faced with the necessity of leaving the farm, most of them felt guilty. While Ewan Maddox stared out at the fallow fields of winter, pondering the difficulties of running his place virtually single-handed, the men finished their supper with unaccustomed speed and sloped off to their quarters to enjoy a freer discussion.

Less eager than the rest, Liam overheard Mrs Maddox's attempt at reassurance. Murphy would stay, she said; and as for Bert, his teeth were so rotten, an army dentist would faint at the sight of his mouth, never mind sign him up. Let them trail down to Melbourne, she advised her husband, and wait and see who came back.

Hiding a smile, for he was sure she was right, Liam closed the door quietly behind him. In the bunkroom, argument and a certain amount of heart-searching was going on. Even Ned, who declared that he would enlist no matter what, seemed less thrilled by the prospect than he had been only a few days ago. Old Murphy had turned sentimental: with tears in his eyes he said he would miss them, but he would stay to keep the farm going with the boss. Arnie was torn between his eagerness for adventure and loyalty to the people who had given him a home, but being less articulate, could only find expression for his anguish in violent movement. When not pacing the floor or thumping the walls, he would fling himself into his bunk and pound the pillows. Liam felt sorry for him. Full of themselves, Bert and Nobby were going to join up and have a great time, doing a Cook's tour of Europe while knocking off a few Germans on the way. Liam had a suspicion that it might not be quite as easy as that.

Then somebody mentioned the elder Maddox brother, managing the place out at Warragul; and Lewis, still at college. What would they do? And if both sons went, what would Ewan Maddox do? The consensus of opinion was that the older one would stay put, while the boss would probably insist his younger son cut short his studies and get himself home where he was needed. After all, somebody had to stay home and keep the country going, so why shouldn't Lewis get his finger out and do something practical for a change?

'What if he wants to enlist, like the rest of us?' Liam asked.

They were nonplussed at that.

If Lewis communicated with his parents over the next few days, nobody heard about it; but they were all astonished when Mary arrived on the Sunday to tell them that she had decided, with half a dozen friends, to volunteer as an army nurse. Ned was overjoyed.

Despite the enthusiasm, for several days there were no facilities for dealing with the mass of men and women eager to do their bit for King and country. Newspapers appealed for patience. Mary had returned within hours to Melbourne, but said she would be home again soon. The men worked badly and found excuses for making frequent trips to town. Mrs Maddox was anxious about everything and her husband on edge. No one heard from Lewis.

Recruitment began on 11th August.

TWELVE

Those frequent trips into Dandenong paid off. Even while they were planning their journey into Melbourne to enlist, Nobby returned from town with the news that Dandenong was setting up its own facility. But Ewan Maddox dug in his heels. He wanted a week's notice, and 11th August was a Tuesday, Market Day, so the only trip into town that any of them would be making, was to market with half a dozen young bulls. As far as he was concerned, they were all employed until Thursday evening; after that, they could please themselves.

There was bitter frustration in the bunkroom, and talk of mutiny, but in the end respect won through. There was also the possibility – remote, of course – that not all would be accepted, and those who were not would still need a job at the end of the day.

Thursday night saw a great polishing of boots and shoes, a clearing of precious possessions from individual shelves and hasty packing of clothes. Over an early breakfast next morning they said their goodbyes. Ewan Maddox was brusque, finding urgent business in the barns, but his wife shed a few unexpected tears over each of them. Ella was inconsolable, weeping floods into the washing up and hiding her face in her apron as they set off down the road at first light. Old Murphy hobbled off to the stables.

Subdued at first, the little group was soon singing down the road to Dandenong, spirits soaring with the sunrise. Early morning mist hovered over the paddocks and clung beneath the trees, standing like fog where the creek became marshy near the town. From a distance it looked like a heavenly city, treetops and chimneys and mock-gothic towers sparkling above a white, sunlit cloud; and only as they drew closer did that impression dissolve into the mundane greyness of mist. People were astir, labourers going about their daily business, one or two women waiting outside butchers' and grocers' shops, and, unusually for that hour, a group of men shifting and fidgeting on the corner by the Royal Hotel. There were perhaps a dozen or so, all waiting for the temporary recruiting office to open.

Liam recognized one of the blacksmiths, and a clerk from the post office; Ned took up conversation with a couple of hands from a neighbouring property, while Arnie seemed to know everybody. It was a cold, shivering wait, but they exchanged cigarettes and jokes and discussed the endless possibilities of the war, feeling superior every time other young males passed by. Some, including Arnie, were unable to resist a few jeers. Two boys from a local German family slunk by on the other side of the street, but a couple of Irish labourers were more than willing to make a fight of it, the situation saved only by the arrival of the recruiting party and the smart opening of the office.

Two burly sergeants ushered them inside, and while a plump young lieutenant shuffled papers at a trestle desk, the men were pushed into something resembling a line. There were grins and coughs and a few self-conscious sniggers before one of the sergeants addressed them briefly on their reasons for being there. Then the local doctor arrived, followed by a corporal who had obviously been detailed to assist. After a hurried consultation, the doctor went through into the next room, closing the door behind him. Names were taken, then there was another wait. After what seemed an interminable time, each man was called to the trestle desk to answer a detailed series of questions, and after that came a surprisingly thorough medical examination.

If any of them thought they could sweet-talk that elderly local man into falsifying his entries, they were mistaken. The army had laid down some very exacting standards and he was under precise orders, despite his civilian status, to comply. The corporal measured heights and weights, bawling out each measurement as though across a parade ground. Liam watched the doctor wince. Six foot tall, 40 inch chest, weight 176 pounds, age 19 years 10 months, it was all recorded for the army's benefit. His heart and chest were sound, feet good, genitals normal, eyesight and hearing perfect, and no history of serious illness. His only anxiety was whether enquiry would be made into his means of arrival in the country, but none was. With his signature appended to a form headed, '*Australian Imperial Force*', Liam was in.

That acceptance was not universal. For various reasons, several were rejected. Bert, despite lying about his age, was turned away; his teeth, as Mrs Maddox had surmised, were his let-down. And little Nobby Clarke was two inches below the statutory requirement of 5 feet 6 inches. Arnie at twenty-two was fit and strong, with just enough schooling to sign his name, and at a stocky 5 feet 10 inches, Ned sailed through all the examinations with ease, to emerge like the victor in a heavyweight contest.

Meeting up with the two rejects outside, it was hard to find any words of consolation. Hurt, when they had been prepared to give their all, humiliated to find themselves less than what their country expected, Bert and Nobby were like children turned away from the party of the year. There was no point in hanging around. After brusque farewells and exhortations to 'knock 'em out' and 'give 'em one for us,' the two men pushed their way through a thickening crowd to return to the farm.

Relieved by that departure, too full of themselves to contain their elation any longer, the three remaining heroes gave vent to their feelings in an orgy of back-slapping and self-congratulation. Returning inside for further orders, however, they were rapidly deflated. Yes, the army was delighted to have their names, but having enlisted its volunteers, did not quite know what to do with them. Victoria Barracks in Melbourne was packed already, so until a decision was made, would they please go home and report back on Monday?

That was not a contingency for which any of them had planned. For several minutes they stood with the other enlisted men feeling very foolish indeed; having left like gladiators, it seemed they must now return like clowns.

And then Ned started to laugh. 'Come on,' he urged, 'let's go and get drunk!'

Arnie was in full agreement. At the risk of sounding a kill-joy, Liam remarked gloomily that as they had nowhere else to go but the farm, they really should try to remember Mrs Maddox and her feelings about strong drink. Ned cheerfully accused him of being lily-livered, a point that Liam did not dispute. Although he had never been much of a drinker, he knew that this was one occasion where Dutch courage was required. They headed for their usual bar, Ned's sense of humour erupting yet again as he spied Bert and Nobby drowning their sorrows in a corner. His laughter was infectious. Within seconds they were all rolling with it, thumping each other's shoulders and wiping tears from their cheeks. One round led to another, and by mid-afternoon they could hardly stand. It was a very sorry group that eventually made its way back to the Maddox farm that evening.

Fortunately, even Ewan Maddox saw the humour in it, and while his wife scolded and commiserated and saw them all to bed, he hid his laughter behind a pipe of tobacco. They could work for their keep over the weekend, he said, hangovers or no. And of course he would consider the two rejects as new hands, they had been good enough for him in the past and would be so again, no matter what the army thought.

Well sober by Monday morning, Liam was able to view the incident with a modicum of gratitude. Leaving on Friday had been wretched, while the farce of their return had injected a much-needed dose of laughter into this second departure. Even Ella was giggling as she kissed them all goodbye. 'See you tonight!' she called as they set off again for Dandenong.

But against all expectation they did not return.

The broad thoroughfare between Flinders Street Station and the barracks on St Kilda Road was thronged as though for a national celebration. Melbourne seemed to be out in force, whole families moving along with groups of men and boys, children skipping beside them, the atmosphere electric with anticipation. Paper boys crying the latest war news added to the hubbub, but here and there amongst the crowds were silent, determined, solitary men, their dusty boots and packs signifying far longer and less convenient journeys than the twenty miles Liam had just made by train.

They reminded him of himself eight months ago, and glancing down at his new tweed jacket, the boots freshly polished that morning, he could scarcely credit the difference; nor the weight in his bag. On the road, the only way to travel was lightly; in settling, things gathered, affections as much as material goods, and they seemed heaviest of all.

Beneath the excitement he was conscious of regret, a sadness at leaving the Maddox farm which had intensified with the journey, and a dreadful suspicion that he might never see it again. He glanced up at the girls waving from high windows and flags fluttering in the wind, and thought of the rolling plains and misty blue hills beyond; but he said nothing. The men who had travelled down together on the train were laughing and joking, enjoying a rare sight of the city and the fact that they were part of a spectacle. For them, Dandenong was nothing much, while for him it represented the life he had always wanted. In that moment Liam felt he had been betrayed by his emotions, betrayed by sentimental attachments which he had thought were severed a year ago. With jaundiced eyes he viewed the Dandenong men who had enlisted with him, all, he could swear, at least two inches taller than they had been last week. Most of them were well-built, fit in wind and limb, but a motley collection of characters, nevertheless. With a sinking heart he feared the army was going to be shipboard life all over again.

St Kilda Road was probably busier, Liam thought, than it had ever been in its existence, with packed trams rattling one way and empty ones back, and men on foot all heading for the barracks. He could see the tall, bluestone building sitting back from the road, but it was impossible to see the gates for the jostling crowd outside. The army had imagined itself geared and ready for an enthusiastic response but was not prepared for this avalanche of volunteers. Although Liam and his companions were already enlisted, they had to wait to be processed and sworn-in. The morning passed in endless queues, men keeping places for others who returned into town for food. New volunteers were still crowding in, more than one weeping with frustration as he was turned away.

'At least we're in,' Ned muttered, 'but I wish I knew what they were going to do with us. It's a bloody circus, this.'

With the lines of flimsy trestle desks across the parade ground, it reminded Liam more of a market place with impatient customers and extremely harassed stall-keepers. Considering the army's reputation for efficiency and organization, he wanted to laugh.

Processed at last, they were formed up in lines of four into a rough sort of company, and under the guidance of a middle-aged sergeant and a couple of veteran corporals, marched out of the barracks towards an exercise ground at Broadmeadows, twelve miles away. It was a bleak-looking expanse of bushland, with a few temporary buildings and a lot of bell-tents. Within days, the weather, which had been remarkably dry, changed abruptly. Broadmeadows dust became Broadmeadows mud, making the next few weeks a miserable existence of endless drilling and lectures delivered in the pouring rain. A first taste, though none of them knew it, of what was to come.

Organizing that mass of untrained, authority-hating individuals into a cohesive fighting force was no easy matter, especially as most of the hastily-promoted NCOs had no more experience than the men they were attempting to instruct. When asked for volunteers to take the rank of corporal, Liam and Arnie pushed Ned forward. He was older, had always assumed the position of leader at the Maddox farm, and they liked him. Rather Ned than some arrogant stranger, Liam reasoned, and that opinion was reinforced by the other Dandenong men. The post office clerk was designated lance-corporal, and while both men were initially reluctant, they took their new positions seriously, particularly once they had their uniforms.

Ned became surprisingly conscientious, attending all the lectures and special courses, and whether it was the fact of those stripes at his shoulder or the weight of a new responsibility, Liam could not have said, but there was a distinct change in him. His laugh was less ready, and his critical streak was suddenly channelled into practical rather than personal matters. Once, after a particularly tough day, he confessed to Liam that he wished he had paid more attention at school.

'You'd walk through this lot,' he said, showing a ream of regulations and instructions that he had to learn. 'I don't know why you didn't put yourself forward, you'd be a damn sight better at this than me.'

Wanting to laugh, Liam confined himself to a wry grin. 'But you can tell the blokes what to do, and they do it. You've been giving orders for years, you know you have – I wouldn't know what the hell to say. Anyway, they'd laugh as soon as I opened my mouth – my lingo's all wrong.'

Ned shook his head and grumbled some more, so obviously over-faced by that mass of army jargon that Liam felt constrained to offer some help. 'Do you want me to go through it with you?' he asked tentatively. 'Two heads might be better than one.'

So he read and interpreted, unconsciously absorbing everything; and when Ned did well in his courses, Liam's satisfaction could not have been greater had the success been his own. Although of necessity they spent less time together than on the farm, Liam was pleased to note that he had earned a measure of respect from Ned, and in return tried hard not let him down in practical matters. It was not easy. Soldiering struck him as a boring, mind-destroying occupation, a constant struggle on behalf of the officers to replace individuality with conformity, to reduce each man to the level of a cog in a vast, smooth-running machine. But the cogs, at this stage, did not want to be forced. Some had poor physical co-ordination, others deliberately made a mess of drill sessions, turning them into tests of endurance. From past experience Liam knew that in the long run it was easier to conform than to rebel, and being blessed with both stamina and ability, often cursed the less willing.

Arnie was one of them. Not only did he seem possessed of two left feet, he hated what he had to struggle to achieve; his moans of regret wore everyone down. On the day of their enlistment Ned had said to Liam that they must 'look out' for Arnie, as he was not one of the brightest. But with Ned having other responsibilities, Liam was left very much alone in that task. Arnie seemed to have a talent for being in the wrong place at the wrong time, and the only thing he liked about being in the army was the uniform. That went to his head. Suddenly he was a success with girls, and at every opportunity was away into Melbourne, along with half the camp, ignoring regulations and having a high old time.

For a while Liam tried to keep steering him away from the worst of the city's attractions, but it was an expensive and exhausting business. Training all day and drinking all night was not Liam's idea of pleasure, and even his stamina was no match for Arnie's. It struck him, too, that most of the girls who made such a play for these uniformed demi-gods, were not much better than the prostitutes who haunted seamen's hotels the world over. He tried to explain but Arnie would not listen, and Liam was too fastidious to enjoy being coaxed and touched in turn by women who were coarse and none too clean. Eventually, unable to curb Arnie's excesses, Liam simply gave up trying. Camp life became no easier, but a full night's sleep reinforced his stoic acceptance.

He had been at Broadmeadows a little over a month when Ned rushed up to tell him that he had just bumped into Lewis Maddox. Lacking a uniform as yet, but shortly to be commissioned into the Light Horse Regiment. Apparently his father had threatened to cut him off without a penny unless he came home immediately, but Lewis was over twenty-one and could do as he pleased. And Mary had been accepted into the Australian Army Nursing Service, so with any luck they would all set sail together.

Liam could not make up his mind which piece of information pleased Ned more: the fact that Lewis had managed to outwit his father, or the idea of sailing all the way to Europe with Mary Maddox close at hand. On small reflection, Liam thought the latter. It made him smile.

A few weeks later mail reached him from England. Two letters, much delayed by the war and a circuitous journey via the Maddox farm and Victoria Barracks. Both bore familiar handwriting: Edward's elegant copperplate and his mother's firm, rounded script. With her letter uppermost, Liam paused in drizzling rain to watch the fine drops make a haze of each clear black line. When name and address were almost obliterated, he stuffed both envelopes into his pocket and strode away.

So completely did he erase them from his consciousness, it was a surprise to him later to feel the crackle of paper when he removed his tunic. Most of the men were either away to town or in the canteen; Arnie was for once collapsed and asleep, his phenomenal strength having temporarily deserted him. Lighting a small candle-lamp, Liam was tempted to burn the letters unread, his mother's particularly. He even held a corner of it over the flame and watched with satisfaction as it began to brown: a little curl, edged by sparks, peeling away from the tight-packed pages within. The charred edges were like a reproach. Beset by sudden fury, Liam dashed it away; he would not read it, he would not!

She had no right to intrude upon this new life, no right to impose herself here.

There were voices outside the tent; Arnie moaned and stirred. Hurriedly, Liam retrieved that heavy bundle of pages and hid them amongst his kit. Edward's missive lay unmarked and unopened beside the lamp. The voices went away, Arnie slept on. Liam doused the light and settled himself down. Sleep eluded him, and sometime before midnight he gave up the struggle and re-lit the lamp. He picked up Edward's letter, weighed it in his hands, the contents less than his mother's. Wanting to read it, some instinct told him to get the worst over first. From his kit Liam extracted the other one, sliding the charred pages from their envelope.

If his brother's letter had given Liam an inkling of what to expect, this direct communication from his mother was worse, pouring the salt of guilt and bitter resentment into wounds which had failed to heal. She wrote of love, love which had broken her heart with his leaving, love which had tried to protect, and succeeded only in deceiving. And with an honesty which scoured her son, Louisa wrote of her early life with Robert Duncannon. Love again, but a very different kind of love, one which was tarnished, in Liam's translation, by overwhelming lust. No matter how hard she stressed Charlotte Duncannon's madness and the impossibility of divorce, Liam refused to believe it, except as a story attributable to Robert Duncannon. After all, he reasoned, the woman could not have been so repulsive: she had borne a daughter to her husband; and that daughter was very beautiful. Robert Duncannon must have loved his wife, if only in the beginning; that he could abandon her so quickly for another woman, said nothing for his morals. It said little for his mother's, either, that with no hope of marriage, she should leave her home and family, and go to live openly with him in Dublin. If anything had driven Charlotte Duncannon out of her mind, Liam reasoned it must have been that.

He read on, his heart hardening with every line. In Dublin, apparently, as the first flush of passion faded, things had begun to go wrong. She said she had become obsessed by guilt, by a realization that life with Robert could never work as a real marriage should. Reading between those lines, Liam guessed that his natural father's attention and affections had begun to wander. Away from home a great deal, driven by the kind of strong sexual needs Liam was coming to understand from the men around him, he had decided that Robert Duncannon had no more idea of abstention or faithfulness than a stallion with his choice of mares in season. And like a willing mare his mother had gone with him, the fact of their continuing affair obvious from Tisha's birth.

Louisa wrote that she had not known, when she left Dublin, that Tisha was on the way, that she had returned to York simply because she had nowhere else to go. Her mother, their old servant Bessie, and particularly her cousin Edward, had made a home for Louisa and her two sons, and supported them. But the hotel on Gillygate, which Liam dimly recalled, had begun to fail as a business, and with Mary Elliott's death it had been necessary to look for somewhere smaller. Louisa, Edward and the three children, had moved to the cottage by the river. She and Edward had married ten months later, in 1899, on Liam's fifth birthday.

Astonishingly, with the day named for him, Liam's memory was both clear and detailed. He had returned from school to find a party gathered: Aunts Blanche and Emily, Uncle John Chapman, and old Bessie, who had gone to work for the Chapmans in Leeds. There was a cake and a table groaning with food; everybody was very happy, laughing and talking and congratulating him on his fifth birthday. There were presents, too. But his clearest, most vivid memory of that surprise party was of his mother looking lovely as a princess, laughter dancing in her eyes, and himself wanting to stay with her to be cuddled and fussed at bedtime. Instead there were tears and disappointment, he and Robin and Tisha being whisked away to Leeds with Aunt Emily and dour Uncle John, to endure the nips and pinches of cousin Elsie, and the whinings of little Johnnie and Harold. Despite its size, the house had no more than a tidy square of garden in which they could not play, and was hemmed in on every side by grimy terraces, all depressingly alike. Liam had visited the house many times in the succeeding years, but never again stayed overnight.

With memory and astonishment came shock at the magnitude of that deception. They had used him, used the occasion of his birthday to cover the reason for that family gathering. It seemed such an abuse of innocence that Liam was outraged, unable and unwilling to see, for all his mother's protestations of love and protectiveness, that it had been done in anything but a calculated manner. He was so irrationally hurt by that revelation, he did no more than skim through the rest, which seemed to him just a lame collection of excuses for her marriage to Edward.

The flimsy tale that they had loved each other all along, yet failed to notice until that summer of 1899, seemed incredible to him. In love himself, passionately and without hope, Liam was sure that if they had been in love all those years, they would each have known about it. His limited experience did not allow for different levels of love at different times, and between people who had been brought up in close proximity to one another.

Disbelieving, sickened by what he saw as self-deception on his mother's part, invented to ease her bad conscience, Liam was also outraged by her temerity in thinking he wanted to know the intimate details of her life. It was enough to know that she had shared another man's bed; he did not want to know that she had done so willingly. Edward was so gentle, so fatherly, it disturbed Liam not at all to imagine him sharing his mother's bed, holding her, kissing her, loving her; indeed he had seen them in bed so often, arms around each other, it was the most natural thing in the world. Or had been. Until that world was shattered. The image of her with Robert Duncannon was altogether different. It smacked of animal-like coupling, and had become more graphic as his knowledge of other men's sexuality increased.

He could not bring himself to read Edward's letter. It lay unopened in his pocket for several days, while his few solitary moments were taken up with self-pity. It seemed he was doomed to be denied all the things which were most important to him: people, places, even a way of life. He missed the Maddox family and their farm with a poignancy akin to homesickness; but he would not admit that he missed York. The army was a poor exchange for all that should have been. When he did allow himself to dwell on Robert Duncannon, the fact that he had willingly chosen the military life only served to underline the differences between them.

No solitude, no privacy, poor food and a succession of days

full of noise, and endless, mindless drilling. That was the army. It amazed Liam that so many of the men seemed to thrive on it. At the end of a crushing week he took himself off into town, eager to shed his depression in any way he could. After several beers in a back street bar, he left the crowd to look for somewhere to eat. Amongst the maze of dark, wet, ill-lit streets, he found a little chop-house quiet in the early evening and tolerably clean. The waitress had seen enough uniforms in the past few weeks to be unimpressed; or perhaps, he thought, glancing up into her expressionless face, she had troubles of her own. Either way, she took his order for steak and fried potatoes without enthusiasm, and slouched back to the kitchen. He drank another beer while he was waiting, slowly this time; and in the stillness remembered Edward's letter. For the first time in a week Liam felt sufficiently fortified to read it.

Its tone was calmer, less impassioned than his mother's, beginning not with recriminations at his leaving, but hope that his new life in Australia would turn out to be all that he was looking for. There was such unintentional irony in that, Liam almost smiled as he reminded himself that this had been written well before the storm-cloud gathered. The news about Robin and Tisha was so old, Liam could not help longing suddenly for more up-to-date information. Especially from Robin. But the letter was not what he had feared. Apart from a passage which begged for understanding of Louisa, and that he would read her words with compassion, Edward made little attempt at explanation. For that, at least, Liam was grateful: he could not have borne another lengthy version of what had gone before, and why. Reading the simplicity of Edward's statement that he had always loved Louisa, but that at one time it had seemed wrong to acknowledge it, Liam tried to view it cynically, and failed. Instead, he was ridiculously touched by the older man's loyalty. Even more so when the next sentence went on to acknowledge Liam's feelings for Georgina.

'I could not speak, because I was not free to do so – yet I watched and feared and prayed that I was wrong in what I suspected. That was why I was so short with you, and because of that, my dear boy, I humbly crave your forgiveness. I understand, in part, what you must have felt then, and indeed what you are perhaps still feeling. There can be no greater tragedy in life. I pray that it will pass, as these things sometimes do, and that your memory of this anguish will fade with time. We see Georgina less often now, but she seems well, if much chastened. She always asks for news of you, but I do not think she was aware of your feelings for her, and we have not enlightened her. Nor, I think, has her father, but I cannot be certain of that point...'

In a sudden mist, the words disappeared. Folding the letter over, Liam coughed to clear his throat. As he found his handkerchief, the waitress reappeared with his meal, and for the moment he set Edward's letter aside. It surprised him that he felt no anger towards his adoptive father, and that those brief lines regarding Georgina should have brought forth such a swell of gratitude. It was little enough, but it was news of her. He had longed for her to understand his feelings all those months ago, but in retrospect it was probably just as well that she had no inkling. She, at least, would be spared this anguish.

The meal was good and satisfying. Afterwards, Liam felt refreshed and suddenly more cheerful. He picked up the letter again and read on. There was not much more, but the last few lines made him glad of his quiet corner with its shadows.

'Although I am not your natural father,' Edward had written, 'I have loved you all as though you were my own. Remember, too, that I am not a stranger – I am your cousin, and we share the same blood.'

The truth of that last statement had not occurred to Liam before. His determination to cut himself off, to stand alone, was temporarily forgotten as the warmth of Edward's words penetrated. He read that letter many times over in the succeeding weeks and derived great comfort from it. Edward's tact and understanding seemed to acknowledge the change in their relationship, projecting them both beyond the narrow confines of father and son, and into the realms of equality.

Previously, he had viewed Edward and his mother as partners in a conspiracy against him, but Liam was now persuaded to reassess the situation. Edward, it appeared, would have preferred to be honest from the start; and it was suddenly blindingly clear that he need not have taken on three illegitimate children all those years ago.

That he should have taken up another man's responsibilities, both willingly and successfully, said a great deal for his qualities as a man. It was also a humbling thought. Liam did not think he would want to do the same. It occurred to him, too, to consider what life would have been like without Edward as their father, and immediately much that had been rich and secure and satisfying fell away. Without him, as children, they would have been so much poorer. Perhaps not in a financial sense, for Robert Duncannon with all his sins would surely not have seen them starve; but spiritually and intellectually they would each have been so much less. Never once, by word or gesture, had he ever intimated resentment of those three children who were as much Robert Duncannon's as Louisa's. Yet Edward had little liking for the Colonel, of that Liam was certain. Theirs, he reflected, had been a happy childhood, and perhaps it was that very fact which made the truth so hard to bear.

If his thoughts of Edward were increasingly more generous, Liam's attitude towards his mother did not improve. Indeed, she suffered by comparison. In his reply to Edward's letter, he made no reference to Louisa's.

Thirteen

Christmas in York that year, Georgina reflected, was going to be a very half-hearted affair. Midway through December, the war was showing no signs of drawing to any conclusion. Indeed, from judicious reading of newspapers and casualty lists, it seemed no better than stalemate. Uniforms in the streets, faces which were either glum with misery or taut with anxiety for absent loved ones; and everywhere a dank, persistent mist. She could not recall a day when the sun had last shone from a blue and perfect sky. She imagined it was in the summer, but summer with its roses and picnics seemed to belong to another age.

The shrouded Minster, as she passed by, seemed shuttered and forlorn, as though God had gone away for the duration. Crossing the road by the south transept, Georgina cut through Minster Gates on her way to meet Louisa for tea. By Coffee Yard her step faltered as she thought of Edward, working away at his beautiful books. For a moment she was tempted to stop by and say hello, but their meetings these days were rare, and while his manner was unfailingly courteous, she had the feeling the sight of her pained him. He was so calm, such a tower of strength, Georgina often wondered whether Louisa understood what it cost him in physical terms. His slender, sensitive face was pared almost to the bone, paler than ever, and, Georgina suspected, showing the signs of incipient heart disease. He needed rest and freedom from anxiety, yet the war imposed additional worries.

The cheery welcome of the tea-shop bell sounded incongruous to Georgina's ears, but it was warm inside and for that she was grateful. Louisa, sitting by the window, raised a hand in greeting. She was thinner, too, but the haggard misery of the last eighteen months had been relieved by Robin's news of Liam. Now all she waited for was a direct communication, some sign that he understood and had forgiven her. Georgina, having to listen to that gnawing anxiety whenever they met, steeled herself.

Today, Louisa's smile was tense, but the pressure of her hand on Georgina's was warm with gratitude.

'I'm so glad you were able to come. Edward's had *two* letters from Liam this week – one from Australia, posted six weeks ago, and one from Egypt. He's in *Egypt*, Georgina! Goodness me, it seems so strange – imagine Liam seeing places like that. Alexandria – it makes you think of the Pharaohs, doesn't it? – and Cairo.'

Beneath the table, Georgina squeezed her hands together to still their trembling, and while Louisa fished in her small leather bag for the letters themselves, forced her stiff lips into the semblance of a smile. How ridiculous it was, she thought, that news of Liam – from Liam – should affect her in this way. It had been worse the first time. Even now it astounded her how she had managed to control that wild succession of emotions. Exultant at the broken silence, at his safety amongst good, honest farming people, she was relieved after months of worry. Afterwards, in the privacy of her room, Georgina had sobbed like a child, knowing only then how much had been pent up since Liam's disappearance.

She had known of it within hours, because they came to her first, demanding to know what she knew, and whether Liam had confided anything to her. But of course he had not, apart from those tentative dreams of his. It had been a slender clue, too slender to provide much hope, but to that everyone had clung. No one accused her of being to blame for his disappearance, but she felt it even so, knowing in her heart of hearts that his feelings for her were what had tipped the balance so drastically. Looking back, Georgina knew that she had deliberately ignored what should have been clear to a blind man, and all for the selfish pleasure of his company.

And because she knew, she did not ask why it was that Liam had reacted so badly to the truth, while Robin had made no more than a token protest and Tisha none at all. And because they were all – even her father – so eaten up with guilt at their own parts in the tragedy, no one thought to question her further.

Past expert that she was at covering her own emotions, Georgina gave nothing away while she listened and comforted and made feeble attempts to reassure. Only Edward looked askance at her. Dear, kind, shrewd Edward, who might suspect, but never accuse.

For the moment, however, there was no need to reassure, Louisa being taken up with Liam's news, albeit as relayed to her husband. She began by reading parts of the first letter aloud, then, as an increasingly quavering voice betrayed her emotions, handed both to Georgina.

'There,' she said, dabbing at her eyes, 'you read them, I can't. I don't mean to be so silly, and I'm delighted to have news of him by any means – I just wish he would mention me...'

Her voice tailed away, and the brilliant eyes stared out over the square. Georgina's heart ached for her, but there was no comfort in empty, unconvincing words. With Liam's letter in her hands she forced herself to relax, to convey an outward impression of calm. There was a trick to it which she had learned as a child and employed to excellent use as a nurse. To herself she labelled it acceptance. Accept everything, even the most bizarre situation as normal; don't question it, don't react to it, and above all don't panic. Laugh, weep, rage, or even break your heart, but not until afterwards, not until you are alone.

The forward-sloping hand was not as elegant as Edward's, but it formed a pleasing pattern on the page, while words and phrases, stilted at first, soon relaxed into a style more mature than Robin's, whose letters rushed on, youthful, ingenuous, eager to summarize a situation in as few sentences as possible. But Liam, once in his stride, was possessed of the telling phrase, the vivid description which brought everything to life. Reading his letters to Edward, Georgina cursed the food, sighed over the boredom of basic training and shared the frustration of not knowing when they were to sail for Europe. The original date, towards the end of September, was constantly put back as the threat of German warships in the vicinity made everyone fearful of losing that vital convoy.

Liam mentioned the fact that his twentieth birthday had been spent in camp, drilling as usual, but that he and a friend had gone into Melbourne that evening for a celebratory meal – 'a good excuse,' he wrote, 'for getting away from the inevitable army stew.'

And two weeks later, on 19th October, the troopship *Benalla* had eventually sailed from Melbourne to join up with the convoy at Albany, Western Australia; and a few days after that they were preparing to set forth across the Indian Ocean.

'... We have a contingent of nurses abroad, most of them from Victoria. One of them is Mary Maddox, daughter of the people I worked for. Her brother Lewis is also aboard, which made for quite a send-off when we left Melbourne. Mr and Mrs Maddox came down from Dandenong, which nobody expected, and while they had not approved of Lewis joining up, he had their blessing at the end. It was a great send-off, with streamers, bands, sirens blowing, but also very sad, so many girls and women crying on the quayside. Mary was crying, too, but had her brother to comfort her...'

Thanking providence for that, Georgina experienced an irrational surge of jealousy. She told herself that this Maddox family was altogether too good to be true, that they had no right to figure so largely in Liam's affections, when his own family were so starved of him.

Of that letter there was not much more. Concerned lest he should not have chance to catch the post, Liam had finished it hurriedly with a promise to write again soon, and the second was penned largely at sea, relating the daily routines of exercise, lessons in signalling, and an exciting brush with the German cruiser *Emden*. The eventual sinking of the German ship by HMAS *Sydney* had cheered them all, making them keener than ever to reach Europe and 'get into the thick of it.'

After all the excitement, the letter ended on a note of disappointment. For some reason they were to disembark at Alexandria, which made Liam wonder whether that unscheduled stop had anything to do with England declaring war on Turkey. He hoped not, 'as the lads joined up to be where the real fighting is, not to be used to mop up some side issue out here.'

The letters begged for news of Robin and Tisha, and in a postscript gave his new address as Mena Camp, which he described as being *'in the shadow of the Pyramids'*. Stricken by that romantic image, picturing Liam escorting some other nurse by moonlight, for a moment Georgina was overcome. He did not ask for news of her, and like Louisa she might have cried, 'if only he would mention me...'

Instead, she slipped the much-thumbed sheets back into their envelopes.

'Well,' she said with as much brightness as she could muster, 'at least he's safe in Egypt.'

'And I thank God for that,' Louisa murmured. Her eyes were suddenly looking away again, over the square, and Georgina knew she was thinking of her other son, in different circumstances entirely.

Robin had been in Flanders since the beginning of October, involved in a tremendous battle to defend Ypres, and in the firing line constantly for almost three weeks. His battalion, which had started out at something like a thousand, was reduced to one captain, three second-lieutenants and less than two hundred and fifty men. That Robin had come through it without physical injury was, Georgina felt, no less than a miracle. While the battalion regrouped they had been moved across the French border to a reserve position. While he was not exactly out of danger, for the time being their collective anxiety was less intense. His letters were arriving frequently again, if a little less jaunty than before.

The last few weeks, Georgina reflected, had been ghastly; it was no wonder that Louisa looked so drained. 'And how's Tisha?' she managed to ask, hoping for a little light relief.

But Tisha, it seemed, was still behaving as though her heart had turned to stone, enjoying her new job as a clerk at the barracks and out with friends almost every night. She was at home for meals, Louisa said, but other than that they rarely saw her. She read Robin's letters when they arrived and wrote to him occasionally, but any mention of Liam was a cue for her to change the subject or leave the room. When remonstrated with, she declared cruelly that she was sick of their anxiety for him, he had chosen his own path, and in her opinion was quite able to take care of himself.

'She's young,' Georgina observed, 'and the young can be very thoughtless.' Privately, she wondered whether Tisha simply felt neglected. Quiet and obedient for months, when she did begin to assert herself again, she did so implacably. No argument or remonstration would turn her from her purpose. Looking back, Georgina wondered whether Edward and Louisa had strength left to exert much discipline. Tisha, it seemed, was intent on going her own way.

As ever before leaving, Georgina mentioned her father, passing on the love and contrition that Louisa always refused to accept.

As expected, she shook her head. 'If he had only stayed away... But your father has never understood anything but *military* duty!' On a sharp sigh she looked away, and for a few moments silence stretched between them. Then, unexpectedly, she asked about him. 'What is he doing, these days? I don't suppose they've sent *him* to the Front,' she added bitterly.

'No, to his regret. He's been requesting it for months, ever since the war began. But, as you may know, his special sphere is Ireland, and has been for some time. They don't want him to abandon that.'

Again, the silence. With a visible effort, Louisa tried to contain her curiosity, and failed. 'And what has he been doing there?'

'I don't know,' Georgina confessed. 'He doesn't talk about it. I don't think he's allowed to.'

A smile which was more derisive than amused passed Louisa's lips. 'Oh, so secret, is it? Ah well, Ireland was always dear to his heart. I wonder,' she added a moment later, 'whether his masters at the War Office know how he really feels about Ireland? If they did, they might be glad to send him to the Front!'

'What do you mean?'

'Ask him, my dear. Ask your father, not me.'

'Yes, I will,' Georgina promised as they parted on Coney Street. Disturbing at the time, afterwards, Louisa's insinuations seemed no more than the product of bitterness. A deep-seated resentment that a man who had made the army his life – and at the expense of so much else – should be kept away from this terrible war, while innocent boys suffered and died.

Afterwards, too, she allowed herself to think about Liam, writing down that new address at the back of her diary, beneath two others she had remembered and transcribed. In what remained of her afternoon off she sat down to write to him, an oft-repeated exercise which had yet to reach her own exacting standards. In trying to achieve the perfect balance between detachment and affectionate concern, Georgina always erred. She was either too cold, sounding like an elderly governess issuing reprimands, or else her warmth set fire to itself, becoming an impassioned interrogation. Why had he gone away like that, without a word? Surely, after the friendship which had existed between them, he could have confided in her? She would have understood, whatever he had to say, and could have helped and comforted him. Knowing the situation, having suffered herself as a child because of it, she was better placed than anyone to sympathize...

Begging for some communication, even a few words on a postcard, then Georgina would remember that his feelings had been those of a boy approaching manhood, and consequently less platonic than hers. Not knowing she was his sister, mistaking her liking and affection for something more, Liam had imagined himself in love. Although in his letters to Edward he asked for news of the family, like Louisa's name, Georgina's was significant by its absence. He had adored his mother, and now it seemed he hated her; perhaps his feelings for Georgina had undergone a similar metamorphosis.

It was the same that afternoon. After an hour of flowing, anguished prose, she was devastated by a sense of futility. This was another letter she could never send. Only if they were to meet could this thing possibly be put right between them. Only face to face could she say what had to be said, explain the past in terms that he would understand, and help him to accept what could not be altered. If only, she prayed, he might survive that long. She could not bear to think that he might die with hatred in his heart. Whatever Louisa's sins, which were surely those of omission rather than intent, she was a good woman and a warm and loving mother: she did not deserve the treatment Liam was meting out.

And if it should prove to be that I am guilty of more than I suspect, Georgina thought, then I, too, need to be forgiven.

A week later, with Christmas a matter of days away, Georgina finally came to a decision about her work. As the war gathered pace in those early weeks, she had wondered whether she should volunteer to serve in a military hospital. The idea of escaping from York with all its emotional pressures and responsibilities was certainly attractive. Lately it had become so insistent that she hesitated; it did not seem a valid reason for leaving rewarding work in a situation so completely suited to her talents.

Several nurses and attendants had left already, and with each publication of casualties from the Front, Georgina imagined that one of them might be Robin, or her Irish cousins from White Leigh, both of whom had lately volunteered. Liam for the moment was safe in Egypt, but with the war lurching along into another year, eating up young lives with obscene relish, those Australians would be needed somewhere, sooner or later. She had heard of horrific injuries, and young men sent almost mad from the noise of those heavy bombardments. If she could bring the separate disciplines of her training together, she might save lives, comfort shattered minds, return some of them whole to their families when the war was over.

Fired by that idealism, Georgina was able to recognize the stalemate of her personal life and set it to one side. She had done all that it was possible to do, and now that Liam was writing regularly to Edward, the Elliotts as a family knew of his movements, and could communicate with her and with each other. Her presence in York, as far as she could see, was no longer vital, whereas elsewhere, her training might do great good.

FOURTEEN

Thirty-eight transports arrived in Alexandria, by degrees discharging company after company, battalion after battalion, for the next stage of their journey to Cairo. From the capital's railway station to their destination on the fringes of the Western Desert, was a hot, uncomfortable march of several miles. When the first of those eighteen thousand men arrived, there was nothing but the looming Pyramids and a cluster of buildings around a country house hotel. The Mena House was requisitioned, and from that, Mena Camp took its name. Tents began to sprout like mushrooms, vast numbers of them, rapidly taking on all the aspects of a city. A city full of men.

Liam had glimpsed Egypt briefly during a passage of the Suez Canal the year before, but at close quarters it made an impact for which he was no more prepared than those who had never seen anything but Australia. Bleached by centuries of sun and scoured by sand, Egypt, he found, was possessed of a vivid beauty that both excited and repelled him. There was light and colour everywhere, and the most appalling poverty he had ever seen. Scented flowers in formal gardens competed with the stench of decay in the streets, while marble palaces on grand avenues fronted a maze of foetid alleys in the native quarters. Electric trams and gleaming motor cars moved alongside biblical forms of transport: donkeys brayed and camels spat, while their owners screamed unintelligible insults at passing, goggle-eyed soldiers.

The open desert possessed a different kind of beauty. For the first day or so after leaving Cairo, Liam found it a relief, although the nights spent on guard duty were unnerving. With moonlight bathing the Pyramids, the desert managed to exercise its own terrible fascination: the empty tombs of those long-dead pharaohs seemed alive with whispers and moving shadows, and the wraithlike kiss of the wind.

Once the sun came up, rising with speed through each magical dawn, there was little time for dreaming, little time for anything but work. With the completion of the camp, those eighteen thousand men were plunged into an excess of drilling and marching and trench-digging that was intended to bring them to a peak of physical fitness. In effect, after the relative inactivity of their sea-voyage from Australia, it brought them virtually to their knees.

As Liam wrote in one letter home, if the hours had been less punishing, if they'd had enough to eat and been allowed even one day off a week, the men could have adjusted. Even Sundays, he complained, were marked by early calls and church parades, and several hours' drilling in the heat of the afternoon. After days spent marching through sand on no more than a bread-roll and a half-tin of sardines, heat-stroke and illness had most of them falling down like flies.

At first, few had energy left to go into town, but resentment breeds its own energy. After almost three weeks without a break, trouble was building like a thunder-head.

Physically exhausted, and as mentally adrift as his companions, Liam listened to the rumble of discontent and felt it echoed in himself. He too began to question the sense of things, not least the reasons for their stay in this outlandish place. With Christmas practically upon them, all he could hear were the calls of the muezzin from distant minarets, so alien compared to York and the clamour of church bells. Swept by a tide of homesickness, he found himself longing for sights and sounds not thought about in months.

The patriotism he had privately scoffed at was burning inside, fuelled by letters from his brother, lucky enough to be in France and really doing his bit for England. Stuck in Egypt, doing nothing but march and drill, drill and dig, Liam was possessed by an envy he would not have thought possible on the day he enlisted. Here and now seemed such a terrible waste of time, while that noble cause, repeated in every lecture, of freeing the world from German imperialist aggression, seemed hollow indeed. Pointless while breaking their backs digging useless trenches in the desert, pointless in the face of endless hours on parade, when every missive from England contained news of great battles going on in France and Belgium.

Every conversation echoed that common resentment. Even the least mutinous agreed that they had not joined up to listen to uplifting speeches by officers who had no more idea of war than a bunch of donkeys. They'd come to fight, not learn a set of petty rules and regulations laid down by a bunch of pen-pushers back home.

Bored and tired and viciously frustrated, with day-leave denied, the troops began to depart each night in ever-increasing numbers, with leave and without it, for the fleshpots of Cairo. On five shillings a day the Australians were the best-paid of all the allied armies, and Liam, particularly, had never been so well-off. Even with half his pay allocated in Edward's name to a York bank, he had more money at his disposal than Robin, and was determined to make the most of it.

Perpetually hungry, Liam's first thought was always of food, and in Cairo the choice was vast, from the glittering restaurant of Shepheard's, to cheaper but less salubrious establishments in the narrow back streets. To begin with, a decent meal with a few beers was all he indulged in, but he was soon infected with the atmosphere of excitement pervading these illicit trips into town.

After weeks of confinement, the realization that it was possible to set fire to the rules and get away with it, went to every man's head. Nightly forays became wilder, tinged by an atmosphere of hysteria as large groups gathered to drink and gamble and fornicate their way through the streets of Cairo. Out of sight of families and employers, with respectable communities left way behind in Australia, they were let loose on a land which had seen everything before, a city which was old in sin and well-used to catering to every conceivable taste.

Liam had been away from home a long time. In the early days, grief had kept temptation at bay, but the licentious atmosphere was beginning to blunt his finer feelings. At first he stuck to Ned on their legitimate nights out, but his friend frequently disappeared without explanation, tapping his nose as he left Liam and Arnie behind. The rest of the crowd assumed Ned the Corp was away looking for sex, too mean to share the delights of a good brothel with them. Liam had other suspicions, but either way those abrupt departures put more distance between him and Ned than rank ever could.

Feeling snubbed, he threw himself into the party. Exhausted by day, at night he seemed to float on a tide of exhilaration, buffeted back and forth against an exotic, lotus-strewn shore. And that shore seemed peopled by half the women of the world. Dark and fair, bold and shy, they inhabited the shadowy back streets in seedy rooms and opulent houses, guarded by ancient, painted Frenchwomen or homosexual Egyptian men.

There were shows featuring eastern belly-dancers and young girls with fans, and there were others more rampantly seductive. On every street corner were postcards for sale and the kind of books that could never have seen the light of day where Victorian morality had gained a foothold. It was a land where sex was for sale, a land where every persistent and importunate native had a 'sister' who would love to entertain each fine, wealthy, good-looking soldier before he went to the war. The fact that such offers rapidly reached saturation point made them easy to resist, but the atmosphere, loaded with sexual invitation as it was, impinged upon them all. As far as Liam was concerned, much of what he saw produced nothing more than embarrassment or disgust; but it was also illuminating, larding both dreams and fantasies with an eroticism that had been absent before.

On innumerable occasions he watched Arnie and those of like mind leave the bars to take their pick of the girls along the Haret el Wasser. Oddly enough, while he was prepared to drink and gamble with the best, and take his part in the wild dashes back to camp via any form of transport, hired or stolen, the one thing he could not bring himself to do was join them in this nightly ritual. Most of the time he wanted to, and could not understand the reticence which had survived the loss of almost every other inhibition. But regardless of either drunkenness or sobriety, and in spite of the good-natured baiting he endured from the bolder spirits, something stopped him.

To begin with it was thoughts of Georgina, constant comparisons which sprang unbidden whenever he thought some girl or woman might be vaguely attractive; then he would look again, and find that she was not. It became a habit. He told himself that if he could just find a girl who looked like her, then everything would be all right. But Georgina's true, pale fairness was as rare amongst these rich, dark plums as snow upon the desert's face, while the fair European nurses at Mena and in the Cairo hospitals were as unattainable as women in purdah. Certainly to humble private soldiers like himself. He did suspect, however, that a few pips at the shoulder might have made all the difference.

Of course, he had his suspicions about Ned, although his old friend still refused to be drawn. Liam saw Mary Maddox a few times, and she was cordial as ever, colouring only slightly when he mentioned their mutual friend. He bumped into her brother quite frequently, and although rank made it impossible to engage in more than a few minutes' conversation, it was always heartening to see the pleasure in Lewis's eyes, and to know that this desert training was as tough on the young mounted officers as it was for the infantry. Lewis had not lost his intensity, but it seemed to Liam had he had grown up a great deal. Catching sight of him one night amongst a group of officers and nurses on the steps of Shepheard's Hotel, Liam thought how relaxed and sophisticated he seemed. Envying him, imagining his dark and not unhandsome friend as a smooth and successful Lothario, Liam wished he could be so fancy-free. Wished too that he had never met Georgina Duncannon; or, having met her, that he could release himself from the obsession she had become.

She was both forbidden and unattainable, and nothing was ever going to change that. He told himself that he was being ridiculous, and several times swore he would tear up that photograph Robin had taken; but it was impossible. In the end, it seemed the only way to cure himself was to find a girl who looked nothing like Georgina Duncannon, and put into practice what he so frequently dreamed of doing.

It turned out to be more difficult than he had imagined. The first time, the sheer squalor of the room quelled his passion. Even as the woman lit the lamps Liam walked out, pursued by shouts and curses. It was a while before inclination and opportunity combined again.

The second time he went about it with more care, choosing

a better-class brothel instead of a casual pick-up. Swallowing his initial nervousness, Liam explained to the *Madame* that he wanted someone young and clean, with fresh sheets on the bed. The woman was old and fat and grossly painted, but for a moment, as her eyes took in his tall, straight frame and the shock of fair hair falling across his forehead, she seemed about to suggest something else; then with a shrug she turned away. A girl was brought forward. Small and pretty in a childish, undeveloped fashion, she had beautiful eyes and a smooth olive skin. Briefly, Liam hesitated; this was not quite what he had envisaged. He preferred women to young girls, but any protest might be misunderstood. Recalling the look *Madame* had cast over him, it seemed more prudent to take what was offered.

The room was hardly fresh, and the noise from the street outside was distracting. The girl quickly slipped off her evening dress and lay back on a wide feather bed, legs spread and awaiting him. As Liam glanced at her, slowly removing his tunic, she reached across to a bowl of fruit and began to peel an orange.

That hardened lack of interest in what they were about to do was off-putting. He paused in the act of unfastening his shirt, aware that his edge of excitement was gone. Nothing about her stirred him; she might have been no more than a slab of meat displayed in a butcher's window. He pictured all the men who had used her, and was no longer surprised by her attitude. Why should she care? He was just one more, and plenty would follow when he had gone. There was a moment's regret for the money already spent, but it was impossible to claim what he had paid for. With a sigh, he donned his tunic and left.

Back at camp, however, with his pity for the girl dispersed, he called himself a fool and a coward, wondering what was wrong with him that he could not perform the act other men found so simple. In an agony of frustration, he flung himself down and gave way to self-pity. Ned, returning refreshed from his night out, indulged in a burst of knowing laughter.

'There's nothing wrong, you bloody idiot,' he declared. 'Nothing a decent woman couldn't put right in no time flat. And for God's sake don't start comparing yourself to Arnie – we all know where he keeps his brains, and one day he'll know about it! Besides,' he added with a cryptic grin, 'you can take it from me that most women prefer quality to quantity, and on that score, Arnie's got no more idea than a second-rate ram!'

'It's all very well for you to talk,' Liam complained bitterly, 'you've got no problems that I can see! It is Mary Maddox you're meeting, isn't it?'

Ned tapped the side of his nose. 'Like I told you before – ask no questions, you'll be told no lies.'

With a derisory gesture, Liam sat up and lit a cigarette. 'Well, I just hope nobody finds out, that's all. She'll be packed off home, and you'll be on fatigues for the rest of the bloody war!'

Ignoring that, Ned simply laughed. 'Find yourself a nice little nurse,' he blandly advised, 'and keep clear of the bloody Wasser. Nothing but trouble there, mate.'

Except as a patient, Liam's chances of meeting up with a nurse were remote; they both knew that. Mary Maddox broke every rule in the book for Ned, but only because theirs was a relationship which had begun before they left Australia. Perhaps not openly acknowledged, but Liam had been aware of it. He did wonder, however, what Lewis would say if he knew; and indeed, how Mr and Mrs Maddox would view such an alliance.

After that, he steered clear of the Haret el Wasser, but not for the reasons Ned listed. In truth, Liam's fear of humiliation temporarily outweighed his desire for sexual experience.

Just after Christmas, when three hundred men were posted absent without leave, one battalion was forced to abandon a parade for the simple reason that there were not enough men present. The next day, a strong picket line was placed across the road from Mena to Cairo, and all passes rigorously checked. Hard on that, training was intensified, longer marches into the desert became the order of the day, and some units – including Liam's – were exiled to garrisons along the Suez Canal.

There, although the food still consisted largely of bread and jam, sardines and bully beef, it was just adequate, and Sunday became at last a day of rest. Church Parade was still compulsory, but apart from that the men did have a free day at their disposal. They began to behave more like tourists and less like vandals, and the numbers going sick from exhaustion dropped dramatically.

But then a different problem began to make itself felt. Until one of their number went down with it, venereal disease had been something of a joke amongst Liam's unit, but after Arnie reported sick they never saw him again. Despite feeling that he, more than most, had 'asked for it,' all were shocked by the treatment meted out. Under military guard he was taken to join the increasing numbers who had 'wilfully' contracted the disease, and as per the regulations, his paybook was stamped accordingly and he was forced to wear a white band on his arm, 'like a leper,' as Liam put it. Arnie had been a fool, that was agreed, but the disease could have been contracted just as easily by a man who had succumbed to temptation only once. Liam felt sick when he recalled his past intentions, and guilty that he had not tried harder to keep Arnie away from prostitutes. Conscious of having abandoned the boy, Ned felt worse. They went down to the barbed-wire compound the next Sunday afternoon, with fruit and cigarettes.

They were turned away. No one was allowed to speak to the patients, not even their guards. As Ned and Liam stood outside in the burning sun, all they had from Arnie was a half-hearted wave. He looked like a dog which had been tethered and penned and does not know why. Liam took a long, bitter pull at his cigarette then stubbed it viciously into the sand.

'A fine way to make an example of us!'

'Come on,' Ned murmured, 'there's no point in standing here, staring. They're like animals in a bloody zoo.'

It was a harsh lesson and one which sobered them all. Rumour had it, correctly so for once, that the VD cases were to be repatriated to Australia along with some of the worst criminal offenders. It seemed an ignominious end to what had begun so hopefully six months before, and the bulk of general opinion gave one reason: Egypt.

With the novelty worn away, even rebellion lost its attraction and the troops settled down to something approaching acceptance. Life, however, continued to provide its irritations. Coarse desert sand found its way into eyes and ears and noses; it was in their food and in their bedding, and the frequent dust-storms were misery for man and beast alike. After four months Liam began to wonder, along with everyone else, if they would ever leave the dirt and grit to get on with the job for which they had left Australia.

Those eight and ten mile marches out into the desert with machine guns and rifles and heavy packs seemed just as pointless and pitiless, but it began to be noticeable even to the least enthusiastic that they were pulling together under their officers and NCOs. For the first time they were beginning to feel like fully-trained fighting men, instead of an ill-directed rabble. Liam, who had always been something of a loner, was discovering the tactical advantages of team-work, the necessity of reliance upon others. He was also finding pride in himself. Training and a seemingly natural ability had made of him an excellent marksman, the best of his platoon, while four months of trench-digging had developed a muscular strength more than equal to his height. He was twenty years old, lean and fit, and he could not wait, as he wrote more than once to Robin, to see some real action.

By the middle of March, with the issue of new rifles, rumours began to fly. Some said they were about to leave for France, others that the Canal was to be defended against an attack by the Turks. But with the naval bombardment of the Dardanelles having failed, there was also talk of an infantry campaign in that area, the object being to capture Constantinople and thus knock the Turks out of the war. Success would release Britain's Russian allies from the Black Sea, where they had been blockaded for months, and seal up Germany's back door into the Mediterranean. With stalemate on the Western Front, it was a success the Allies badly needed.

Back at Mena Camp, keyed up by the knowledge that they were going somewhere, and soon, the atmosphere was taut with anticipation. Within days their destination was known: it was to be the Dardanelles after all, their jumping-off point an island in the Aegean, Lemnos.

The 8th Battalion was one of the first to receive marching orders. It was to be within thirty-six hours. After four long months of waiting, the news came both as a relief and a shock. Other battalions would follow by train to Alexandria, and thence aboard ships sailing singly across the Mediterranean. A convoy might have attracted too much attention.

In a wind which stirred the atmosphere over Mena into the consistency of soup, the 8th packed their tents on the morning of 4th April, and marched the ten miles into Cairo, none of them sorry to be seeing the last of it.

'And if I never see the bloody Pyramids again,' Ned remarked bleakly, glancing over his shoulder, 'it'll be too bloody soon.'

At the station, it was a different tale. On one of the platforms, surrounded by a small group of nurses, Mary Maddox was waiting to say farewell. Her kind, distressed face touched Liam's heightened emotions, especially when she came to speak to Ned before they climbed aboard the long line of open trucks. Liam tried, tactfully, to move away, but was stayed by the light pressure of her hand and a half-whispered plea. Bemused for a moment, it suddenly dawned on him that Mary needed his presence as cover. He too belonged to the Maddox farm, sufficient reason for her saying farewell to both of them, but not to Ned alone.

Amidst pithy comments from all sides on the standard of accommodation for their hundred-mile journey to Alexandria, Mary exchanged a few words with Ned, before turning to Liam. To his astonishment she reached up and kissed his cheek.

'God be with you,' she whispered.

He did not catch what she said to Ned, but their lips met, and for a second he embraced her passionately; then, as though ashamed of that weakness, abruptly turned away.

Liam glanced over his shoulder; but the men milling about were his own platoon. A couple of winks and sly grins told Liam all he needed to know. With a sigh of relief he turned to tell Mary not to worry, he would look out for Ned; but she had slipped away into the crowd.

From the vantage point of the truck he could see her with the other nurses, all come to wish 'their' boys good luck. The 8th Battalion was the State of Victoria's own, and for many of the nurses at Mena House the interest was personal. If the little group with Mary Maddox all looked stricken, so did Ned. Wanting to sympathize, Liam found it hard to say anything at all. A sudden longing for Georgina overwhelmed him, and he was envious of the scene he had just witnessed.

Watching the nurses sheltering from the dusty wind, he wondered whether Georgina would be wearing a red cape too. According to letters from home she was no longer in York, but nursing the wounded in some unnamed military hospital in London. That knowledge made him bitter about not going to France, dulled the edge of his excitement now. The likelihood of him seeing her again was nil. Their cheerless Brigadier had told them that in a month's time, most of them would probably be dead.

He envied Ned the hours he had spent with Mary, even the enforced brevity of their parting. With sudden insight, he realized that outside the peculiar circumstances of Egypt and wartime, Ned might never have pursued Mary Maddox, and outside the bonds of marriage, such intimacy as they had no doubt shared would have been impossible. Was that a good thing, or was it as morally wrong as he had always been led to believe? It was an uncomfortable question, one which opened avenues he had no wish to explore. Amidst that noisy, jostling throng, Liam suddenly felt alone. He was glad of the locomotive's shrill whistle, and the lurch which set them all scrambling and laughing. They were off, and a cheer went up immediately; hats were waved and thrown into the air, and the little band of nurses smiled bravely, handkerchiefs waving, red capes flapping like flags against the wind.

They left Alexandria four nights later, in winds which were strengthening to gale force. The old troopship rolled and pitched its way across the Mediterranean in some of the worst weather Liam had ever experienced. It was no consolation to the seasick men that the weather was just as bad for enemy submarines. Quartered in cargo holds, packed as close and tight as sardines in a can, the sick groaned and vomited for two days and nights, and prayed for death to claim them. The stench was enough to turn the most hardened stomach, and despite the coldness of the nights, Liam spent as much time as possible on deck, huddled in a greatcoat.

With the second night the weather subsided, and they arrived off the island of Lemnos to a glorious April morning. Liam thought he had never seen anything so beautiful. Against a curving sweep of grassy, flower-strewn hillsides, the sea was a calm, pale turquoise, reflecting the simple whitewashed village of Mudros at the head of the bay. A vast array of ships lay at anchor, dreadnaughts and destroyers which had taken part in the earlier attack; among them were the flagship *Queen Elizabeth* with *Agamemnon* and *Lord Nelson*. Between were black-hulled cargo boats, white hospital ships and little sailing vessels. Their design must have been old, Liam thought, when the ancient Greeks were young.

It was impossible to set up camp ashore, there being too little water to satisfy the thousands of men gathering for the coming assault on Gallipoli. Instead they lived aboard their transports in the same cramped and insanitary conditions which had been their lot from Alexandria, and waited for others to join them. For two weeks, training was continued, although much of it was novel enough to pass as fun. Every single day they practised climbing up and down rope ladders with full packs, over the ship's side and into lifeboats. The best rowers were trained intensively, races across the bay being one of the highlights of the week, while trips to Royal Navy ships were organized for afternoons off.

Route marches across the island were part of the agenda. Thankfully, in the rest periods, they were also allowed to bathe. After the dust and dirt and stench of Egypt, Lemnos was like a holiday camp, with warm sun, fresh breezes and shy but hospitable islanders. Curiously dressed, like characters in some eastern fairy tale, they seemed bemused but friendly, selling food they could spare at a fair price. None of them, Liam noted ironically in a letter to his brother, had sisters for rent.

In the warm, gently lapping sea, Liam swam and dived like a porpoise, revelling in its clean, salt taste, enjoying the fresh tingle of his skin in the sun. His body was hard and brown, his spirits elated once more by the thought of the coming action; keyed up by expectation, he had no fear of dying. His fears were reserved for the pain of serious wounds. If that should be his fate, Liam hoped he would behave with dignity and not be a whimpering burden.

On the evening they left the safety of Mudros Bay, he was suddenly beset by doubts. As were the majority of those aboard. Everywhere men were scribbling notes, and in quiet asides asking their particular friends to be sure to pass on certain possessions if they 'bought one on the way in'.

'Bet my sister'll be checking out the will when she reads this,' Ned joked, showing Liam the envelope with a Melbourne address. 'Who're you giving the benefit?'

'My people in York,' Liam said shortly, pen poised over a blank sheet of paper. Ned carried on talking, about his sister and her family, about the broad acres they had left behind in Australia. It was a topic which had drawn them closer, a shared ambition to own land one day, to farm a spread like Ewan Maddox. Now he gave vent to hopes for a future with Mary, if she would have him once the war was over.

'Course, her father might not approve, me being just a hired hand and that. But she's not a kid. Old enough to make up her own mind, Mary is. And I think she'd have me...'

He continued to muse aloud, while Liam wished he would be quiet.

Taking a sealed envelope from his breast pocket, Ned nudged his friend. 'Just make sure Mary gets this, will you? You know, if anything should happen to me. I don't want to *post* it,' he added with a surprisingly bashful smile, 'in case I come through – I'd look a prize dill, wouldn't I, saying all that and not a scratch on me.'

With a smile, Liam nodded. He thought Ned should post it anyway, but part of him understood the reluctance: after all, he had already written something to Georgina that he did not intend to send through official channels. That letter, addressed via Edward, lay between the pages of his notebook, and if he should survive, it would not be sent at all.

His pen still hovered. As Ned lapsed into reverie, Liam sighed, leaning his head wearily against his pack. Lights were dimmed to a minimum, and in the unaccustomed quietness the steady pulsing of the engines was like a heartbeat, the slight roll of the ship across calm water no more than the gentle rocking of a cradle. The faces all around him were heavy with apprehension, some still writing, many smoking as they lay propped against packs and equipment.

It took no great leap of the imagination to suspect that most, like himself, were thinking of homes and families so far away. It was months now since he had received that first letter from his mother and there had been others since, innocuous enough, as though she realized her mistake. But he had never replied. Now, with the unknown awaiting him, conscience was dictating its own terms. In truth, Liam knew that given his time over again, he would not – could not – have behaved in any markedly different way; but he did regret the pain he had caused. Ever since Robin's letter, he had regretted that. And if he were to die with the dawn, her pain would be even greater; it would be too cruel to add silence to the burden, to let her feel that he had gone to his grave not forgiving her. He just wished that he could find true forgiveness in his heart, but even now it eluded him. There was still that hard lump of anguish whenever he thought of his mother, and to mention the reasons for his going would have brought forth a flood of recriminations. That would not do.

In the end, he wrote only a few lines, begging her forgiveness for the grief he had caused, and telling her that she was in his thoughts. He added that she was not to worry about him, as he was not afraid of dying; and anyway, he had some good friends, and they would stand or fall together.

Hurriedly, before he could add more, or change his mind completely, Liam folded the single page and thrust it into an envelope. Come what may, his mother would have something from him, and if it was only halfway to reconciliation, then it was better than nothing.

Just after one o'clock, having slept fitfully for a couple of hours, Liam went up on deck. Sailors were moving silently between the troops, handing out mugs of cocoa; he accepted one thankfully. Beneath a moon which shone a path across the glassy sea, he could make out the hulking shapes of other cargo boats; the group of warships and destroyers which had passed them at sunset would be well ahead by now, poised and ready for the landing. Those warships carried men of the 3rd Brigade, those who would be first ashore; Liam envied them. They would have the advantage of surprise, while the 1st and 2nd Brigades must face a roused and implacable enemy. As far as he understood, the 8th Battalion would be one of the last to land. It was a daunting thought.

Time passed with dragging slowness. By three o'clock they were passing the southern tip of Imbros Isle, with possibly a dozen miles to go to the Peninsula. They were to land where it was not much more than four miles wide, where the long, mountainous backbone was broken by gentle uplands. The aim was to push inland and cross the Peninsula to a high point commanding the Narrows. At the same time the British would be landing at Cape Helles on the southern-tip, and the French on the Asian shore, directly opposite. Hearing the objectives put as simply as that by their CO, Liam thought it sounded deceptively easy, but there had to be hidden snags, else why that dire warning before leaving Egypt?

The moon was setting behind a thick veil of mist. Orders came from the bridge to extinguish all lights, and Liam reluctantly nipped out a cigarette lit only moments before. It must have been his tenth since coming on deck. As he returned the stub to its packet, he noticed his hands were trembling. In the pit of his stomach, the hot breakfast eaten too recently was churning, threatening to disgorge itself. Then a murmur distracted him from that unpleasantness. There was a light, white and hazy, behind land away and to the right of them. Someone said it was a searchlight. The light moved jerkily to left and right, then disappeared. The men around him began fidget. Liam craved another cigarette; beneath his greatcoat, despite the night's chill, he was sweating profusely. In the first, faint, greenish light of dawn, he could see the high, broken ridge of the land, make out the shapes of three other transports around them, moving into line. In a whisper, someone asked the time: it was almost half past four. The suspense and the silence were terrible. Liam found himself longing to get there, for something to happen, anything to break the tension.

It came a few minutes later in the form of a bright yellow light way to the south. A moment later there was a peculiar sound of knocking, isolated small-arms fire which rapidly became continuous.

They'd landed! The first wave was in there and fighting!

Awareness rushed over and through them like a sigh. In the brightening dawn, faces were suddenly smiling, fingers clenched on rifles, all eagerness to join the fray.

The knocking grew louder, brilliant flashes began to appear from a point on the shore; a shower of rain made the sea boil on the starboard side. Surprised, Liam realized it was too local for rain: shrapnel falling. From one of the battleships close by, a thunderous explosion rent the air. He saw the gun's recoil, the great curl smoke which followed, and wanted to cheer. Destroyers which had been close in to the beach began to come alongside the transport, ready to collect the next wave of men.

'Must be our turn next,' a man beside Liam muttered, 'the jolly jacks are here with the rum.'

Shells were falling near the ship. The massive naval guns retorted, flash and boom, flash and boom; a whistling scream and great fountain of water rose beside the old *Clan MacGillivray* making her roll and sag like an old woman. Liam staggered, the sailor beside him almost lost his footing, but saved the rum, handing it out with twice his previous speed. Liam downed his tot in a second, coughing as the thick, treacly spirit hit his throat and burned its way into his chest. He felt better for it, had cause to be doubly glad when their destroyer moved in alongside.

In the first rays of the early morning sun, her decks were like a scene from hell, littered with maimed and wounded, running with blood. Liam was aghast at the numbers, could not believe so many in so short a time. Fear clutched at his guts. Waiting while the wounded were transferred was torture. He tried not to look, tried not to hear the cries so clear against the scream of the shells. The platoons took position, the routine of scrambling over the ship's side and down the ladders going without mishap. Tension again as the destroyer sped towards the beach, men packed like toy soldiers on her decks; then down rope ladders and into the boats, more like barges, Liam thought, wondering how the rowers would handle such large, unwieldy craft.

They were about two hundred yards from the shore, with shrapnel bursting around them; an oarsman was hit and lost his oar, another fought to take his place, pulling out of time with the rest. 'In, out – in, out,' their officer yelled, for all the world like a coxswain in a boat race. Liam wanted to laugh.

The boat grounded on shingle. 'Right, chaps, this is as far as we go – everybody out!'

Overboard into four feet of water, he gasped with the shock, holding his rifle up and clear, determined not to lose his footing with the heavy pack on his back. On a narrow strip of beach he saw huddled shapes like bundles of rags and wondered what they were; then bullets danced in the sand and more fell. Something sang past his ear, the sea was suddenly hissing around him; a man with two stripes turned at the water's edge, urging his platoon on. Liam saw that it was Ned and struggled to join him as a shell burst on the rocks ahead. He had time to register the blinding flash before the shock wave knocked him flat. Deafened, half-drowned, aware of nothing more than a need to reach the shelter of those cliffs beyond the beach, he rolled, cursing the pack. A man behind caught his arm and dragged him clear.

Liam looked for Ned and could not see him. From the shelter of the cliffs he scanned the beach with mounting panic. Wallowing at the water's edge was a body; soldiers from another boat tripped over it, revealing the stripes on the sleeve. It was Ned; Liam knew it was Ned. Shedding his pack he staggered to his feet, only to be grabbed by the man beside him. What was he thinking of, the stranger wanted to know; they had to get *off* the beach, leave casualties to the stretcher-bearers.

'There aren't any bloody stretcher-bearers. And he's my *friend,* for Christ's sake – I can't just leave him to drown!'

He leapt forward, and to his credit, the other man followed. Between them they hauled Ned out of the red waves, getting in the way of the next boat-load coming ashore. Liam cursed them as he tried to cut Ned's pack free. He was alive but only just, blood pumping from a wound in his neck. Amidst a hail of shrapnel they dragged him to shelter.

Conscious enough to recognize Liam, Ned smiled. Minutes later, with his blood seeping through a hastily-applied field-dressing, he died in Liam's arms.

Wet through, with sea-water dripping from hair and clothing, Liam was not aware of the tears he shed. His companion's urgent demand as to what they were supposed to do now, went unheeded for the moment. From the back of his numbed mind, Liam recalled instructions dinned into each of them on exercise.

'Report to the nearest officer. We have to remember the dead man's position and report.'

'Sod that! We'll be dead ourselves if we don't get off this bloody beach. God knows what's happened to my mob – they'll be halfway to Constantinople by now. Come on!' The stranger started to scramble upwards, then looked back. 'What the hell are you doing now? Let's get moving.'

Liam was searching Ned's pockets. 'There was a letter he wanted me to post...'

'In this lot? Are you crazy?' He slithered down to Liam, grabbing his arm as he found the wet and crumpled letter, and dragged him upwards. 'Get moving, you stupid bugger, before you get us both killed.'

Numb with shock, his mind operating on a different plane altogether, Liam did not resist again. He was only vaguely aware of scrambling upwards amongst a group of gasping, cursing men; hands and knees were gashed and scraped on sharp rocks, but he was not aware of it.

'Where the hell are we?' a voice demanded from the left. 'This ain't the place we was supposed to be. Flat, they said – they said the sodding landing place was *flat*!'

'Tide rip,' somebody else gasped, 'took that first lot north, I reckon. Should be down there, where that bloody fort's firing from.'

'Stupid bastards,' another voice commented. 'You'd have thought the bloody navy could bloody navigate!'

For the first time, Liam looked down the way they had come. The narrow strip of beach below them was still in shadow, curving from a peaked headland on the left to a smaller one on the right. Beyond that it broadened considerably, reaching gently inland to where a distant wheatfield looked like a patch of pale green silk. A rocky headland overlooked that longer beach, and from the promontory came a series of flashes which indicated the source of those shells exploding with such deadly accuracy over the landing craft still coming ashore. Privately, Liam thought they would not have been any better off had they landed down there; the Turkish defences were obviously concentrated at that vulnerable point, any attacking force likely to be mown down immediately.

From the sea, at least two of the destroyers were pumping shells at the fortress in an attempt to silence those deadly guns; it was a heartening sight for the men on the cliffs, but did nothing to halt the equally deadly machine-gun fire coming sporadically from above.

Just below the summit they came across a group who had paused to gather breath. Some bore the red and white shoulder flashes of Liam's battalion, but none were of his platoon. Where were they? With a flash of panic, he knew they could all be dead.

With an effort, he quelled the thought. Along these cliffs they could be anywhere.

An officer of the 9th, whose men were scattered in a ravine to the right, was trying to organize all the odd members of other battalions who had been separated in the chaotic advance. He kept saying it was important to reinforce the line, while Liam wondered how he could know where the line was. From here, it was impossible to see what was ahead; below, it was all too clear. Men were still landing, still being fired upon; the dead lay huddled among discarded packs on the shingle, while a few brave souls struggled to get the wounded back into the boats and off the beach. Seeing the terrible numbers, Liam forgave the man who had dragged him away from Ned. He had saved Liam's life, while Ned was gone and nothing more could be done for him.

Except the decency of burial. That was not possible here and now, but Liam swore he would not rest until he had found his own company and an officer to whom he could report the details.

If that had been me, he thought, Ned would have done the same.

Looking to right and left, for the first time he saw they were not alone on the cliffs. Half-hidden by the thorny scrub, working their way up in groups of three of four, were scores of men. Every now and then one would fall. With a shock, Liam realized they were being picked off by snipers hidden amongst the dense, low-lying vegetation.

The officer was talking quietly, rallying the scattered force for concerted attack on the machine-gun post above them. As they fixed bayonets, Liam kept thinking of manoeuvres, the rushing and yelling before the carefully balanced thrust into the gut. When it came the reality was nothing like that.

It was far from easy to rush the crest through that terrain, over rocks that crumbled and rolled with every footfall, but somehow they achieved it. On the right flank, Liam stumbled into a hidden trench, almost on top of a Turkish soldier struggling to escape. For a second he hesitated. The man levelled his rifle and Liam went at him awkwardly; there was no room for the balanced thrust, the bayonet shuddered as it went in and the Turkish soldier fell forward, his scream ending in a froth of blood. Shocked, Liam jerked back, narrowly avoiding a bullet. A sergeant silenced that man, while others loaded rifles and shot at the retreating enemy.

The men were jubilant at their success, putting forward a dozen ideas as to what their next move should be. The officer thought they should man the gun and use it against the Turks; their own guns had yet to arrive, and would be the very devil to manhandle from the beach. But no one knew how to operate the one they had captured, so it had to be disabled. Liam drank from a Turkish water bottle and tried to avoid looking at the man he had just killed. In little more than an hour he had watched his best friend die, and killed a man at close quarters. He was shaking so badly he could hardly light a cigarette, and beneath the constant whine and crump of shells to the right, his ears were still ringing from that explosion on the beach.

With an effort he forced himself to concentrate on what the sergeant was saying. They were to make their way carefully across the ridge and down into the next gully, where some sort of rendezvous was being set up. From there they might find their own units.

It was vicious, unfriendly country, full of jagged rocks and hidden holes, perfect for snipers; a country ideally suited to defence, but hostile to attack. Unexpected scree slopes sent the unwary careering down into thorny, dried-up stream-beds, and in a couple of hundred yards Liam counted three exposed ridges and as many hidden gullies. Reaching the rendezvous in the deepest and broadest, which ran at an angle up from the beach, was a nightmare journey, unrelieved by what seemed even greater chaos when they arrived. Hideously wounded men were being ferried by stretcher-bearers down the rocky slope, while active companies struggled to climb in an attempt to reinforce a thin line spreading out along the ridges. Brigadiers were holding hurried meetings in rocky ravines, messengers dodging stray bullets, while the NCOs of a dozen different companies transmitted garbled orders to their men.

Liam and his friend from the beach searched for the red and white square of their battalion, finding several men in the same position as themselves but no NCOs. During that short delay on the beach and their subsequent scramble for the first available cover, it seemed as though the main body had advanced without them. Accosting a harassed adjutant, Liam asked where they were likely to be; in a vague gesture, the man indicated the hills to the right, and equally vaguely gave Liam permission to go in search of his missing company.

'Might as well,' one of the men said in answer to Liam's question, grinding out a cigarette. 'We're like a pack of bloody dills, standing here.'

The man who had dragged him off the beach was less keen. In the gully they were far from safe, but the odds against survival on the ridge were vast; he was for waiting on direct orders. Impatiently, Liam took a vote and found that they were evenly divided. Sadly, for he felt he owed the man something, Liam said goodbye, and squaring his shoulders, set off with his small group.

Implicitly they followed his lead up and across another series of crests and gullies, benefiting from a lull in the firing. Within the hour they spotted a large body of Australians ahead of them on the next ridge. Without field glasses it was impossible to tell whether they were men of the 8th, and a sudden increase in shelling over the beach made shouting useless. Scanning the intervening valley, Liam paused for several minutes. It seemed to him that the body ahead must have come this way, and the absence of gunfire below suggested that any lingering Turks had been flushed out. The greatest danger, as Liam was beginning to understand, would inevitably come from above. Nevertheless, it was a chance that must be taken.

Exhausted from their exertions, with little water and no food since well before first light, the others wanted to stop and rest. Liam, sweating just as freely in the hot sun, was anxious to press on before the group ahead moved out of sight. He pointed to the scree slope and told his companions to dig in their heels and slide down; from there it was but one more climb.

'Yeah,' the most aggressive of his companions muttered, 'just one more bloody climb through that lot!' His hands were torn and bleeding, his breeches, like Liam's, already in tatters. 'I say let's rest: we can catch them later.'

The rest were wavering; hesitation, Liam felt, might well prove fatal for them all. The bayonet which had wrought such damage a short while before, was in its sheath. Threateningly, he pulled it free. Although not aware of it, he was a daunting figure with blood all over his breast and sleeve, face scratched and filthy, blue eyes glittering beneath the broad-brimmed hat jammed firmly over his brow.

'If they're advancing,' he said tersely, 'they need every man they can muster. I say we go now – and we stick together. Right?'

'All right, mate, keep your hair on. You want to go now, fine, we'll go now.'

'We will indeed – you first!' With that he shoved hard and sent the other man careering down the slope. The others went of their own free will, while Liam followed, bullets from some hidden point flying round his head. The others scrambled for shelter in the gully, but Liam had grown immune to the noise. It seemed to him there was little point in being afraid of bullets, it was more important to discover their source. From the cover of a scented myrtle bush he looked for the hidden sniper; a movement from above brought two more flashes from across the gully, only a hundred yards or so from where they had passed. With great care he levelled his rifle and waited; not long and there was another flash and a report; an instant later he pressed the trigger. As the butt thudded back into his shoulder, he saw the barrel of a gun jerk upwards through the scrub. He fired again and a body fell like a broken puppet. Gripped by elation, he wanted to jump up and cheer his own success; instead he kissed the barrel of his Lee Enfield and scurried to join the others.

For a moment they were speechless, then, clapping him on the shoulder, resumed their climb. There was a short whistle and one of them dropped like a stone. Shocked, Liam realized another sniper was at work, something he should have known from the shots that had rained around him as he came down the scree. This time, however, the sudden fire attracted attention from the company above them. Within minutes a regular battle was going on, while the four remaining men climbed like beings possessed.

They found men as shattered and exhausted as themselves, almost unrecognizable as the smartly-uniformed troops which had mustered on the boat-decks before dawn. Of the gathered companies, one was Liam's, but of his platoon, only a handful remained. His arrival caused a stir, because the shell that killed Ned had taken out several others. They thought it had finished Liam, too. Their young officer, exhorting them all to pull together, had met his end beneath a burst of shrapnel fire in the first gully; others had been killed or wounded by snipers and machine-gun fire in the subsequent advance. Amongst so many, Ned's death made little impression, and it struck Liam strangely that his own survival should be the cause of such rejoicing. He had not thought himself so popular.

There were, apparently, several companies of different battalions gathered on that long, southerly spur; separated by thick scrub, but under the general command of Colonel Bolton of the 8th. It seemed they were on the extreme right flank of the line. Although orders were confused and conflicting, it filtered down that the advance had been stopped by concerted enemy fire, and that they were to dig in and hold their position on the heights.

During a break in the trench-digging, Liam shared out water and biscuits with the remaining men of his platoon. It was hardly a feast, but the food and the respite from constant action put heart into them all. It was pleasant, suddenly, to be there; the sky was blue above and birds were singing, and in the noonday warmth they were surrounded by the mingling scents of myrtle and thyme. Before them and to the left, where the hilltop widened before dividing into another ridge, was a small wheatfield, scattered with scarlet poppies, the field Liam had seen in his original climb from the beach.

With familiar faces around him, for the first time that morning he felt safe. Relaxing with a cigarette after that small but satisfying meal, almost idly he watched a destroyer closing into the long beach below them. Peace was abruptly shattered as *Bacchante* fired shell after shell at the fort of Gaba Tepe on the promontory. The men cheered as shells burst into great gouts of flame, cheered louder still when one of Gaba Tepe's massive guns was flung into the air and broken like matchwood.

The cheering came to an abrupt end when shelling from inland interrupted their high spirits with crumps and booms close by. A company of the 6th Battalion, ordered to dig in on the wheatfield, had been spotted by the Turks. The pale green corn made an easy target, and salvo after salvo descended on that small patch of ground, while those who watched were helpless to defend the men lying low before them.

Ducking into a trench while those shells thudded into the soil and scrub around them, Liam was close enough to the command dugout to catch something of their officers' frustration. As yet they had no artillery, but with those huge naval guns so close, if that Turkish battery could be located, it could be stopped. Runners were sent out to make contact with the forward lines to the north, but none returned. Meanwhile, as troops moved on or near the wheatfield, the enemy reopened fire. Other runners were sent back to headquarters in that gully off the beach, returning with the anxious news that the forward line was opening as it continued to advance across the main plateau. If it were to hold, the main body must be reinforced, therefore some of Colonel Bolton's men must be relinquished in support.

Overhearing some of these exchanges, and shrewd enough to guess the rest, Liam began to wonder whether this was the right place to be. He watched a man detach himself from the party on the wheatfield and sprint up the hill towards them, attracting another salvo as he did so. Wincing, he ducked again, while the man fell in a gasping heap beside him. Even as Liam reached out to help him up, he was scrambling away to deliver his message.

Permission was granted for the men below to advance, anything better than lying prostrate beneath those shrieking salvoes. Orders were hurriedly given, and as hurriedly carried out. Together with several other sections of the 8th, Liam's platoon was detailed to accompany that party in their attempts to reach the forward line. They had to cross the open field, while shells screeched and thudded beside them. Knowing the Turks had the range wrong did not ease that nerve-shattering dash. With no casualties, they reached the body of men in command of a young lieutenant, from there wriggling forward on their stomachs until they reached the scrub at the field's far edge. From there it was a steep drop into the gully below.

At the far end of the next spur, they came across another remnant of the 8th, with only one surviving NCO. Hard pressed in that advance from the beach, they were exhausted. Someone asked whether they had eaten: in the heat of battle food had been forgotten. Again, as had happened with Liam, the combination of food and friendly faces put new life into them. After a short spell they set to work digging themselves in.

It was essential to keep on the alert, but apart from the shells still screaming overhead, it was a surprisingly quiet afternoon. Liam found himself counting the salvoes, pitying the men still holding the ridge behind them, for the Turks knew exactly where they were. Detailed for this party, he had been convinced he would not survive that dash across the field; but he had, and this was a better position. But it seemed a strange sort of battle to him, a series of mad dashes with no more than rifles and bayonets, against an enemy entrenched with artillery and machine-guns. As yet the Australians had neither.

At about five o'clock, large numbers of Turks were seen on the skyline, advancing from their positions on the highest ridge, towards the pine-covered spur immediately in front. Silhouetted against the sky, they were a perfect target, but as yet too far off to be reached by rifle fire. Suddenly shells screamed over from one of the warships, but although many men went down, more continued to come on. The joint company prepared themselves for action, and within the half hour, as the Turks crept through a line of pines across the little valley, they opened fire. Heavy and continuous, it was also unexpected, and the enemy fell back; elated, the Australians yelled and whooped for joy. The young lieutenant leapt to his feet, directing fire, and at once a Turkish bullet felled him. Wounded in the chest, for a while he could barely speak, but insisted his company held on until nightfall. Determined to hold back the Turkish advance, they did so, but it was a costly, exhausting action.

His hands blistered from loading and firing, Liam wondered how much longer they could hold on. But then, as the light began to fail, the attack ceased. He could hear isolated battles going on all around, but it was impossible to tell friend from foe. At last the noise faded away, and after dark the runner who had gone to report their situation, returned with orders to retire to the ridge overlooking the wheatfield.

Liam had never envied an officer, never wanted to be one of them. In his mind they were associated with Robert Duncannon, and as such to be held in some sort of contempt. But that day he conceived an admiration for this man, no more than his own age, who had kept his head under terrifying conditions. More than that, the young lieutenant seemed to know what to say and when to say it. Despite his wounds he had, in effect, held the men together.

After the unremitting ordeal of a day which had begun some twenty-hours before, they were each on the point of collapse. Some had simply fallen asleep in the shallow trench, rifles clutched beside them. With the return of the messenger, Liam went forward to their acting commander, a corporal he remembered from Cairo. He was a big, muscular Queenslander, and a badly broken nose testified to more than one vicious pounding from fists as big as his own. But he and Liam were of a similar height, bigger than most of the survivors; it seemed only sensible that they should carry the lieutenant between them.

They made a seat for him from their crossed hands, and with great difficulty descended into the valley. Although he was not particularly heavy, in their exhausted state his weight seemed like lead, and the sheer awkwardness of negotiating a steep slope in darkness, over loose rocks and spiny scrub, called for a strength and control which drained them both. By the time they reached the narrow valley, Liam was sweating and trembling in every limb, his arms burning in their sockets. Faced with the scree slope, terrified of dropping the lieutenant and making his injuries worse, Liam suggested carrying him across his back.

Between bouts of agony, the lieutenant objected thoroughly and colourfully, insisting they leave him. But rumour had it that the Turks mutilated their prisoners and that was a risk that Liam was not prepared to take.

The Queenslander ordered Liam to hold the lieutenant upright.

With difficulty he did so, wincing at the groans of agony, easing him as gently as possible onto the other man's shoulders. With Liam guiding and pulling, they managed perhaps twenty paces. Then Liam took over the burden, and with another man pushing and the corporal guiding, he managed half the slope before collapsing, his lungs on fire. Suddenly, he heard voices raised in argument above. The corporal heard them too, identifying himself before they could be mistaken for marauding Turks.

Help came quickly. Relieved of his burden, Liam found himself incapable of movement. To his shame, he had to be supported up the rest of the incline and across what appeared to be a ploughed field. With something of a shock he realized it was the wheatfield, dotted with poppies, which had looked so beautiful in the rising sun.

Fifteen

Having checked the course for the Dardanelles, Stephen took his coffee outside, yawning in the warm air, pleased by the touch of the sun on his skin. It was another limpid blue morning, with the azure hills of Imbros Isle poised between sea and sky. The kind of morning to satisfy every holidaymaker on every island in the Aegean; and after all, this was what they saved for, assiduously, all year round. Responding to it, he smiled, counting his blessings, glad that he did not have to earn his living cooped up in an office. If this job had its drawbacks, then it also had its advantages, and moments like this were blessings indeed.

Spring, and the weather was beautiful; it must have been a day like this that saw the initial attack on Gallipoli. Anzac Cove, named for the Australian and New Zealand Army Corps, had passed into legend, and the debacle of the whole campaign faded to nothing beside the bravery of those men who endured it.

Transcribing Liam's diary, Stephen had begun by separating the notes relating to different years. 1914 was rapidly dealt with, while the memoranda for 1915 was fuller, but still frustratingly sparse on detail. With his eyes taking in the harsh skyline of mainland Turkey and the tip of the Peninsula ahead, Stephen wondered whether Liam had made notes at the time of dates and places and particularly violent exchanges, or if, in that depressing return to the desert in early 1916, he had checked details with others who were on Gallipoli, entering noteworthy dates in his new diary sent out from York at Christmas.

It was difficult to say. Possibly it was a combination of both, since Liam seemed the kind of man who liked to keep a tally of what was happening. But if the notes for that period were disappointingly brief in comparison to the following year, they were also shocking in their terse accounts of attacks, gains, and casualties. Set against his own general knowledge of that campaign, the diary made him wince.

Studying the chart last night, he could see why the planners in London had thought it such a good idea. It looked easy. The Gallipoli Peninsula, at the point where they had attacked, was only about four miles wide. Capture the forts either side of the Dardanelles, hold enemy shipping to ransom, and while you're at it, lads, just nip up and take Constantinople...

But with no first-hand knowledge of the terrain, and without taking into account the weeks of foreknowledge given to the Turks, it had been a disaster. Those forts were never taken, and they were stuck there from April to December, lobbing home-made bombs into Turkish trenches, dying from the heat and flies in August, and frozen to death in November, when it snowed. No fresh food or water, and supplies had to come by ship from the island of Lemnos.

The idea that ignorant men in comfortable offices in London could send other men across the world to die in conditions like that made him angry. It made him angrier still to think that little had changed.

His anger was so at variance with the beauty of the morning, it was unbearable. He went inside. An hour later, with the Dardanelles looming, he was back on the bridge, checking course and radar projections, scanning the shoreline with powerful binoculars. The Peninsula, low at its southern tip, rose in a series of ochre hills, in parts densely covered with evergreen scrub. From the sea, it had a certain rugged beauty, but the vivid pictures in his mind's eye made him shiver. The Anzacs had landed way up on the seaward side, but what Stephen was seeing now would have been seen by Liam as he took part in the second assault on the Peninsula.

Just ten days after the original landings, he had been part of a combined British and French assault on Cape Helles at the southern tip. Stephen guessed that it must have been reasonably successful, because somehow, in the wake of hideous fighting, Liam had found time to explore the ruined fort of Sedd el Bahr. He had examined some crippled French artillery, had a swim in the sea, and the day after, '*Had a yarn with Commander Sampson about his plane, named Dragonfly.*'

Two days later, on 8th May, came a salutary note: '*Took part in the second attack on Krithia. Gained 800 yards, lost 2,000 casualties.*'

On 15th May, Liam was back at Anzac Cove, again landing during a concentrated shelling; and by the 20th he was fighting in the hell of Quinn's Post, where the trenches were no more than a few yards apart. In that small area the dead lay unburied in their thousands, so numerous and so offensive that – as Liam again noted – an armistice had to be arranged for their interment. There seemed a dreadful irony in that.

Although he never remarked on minor injuries, considering the terrain, the intensity of constant warfare, Stephen could not imagine that Liam had remained unscathed. And if he had, there was always dysentery to contend with, which had been endemic, made worse by the lack of sanitation and the hordes of devouring summer flies.

What amounted to a starvation diet had also taken its toll. For eight months those men had lived on the kind of iron rations meant to support a man in the field for no more than a few days. By the beginning of September Liam had been seriously ill. Not dysentery – although he had probably had that too – but pneumonia. He left Anzac on a hospital ship for Alexandria, arriving at the Palace Hotel, Heliopolis, on the 10th. On that date, the tall, fine-looking young man noted that he had weighed only 130lbs. In four months Liam Elliott had lost more than three stones in weight.

Six weeks later, however, he was pronounced fit for action, and with a promotion to acting corporal, was returned to Anzac with a new uniform, an advantage many of the others would not have had. Winter came early to the Peninsula that year, and the last two months were bitter, with temperatures well below freezing. In their pathetic holes in the ground, many of the emaciated troops died of exposure.

After that, just before Christmas, had come the evacuation. A creeping retreat so that the Turks would not realize it was over and that their foes were leaving. Liam, in the firing line to the bitter end, had watched stores and food being burned on the beach while those beside him went hungry. The next day, after a bombardment which lasted six hours, he and his compatriots left

Anzac Cove without another shot being fired. Within twenty-four hours, he noted, they were back on Lemnos and drilling again, three hours a day.

That terse comment was echoed, day after day, throughout the next three months. Egypt had not changed when they returned to it, but the men had. They were weary and depressed, had suffered an ignominious defeat and had watched their friends die for nothing. That they themselves had fought like the Trojans of old, that they had endured and ultimately survived, was not enough to raise spirits crushed by the experience. That those in command seemed not to care only added to the burden.

The entries in Liam's diary for that period at the beginning of 1916 were short and monotonous and full of complaint. It was so indicative of malaise, Stephen's anger had been choking as he typed up days and weeks of the same thing. '*Drill again, food still scarce,*' was typical, as were complaints at lack of leave for the men, while officers were allowed plenty.

Later, from an active post by the Suez Canal, Liam had written over several days: '*No food, nowhere to buy any... Digging gun-pits and trenches... No issue of water for over 48 hours, one loaf of bread between three men... Lecture by our Colonel on whether we are fit to go to France...*'

Those entries in Liam's diary were, Stephen thought, a terrible indictment of all that had passed in the name of organization. All inflicted by those at the top, men of their own nationality, on their own side. That was the worst part: it might have been more forgivable had those deprivations been suffered under an enemy hand.

With the diary in his pocket and his eyes on that brooding neck of land, so intent was Stephen that he barely noticed the arrival of the Turkish pilot. It was with something of an effort that he brought his thoughts back to the present and the job in hand.

Some hours later they dropped the pilot at Gelibolu, where the Dardanelles widen into the Sea of Marmara. They passed much Soviet and Romanian shipping, most of it merchant trade, although there were a couple of naval vessels, bristling all over with the latest military technology. Stephen photographed them just for the hell of it. Watching them slink past like greyhounds on a leash, he thought how ironic it was that Liam had fought, ostensibly, to release the Tsar's navy from the Black Sea. But the plan, ill-conceived and unprepared for such resistance from the Turks, had failed. At this distance in time, Stephen could not help wondering what difference it would have made to the war – and the world – had they succeeded. Probably not very much. Russia had been heading down the road to revolution, even then.

After dark, Istanbul and the Bosphorus slipped by like a jewelled stage-set for the *Arabian Nights*; by comparison, Stephen thought, Odessa at noon was about as alluring as a banana republic on the eve of a coup. But it would have been all the same had their loading port been the best place on earth: he was too busy to go ashore, and except for Sparks, the Radio Officer, that went for his officers, too. Not so the Filipino crew. Most of them managed to spend some time ashore, and while handing out roubles before they went, Stephen stressed the need to obtain receipts for everything purchased.

Two days later, eager to get away from the armed guards and that depressing townscape, before the ship sailed, he called each of the crew to his office to collect the unspent currency.

'You may not keep any roubles,' he explained. 'All you have left must be returned to the agent. And I must have your receipts.'

The first three shook their heads in some confusion. 'But they do not give receipts, sir.'

As the young steward outlined a female form with his hands, the two cooks dissolved into helpless laughter, and suddenly Stephen understood. But he could hardly credit it. 'You mean Russian girls?'

'Oh, yes, sir – very good!'

The situation afforded him the first hearty laugh for several days; nevertheless, he did wonder how to explain their purchases on the forms before him. He was left with a dual sense of admiration: for the crew's determination and prowess, and also for the spirit of free enterprise at work in that grim Communist city. He was, however, glad to leave it.

Approaching the Bosphorus on the return journey, he related the tale in a letter to Zoe; although with Liam still on his mind, the majority of what he had written was concerned with the diary and his enclosed transcript. Only as they anchored, awaiting the boat to collect the mail, did he feel the need to add lines which were lighter and more personal. With mosques and minarets reflected in the still water, and the huge dome of Aghia Sofia rising above the city, it was impossible not to be touched by the romance of Istanbul. It was Byzantium and Constantinople, the seat of popes and sultans, a meeting place of past and present, sacred and profane; Europe and Asia facing each other across a narrow strip of water. The evening air was like velvet against his skin, perfumed and spicy, making him long for things which seemed forever destined, like the city itself, to remain just out of reach.

Describing the view and the atmosphere, Stephen was tempted, suddenly, to make her smile.

'I have this private fantasy,' he wrote, 'about sailing ships and warm wooden decks beneath the stars – and this would make the perfect setting. But then I look around me, and there are no tall masts and spars, no furled sails and scrubbed wooden decks. Only functional painted steel, complete with squared-off afterdeck and bulbous bow – these days ships don't even look like ships!

'Why am I here? I ask myself that all the time. And if I have to be here, which it seems I must, why are you so far away? I wish we could be together again – here and now, with a good meal awaiting us at some tiny candlelit restaurant, and my very comfortable, but oh, so empty bed, to return to. So I say to hell with the warm wooden decks – better in imagination than reality!'

Reading through the last few lines before he sealed the envelope, Stephen wondered what he was saying. That he wanted her with him? There had been moments in the past when he had longed to share the delight of an experience with someone else, but never before had there been a woman with Zoe's depth of understanding, a woman with whom he could share such things so completely. Most particularly, he could think of no other woman who would appreciate how he was beginning to feel about Liam Elliott.

His desire to talk to her on that very subject was reinforced within the hour. The boat which came to collect their letters also bore a package of mail from London. Sorting its contents into piles for different officers, Stephen's heart gave a pleasurable leap at the sight of Zoe's handwriting on two envelopes. Unable to resist opening them there and then, he quickly scanned the contents, gratified by her admission that life was not the same without him, that she missed him even more than she had anticipated.

But as though that path was fraught with danger, she had rapidly abandoned it for safer ground. Disappointed, Stephen returned to those comforting few lines and read them three times. He skimmed the part about some new work and her agent's opinion, slowing as he reached a most unexpected piece of news. She had, she said, found amongst Louisa's letters, a whole bundle from Liam, written during the war. Addressed to Edward, they covered the period spent in Egypt, Gallipoli and then France, the early letters full and vivid, later ones terse with weariness, giving the impression that much was left unsaid, and not just for the censor's sake.

Her enthusiasm at this find sprang off the page; and also her sadness. Like Stephen himself, she was angered by the almost unimaginable horror of Liam's experience, a horror which led him to edit his own sentences before they were written, to couch all but the lightest moments in bland phrases.

'The strange thing is,' Zoe had commented in her neat, italic hand, 'that despite his obvious attempts to hide things, I feel as though I know what it is he's hiding, and why he's hiding it. I'm starting to feel as though I know him.'

Me too, Stephen silently agreed, drawn closer to Zoe by that common awareness. In the next sentence, as she confessed that she had even begun to dream about Liam, Stephen's heart skipped a beat. Despite the warmth of his office he shivered, wondering whether her dreams had been as disturbing as his own. He hoped not, but for the moment he was unnerved by the coincidence.

With daylight and the return passage through the Dardanelles his reaction seemed extreme. He told himself that what they were investigating had very quickly ceased to be a mystery; identities and ambiguous relationships had been sorted out, providing clear motivation both for Liam's abrupt departure and Tisha's later eccentricities. Regarding Robert Duncannon's paternity, Stephen could sympathize with those closest at the time. Even with two generations between, for him there had been an odd, almost drunken shift of perspective; which seemed strange because he had never known Edward Elliott. He could only imagine it was something to do with identity, with the assurance that came from knowing who you were, and where you had come from. It was not something people examined every day, but it was there, like childhood. And there must have been a world of difference, he reflected, between Edward Elliott, the poet, and Robert Duncannon, the professional soldier.

It was different for Zoe. She had experienced no sense of shock at their discoveries. Having known nothing about the family, she came to it clean, with no preconceived ideas; yet having said that, even her detachment crumbled when it came to Liam, just as his own was doing. Why?

It was a question to which there was no ready answer; or rather too many answers, all facile, none of them touching the heart of the matter, none of them explaining the long chain of coincidence.

Once out of the Dardanelles, Stephen made a concerted effort not to think about it. Since Mac was growing anxious at what seemed an obsession, Stephen dutifully accepted every invitation to darts in the bar, and even arranged a general knowledge quiz for Saturday night. At one time, he reflected nostalgically, social evenings had been organized by junior officers, the old fogies invited along purely from courtesy. But nowadays, the youngsters organized very little. A diet of television and videos had apparently made them too sophisticated for games, but games were more than simple entertainment, they made people talk. And social intercourse was important, welding bonds between strangers, easing some of the strains of the working relationship with humour. Stephen needed to know his officers, needed them to know each other; the job itself was hard enough without the added stress of isolation and poor morale.

Initially it was difficult to promote enthusiasm; only afterwards, having had a better time than any of them imagined possible did they suggest more. Stephen felt he had made a breakthrough when the 3rd Mate asked whether he might arrange another quiz for the following Saturday.

'Providing we're not in port, you can. We'll get Saturdays organized yet – Board of Trade Sports in the morning, Quiz Night after dinner...'

The lad looked blank. '*Board of Trade Sports*, sir?'

'Old joke, Marcus,' Stephen explained with a grin. 'I mean boat drill and fire drill.'

En route for Augusta, Sicily, Stephen's main concern became that of their next destination. He was not at ease when charters and cargoes were difficult to come by in London. With the war in the Gulf, he dreaded the kind of desperation for work which might send him and his ship running the gauntlet through the Straits of Hormuz.

Their cargo of Russian oil was discharged in Sicily without too many problems, but as the last marine surveyor drank his beer and said his farewells, a telex came through from London. The instructions were to proceed in the direction of the Suez Canal.

'Oh, wow,' Mac said in an acid impression of a gleeful schoolboy, 'haven't seen Port Said in years. Wonder if it's changed any?'

'One can always hope,' Stephen responded. 'Thank God we're only passing through. Can you imagine the crew ashore? They'd come back bankrupt!'

Mac chuckled. 'After Odessa, I think we should telex ahead to every port, telling them to lock up their women. Our lot might not speak the lingo, but they can certainly make themselves understood! Mind you,' he added slyly, 'we didn't do too badly when we were younger, did we?'

'Not in bloody Port Said, though!'

'No, not Port Said – Singapore was the place then. And Japan,' he added nostalgically. 'I remember a girl in Osaka-Ko...'

'Mac,' Stephen interrupted, staring at the telex. 'They're not telling us something. Why are we heading for Suez? Going through there costs money, and we're in ballast, earning not a brass farthing. Whatever they've got in mind for us east of Suez, must be pretty bloody lucrative...'

Picking up that sudden, overwhelming conviction, Mac slowly shook his head. 'Oh, no – come on, Steve, they wouldn't!'

'Wouldn't they bloody just!' He slammed the paper down and

quickly lit a cigarette, pacing Mac's cabin like a caged tiger. 'I bet you – I bet you anything you care to name that that's where we're going!'

Mac stroked his beard. 'Indonesia?' he suggested hopefully. 'Singapore? We are due for dry-dock.'

'Stuff the bloody dry-dock, Mac – we're going to the Gulf!'

A few days later, told to proceed towards Singapore for further orders, Mac was convinced he would get his dry-dock after all. But as they cleared the Red Sea the telex came in which confirmed the worst of Stephen's fears. Not just a single trip up the Gulf, but a charter which would have them in and out every week. For a limited period, the message said; but that could mean anything from six weeks to six months, as Stephen well knew. Furious that such orders had not warranted a personal telephone call via the satellite, he simply acknowledged the telex without comment. It was midday in London, so let them call him if necessary. If he spoke to the company now, in the heat of his anger, he might live to regret it.

Over the internal telephone, he called the Mate's cabin. He was off duty; as expected, he was in bed. Mac and the Second Engineer were in the bowels of the engine room, but within ten minutes all four were gathered in Stephen's cabin with the outer door shut. The Radio Officer, with his professional commitment to keep the contents of telexes to himself, had already been sternly reminded of it. In deliberately neutral tones, Stephen read out the contents of the message to his senior officers. The Mate, unexpectedly, gave vent to a string of obscenities which were echoed, to a lesser extent, by the Second Engineer; Mac simply stared, his brown eyes hurt, as though Stephen had personally arranged to prove him wrong.

With a defensive shrug, Stephen skimmed the paper across the table so that they could read it for themselves. He went to the fridge for four cans of beer and set them on the table. It was hot in the cabin and he was sweating, his shirt sticking to his back like tissue paper.

'Technically speaking,' he said slowly, 'we are not obliged to carry on our occupation in what is officially termed a war zone.

Technically, I could send a telex back, demanding reliefs for all of us...'

'And we all know what sort of a reaction you'd get to that!' Mac commented, red whiskers bristling. He took a long pull of his beer.

'True, but I can try. However, we need to anticipate a refusal, no matter how it's couched, and plan accordingly. Because no matter what pressure is brought to bear, certain people will want off, regardless.'

'If they pay me enough,' Mac growled, 'I'll sail the bloody ship for them – right up the main street of Tehran!'

Laughter broke the tension, and for a few minutes they discussed money, and what should be demanded in return for their 'loyalty' to the company. Stephen let them carry on, knowing that certain figures and percentages would be offered, and that it would be up to him to negotiate the best deal. He had few illusions about the attitude to reliefs.

Only the Mate seemed particularly unhappy. 'I've got a wife and three kids, and as far as I'm concerned, they're more important to me than any bloody job. What's money if you're blown to bits?'

Stephen was inclined to agree with him, but forbore to do so. 'I don't have a wife,' he said, 'nor do I have children. My objections are those of principle. I hate war and I loathe what they're doing.' In the ensuing silence, his breathing sounded ragged, at odds with the chill in his voice. 'However, what we have to face is our own economic reality. And I think – before we start telling the company where to get off – we have to consider our positions seriously.

'I also think,' he went on a moment later, 'that those of you who are married should try to get in touch with your wives. In a sense, they're just as involved as we are. But please, not until I've had a word with the office, and we have the official line on what the choices are.'

Stephen took copies of the telex, had one posted in the bar, another on the bridge, while a third went down to the crew's quarters with a message for the Bosun to contact him as soon as possible. Part of him wanted to break his own rule and telephone

Zoe at once, but although he had a good idea of what the official line would be, he felt he must await its confirmation. And when it came, shortly after seven that evening, the voice of his respected ship-manager was hardened with a deliberate chill, like that of a 1916 officer informing his juniors of the next big push.

The slight pause inflicted by the satellite link distanced them further. We were friends, Stephen thought, united by many a previous difficulty, mutually solved; and now we sound like enemies.

'I'm sorry, Jack, but feeling here is running strong. Nobody wants to risk his neck just to keep a bunch of Muslim fundamentalists in Exocet missiles!'

The voice, after a second's delay, was colder than ever. 'This charter is to the Kuwaitis, Captain – the oil is Kuwaiti oil!'

'Balls!' he retorted, infuriated by that insistence on something they both knew was little more than a technicality. The oil might be coming through Kuwaiti pipelines – it might even be from their own fields – but the money it was earning, that was a different matter. In a biased neutrality, the Kuwaitis were feeding financial aid to their war-torn Iraqi neighbours; and the Iranians, knowing exactly what was going on, were intent upon stopping the trade.

Again the delay, but this time the voice had softened to a cajoling note. 'Look, Stephen, I'm giving it to you from the horse's mouth. We *need* this charter, it's worth a lot of money to the company – we're on the edge, believe me, and it might just tide us over till things improve. If they improve.' There was an eloquent sigh. '*We can't afford to turn it down*. Nor can we afford the delay while you and your crew prat about making up your minds. If we have to do a complete crew-change, I'm telling you the Filipinos will never work again – not at sea, anyway. And there'll be that many black marks on the officers' files, it won't be worth their while applying elsewhere. The company has long arms and much influence, you know that.'

Stephen did know; nevertheless he could not believe he was hearing it stated so unequivocally. He had expected pressure, but not a deadly determination underlined by Jack's confidential tone. Had it come from anyone else, even the Chairman, he knew he would have been tempted to lay down the gauntlet of challenge. But he knew Jack, and Jack knew the company inside out. In the intimate world of shipping and ship-owners, these people were akin to the Cosa Nostra. How else had they survived, when almost every other British company had gone to the wall?

Stephen knew, too, that however highly he was regarded, they would be prepared to fire him over this issue, and at the end of the day, when he needed a reference, his file would be marked unreliable, and there would be a tactful disinclination to comment. They had him over a barrel, and they knew it. Rage coursed through him. The iniquity of blackmail offended his principles and integrity even more than the nature of what he saw as being a very dirty job indeed. Biting back the urge to tell Jack what to do with it, Stephen shut his eyes and clamped his hand across the mouthpiece.

It took all his self-control to remind himself of the vow made years ago: *when you pack it in, Elliott, it'll be when you are ready, and not before.*

This was not the time to call the odds.

While Jack Porteous dotted the i's and crossed the t's of all he had said already, Stephen shuddered, as at a mouthful of bile. Releasing his cramped fingers, he said bitterly: 'It's a pity the company can't use some of its fabled power to lobby the bloody government. If British shipping had more support from that quarter, Jack, maybe we wouldn't be in this situation in the first place. Tell that to the bloody Chairman!'

It was, he felt, a suitable last word. Abruptly, he severed the connection, and it was some minutes before he had calmed down sufficiently to speak to anyone else.

In the radio room, Sparks was lounging like a disc-jockey before the banks of electronic equipment. 'So what are they going to pay?' he asked laconically. 'Over and above, that is.'

'Not enough,' Stephen answered tersely. 'And if it was a couple of million in a Swiss bank account, it still wouldn't be enough.'

It was, however, a question asked by all the others. The bonus was to be a percentage of their monthly salaries, not ungenerous when considered in isolation, but worth little in the light of insurance policies made invalid by the war zone. Death or disability thus incurred was not standard cover.

The Mate was the first to use the satellite phone. His wife apparently echoed his sentiments, because he repeated his request for a relief. Wearily, Stephen nodded. The younger officers, however, were oddly exhilarated by the thought of danger and the chance of extra money; the older ones resignedly counted the weeks still to run before they could legitimately apply for leave. Mac and Stephen, having been last to join, had something like four months ahead of them. The Third Engineer, with three months yet to do and a wife and baby at home, requested a relief.

'I'll get a job on the rigs,' he said defiantly, 'and stuff the bloody company.'

Stephen rather admired the belligerency. Contrary to his expectations, the crew were unperturbed by the situation. He was not sure whether it was fatalism or greed on their part, but every one elected to stay. That should please Jack Porteous, he thought, returning to his cabin to make another call. With the receiver in his hand, however, he paused before dialling the London office, deciding to speak to Zoe first. He had some vague hope that she might persuade him otherwise, bring forth a string of incontrovertible reasons as to why he should say, like the Mate and the Third: 'Stuff the company, I'll find something else...'

But deep down, at the heart of him, he did not want to say that, not yet...

She was not at home. Envisaging the empty flat, he let the telephone ring and ring, willing her to dash up the stairs to answer it. Dejection gripped him; he had wanted, so much, to hear her voice; then he was furious, wondering where she was, and what could be more important that she must be out when he needed her...

Still in that spirit of anger, with a sense of having all his exits cut off, Stephen called Jack Porteous, and their communication was terse and to the point. *Now we know where we stand*, Jack seemed to be saying, *we can organize with lightning speed*. As indeed they could. Nevertheless, Stephen did wonder who would be sent to replace the men he was losing.

It was not until he tried to call Zoe again, later, that he realized something was wrong with the satellite link. He tried the telex and that too was down. Impotently furious, he was further incensed when Sparks, having checked everything and risked his neck up the mast, announced that it would take specialist engineers to cure the fault. For the next few days they were forced back to what seemed a prehistoric means of communication: morse code over the shortwave radio.

The ship put into Fujairah, outside the Straits of Hormuz, landed the two officers and took aboard their replacements, together with the electronics experts. The only joyful moment for Stephen was in greeting the new Mate, that same John Walker with whom he had served aboard his last ship, the ill-famed *Nordic*. He had a feeling that Johnny's irreverent humour was going to be a tonic they would all savour.

'What the bloody hell made you agree to all this?'

'I dunno, Captain – I think my bank manager said I could do with the money. Mind you, I was a bit pissed at the time, so don't quote me.'

Stephen laughed. 'And what about the girlfriend?'

'No problem – last time I saw her, she said she'd like to see me in hell anyway.'

'Oh. All off, is it?'

The long, lanky Mate shrugged, his nonchalance that of the seasoned campaigner. The new Third, unmarried, uncertificated, and well into his fifties, seemed to regard the situation as normal. Their combined attitudes put new heart into Stephen. They had been at home, living with the television news, and must know what they were getting into.

At noon Stephen went ashore with the agent, his chest struggling against heat which pressed like a hot iron. About to phone Zoe, he was apprehensive at the thought of having to explain where he was and why; and awed by the commitment he was about to make. This time, the need to tell her that he loved her had not come from outside himself, but from deep within; and it was suddenly the most important thing in the world. He wanted desperately to say so, and to hear the same words from her lips.

The thought of dying, Stephen realized, clarified the mind wonderfully, identifying priorities with the speed of a computer.

Having accepted the situation as unavoidable, all he wanted to do now was get on with the job. He was still angry, but he treasured the anger, like his love for Zoe, as a talisman against fear. And when the job was over, please God, he would go home, sort out his life, and make proper plans for the future. He had drifted too long; it was time to set a definite course.

Like a man with a terminal disease waiting impatiently for a solicitor to draft his will, Stephen drummed his fingers on the agent's desk, a telephone within reach, while the agent complacently sorted business of his own. At last the man left him alone to make his calls. Time demanded he contact the office first, and when that lengthy business was complete, he dialled Zoe's number. There was a silence, then interminable clicks and sighs; the phone rang four times and was then picked up.

A man's voice answered, light, cultured, faintly amused.

The unexpectedness stabbed like a knife in the breast, stopped his breath for a moment. The voice at the other end was impatient, became peremptory. Almost stammering, Stephen asked for Zoe.

'And *your* name?'

'Elliott,' he snapped back, barely controlling the urge to demand the other's name, and the nature of his business at Zoe's flat at ten on a Saturday morning.

Muffled words, a voice – her voice – suddenly clear in the background; a rustle of movement which made him wonder where she had been, what doing; then flustered, breathy intensity.

'Stephen – where are you calling from? This is a surprise!'

Racked by the most painful suspicion, for a moment he almost hated her. It was with great difficulty that he controlled his words, his voice. 'Just thought I'd ring – see how you were.'

'I'm fine – just fine,' she claimed, while a nervous laugh escaped her. 'But how are you? You sound *different*. Is anything wrong – or is it just this awful line?'

'I'm fine.'

'Well, good, I'm glad to hear it. Where are you?'

'Some place you've probably never heard of. Fujairah – it's part of the United Arab Emirates.'

There was a pause on the line. Stephen could almost hear her thinking, raking over world geography, trying to place it exactly.

'Zoe,' he said with mounting urgency, aware of time passing as he was of the man in the background, and unable to ignore either, 'we're going into the Gulf. We'll be in and out for the next few weeks, between Kuwait and Karachi. It's annoying, and I can't say it's something I relish – but frankly, there's nothing to be done about it. I just wanted to say…' He broke off. 'I just wanted to tell you where we are – in case you don't hear from me for a while.'

'The Gulf?' she repeated faintly. 'Not the *Persian* Gulf?'

'The very same.'

'But – there's a war going on. I keep seeing it on the news – missiles, minesweepers…' He could hear her breath coming sharp and deep. 'Stephen – they *can't* send you there.'

'Why not?' he demanded. 'The rest of the world wants to buy what they're still selling – and fools like us have to do the dirty work!'

The muffled exclamation of her distress cut through his anger. The iniquity of his position, Stephen reminded himself, was not her fault. Apologizing, knowing the conversation was not going the way he had intended, he rubbed his forehead wearily. He would have liked to start again, but the presence of the other man in Zoe's flat was as tangible as the heat on the window behind him.

'I'm sorry, Zoe, I have to go. I'm phoning from the agent's office and it's a courtesy call. I'll write as soon as. I can. By the way – did you get my letter from Istanbul?'

'Yes,' she said eagerly, 'I did, last week. And your transcript of the diary…'

'Good, well, I'll write again soon – let you know more about what's going on.' For a moment he was tempted to end the conversation there, but his need to know about the other man was too great. Tersely, he said: 'Who's your friend, by the way? Or shouldn't I ask?'

There was a short silence. Her response, when it came, was just a shade too dismissive. 'Oh, it's only Philip. He – well, my car's playing up again, and he offered to give me a lift down to Sussex. It wouldn't have mattered,' she added with a false little laugh, 'but I've got an appointment this afternoon to see Tisha's old house…'

'I see.' It sounded plausible and he would have liked to believe her, but not even the mention of Tisha's name could overcome a hot surge of jealousy. So Philip Dent was on the scene again. 'Well, I hope he's a good driver. Have a nice weekend.'

She seemed nonplussed by his acidity. 'Stephen, it's not like that. Please don't...'

But he never could abide lies. Quite deliberately, he cut the connection, hating the false intimacy of telephones, the emotions stirred by the sound of a voice, the sheer impossibility of closeness that they underlined. And to the recipient, he thought sardonically, a call could be such an unwelcome interruption.

Standing by the window, with sunlight filtering through the young leaves of plane trees outside, Zoe listened to the empty hum of the line and knew the disconnection was not accidental. Angry, hurt, disappointed, and most of all frustrated, she turned on Philip.

'There now – see what you've done!'

'Hey, just a minute, Zoe – you did ask me to take it.'

'I know – but now he's got entirely the wrong impression!' She slammed out of the room and began to gather her things in a fury, dumping them in the tiny lobby.

'Oh, *damn and blast!*' she ground out between gritted teeth. 'Damn him – damn you, Philip – and damn the blasted car! If it hadn't been for that, this would never have happened. And if you hadn't been so ridiculously early...'

Severely put out, Philip of the perfect looks and elegant manner paced the room with less than his usual composure. 'I'm beginning to wish I hadn't offered to take you down to Sussex,' he declared huffily.

'Me too. But as you did, perhaps we'd better get going.'

Without another word he picked up the lightest bag and set off down the stairs, keys jangling irritably between his fingers. Left behind to lock up, Zoe hoisted the paraphernalia of bag, camera and sketch-book, in that moment regretting everything to do with Philip Dent. Sliding into the front seat of his open-topped Saab, she wished she had taken the train to Brighton, and had her mother collect her from there.

But two days ago, when they ran into each other, he had seemed pleased to see her, keen to treat her as a friend and not an ex-lover. When he mentioned Clare – met only once since that unfortunate evening with Stephen – Zoe was consumed by curiosity. She wanted to know what was happening, and Philip seemed to need to talk. He had mentioned a drink at the weekend, and she had mentioned Sussex, and here they were...

That Stephen should have chosen that moment to telephone! Half an hour earlier or later, and he would have been none the wiser, and because there was nothing for him to worry about, she would have had nothing to explain. It really was too bad.

Fretting and fuming, she answered Philip in monosyllables, but it dawned on her at last that there was an edge of malice to his probing, and now that he had recovered himself, a certain smug satisfaction at her discomfiture. She was too upset to hide her feelings; wanting to hurt him, too, she answered with brutal frankness.

'Yes, Philip – Stephen is important to me. He's the most vital man I've ever met. Being with him is like being alive to your fingertips – and yes, I'd dearly love to spend the rest of my life cooking his meals and darning his socks. Are you satisfied?'

'So much for feminism,' he replied contemptuously. 'I thought you wanted to be a free woman, devoted to your art.'

'I've changed.'

'All the nice girls love a sailor, eh?'

'Oh, don't be fatuous!'

'But he doesn't trust you, does he? Not that I blame him – after all, you threw me over for him, and now he thinks – '

'I did not throw you over for him! Clare's a liar if she said that – I hadn't even met him when I said goodbye to you!'

'But if he trusted you,' Philip went on, regardless, 'my being in your flat this morning wouldn't have meant a thing.'

That hurt, because it was uncomfortably close to the truth; hurt more, because such lack of trust was unjustified. She could have wept with fury, but would not give Philip the satisfaction.

'Do you have to be so hateful, Philip? So gloating? You've got your revenge on a plate – I hope it tastes good.'

He pressed his foot down on the accelerator, and after that, neither of them spoke. In the glorious weather of early June, trees in full leaf zipped past overhead; Zoe had glimpses of vivid colour in gardens and forecourts, but they were travelling too fast for appreciation. Only as they slowed behind the massive, tubular bulk of a road tanker did she find her self-obsessed thoughts suspended. With an anxious glance at the speedometer, she realized the tanker was doing something like fifty miles an hour in two-way traffic along roads which were far from straight.

Philip was clearly anxious to overtake. Zoe held her breath. The chemical symbols for petroleum spirit loomed large. Afraid to look at the road ahead, she glanced sideways, seeing massive double wheels too close for comfort and an unfamiliar logo, Q8, emblazoned on the tank above. Q-eight, Q-eight, Q-eight, drummed menacingly through her head until they were safely past. In relief she involuntarily murmured it aloud, and instantly the hidden meaning became clear. Not Q-eight petrol, but petrol from *Kuwait*!

'Kuwait,' she repeated, stunned by the connection with Stephen. It was oil from Kuwait that he would be transporting out of the Gulf, and for which he would be risking his ship and his life. Guilt washed over her. Hung up on her own frustrations after that telephone call, Zoe had all but forgotten the reason for it. All but forgotten Stephen and the knife-edge of his situation.

'Yes,' Philip said, obviously glad of a neutral topic with which to break the silence, 'it's a new company. Prices seem reasonable, though.'

'Reasonable?' she repeated, a shrill edge to her voice. She thought of the twenty-six lives aboard Stephen's ship, the hundreds, possibly thousands more who were engaged, at this very moment, in the same trade. 'I suppose anything's *reasonable*, if you don't count the human cost...'

Sixteen

Zoe borrowed her mother's sports car to meet her appointment near Worthing, and despite the persistent anxiety of her thoughts, had to admit that it was fun to be driving the old Triumph Spitfire, its engine and gleaming red bodywork kept in excellent repair, and at enormous expense, by Marian's 'little man' in the village. It typified her mother. She loved anything with a smart label, preferably antique or vintage, and in prime condition.

That element of perfectionism extended to her personal life. With two failed marriages behind her and a number of relationships which had, at some stage, been 'meaningful', Marian seemed to have resigned herself to the fact that she was better off as a single woman. This was something of a relief to Zoe, who over the years had lost track of the different partners and the innumerable houses to which she had been invited during breaks from school and college.

As women, Zoe and her mother were temperamentally opposed. Having recognized and accepted that, it was easier now to set it aside, to concentrate on the things they had in common. They shared an interest in the history of art and furniture, but where they diverged was in this matter of genealogy. Marian found it hard to be rational about her own past and had a tendency to lay most of her considerable problems at Letitia's feet. She was bitter too, about her relationship with Zoe, maintaining that Tisha had managed to alienate Marian's only child. There was no point, Zoe had discovered, in repeating that one swallow did not make a summer, or, in this case, that one summer did not make an alienated child, because Marian pegged all her guilt on that.

Nevertheless, she was intrigued by Tisha's past, wanting to know, if not to discuss, the reasons for the old lady's secrecy. But every time the subject came up, Zoe had to steel herself for the usual epithets of *cruel, paranoid, mean, selfish,* when applied to Letitia Mary Duncannon Elliott. And every time, Zoe had to remind herself that her mother's story was both sad and unfortunate for all concerned.

So, it had been something of a surprise to receive a call from her mother, last week, to say that if she was interested, Tisha's old home was again up for sale.

'I was just glancing through the property pages, and I happened to see it. Gave me quite a shock, darling, but there we are. I rang the agents, by the way,' she had added distastefully, as though it went against principle, 'and they informed me that it's been for sale for some time. It's empty, too.'

If it had given Marian a nasty turn, the news provoked in Zoe a queer leap of the heart, bringing back memories of childhood, of that awful, uncertain time of her parents' separation, and the summer spent with an eccentric old lady she hardly knew.

She recalled her father's protests, but Marian had had her way; and while the two adults sorted out their tangled emotional affairs, Zoe had been sent to that strange, ugly, Victorian house with its overgrown garden and empty rooms. It might have been the stuff of nightmares, but Zoe's disposition had always inclined towards the adventurous, rather than the timid. And as it transpired, in comparison to the months which preceded it, and the misery of boarding school which followed, that summer had been heavenly.

Unable to resist a desire to see the old place again, Zoe had telephoned the estate agent and, trying to sound like a serious buyer, made an appointment to view. She hated lying, but knew that no self-respecting agency could afford to indulge a matter of idle curiosity. With her age against her, Zoe hoped the vintage sports car would give credence to her tale that she was looking at property on her father's behalf, with a view to investment. It was so typically her father, she felt the tale was one she could carry off.

But she need not have worried. The young man who waited with the keys was singularly uninterested in who or why; so many had been and gone, it seemed that this was no more than another waste of a glorious Saturday afternoon. He did not even offer to show her round, but simply sat on the steps of the south-facing terrace with sleeves rolled up and collar open, taking in the sun.

'If I really wanted to buy this place,' Zoe remarked with amusement, 'I think I might report you for indolence.'

He glanced up, sharply, uncertain as to her meaning, and for a moment looked faintly alarmed; then Zoe smiled, and he grinned back, relieved. 'You mean you've no intention of buying? Well, I don't blame you – it's a heap. And it'll take a fortune to repair. But we live in hope...'

He was lazy and unprofessional, and Zoe could have told him that he was in the wrong business; but at least he was honest. She smiled again. 'It might surprise you to know that it was not markedly different when I last stayed here, sixteen years ago. My great-grandmother had the house then, but she died the following winter, and I haven't been back since. It passed to my mother – I seem to recall she sold the place pretty quickly, but I don't know who bought it. Do you?'

'Fifteen years ago?' He pursed his lips. 'Could be the people who are selling now. Same family, I mean. An old chap lived here – a widower. After his wife died, seems he lost interest, let the place go. His family live abroad. One son's in South America – he's the one we're dealing with – and the other's on an Antarctic expedition.'

Zoe laughed. 'So nobody's breathing down your neck?'

Beneath that attractive tan, he had the grace to flush. 'Well, no, I mean...'

'Never mind,' she said easily, 'I'm here under false pretences anyway. I tell you what – you just sit here and enjoy the sun, and let me have a browse.'

Inside, so little had changed. Different wallpaper, perhaps, but fifteen years ago many of the rooms had been as empty as they were now, so nothing seemed strange. Although Zoe had said that the house passed to Marian after Tisha's death, that was not strictly true. The house had never belonged to her. The circumstances of her residence here were complicated by untimely deaths in two wars.

Tisha's in-laws, the Fearnleys, had owned the house and willed it to their grand-daughter, Edwina. After their deaths, a firm of solicitors and a distant Fearnley cousin had acted as trustees. Meanwhile, Edwina had grown up and married young, a naval lieutenant. Their child, Marian, had been born in 1940, just two years before Edwina and her dashing young husband were killed during one of the many raids on Plymouth. At the time, their little daughter was safe at home in Hampshire with her nanny. Nanny had bestowed her charge on the closest relative – grandmother Letitia – and Tisha had been forced to don the mantle of motherhood for the second time.

There had been money from the naval officer's side of the family, but it had all been tied up for Marian; as was that rambling great house in Sussex. For years Tisha had been selling *objets d'art* to keep herself in little luxuries. With her daughter's marriage, Tisha had closed up the house and taken a small flat in Pimlico, her old stamping ground. It had been such fun, she said, until Edwina's death, but London was no place for babies and nannies, so it was back to dreary Sussex and this insufferable old house.

Zoe could hear her saying it, hear Tisha's voice as plainly as though she had been standing there, gazing bitterly from the window. No, not bitterly – resignedly. She might have been bitter once, but Tisha had outlived strong emotion, it seemed, and survived on a diet of cynicism. She had been allowed something from the child's inheritance, but it had never been enough. When old man Fearnley's collection of *objets d'art* ran out, she had started selling larger pieces: paintings first, then furniture. By the time Zoe arrived here, there was little left, and Tisha was reduced to living in two or three rooms. Not that she cared. As long as she had enough to dress well, and to take a trip up to town once a week to meet a few cronies for tea at Fortnum's, she was happy.

She enjoyed playing Letitia Fearnley, *grande dame*, and did it on very little. Her immaculate outfits were always set off by one or two items of good jewellery and a mink stole; and she had enough hand-made shoes to survive any fluctuation in fashion. 'There's nothing new, darling,' she used to say, 'just the same old styles made over to look different. Keep a thing long enough, it comes back again.'

And keep things she did. The furniture might have gone, but clothes remained, hoarded in trunks and wardrobes, packed between tissue and moth-balls. Zoe had had a wonderful time with flapper dresses and feather boas, hobbling about in gilt and silver sandals, purple satin slippers, and velvet mantles fit for a queen. For a ten-year-old little girl, it had been paradise.

In the first-floor bedroom with its long windows and balcony outside, Zoe smiled, remembering. In those days this room had been stripped bare except for the wardrobes and a long pier-glass, and an ancient chaise-longue by the window. Excellent for dressing-up. And Tisha had sat in the sun with the French windows open, watching her great-grand-daughter through half-closed eyes, an almost feline satisfaction in her smile. She had never much liked her grand-daughter Marian, and seemed to derive pleasure in telling Zoe that she had not allowed her mother to rummage through those precious things when she was a girl. But as Zoe had not much liked her mother at that time, the pleasure was mutual. Only in retrospect did that seem shameful.

There had been added pleasure in the reminiscences the clothes provoked. Tisha might never have mentioned her early life in York, but she obviously enjoyed reliving the high points of her young womanhood, the parties, the people, the cafe society of the twenties and early thirties. And every outfit had a story; in one slinky black number by Schiaparelli she had danced with the Prince of Wales.

'He had a taste for slim, dark women, even then – and in those days, darling, I was very slim and very dark.' She had patted her short, chic, silver curls. 'And of course people always said I had such marvellous eyes.' She had peered closely at Zoe then. 'A shame, darling, that yours lack colour...' And then, back to the original tack: 'He should never have married that Simpson woman – she had hypnotic eyes, did you know that? She mesmerized him, like a stoat... Of course,' sighing, 'I couldn't keep up with their set – didn't have the money, more's the pity. And with poor little Edwina to think of, here, in this place, with those dreadful Fearnleys – I had to keep coming back, you see...'

And while Zoe gazed at her, agog in childish innocence at this talk of princes and house-parties and love-affairs, she had suddenly grown sad.

'Edwina was a dear little thing. Very affectionate, very trusting, just like her father. Poor Edwin.' Another deep sigh, and at Zoe's question, she said: 'He died, darling, in the First War – he was wounded, rather badly I believe, and then he died. We'd been married just over a year, and he never saw his baby daughter...' Gazing from the window into the sunny, overgrown garden, Tisha seemed lost in memory, and Zoe had been almost afraid to breathe; but then those thin shoulders shrugged, and with a smile she said: 'What is it they say? *Only the good die young...*'

There had been no need to ask about Edwina. Even then, Zoe had known that her mother's mother had been killed when Marian was too young to remember her. But she had been sad, and hugged Tisha, and her great-grandmother had wiped away a tear and said: 'Well, darling, the tragedy is that I was never cut out for motherhood...'

But a moment later her eye caught the sweep of brilliant red silk spilling from one of the trunks, and she had launched into a tale of some exiled Russian count met in Paris just after the war.

Zoe smiled at the memory. For all its bareness, the house seemed full of her; she had impressed her forceful, independent spirit upon every red Victorian brick, giving a damn for nothing and nobody, least of all the remnants of her family. Vain, selfish and egotistical, by the standards of everyday society, Letitia Mary Duncannon Elliott had not been an admirable woman, and yet she had fascinated Zoe; and beneath that carapace of cynicism, something in her had warmed to the child. Was it the recognition of kindred spirits, or a heavy measure of nonconformity passed down in the blood? Or was it simply a matter of lonely old age reaching out to a solitary and misunderstood child?

With a sudden flash of insight, Zoe realized that it was probably a combination of all three.

Certainly Zoe had enjoyed every minute of those few weeks, loved the air of 'camping out' within the house, the irregular meals and what her mother would have called 'unsuitable' food. One day when the grocer neglected to call, they had lived entirely on strawberries from the garden; another time, after a trip to Fortnum's, it had been quails eggs for breakfast and pâté de foie gras with toast for tea. And the trips to town, after lengthy preparations the day before, had been the most exciting occasions of her young life. The three old ladies and their gentleman friend had gossiped unashamedly before her, stuffing her full of cream cakes and giving her sips of wine to drink. Witty and world-weary, dry and brittle as autumn leaves, they were relics of a time between the wars; how she wished she had been older, or that they were still alive.

It had been a fabulous, fantasy time; the weather had been glorious that summer, the towered and turreted house sleeping in the sun like a fairy-tale castle, the garden an overgrown mass of peonies and roses and wild honeysuckle. In the orchard a Russian vine had spread like a canopy through the trees, strangling everything with its winding tendrils and pretty, lacy blossom. Despising gardeners and gardening, Tisha had said she preferred it like that.

A perfect place in a perfect summer, and for years it had been encapsulated in her mind as the idyll of childhood, with Tisha the benevolent white witch who made everything possible.

But the adult who looked at those great high rooms also saw rising damp in the kitchen quarters and dry rot in the attics; she shivered involuntarily, wondering what winter was like. The central heating looked prehistoric and the fireplaces were huge; Tisha would not have spent money on fuel. The winter following that idyllic summer had been harsh; Zoe recalled shivering every night in her boarding school dormitory, and did not wonder at Tisha's sudden death. The certificate recently unearthed gave hypothermia as the cause.

Suddenly, needing the direct heat of the sun, Zoe hurried downstairs and out onto the terrace. Summoning a smile, she handed the keys back to the indolent young man.

'You can lock up now, if you like. I've seen all I want to see inside. If you don't mind, I'll just have a wander through the garden.'

'I'll go, then.'

'Yes, you may as well.'

He hesitated, gave her a smile. 'I don't suppose – you wouldn't care for a drink down at the village pub?'

Zoe shook her head. 'No, thanks all the same. Another day, I might have said yes – but right now I don't think I'd be very good company.'

'Sure?' He met her steady gaze and sighed regretfully. 'Oh, well, never mind. Some other time, perhaps?'

'Yes, perhaps.'

She watched him lock and test the doors, saw him stroll back to his car and give Marian's little Spitfire a look of envious admiration. With a final wave, he swung his modern saloon round on the gravel drive, and disappeared between the shrubberies.

Like everything else, the gravel was overgrown with weeds. In the orchard the vine had gone, while at some stage the old trees had been pruned back to some kind of life, although it was impossible to tell whether they would ever bear fruit. Zoe suspected not. Since Tisha's day, the garden had obviously been cleared and tended, but more recent neglect had again allowed the vigorous growth of climbers and creepers to smother less hardy plants. There was a certain wild, ragged beauty about it, but the place had lost its magic. She paced a winding path through the shrubbery; as a child, this garden had seemed endless, the paths like tunnels which went on for miles.

Back at the terrace, Zoe sat down on the steps and glanced back at the house. Afraid that it too might seem suddenly diminished, she averted her eyes, wanting to preserve the memory as it had been. But the memory that was Tisha was crumbling in the light of recent knowledge; secrets had been revealed and personal traumas guessed at, clarifying motives which had been hidden for more than half a century.

That happy, smiling family group, photographed in the garden of a cottage in York, was no sham; but Edward's face and the presence of Robert Duncannon presupposed tensions which were about to erupt into tragedy. How the truth had come out, it was impossible to say; but that it had come out, and blasted them all in the shock, was certain. Letty Duncannon's correspondence bore that out. Tisha had stayed on at home for two more years, but Zoe gathered that it had been an uneasy truce, that her acceptance had been borne of necessity, as was so much else in her life. Never one to bemoan her situation, she had simply bided her time, like a half-wild cat awaiting its opportunities; and at the first opening of the door, she was gone.

The war provided her opportunity. With trained men off to the Front or needed for training others, women had been taken on at the barracks as clerks; from York she had transferred to the War

Office in London, and there, presumably, she had met Captain Edwin Fearnley, a regular soldier some years her senior. Had she loved him? Zoe wondered, gazing at the garden his parents had once so carefully tended. Perhaps she had, in her way, for she had spoken of him in affectionate terms. Perhaps he represented the security she had lost; the security destroyed by Robert Duncannon. And what, Zoe wondered, was her opinion of *him*?

As ever, the more questions were answered, the more others arose. It was a frustrating exercise, particularly when undertaken alone. Together, she and Stephen had tossed ideas around, reasoning, speculating, sifting the evidence and looking for logical conclusions to every question. And it was exciting, because their minds complemented each other, hers quick and instinctive, but not always leaping in the right direction, and his slower, more methodical, following the line of reason. Between them, they usually reached solid and satisfactory conclusions.

She missed him. Missed his company and his affectionate teasing; and most of all in that moment she missed the passion they had shared. Her body, as much as her lonely spirit, ached for him. If that lengthy and beautiful letter from Istanbul had perfectly expressed his yearning, then Zoe could have echoed it here, in this garden, at the fall of evening.

Across the lawn's soft grass, long shadows were creeping, indigo beneath the trees, dove-grey where they touched the rounded shape of a cherub in the dried-up lily-pond. The past was no longer perfect, and the present less so; she wanted Stephen, needed him now, not in three or four months' time. She wanted him to be here, seeing all this, sharing her past, helping to exorcise the devils of memory which held her in thrall.

It was hard to leave, because the last time she had done so it had been to discover that her own world was crumbling; like Tisha, she had had to face some very unpleasant truths. Her parents had parted and it seemed they no longer wanted her. James Clifford was in London and managed to see her only once before Marian was taking her to a huge, horrible place full of strangers. It was like a prison. That had been her first impression, nor had it changed, despite the beautiful grounds, the tennis courts and hockey-pitches, the neat village beyond the walls. After the freedom of this house and Tisha's own brand of magic, boarding school had represented endless years of punishment for some obscure crime she could never recall committing. And with Marian constantly moving house, the holidays were no remission. She saw little of her father, and Tisha was dead.

The drive back through summer twilight was not easy. Unfamiliar with these country lanes, Zoe had to force herself to concentrate on what she was doing, where she was going. When she finally arrived at her mother's cottage, Marian came out straight away, as though she had been waiting by the door.

'Thank heavens you're back – I was convinced you'd had an accident, or worse. Picturing you locked up in that awful house with a madman, or something!'

'Oh, Mummy, I'm sorry. I should have phoned, I didn't think – '

Anxiety turned to anger. 'Don't tell me you've been chatting up that estate agent in some pub, Zoe?'

'No – no, I haven't.' On the verge of tears, Zoe dissolved instead into weak laughter. 'But oddly enough, he did offer...'

Inside, with the lamps lit and a bottle of chilled wine on the low table between them, Zoe explained, as best she could, why she was so late; but the wine loosened her tongue, and for once she was not so inclined to spare her mother's feelings and keep things to herself. Ignoring Marian's deepening frown and her occasional exclamations, Zoe let the whole day come pouring forth.

She talked about the girl, Tisha Elliott, and her relationship to Edward and Louisa and Robert Duncannon. She talked about Letitia, the old lady her mother had known, and about the house and the summer Zoe had spent there as a child. And about herself, the years at boarding school, the feeling she had then, that her parents no longer wanted her. The wine loosened something else, so that by the time she came to the end of the tale, which rested where it had begun that day, with a telephone call from Stephen, Zoe could no longer control the accumulation of grief. Huge tears poured down her face, running along her jaw and soaking the front of the thin blouse she wore. As Marian handed her a box of tissues, Zoe apologized again.

Marian seemed more confounded than upset, as though she were trying to sort out that mix of tragedies old and new, as though she could not find words to say or even a place to begin. Eventually she patted her daughter's shoulder and swept the damp hair from her face; physical affection had never come easily to her, and it was almost as though she were afraid to embrace her grown-up child.

'I'd no idea you were so unhappy,' she said at last, wonderingly, and it seemed to Zoe that she spoke no less than the truth. 'You were always so self-contained – no tears, no tantrums, quite the perfect little girl in those days.'

While Zoe sobbed afresh, recalling the tears she had shed in private, the secret world she had inhabited, Marian said: 'I'd no idea I was such a poor mother. I liked school, you see, when I was a child. Everything was so ordered, so safe. There were rules and you obeyed them, and if you did well, people liked you. And I wanted to be liked, so I did well. But it wasn't like that at home. Home!' she repeated bitterly. 'That great, empty mausoleum – you've no idea how I hated it, how unhappy I was in the holidays. No friends and nothing to do, and Letitia off gallivanting most days up to town...

'I only sent you there in utter desperation that summer,' Marian confessed. 'I thought, well, the poor lamb will just have to put up with it for a few weeks – even that was better than the ghastliness of the separation. Rows, bickering, up to town to see solicitors – oh, it was awful. I had to spare you that.

'But you enjoyed being with Letitia, didn't you? I couldn't understand it. And you were so difficult after that, Zoe, I'm afraid I blamed it all on her. I was convinced she'd turned you against me. We never did get on.'

'I know,' Zoe said bitterly, 'that was obvious, even to a child.'

'She resented me. Resented my existence. I dragged her back to Sussex, and she hated it. She couldn't wait to get me off to school so she could resume her rounds of friends and men and parties. And in the meantime, she sold everything of any value in that house – things that should have belonged to me.'

Zoe had heard it all before; but now she was seeing it differently. Suddenly, she felt sorry for her mother. Tisha had managed to embitter her grandchild, and through Marian her selfish behaviour had somehow managed to colour Zoe's existence. There was a degree of blindness in both women, a limitation of spirit somewhere that made it difficult to judge the effect of their behaviour on others. Wondering whether that was, in part, everyone's problem, made Zoe anxious. She was aware of wanting children, Stephen's children, and yet it frightened her to think that she might behave in the same blind, selfish fashion.

It frightened her more to think she may never have the chance.

Nothing was resolved. Nor did her mother seem to understand about Stephen. His profession seemed so entirely unsuitable, she could not imagine what had attracted Zoe. Knowing that her mother would never understand the special links forged by their common inheritance placed a clamp on Zoe's need to talk about him. She said her farewells after lunch the next day, and took a train back to London.

Because much had been said about her father, she found him still very much on her mind. Marian's claim that James Clifford was more interested in money than people was simply not true, but Marian would never believe that. It was not money as such that interested him, rather the excitement of making it; and with his wide-ranging business interests, his time and attention were immersed. When Marian said that he could not have looked after a little girl, even one at boarding school, Zoe knew she was right. It did not, however, ease her sense of regret, for she liked her father and there was a level of affection between them that she had never shared with her mother.

When he was not abroad, they met for dinner fairly regularly, perhaps once or twice a month; and occasionally he would drop in to see her at the flat on his way home from the office. He always enquired about his ex-wife, but James Clifford rarely talked about the past. The present and the future were what interested him, not the whys and wherefores of a failed relationship, even one that had produced a daughter as dear to him as Zoe.

He knew about Stephen, and was sorry not to have met him; he was also rather intrigued by the blood relationship.

'Although I sincerely hope,' he had said with a laugh when

she explained the connection, 'that these Elliotts you speak of are nothing like their late and unlamented relative!'

Letitia had earned his grudging respect, if not his liking, for nerve and sheer tenacity in clinging to a way of life that she had made entirely her own. The facts Zoe had unearthed about her origins amused him.

'Well, she always claimed a connection with the Irish gentry,' he said, 'and it seems she was telling the truth. I have to confess I didn't quite believe her at the time.' But in the light of her illegitimacy, he said he was not surprised that the old lady had been so secretive about her family.

James Clifford was currently abroad again, but not even his sympathy could ease the problem of Stephen. Thoroughly miserable by the time she arrived home, Zoe sat and stared for a while at the ominously silent telephone, then went to invite her neighbour Polly down for a drink.

Their friendship was one that had grown over the years, born of the fact that they were the only single women in the building, and, as far as they were aware, the only two regularly at home during the day. But if it had begun in the realms of convenience, their relationship had become a true one, full of warmth and honesty. As a friend, Polly had proved to be more steadfast than others in more conservative professions. She was an actress whose rich, throaty voice was much in demand for radio plays and television voice-overs, but her vibrant personality masked a practical nature, and her concern was generally expressed in forthright terms.

Faced with the problem of Tisha and the past, she said quite bluntly that nothing could change it, so worrying was a waste of time. 'Look back if you must, Zoe, but only to check up on things. It strikes me that the template was a pretty poor one, and the best thing to do is break it.'

Which was virtually the conclusion Zoe had come to already, but it helped to hear it from someone else.

'And as far as your beautiful man's concerned,' she went on, 'why don't you just write and tell him the truth about Philip?'

'But I could be doing Philip a grave injustice. I mean, just because he wasn't a great lover, doesn't mean to say that he's gay.'

'Oh, come on, does it matter nowadays? All right, it obviously matters to him, and for his own sake, the quicker he gets himself sorted out, the better. As far as Stephen's concerned, I think you should be honest. I'm sure Stephen's mature enough to understand. Let's face it, he lives and works in an all-male environment – he must have seen it all before.'

'But how did Philip strike *you*?'

Polly threw up her hands in despair. 'For goodness' sake, why does everybody think, because I'm an actress, that I should be an expert on gay men? It doesn't say a lot for my reputation, does it?' She shook her head and laughed. 'Anyway, you've asked me that question before – and as I said, he simply struck me as being not your type. Too uptight, somehow. I know you thought he had hidden depths,' she reminded Zoe with a gurgling laugh, 'but to me he was just plain boring.'

Zoe chewed her lip. 'You're sure?'

'No, I'm *not* sure. How do I know what turns him on, or what his hang-ups are? You went out with him for three months, and even *you* don't know! But I'll tell you this,' she added firmly, pouring herself another glass of wine, 'that man is getting out of all proportion. He's not important to you – Stephen is. So why don't you write him a searingly passionate letter, telling him how much you love and adore him, and you can't wait for him to get back to warm your lonely bed. That should cheer him up no end.'

But that was what Polly would have done. In and out of love with amazing regularity and unflagging enthusiasm, Polly was passionate about most things. Zoe's feelings, however, were more tender, and, where Stephen was concerned, infinitely more vulnerable to pain. In her present mood of uncertainty, she was far from sure what it was that Stephen wanted to hear. It was all very well for Polly to maintain that he had telephoned simply because he cared, and that his sharp manner had been prompted by jealousy. It might be true, but he was set against commitment on either side, and in Zoe's book, a declaration of love was a serious matter.

In the end, having slept on the matter, she chose the lesser of two evils and wrote a letter explaining Philip Dent, from the circumstances of their first meeting to the moment of realizing it was all a waste of time. She would have liked to be frank and say, 'and furthermore, I don't think he really fancied me,' but it sounded as though she judged men on their performance, while that aspect was merely the final nail. In the end she settled for, 'There just wasn't any magic in Philip, and other than our mutual friends, we had little in common...'

She hoped Stephen would now understand that Philip was well and truly in the past, and not likely to be resurrected by chance meetings or the offer of a lift to Sussex.

Suppressing a desire to tell him how much she loved and needed him, Zoe gave vent instead to the awfulness of that moment on the road when they had overtaken the tanker. She did not hold back in describing her reactions to that.

Although she laboured over the first half of the letter, the rest, comprising a description of Saturday afternoon, almost wrote itself. Despite her efforts to contain it, emotion crept in as she wrote about Tisha's house and the memories stirred by her visit.

'It was probably the wrong time, in one sense. In another, maybe it was needed. But after what turned out to be a thoroughly miserable weekend, writing all this to you has acted like a purge. And having raked over the ashes of those years and really looked at them, I find they are less dreadful than they appeared to be.

'And I think I must say the same about Philip. I'm sorry I didn't tell you at the time – I wish I had, but I felt so badly about it. The silly thing is, Polly put it all in perspective for me when she said he was boring. He is, although I didn't realize it at the time. Looking back on that episode, even talking to him the other day about Clare and David, it strikes me I don't need that kind of thing in my life. And after the row we had in the car, he won't be offering again.

'My one regret, as I've said, concerns your phone call. It was so wonderful to hear your voice, I just wish we had been able to talk – really talk, I mean. But I was shocked by your news, and you were so obviously wondering about Philip...

'Anyway, you have the truth of it now – I just hope you can understand...'

Zoe paused and read her letter through. The more she wrote about Philip, the more she wanted to go over and over it, like a criminal obsessed by his crime. Which was silly, because as Polly said, it was giving him an importance he did not deserve. There was no need to say more. Hesitating over how to close, instead of her usual '*love Zoe*' which was affectionate but casual, she wrote, '*All my love to you...*'

For a moment, its straightforward honesty made her feel better; but then uncertainty over his reaction attacked again, and she stared at it helplessly. She could hardly cross it out, and she did not want to write the whole page again, so in the end she let it stand, bestowing a sentimental kiss before she sealed it into the envelope and took it to the post.

It was a bright morning, invigorating, with a sly breeze that made her shiver a little as she returned from that short walk. She had a sense of fragile hopefulness, as after a brief but debilitating illness; not a conviction that things would turn out well, but an awareness that the only way forward was with one step at a time. Stephen's wrong impression the other day still bothered her, and she hoped that when he read her letter he would understand that the last thing she wanted to do was to play fast and loose with either his emotions or her own. She hoped too that he could sense the love between the lines, because she knew, more certainly than anything else, that he needed love, whether he was aware of it or not. When he came home, they would have to begin again. It was as far as she could think, but it was enough. It had to be enough.

That letter, however, and the weekend's reflections on motherhood, brought something else to mind. In the act of analyzing Tisha on paper, it struck Zoe that in all Louisa's correspondence, she had so far come across nothing from her daughter.

In a large cardboard box resided all the as yet untouched bundles, now much depleted. In another were letters identified but still unread, and, filed in a series of smaller boxes, the ones already dealt with. Each envelope was numbered in pencil, each number corresponding to a series of notes Zoe was making in a large, stiff-backed notebook. It was a mammoth task and there were cross-references everywhere; but as she had so recently remarked in her letter to Stephen, it kept her occupied and interested, and left little time for anything else. Particularly a social life.

Not that she regretted it. Indeed, the task was becoming something of an obsession, since most of her spare time was spent reading and making notes, the rest of it searching for books in the reference library. Reminiscences, retrospectives and official histories of the war had, together with the letters and Stephen's transcript of the diary, formed her staple diet for weeks, to the extent that she thought of little else. It was perhaps fortunate that she had no important commissions to undertake, for all her recent doodles were of crosses entwined with poppies and barbed wire, which seemed, like recent odd and disturbing dreams, to be the result of that extensive and sometimes distressing research.

Now, eager to get back to Louisa's correspondence, Zoe was glad of a need to look for something else, something lighter which might provide a clue to Tisha's early life, form a bridge between the difficult girl referred to by Letty Duncannon, and the sophisticated woman she had become.

That Tisha had been a source of much anxiety to her mother, was evident in the replies Louisa received from her old friend in Dublin; although once the girl had left for London, Letty's advice had been sound if unsympathetic. '*You really must stop worrying about her now. Robert will keep a discreet eye upon her, and despite your present hard feelings towards him, he will not allow her to come to any harm.*'

In the next sentence, Zoe recalled with much satisfaction, had come the confirmation that she and Stephen had been seeking for so long: '*After all, Robert is her father.*'

Good old Letty, she thought with affection, having grown fond of Robert Duncannon's sister with her quirky opinions and eccentric interests; and that little tit-bit would be an unexpected present for Stephen when he received his letters in the Persian Gulf.

That striking photograph of Robert, taken in full uniform when he must have been in his early thirties, stood on her bookcase along with other copied pictures of the family. It caught Zoe's eye as she crossed the room. Almost a hundred years stood between that moment and this, and yet she could feel something of the power of the man. It was in his face, in the way he held himself; not the arrogance at first suspected, but confidence. He knew himself very well. It seemed to her that he was a man who would make few apologies.

Like Stephen.

That thought came unexpectedly, sending little shock waves through her awareness.

But after all, she reasoned, his blood ran in Stephen's veins and genetic inheritance was a strange thing, often skipping generations to reappear in unexpected quarters. Physically, they were not alike, except perhaps in height and build. Stephen favoured Liam in looks, apart from his hair, which was curly, and Liam had favoured his mother more than Robert. Zoe was already aware that she bore a strong resemblance to Tisha, but who did Tisha resemble? Studying the gathered photographs, it seemed to Zoe that her great-grandmother had Robert Duncannon's Irish colouring of dark hair and pale skin, while the shape of her face was Louisa's. Broad forehead, high cheekbones, round, determined chin. Only Tisha's mouth was different: small and cherubic – how misleading that was! – where Louisa's smile had been both wide and generous.

And what was it that Stephen had said? That she had Louisa's mouth. The memory pleased her, made her smile even as she touched her lips with a fingertip. Perhaps she was not so much like Tisha after all; perhaps she had more of Louisa in her than she had suspected.

Poor Louisa. For the first time, in her own uncertainty over Stephen, in that longing for him which could not be assuaged, Zoe felt something of Louisa Elliott's pain. Robert could never be hers, not in the way she needed him to be; so she had turned her back on him and married Edward, and as far as anyone could know, they had been happy together. But had she ever stopped loving Robert? In spite of everything, all the sadness and misfortune, all the terrible things that had happened over the years, could the ties be cut, irrevocably? Zoe thought not. However much Louisa might have wished otherwise, the children held those links, and not even death could dissolve them.

In leaving York for London, Tisha had, willingly or not, been placed in the care of her natural father, which meant that by 1916 he had had two daughters to keep an eye on, one the dedicated nurse, the other perhaps already showing signs of what she was to become. Zoe wondered how he dealt with them, and, in his apparently frequent absences from London, how he managed to supervise Tisha's life. Letty's confidence that her brother *'would not let her come to any harm'* gave rise to a wry smile. It was obvious to Zoe that Letty had not known her niece very well.

She had never been familiar with Tisha's handwriting, so her search through the box that day was for the unfamiliar, a difference of style that would declare itself. She knew Liam's hand at a glance, despite the variety of inks he had used, and Robin's too, while Letty Duncannon was characterized as much by the quality of envelopes and paper. In each beribboned package most of the outer envelopes had yellowed with age, and some were scuffed and faded which made identification difficult, but at last Zoe came to a bundle addressed in an ink that had paled to beige, in a hand that was not dissimilar to her own. Convinced by the London postmark that she had found what she was looking for, Zoe retired to the sofa, tucked up her legs and prepared herself for an interesting hour or so. Very carefully she untied dusty ribbon which held perhaps a dozen letters.

Unlike Zoe, Louisa Elliott had never, in haste, ripped open an envelope with her thumb. Each one had been slit with a paperknife, each letter carefully refolded into its original pattern, making every one look as though it had just arrived.

Opening the first letter, she glanced at the last page for the confirmation she expected. But this letter was not from Tisha. It was from Robert Duncannon's other daughter. Registering the fact of Georgina's signature, Zoe was first disappointed and then annoyed; she almost thrust the pages back unread. But in the act of refolding them, an address, engraved at the head of the first sheet, leapt out at her. It was her address. This house in Queen's Gate, London.

For a second she thought she had imagined it, that it was some kind of hallucination. She rubbed her eyes and stared at it; touched her finger to the lettering and felt its slight indentations. She looked again at the signature and then the heading. It sank in slowly. Georgina Duncannon was living here, at this address.

Feverishly, Zoe opened all the other letters, trying not to tear the pages in her trembling, fumbling haste. Not all were written from here; some were on cheap notepaper, from a hospital in south London.

Was she nursing there? She must have been, Zoe thought, noting the irregular dates. Living in, while this was her real home. Or was it? A vague recollection of something Letty had written sent her scurrying for the thick notebook with its listed references. What was it that Letty had said about her niece?

Yes, that she was sharing her father's apartment in Kensington. And in brackets beside that note, Zoe had added a query as to the address. Well, now she knew. But which apartment? What floor? A sudden thrill of instinct told her that it had to be here, this floor, these rooms, and a dozen strange dreams slipped into place like pieces in a jigsaw puzzle.

But there had to be a way of proving it, of finding out who had owned this house at that time. Halfway to the telephone to speak to her father, Zoe stepped over scattered pages which had fallen to the floor. Guiltily, she scooped them up, noting a date, *March 29th, 1916*, and in that neat script Tisha's name in the first paragraph.

Seventeen

Georgina's bedroom was not very big. It contained a three-quarter bed, a small wardrobe, a chest of drawers and a wash-stand, and those items almost filled it. Overlooking the mews at the back was a tall window draped with lace and a pair of gold brocade curtains, and on the floor, between one side of the bed and the wall, a warm Turkey rug. The room was small and overcrowded but, compared to her spartan quarters at the hospital, luxurious. The feather bed was soft, the eiderdown matched the curtains, and a triple mirror stood on the chest of drawers. It was a haven of comfort and privacy.

As always before making the effort to rise, she looked round, appreciating every item, the row of novels on a shelf, and photographs of the family within reach. As always, she blessed the day her father had insisted she make this place her home. At first, unsure whether she wanted to commit herself to such an arrangement, she had hesitated. But he had pointed out that his absences were frequent and often protracted, and Georgina had remembered the blessedness of escape from hospital life, even when she was in York. Then, the cottage her been her haven; now the refuge was her father's apartment.

Originally, before the army purchased it, the building had been one house, tall and deep; a nightmare, she often thought, for the servants constantly up and down ten flights of stairs from cellars to attics. This floor comprised two large rooms, a lobby, and two other rooms which might have been dressing rooms, or even part of the nursery quarters. One room had been converted into a sort of butler's pantry, with sink and gas oven and cupboards; it could hardly be called a kitchen, although it served as such. And the other, which for a few years had been her father's dressing room, was now her bedroom. Robert's servant shared quarters two floors above, and there was a communal bathroom on the floor below, for the use of the four staff officers who lived there. One had a wife who stayed occasionally; the others were single men whom she passed occasionally on the stairs.

There was no sense of community, but she had enough of that at the hospital. Here was privacy, a peace and quiet which reminded her of Dublin before the war, of home and luxury and all the things she had then despised and since come to long for with all the passion of nostalgia. Here were no bells, no demands, no broken bodies to care for, no shattered minds to soothe, no sudden deaths to sweep away before the next batch of wounded arrived. Here was peace where she could write letters, read books, or simply sleep the sleep of exhaustion, gathering strength and wits in a brief respite from work.

It was pleasant, too, to see something of her father. She found him much changed from the man who had once opposed nursing as a career. If there was often anxiety in his expression when he looked at her, there was a measure of pride, too. He knew what she did, and while he might regret the hours she worked, he saw its necessity. He also seemed to appreciate how valuable had been her training at the Retreat.

Army doctors were not renowned for their embrace of new ideas, but just occasionally one of the more enlightened would, in a roundabout way, seek her opinion; and when it was not sought Georgina did what she could within the limited sphere of her time and influence. More and more did it seem to her that one day, when this war was over and there was time to understand, special hospitals would have to be set up, or units within hospitals, simply to treat the injured minds.

Lacking in moral fibre was no way to describe a volunteer whose spirit had been battered beyond endurance; and while shell-shock was kinder, she was beginning to realize that it was more than just the sound of shells firing and exploding that destroyed a man. It was the sight and sound and smell of death, sudden and ever-present, sweeping down with a scream to gather friend and foe alike.

What astonished her, seeing the results of what was going on across the Channel, was the resilience of the human spirit. Not all succumbed to fear; most managed to thrust the horror aside, while some could still laugh and joke, still talk of excitement and comradeship and patriotism. They were the ones she found hardest to understand. Georgina was no longer patriotic. She did what she did because it had to be done and she was trained to do it; but from that well of compassion which refused to dry up, she thought of all the others in German hospitals, tended by German nurses who were as tired and stretched and heartsick as herself. The war for her had been reduced to exhaustion, to an aching back and sore, calloused feet, legs that continued to walk, stand, bend, far beyond what she considered to be their ability to do so. And her hands, constantly in and out of hot water, were like those of a maid-of-all-work, chapped and chilblained, their touch, she knew, like sandpaper on tender skin.

All winter Louisa had been sending pots of cocoa butter mixed with scented, soothing herbs; but while that preparation helped, it had no chance to cure. Robert joked about those little pots, made occasional acerbic comments when Georgina read Louisa's letters aloud, although he wanted to know what she said, what she had been doing, what life was like in York. And while his guilt was less acute these days, he always said, when Georgina was writing back, that she must enclose his love and sincere regards.

At Christmas, Robert had managed to use his influence with certain people at the War Office to obtain a week's leave for Robin. A lot of string-pulling, but with the news so bad from Gallipoli, and Liam completely outside Robert's sphere, he had been determined to do something for Louisa, anything to lighten the load of their collective anguish. They had managed to see Robin on his return to the Front, just an hour between trains in a dismal tea-shop near the station, but it had been worth the effort involved. He was cheerful, but he was older, much less buoyant. Georgina remembered touching him, holding his hand, thinking of Liam.

Afterwards, despite Robert's instructions to the contrary, Georgina wrote to Louisa, telling her that she had him to thank for Robin's leave; and although it was not directly acknowledged, since then Louisa had enquired after him in most of her letters. It warmed Georgina to think that her father was in some respect forgiven for that spilling of the truth.

But if Robin and Liam had both survived almost two years of war, her cousins from White Leigh – one older than Georgina, one younger – had both been killed at Loos. She had seen neither of them since her mother's funeral and it was hard to comprehend that she would never see them again. It seemed they would be preserved for ever in her memory as two young, high-spirited boys with whom she had played and danced and gone hunting. Like so much else, they were part of the past; only if she went back to White Leigh would she feel their absence and be able to grieve for them.

Glad of the impossibility, Georgina grieved now for her father, who had just returned from there. His visit, coinciding with official business, had distressed him. William, he said, had lost interest in everything; the estate was neglected, the tenants close to mutiny, the house no better than a mausoleum. His brother seemed set on drinking himself to death, while Anne, William's wife, had grown patriotic to the point of mania, working for the Red Cross, organizing sewing circles and knitting bees, and urging every man and boy within a twenty-mile radius to join arms against the evil Hun.

'She should be careful,' Robert had confided last night over a large measure of brandy. 'In spite of the war, public feeling in the south is not entirely pro-British...'

It was an informed comment, one that sent a chill through her as she stared at a photograph of her cousins on horseback, taken in front of the steps at White Leigh. There was another of Robert as a young man, standing on those steps which led to the main entrance, with Georgina aged three in his arms. She was hugging herself close, her round cheek pressed to his, and he was smiling. One of the rare times that he had been at home...

That picture always aroused a plethora of memories, not all of them good: her mother, like a mad ghost at White Leigh, then the move to Dublin with Aunt Letty, and the happy years when Louisa lived with them. All too brief. And with Louisa's departure her father had abandoned them all for a war in the Sudan; and it seemed no time at all between that war and the next in South Africa. After that he had gone with his regiment to India, leaving his daughter to Dublin and Aunt Letty, and summers spent at

White Leigh.

She had loved him, as one worships heroes, but she had never really known him; and until recently, what she had known about him – what had been revealed in the harsh glare of impatient youth – had been difficult to like or understand.

Only in this last year had she come to know him better. They conversed now as adults, discussing her work and his, affording each other a respect born of new understanding. It seemed he was glad to have her there, and she wondered whether he was lonely. If he had women friends Georgina never saw them, and with his life torn between London and Dublin, she thought he was probably too busy, never in one place long enough to form new relationships. It seemed, too, as though what had happened in York that summer of 1913, had killed something in him, a spark of wilful carelessness perhaps; or rekindled a different flame, one that burned deeper than even he suspected.

He never spoke of it, so she could not be sure, and it was not a subject Georgina cared to probe. Instead they talked of Dublin and Letty, and the work, which, since 1910 and his return from India on half-pay, had been largely concerned with Ireland. With his knowledge and extensive family connections, the government had employed him in an advisory capacity pending the settlement of the vexatious Home Rule question. But the militant resistance of Ulster Loyalists had managed to drag out negotiations interminably, and with the government's reluctance to come into conflict with the industrial north, public opinion, which had been favourable, waned yet again. Robert was sickened by a situation which seemed destined never to be resolved, and after four years' hard work, with all his arguments in favour of Home Rule set aside, had wanted no more of it.

On the outbreak of war in August 1914, he had volunteered immediately for active service, but the War Office continued to refuse him, even as an administrator of Kitchener's new battalions. With what he saw as stubborn pig-headedness, his new masters insisted on sending him back to Ireland, using the connections he had built up to provide them with essential information on what was going on within Sinn Féin and the Irish Republican Brotherhood.

Ostensibly, he was still employed on the Home Rule question, fostering the implicit belief that it would be granted with the cessation of hostilities. But the question had been debated during the whole of Robert's lifetime; he had seen it come to Parliament twice and fail, and now no longer had faith in a third time.

Georgina knew her father loathed the duality of his role, the necessity for secrecy; knew too that until recently he had felt most bitterly that his abilities and vast experience in the military field were being wasted. Only in the last few months had he begun to see the necessity for himself. England's other island might have set aside her antipathy during 1914's surge of patriotic fervour, and Irish mothers might still be sending their sons to die upon England's behalf; but as Robert had been at pains to explain, other, smaller, more determined forces were now at work.

Tension was in the air, and he was suddenly very much afraid that what could not be wrested from England politically, would be attempted by force of arms. And that was something Robert could not condone. He held the King's commission still, and as a Dragoon officer in Ireland before the Boer War, his role had always been to preserve law and order. Even now, to oppose the rule of the gun, Georgina knew he would shelve his own ideals for ever.

Certain elements, he had remarked the night before, saw death and destruction as the only path to political freedom; and what alarmed him now was the potential reaction.

'The government won't stand for it,' he declared. 'Not with a war going on. That's what these hot-heads don't seem to grasp. They think they might just conceivably wrest power while our backs are turned – they don't believe me when I tell them what will happen.'

'And what will happen?'

'Oh, my dear girl! Any such action will be regarded as treason – and it will be stamped on, quickly and effectively, no matter how many troops it takes to do it. The Fenians can't win – I've told them that in Dublin and in Waterford, and I've told them to pass the message on. But they don't believe me. And the stupid thing is, they keep denying it! But I know something's up – I can feel it in Dublin, brewing like a summer storm. I've told Letty to get down to White Leigh and stay there. Of course, she doesn't want to go...'

'You could be wrong,' Georgina had ventured.

'No. Although I wish I could say I might be...'

Tired though he was by his journey from Dublin, her father had not wanted to go to bed. Knowing that mood, Georgina would have liked to sit up with him, but with exhaustion dragging at her eyes and limbs, she had been forced to leave him to solitude and his bottle of brandy. Sighing now as she washed and dressed, she wondered how he was feeling, what reports he was composing, and how they would be acted upon.

Lost for a moment in a gloom of anxiety, the telephone's ringing startled her. She guessed it would be her father before she picked it up; apart from Tisha he was the only one who used it. The hospital had no idea that she could be reached by such instantaneous means, and she was determined never to reveal it.

He sounded weary and his message was brief. Knowing he was back, Tisha had called in to see him, wanting to come to tea. She wondered also whether she could bring someone with her?

'Who?' Georgina demanded, knowing she sounded ungracious and unable to control it.

'Oh, some young fellow from my department – Fearnley. You know, the one who will keep pestering for active service. He's invited her out a couple of times, and now she wants to return the favour.'

'Impress him, you mean.'

'Well, perhaps so. But he knows me well enough, he's not likely to be impressed. Do your best, Georgie, will you? Make some of those delightful scones of yours, and see if we can't be jolly for an hour or so.'

'You don't sound very jolly.'

'Nor do I feel it. Never mind – I'll tell you about it later.'

Replacing the earpiece, Georgina swore, softly and eloquently. Nursing soldiers had extended her education in many directions, not least those of language. No doubt her father meant well by Tisha, but Georgina resented her half-sister's intrusion. Since her arrival in London at the end of January, life had not been the same. The thought of having to relinquish the novel she was enjoying, bind up her hair and put on a pleasant company face, was not one Georgina relished; and the idea of having to listen to an enthusiastic rendition of what a wonderful time Tisha was having in London, was daunting.

Checking the contents of the little store-cupboard, she was thankful that enough was there to make a passable wartime feast. Pathetic by peacetime standards, but everyone was experiencing the same difficulties, so whatever was offered was praised. The scones were to Louisa's recipe, which was why her father loved them, and even the blackberry and apple jelly had been sent from York the previous autumn and hoarded for special occasions. It was so difficult to buy anything good, and Louisa always remembered them.

Having prepared everything to her satisfaction, Georgina went to change her clothes, trying to find something smart, anything that might stand up to whatever modish creation Tisha would be wearing; but all Georgina's clothes were practical and well-worn. Eventually she settled on a grey skirt and pink silk blouse, and a string of pearls her father had bought for her twenty-first birthday. Not very exciting, but it was the best she could do.

They arrived just after five, cold after their journey by taxi-cab from Westminster. Robert's servant had made up the fire and the room was welcoming in its dark, glowing colours. Outside, beneath a wild grey sky, it was more like winter than spring, with the window panes rattling and plane trees tossing in a blustery gale. Georgina drew one set of velvet curtains against a sneaky draught and sat down in her chair beside the fire, leaving Robert's servant to serve the tea she had prepared.

Fortunately young Captain Fearnley knew Robert well enough not to be overawed. Had he known that the girl he escorted was Colonel Duncannon's natural daughter, rather than the niece she purported to be, Georgina thought he might have been considerably nonplussed. But Edwin Fearnley did not know. Along with everyone else in their respective departments, he had remarked upon a shared family resemblance. But Robert's relationship with Tisha had always been that of a rather distant relative, and her present attitude towards him – which Georgina always thought a shade too coquettish – did not appear to be amiss. Robert treated her now with the kind of fond indulgence which might be expected of a doting uncle, and only occasionally did Georgina detect a certain irony in the girl's response.

At such times she was possessed of a very unchristian suspicion that her half-sister was using their father's affection and generosity to the upmost. She played up to him, just as she was playing up to both men now, exercising her pretty, kitten-like charm. But the kitten was growing up, she had claws with which to defend herself, and she could snarl and sulk with the rest. Robert had never seen that side of her, but Georgina had, and would never forget the wounds she had inflicted on others. For the moment, however, she was determined to be pretty and amusing, charming both men with her talent for mimicry, one minute a blustery old colonel from the War Office, the next a mouse-like secretary.

And Robert, a colonel himself, though far from blustery, lapped it up, while young Edwin Fearnley was almost helpless with laughter.

'You're a very naughty young lady,' Robert said with mock severity, while Tisha pretended contrition, called him Uncle, and passed him another of Georgina's scones.

Taking note of her sister's stylish outfit and pretty shoes, Georgina experienced a twinge of envy that she knew was as silly as it was unpleasant. But it seemed that their father could refuse her nothing, that had she asked for the moon, he would have endeavoured, somehow, to obtain it for her. He said, shamefacedly, that it was because his other daughter asked for nothing, that she refused him the chance to spoil her with pretty clothes and entertainments, and always had. There was, Georgina supposed, a certain amount of truth in that, but it did not cure the resentment. She felt so plain and dull beside Tisha, could not make witty conversation and make people laugh. Even her funniest stories seemed out of place, because they related to the hospital, and brought the seriousness of war into the conversation, changing its tone completely.

She laughed politely at Tisha's lively chatter, made the right comments, asked the right questions, and all the time wondered what was going on behind those bright but rather calculating eyes. Edwin Fearnley, clearly besotted, spared barely a glance for Georgina. From observation and certain casually-phrased questions, she did manage to elicit a few details, however. He was older than Tisha by some ten years, a regular commissioned officer who had been attached to the Staff College before the war in a minor, administrative capacity. He claimed, jokingly, that every time he had applied for active service since then, they had promoted him and sent him elsewhere; so he was forced to the conclusion that his superiors thought he was not much good at anything, and only wanted him out of the way.

'If they'd thought that,' Robert chipped in, 'you'd have been in France with the first wave – the second, anyway!'

Edwin grimaced at that, and with a laugh said he was thinking of applying again for active service; that way, he would perhaps get his majority and a nice increase in pay.

'Don't be too hasty,' Robert warned. 'They might accept your offer, and I would lose an excellent brain from my department!'

Wondering what it was he did, Georgina knew better than to ask; but he certainly had an intelligent face, and eyes which, when they were not looking at Tisha, were alive with shrewdness and good humour. He was not very tall nor particularly good-looking, but a lively personality made him attractive. It came out in the course of conversation that his people lived in Sussex, his father having retired some years ago from lucrative business in the Midlands. It transpired, too, that he was an only son. Georgina began to see what it was about this man that made him so attractive to Tisha. For her, looks and personality would be important, but never quite enough.

Warming to him, Georgina felt a small stab of pity. He would probably make Tisha an excellent husband; but she was too young to appreciate good qualities in any man. She was a manipulator, out for her own ends. It was possible she would ruin him.

It was also possible, Georgina told herself, that she was making too much of this visit. Tisha was busily enjoying a freedom she had longed for; Edwin Fearnley might be no more than a pleasant interlude. If he proposed marriage, she would no doubt drop him and move on to someone else.

Before they left, he was already talking of a run down to Sussex in the near future, so that Tisha could meet his parents and see something of the beautiful coast and countryside. Pleased by that,

Robert even went so far as to pat young Fearnley on the back and address him as my boy. Georgina could have kicked her father.

Her antagonism, however, was put to flight minutes later by much stronger emotions, ones more difficult to hide.

'Oh, by the way,' he said gently to Tisha as she stood to leave, 'I heard something today about the Australians. They've left Egypt. Liam's on his way to France.'

Georgina went cold. Her blood pressure fell so rapidly she thought she might faint. As she clung to the mantelpiece, Tisha gave a tight little smile and said something to the effect that Liam would be pleased about that, he had never cared for Egypt.

Then, as a particularly violent gust shook the windows behind them, she indulged in a dramatic shiver. 'But he won't like the weather much, will he?'

How Georgina controlled a violent response, she could never afterwards imagine. But as she turned away, her father said with soft reproof: 'I think he may find something more than the weather to worry about.'

'Yes, I imagine so,' Tisha agreed without interest. 'Well, Edwin, we really must go, else we'll miss that concert at the Palladium – everyone says it's very good...'

Robert saw them out, and with a quick glance back at Georgina, said he would walk downstairs, and see them to the front door. Clearly startled by her expression, for a second he hesitated; then his eyes dropped away and he pulled the lobby door shut behind him.

Georgina sank into her chair, as grieved by that news as she might have been by his death. France for her was no longer a foreign country, it was in her heart and on the hospital wards; it had become a place where men went to die. Only then did Georgina realize how much she had depended on Liam being kept in Egypt indefinitely. Miserable for him perhaps, but so much safer there! By some unexplained miracle he had come through the hell of Gallipoli and survived; why must he come to France?

Her father's servant came in to mend the fire and clear away the tea things; with an effort she composed herself and picked up a book, pretending to read. When Robert returned she was almost her usual self.

He poured drinks for them both, handed her a sherry and lowered himself into the chair facing hers. Under his scrutiny she felt exposed.

'I'm sorry,' he said at last. 'That was the news I've been sitting on all day. I thought I must tell Tisha. I didn't mean to shock you.'

'He's my brother, too.'

'I know. Sometimes I almost forget.'

'I don't,' she declared, looking straight into her father's eyes. 'I never have.'

'Good. I'm glad to hear it.'

Aware that this was dangerous ground, she answered him with a certain amount of challenge. 'But I do care about him – very deeply. Tisha doesn't. Robin perhaps – but not Liam.'

Robert sighed and looked away. 'Jealousy. Louisa made too much of him. Liam was her firstborn.' After a long moment, he said: 'She never wanted Tisha.'

His honesty shocked her a little. 'Why not?'

'Tisha was the end of our relationship,' he answered painfully, 'the result of conflict, not love. I've always blamed myself for that...

'Oh, I know you think I don't see how she really is, that I indulge her because she's pretty and amusing and knows how to flatter a man. You think I'm an old fool, Georgie,' he went on, pouring himself another drink. 'But I'm not in my dotage yet – and I've known enough women of that ilk to be able to spot another one. But she's young, and she's had a difficult time of it in recent years. I feel sorry for her – and I'm fond of her. She may change.'

For some minutes, digesting those unexpected revelations, Georgina said nothing. She wondered at the nature of the conflict, but dared not ask. Instead she questioned him obliquely.

'Are you sure it's pity you feel? Or is it guilt?'

The question angered him. 'She's my daughter, for heaven's sake – just as you are. Yes, I'm sorry for what I see in her – and yes, I do feel guilty. I can't help it.'

'But she knows that, Daddy – and because of it, she's using you!'

He faced her squarely. 'I know.'

'And you'll let her carry on?'

'Yes. For as long as it's necessary.'

'Why?'

'Because I don't think Louisa ever understood her. I do, in a peculiar sort of way. She needs fussing and spoiling for a while – and then, perhaps, a steady, level-headed man to love her. She could do a lot worse than young Fearnley – and if he stays put and keeps his mouth shut, he could see this war through. Which is more than can be said for most of the others out there.'

Wincing, thinking of Liam – and Robin, she must not forget Robin – Georgina shook her head. 'Oh, Daddy – I think you're wrong. She'll break Edwin Fearnley's heart – yours too if you're not careful.'

He smiled and tapped his chest. 'This old heart of mine's tougher than you think – but thank you for thinking of it.'

They dined together at home, then spent a quiet evening, Robert studying papers at his desk, Georgina writing letters and thinking. Although she had long ago ceased in her attempts to communicate with Liam, she always mentioned him in her letters to Louisa. Detached, careful phrases, but they ensured a good response. And knowing that Tisha rarely sent anything more comprehensive than a postcard, Georgina included her father's news.

'*No doubt you will soon be hearing from Liam. Indeed you may have done so already, from Egypt. The post is so peculiar these days. I've already written to Robin – you never know, they may meet up.*'

It was a feeble attempt to be cheerful, a single straw of hope in what she saw as a sea of despair. Addressing the envelopes, she laid them on her father's desk, ready for posting.

'Try not to worry,' he said softly, squeezing her hand. As she turned away he rose to stand beside her. 'Tisha's a born survivor, you know – and so, it seems, are your brothers. Perhaps it's something they inherited from me!' He smiled; then suddenly, impulsively, hugged her close.

'Oh, darling girl,' he whispered against her hair, 'you're the one I worry about. Do take care of yourself – I couldn't bear to lose you.'

Tears welled for a moment and she clung to the unfamiliarity of her father's arms. He felt strong and safe and she wished she could have been a child again, just to have him go on holding her.

Eventually he let her go. Tucking back a stray lock of long blonde hair, he said: 'You'll be gone in the morning, I expect. If you have a free afternoon at any time, telephone the office. I'll send a car and we'll go out.'

She nodded, clearing her throat. 'When do you go back to Ireland?'

'I don't know. I dare say I could be there and back several times before they allow you another couple of days off. However, I'll keep you informed.'

Reaching up, Georgina kissed his cheek. 'Thank you, Daddy.' Unable to risk another word, she hurried off to bed.

Eighteen

The next morning, about the time Georgina was setting out in wind and heavy rain for her hospital in Lewisham, Liam was sheltering from the weather on the afterdeck of a Union Castle Line transport in the Gulf of Lyons. He had been on submarine watch since four and was cold and tired and wet through. Every now and then he would cease his scanning of the seas on the starboard quarter and glance forward, to where he could see land looming on the horizon. It was probably the French coast: he knew Marseilles could not be far away.

The thought of it was strange after all this time, not quite believable after all the promises and diversions, after two stretches of the purgatory that was Egypt, and stoking the fires of hell in between. Getting on for two years since joining up, and there was a dreadful irony when he remembered the names and faces of all those who had been so desperate then to get to France, and would now never see Australia again. The greater part of them gone, and he could hardly believe that he was still alive. For long enough after Gallipoli his hands would indulge in a moment's automatic exploration each time he awoke, checking all the vital parts of his body before silently praising God for safe deliverance into another day; then praying for the guts to see this one through.

He had abandoned the physical checks, but not the prayers; the prayers would always be important. When he thought of what he had survived, the narrow squeaks of every day on the Peninsula, shells, bullets, shrapnel which always seemed to strike the next man, never himself, and the massive miracle of coming unscathed through battles which went on for days and in which thousands died, he could not take that survival for granted.

He should have died that August. He should have, everybody said so. From the dysentery which had racked his body for weeks, and from a bout of influenza that had turned to pneumonia within a couple of days. Everyone said how lucky he was to be alive, including the doctors in charge at Helouan and Heliopolis, and the nurses who had brought him through. For a while he had enjoyed a certain fame, with even the oldest, toughest sisters beaming at him like head teachers with a particularly bright and well-mannered child.

But Liam had not needed to be told. There was a moment when he thought he had died, and the strange thing was that he was able to remember it as clearly as when it actually occurred. Memory had dimmed nothing of that grey mist and his sense of floating detachment, nor of the path which appeared between shrubs and trees of an unearthly, indescribable beauty. He had come to a meadow of brilliant flowers, and beyond that was a stream with a small bridge. Liam's sense of exaltation seemed complete when he saw Ned coming towards him with hands outstretched in welcome. A Ned no longer in uniform, but as he used to be, in boots and old moleskin trousers, with his shirt open and sleeves pushed back. No words were exchanged, but they embraced; then Liam knew, looking at his old friend, that he must not cross the bridge. Ned took his arm, and gently urged him back the way he had come.

And for a second, when he awoke from that dream which was not a dream, he was looking down at himself in a narrow hospital bed, surrounded by a sort of tent with two nurses standing by. His next awareness was of being in that bed, fighting for breath and to open his eyes. He saw the nurses, very hazily, above him; then slipped back into unconsciousness.

Meeting Mary Maddox when he was convalescent, talking of Ned's death on the beach at Anzac Cove, he had been aware of a need to comfort her, to give her something to hold on to in her loneliness and grief. During her third visit he tried to explain what struck him as being a glimpse of life beyond the physical present, but either she could not, or would not, understand.

Until that moment, Liam recalled, there had been something between them, sympathy and a shared love for Ned which might have drawn them closer still. Sadly, afterwards, she became a nurse again, assuring him with professional detachment that what he had experienced were no more than feverish hallucinations. She even told him that such hallucinations were quite common, which, far from denting Liam's convictions, merely reinforced them. He wished he could have explained to her that Ned, who in life had always been so brusque and prosaic, was almost radiant with love. It was not, however, something Liam could put into words; it would have embarrassed him, and she would not have believed him anyway.

He did not see her again. That she thought him foolish, even slightly mad, was a shame. He felt he had lost yet another link with Dandenong, and as each link parted, it seemed less and less likely that he would ever return.

Lewis was still in Egypt with the Light Horse, constantly on the move, but he did manage to see Liam a couple of times, and then again before the battalions left for France. He was much thinner, much harder, and sad at the loss of so many old friends. It was obvious, too, that he carried a sense of guilt at having missed Gallipoli. Egypt had been no picnic in the last year, but still, it had been relatively safe.

'I should have joined up with you lot,' he said as they were parting.

'Oh no,' Liam had softly replied. 'Somebody's got to go back to the farm, Lew, and you belong there. So take good care of yourself.'

And in watching him mount one of the sturdy Australian walers, Liam had felt the pull of another parting, could not help feeling that they would never meet again, and that was upsetting. He liked Lewis. However briefly, they had been friends.

Almost anywhere was better than the desert, and when it came to fighting, France could not be worse than Gallipoli. In Egypt, with two stripes at his shoulder, Liam had tried hard to be worthy of the responsibility. There had been little opportunity for foolishness, anyway. Reorganization, retraining, new recruits from Australia, new units with new tasks to perform, all required time and thought and care under a regime which was harsher than ever.

Liam was now in charge of a machine-gun team, under an older and less experienced sergeant, a man who very much resented the hero-worship afforded to his twenty-one-year-old corporal. Keenan referred to him sardonically, in accents which still betrayed his Belfast childhood, as *the golden boy*, or, *my blue-eyed Billy*. Liam hated the sarcasm, and in the man himself found little to respect, even though he could understand what it was that so irritated Keenan, whose experience of Gallipoli was restricted to the last few weeks. Liam was one of the originals, a man who had survived the landings and illness and eight long months of fighting on the Peninsula. He was a lucky man, a man to touch and stay close to, a man protected and revered by his companions. Keenan could lay claim to none of that.

The ancient port of Marseilles with its docks and factories and forts was a source of great fascination during the hours which elapsed between their arrival and disembarkation. Liam would have liked to explore, but shore leave was not allowed. Guards patrolled both gates and gangways, keeping the ship's volatile cargo well confined and under constant surveillance. It was as though higher powers, remembering Cairo, were terrified of sudden outbreaks, drunkenness on a massive scale, and complaints of rape and pillage from the local population.

The Australian troops, however, had been well lectured before leaving Egypt, their finer feelings appealed to. Most of them, Liam knew, would try to live up to those expectations, but the girls, lining the streets next morning as the troops marched through, were so appealing. Smiling, waving, pressing flowers into the men's hands, shouting encouragements in a musical but incomprehensible language, they were temptation personified. Laughing, his hand kissed by warm lips, Liam pushed a twig of cherry blossom into his rifle, and thought it just as well that none of them had been let loose in this hospitable city, or few would have reached their destination.

The train journey north from Marseilles took four days. Not in cattle trucks this time, but third-class compartments with seats and windows. It was an unaccustomed luxury and the men were lively as holidaymakers, waving and cheering to people on stations and in fields beside the track. Word seemed to have gone ahead and all along the line people were waiting to cheer, or press gifts upon them at wayside halts. French soldiers were everywhere, some of them in red trousers and kepis, most of them wounded. Those Australians who had a smattering of French tried conversation, returning with an impression of fiery encouragement for what lay ahead.

From the rocky coastline they meandered slowly up to Avignon, halting in a siding for the night; then slowly up the Rhone valley, with pauses in other sidings while express trains rattled past. They crossed the winding river on a series of girder bridges, the dramatic scenery of such delight that Liam exploited his rank to hug the open window. He felt like a child travelling for the very first time, wanting to ask questions, longing to stop the train, explore that tiny, sun-baked village suspended, it seemed, between cliffs and riverbank.

As the train passed through Lyons and chugged on north, he longed to walk and run along the dusty white road to where woods were veiled in their first flush of delicate green. Early next morning the air was frosty and clear, the open countryside so evocative of England in the spring that he was suddenly, desperately, homesick. He could even identify some of the trees beside the line, repeating their names like a litany from childhood.

Dozing as night fell, leaning into his hard window corner with feet propped on the opposite seat, Liam dreamed of home for the first time in months. He was in the kitchen with his mother, trying to make his peace; but she carried on baking, rolling out pastry with that familiar click, click of her wedding ring, and did not seem aware of his presence. He spoke to her gently at first, then became agitated; when she did not turn round he shouted out...

He woke with a start, to find the train stopped and in darkness, a man's weight against his shoulder and a body beneath his legs, stretched full-length along the floor. Aching and cramped, Liam tried to move without waking them. He longed to move, to get away; to go home and leave all this behind. He wanted no more of these men, the weight of their lives, the press of their bodies. It was too much. He was no older than they were: too young to be responsible, telling them what to do, wiping their noses and writing their letters – what would he do when they got themselves killed?

For a moment he almost panicked.

Flexing arms, fingers, a leg, he took a deep breath and reached for the window sash. With difficulty he lowered the glass and struggled to his feet. Amidst moans and groans of protest, he dragged sweet, cold air into his lungs.

Someone demanded to know where they were: Liam had no idea. A town, the shapes of houses, dark against a less-dark sky. Another voice suggested, forcefully, that he shut the window; he ignored it. Gradually the shuffles and protests subsided again into whistles and whimpers and heavy, stertorous breathing. Liam lit a cigarette and began to feel better.

In the stillness he heard the swish of steam, a reedy whistle and the sudden grunt of power from their locomotive; the long line of carriages gave a convulsive jerk, waking everyone, and they were on their way again.

They passed through the dismal outskirts of Paris in the early hours, changing course again to head directly north. Again it was a beautiful morning, hazy with a hard frost. In the hedgerows were partridge and pheasant, and across a whitened field he saw a fox make a guilty dash for cover. The land was rolling, heavily wooded, more like home than ever. He thought of the Wolds and the Vale of York and knew it was a lifetime past, that even if he went back now it would not be the same, because he was different.

All that – York, its surrounding countryside, the Wolds, the rugged sea coast beyond – was an extension of home, part of his childhood, part of his mother. To go back now would mean facing her, letting her claim him again, letting the past claim him, and he was still determined to stand apart from that. If he was honest, too, Liam knew that in one small corner of his secret being, he was still afraid of what had happened three summers ago. He had not forgotten those wrenching, tearing, gut-churning emotions; nothing since had approached that pain, not even Gallipoli. The horror of that had been an external thing, which after a while lost its impact. Friends died, and if you could, you buried them; if not, you used their bodies as sandbags, knowing that even in death they would be pleased to protect you. He had come to terms with that; what he could not come to terms with were the facts of his own existence.

Approaching Calais in the afternoon, they passed it by, turned south again, then stopped for several hours in a siding at St Omer, the old British headquarters. Eventually the train moved again, east to Hazebrouck, then north-east towards Ypres. Finally, just after midnight, when they were convinced they were heading straight for that battered medieval city, the train stopped at a village just short of the Belgian border. The boom and flash of the guns seemed horrifyingly close. In spite of himself, Liam was afraid.

Ypres, however, proved not to be their destination. As one hard-bitten British Tommy informed them, they were not fit for *Wipers* yet; the nursery at Armentières was bound to be their destination.

Liam bristled at that, felt his fists clench as Gallipoli flashed through his mind, but he bit back a scathing reply. In a way the man was right: they were the new boys here, and needed to learn how things were done. Already he was aware of differences, vast areas behind the lines which were untouched by war. Here was room to manoeuvre, whereas on Gallipoli once you landed, you were in it, right up to your neck. No time to learn the basic facts of life: you acted instinctively, and if you made a mistake, it was very likely your last. Here, in Flanders, the British were more relaxed.

There was nothing relaxed about their first route march. Eight miles of cobbled roads, on soft feet in relatively new boots, was painful. Their journey was south-east this time, through the town of Bailleul to billets in a series of farmhouses off the Armentières road. With fifty other men Liam was directed to a walled enclosure of house and farm buildings. In the midst of the yard, assaulting their nostrils even in the crisp, cold air of that frosty afternoon, was a midden, a huge, sunken pit full of manure. It was something of a shock, as was their accommodation in the nearby barn, especially to those naive enough to have expected beds and clean sheets in the farmer's best rooms. Whatever spare beds existed in the farmhouse were allocated to their officers.

Remembering Gallipoli, Liam laughed at the twitching noses around him. 'Better than a hole in the ground,' he declared, shrugging off his weighty pack, 'and at least the straw's clean.'

Although it had seemed a temporary resting place, they were

at the farm for ten days, days which were given over to intensive training. There were lectures on gas attacks and a necessary exercise in the use of gas helmets. Tear-gas bombs were exploded to illustrate the effects on the unprotected, and then to give the inexperienced confidence in those hideous face-masks, a cylinder of something more deadly was opened in a trench while the helmeted troops walked through it.

The machine-gunners were put through a fresh series of courses on the stripping, mounting and firing of the heavy Vickers machine-guns. Their instructor was at pains to remind them, frequently, of the importance of care in filling the belts. Unless every cartridge was correctly in its place, he said, the gun would jam; and as Liam well new, that kind of carelessness cost lives. Once a gun stopped firing, and the enemy had its position, no quarter would be given. Machine-gunners were not taken prisoner: they were killed.

Amidst the hectic activity, the lectures, demonstrations and tests, Liam thought often of Robin and wondered where he was.

It was some time since letters had reached him, and he was alert for news of the Green Howards. He missed his brother, was aware as never before of a need to see him face to face, to touch him, even hold him for a moment. It was, he supposed, a reflection of the loneliness he had felt since losing his companions from Dandenong. They had been like family, and since then he had had no particular friends. He was closest to the men of his machine-gun team, and his affection for Matt and Jack, Smithy and Carl – and even for Vic, the cocky youngster who made up the sixth member of the team – was general and undiscriminating. For any one of them he would have risked his life, but personal attachment was a thing of the past. Liam could no longer say, as he had once done of Ned, *this man is my friend*. Since Ned there had been too many deaths.

His frustration was Sergeant Keenan. Mostly, Liam tried not to provoke him, because the older man had the power to retaliate in dozens of irritating ways, and small irritations were always the most maddening. But the antipathy between them was strong, and much as Liam tried to contain it, Keenan seemed determined to draw it out. At times, Liam wanted to hit him hard, to drag him to his feet and tell him that there was a war going on and they were supposed to be fighting on the same side; if they could not pull together in a common cause, how on earth could they hope to win?

But he knew it was pointless. Keenan, with three stripes on his sleeve, had the upper hand.

He was so disliked, Liam began to wonder what would happen when they got into the trenches; in the heat of battle it was not unknown for old scores to be settled permanently, and who was to know whence the bullet came? Despite his loathing, Liam was not even tempted. When the time came for Keenan, fate would decide his end, and if there was any justice at all, he thought, it would be sooner rather than later.

By mid-April, they were on their way to billets nearer the front line. The weather, which seemed to have been warming up for spring, changed its mind that day. Cart tracks and unpaved country lanes were quickly churned to mud, while from a leaden sky the wind whipped cruel flurries of sleet, stinging their faces, making what might have been a pleasant journey across country into a bitter slog.

Erquinghem seemed a haven of civilization after that march. It was a small but busy industrial town, all slate roofs and tall, red-brick buildings, its broad streets boasting a plethora of small cafes and restaurants. As soon as the men were billeted they were out again, eager to sample whatever was on offer.

Gun drill and firing on practice ranges was interrupted only to familiarize the men with the trenches. Over the following week they went in small groups to view the front line in several places, and as a bonus came to know the string of villages and small towns which followed the course of the meandering River Lys.

Easter came late that year, not until the third week of April. Good Friday had been as wet and miserable as its predecessors, but the Sunday dawned like a promise of summer. Church parade, on that glorious Easter morning outside a ruined farmhouse on the edge of Fleurbaix, was attended by most of the battalion. Once the service was over, Liam was aware of nothing more than a need to escape.

He had money in his pocket and the rest of the day free.

With barely more than a glance and a wave at his companions, he crossed the bridge and set off in a westerly direction along the riverside. The sun was warm, releasing all the heady scents of spring. In his old life that yearly miracle had been taken very much for granted, but with the scorched, dry memory of Egypt still clear in his mind, Liam found a sensual pleasure in this subtle fragrance of earth and flowers and new leaves. In the midst of destruction it was like a blessing from God, a blessing he was not sure anyone deserved.

After almost a month, it still amazed him to see fields like the one beyond the hedgerow, recently ploughed and sown, and in meadows nearby, cows munching contentedly while shells ploughed fields just a few miles away. Here people lived on the brink of death, tending their farms with sandbags stacked against the direction of the guns, and windows shuttered against the blast. Just up the road to the east, half of Armentières was devastated, while in the other half lived families who still went to work, to school, to church on Sundays. It lent an incongruous air of normality to what was surely a highly abnormal situation.

He supposed the war had become a fact of everyday life to local people; but there was danger in that acceptance, and danger to the new soldiers amongst them. No matter how strongly they were urged to remember the close proximity of the German guns, and the keen eyes of enemy spotter planes crossing the lines, it was easy to be lulled into forgetfulness. In this lush land full of food and water and friendly faces, it was too easy to relax, to march, singing, down the centre of a road to billets in nearby houses, to stand outside smoking and talking, and forget the eyes that watched and marked every movement.

Yesterday, Easter Saturday, two billets near Fleurbaix had been shelled to oblivion.

He found himself in Sailly, amongst villagers returning home from Easter services and idling soldiers from other parts of the line. He nodded, exchanged the odd greeting, and continued on his way. Beyond the village, where he had never been before, he found a small military cemetery beside the road. Most of the graves were British ones, but already there were Australians too. Between the rows of wooden crosses were flowers, wild hyacinths and narcissi growing by the older graves, and on some of the most recent, bunches of daisies and anemones. Taking off his hat, he walked the rows, reading every name, softly repeating each one like a litany of prayer.

When he returned to Erquinghem it was late afternoon. The place where he had eaten the night before was quiet. Two British soldiers were drinking themselves into a stupor in the corner, and a group of Australians, having finished their meal, were preparing to leave. There was no one behind the bar, and he did not expect to see the girl who had been serving last night.

When she appeared to take his order, something inside him responded instantly. Although he was hungry, he ordered a beer first, and begged her to sit at his table. For a moment she hesitated; then, with a glance over her shoulder, poured herself a mineral water and sat down.

He felt ridiculous then, with nothing to say; at least, he could think of plenty in English, but nothing he could translate, adequately, into French. So he drank his beer and looked at her. She was fine-boned, with a delicate, pointed face and a certain pertness about the mouth and eyes which offered challenge. For the first time since those early days in Egypt, Liam was ready to accept it, was possessed of a need and a confidence which far outstripped anything felt before. He wanted her. His body was on fire with the need to know and touch and conquer. He longed for the ease of softness and release.

His thoughts were so violent that a corner of his mind, still coolly detached, was appalled. He dragged his eyes away, shading them with his hand lest he terrify the girl into leaving.

But she was older and wiser than that. Protected she might be – he had seen her mother glowering at him the evening before – but intuition and two years of passing soldiery had ensured a certain loss of innocence. She took his trembling fingers between her own, and made him look at her. Dark hazel eyes softened into sympathy. With a mixture of broken English and slow, clear French, she told him that she understood; she was sorry, it was not possible, but she understood.

'I'm sorry,' he murmured, softer now, the violence abating, his desire for her still there, but under control.

'No. No regret.' Slim shoulders shrugged, and she smiled, eyes twinkling. 'Beer?'

'Yes – please.' He lit a cigarette, sucking the smoke in hungrily. It helped a little.

With the glass on the table she faced him, fingers interlaced, her eyes reading his expression more clearly than the words he longed to say.

'You are sad.'

Liam almost laughed at that. 'Am I?'

'Yes. Today – where?'

'Where did I go? Walking – to Sailly.' And then he remembered and his smile disappeared. 'To the cemetery.'

'Your friends?'

Liam shook his head, dragging more smoke into his lungs, aware, now that she had pinpointed it, of the utter desolation which had possessed him then. He knew now, as she probably did, why he had wanted her so violently; why, if he was truthful, he still wanted her now. It was to prove that he was still alive, and more than that, to know the joy of making love to a woman before he quit this world forever. Except he did not love her, he hardly knew her. She was just a pretty girl with a come-hither smile.

Monday was fine and devoted to training; Tuesday, the 25th, was the first anniversary of their landing at Anzac Cove. The Brigade mustered that day for an inspection by General Walker, and as though to remind the Australians of what had been their fate a year ago, the German artillery shelled some billets outside Erquinghem, wounding ten men. A couple of nights later, after a gas alert, the Australian artillery opened fire for the first time, laying a barrage across the enemy parapets amidst rousing cheers from their own side.

Standing outside their billet, drinking vast quantities of the farmer's homemade beer, Liam and his companions whooped and yelled at every explosion, at every flare that soared with a trail like a rocket and burst into a graceful, brilliant white star. With the red and yellow flashes of the guns it was like the celebrations of 5th November; and Guy Fawkes, Liam thought with childlike joy, must be cheering from his traitor's grave.

'*Vive l'Australie!*' the farmer shouted in his ear, skipping like an ancient gnome as he hoisted a jug of beer and refilled all their mugs.

Drinking his health, Liam tried to explain the excitement of Guy Fawkes Night at home. But the traditions of the eccentric British were lost on that son of Flemish soil, and the finer points of a Catholic plot to blow up Protestant King James as he opened Parliament in 1605, were seemingly appreciated only by a very small boy, who gazed up at Liam in open-mouthed amazement.

'And he was born in York, you know,' Liam announced, 'so he can't have been that bad, even if he was a traitor.'

'Who was?' an Australian voice asked.

'*Guy Fawkes* – weren't you listening? And he might have had a point, at that,' Liam went on, slurring his words. Draining his mug, he held it out for more.

'Don't you think he had a point?' he demanded a moment later. 'I mean to say, just look at all that...' He waved towards the brilliant sky, shouting above the din. 'It's a wonderful firework display and – and I'm sure it's very good of them to put it on for us – but what is it all for?'

Swaying towards the man in front of him, Liam grabbed him by the collar. 'Men are getting killed under that lot. Tomorrow – tomorrow, it might be us. I ask you, mate – *what is it all for?*'

The answer was briskly sober. 'Shut up, Corp, you're plastered. Let that bastard Keenan hear you, and if he don't have you shot, he'll have them stripes off you right sharpish!'

'Bugger Keenan. We should take a leaf out of Fawkes's book,' Liam declared in a confidential whisper, 'and turn that bloody artillery on Haig and Walker. See how they like it!'

'Come on, mate, you're drunk – '

'Am I drunk?' Liam asked in surprise. He stared at his tin mug, empty again, although he did not recall drinking, and then up at the sky as a continuous volley rent the night in two. A great white star exploded and fell to earth in a sweeping arc, all the buildings and men around him seeming to move with it; without the support of his companion, Liam would have keeled over into the mud.

'Yeah,' he mumbled, 'I am drunk. What I was saying – stupid.

Forget it.'

'It's all right, Corp,' the other man sighed, 'if I'd been at the Landings, I might feel the same.'

His hangover the next day was of Cairo proportions, made worse by the shame of recalling every single word he had uttered; what he could not recall was the identity of his companion. Not one of his own team, he was certain, and that was unfortunate. He felt a fool. It alarmed him to realize that he had said such things while not even conscious of having thought them. At least, not for a very long time.

That, coupled with his reactions in Erquinghem on Sunday afternoon, conspired to worry him. He felt he was losing control. In an attempt to regain mastery, he threw himself into the training and prayed for action soon.

They went, a few days later, into the trenches at Bois Grenier, and apart from the unpredictable weather and the brazen activities of their constant companions, the rats, Liam was able to report in his letters home that he was quite enjoying himself. It was good, he said, to be in the thick of it again, to be doing something useful at last after months out of the line. Even in the trenches, after a week or so, they were able to have their rest periods away from the fighting. There had been no such respite on Gallipoli.

In his diary he recorded the events of everyday life, a sudden improvement in the weather in May, the welcome presence of a cat about the place. He described the planes soaring overhead, the dogfights and the daily bombardments, sniping from enemy trenches, and his own satisfaction in returning such fire.

Their gun-pit, he wrote, was in a ruined house, their living accommodation a hut set into the ground and protected by sandbags. But the house lay beside a road which attracted constant attention from the enemy, and the Germans used it as a target for their artillery. Supplies of food and ammunition could only be obtained at night; and at night machine-guns played with devastating accuracy upon the road. Several times he'd had to run for shelter, or simply lie flat in the mud until the enfilade ceased. The sniping at their hut, both with rifle and machine-gun fire, had suddenly become less haphazard and more wickedly accurate, as though their own activities had finally stirred a crack shot into determined action.

Next day he asked permission from Keenan to move. It was refused. But then Keenan left to attend several days of an instruction course. After a few hours in which the hail of bullets had his men dancing every time they wanted to leave the pit, Liam sent a message up the line to their officer. He thought he would have to wait until after dark, but one of their own howitzers started firing into a wood on the German side, and under cover of the smoke, he was able to get out.

Permission granted, they worked all night to build a new gun pit some few yards up the road. With daylight, during a bombardment of the German trenches, the team moved out of the ruined house. None too soon. During the German return attack, four guns, firing as one, managed to take off the sandbagged roof of their old hut; that night, improving the new dugout, the men piled eighteen inches of earth across its top. The following afternoon, he watched their old home disintegrate beneath a volley of high-explosive shells.

'Then they burst shrapnel overhead with the hopes of getting anyone running about,' he jotted into his diary. 'As if anyone could have survived the shelling. But Fritz is very thorough. Thank God we moved in time. If Keenan had been here, I suppose we would have been under that lot.'

Bitterness and a certain amount of vindictive crowing prompted Liam to keep up the fire from their new emplacement. Having sighted the position of those four enemy machine-guns, he was determined to make them suffer. His efforts attracted the artillery again, setting all of them hopping as they dashed back and forth to their tiny cookhouse, trying to get something to eat. They were all laughing, but that afternoon, when news came that they were to be relieved, Liam was more than thankful.

After twenty-four days' subjection to shelling and machine-gun fire, it was good to be behind the lines again, even if only for a few hours. Liam and his team went to the baths at Sailly, and then on to the battalion post office. Apart from one letter from Australia, for some reason there had been no mail since coming into action; he was overjoyed to see a pile of letters and two parcels of newspapers awaiting him.

It was a pleasant afternoon and the six men ambled down the road, reading their mail as they went. Liam flicked through the collection of envelopes, mentally identifying each writer. Three from York, one from his cousin in Leeds, two from Robin, and one with a blurred postmark and writing he could not believe he recognized. He stopped in the middle of the road, staring at that distinctive hand.

Georgina.

Although he had deliberately not thought of her for a long time, her face, smooth, fair, serene, appeared before his mind's eye as clearly as though she smiled for him.

For a minute or two his feelings were so jumbled he could not have said whether he was delighted or dismayed. He was certainly shocked. Why had she written? After all this time, why now? Was something wrong, had somebody died?

But no – he had letters from all who were important to him, it could not be that. Her father, perhaps? His father? He stared at the envelope as though it might tell him itself. Perhaps it was something else – perhaps she was getting married.

His jaw clenched on that thought. Liam slipped the envelope into his breast pocket. Whatever it said, he could not bear to read it now.

The others were already some distance down the road, seated outside a little *estaminet*, beers on the table in front of them. He lit a cigarette before joining them.

'All right, Corp?' one of them asked, glancing up with concern in his eyes. 'Not bad news, is it?'

Liam shook his head. 'No. Just something from somebody I never expected to hear from.' He laughed, a little shakily.

Another one grinned. 'She's heard you're a hero, Corp – wants to know you now.'

'Rubbish,' he muttered, and stuck his head into one of the York newspapers. The letters – all of them – would have to wait until he was alone.

The others read their mail and ordered more beers. Liam's newspapers were passed around. Lighting a fresh cigarette, he read the war news in the most recent paper and then immersed himself in the more local tit-bits. Although he was barely concentrating, the graphic description of a tragic drowning at Bishopthorpe caught his attention. Whether it was solely that or the effects of the letter in his pocket, he could not have said; but he was suddenly reliving the agonizing emotions of his last day at home. Robert Duncannon's voice, which he thought he had forgotten, surfaced unbidden, banishing the flicker of hope that letter inspired.

A sudden exclamation from one of the others disturbed his anguish.

'Well, of all the dirty, low-down tricks! Have you seen this? I never heard about this, did you? Where the bloody hell have we been for the last month?'

'In the trenches, mate – have you forgotten?'

They all wanted to see, but the newspaper was passed to Liam. Reluctantly he took it, scanning the headlines several times before the meaning sunk in.

In Dublin, a month ago, there had been armed rebellion on the streets. On Easter Monday a republic had been declared, and for several days the General Post Office on Sackville Street was occupied by forces opposed to the Crown. After five days of fighting the rebellion was crushed, but British field guns had destroyed much of the centre of the city.

It seemed incredible. A stab in the back. Like the others he was disgusted, on reading further, by the apparent connection with Germany. An ex-British consul, Sir Roger Casement, had tried to enlist enemy aid, but had been arrested after landing from a German submarine. He was to be tried for High Treason. The Irish rebels had been shot.

He stopped reading, handed the paper to someone else and took a deep breath. Without that letter in his pocket, he knew he would have been frantic by now, wondering whether Georgina might have taken an Easter holiday to be with her aunt in Dublin, wondering whether she was still alive...

But where had that letter come from? And when? Oblivious to his companions, he whipped the envelope from his pocket and tore it open. The letter, dated 30th April and sent from a hospital in London, was almost a month old. 'Dear Liam...'

Dear God, he thought, closing his eyes, seeing her face, hearing her voice; how long since he had heard her speak his name!

'… Just a few lines to let you know that we all are well. With the dreadful news from Dublin this week, I fear you may be wondering about us, and although I know your mother writes regularly, I wanted to be sure you were not anxious.

'Father has been in Dublin since Monday. His letter today says the fighting is over, although he is deeply grieved by the destruction to the city. Not his responsibility, thank God, but he is bitterly angry with those who ordered it, and now fears for the safety of all those involved. It will not stop here, he says.

'The strange thing is that I applied for leave to go home for Easter, it being so long since I saw Aunt Letty. Father was against it, but in the end Matron could not spare me, so it was just as well. Apparently Aunt Letty refused to stay at home, and came close to being arrested for trying to help the wounded. All this in spite of her arthritis! What a family we are!

'I hope you are well, dear, and that things are not too terrible for you in France. Your mother writes often and keeps us up to date with your news, but it would be nice to hear from you personally, if you have time to write. If not, then I understand.

'With affectionate regards – Georgina.

'Oh, you beautiful girl,' Liam whispered, crushing the page in his hand.

In June's early summer dawn, birds were warbling an enthusiastic chorus from the hospital grounds. Roused from a momentary reverie, Georgina stood before the open window of her office, wishing she could be as bright as they were at this hour. It had been a long and wearisome night, not very busy but the last of several weeks without a proper break. She could not wait to have the next couple of hours over, to be away from here and going home to sleep. Three days! Three whole days to relax and do nothing. She needed it.

Voices were stirring on the ward. A young VAD nurse knocked on the open door demanding her attention. The amputation in bed four was severely distressed and would not be quieted; would she come?

'*Names*, nurse,' Georgina repeated wearily. 'He's not just an amputee, he does have a name. Please remember that.'

'Sorry, Sister – Private Hopkinson. It's just that – '

'I know – when you were in France, they were in and out so fast there was no time for names.' Georgina had heard that too many times from this young woman. 'Here we have time – here, names are important.'

The nurse bowed her head in acknowledgement, but could not control an irritated sigh. She was thorough, but Georgina wished she would give some evidence of caring for these boys who were here, often for several months. They needed more than medication and clean dressings, they needed interest and reassurance: she had learned that much from the Quakers and was determined to have it here. Once the euphoria of survival had worn off, many of them became despondent. Some had families close enough to visit, but too few knew what to say. It was as though the experience of war and terrible wounds had set insurmountable barriers between those boys and their loved ones.

Georgina was convinced that men who felt they were cared for recovered more quickly than those who imagined themselves a burden to the staff. For some nurses affection was hard to give without great personal cost to themselves; and the inexperienced sometimes erred by giving too much. It was a narrow, difficult line to tread, always with the danger of provoking passionate adoration from this one or that. Georgina had found herself, from time to time, the object of both lust and fantasy as well as gratitude masquerading as love. The young officers were more susceptible, for some reason, than their men. She explained to each that what they felt was natural, if temporary; they would recover in a surprisingly short space of time. Few believed her, asking if they might write. In spite of her discouragement some did, from home, from convalescent hospitals, from France. But rarely more than once. She kept their letters.

The ones who broke her heart were the ones who died.

It was perhaps because their future had been full of a potential which would never now be realized; or perhaps each death represented, to her, a personal failure. It was not something she could adequately explain. It might have been simply the sight of those young, beautiful bodies, which should have been warm and passionate and full of life, and were suddenly so cold and grey in death. If only briefly, she loved them all, and grieved for them like children. Only the detached nature of her love, the fact that she had never explored its physical possibilities, saved her from personal involvement. It was something she was but dimly aware of, yet she clung to it as a nun clings to her marriage in Christ.

Most of the Medical Officers were older, married men, too grossly overworked to indulge in more than the mildest flirtation. There had been one on temporary attachment, however, who had been attractive and single and barely older than herself. He was abrasive with the staff but unusually kind to the patients. For that alone, Georgina had liked him, until in his odd way he had tried to pay court to her. That he was doing so had not occurred to her until one morning over coffee, when he had declared with blunt frustration that she was one of the best nurses he had ever worked with, and by far the most beautiful. It was such a pity, he added, that she never raised her eyes to the level of whole, healthy, normal men; but if she did, he supposed she would not be the excellent nurse she was.

Dumbfounded by that declaration, she had not even blushed; simply stared at him. Finishing his coffee, he had turned to leave.

'I thought you were perfect,' he said from the doorway. 'But you're not – you lack a woman's heart.'

That had hurt. Thinking of it now, she wondered whether that careful schooling of her emotions – so hard won, over so many years – had atrophied all feminine inclinations, leaving her as sexless as a machine. And yet, with her background, marriage would have been folly and as marriage generally followed on love, she had always been careful not to seek it, not to encourage in any way. Instead, like a nun, everything had been channelled into her vocation.

But still, that accusation from a man – a man she had liked and respected – cut to the quick. By way of compensation she drove herself and her nurses even harder, trying to instil her philosophy into all of them. But mostly they were too tired, too overworked, too desperately in need of kindness themselves, to be able to summon the necessary response.

Which was how she felt now. But the words would have to come, the sincerity have to be found, the encouragement expressed.

Leaving the hospital at eight, Georgina was exhausted almost to the point of tears. When the porter called her back, she was tempted to ignore him. Even the small bundle of letters failed to lift her spirits. With a brief word of thanks she pushed them into her pocket.

On the tram she fell asleep and had to be roused at the terminus. A motor bus across the river, and yet another to take her to Kensington Gardens. She was home by half-past nine. The flat was deserted, her father and his servant away, yet again, in Ireland, where executions were the order of the day, and rebels with whom few had sympathized were being raised to the level of martyrs.

It was a bitter, heartbreaking situation. Like her father, Georgina could see no sense in it. It seemed the crowning folly of years of mismanagement, years in which the famous English sense of fair play had been remarkable only for its absence. If only, she often thought, the government would not persist in treating Ireland like a recalcitrant child. Such arbitrary punishment was less likely to hammer evil out, than temper it to greater strength for the next attempt. And there would be other attempts, of that her father was sure; his prognostications for the future were dire indeed, and the smaller tragedy was that his present sympathies were in direct conflict with his sense of duty.

He had tried, yet again, to resign, but short of laying himself open to a charge of treason, it was impossible to reveal that depth of antagonism to his masters at the War Office. Georgina had never seen him so desperately low in spirit, and there was little she could afford in the way of comfort. Ireland was her country too.

Only one thing had cheered her father in recent weeks, and that had been the arrival of the Australians in London. The first contingent had marched to Westminster Abbey on 25th April to commemorate the anniversary of the landing at Gallipoli. Since then others were to be seen everywhere about the town, handsome, muscular, sun-bronzed men on leave, engagingly friendly if curiously disinclined to salute the many British officers at large on the streets.

That aspect afforded Robert Duncannon a certain amount of perverse satisfaction, and in the midst of his despair over what was happening in Dublin, he had related to Georgina a story that was currently being repeated in shocked tones throughout the War Office. While in Egypt, apparently, a young Australian officer had been accompanying a visiting brigadier on a tour of inspection. Coming upon a soldier on guard duty engaged in eating a pie, the horrified young officer immediately ordered him to present arms, whereupon the soldier calmly requested the brigadier to hold his pie while he did so.

True or not, that story amused Robert enormously, as did the legend of those rare salutes. These wild colonial boys were idiosyncratic when it came to one of the prime rules of British army life, and would apparently only afford that civility to those officers known to them and respected.

'Which must cut out the entire General Staff,' Robert had commented with acid appreciation. 'No wonder Haig loathes them – he was always so particular about his status!'

But when Georgina had gently teased him with the question of how he would feel if the Australian soldiers did not salute *him*, Robert had lapsed once more into bleak despondency.

'Well as I don't have much respect left for myself at the moment, how on earth could I complain?'

That comment, Georgina felt, mirrored her father's attitude with disturbing clarity. She was anxious about him, on top of all the other constant, pressing anxieties which made up her life these days. Ireland, the war, her work, all intruded into every waking hour, and often the sleeping ones as well. She dreamed sometimes of Liam, a recurrent nightmare in which a faceless, mutilated body on her ward turned out to be him.

It was not necessary to ask her father whether any of the Australians currently in London included Liam. Robert Duncannon had made a contact on the Australian staff in London, who was primed to tell him the instant Liam's name came up either for leave or as a casualty. Nevertheless, that did not prevent her heart leaping every time she saw one particularly tall, fair soldier in the by now familiar slouch hat. But it was never him and the disappointment was always acute. Her need to see him, to have some word from him at least, grew out of all proportion, becoming for her a touchstone, the one thing that would relieve all other anxiety. She did not ask herself why that conviction had taken root, nor question its logic; she knew, quite simply, that it was so. She was also aware that Liam was unlikely, after all this time, to write to her. If she wanted to hear from him, she would have to be the one to break the silence. And by that time Georgina was incapable of weighing the issues involved.

But it was a month now since she had set pen to paper, using the flimsy peg of what had happened in Dublin as the excuse for writing, four weeks in which she had searched assiduously for his hand on every missive which arrived. Mornings of disappointment had given way to night hours in which she cursed herself for trying to break those silent years. She told herself that there was no reason why, after all this time, he should want to hear from her, or care whether she was in London, Dublin or Timbuktoo; and in the greater hell of imagined rejection, it seemed to her to have been better to leave things alone.

Quite deliberately, a week ago, it being the only way to do her work and retain her sanity, Georgina had put him out of her mind. Now, glancing at the army-issue envelope, she assumed that it was from Robin, and dropped it on the bed. Unpinning her stiff white collar, peeling off the grey nurse's uniform, she peered down at the writing and realized it was different. Needing a better light she hurried into the sitting room, thrusting back the heavy curtains to let in the morning sun.

Hardly daring to believe that it might be from Liam, she tore at the envelope with trembling fingers. Her eyes ran down the single page, taking in formal, stilted, uncharacteristic phrases to the signature at the end. For a second she was torn between delight and pain; and then she smiled, remembering her own difficulties, the strain of finding words to overcome the years between. It must have been the same for him.

He did not apologize, as she had not, for the years of silence, but simply thanked her for writing, said he was glad to have her letter and relieved that she had not been in Dublin during the riots. He had been in the line for weeks, and mail had been delayed, which was why he had not replied earlier. Life in France was better than he had imagined, and they had not been involved in anything serious. The following sentence had been obliterated by the censor, so Georgina assumed it must have contained some reference to where they were or about to be. She held the page up to the light, but that thick black line was all-encompassing and she swore with frustration. After all this time every word of his was precious to her; she could not bear to be so denied.

The letter ended on a note of hope. Liam said he looked forward to hearing from her again; he would like to know something of what life was like for her in London. His signature, strong and forward-sloping, was underlined by a single flourish.

Pleased beyond all reason, Georgina burst into tears.

NINETEEN

At the end of June, three weeks after posting her letter to Stephen, Zoe was still waiting for a reply. The letter received the previous week was not in answer to any of hers, in fact it was little more than a note, outlining where the ship was and why. The apology for his brusqueness over the phone was brief. There were few allusions to his own emotions, either with regard to her or the situation out there, although he did say in a postscript that she was not to worry about him, the media made far more of isolated incidents than was necessary.

Hardly knowing what to make of the letter itself, Zoe read the last sentence with grim disbelief. She took a respected daily newspaper and could hardly avoid the BBC news, either by radio or television. Misplaced or not, her faith in such institutions was not easily broken. Only a few days before, a journalist reporting from Dubai had helpfully analyzed the score of shipping hit in the preceding three years, and of those 227 ships, most were tankers, and most, like Stephen's, were registered in Liberia. The total of merchant seamen dead was equally devastating, especially when one considered that this was supposed to be a local war, the merchant ships unarmed and their crews 'just doing a job'. In the interests of world trade – and somebody's fat profit, Zoe thought bitterly – 211 non-combatant merchant seamen had lost their lives.

The article did not list the numbers of maimed and wounded. It did, however, report that many ships' masters were breaking international law and the rules of safe navigation by running close into the coast of Oman and the United Arab Emirates: two fully-laden tankers had recently gone aground in their attempts to avoid attack by Iranian gunboats.

It did not make reassuring reading, and with those figures

buzzing in her head as she pored over the latest international news, Zoe wished she had remained in ignorance. Pushing the newspaper aside, she cleared her breakfast things and set out the morning's work. The radio was playing a track from a Dire Straits album, one of Stephen's favourites, and she smiled, remembering; but at the following news announcement she felt herself tense, as always now, expecting the worst.

Another bomb had gone off in Belfast, killing two soldiers, but even as she winced, wondering whether Ireland's problems would ever be solved, the voice ran on, outlining Washington's plans for protecting American-flagged ships in the Gulf. And in the Gulf itself, Iranian gunboats had launched missile attacks on two tankers sailing out of Kuwait. The detached, unemotional voice of the newsreader went on to state that the Chief Engineer of one ship had been killed, two crewmen injured on the second.

Poised over her drawing board, listening with every nerve and muscle tensed, Zoe was still unsure of what she had heard. Doubt crept in. Had they really said Scandinavian, or was it Liberian? The news had been brief and no names announced. Perhaps they had made a mistake, perhaps only one ship was Scandinavian, and the other...

Abruptly, she pushed back her chair and reached for the telephone; got the number from enquiries and dialled the BBC. Eventually she had the names of both ships, neither of them Stephen's. Trembling like an aspen, she went up to call on Polly.

'Oh, God, I can't stand this,' she whispered, following her friend into her tiny kitchen. 'I can't work, I can't sleep – after three weeks, I'm a nervous wreck. What am I going to be like after three *months*, for God's sake?'

'Stop listening to it – cancel the papers.'

'*I can't.*'

'You must,' Polly said practically, lighting a cigarette. 'Put it out of your mind, Zoe, it's the only way.'

'That's easier said than done! I'd have to be a stone wall, for heaven's sake, to ignore what's happening out there, when Stephen's part of it.' She hugged her body, rocking back and forth as though in physical pain. 'Oh, hell!' she exclaimed, 'if anything was ever guaranteed to make me start smoking again, this is it!'

'Well, you're not having one of mine,' Polly declared. 'Have a glass of water, instead – it's supposed to dull the craving.' Turning on the cold tap, she doused her cigarette and opened the window. Filling a glass with water, she stood over Zoe until she drank it down. 'There now – better?'

'No,' Zoe grinned, but she was just as anxious. 'What if anything happens to him? What will I do?'

'Nothing will happen to him – and if, God forbid, it should, you'll help nobody by worrying yourself silly anticipating it. Look, why don't you ring that auntie of his? Or that couple you stayed with? You know – didn't you meet the wife aboard Stephen's ship? She must be worried sick, too – maybe she'd appreciate a call.'

Zoe nodded. 'Yes, yes, I will – I've been keeping in touch with Joan, but I haven't spoken to Irene for weeks. I'll give her a ring this evening.'

'That's the thing. But in the meantime, turn off that bloody radio, and listen to some music. Forget the news!'

An hour later, Zoe left. But she could not get Stephen out of her mind, and while it was a comfort to talk to Irene that evening, to hear her calm, sensible voice saying much the same as Polly, once she had put down the phone, Zoe was racked by nerves. Worried for him, wanting him desperately, she almost wished they had never met; she certainly cursed herself for falling in love with such a man.

She spent a poor night and slept late the next morning; it was with misery dogging every movement that she washed and dressed in jeans and an old shirt, and went down to see whether there was any post. The airmail envelope with Karachi on the postmark sent her spirits soaring.

Clutching the letter like a lover, she ran back upstairs, set the kettle to boil and reached for a chocolate biscuit. Had there been a box of chocolates in the flat, she knew she would have eaten the lot.

His letter was in answer to hers of three weeks ago, the first, stilted words of its beginning bending, almost reluctantly, she thought, into tenderness. Zoe's personal history seemed to have touched some chord in him that he could not disguise, as though having known a largely happy childhood, he could not bear to think of her endurance through unhappy years. His concern touched her, to the extent that she half-regretted that outpouring of old sadness – he had the power, even with a word, of making her so happy, she found herself wondering what all the misery had been about.

What he thought about Philip Dent, Stephen did not say. Other than to tell her to forget the incident, he made no reference to that half of Zoe's letter, and she was left wondering whether too much had been divulged. It was hard to judge if her honesty had caused him pain, or whether he was pleased to know that Philip no longer posed a threat. His reticence nagged at her, chilling the warmth she had felt initially. She read the letter again, looking for evidence of coolness, and managed to find something in his suggestion that she should get out and about more often, see friends, and spend less time on the past.

Was he saying she must not rely on him, not bank on that mutual interest at the expense of other possibilities?

She wished so much that she could make him understand that a wholesale takeover of his life was not on her agenda; that she valued her own independence sufficiently to respect his. She wanted to share his life, not own it.

Dogged by uncertainty she returned to her desk, automatically switching on some music she had been playing the day before. It was Richard Rodney Bennett's film score to *Far From the Madding Crowd*, the introduction washing over her like the gentle rain it simulated, suggesting dripping trees and country lanes, and reminding her – as it always did – of the very first time she had heard it, that night in Stephen's flat. They had stood together, looking out at the floodlit Minster, talking about that night in the mist. Remembering their closeness, then and afterwards, she found herself longing for Stephen with a passion which shook her, and was suddenly tempted to write, at once, telling him all that she felt, her growing conviction that they were destined to be together.

Evocative of time and place, the music seemed to epitomize Hardy at his most poignant, gentle, plaintive melodies overlaying violent passion beneath; and interspersed throughout the score, the country ballads with their telling words. Laying Stephen's letter down, Zoe was about to set pen to paper when the words of one particular song stayed her hand.

> I overheard my own true love
> His voice did sound so clear:
> 'Long time I have been waiting for
> The coming of my dear.'

> Sometimes I am uneasy
> And troubled in my mind
> Sometimes I think I'll go to my love
> And tell to him my mind.

> But if I should go to my love,
> My love he will say nay;
> If I show to him my boldness,
> He'll ne'er love me again.

Old-fashioned words, she thought with a sudden surge of bitterness, but in spite of feminism and the lip-service paid to equality, had very much changed between men and women since Hardy's day? She thought not. Let a woman talk of love and commitment – and by implication, children, too – most men would back away. It was not selfishness particularly, nor was it immaturity; it was simply the way they were made. Crawling up the ladder of civilization might have refined a few things, but the basic differences were still there.

On that thought she experienced a moment's pity for Stephen's ex-wife, and knew that in spite of her own love of independence, basically she wanted the same sort of commitment. She wanted to know that Stephen loved her, that he wanted to father her children; because to Zoe the thought of children, of continuation, was becoming increasingly important. But not just any man's children: Stephen's.

But he must come to her. He must be the one to speak of love and unity, he must be willing to acknowledge the ties that bound them. She was sure he was aware of those ties, but as yet they could be broken. And with such physical distance between them, they might simply drift apart. And in this situation – oh, God, *this situation* – death could intervene in one swift stroke, leaving her here, in Georgina Duncannon's flat, stranded and alone.

That thought chilled her.

Polly was right: she must not think of these things. Abruptly, Zoe switched off that haunting music and went out for a walk in the park.

Having loaded a mixed and highly flammable cargo of aviation spirit, diesel oil and motor gasoline, the *Damaris* was ready to sail in the early afternoon. With no intentions of leaving before nightfall, Stephen left watchmen posted and told his officers to get some rest. He went below himself but found it difficult to sleep. When he did eventually doze, it was to dream again of Liam Elliott, lurching towards him out of the mist. Although he had experienced the same dream two or three times before, it was no less disturbing: Stephen woke in a cold sweat.

'For Christ's sake,' he muttered into the gloom, 'what are you trying to say to me?'

Glancing at the clock, he realized he had slept for not much more than an hour. There was no point in trying again: it would soon be time for dinner, and he must eat. Lighting a cigarette he went through into the dayroom to make a pot of tea. It was hot and sweet and refreshing, and he began to feel a little better. A long, cool shower completed the process of dragging his reluctant body into wakefulness.

Pulling on a pair of shorts, his eye caught Liam's diary lying innocently on the bedside chest.

Sighing, he said aloud: 'I can't think about it now. I haven't time.'

Like an unexpected reply, the telephone rang, startling him. He snatched at it, his answer terse. 'Yes, I'm awake – I'll be down in a minute.'

He reached for a clean shirt, fastening the epaulettes with their four gold stripes to the shoulder tabs. For a moment he stared at the mark of rank, wondering whether ambition was worth it. Minutes later he was down in the saloon, sipping at a glass of iced water. With a long night ahead, Stephen ordered soup, salad, fillet steak and chips, and cheese to finish. He was not ravenously hungry but forced his way through everything: for the next twelve hours he would exist on black coffee and cigarettes, with perhaps a sandwich to take him through to breakfast.

He exchanged a few words with the Mate and then they went together up to the bridge. It was Johnny's watch, but until they cleared the Straits of Hormuz in something like seventy-two hours' time, Stephen would remain on the bridge, resting in the sea-cabin behind the wheelhouse during the necessary anchorages. Safe anchorages, supposedly, but in the Gulf safety was a relative term: anchoring close to neutral territory, a centre of population or major oil installation, simply made the risk of air attack by day less likely. In the daylight hours helicopters were buzzing around and Iranian jets screaming back and forth; while at night gunboats crept out, hiding amongst the fishing fleets of Arab dhows. Less than a month of running the gauntlet every week, and already the strain was making itself felt.

The tugs were away just before seven. Stephen telephoned the engine room. 'Right, Mac, let's get this show on the road. Full revs as soon as you can.' He gave a short bark of laughter at the Chief's answering comment. 'Too bloody right – we don't stop for anything. Particularly small boats wearing missile launchers!'

The last lingering glow of light over the desert was soon gone, and at full dark the ship was making sixteen knots away from the Kuwaiti terminal and directly out into the Gulf. Apart from the narrows at Hormuz, this was one of the worst stretches, the vast oilfields off the Kuwaiti and Saudi coasts making it impossible to hug the safety of neutral territory. At the furthest point, before turning south for Ras Tannurah, they were only sixty miles from the Iranian coast, frighteningly close to the place where the Scandinavians had been attacked a couple of nights before. The gunboats were getting bolder.

Stephen checked charts and radar constantly, and with the changing of the watch at eight, had the Third Mate on the port bridge wing and a seaman to starboard. He moved all the time between the two, every nerve stretched taut, carefully plotting every blip on the radar, identifying each approaching ship through night glasses.

At midnight, with the arrival of the Second Mate it was time to change course away from the centre of the Gulf, back towards the Saudi coast. After that he took a short break for a sandwich and a cup of coffee before resuming his pacing. His mind was clear, concentrated totally upon surveillance; he did not allow himself to wonder what he would do in the event of an attack. He had to trust himself and the years of experience behind him; had to trust that his reactions, which had never failed him yet, would be the right ones. To doubt that would be to fall apart.

With the Mate's re-emergence at four, and the anchorage at Ras Tannurah no more than a couple of hours away, Stephen felt able to relax a little. Once Johnny had taken over the watch Stephen eased himself into the high pilot's chair, aware of aching knees and ankles.

Lighting a cigarette, the last of a packet opened just before dinner, he said: 'Did you sleep?'

'After a fashion.' Silhouetted against a faintly greying sky, Johnny was following the movements of three tankers, like themselves all running for the safety of the anchorage. He checked their courses against the radar plot, then said: 'I kept thinking about those poor bloody Scandinavians.'

'Me too.'

'Quiet night?'

'Plenty of tonnage going up, and we overtook a couple coming down.'

'No nasty little men in boats, then?'

'Well there was a bunch of fishing boats just before we changed course – made me sweat for a while, I can tell you. But nobody asked us to stand and deliver, so we just kept going.'

Johnny grinned and continued his surveillance. Stepping down from the pilot's chair Stephen made some coffee, relieved, after eleven hours of solid concentration, to let it lapse a little, to know that his senior officer was alert and capable. The worst of the night was over, and in the east the first glow of dawn was spreading like the fan of a peacock's tail. The sun rose rapidly, shooting a path of gold across the sea and casting long, dramatic shadows from the ships ahead. They were drawing closer to the three tankers now, with another, very slow-moving pair ahead of them. But were they tankers? Stephen wondered, trying to discern shape and form through the glasses.

Impossible: another ship was in line of sight. He studied the radar and thought it might be one ship under tow. 'Never mind, they seem to be heading for the anchorage – we'll see them soon enough.'

He glanced at his watch. Six o'clock and he was hungry, more than ready for the breakfast that would be waiting once they were in position and securely anchored. One by one the ships ahead of him altered course and slowed for their approach, and as Stephen prepared to do the same, he noticed the furthermost vessel holding its original course. Once again he studied it through the binoculars, and the thing, whatever it was – an enormous barge, Stephen thought at first – was attached to an ocean-going tug. It took several seconds for him to register what he was seeing, and when he did, his hunger disappeared.

'Have you seen that?' Johnny murmured, and there was horror in his voice.

'I have indeed.'

The two vessels were travelling so slowly, the *Damaris* was soon abreast of them, perhaps half a mile distant. With the glasses pressed to his eyes, Stephen was only dimly aware of Mac joining him on the bridge wing. The 'barge' was a stricken tanker, her name and port of registry just visible beneath burned and blistered paint on the stern. Other than that, Stephen thought, she was barely recognizable as a ship, more an obscene caricature with plates ripped and curled, and pipes twisted across the remains of her foredeck. There was no superstructure, no accommodation, no bridge; only two bent uprights that had once supported the wings.

In the Gulf these days, damaged ships were commonplace, most with holes in either bows or stern, temporarily crippled and waiting at every anchorage for their turn in the crowded repair yards. But Stephen had never seen anything like this. Whatever had hit her, either Exocet or high-explosive shells, had hit the after-end accommodation, and presumably fire and a series of explosions had done the rest. Had anyone survived? Had there been time to jump clear? It seemed unlikely that there could have been chance to man the boats. When had it happened? And where? They had heard nothing during the night, and no word had come during their two days in Kuwait. It was a mystery but not one on which he wanted to dwell.

They were all subdued after that, and Stephen nosed his own ship's 870 foot length carefully between a motley collection of the world's shipping, to find a comfortable space where the *Damaris* could swing around her anchor with ease. There were tankers of all sizes and all ages, Greeks, Kuwaitis, Japanese, Norwegians and at least a dozen carrying the Liberian flag. Some were in a sorry state, dented and battered, but none like that stricken thing on its way down towards Bahrain and ultimately the knacker's yard.

All, without exception, were showing signs of wear, their hulls streaked with rust, decks and accommodation patchy. On runs like this Stephen knew there was no time for cosmetics, no time to do any but the most essential maintenance. It hurt his professional pride that after only four weeks on this run the *Damaris* was beginning to look like an old tramp. But what were a few streaks of rust compared to structural damage and loss of life? The important part was the engine room.

With a familiar twitch of alarm, *Nordic* and her old tricks sprang to mind. But this was a relatively new ship, and thanks to Mac, the engines were tuned like Her Majesty's Rolls-Royce, every valve and pump in excellent order, fire-fighting equipment and breathing gear in a state of constant readiness.

Fire drill and boat practice: no longer exclusive to Saturday mornings, no longer a light-hearted run-through to comply with regulations. Outside the Gulf Stephen insisted on the full emergency drill every trip. He even had the crew blindfolded. Search and rescue were all very well in practice, but in reality, with generators gone, no lights, and the accommodation full of smoke, it would be hard to see anything. So he made them all pretend. So far to the crew it had been a great game occasioning much merriment; having seen that blitzed tanker, he wondered whether they would laugh next time.

They spent the day at the northern holding anchorage off Ras

Tannurah, a day in which a hot, searching wind blew dust off the desert's face and the sun could have fried eggs on the steel decks. A day like any other, with the sudden, heart-stopping scream of low-flying jets and the more sustained anxiety of reconnaissance aircraft.

Aboard the ships, nothing stirred until sunset, when there was a sudden flurry of activity. Like lizards that have been as dead as stones in the heat of the day, once the sun had gone those ships began to slip away, one after the other, on their various journeys through the night. Another twelve hours of anxiety, with the safety of Dubai just after dawn; then a day and a night of heat and inertia, of eating and dozing and reading in the sea-cabin, while the officer of the watch paced back and forth across the bridge.

Stephen tried to write to Zoe, but there was so much that could not be said, it left little to describe. With the imprint of that stricken tanker still on his mind, it was hard to avoid mentioning the dangers, and an hour later, reading the letter through, his observations of Kuwait sounded almost childishly resentful. In three pages he described the numbers of Soviet supply ships off-loading arms, presumably en route to Iraq, and went on to complain about the nitpicking levels of bureaucracy – worse than anything he had ever encountered – and the fact that no one from a foreign ship was allowed ashore in Kuwait. None of it endeared him to that tiny country, and the fact that he was risking his ship and his life to maintain the war and the oil-sheiks' riches, made him hate everything connected with it.

Anger and a sense of his own inadequacy depressed him. He would have liked to tell her how it felt, being here, but that was somehow too frightening to contemplate.

They left again after dark, part of a general movement of ships that clustered together for safety like an old Atlantic convoy; except that here were no corvettes or destroyers to protect them. Only a bevy of little minesweepers doing their bit by the Straits.

The air was heavy and close, visibility poor with dust in the atmosphere. In another few weeks the monsoon winds would be blowing in earnest, creating yet another hazard. He longed for news from London which would release him from this hellish contract, but did not seriously expect it before his leave was due.

This run was too lucrative. One thing was for sure, he promised himself: they could beg, plead and threaten, he would not accept another posting to this hell-hole until every other Master in the company had taken his turn. And at that rate, Stephen calculated, he should be ready for retirement.

Just before dawn they gathered themselves for the final, nerve-shattering dash through the Straits of Hormuz in broad daylight. Even hugging the coast of Oman, the Straits were too narrow, too uncomfortably close to Iran and all those ferocious heroes of the Islamic Revolution for anybody to risk going through at night. With the thought of Exocet missiles for breakfast, however, Stephen was hardly comforted by the Radio Officer's news that three men aboard that ravaged tanker had been killed and two injured.

An improvement upon his imagination's score, but that was all. Unarmed men, part of nobody's war, they were victims of murder. And for what? Politics? Religion? Profit? Was the reason so important? He thought not. All that mattered was that they were dead.

And there but for the grace of God, thought Stephen, go I.

TWENTY

On 1st July 1916, on the slopes of rolling chalk hills north of the River Somme, more than 20,000 British soldiers met their deaths in flower-strewn meadows, mown down by machine-guns, trapped by giant caterpillar rolls of barbed wire.

At Fricourt, three miles from the little country town of Albert, Robin Elliott advanced with the 7th Battalion Green Howards and watched his friends fall around him. In the shelter of a shell-hole just before the German line, pinned down by a ferocious hail of bullets, he applied inadequate field dressings to the wounds of one man, and a rough tourniquet to the arm of another. He comforted them, fed them sips of water, and waited for the day to pass.

It was long and hot and cloudless, a day to sear the memory, the sun like a branding-iron, the air thick with the smell of lyddite and blood. The cries of the wounded were harrowing. One of his companions, the one with abdominal wounds, died just before sunset; the other, with his hand a mangled mess of bone and tissue, moaned constantly. At full dark, which was not until after eleven that night, he hoisted the barely-conscious man out of the shell-hole and proceeded to crawl with him back to the point from where they had set off. It was not very far, perhaps a little over fifty yards, but it took him more than two hours to reach the safety of their own lines.

Under fire in the trenches opposite Messines in Belgium, Liam knew nothing of it. The Germans facing them were not only alert but intensely serious about the business of killing.

It was a long time since Liam had been quite so nervous, and when, after another ten days of noise and rain and squelching, stinking mud, the company was relieved, Liam could have kissed the incoming British troops. But one man was killed going out that night, and the fifth member of Liam's team, Jim Smith, was caught by the same scythe of fire. Half-groaning, half-laughing, with the fleshy calf of his leg in tatters, he hung onto Liam and Jack, the Number Two, while they dragged him through the mud to safety.

'The bastards got me,' he kept saying, 'the bloody bastards got me!' Then it seemed to dawn on him that he was wounded, and he said delightedly, 'But it's a Blighty, this one – it's got to be a Blighty! I'll be out of this bloody mess for a bit, won't I?'

'Oh, he's a lucky sod, this one,' somebody else remarked. 'Clean sheets for him, and angels with wings waiting on his every whim!'

'You're getting quite poetic, Vic – careful, they might give you a commission.'

'Heaven forbid, Corp – I'm staying with you!'

But that wound put a slight dent in their feelings of invincibility. They had been together as a team since the early days at Bailleul; as Smithy was handed over to the ambulance team it occurred to all of them that they were one less, that for the first time they needed a replacement.

Euphoria at leaving the line was further dampened by the weather. In the midst of an electrical storm they marched back to camp to find it flooded out. The morning was spent digging drainage ditches round tents and canvas bivouacs. Too tired to sleep and needing suddenly to get away from the press of other human beings, Liam went for a walk. The storm had cleared the air, leaving the sky pale and fragile, reflected like a string of pearls in puddles along the road.

Beyond the woods which flanked the camp he heard strange noises, hammering and tapping which bore no resemblance to gun-fire. Investigating, he came across an army of engineers laying track-beds and rails at a tremendous rate. Fascinated by their activity he stood and watched for a while, noticing as he did so that much horse-drawn artillery was moving south on a road close by.

Sauntering past a group of pioneers who had stopped to brew up, he asked what was going on.

'Don't you know, mate? It's for the advance. All that lot's going down to Amiens, and this here track's for the armoured trains.'

'What advance?'

'Lord, son, where 'ave you been? Australia?' The old sergeant cackled at his own humour, while his men shook their heads. 'Big push north of Verdun. Helpin' the Frogs out, we are – doing all right too. We'll soon 'ave Fritz on the run!'

Against a hard little kernel of disbelief, Liam's spirits lifted; because he wanted it to be true, he laughed, said it was tremendous news, and wished them well with their task. On the way back his step had a spring to it, and almost in spite of himself he repeated the story as though it were gospel fact. It certainly fitted with what they knew already, that the Germans locally had been rattled into vindictiveness, and probably by the news that they were being defeated elsewhere.

Next day the machine-gunners were issued with revolvers for range-finding, it having been decided at long last that rifles were too cumbersome to carry along with gun barrels and tripods and heavy boxes of ammunition. They had some fun practising, and even greater fun later at the baths in Neuve Eglise. Cleanliness and a fresh change of clothes worked wonders; tiredness evaporated and suddenly life was worth living again. Pay and an issue of mail completed everyone's satisfaction.

Liam returned to their camp in the grounds of an old moated manor house, his disappointment that there was nothing from Georgina intensified by an awareness that his weeks-old request for leave was hardly likely to be granted now. Artillery was still moving down that road beyond the woods, and if the push was as big as was rumoured, no doubt the Australians would soon be moving with it. On these sombre considerations he settled down with his back against a tree-trunk, lit a cigarette and prepared to read his mail. Most unexpectedly, there was a letter from Tisha, which in her hurried scrawl announced the fact that she was married.

It had been very short notice, she wrote, because Edwin was about to leave on active service, something for which he had been applying regularly, but not really expecting. At her description of his rank and background, Liam felt his lip begin to curl, and not even a lingering affection for his sister could prompt much sympathy for their situation. He knew already, from Georgina, that Tisha had landed on her feet in London, and suspected she took as much advantage of people there as she had always done.

It was a shock, however, to read that Robert Duncannon had given her away at the short ceremony before a registrar.

'Mother and Dad weren't able to travel down, you see, as Dad's not been so well lately. I'm writing to Robin, too, but if you should see him give him love from me and Edwin. Edwin is just longing to meet you both, but I don't suppose it will be until this dreadful war is over. We really must get together then, don't you agree?'

Liam swallowed hard, wondering why Tisha should still, after all this time, have the power to infuriate him. All those throw-away lines, no real news, just a series of by the ways. 'Dad's not been so well lately.' What did that mean? There was nothing from Edward this time, only a brief note from his mother.

He scanned it quickly, looking for any reference to illness, but there was none. She said Edward was very busy at work, and what with that and the difficulty of travelling at short notice, they had not been able to go to the wedding. 'But I don't expect that will have upset Tisha very much,' was added in a telling statement, 'and I gather the young man's parents were also unable to be present.'

There was nothing surprising about the letter, yet for some reason it made him uneasy. Why should Tisha refer to illness, and his mother not mention it? If either of them suffered so much as a cold, she usually saw fit to remark on it. What was so wrong with Edward that it must be hidden? Or that – God forbid! – he was unable to write? Disturbed, Liam promised himself that he would ask some searching questions in his next letter home. And he would ask Georgina, too. She communicated with his mother; she would know.

Suddenly, they had orders to pack up and leave. The fairy-tale beauty of the old manor house, reflected with such purity in the glassy waters before it, slept on in the morning sun, oblivious to the activity around. The men packed limbers and field kitchens, hitched horses, filled in latrines, folded tents and prepared for a lengthy march to Bailleul, their original base near Armentières. From there cattle trucks took them overnight to Doullens, where everything had to be unloaded from the train for a rapid march south through Picardy.

It was beautiful country, a place of misty woods and hidden valleys, of winding country lanes and thatched, half-timbered villages. Gentler than Flanders, more secretive somehow, and less intensively farmed, it was also much poorer. The people had little to sell and nothing to give. Two years of war had destroyed their harvests, and the troops moving back and forth had consumed everything else. Bread was a luxury and fresh meat a legend. Liam had the impression at every halt that despite their forced smiles, the locals could not see much to choose between the marauding Boches and defending British. Their own sons were dead and dying at Verdun, and for those few who returned, a pathetic inheritance of shell-holes and fallow fields would be all that was left.

That atmosphere of sadness seemed to colour the landscape, beauty and tragedy mixed, as in some old romantic poem. Lovely but neglected chateaux, their gardens a wilderness of roses in full bloom, and picturesque old farmhouses whose quaintness hid emptiness and hunger within. Ponds without ducks, barnyards without geese, watermeadows which supported no more than a wealth of wild flowers.

Standing outside one of those ancient barns at sunset, Liam heard the guns and imagined the destruction. He was a lover of beauty and solitary places, of land that was fruitful and lovingly tilled, and to him this march of men, of guns and battle and sudden, violent death was like rape. And he was a necessary part of it; that was what hurt, what made him long with a force that shook him for this battle to succeed.

The English newspaper he had bought in Bailleul claimed that it was going well, although as they came closer to the town of Albert, the sight of so many exhausted and dispirited British troops made him wonder at the truth of it. Next day, with his first letter from Georgina in almost three weeks, Liam knew that much was being withheld.

Her note was little more than a brief apology. There was no time to write at length, little time to breathe with convoys of wounded coming in almost faster than they could be dealt with. Staff working ridiculous hours, wards full with more beds being added every day. She prayed that he was still in Belgium and safely out of what was happening on the Somme. Had he heard anything from Robin?

Louisa had received the usual printed card, ringed where it said, 'I am well,' just three days after that first terrible day of battle. But other than that, nobody had heard a thing.

That first terrible day. Georgina's words had the ring of doom about them, flaring the ever-present embers of his anxiety over Robin. Sixteen days had passed since the initial advance, and the battle had not stopped. It was still going on, he could hear the boom of the guns like thunder just a few miles away. The whole of the Australian 1st Division was on the move, and the battered remnants of the British 29th, with whom they had fought at Gallipoli, were resting in the next village. The ones he questioned all told the same tale: that the Yorkshire regiments had taken the most dreadful battering, some battalions virtually wiped out. And his informants did not seek to shock; their words, like their eyes, were without any discernible emotion.

Recognizing the symptoms, Liam felt a chill enter his soul. He did not ask what the battle had been like, there was no need. He had been there, at Quinn's Post and Lone Pine and a dozen other places on the Peninsula. So he was gentle with them and shared his cigarettes and patted their shoulders when he left. Their band was playing that evening in the village street, but those rousing, popular tunes were as inappropriate as dance music at a funeral. The lament of a solitary piper would have been more fitting.

They were held outside Varennes until the 19th, and the move, when it came, was sudden. Kit was donned for fighting order, packs marked and handed in, felt hats exchanged for the new steel helmets. Marching through Senlis later that day, Liam saw a group of German prisoners unloading stores under guard, and was astonished by their youth. Such boys they looked, their faces pale and bewildered; then he thought of his brother, and pity evaporated.

Camp that evening was in the open, in a field outside Albert, beside the shell-pocked ribbon of the Bapaume Road. It was a broad path first built by Romans, not curving around hills but tackling them head-on; now it climbed the long slope of 'Tara Hill' like a smudged white line disappearing over the crest to rise again in a series of small swells, beyond their immediate sight, to a high point some four and a half miles away, on which stood the village of Pozières.

To left and right of the road, in an arc around the town, stood several other villages from which the Germans had largely been beaten back. In that bitterly defended action, however, they had retrenched themselves on the higher point of that rolling chalk downland, from where they commanded views north to the ridge at Thiepval and south towards the valley of the Somme.

The aim of this push, their officer told them, was to make a break in the line – that never-ending line which ran from the Channel port of Ostend all the way to the Swiss border – so that the German forces could be outflanked at last, rolled up like a human carpet. The Australians' task, he revealed with awe and pride in his voice, was to dislodge the enemy from Pozières.

The 1st and 3rd Brigades would be going in first, with the 2nd, the Victoria Brigade, held in reserve. The young officer, who had joined them in Egypt, sounded regretful as he imparted that information; hearing it, Liam groaned with the rest. Like them he was keen to get in there, keen to deal the swiftest, most lethal blow, so they could finish the war quickly and go home. But it seemed they were destined to wait on the sidelines, dodging shells, chewing their fingernails, wondering when and if they would be needed.

The Roman road, bearing its evidence of craters, was too exposed for these latter-day legions; all approaches to the ridge were made via two shallow valleys, 'Sausage' to the south of the road, and 'Mash' to the north. The Division moved in stages to the southerly approach, through the ragged remains of Bécourt Wood and along tracks which led to the shallow dip of 'Sausage Gully'.

High on the ridge beside the Roman road was the chalky detritus of a massive crater, blasted by mines on the first day; below it, criss-crossing the vale like the string of a cat's cradle, stretched dozens of white lines. The whole area was scarred by shell-holes and old trench-systems: by a chaos of men and horses and transports, field ambulances, kitchens and guns. Amidst the intermittent blast of their own artillery came the distant crump of other guns. At the head of the valley, where the stumps of Bailiff Wood stabbed the skyline, great gouts of smoke regularly obscured the cloudless blue beyond.

Warned to be ready on several occasions, on 22nd July Liam's unit moved from field to wood to old German trenches overlooking the crater.

The British bombardment began at seven in the evening. It went on for five hours.

In the old, well-dug German trench Liam curled himself against the crushing reverberations, stuffing lint in his ears to block the din. The roars and the shocks were continuous, like being bowled along in a steel drum, hour after hour with no escape. It was worse than anything he had ever experienced. For a while, before his ability to think was eradicated, his pity went out to the attacking battalions, waiting so close to where those shells were landing. They must be going mad with it. How would they gather themselves to attack when the barrage lifted?

And what about the Germans? Were they safe in their deep chalk dugouts, as they had been on 1st July? Or where they being slowly pulverized to oblivion, dying, one by one, from concussion? Eventually his pity extended even to them.

Hour after hour through the long summer twilight the bombardment went on, great pink clouds of dust erupting over the horizon. When darkness came, the night was lit by a continuous flickering band, with star shells bursting and shrapnel twinkling, and red and green rockets curving away into hell. And always the noise, the everlasting noise...

When it stopped, the silence was palpable, eerie, the only sound inside Liam's head, a dreadful, continuous ringing. For a while he thought he must be dead. As sensation returned, he jerked into life. His men were alive but stunned. Mouths open, eyes flickering, no words. The sharp ripping of machine-guns, the crack of mortars, were crackling insect noises. At last it came to him that the battle had begun.

It was a cold night with a heavy dew. Huddled inside a couple of old German overcoats, Liam dozed towards dawn, half an ear cocked for the call that would rouse them all to action. But none came. At sunrise he went down with three of the team for water and provisions, and saw the stream of wounded coming in. Most of the injuries were slight, in legs and arms, and in spite of the pain the men were jubilant, the battle was going well, they had

Fritz on the run. The claim was borne out by the numbers of prisoners being taken down the valley, most of them so dazed they looked like sleepwalkers.

'Poor buggers, I bet they were glad to surrender,' the new man, Gray, remarked and Liam was bound to agree. But their own walking wounded were singing.

It was a day of inactivity for the machine-gunners in reserve. Liam obtained permission for his men to explore the nearby deserted village of La Boiselle and went with them to explore the deep dugouts which had enabled the defenders to withstand the initial bombardment of 1st July.

Flights of steps led deep into the chalk hill, with sizeable rooms beneath, all fitted out with wire-sprung beds and dressing tables and electric lights. Awestruck by these creature comforts, they were ill-at-ease down there, feeling like voyeurs, intruders into a temporarily abandoned home. Tunics were still hanging on pegs, underwear in drawers; a broken powder compact beside a very feminine shoe gave shocking reality to the evidence of female names on a duty roster. Apparently women had worked here as telephone operators.

The men were shocked; having women in the front line seemed to verify the Germans' barbarism. But they were envious too. Perhaps this was the way to go to war, with pretty faces and trim ankles to alleviate the boredom, and a warm pair of arms to welcome you at night. But beneath the coarse jests were gentler longings, an awareness of home and their own women, so totally out of reach.

It was damp and cold underground; the afternoon sun struck Liam pleasurably as they returned to the surface. For a good half-hour he lay sprawled with his team on the warm earth, watching the clouds of dust rising and falling above Pozières. Passers-by related the state of play in cricketing terms. The home team were in and scoring well, pushing through the village, aiming for the cemetery at the northern end. The British 48th would join the game there. Artillery was bowling an isolated outpost of Huns on the western border.

He sat up to identify the spot, amused by the idle discussion of tactics and positions. It seemed, disappointingly, that the reserves would not be needed. Above them planes were buzzing round like gnats, and behind the British lines he counted sixteen observation balloons like silver clouds against a cerulean sky.

Returning, he heard that the 8th Battalion had been called up to reinforce the 1st Brigade. Good news in one sense, but it meant another night of anxiety, wondering whether they would be called in support. They were not. By morning news came through that the village of Pozières had been captured, that the 8th had cut a swathe through enemy opposition and pressed forward to the cemetery. It was tremendous news; the men in reserve cheered and yelled, dancing like cannibals round the field kitchens. But it was by no means over. There passed another twenty-four hours of uncertainty, ferrying supplies up the valley, questioning every stretcher-bearer and runner whose anxious, gasping breaths would allow of a reply. The Australians had the village, so why were they not pressing on? What was the hold-up? But nobody seemed to know.

In the early hours of the morning of the 25th, uneasy sleep was broken by the din of a fresh bombardment, German guns this time, which seemed to be finding their marks. Liam saw many wounded coming down at first light, all of them in a poor way. From what he could gather, the 8th had lost two-thirds in death and injury, the 5th even more.

All through that beautiful day a constant fume of fog hung over the ridge; the Germans were having their innings now, seeking to regain lost ground, and flinging everything at it in the attempt. The bombardment continued intermittently, intensifying at sunset, throwing back the most glorious colours to the watchers in the valley. Elsewhere the front line was quiet.

It seemed to Liam that the world had paused to watch that duel on the hill.

At dusk, the full company of machine-gunners moved up to Bailiff Wood. It was impossible to see Pozières, although no more than a small field lay between the wood and the tiny hamlet of Contalmaison. No longer inhabited by the living, its walls had collapsed into paths and gardens, the orchards torn limb from limb.

Like the dead, he thought. Unburied bodies, in the grotesque attitudes of death, lay strewn where they had fallen, Saxon and Yorkshireman side by side amongst the rubble. Covering his mouth against the stench, Liam searched while the light allowed for any sign of his brother. Fricourt lay less than a couple of miles away down the valley; there the Green Howards had fought to a standstill, and then come back a week later to try again. Had Robin been here? Was he amongst the dead?

But nothing remained which suggested the slender body of his brother. Alone, with one of the team watching out for the signal which might come any minute, Liam stopped for a moment in the shelter of a warm farmhouse wall. A few half-ripe apples were scattered amongst debris underfoot; a butter-churn, undamaged, lay beside the mangled remains of a baby's high-chair, while beneath it, staring up at him with bland, unblinking eyes, was a china doll with a broken face.

Suddenly, he was weeping uncontrollably, broken by this evidence of family life, its senseless destruction. This had been a man's home, the place to which he returned each night after work in the fields. War had made of it a charnel house.

Anger shook him then. He walked through the stink of death and raged at its indignities, seeing his brother in every distorted face. Why were they not buried? Why were they left here to rot?

He knew the answers to those questions, but the anger sustained him. As he rejoined the group in the wood, Sergeant Keenan strode up, angrily demanding to know where in hell he had been. Bitterly amused by the term, Liam turned away and was threatened by a charge. 'Looking for my brother,' he said, and something in his eyes quelled the other man.

Evening deepened into darkness, and from the valley behind them the British artillery opened up again. Watching red-hot shells passing overhead, Liam was sure the call would come soon. From time to time his body winced and shivered, but he was less conscious of fear than of physical tension, a coiled spring which when the order came, released itself in a grunt of praise.

Of the two machine-gun sections to go up, theirs was the first. With his gear already strapped about him, Liam hoisted the 50lb weight of the gun's tripod and waited for the nod from Keenan.

When it came he led his team down past the crossroads at 'Casualty Corner' and along the partially sunken road which led eventually to the ridge. They had a guide, for which Liam thanked God; without him in the darkness they might easily have gone blundering on into the German lines. According to directions, they were to take up a position at the south-western corner of the village, relieving two sections of the 1st Brigade who were both undermanned and exhausted. They found the men they were to relieve in a shallow, crumbling trench, but of a village there was no sign.

They dug in as best they could, filling sandbags to support the gun. With the sunrise they were able to distinguish bricks and rubble, the low remains of walls which roughly marked the line of the Roman road; in places where there should have been trees, were uprooted stumps and splintered branches. The farmhouse on the corner which had been fortified by the Germans appeared as no more than another hump on a plateau piled with rubble. In its cellars were the headquarters of the 7th and 8th Battalions.

It was quiet for some time. Unnaturally so, without even the sporadic bursts of gunfire which marked dawn and dusk. In the silence, the sound of birdsong carried clearly from woods behind the lines; a lark, unconscious of the tragedy below, went trilling up, up, up into the blue, praising the sun and its own ecstatic freedom. In their holes in the ground, the men sipped water and chewed on hard biscuits. Matt, the team's Number Two, had managed to procure a section of hard, dark-brown sausage which he pared into slices and handed round. Spicy but satisfying, Liam thought. He had barely swallowed when with a sudden, head-splitting, synchronized crash the German bombardment began.

The new front line dug by the Australians in the past couple of nights had been located by artillery far to the east. On the stroke of seven those heavy guns exploded into action, firing salvo after salvo, rending the air with hurricane force, sucking up dust, lashing down grit, throwing out chunks of chalk and brick. The men were buffeted by the concussion, it pulled air from their lungs, squeezed chests and ears and noses; it made their hearts pound to the point of bursting.

Overhead, shells screamed and shrapnel exploded like deadly rain; below, the earth groaned and shifted in protest.

It went on, with barely a cessation, for more than sixteen hours.

The Vickers, which had been set up against the parapet, was soon covered in rubble. Expecting an attack as soon as the bombardment lifted, Liam struggled to clear it. As he did so a shell landed not a dozen yards away, lifting two men like rag dolls and dropping them back, dead. A moment later another landed just short of the parapet, caving it in, burying several infantrymen close by. The team rushed to dig them out, scrabbling in the dirt with bare hands; four were alive, shaking and jibbering like idiots, but the fifth was dead, concussed or suffocated, none could tell. Then young Vic caught a blast, knocked flat in the trench by a hundredweight of rubble. Seeing it happen, Liam dived straight for the boy's head, digging like a dog until he had cleared a passage of air, scooped dirt from his mouth. Alive and crying, choking on earth and grit, he was hauled free and Liam held him fiercely, rocking with the shocks, thumping his back while the boy coughed and sobbed and wept for his mother. With shoulders pressed to what remained of the parapet, and the team forming a protective arc around them, the two men clung together, and then that concentrated storm of death began to pass away to their left.

For a while Vic moaned with shock, burying his face against Liam's neck. As realization dawned, there came the rising wail of hysteria, the desperate need to get away.

Clamping his arms, Liam held the boy and shook him. 'You're all right! There's nothing wrong with you, Vic – you're *alive!*'

Twitching and shuddering, the boy still struggled. Liam slapped his face, hard, and jammed a steel helmet onto his head. 'It's moving – the barrage is moving – the shells are dropping somewhere else!'

Livid marks stood out against the bloodless cheek; the eyes were terrified, but registered Liam's presence, the presence of authority. Before he could slip back into panic, Liam said harshly: 'Pull yourself together, Number Six, and dig that bloody gun out. As soon as this lot lifts, we're going to need it! Now move yourself!'

They all jumped to it, entrenching tools clearing the dirt, experienced hands examining the barrel and mechanism for signs of damage. The boy, white-faced, still trembling, did what was required of him while Liam surveyed their position, tried to assess what was happening. Men were still alive, digging out caved-in sections of the trench, giving first aid to the wounded and taking advantage of the lull just here to send messages back to base. He caught sight of Keenan, with another section facing the road, and had the satisfaction of watching him disappear as another salvo lifted clouds of dust behind him. With any luck, Liam thought, he too would know the terror of being buried alive. Moments later, however, his head was bobbing about again. Liam took a sip of water, swilled it round his gritty mouth, and spat.

Within minutes they had the Vickers stripped and cleaned, the tender mechanism oiled and a fresh belt of ammunition locked into place. Liam aimed at a tree root two hundred yards away and fired off a few rounds; it was working perfectly. Moving further down the trench they consolidated their position just as a fresh wave of heavy shells crept closer from the right. Supposed to stay apart during a bombardment, they all drew inexorably together, hanging on against the dreadful buffeting, needing the comfort of physical contact while the earth rocked and thudded beneath them. The noise was horrific. The boy who had been buried edged up to Liam and held his arm, his grip tightening convulsively with every ear-splitting explosion. Needing a hold on sanity himself, Liam started counting, totalling fifteen to twenty heavy 5.9s every minute.

Those concentrated bursts at the south-western end of the village continued all day. The entrance to 'Gibraltar', the fortified cellar on the corner, was blown in, and across the road the 6th Battalion's headquarters in a log hut was buried several times before taking a direct hit. Officers were killed and wounded, runners and stretcher-bearers travelling the sunken road ran races with death; the infantry in the line crawled out of it and took shelter in shell-holes.

As darkness fell, the German bombardment ceased. The ground was pulverized, the trenches dug so painstakingly had ceased to exist; a thick fog of dust swirled constantly, obscuring everything.

Concussed and beaten, they waited for the attack. Waited to die.

Afterwards, it seemed a miracle. Had the attack come that evening, it could not have been repulsed. But it did not come. All the

Australian positions held, and with the cessation of the barrage sometime after eleven that night, the 1st Division slowly gave way to the 2nd coming up from the valley.

Hardly able to believe they were still alive, hardly able to stand, the machine-gunners were relieved just before two o'clock in the morning of 27th July. Another bombardment was going on, this time by the British artillery, but the noise and reverberations were just the same. It took a couple of hours to reach their old billet near the crater of La Boisselle. Two staggering hours weighed down by gun-barrels, tripods and equipment, on limbs that felt like jelly. On the point of collapse, longing for sleep, Liam could not believe what he saw. A row of massive sixty-pounder guns had been moved up from the wood, and their trench was just beneath them.

'Can't we go somewhere else?' he demanded of Keenan.

'There is nowhere else, sonny. All the billets are taken. Put up with it.'

In the end the team collapsed into dug-outs just yards from those guns. The constant flash and crash and thudding recoil continued all night. Haggard, deaf to normal sounds, they emerged at first light to find the warm metal monstrosity of the battalion kitchen. Taking pity, one of the cooks brewed tea. Cupping cold, shaking hands around his enamel mug, Liam felt like the walking dead, his heart beating erratically, limbs so heavy he could scarcely move. Inside his skull the noise was still trapped; he wondered whether it would ever go away.

Nobody spoke. When he could raise enough interest, Liam looked at the faces around him, all grey, all filthy; all, like himself, unutterably weary. No jubilation this morning.

The tea was hot and sweet with condensed milk; after three mugs and several cigarettes, he began to feel a slight improvement, enough to respond to the smell of food. After twenty-eight hours of nothing but water and hard biscuits, he was suddenly ravenous. There was cold boiled meat and hot new potatoes, with bread and jam to finish. Breakfast at the Ritz, he felt, could not have been better.

TWENTY-ONE

After breakfast they moved down to Bécourt Wood at the mouth of the valley. From his issue of water, Liam drank long and deep, and then he washed as best he could before spreading out his greatcoat in the shelter of a grassy mound. He slept then, dead to the world and all its noise, for most of the day. As the sun was beginning to set in the peaceful west, the survivors of the 1st Division moved back to that field just outside Albert.

Most of them went down to the river to wash and swim. Stripping off, plunging in, relishing the cold shock, Liam ducked down into the cloudy depths, needing to rid himself of the filth of battle. Afterwards he swam lazy strokes and floated, staring up at the pink-streaked sky, letting the water block his ears to noise. But it felt strange to be out in the open again, not to be grubbing for cover in some pathetic hole in the ground.

Despite the warmth of the evening, when it came time to settle down, he found it difficult to sleep. When he did, his dreams were disturbing, too well-connected to the thunder on the hill. Waking just after dawn he was glad to rise and move about. His insides still felt mangled, but he was glad to see that the violent tremors of the day before had abated. Forgoing breakfast, he sought out Keenan for permission to go into town. The sergeant looked sick, still too bemused by that pounding at Pozières to have the wit to question him closely. With an admonition to be back before noon, permission was granted. Liam returned to his team only to tell them to cover for him should he be delayed.

'But what if we've moved on?' Vic asked anxiously; like a child he seemed afraid to let Liam out of his sight.

'I'll find you.'

Albert at that hour was practically deserted, ruined buildings in dusty, shadowed streets the haunt of sparrows and starlings and stalking cats. On a sunny doorstep a brindled dog lay curled, muzzle between paws, too lazy to stir as Liam passed by. The town was badly damaged, but people seemed to be carrying on their lives, much as they were further north. Had the villagers of Pozières taken refuge here or further west, he wondered; and with nothing to go back to, what would they do when the war was over?

The open, cobbled square was pocked by shell-holes, the tower of its massive basilica badly knocked-about. He stared up at it, marvelling at its size for such a small town, but finding the red and cream brickwork too garish for his taste. He longed, suddenly, for the mellowed stone of English village churches, a game of cricket on the green, the faint rustle of applause from watchers outside the village inn. He could see it in his mind's eye: the inn was called 'The George', the landlord large and jovial...

Liam smiled, mocking himself. An illusion, a memory, a dream. Was England really like that? Had it ever been so perfect, except on the surface? The church with its square tower, the medieval pub, the village green; and the local squire in his manor, tenants tipping their caps, agricultural labourers living in ever-increasing poverty. A way of life from which he had escaped, a place where common men did not own the land, but tilled it for the gentry. Even his parents, comfortably-off though they were, did not own their cottage, nor the land his mother utilised so productively. They paid rent to the man who owned it.

Reality. What was it? A place – a moment in time? This was real, this town square with its piles of rubble, its foreign-looking church, the Blessed Virgin knocked sideways, apparently throwing the Holy Child to his death...

And death was real, he could testify to that.

Was Georgina flesh and blood, he wondered; or just a product of his imagination? He dreamed so often of leave in England, of seeing her, talking to her honestly with every barrier swept away. What would he do, though, if that opportunity was ever granted? He would have to remember, every waking moment, that he was her brother, not her lover. That thought seemed most daunting of all. Perhaps it was better that she remained the stuff of dreams.

And Robin, flesh of his flesh, blood of his blood; he was here, somewhere in this small corner of France. He had to find him, dead or alive; he had to know, feel his reality, before he too became no more than a dream, a memory, an illusion.

Liam went into the church, trying to pray his English Protestant prayers amongst gilded frescoes and damaged plaster saints, but he was uneasy and not at all sure that the Almighty had ears left to listen. With all that noise at Pozières, all those men calling out from either side for Him to save them, God was probably weary or deaf or in retreat. While the Devil was rejoicing.

Stepping over the rubble, Liam came upon an undamaged statue of St Anthony. He paused, clutching at a straw of memory, almost sure that someone – a Catholic boy he had been friendly with, years ago – had once told him that St Anthony was the patron saint of missing things. Of course it might have been another saint entirely, but Liam felt it was worth a try. With a smile that was only slightly cynical, he took a candle, lit it, and set it in the sconce before the saint.

'Please,' he whispered, 'help me find my brother.'

Leaving an offering in the poor box, he went out into the sunlight. People were crossing the square, an old lady in black approaching the church for her morning devotions. Shopkeepers were taking down shutters, and outside a small *estaminet*, the elderly *patron* was setting out tables and chairs. Liam strolled across and sat down, ordering coffee and rolls.

'*Avez-vous du fromage? Un peu, s'il vous plâit.*'

The cheese was strong, goats' milk, he guessed, but the bread was deliciously fresh and the coffee excellent. The luxury of the meal, as much as its sustenance, put new heart into him. Lighting a cigarette afterwards, Liam felt better than he had for some time, almost relaxed, almost at peace. The *patron*, charmed by his attempt at the language, fussed a little, bringing fresh coffee, offering extravagant compliments as to the Australians' exploits over the past few days. Slightly embarrassed, knowing that he personally had done nothing to further the battle's progress, Liam was glad that the arrival of other soldiers demanded attention. They nodded to him and Liam peered at their regimental insignia, his heart twisting a little as he identified the arc of letters at the shoulder, KOYLI – the King's Own

Yorkshire Light Infantry – which had always done much of its recruiting in York.

They were young and fresh, their uniforms too clean to have seen much action, if any; and they had about them the excitement of youth. Beside them Liam felt old and weary and indescribably soiled. Their eyes were on him, noting the shoulder badge of crossed machine-gun barrels, his loose and comfortable Australian tunic with sensible bone buttons, the non-regulation leather gaiters he wore. He was big and blond and tanned; he looked so absolutely a son of the outback that it amused Liam to stress the flatness of his vowels in situations like this. With Australians, he could sound quite like them; but he could also revert to the accents of his childhood. He thought he would surprise these youngsters.

Deliberately knocking the aitches off, he said: "'Ave you seen any Green 'Owards about lately? I'm lookin' for me brother.'

One started to answer before it dawned; then he laughed and said: 'You're a Yorkie! Whereabouts do you hail from, then?'

Evasively, Liam gave a street name not far from his home.

'Oh, me auntie lives down there. Mrs Dane, do you know her? Big woman, all mouth – everybody knows *her*!'

Liam laughed, shaking his head. 'No, sorry – it's years since I was last home.' But it was so typically York, more an overgrown village than a city, full of people whose relatives never moved. It brought a hard lump to his throat. He smiled and listened while the boys chattered on about people and places he might know. Eventually they got back to his question: yes, they had seen reinforcements on the way down from Doullens; in fact they had travelled more or less together, overtaking each other through the villages between there and Amiens. If he hung about, they said, he was bound to see them coming through the square.

Glancing at the sun, Liam said he had not much time to spare; thanking them for their information, he set out to look for those other reinforcements. They would know where they were heading, know where the main body of the regiment was camped.

He crossed the square towards the Amiens road, intending to walk out in that direction in hopes of meeting them coming through; but within a few hundred yards he spotted the Green Howards' badge on a group of three NCOs. Obvious veterans, these, with hardened eyes and uniforms that had seen better days, despite the brilliant brassware glinting in the sun.

He stopped, asked where they were camped, and did any of them know of a lad by the name of Elliott? He gave Robin's company, but they shook their heads.

'I'm his brother,' Liam said, 'and I haven't much time. We're moving out today – I don't know where – and I need to find him. If he's still alive,' he added wearily.

'Aye, well, "B" Company lost a lot of lads,' one said flatly. 'But I tell thee what, I'll come back with thee, show thee the way, like. If he's alive, we'll find him, lad, never fear.'

The old sergeant was from Rotherham, a miner whose wealth of blue scars told of years below ground and innumerable pit accidents. He looked hard, but his kindness was palpable. He had lost his eldest son, a regular soldier, at Mons.

'Didn't want him to go down the pit, see? Shoved him in the army – peacetime it was a good life. Bloody daft, eh?'

'But you joined up.'

'Aye, well, felt I had to, somehow. Felt I owed it to my lad.'

Liam sighed.

It was perhaps just over a mile to the camp. The sergeant enquired at Headquarters for the company's location, and asked whether Liam's brother was still listed. His leathery old face was wreathed with smiles as he came out.

'He's all right, lad – fit as a fiddle, and should by rights be with the rest of 'em.'

They went down together, past a forest of bell tents and canvas huts, to where 'B' Company was camped. Liam's heart seemed to be performing somersaults, his eyes scouring every tall and slender figure, every man with crisp dark hair. In the end Robin saw him first.

Poised in braces and shirtsleeves, he stared with open-mouthed astonishment across a mess of kitchen fatigues.

Meeting his brother's eyes, that familiar open smile, Liam felt his own mouth curving, laughter swelling his chest as Robin bounded towards him, swinging them both in a joyful embrace.

Liam hugged him, lifted him off the ground, spun him round; and, as he set him down again, met the broad, delighted grin of the old sergeant.

'Nice to 'ave an 'and in some good news, for a change,' he said, turning away before Liam could thank him properly. He shouted his thanks to the retreating figure, and had the satisfaction of a wave. Then he turned to Robin and hugged him again.

'Why haven't you written home? They're worried sick about you!'

'I have written – last week and again, yesterday.'

'Why didn't you write immediately – as soon as you came out of the line?'

Robin's eyes looked hurt, shifted suddenly away. 'I – I couldn't.'

'Why ever not?'

'Because,' he admitted, shamefaced, 'I *couldn't*. Didn't stop shaking for nearly a week.'

Liam winced. 'Oh, dear God,' he breathed, ashamed of his own lack of tact. 'I'm sorry.'

'Oh, I'm all right now,' he declared, laughing. 'And all the better for seeing you. What shall we do? Go into town? Come on,' he said eagerly, 'I'll just clear it with the Sarge, and we'll go and paint the town red!'

As Robin returned, pulling his tunic into shape, fastening buttons that gleamed with parade-ground brightness and straightening his cap, Liam was amazed at the change in him. Even in his old, battle-scarred uniform he looked every inch the soldier, his bearing so upright he might have been a young officer in disguise. He had grown at least an inch, Liam guessed, and put on muscle, although his face was thinner, with the shadow of a dark beard along his jaw and upper lip.

'And you're a fine one to talk about writing,' Robin said as they cleared the camp. 'Almost a year, it was, before we heard from you. We were all convinced you were dead.'

'Do we have to go into that?'

'No.' He grinned, suddenly the boy again. 'How strange, you turning up today. You won't believe this, but we didn't come back down here till Saturday, and we've only been in this place for a couple of days. I heard your lot were up at Poz when we arrived, and I've been looking for you ever since. Into town, morning and evening, hoping you might be passing through – but today I got stuck on fatigues.'

'We came out of the line yesterday, but we're moving on this afternoon. I haven't got long.'

'Were you in it? That lot at Poz?'

Liam nodded. 'Twenty-four hours, that's all. The battalions were in for four days.'

'We were watching it.' A muscle twitched in his face. 'I kept thinking about you. All the time.'

'I was thinking about you, too.'

They walked on in silence, very close, arms touching, needing the reassurance of physical contact.

'We heard about that first day,' Liam said at last. 'Sounded like a bloody shambles.'

With a sharp bark of laughter, Robin agreed. 'It was. And we walked straight into it.' For a moment he was silent, and when he spoke again, his voice was breaking with emotion. 'The bloody sun was well up by the time the barrage stopped. We thought, this is it… couldn't understand why they held us back for another half-hour.' He sniffed, fumbling in his pocket for cigarettes. 'And when we did go,' he added, lighting up, 'they were just waiting for us… that bloody barrage hadn't changed a thing…'

'Deep dug-outs,' Liam murmured, picturing the crater at La Boisselle.

'I know. Can't believe I'm still here…'

At that, Liam put his arm round his brother, gripping his shoulder, not caring if they were seen. He knew what Robin had been through, had been through similar himself. But neither of them wanted to talk about it. After three years apart, it seemed strange that there should be so little else to say. Or rather there was too much; and being so conscious of each other, it was hard to say anything at all.

They made for the *estaminet* in the square, the *patron*, delighted by their reunion, insisting on two beers on the house. It was nothing like English beer, but it was cool and thirst-quenching, and after two or three apiece, their tongues were loosened, the barriers down. They talked about home, about Tisha and her marriage; and in a general way about Edward and their mother. Liam wanted to know if Edward was ill, but beyond recalling a certain frailty last Christmas when he had been home, Robin knew nothing more than his brother.

'I just thought he seemed very tired,' he said. 'And worried about the business and the war. Same as everybody else, I thought. I didn't think he was ill.'

'Well, he may not be. Perhaps they just told Tisha that, as a sort of face-saver, so they didn't have to go to the wedding.'

'You could be right. Mother always did hate dressing up, having to put on a company face.' After a pause, he said: 'Did you know the Colonel gave Tisha away?'

Liam felt his face muscles tighten. 'She said so in the letter.' Under scrutiny he looked away, narrowing his eyes as he appeared to study the hanging Virgin across the square.

'You haven't got over it, have you?'

There was no need to elaborate; they both knew what he was talking about. With a shrug, Liam affected nonchalance. 'Not entirely, but it's not something I want to discuss.'

'I wish you would.'

Briefly, Liam looked back at his brother and smiled. 'All right, we will – one day. But not now. Don't let's spoil this time we have.'

'There may not be another chance,' Robin reminded him, sombrely. 'Does that never occur to you? That each day might be your last?'

It did, but those sentiments, coming from his younger brother, caught Liam by surprise. Looking at him, really studying him, he could see how deeply the war had marked Robin. The joy of their meeting had covered it, given him the gloss of boyishness, but he was a boy no longer. He had seen too much of death, felt its brush too closely and on too many occasions. Liam thought how frequently he must have been under fire, and how much, very recently, he had taken of bombardments like the one at Pozières. Robin had seen too much, experienced too much, and it had taken his boyhood away.

The lines of his face, that bruised look about the eyes, were so common these days they generally went unnoticed; and because they were all of them in it up to their necks, with no escape, it was no longer worth discussing. Gallows humour prevailed instead. It was the only way to survive.

So he was unprepared for this seriousness. He felt exposed and horribly naked, and for a moment could have broken down, just like young Vic. But the moment passed. Blinking rapidly, he looked away.

'Yes,' he said softly, 'it occurs to me all the time.'

'Then why don't you do something about it?'

'Like what, for heaven's sake? Dash home right now and tell them all is forgiven? That I'm sorry I rushed off like that and I won't do it again?' In the ensuing silence he fumbled for cigarettes and lit one, his fingers trembling over the match. 'I do write, you know. I have, regularly, ever since that first letter I sent to you.'

'But have you really made things up with Mother? That's what I'm talking about. You can write nice, cheery letters till the cows come home – or until this bloody war's over! – but until you say the words she wants to hear, she'll never rest. It's destroying her. Do you want that on your conscience?'

'Oh, for Christ's sake, Robin! What words? What?'

His arm was gripped with painful urgency. 'She wants to know that you understand – that you forgive her.'

Liam looked at his brother's hand, then up into his face. He could have struck him. 'But I *don't* understand,' he declared in an undertone. 'I never have and I doubt if I ever will. Now leave it alone, Robin, and get your hand off my bloody arm!'

Moving back, Robin sank the rest of his beer in one swallow, found his own cigarettes and lit up. His hands were not quite steady. He ordered two more beers with a calm pleasantry for the *patron*, but there was tension in every muscle. With sweat standing out on him and heart racing, Liam felt as though he had just been under fire. He was distressed, too; arguing with the only person he could love unreservedly, the one he had longed so desperately to see. On the point of apology, he heard the words from his brother.

'No.' Liam shook his head. 'I'm the one who's sorry. I'm sorry for this – I didn't want to talk about it because I knew what it would come to. And I'm more grieved than you can ever understand about the whole bloody sorry situation. Really I am.

I do know what you're trying to say to me. I've thought about it so many times, don't think I haven't. But I can't resolve it.' He sighed, shook his head. 'It's impossible.'

'But *why*? What is it you don't understand? I mean it happened – years ago – why can't you just accept it? What difference does it make? Especially *now*, with all this...' His gesture encompassed the shell-pocked square, the whole of the war. 'How can it be important, in the face of all this?'

Liam turned away, afraid to show his pain, afraid that somehow, with that uncanny intuition of his, Robin would see and understand what it was that still gripped him. That he could not think of the man who was his father without loathing, nor the woman who was his sister, without desire.

Eventually, to deflect the subject, he said sardonically: 'And our *father* – how is he? Where is *he* in all this? I don't see him in a sweat-stained, lousy uniform, do you? Where was he when we were sitting in our holes in the ground, going daft with the noise? He didn't sweat and tremble and cry, expecting death by the second! And when you stormed the trenches at Fricourt, and saw all your mates mown down like grass, where was he?

'I tell you where he was,' Liam added, stabbing the table with a finger that was scabbed and torn, 'he was sitting in a comfortable office in Whitehall, or reading papers in his flat, or taking the boat-train to Dublin. *That's* where he was. Not here. Oh, no – not here.'

'You're very bitter.'

'He's a professional soldier, for God's sake! A fucking staff officer! He got medals for being so bloody clever in South Africa and the Sudan – he's an old mate of Haig's, did you know that? Oh, don't look so surprised,' he added quickly, covering up for the source of that information, 'I looked him up a long time ago.'

'I don't think *mate* quite fits his relationship with Haig,' Robin said stiffly. 'He knew him, but they never got on. In fact I got the impression that he disliked him intensely.'

'Oh, you did, did you? And when was that?'

'Last Christmas, when I was coming back from leave. He met me at King's Cross with Georgina.'

Her name was like an arrow to the heart. Unable to trust his voice, Liam simply shook his head.

'I wish you could understand how deeply he cares, how bitter he is at being kept in Ireland. It's not his doing, you know.'

'Isn't it?'

'No, it damn well isn't! I know you dislike him, but I wish you wouldn't despise him so. He doesn't deserve that. For all his faults he's very straight, and says what he thinks. Which is why he'll retire as a colonel, while Haig will probably end up with a bloody sainthood!'

'He's drawn you to his side, I see that.'

'It's not a question of *sides*. I like the man, I admit it. I always have.' He softened suddenly. 'It's strange, but I remember him so well from when I was little. You don't, I know, although I can't imagine why. In fact one of my earliest memories is of sitting on his knee and eating humbugs. And then we had a game, and he let me slide down his legs – and I swallowed the humbug whole!' Robin laughed at the memory. 'I suppose I must have been about two or three.'

'And you've been swallowing humbugs ever since,' his brother remarked acidly.

'Oh, thanks! And what have you been doing that's so much better? Running away from things, burying your head in the sand, just like you always did! You can hurt other people, but nobody must hurt you. Is that it? Tisha always said you were spoiled – I'm beginning to think she was right.'

Liam winced at that.

'You're my brother and I care about you. I'm taking nobody's side against you. But just because you're the eldest doesn't mean to say you're always right. In this case, I think I am. You can't change what happened, Liam, but you can change the way things are now.' He paused and leaned across the table. 'It would do Mother and Dad so much good. Get some leave, if you can. Go home and see them. Please, Liam.'

How the old name affected him! It touched so many chords, brought forth a softness in him that could well have dissolved in tears. Was he really so selfish? Was that how it seemed to others? Had his behaviour been interpreted as that of a spoiled, wilful child? Surely not. His name, the thought of home, the memory of his mother placidly gardening, lovingly ruffling his hair, all flooded his mind and weakened that stony resolve. He wished with all his heart that he could go back, that the past with all its tragic mistakes could be wiped out; that truth could have come gently. Perhaps, if he went home, he might see things differently; perhaps the pain would ease...

Briefly, he gripped his brother's hand. 'All right, all right. If it will satisfy you, I'll go home. If I get the leave I've applied for, I'll go.'

There was joy in Robin's eyes and a sudden warm hand-clasp which said everything was all right again between them; what had been said was harsh, but they were brothers and it did not matter. It did, because Robin's words, despite their sting, had given Liam something to ponder over. But that extracted promise left him feeling curiously relieved.

The atmosphere lightened, became rather silly. They ordered more beers and something to eat. More than a little drunk, with the hour of noon well past, they decided to have their photographs taken.

'Looking like this?' Liam demanded. 'I haven't even got a bloody hat – only this tin thing.'

'We'll borrow one. Look – there's some of your mob killing time – go and ask.'

Concerned that he should be on his way back to camp, Liam was reluctant to draw undue attention; but he knew why Robin wanted photographs, knew why he wanted them himself. They were a kind of proof, something of this day to hold on to. Otherwise it would slip away, become dreamlike, unreal.

He borrowed a hat and stood the soldier a beer at the *estaminet*. Half an hour later, with Robin promising to collect the photographs and send one on to him, they were walking back towards Liam's camp, when, rounding a corner, they spotted the whole contingent coming towards them. With a sharp about-face, Liam dragged his brother back to the square, into the shelter of a recessed doorway. There was no time for more than a hurried farewell.

As his company appeared, he slipped out to march alongside them; somebody moved over and he was roughly in place, two rows behind Keenan. Looking back to wave, he saw Robin sprint forward, grinning from ear to ear as he kept pace alongside. His eyes were sparkling – with laughter or tears, Liam could not be sure – but for a moment he looked so much the mischievous boy, that Liam was disoriented, wondering what on earth they were doing here.

They passed the church, but Liam's view was blurred; he put out a hand to wave his brother away and felt it grasped in an iron grip. Then Robin released him, said good luck, and fell back.

At the corner, turning his head, Liam saw him shadowed against the sunlight, tall and dark and straight, raising his cap in a final wave.

Twenty-two

The photograph took just over a month to reach him. Holding it, Liam had the sense of a moment captured, preserved forever in time; a moment which seemed to have been amusing, although he could not imagine now what they had found to laugh about. Still, he was glad to have it; glad, too, to have Robin's letter, despite its age. Was he still alive? He supposed so, he still had news of him from York, but it was one of the frustrations of war that letters took so long to cross a battlefield.

Aware that he should write to him, Liam shied from the task. Feeling as he did, he was in no fit state to communicate with anyone.

Instead, he turned to his diary. '*Poperinghe. Tomorrow, or the next day, Ypres. A sea of mud, probably, after a week or more of storms and torrential rain. Flooded out yesterday from the camp outside town, and today we are billeted in an old warehouse. Not much better, the roof leaks. Spent afternoon cleaning gun and filling belts. Had the usual silly orders read out, about smartness and saluting. As if it mattered.*'

He sighed and tucked the diary back into his breast pocket, found his cigarettes and went to the huge warehouse doorway to smoke. The rain was passing, a pale evening sun making high drama of thunderclouds in the east. Across the canal everything was sparkling, so green after the dearth of Pozières, so untouched. And so quiet; although that was probably deafness. He felt as though his ears were permanently stuffed with wool, and it had been growing worse with every bombardment.

Swallows were swooping low over the water, and on a sudden stirring of the air Liam caught the invigorating smell of rainwashed fields. He felt his nostrils flare as he followed it, dragging deep breaths into his lungs, filling his chest with clean, ionised air. He had forgotten its intoxication, had imagined he was filled forever with the sour-sweet smell of death and the acrid reek of chemical explosives. Even now, with the freshly-washed streets of the little town before him, soldiers and black-clad women passing back and forth, Liam still had a vision of hell imprinted at the forefront of his mind. It was a wasteland of shifting grit and ashes, a place so thoroughly obliterated that no sign of human habitation remained.

Only the dead remained, only those rotting carcases of men. Their mangled bits of arms and legs, sometimes attached to a piece of khaki, sometimes tangled in strips of barbed wire, were thrown up with horrifying regularity, to remind those who were still alive of those who had gone before. There were moments when he thought that no one could convey the moonlit horror of those journeys across the ridge, when the sudden explosion of flare or shell would send men flat, to come face to face in the dirt with gnarled, disembodied hands, or the blackened eyes of a rotting skull. Who would willingly describe the days of sweltering sun, lying in shell-holes which were alive with fat, buzzing flies and the sickening miasma of corruption. Or the rain, which turned everything to greasy, slithering, stinking mud.

In the four days that it took to take and hold Pozières, and in the ten days which had just passed, the 1st Division had lost almost 8,000 men. Between times, the 2nd and 4th Divisions had held the village and pressed northwards a further thousand yards to the stronghold of Mouquet Farm. Eastwards, they had taken the position at the windmill beyond the village, and pushed the Germans back a few hundred yards along the Bapaume Road. But each attack had been on such a narrow front, like driving a wedge into a hardwood log, each blow less effective as the wood became harder, more dense with resistance.

Knowing what was coming, knowing too well the aim of those blows – which were to cut off the Thiepval ridge – the German commanders had thrust all their reserves into that same small area. As for the British Commander-in-Chief, Sir Douglas Haig, he let the Australians get on with it. There was some assistance at Pozières, most notably, in Liam's experience, from the Black Watch, who had managed to earn his wholehearted admiration. The British artillery, alongside their Australian cousins, had kept those guns going night and day. But elsewhere on the front line the attacks were no more than skirmishes. Haig's troops had taken a terrible battering in those first two weeks of July, and instead of flinging everything in, all along the line, he had held them back for rest and recuperation. Now, with each passing day, he was losing the chance to follow up that hard-won victory on the hill.

In bitterness they had all discussed it, all the amateur strategists repeating what this or that officer had said or been overheard to say. Liam agreed they were right to feel badly let-down. The costs were incalculable. But after being with his brother he had a fair idea of how badly beaten the British troops had been. And yet, had those good, brave men not been so utterly wasted on 1st July – if that initial attack had been at dawn, instead of in broad daylight, surely surprise would have been on their side!

But as Robin said, at half-past seven, attacking into dazzling sunlight, long after the barrage stopped, they had not stood a chance.

And who was to blame for that?

The waste of it ate into his soul. And still it went on. The Australian divisions were still hammering at Mouquet Farm, trying to push through, trying to cut off the Germans at Thiepval. It was a lost cause, they had all been through it twice, and nobody wanted to go back again. Not there.

Heartsick, despairing, Liam could not summon so much as a sense of relief at being out of it. After five days travelling on foot and by train from Pozières, they were relegated to rest and recuperation at Ypres, to take over from the Canadians, who were slowly moving down to the Somme. *Rest and recuperation at Ypres!* The Canadians he'd met had laughed at that. To be sure there was no big push to contend with, but it was hardly a place in which to sit and lick wounds.

In one explosion out of the millions that had churned the earth at Pozières, Liam had lost Jack, his Number Three. That big, cheerful, reliable man had fallen beneath a direct hit which Liam could still see in horrifying detail. There had been nothing left to bury, or rather, too many bloody pieces, and no chance, under that bombardment, to do the decent thing. That side of war, the impossibility of burial, of necessary prayers and time for grieving, could still hurt him; all the friends lost, and on no more than an indrawn breath, the business of war went on.

Young Vic, the railway clerk from Melbourne, had finally succumbed to horror and had to be sent out of the line, his reason gone completely. Liam prayed it was only temporary, but did not expect to see him back. One burly sergeant had gone quite mad with the noise, attacking everyone in sight; it took four men to restrain and disarm him. Keenan, however, had survived, like the bad penny he was; twitching visibly by the end of it, but then they all were.

One night, after a relief of twenty-four hours, the team had carried up, between them, 32,000 rounds of ammunition. It was all used up by morning. A bad night that, Liam remembered, in which the 2nd Brigade had attacked after a heavy bombardment, but by some mistake got into their own artillery barrage, losing many men. It was a bitter tragedy, but understandable in that shifting sea of dirt, where there were no landmarks to establish, even from the air, the correct position of the line.

On a very trivial scale, that same night he had been struck on the heel by a flying shell-splinter, which had sliced the heavy leather of his boot but missed his foot. Looking back, he was unsure whether to be happy or sad about that; like his old mate Smithy at Messines, he felt it might have sent him home.

Home. Strange word. Did he know where it was, could he identify it? When his mates said home, they meant Australia, but Australia had become, for him, no more than a distant dream. When he thought of it, which was less and less often since he had come to France, he could hardly believe that he had spent eight months there. It seemed so brief, a moment from another lifetime; while York, which he had left so bitterly, loomed large on the edge of his awareness. Recalling his conversation with Robin, the extracted promise seemed no more than academic. Convinced he must die at Pozières, Liam found it hard to come to terms with his survival. He had no faith in the future, no belief in anything but death.

The guns were booming at Ypres. Was one destined to bring death to him? If so, he hoped it would be soon, direct and instantaneous oblivion, not the drawn-out agony of disembowelment, or wounds that turned gangrenous, or the burning, blinding, retching end of poison gas.

With no particular aim he ambled wearily towards the centre of Poperinghe, surprised to see people strolling along pavements, taking the evening air. Leaning against a wall, lighting a cigarette, Liam heard muffled thuds and wondered if he was imagining them. Everyone else seemed quite oblivious, heads nodding in conversation, lips smiling. A sudden burst of laughter penetrated his deafness, and he could have turned and yelled at them to be quiet.

He moved on, vaguely aware that he had missed a meal; he would have liked a drink, but had no money. No pay since before Pozières. Had he been able to think where he might go to escape all this, Liam was aware that he would have gone. Just walked away. But he was beyond making decisions. He felt as empty and useless as a spent shell. There was not even enough in him to be afraid, although he had an uneasy feeling that he was unfit to carry out a corporal's duties. How he would deal with any new men coming into the team, he had no idea.

Having made a circuit of the town, Liam found himself once more in the square. He supposed he should return to the billet and try to sleep. He was certainly tired. So tired he was no longer sure of the way back. Dragging his feet across uneven cobbles, he headed for the far corner, hoping it was the right direction.

A small man in the rather shabby uniform of a British officer stopped him. Liam tensed, expecting a dressing down for his lack of a salute; but the man was smiling. He was also wearing a clerical collar.

'Excuse me, Corporal – you don't have a light, do you? I seem to have lost my matches.'

As Liam fished in his pocket, the man produced a pack of cigarettes and held it out. 'Bet you could use a smoke, couldn't you?'

Liam hesitated, not wanting to be engaged in conversation, especially by a Padre. But the man pressed him, seeming determined to have his chat, even though Liam explained that he could not hear very well. Undeterred, he accompanied Liam across the square, asking where he was billeted, and had he just come up from the Somme?

'Pozières,' Liam answered, convinced it would mean nothing.

'Ah, I see.' There followed a noticeable silence. Then the Padre turned to him and said clearly, 'Come back with me to Talbot House. It's just along here. Have something to eat and a cup of tea. And if you'd prefer to sit quiet for a while, you won't be disturbed.'

It took a moment for the man's words to sink in. There was such kindness in his face, such unspoken depths of understanding, Liam felt his resistance crumble. Clearing his throat of a sudden obstruction, he said, 'We haven't been paid for weeks. I haven't any money.'

'No need. We ask only what a man can afford. And if he has nothing, we ask nothing – as simple as that.'

The tall white house was on a street Liam had walked already. Seeing the open door, the sign outside, he wondered how he could have missed it. In the depths of the house he thought he heard the notes of a piano, and voices raised in song, but the Padre steered him through to the garden, long and deep and still wet with rain.

Shrubs and climbing plants made silent arbours, hiding seats and benches set back from the paths. Against the wall, roses were in bloom, nodding heavy heads, shedding drops like tears from velvet petals. A soothing place, a million years, surely, from the shifting sands of Pozières. Hardly noticing that he was alone, Liam slowly lowered his numb, unfeeling body into a seat and closed his eyes. Not to sleep, just to breathe the scented air, to feel its moist sweetness against his skin and taste it on his lips. And when he opened his eyes it was to look at everything, each tiny leaf and tendril, the dazzling intensity of colour in every bloom.

It was so perfect it was almost unbearable.

A woman came with a tray of food. Potatoes and tiny green beans, and some sort of chicken stew, the whole meal a feast of delicate flavours, as perfect as the garden. He had barely finished when the Padre came out to join him, smiling, bearing two mugs of tea.

'How was that? Good? We have an excellent cook – she can make something out of nothing, believe me!'

Watching him, almost lip-reading because of his deafness, Liam found himself smiling in response. It felt strange – he hadn't smiled for a long time. 'I believe you, Padre. Thank you.'

'No need. Glad to be of service. You know,' he continued,

accepting one of Liam cigarettes, 'you haven't told me your name, or where you come from. I'd lay bets you're not Australian born. Let me see now – don't tell me – you sound as though you might be from Lincolnshire or perhaps further north. East Riding of Yorkshire?'

'You've a good ear, Padre. I'm from York.'

'Ah, a lovely city – I know it well. The Minster, the walls, the river – what a combination. Some lovely old churches too.' He mused for a moment, smiling. 'I don't expect you've been home for a long while?'

'No.'

'Have you applied for leave to England?'

'I have, but I shouldn't think I'll get it.'

'Why not?'

Liam shook his head, words beyond him.

After few moments, very gently, the other man touched his arm. 'My boy, if you'd rather I left you alone, just nod your head and I'll go. But if you'd like to talk then we'll go inside, where there's less chance of being overheard.'

He wanted to say no, he was fine. He was not fine, he knew he was touching the edge; but somehow, words were more frightening than the war. Even as he rose to his feet, with every intention of leaving, Liam found himself following the stockily-built little man. He was not old – indeed Liam would have been hard put to guess his age – but there was a quality of fatherliness in him that drew a response, a warmth difficult to resist. He entered a room on the first floor and held the door for Liam; above it, there was a sign which read: 'Abandon rank all ye who enter here.'

Despite himself, Liam smiled. The Padre chuckled. 'Yes, some people do need reminding! But sit down – make yourself comfortable. You know,' he added, settling himself into an easy leather chair, 'you still haven't told me your Christian name. I don't want your surname, rank and serial number, that doesn't matter, but I would like to know what to call you.'

'My mates call me Bill, but my family always called me Liam. It's short for William.'

'And what would you rather I called you?'

For a moment he hesitated. 'Liam, I think.'

To begin with, it was a terrible effort to speak, but the Padre kept talking, facing Liam, lifting the pitch of his voice so that he could hear. With the odd question here and there, it soon became clear that this was a man who *knew*, who understood all the terrors to which Liam had been subject, the effort it cost to stay calm under fire, the energy required to transmit that calmness to men who were on the verge of panic. He knew, too, of the terrible cost afterwards, even to men who were otherwise strong, otherwise unmarked. And he understood the despair.

He neither defended nor condemned the war; and other than a gentle reminder that the General Staff were men too, as fallible as the rest of humanity, he offered neither praise nor blame in that direction; but he did listen, and he did try to penetrate the despair.

To a certain extent he succeeded. Liam was unaccustomed to sharing burdens, and the enormity of what he felt about the war was difficult to express; but once the first words were found, the rest came tumbling out like water from a broken dam. The sense of release was curative in itself, and although the Padre commented that he wished he could do more than simply listen, Liam was acutely aware that having such a listener was as much, at that point, as he needed. The suggestion that he should report sick, however, was dismissed with a sharp laugh.

'Begging your pardon, Padre, but that's a joke! I'm no more sick than any of my mates – and if I'm sick, they're all sick, every last one of them!'

The chaplain shook his head, insisting that Liam should continue to press for leave, that he needed time away from the war, time to recover his spirit.

Liam's response to that came without thinking, and it shocked him. 'I don't want to go home.'

There was a long silence. 'Do you want to tell me why?'

He shook his head, aware of a hard lump in his chest. 'Not really.'

'Is it to do with why you left home in the first place – why you went to Australia?' At Liam's abrupt nod, he said: 'Was it a crime you committed?'

Laughter released the hard lump inside him, but it threatened to get out of hand. With an effort, Liam calmed himself and apologized. On a deep breath, he said: 'I discovered, in a very shocking manner, that my father was not who I thought he was. That is, not my mother's husband. I have a brother and a sister, and the man who fathered us was someone I thought was just a distant relative.'

For a moment, it was impossible to say more. He tried to light a cigarette, but the trembling which had begun with talk of the war, had gone beyond his control; the Padre lit two and passed one across to him. Liam smoked in a short, angry fashion, leaning forward, forearms pressed against his knees.

'It wouldn't have been so bad,' he said, 'but I'd fallen in love with his daughter. I thought we were no more than – oh, I don't know, second cousins, I suppose – it was never clear. She was older than me, and I never really thought it would come to anything, but...' He coughed, sharply, and shook his head. 'Oh, God, I was eighteen years old and I loved her...'

'Was she aware of it? Did she encourage you?'

'No. No, she knew what the relationship was – she was just fond of me, I suppose.' On a short, sardonic laugh, he added: 'Like a sister should be.'

For a while, digesting that, the other man said nothing. Then, 'What about your mother?' he asked. 'And the man you thought was your father? I presume he raised you?'

'I can't forgive her. I've tried, but I can't. Oh, I write home, I write to them regularly – and I've even promised my brother that I'll go home when I get some leave – but I dread seeing them. I dread having to see my mother again.'

'Were you very close to her? Before all this, I mean?'

Liam's voice failed at that. Eventually he nodded. 'But still I can't forgive her for what she did to me. The lies, the deceit – letting me think...' He broke off. 'I can't tell you what it was like...'

'You don't have to. I can imagine.' After a little while, the Padre said: 'And what about this sister of yours – the one you love. Are you afraid of seeing her, too?'

'Yes. But I want to see her, that's the terrible thing.' Inhaling deeply, stubbing out the remains of his cigarette, Liam sat back, aware, now that he had given voice to the core of it, of a sense of exhaustion. There was nothing to be done, just as there was nothing to be done about the war; but he felt so much lighter, the trembling had abated, and, quite suddenly, he could have slept.

After that the conversation seemed at one remove, and Liam could not recall, afterwards, what he had said. A great deal, he suspected, since he was in that quiet little study for almost two hours. He did remember the chaplain saying to him that he should press for leave, should see his mother; that only in facing her would he be able to achieve the forgiveness he was looking for. And then, perhaps, he would be able to see his sister in the proper light. The chaplain's kindness, and his sense of conviction, penetrated that haze of tiredness and stayed with Liam. He made his promises and gave his thanks; then, with a short prayer and blessing, was sent on his way.

In the doorway, however, that same doorway which insisted that before God and in this room all men were equal, Liam paused for a moment.

'Padre, why did you stop and speak to me this evening? You didn't really need a light, did you?'

The round, cheerful face beamed. 'Not really, no, but it's a way of getting into conversation. Most soldiers smoke, most will accept a cigarette even from a man of the cloth!'

'Why me, though?'

'Why not you? God hears us, even in our despair. *Especially* in our despair.'

Liam hesitated. 'And do you really hear His voice?'

The other man chuckled. 'Well I don't know about a voice – not like yours or mine, anyway. But quite often He gives me a nudge – a little prompt, if you like, to do or say something. I don't always know why, and I certainly don't think it's exclusive to me. Perhaps you've felt it yourself – that urge to do something out of the ordinary, or against what you think is your nature?'

With a regretful sigh, Liam shook his head. 'No, I can't say I have.'

It was only when he was outside and alone in the darkness that truth dawned. He had done something extraordinary; he had acted against his nature. In following the little Padre, in listening to him, and most especially in talking to him, Liam had stepped aside from his usual path…

There was trouble to pay when he got back. The remaining three members of his team were on guard duty outside the warehouse, their faces eloquent as he approached. He remembered instantly, and his heart sank; how on earth could he have forgotten that it was his section's turn to mount guard that night?

'Keenan's hopping,' Matt hissed from a corner of his mouth.

'Where is he?'

Carl jerked his head. 'In the office. What're you going to do, Corp?'

'Get it over with, I suppose.'

Squaring his shoulders, Liam marched inside. At a temporary desk inside the old foreman's cubbyhole, Sergeant Keenan was going through some papers, cigarette burning, a mug of greasy tea beside his hand. He looked up as Liam entered, gooseberry eyes narrowing dangerously.

'Oh, *Corporal* Elliott – you're back! This is a surprise – thought you'd gone for good this time.'

'Not me, Sergeant – you know me better than that. I went out for a walk – and completely forgot it was my guard tonight. I'm sorry.'

'Forgot? You *forgot*? That's no excuse! Corporals aren't paid to forget, corporals are paid to *remember*. And why? It's so they can round up all the skivers and lead-swingers and get them to the bloody church on time. Or in this case, the picket-line! Oh, your mob turned up all right, ten minutes late, half-dressed and no credit to you!'

He paused for breath, but Liam knew better than to interrupt. Better to let the flow go on, until Keenan had worked the ire from his system.

'I could have your bloody stripes for this, Elliott. It's not the first time you've wandered off, God-knows-where, and taken your bloody time about coming back. You're not here on a Cook's bloody Tour, you know – you're here to fight a bloody war, and somebody's paying you over the odds to do it!'

He strode round the desk, coming up short a foot away from Liam.

'And let me tell you this,' he declared, emphasizing each point with a jab of his finger, 'if it weren't for the fact that we're going back into the bloody line the day after tomorrow, with about half the men we should have, I'd have you up on a charge right now!'

Knowing the truth of that, Liam stiffened his jaw and stared over Keenan's head. On the wall opposite was pinned a map of the trenches in the Zillebeke sector, south-east of Ypres. Concentrating on that, he winced as the sergeant's voice rattled his ears again.

'One more little stunt like this, Elliott, and I *will* have you, good and proper, you see if I don't!' With a final jab into Liam's chest, he returned to his seat, eyes gleaming maliciously. 'Tomorrow you're on fatigues, sanitary, along with the rest of your team. I want those bloody latrines filled in like they were never there – and new ones dug at least six feet deep!'

The latrines were perhaps a hundred yards from the warehouse, in an open field. They had been dug hurriedly the day before, and were not very deep; owing to the storm and the saturated nature of the land, the pits were half-full of liquid, which overflowed as they were being filled in. The stench was unbearable, and Liam waved his men away from it, knowing that this punishment was entirely his fault, brought about by his absent-mindedness, not theirs. He had left them sleeping.

Getting the turf back was no easy matter, and beneath that deceptive greenness the filled-in pit squelched like a quagmire.

'Maybe we should get Keenan to come and take a look,' Gray suggested, leaning wearily on his spade. 'If he tries to tamp that little lot down, he'll end up in it – up to his flaming neck!'

The others laughed. Liam was less amused, anxious to get them away and cleaned up, now that the job was done.

'I wonder what he'll find for us to do this afternoon?'

'I don't give a damn what it is,' Matt declared, 'the other poor buggers are off on a bloody route march. Anything's got to be better than that!'

There was more heavy rain that afternoon, which made a joke of Matt's convictions, as the punishment detail was set to unloading heavy boxes of stores from a series of motor lorries. Within half an hour they were aching and soaked to the skin, in no better state than the rest of their company, taking foot exercise. The only consolation was that they were finished well before the others returned, clothes drying over a feeble stove in the draughty warehouse, while they sat huddled in blankets, trying to keep warm.

The chill, north-easterly wind had veered round to the west by the next morning. Warned to be ready by two o'clock, Liam had the gun stripped and cleaned first thing, and damp overcoats set out to air in the morning sun. Dinner was a nondescript stew consisting mainly of vegetables in a greyish liquid, and a small portion of matching potatoes. He forced it down, thinking of the delicious meal he had been given at the Talbot House and wondering how it was that army cooks could destroy food so thoroughly.

By mid-afternoon the battalion with its supporting company of machine-gunners was ready to move to the station at Poperinghe. A short rail journey took them to the outskirts of Ypres, to a little halt near an asylum. Hanging about, waiting for orders, Liam had plenty of time to remember the Retreat and the evening he had cycled up to meet Georgina. The last time he had seen her, spoken to her: the last hour of innocence.

Odd snatches of conversation returned to him, no longer painful but curiously poignant. He recalled giving voice to his dreams, so broad, so ambitious; and the joy of her understanding. Remembered, too, that he had said he would write a book one day when he settled down, when he had done all he wanted to do. There was irony in that when he thought how little he had managed to achieve; how, without knowing it, time had been loaded against him.

It still was. Not one man on this battlefield could look forward with any reasonable expectation to a comfortable old age; *if I get through it* was as far as it went. Forty-eight hours ago Liam had been in despair, preferring death to life; back on the side of the living, he was still weary, still unsure of himself, full of vague apprehensions which seemed to be making themselves felt in a physical way. His stomach was churning unpleasantly, and it was hard to tell whether it was simple fear or the greasy stew he had eaten earlier. In an effort to divert his mind, he kept thinking about Georgina, about what they had talked about that evening. It seemed important, suddenly, not to lose sight of those old ambitions.

Above the western horizon, rain clouds threatened, rising, gilt-edged, to swallow the sun before it set. Its disappearance was like a signal from HQ; moments later orders were given for the troops to form up and proceed.

Within the first mile the rain began, drenching haversacks and overcoats, turning already muddy roads into glutinous slime. Treachery lurked with every footfall; shell-holes gaped, full of the detritus of war, rain spattering like shrapnel-fire from the surface of every puddle. In the fading light, the bloated carcases of horses loomed hideously by the wayside, twisted bits of guns and limbers their permanent companions. Up ahead, the ruined towers of Ypres formed stark silhouettes against the flickering glow in the east. It was a place of gothic horror, a place to strike a chill even on the warmest night. With rain seeping through his greatcoat, Liam shivered, wondering what it must be like in winter. If this was the end of August, what would January bring?

By the shattered ruins of the great medieval Cloth Hall, the battalion turned right, to leave Ypres by a gap in the ramparts known as the Lille Gate. They crossed a battered bridge over an ancient moat, ran the gauntlet of shell and mortar fire at 'Shrapnel Corner', and found their way, eventually, to the Canadian trenches north of the Ypres-Comines Canal. The line, what they could see of it in occasional illuminations, was a boggy, meandering maze of duck-boards, sandbags and wire. Shallow communication trenches and battered parapets glistened with rain and mud. The dug-outs, such as they were, were in poor repair. Apart from defending this particular sector, it seemed the Division would also be making some extensive alterations.

It was past midnight when they arrived, some five miles from the little railway halt; limbers were unpacked, stores, guns and ammunition carried a further three hundred yards to the front line. With the Vickers and fourteen boxes of ammunition, Liam's team were directed to a muddy, sandbagged gun-pit, still containing all the litter of previous occupation.

Chilled to the bone, shivering despite his exertions, Liam set about clearing the mess of empty tins, cigarette packets and used cartridges. Warned not to move or light fires by day, and desperately in need of something warming now, he ordered a brew-up of tea, and from their store of rations, took a tin of Maconochie's meat and vegetables. It seemed to take an age to heat through, and his stomach felt hollow and queasy, but he thought it might improve with food. Carl and Matt shared it out, the three of them huddled in the confined space of the gun-pit, with barely enough head-room to sit up. It seemed strange, being reduced to three; with no reinforcements as yet, Gray had been sent to make up numbers in another team. It made Liam feel very vulnerable. One man to fill the belts, another feeding them into the feed-block, and himself firing the gun, three was the necessary minimum. Looking at these poor defences, and with the Canadians' warning about sniper-fire still ringing in his ears, it was not a comfortable thought on which to sleep.

With his stomach issuing painful threats after that meal of Maconochie rations, Liam offered to take the first watch, but Matt was concerned about him and said he should rest. He tried to, but the pain grew worse, sending him out to find a latrine. In the hour before dawn, he was up and down several times, crawling along the shallow trench, wondering what he would do in daylight. No-man's-land was a wired stretch of some two hundred yards – with Fritz on the other side. He could see it in his mind's eye, every bobbing head presenting a target, like wooden ducks at a fair.

After periods of short relief, in which he shivered and shook and felt as weak as a baby, the cramps intensified; he drank water and was violently sick, munched hard biscuits in an attempt to absorb the fiery liquid in his guts, and was forced by daylight to crouch just outside the dugout, using a make-shift latrine the others had dug. Even lying down he was in agony, trying not to moan as the fever gripped and chills racked his body.

Bursts of gunfire from the German trenches kept the others busy. They dared not abandon the position, nor cease to keep up a sporadic response. From time to time mortar bombs whistled across, exploding with deadly crumps up and down the line. It was a nerve-racking place in which to rest after all they had been through at Pozières, and it was no place in which to be ill. In between filling belts, Carl, the broad-shouldered, slow-talking Dane, wiped Liam's face with damp cloths, and murmured reassuringly. They would get him out at nightfall, get him to the medics, and make sure he got some treatment. He mustn't think of staying in the line, he wouldn't be letting them down, they'd find a replacement from somewhere.

But by mid-afternoon, when he was passing nothing but blood, and vomiting even on sips of water, Liam was beyond protest. He thought he was dying. Slipping in and out of delirium, he lost track of time; lucid for a while, he was aware of lying in his own filth and being unable to move. All he could do was apologize for his weakness. From his position crouched over the gun, Carl was suddenly brusque, telling him to save his breath; Matt sponged his face and tried to persuade him to drink.

As soon as it was dark, they got him to the 8th Battalion HQ, carrying him between them and bundled in greatcoats. The MO was busy dealing with a series of both major and minor injuries. Liam had to wait. Seen at last, he was diagnosed as being just another victim of dysentery, albeit an unusually virulent case. In a painfully conscious moment, Liam wondered whether the MO was right; on Gallipoli, in company with almost every other man, he had suffered from dysentery most of the time, but never like this. Never before had it attacked with such ferocious speed.

On Gallipoli he would have been given arrowroot and left to suffer; here, blessedly, he was ordered to the 2nd Field Ambulance Dressing Station. A lack of stretcher-bearers meant his friends had to carry him, staggering over duck-boards and through the mud in pitch darkness. They found the place eventually, just behind the second set of lines. About midnight, half-conscious, he was bundled into a horse ambulance. Matt and Carl pressed his hands, said goodbye and set off back to the front line; the horse ambulance trundled off on its rough journey to Ypres.

A motor ambulance conveyed him to an Australian Clearing Station, where someone had the sense to mark him *infectious* and keep him apart from the wounded. Morning brought another journey, this time as far as Poperinghe, to a Canadian Clearing Station which could offer a clean bed and a vast amount of pills.

A nurse gave him a cup of milk to drink, but that started a bout of vomiting which continued, on and off, all night. Next morning brought a doctor who paused to ponder at the foot of his bed, and that afternoon Liam was on his travels again, this time by hospital train to the base at Boulogne.

He was there for a week, seven days and nights of pills and blood tests, medicines and various liquid diets. As the cramps and vomiting lessened, Liam slipped into natural, healing sleep. He slept for hours each day, woke to be washed and fed and dosed, and slept again. In the evening of 11th September, which Liam remembered was his mother's birthday, the doctor returned to mark his card with just one word: ENGLAND.

TWENTY-THREE

People were kind. Extraordinarily kind. He kept thinking that all the way home. Home, that word again. But England was home, even if London was not. British troops were afforded the choice of hospitals in their native counties, while the Australians had but one destination, London, and for that Liam had no real regrets. Despite advice and entreaties and promises made, for the moment he felt unable to face his mother, and more desirous of Georgina than ever. She was somewhere in London, and as soon as she knew where he was, would probably come to see him. With the decision made for him, he allowed anticipation to outweigh all else.

Of his old uniform, only his hat remained. He had managed to hang on to that, while everything else had gone to an incinerator. The new uniform was fine, if a little stiff, but he was glad of the hat, it had been with him since Gallipoli. To lose that would have been like losing a friend.

It was good to feel clean again, to meet smiling faces on the dock at Portsmouth, to accept small gifts and blessings, to feel kindly hands assisting him from place to place. Although he was classified as walking wounded, he was still very weak, and standing for more than a minute or two produced debilitating waves of nausea. But hospital trains, at least in England, seemed to run to better time, and they were soon on their way to London and Waterloo.

What looked like a fleet of private cars awaited them. While the stretcher cases were transferred to another train, those who could walk were directed to the cars. A middle-aged lady in black drove Liam and two companions to the Australian hospital at Wandsworth. She chatted amicably as the car bounced over tramlines, requiring little in the way of reply. Just as well, Liam thought, because one of the men was close to passing out, and he felt horribly sick with every jolt. Had she asked what the problem was, he would have hated to embarrass her by telling the truth.

She pointed out various places of interest along the way: Lambeth Palace and, across the river, the Houses of Parliament; Vauxhall Bridge, and, further on, Clapham Junction, nerve centre of London's railways.

'The Zeppelins keep trying to bomb it,' she announced in her well-bred, penetrating voice. 'Oh, yes, we've had some fireworks in Wandsworth, you haven't had it all to yourselves over there, you know!'

The very sick man looked at Liam and managed a feeble smile; the other muttered something about it making them feel at home. Despite the fresh air whipping into his face, Liam knew that if they did not see the hospital soon, he would have to ask her to stop, his stomach was threatening to disgorge itself.

'How far to the hospital?' he managed to ask.

'Not far – we're almost there.' She indicated the broad green common ahead of them, and beyond the trees the great sooty mass of Hospital No. 3, London General, which had been set aside for Australian soldiers.

Apart from the blackened stonework, Liam thought it looked out of place with its turrets and towers. Like a grand French chateau standing in its own grounds, with the dip of a railway cutting for its moat. Through waves of nausea, he had a moment of wondering what it might have been before. As they bounced through an imposing gateway, their lady driver informed them that it used to be a school, a girls' school, the pupils now evacuated to the safety of the countryside.

In the warm, early afternoon sun, convalescents were walking the grounds in the company of nurses, friends and volunteers. Mildly curious glances were cast in their direction as they pulled up beside other cars at the main entrance. A bevy of young nurses, all bearing red crosses on their aprons, all looking like angels, were waiting to assist them inside.

'This is more like it!' someone was heard to declare, and a little ripple of laughter touched the gathered arrivals. They were ushered into a vast assembly hall, where names were taken and wards allocated; and then, at last, a ward with long rows of beds, a hot bath, clean towels and the soft blue drill of hospital uniform.

But to Liam's consternation the nurse who handed him these things insisted on staying.

'We don't want you passing out in the bath, now do we?' she declared briskly, and with that proceeded to unfasten his tunic.

'I can manage,' he protested feebly as her fingers reached his waist.

'I'm sure you can, but I haven't got all day.'

After that, he let her get on with it. At the base hospital in Boulogne, he had been given sponge baths, in bed, and the nurses there were stony-faced, far too busy to give more than perfunctory attention to basic needs. It seemed very strange to be standing naked in front of a pleasant young woman of his own age, one who helped him into the bath and stood over him while he soaped himself; stranger still to feel those firm hands scrubbing back and neck and the base of his spine. But it felt very good. Sinking back into the water, all embarrassment gone, Liam was aware of faint relief that he had not disgraced himself. Although with towels wrapped around him and her hands rubbing him dry, he was thankful that she left the intimate parts of his anatomy to himself.

Assigned to a bed at last, it was bliss to crawl into it, to feel the cool, fresh linen surrounding him and the softness of pillows beneath his head. Within minutes he was dead to the world.

He was woken for tea, and again for supper, both meals consisting of toast and a hot drink, and then he slept again, ten solid hours until six the next morning. Another nurse came to check his pulse and temperature, bringing water and a towel so that he could wash, and later, a lightly-boiled breakfast egg, with tea and more toast.

A man from further down the ward brought over a selection of books, but beyond introducing himself and a few others, did not stay to talk. Liam was grateful for that. He glanced through the books, read a little, and dozed again. The doctor came, asking the usual questions, giving the usual answers that he was in good hands and recovery was just a matter of rest and time. The problem of his deafness, however, was something that would be attended to just as soon as Liam was fit to be out of bed for a few hours. It was probably nothing more than a severe build-up of wax, the body's natural defence against noise. Reassured, for he had no pain in his ears, Liam thanked him and settled back against his pillows. The doctor, with the ward-sister in tow, moved on to the next patient.

The Sister in charge was a buxom, middle-aged Australian woman with a weatherbeaten face and a map of lines which suggested great good-humour, but enough steel, he guessed, to keep a firm hold on the motley collection of men beneath her rule. Liam tried to picture her in civilian life, and imagined her nursing at some small medical station in the outback, at a mine or logging camp, perhaps, or serving a vast area of small settlements. She was not a city woman, he was sure of that, and wondered how she coped with London.

The ward, once the doctor had gone, erupted into its usual buzz of chatter, bursts of laughter from men who had been ill and were recovering well; a medical ward, this, with none of the hush and incipient tragedy attached to surgical cases. There were perhaps thirty beds, not all of them occupied, and most of the men were up and dressed. Liam's bed was nearest the door, and he recalled from his previous spell in hospital that as he improved he would move further down. The man next to him had come in two days previously, and a couple of others across the way had arrived by the same train as Liam. All bore the same hollow, dark-eyed look, a look he had come to associate with utter exhaustion. He supposed his own face must tell the same story, and no longer wondered at that overwhelming urge to sleep.

He managed to stay awake until lunchtime, looking out of the opposite window at a hazy sky above the line of slate roofs and chimney-stacks. Down the centre of the ward an array of lacy ferns stirred in a slight breeze from the open window at his back. So peaceful, it was like heaven. To be here, away from the war and the constant presence of death, was enough to prompt an overwhelming surge of gratitude. As tears welled, he had neither the will nor the strength to check them. He told himself that he had been terribly ill, but the worst was over and now he would get better. He had all he required, and could ask for nothing more. When he felt a little stronger, he thought before slipping off into sleep, he would write and let people know where he was.

Visitors arrived that afternoon, but Liam was only dimly aware of them. Rolling over onto his side, protected by his deafness, he drifted back into dreams.

Something stirred him. Not a sound but a touch, light and cool, against his wrist. Through half-open lids he saw the outline of a nurse beside his bed, stiff white wings of a headdress, a short shoulder-cape of grey edged with scarlet, starched cuffs above a hand which held his own. Another nurse come to check pulse and temperature, he thought, closing his eyes again, wishing they would leave him alone. He drifted for a moment, expecting the brisk word, the sharp prod of a thermometer against his lips; but a minute passed and none came. The fingers against his hand tightened perceptibly, then relaxed and lifted.

He opened his eyes more fully, but the nurse had not moved away, she was still sitting there, head bent, her fingers busy with a handkerchief. She was dabbing her eyes.

Frowning, he blinked several times, trying to muster sight and sensibilities, trying to find a logical reason why a fully-fledged sister of the military nursing reserve should be sitting beside his bed, crying. The answer came to him even as she glanced up, even as he recognized the pale oval of her face and met the deep, dark blue of her eyes. Like cornflowers, he thought, noting the wet, spiky lashes; and her hair, what little he could see of it, was still the colour of summer wheat. He saw her lips curve into a hesitant smile, and he felt his own mouth responding, broadening as he whispered her name.

'Georgina?'

She nodded and he pressed her hand, not really believing it, sure the image was just a dream and that in a moment he would wake to emptiness and disappointment as had happened so often in the past. But he felt her responding pressure, heard a little sound, between a sob and a laugh, and experienced the wonder of seeing two fat tears escape her eyes and roll, unchecked, to her chin. Was she really crying for him?

She said something then which he did not catch, shook her head and dabbed again at her eyes, more forcefully this time. Although he could have watched her, contentedly, for the rest of the afternoon, he realized she was asking questions but apart from the odd word, he was at a loss.

'Come closer,' he begged, with a little tug at her hand. 'I'm very deaf.'

Concern clouded her eyes, and she edged the chair forward, leaning her elbows on the high bed. She was close enough, almost, to kiss.

'Can you hear me now?'

'Oh, yes,' he breathed, knowing that if he raised himself even a little, he could press his mouth to hers, and who would object? She would. She most certainly would. But the idea delighted him, that she should be here, close enough for him to touch, to hold, to kiss. And so soon! With a little laugh in his throat he glanced away, pressed his lips together in a smile, and looked back into those beautiful, concerned, compassionate eyes.

'How did you know?'

'Casualty list.' She glanced down, at the scars on his hands, the trimmed but badly-damaged nails. 'I got to hear about it this morning.'

There was a vague question in his mind as to how she had come by the information, in her hospital at Lewisham, but he was too enthralled by her presence to express it. 'What time is it now?'

'A quarter to four. I managed to get an early break. Usually I take a couple of hours from four till six, but I changed it.'

'And came straight here.'

She laughed, softly. 'I wanted to be sure you were all right.'

'I'm fine, just fine.' Although his hands were a mass of scars that he tried to hide, she seemed to find some fascination there, smoothing the rough and dented knuckles with her fingers. He was supremely conscious of her touch, every tiny movement sending echoes into his heart. For a while he watched her fingers, long and fine, whiter than he recalled from her days at the Retreat, but still those of a working woman. The nails were short, neatly filed to cause no pain, the skin across her knuckles slightly rough from constant washing. He wanted to touch them to his lips, which suddenly, like his throat, seemed terribly dry.

Huskily, he said: 'It's wonderful to see you,' and she smiled then, shyly, and said it was wonderful to see him, too; everyone had been so worried.

But Liam did not particularly want to know about *everyone*, just her.

'How are you? I know you've been very busy, I had your letters – '

A bright smile dismissed her own problems. 'Oh, I'm very well – really. Looking forward to a break, soon, but otherwise all right. Things have calmed down a little, I'm glad to say.'

'Not before time.'

'Mmm. But I know they've been busy, here.'

'Still are, I should think,' he murmured, and felt the tension along his jaw. 'But I'm out of it for a while, thank God. Just so pleased to be here, you've no idea.'

A smile touched the corner of her mouth. 'Oh, I think I have,' she said.

Dark, ash-grey lashes cast flickering shadows beneath her eyes as she looked away, and along her cheekbones, he noticed, was the faintest blush of colour. It seemed to deepen even as he watched, but he could not tear his eyes away: she was so beautiful, even the tiny frown lines between her brows seemed perfect to him.

That she could abandon great responsibility, just to see him; that she could care, even a little, were thoughts that swelled his heart with such love, such gratitude, it was overwhelming.

She seemed to sense it anyway. Her fingers tightened and she bowed her head, and when she looked up her smile was a little too brave, her eyes a little too bright.

She whispered his name; tears sprang to his eyes. Blinking them away, he swallowed hard to clear his throat.

'I didn't expect visitors,' he said at last, biting back the words he longed to say. That he loved her, had always loved her, and how much her presence underlined it. He had not been wrong; he had not harboured false illusions; his youthful sense of her affection for him was true. Time had changed nothing.

Time had changed nothing. The words repeated themselves, but with a different meaning. Even as he raised his hand, touching blunt fingers to the softness of her cheek, he knew that what he felt went far beyond what could be acceptable to her. She was his sister. His older sister. In the past three years, who knows what other loves and loyalties had claimed her? He knew men, knew that beauty as remarkable as hers could not have failed to attract attention, and anyone who knew her well must surely love her. Whom did she love? Was there a man somewhere, a young officer, probably, whose life she had saved? Or a doctor with whom she worked?

She held his hand to her face, then, very gently, took it away. 'Should I write to anyone?' she asked. 'Tisha, perhaps – or your mother? I'm not sure either of them know yet.'

The question brought him back to reality, setting different considerations running like hares. Like hares they scattered, leaving him empty-handed and panic-stricken.

Abruptly, he shook his head. 'I don't want anybody to know. Not just yet.'

She stroked his hand. 'That's all right, I understand. But I'm afraid that as next-of-kin, your mother will be informed soon, if she hasn't been already.'

Heart racing, he closed his eyes, imagining his mother distraught, flying to his side instantly, now that she knew where he was. 'I don't want to see her. Not yet.'

He heard Georgina sigh. 'Very well, don't worry. Would you like me to write to her anyway, putting her off for the time being? I know travelling can be difficult these days – detours, endless delays, changes in the middle of the night – she might be quite pleased not to have to rush the visit.'

'Would you do that?' In the rush of relief he was almost weeping again. 'Tell her I'll write to her myself, very soon.'

'I will. And I won't say anything to Tisha until you feel more up to seeing her. How's that?'

'That could be a long time,' he muttered in an attempt at a joke; but he was thankful. Having thought of no one but Georgina for days, he was beginning to realize that the ramifications of being in hospital in London were endless.

The sudden ringing of a bell in the corridor rattled his eardrums; wincing, he saw Georgina glance at her watch. At the far end of the ward, some visitors were standing up, pushing chairs back into place.

'I've got to go.'

'So soon?'

She smiled. 'It's the end of visiting time. I was late arriving.

Anyway,' she added, patting his hand like a nurse, 'you've had quite enough talking for one day. Time to rest.'

'That's all I do,' he protested.

'And all you should be doing,' she said firmly, but she was smiling, too. 'Don't worry, you'll soon be on the mend – soon be up and around, chasing all the nurses!'

He laughed. 'Is that part of the cure?'

'It certainly seems to be,' she admitted ruefully. 'I can usually tell when a man's feeling better, by the blushes on my girls' faces!'

Laughing again, feeling good because of it, he enquired teasingly: 'And what about you? Do they make you blush, too?'

'Oh, no! They don't try anything with me – I'm the one who cracks the whip!'

'I don't believe it.'

'It's true,' she insisted. 'I don't stand any nonsense.'

Although she was laughing too, Liam believed her. It cheered him immensely.

'I really must go, or Sister will have my head for outstaying my welcome. But I'll come again soon, if I may? Is there anything you need? Anything you'd like me to bring?'

He shook his head. 'Just yourself.'

Her lips parted, and he thought she was about to say something else. With sudden warmth she pressed his hand and bent, quickly, to kiss his cheek. Brief, light, the touch of her lips was hardly there; but once she had gone he pressed his fingers to the place and then, lingeringly, against his mouth.

Coming off duty later that night, still basking in the afterglow of that reunion with Liam, Georgina had to force herself into professional briskness before telephoning her father. It would not be wise, she thought, to reveal the depth of happiness and relief occasioned by that visit.

Robert Duncannon's first concern, as it had been that morning, was for his son, and his sigh of gratitude, followed by a lengthy silence, was eloquent indeed. Giving him a factual report on Liam's condition, Georgina could not hold back her sense of satisfaction.

'He's still very ill – I looked at his notes. But I must say he looks better than I expected. And remarkably cheerful.'

'How long before he's well again?'

The question jarred, driving her thoughts ahead to where they did not want to go. 'Before they can send him back again, you mean?' It was bitterly said, but she made no apology. 'I don't know. He's back, he's safe – can't you be satisfied with that for the moment?'

'I need to know.'

'Well I can't tell you.' Without thinking, she was suddenly the professional nurse, lecturing a subordinate. 'It depends on the severity of the infection and the constitution of the patient. The germ has a nasty tendency to linger, even when, to all intents and purposes, the patient seems quite well. It could be two or three months, or it could be more. Why do you want to know?'

'Then there'll be convalescence,' her father said, ignoring the question, 'followed by retraining. So I imagine,' he mused over the crackling line, 'we're looking at five or six months. That should give us plenty of time.'

'For what?'

'Why to get this mess sorted out, of course. It's been impossible so far, and this is the first chance anybody's had to get that young idiot on one side and really talk to him. I'll be honest, Georgie, now I know he's all right, and not about to peg out on us, I'm glad he's ill. It keeps him in one place, and for long enough, to try and get him to see some sense.

'It's bothered me, you know,' he added gravely, 'all these years it's bothered me. Perhaps now we can take steps to resolve it.'

Georgina sighed again, hearing it echo over the intervening miles, and for a long moment said nothing. She understood what her father was saying. He was concerned, mainly, for Louisa; if he could effect a reconciliation between Liam and his mother, it would also expiate some of his own guilt. Not a bad aim, and one with which she concurred, but she had other loyalties too, and other sympathies; and as a nurse she was concerned for the well-being of a man who needed to recover mental as well as bodily strength. After all he had recently undergone, she could quite understand why Liam felt unable to cope with the emotional problems his family represented.

'I think we're going to need a lot of patience, Daddy. We're going to have to give him time. Yes, I know he's had three years,' she said quickly, in response to Robert's exasperated gasp on the line, 'but I'm not talking about that. I'm saying he needs time to get over the last few months. He's been through so much – if you'd been able to talk to the boys on my ward, you'd know how much – and he's been very ill. He needs time to get over that.'

There was a long sigh. 'All right, I understand. Louisa isn't going to be able to get here straight away, so perhaps it's just as well.' On a note of weary resignation, he said: 'I know you said you'd write to her, but I'm beginning to think I should go to York myself, before they get an official envelope and think the worst. That might finish poor Edward completely. And that wouldn't help at all.'

'Oh, Lord.' In the excitement of the day, Georgina had barely considered that aspect. 'But what if they've heard already?'

'I doubt it. The wheels of bureaucracy turn slowly, my dear, and that list I received this morning from Horseferry Road had only just come in from Boulogne.' After a short pause, Robert said heavily, 'I'll go to York first thing in the morning. Break the news gently, and persuade Louisa to stay where she is for the time being.'

Assuring her that he would also speak to Tisha, he told her that she must leave the family matters to him, and get some sleep; she worked far too hard as it was. On a grateful farewell, Georgina replaced the earpiece and stood for a moment, thinking about him. Although her concern was primarily for Liam, her father's, genuinely, encompassed them all; even Edward, of whom he was not inordinately fond. But as he said, to lose Edward now would only complicate matters, negate even further what small chances there were of settling things.

Edward's illness was rather more serious than Louisa cared for her children to know. They could do nothing, she said, and knowing would only make them worry, so she had asked Georgina to keep the information to herself. But Edward had suffered two minor heart attacks already, and any major shock was likely to be detrimental to his precarious health. Possibly even fatal, so it was important to play things down. Important, too, for

Liam, who needed to regain his balance.

If her presence was a comfort to him, Georgina thought as she made her way back to her room, then she would do her best to visit regularly, even if it meant changing shifts and begging favours. That way she could keep a check on his progress, and as soon as he was in better health, press him to apply for temporary home leave. It seemed to her that it would be preferable to have Liam meet them again on old, familiar home ground, rather than have Louisa trailing here, to London. But that would be something to discuss later, with Liam. Much later, she told herself sharply; for the time being it was enough to have him safe.

And accessible, she thought with warmth and pleasure later, when she was in bed. Despite his illness, despite the exhaustion written into every line of his face, it had been so good to see him. That pleasure would draw her back, no matter how she tried to disguise it. Devotion to duty, to other people's needs, the habit she had acquired of always putting others first, was not a bad thing, except where it divested her of the ability to please herself. In the course of the war, her own happiness had been neglected, if not altogether forgotten; it seemed strange now, to look forward to something so mutually enjoyable.

By Friday, however, warned to expect some serious cases on her ward, Georgina realized that Sunday afternoon visiting would be out of the question. Disappointed, she wrote to Liam what she hoped was a cheerful letter, saying that she had managed to exchange her day off for visiting day on Wednesday, which would make the journey to Wandsworth so much easier. And she would be due a short break of three days at the beginning of October. By then, he should be feeling well enough to enjoy a day out.

It was all very vague, but she felt it important that he should have things to look forward to; the mundane routine of hospital life could so easily become depressing. She did not tell Liam that her father had decided to pay a visit to York on his behalf, nor did she mention its successful outcome. Robert had telephoned her from the hotel to say that Louisa was tearfully relieved by his news, and that Edward, on his feet at last but still having to take life easy, had actually thanked him for coming to tell them.

It seemed that Edward, unlike her father, felt very strongly that the boy should take his time. 'He'll come to us when he's ready,' was a phrase that had apparently been repeated several times. Georgina loved him for his wisdom, was immensely relieved that Edward would keep some sort of rein on any wild impulses of Louisa's. Robert's, she would have to restrain herself.

Wednesday was a free day but she was awake as usual at six. She would have tried to sleep again, but a flutter of excitement set her mind rushing over the day ahead, thinking of Liam, what he might say, what she would say to him, and within minutes further sleep was impossible. Pulling on a dressing gown, Georgina went down to the kitchen to make tea and toast. Another sister was fumbling through the same routine, only half-awake and bitterly resenting the beginning of another day. She greeted Georgina grumpily and stomped off down the corridor. Watching her go, smiling a little, Georgina suddenly realized that she was like that herself most mornings; and most days off, unless she had shopping to do, she stayed in bed. She was surprised to find herself not at all tired and looking forward to the day ahead.

It was a pleasure to bathe and wash her long hair, to sit by the window in the sun, drying it; the only annoyance was having so little choice of clothes. Apart from her uniform, she kept only one outfit here for emergencies, a navy-blue skirt and jacket and matching hat, and a cream silk blouse. It was serviceable for most occasions, and yet she would have preferred something more frivolous, a pretty pastel dress, a hat trimmed with feathers, and silly, high-heeled shoes. It was that kind of day. And then she smiled at herself; even in her wardrobe at Queen's Gate, she possessed nothing of that description. Most of her clothes were plain and practical, tailored to fit her personality; her shoes were good, with small, neat heels, hand-made by her father's bootmaker.

'While Tisha buys hers ready-made on Bond Street,' she muttered aloud to the caretaker's cat. 'Perhaps I should do the same. What do you say, Puss?'

The cat purred and nodded, settling herself down on Georgina's knee.

'Or am I being foolish?'

She lunched early and alone in the communal dining room,

then went along the High Street to buy something for Liam. Although the boys newly arrived from France loved nothing better than fruit, she suspected that Liam's diet would not yet allow for pears and plums. After trying several shops, Georgina eventually found what she wanted: a little box of peppermints and another of chocolate neapolitans, both made by *Terry's of York*. She hoped the memories evoked would be happy ones.

The journey by public transport to Wandsworth took longer than expected, and it was almost a quarter past the hour for visiting when she arrived outside the hospital gates. People were still streaming in, being met by convalescent patients before heading straight out again and up the road for town. Expecting Liam to be on the ward if not actually in bed, Georgina paid little attention to those passing faces, and had covered perhaps twenty yards when her name and the touch of a hand on her arm stayed that eager progress.

She turned and he was there beside her, so much taller than memory served, with his hat set at a rakish angle and laughter dancing in his eyes.

The hat was swept off in greeting. 'I was by the gate, waiting, and you walked right past me...'

Standing so close, looking up into that open smile which seemed to embrace her with such warmth and delight, Georgina could have sworn her heart turned over. Unprepared for the impact of his presence, she suddenly felt quite weak. A little breathlessly, staring up at him, she laughed and shook her head. And had to look away.

Recovering her voice, she said, 'What on earth are you doing out of bed?'

Shrugging, laughing, spreading his hands in a gesture of innocence, Liam said he was fine, that he had been up and about for the last three days, and allowed out that very morning.

'You've never been out since this morning?' She thought it far too soon, would have ushered him back to bed had he been her responsibility,

'Well, not entirely,' he admitted, taking her arm and walking with her along the gravel path. 'I had to see the ear specialist first thing, to have my ears syringed.' He pulled a face. 'It wasn't pleasant, but it seems to have done the trick. My hearing's improved already – I can hear the birds singing, and trains chugging up the incline, and people's voices. It's amazing, everything was so muffled before – as though my ears were stuffed with wool.'

His pleasure was infectious. With a little squeeze of his arm, she said she was pleased for him, glad that there had been no permanent damage. With small, shy, darting glances, Georgina felt the need to reassure herself that he was indeed whole and undamaged. She saw so much of injuries, both small and horrific, that it seemed no less than a miracle to have this beautiful, unmarked man walking beside her.

As they came to a vacant seat and moved towards it, Liam's eyes followed the passage of a legless man in a wheelchair, and suddenly, all his euphoria disappeared.

'Deafness isn't much to complain about, though, is it? Here I am intact – with a couple of months' peace ahead of me.' He looked at her intently. 'What more could I ask?'

'What more indeed,' she murmured. There were men hobbling on crutches, others with bandaged heads and arms. Nevertheless, by the smiles and light voices, it seemed everyone that day was conscious of the joy of being alive.

She pressed his hand. 'You've been so lucky.'

'I know.'

He would have kept hold of her hand, but she withdrew it, too conscious of his closeness, his adult masculinity, to be entirely at ease. In bed the other day, like the boys on her ward, it had been easy to relegate him to the role of patient; seeing him fully dressed changed her perspective. In her memory he had remained a boy; she had not allowed for those missing years, nor the maturity induced by years of war.

Dark shadows beneath his eyes told their own tale. Her professional glance discerned pallor beneath that weather-beaten skin, a paring of the flesh which lent the lines of nose and cheek and jaw a severity they had not possessed before. That boyish softness was now entirely gone. He was very much his own man, she thought, and only he knew what experience had shaped his thinking.

For a while they sat in companionable silence, but he kept

glancing at her, frowning a little and smiling, as though something about her intrigued him. She was on the point of asking what it was, when he said: 'You don't seem to have changed a bit. Seeing you out of uniform reminds me of how you looked the last time we met – do you know it's more than three years ago?' He smiled. 'It seems like yesterday.'

Surprised, because her own thoughts had been concerned with change and the passage of time, Georgina shook her head. Half-tempted to make some flippant remark about how old she felt, she discarded it and said gently that a lot had happened in the interim.

That made him frown. 'Yes, I know.' A moment later, he said: 'But I can't quite believe it. It seems so unreal.' His eyes, shadowed, moved away from her, ranging beyond the gardens to a place of his own imagining. 'I don't think I know what reality is any more.'

Alerted by that change in tone, she searched his face and saw the fear within. She knew it well but in him it frightened her. She bit her lips and clasped her fingers tight, fighting the urge to drag him back from whatever brink of horror claimed him.

But with a deep breath he brought himself back. 'I can't believe I'm here with you,' he said softly, and with a gesture that encompassed the neatly-trimmed lawns, the tennis courts and shrubberies, he added: 'It seems no more than a dream...'

She placed her hand in his, and felt warm dry fingers close over hers. 'I'm real enough – does that help?'

He nodded. 'It's strange, though. From here the war seems so far away. I find myself wondering whether it really happened – if it's still going on. And that's the thing,' he added, turning to her, 'I can't believe it's going on without me...'

Georgina swallowed hard. 'It does, I'm afraid.'

With a bitter smile he turned away. 'I'm sorry. That sounds like vanity.'

'No. It's a very common feeling. It goes, after a while.'

He said nothing to that, but she saw his eyes were suddenly brimming. He rubbed a hand over his face. 'I'm sorry. I was so happy to see you...'

Hurt for him, aware that his whole body was trembling, Georgina clasped his arm and tried to find the right words to comfort him. She thought perhaps it was time to be professional, and wished she had worn her uniform after all.

'I'm a nurse, Liam,' she reminded him, 'as well as your – your friend.' But there was a tight constriction in her throat and it was so hard to express cool detachment when all she wanted to do was hold him in her arms and let him weep. Clearing her throat, she said: 'Give it time. You're still not well – at least not as well as you think you are. And you're still suffering from reaction...

'There's nothing to be ashamed of – it happens to everyone – you must have seen it yourself on the battlefield. The bravest suffer most when the danger is past.' Unsure whether he was really listening, she tightened her grip and gave his arm a little shake. 'But you will get over it. You will. It just takes time.'

Pausing, softening her voice, she added: 'And don't think you have to apologize – I've seen enough, believe me, to know something of what you're going through. It's a little like grief, coming in waves – fine one minute, in tears the next.'

The swings in mood could be alarming, Georgina knew that; what he needed was her reassurance. Stroking his hand, she said: 'And don't try too hard to bottle things up. Whatever you want to say, say it – I'm not likely to be shocked, Liam, I promise you that.'

'Thank you,' he said gruffly, not looking at her, 'I appreciate it. But you see, I don't want to hurt you.'

What should have been the nurse's bright, confident answer – *you won't hurt me* – was in this case neither appropriate nor true. She wanted to say, *your pain is my pain, and for you I'd suffer willingly*, but that, too, was out of place. In the end she said softly: 'I think it's more important that you tell me, than that you worry about how I feel.'

As he turned to look at her, she was rewarded by the faintest curve of his lips; he was regaining his equilibrium, for the moment, at least. With a little sigh she patted his arm and judged that it was time to change the subject. 'Anyway, tell me about Australia. That's something you didn't mention in your letters to me. Was it all you expected it to be?'

'Oh, yes,' he murmured, and the warmth of his response set her wondering, as it had three years before, how many young women had longed to see him smile for them. But he seemed charmingly unaware of his own appeal as he talked, describing the young, growing city that was Melbourne, and the richness of the country beyond. His words painted a vivid picture of Victoria's hills and forests, exotic birds and animals, and revealed a deep admiration for the people. Georgina wondered – could not help wondering – whether there was one special person amongst them.

'And when the war's over,' she said slowly, 'will you go back?'

His answer seemed a long time coming. Like a sudden shadow, pain passed over him. He shifted position, drawing slightly away from her. 'I don't know. I'd like to, yes.' His tone had an edge to it, suddenly, and his eyes were distant. '*When the war's over...* We keep saying that, you know. We all say it. Or we did. But nobody quite believes it any more. You look back, and war is all you can remember – the blokes talk about Gallipoli as though it was ancient history – and you try to look ahead, but all you can see is more of it. And no matter what you do, how hard you fight, how many men you lose, that's all there is ahead of you.'

Georgina winced. 'It will be over, one day. We have to believe in that.' But she heard the desperation in her own voice, and wished she had never mentioned Australia.

'I'm sure it will – one day. The question is, will we be there to see it?'

It was cynically said, and, searching his pockets for cigarettes, Liam did not notice the pain it caused. A moment later, finding them, he said: 'If I come through it, yes, I'd like to go back. It's a wonderful country – paradise. You'd love it,' he added with a quick glance into her eyes as the match flared into life. He cupped broad fingers round the flame, drew deeply, and released a cloud of blue smoke.

A moment later, with a soft smile for her, he said: 'And you, Georgina – what will you do when the war's over? Will you go on nursing, or what?'

'What else is there?' The words came out bleakly, unexpectedly, and frightened her a little. She had never before been aware of a lack of conviction, but it seemed to be there, nevertheless. She wondered whether Liam had released it, with his talk of that clean, new land.

Catching the bleakness, he shot her a quizzical glance. When he spoke, his words had the air of being carefully chosen. 'You've never thought of marriage, then?'

The question was so unexpected, the idea so unlikely, that she was torn between laughter and astonishment; but something in his tone brought colour to her cheeks. She had to look away.

'Marriage?' she repeated, laughing and shaking her head. 'No, never.'

He was surprised. 'Seriously?'

Glancing up, she saw disbelief in his eyes. 'Seriously – it's always been out of the question.'

He doesn't know, she thought; or has never considered it. But why should he? His life and experience did not encompass madness. But suddenly it struck Georgina that the truth of her own background might shed light for Liam on so much more.

She stood up. 'Shall we walk a little way? Do you feel up to it?'

As they strolled across the lawns, skirting tennis courts where a couple of desultory games were being played, Liam slipped off the jacket of his blue hospital uniform and loosened his tie. In the warm sun Georgina removed her gloves and hat, aware as she did so of a sense of freedom, and a lifting of the oppression brought on by thoughts of her mother. It was not a subject she ever discussed, but somehow, being with Liam made things easier. All at once she wanted to tell him about the past and a childhood that was so inextricably involved with his own.

They had talked about Charlotte Duncannon that last evening, when he had insisted on coming to meet her at the Retreat, so he knew that she had died in a similar place in Ireland. What he did not know was the history of that illness, its insidious progress down the years. Georgina felt instinctively that Liam's antipathy to her father might be alleviated to some extent if he knew what Robert Duncannon had suffered because of it.

Putting together what she had gleaned over the years from various relatives, and adding her own professional knowledge, Georgina described her mother from adolescence to grave. As a girl Charlotte had seen her parents murdered in Ulster, been adopted by her uncle's family in Dublin, and introduced into society at the age of eighteen. Georgina described a beautiful young woman whose aloof, mysterious personality had attracted her father from the start.

'Much to his surprise,' she went on with a smile, 'Daddy's suit was favoured. I gather the wedding happened so quickly, even he thought it was rushed!

'But not until after they were married did he start to understand why.' She paused for a moment, to explain that her father almost never spoke of his marriage, that most of her information had come from his elder sister, Letty.

'My mother's behaviour became downright odd, even bizarre at times. She heard voices and conversed with people who weren't there. By the time she was expecting me, she'd become so unpredictable that Daddy was afraid to leave her alone. He was due to go to England with his regiment, but he was so afraid of what might happen, he took her to White Leigh instead, to be cared for by my aunt and uncle.

'Unfortunately, after I was born, my mother became much worse. She became violent and unpredictable. I gather one of her most obsessive delusions was that my father was the spawn of the devil, and that it was her duty to kill him.'

Glancing sideways at Liam, she saw him start. 'It can't have been easy to be on the receiving end of all that hatred, especially when he cared so much.

'And he did care, Liam, I'm not just saying that. He always did his best for her, and he was determined to keep her out of an asylum. He didn't want her abused and ill-treated, so he insisted on her staying at White Leigh. But he was away most of the time, so that was hard on the family...'

She sighed, remembering those days more by repute than reality. Nevertheless, one incident did stand out and she forced herself to relate it to Liam.

'It was Christmas Day. I was three years old. We came back from church to find the servants in uproar. I escaped from my aunt and raced upstairs to find Daddy. He was in his room – sprawled across the bed and covered in blood.

'I thought he was dead. I screamed and screamed, and they tore me away, shutting me up, alone in the nursery. I had nightmares for years after that.'

As she shuddered, Liam slipped an arm around her shoulders and for a moment held her close to his side. Muttering something derogatory about the wisdom of adults, he said: 'She'd attacked him, I suppose?'

'Oh yes. He'd gone to see her while we were out, and she went for him with a pair of scissors. He wasn't badly hurt, as it turned out, just bleeding profusely and in a state of shock – but as I say, I thought he was dead.'

She paused, glancing sideways, before going on to tell Liam that sometime after that incident her father had met Louisa, and when he returned to Ireland with his regiment, persuaded her to accompany him. 'It was the beginning,' Georgina said briefly, 'of three very happy years. I always think of those years as my childhood.'

She waited for Liam to take her up on that, to ask questions about that time, about when he was born and the early years they had spent together as brother and sister; but he did not. Silent for a while, he went back to the subject of her mother. 'What I don't understand,' he said slowly, 'is why your mother agreed to marry him, if she hated him so much.'

Georgina sighed. 'I shouldn't imagine she did hate him, not to begin with. But I'm not saying she loved him, either. I've discovered since that people like that are very strange, often devoid of ordinary human affections, totally wrapped up in themselves. Things happen around them, and half the time they don't seem to notice.

'How my mother took to being married, I've no idea, but she couldn't ignore childbirth, could she, poor woman?' Half to herself, Georgina murmured, 'She must have been terrified, wondering what was happening to her. Perhaps she blamed him for that...'

Her own birth, and the effects of it, ever since she had been old enough to understand, had never ceased to horrify Georgina. That she had gained life at such an expense, was a hugely sobering thought. She knew, but did not say, that after giving birth, Charlotte Duncannon had tried to kill herself. Had her mother died then, Georgina felt it would have been better, more just, easier to bear. But to know that she had lived on, suffering in her insanity, bringing constant anguish to so many other lives – including her own and Liam's – was a hard cross to carry. Nor had it ended with Charlotte's death. Within her, Georgina carried the seeds of her mother's insanity. Or that was how it felt. Seeds which might never come to fruition in her own life, but which might be carried on into her children's lives, and the lives of their children after that. Like fair hair, or blue eyes, or a birthmark on the hip.

If she ever married.

She never would, of course. That decision had been taken many years ago, before men as potential husbands had entered her awareness. And having taken the decision, she had cut herself off emotionally, halting any advance before it became necessary to explain herself. How odd that she should be faced with explaining it now, and to Liam.

'So you see,' she went on, matter-of-factly, 'that I could never consider marriage. Once upon a time I thought I might end up like that myself.' She gave a kind of laugh, as though the matter was one for joking, but it was the only way not to shudder. 'However, it seems unlikely now. After all I've seen of this war, Liam, I'm sure that if I was likely to lose my reason, I'd have lost it already.

'But I might pass it on, you see. If I married and had children,' she repeated quietly, not laughing now, 'I might pass it on...'

He stopped suddenly and turned towards her; and when she looked up at him, his face was taut and hard with suppressed emotion. All the diffidence was gone. She thought he was about to speak, to utter some fierce denial, but he raised his hand to cup her face, and bent to kiss her forehead. It was a warm, firm kiss, not at all lover-like, yet it expressed so absolutely his love and compassion, Georgina felt her own heart leap in response. She was at once humbled and exalted, feeling like a child in the presence of some tremendous wisdom, a warmth that encompassed her and held her safe. She could have clung to him and wept.

They had walked on a small distance when he said tersely: 'I didn't know. I remember you telling me about your mother, but I never realized – I mean, that side of things never occurred to me. I am sorry.'

She tried to make light of it, and found herself almost stammering. 'Don't be. I mean, well, it's one of those things, isn't it? Unfortunate, but one accepts it – that's the way things are, after all...'

394

'But is it? Do you know for certain that the illness is inherited?'

'It hasn't been proved, if that's what you mean. But I *feel* it. I know it's there.' Confused in the face of his intensity, she felt herself reduced to emotion rather than fact. 'I can't explain,' she finished lamely, 'I just know it and it frightens me.'

He regained her hand, and she was aware of its hard dryness, the callouses on the palm, and a warmth flooding between them. It seemed to take away all the pain. Instead of arguing, he asked bluntly: 'So you've never been in love? Never wanted to marry?'

'No, never. It was always – well, something I avoided.'

'I don't think people *choose* to fall in love,' he remarked, and something in his expression as he looked at her made Georgina feel very gauche, very vulnerable. Too conscious of his hands and his smile and that tingling, spreading warmth, she eased herself away, suggesting a halt.

On the far side of the trees, where it was sheltered and sunny, he sat down, spreading his jacket for her on the grass. Kneeling beside him, she remembered, belatedly, the little gifts she had brought, and as he opened the wrapping, tracing the trademark of palm trees with his finger, she saw him smile with wondering pleasure. He leaned back, stretching himself full-length on the grass, holding up the little packets before him.

'So,' he murmured, 'they're still making these, are they? My old favourites – how did you know?'

She was able to laugh, then. 'I must have remembered.'

Not consciously, she was aware of that, but once said, it did come back, like so many other things. Seeing him there, lying on the grass, long legs looking longer still in the narrow blue trousers, shirt-sleeves pushed back over brown forearms, she was reminded again of that last evening before the storm broke, when he had talked, so innocently, about leaving. She had thought him beautiful then, a lovely boy with all the world at his feet...

And now he was a man.

It made her shiver, as did the thought of all that had gone between. He had changed, she could see that, but despite weariness and bitterness bred by the war, he was still, miraculously, the same person. A little wiser perhaps, and with less polished ideals, but a gentle man for all that, not brutalized, as some were, by the hard school of experience. Sensitivity was still there, and that he still cared for her, very deeply, was evident by all that had passed between them today.

But perhaps, she reflected, that was less good than it seemed. For a moment she experienced a faint twinge of unease; and then he smiled at her, and it was gone.

TWENTY-FOUR

Liam had good days and bad, bursts of energy which led him to believe he was quite well, often followed by several days in which he shivered with weakness and misery. His nights, too, were mixed, sometimes tense and wakeful, listening to rain pattering on the windows and trains chugging up the incline, as often full of nightmare and horror as they were of relaxed, health-giving sleep. The ward-sister who had been in charge when he first arrived, moved back to her regular night slot, which Liam had cause to be glad about. Often when he woke in fear, unable to sleep again, she would make him a hot drink and let him talk for a while until the anxiety passed. She did that with all of them. She was very kind.

He imagined Georgina doing the same, and he would think of her, years hence, wondering whether she would always be devoted to the suffering of others, living for them, never having a life of her own. Nursing was a demanding if noble vocation; no doubt it had its rewards, although as a mere patient suffused with gratitude, he could not imagine them.

Each of these women, he reflected, could marry and leave the profession, but that choice was not open to Georgina. Although she could leave, and no doubt live on the income from her mother's inheritance, he could not imagine her doing so. No, she would carry on, probably for the rest of her life, never knowing a man's love, which seemed a tragedy to him, a sin against the natural order of things. She was a woman who deserved to be loved and cherished, yet he could not deny the surge of relief when she declared that love and marriage were not for her. The reasons were tragic, although in a strange way they eased his conscience; he felt less wrong in loving her, less guilty in looking for her affection. With the surety that he was detracting from nothing and no one, it seemed to Liam that he might freely enjoy her company and give whatever degree of love she might accept.

Despite the insurmountable barriers, he felt there was no real reason why they should not share a tender friendship and the comfort of knowing that each cared about the other. It was not a love which could be consummated, but then he had never expected it to be, so experienced no particular sense of loss. With no demands, there was even a strange comfort in it, a sense of knowing, without being told, exactly where he stood. It was one of the few things in his life with any foundation.

What caused him some unease, was the image she had presented of Robert Duncannon as a loving father and tormented young husband. It sat awkwardly against his fixed impression of a middle-aged philanderer who cared everything for his own passions and little for his offspring. What age had he been then? Mid- to late-twenties, probably, not much older than himself: no doubt hot-headed, and inexperienced in the ways of the world...

No, it would not do. If he stopped hating Robert Duncannon, everything else would fall apart. If he stopped hating the man who had brought all this about, then who was there left to blame? And it must be somebody's fault, this crazy situation; it had to be somebody's fault.

He stopped thinking about it altogether, wrote his mother and Edward a few bland missives, said he hoped they were well, and he would see them as soon as he was fit to travel. There was no point, he argued, in their coming to London; he would travel free on a rail pass as soon as he could obtain leave, which was bound to be quite soon.

As the September days shortened with fog and rain, he spent much time in the library, a place of endless fascination. The hospital had been a school, an orphanage, the history of which he read one dark afternoon when the ward was crowded with visitors and Georgina unable to come. It had been built on a wave of patriotism after the Crimea, for the orphaned daughters of veterans of that campaign. Public subscription had raised more than a million pounds for its erection, and it was grand indeed, the great hall decorated with banners and arms of the great cities of Britain and the Empire. Like the whole building, it had something medieval about it, an air of masculine romanticism, upon which several hundred little girls had failed to leave an impression.

The present wards had been dormitories and schoolrooms, built around quadrangles which reminded him of cloisters. Often, hanging about the rear entrance on wet afternoons, smoking, he would look back across the brick-paved cloister and watch the passage of nurses up and down, up and down. He noted the men too, the men, hundreds of them, from whom the women were professionally separated.

There was an air of other-worldliness about it, romantic, medieval, monastic, which fitted the place exactly. With its high, gothic walls, quaint arched windows and communal living quarters, it seemed part of Chaucer and Malory and the romantic poets of old. That sense of celibacy, enforced and upheld, seemed natural rather than irksome. He was not, he was sure, the only one to feel that; it seemed to affect other men, too, even the ones on his ward, who were mostly less ill than the rest. Each new nurse had her followers, men who fell romantically in love at the first kind smile; but there was less coarseness than might have been expected. Worship, adoration and respect were the order of the day, and in that atmosphere Liam's relationship with Georgina seemed not at all strange.

He was teased, of course. Georgina was referred to as his private nurse, and he was asked several times when he was going to do the decent thing by her and name the day. All the men were convinced she was in love with him and just waiting for Liam to pop the question. If it was flattering, it was also highly embarrassing.

He had become practised at fending them off, but two of the men had asked the same question. 'Is she your sister, or what?' To which he had said they were cousins, a point which had been agreed, early on, between himself and Georgina. But each response had been similar, words to the effect that his answer explained a certain resemblance. 'Mind, she's a bloody sight prettier than you!'

Liam took the teasing in good part, while finding much irony in those comments. Except in colouring, and possibly something about the eyes, they were not alike. He was heavy-boned, while she was as slender as a willow; and if he had inherited his fairness from the Elliott family, she had hers from her mother. Robert Duncannon had passed on nothing of his dark Irish looks to either of them. Robin was the one who had inherited the colouring and bone structure; and Tisha, who was not tall, bore her resemblance in hair and eyes. It was odd too, that when his sister did arrive on a brief visit, no one recognized her as such.

Liam was more pleased to see her than he had expected to be; but they had so little to say to each other that the visit was something of an embarrassment. The only matters they had in common were York, home and the past, and as each had private reasons for not wanting to discuss these things in depth, it left little to talk about.

Tisha did, however, manage to shock him. She revealed the fact of Edward's illness in such a casual way that at first he thought he had misheard. When pressed for details, she said airily that he was quite well again, there was nothing to worry about, and their mother had everything well in hand.

More upset than he could say, Liam was aware of his own heart pounding painfully, that erratic, uneven beat which had become more pronounced since those last bombardments at Pozières; he was sweating too, although it was not a warm day.

'Have you seen him?' he demanded. 'Did you go home?'

'Well, no. I've been very busy since I got married. Edwin went off training and then he came back on embarkation leave, and I knew Mother couldn't do with visiting when Dad was ill, so I thought it better to leave it for a while.'

'But he might have died!'

She clicked her tongue. 'Oh, Liam, you always did exaggerate! They were only mild attacks, and Mother particularly impressed upon me that I was not to worry.'

'So you didn't?' he asked sardonically. 'But do you think you might? Go home, I mean?'

'Not just yet,' Tisha replied, smoothing the seam of her stockings. 'Mother's got enough to do, without looking after guests.'

'You're hardly a guest – you're her daughter, for heaven's sake! Or doesn't that mean anything to you?'

His sister looked up, fixing him with a cold stare. 'Since you ask – not a great deal, no.'

He was stunned. Almost stammering, he said: 'But Tisha, you should go home.'

'And so should you,' she retorted. 'And perhaps when you've been and settled your differences, then I'll go. Perhaps. Until then, dear brother, don't try to tell me what to do. I'm a married woman, now, and I can please myself.'

With that, she swept out, as elegantly as she had come in, on a wave of French perfume and a swirl of silk.

Guilt washed over him, and a helpless feeling of frustration. Three years! What had happened to her in that time? She had been a child when he left, and now she was every inch a woman, smart, hard and sophisticated. On the surface at least. What was she beneath, though? A childish, vindictive little monster. Married woman, indeed! Liam pitied her husband.

When he had eventually calmed himself, he wrote to Edward, a letter less carefully phrased than usual, expressing his deep concern and need for assurance. He would come home, he said, just as soon as he was able to do so.

It was several days before he saw Georgina, and by that time his anger had abated; nevertheless, at the first opportunity he took her to task on the matter, demanding to know why, since she was aware of Edward's illness, she had neglected to tell him.

'You were in France,' Georgina said stiffly, 'facing rather more immediate dangers. Louisa knew – and I agreed with her – that a matter of a mild heart attack did not mean that Edward was at death's door, although you and Robin might have jumped to that conclusion. And if you had, what good would it have done? Could you have obtained leave at that time? I doubt it. And when you arrived here, and the opportunity to tell you arose, it was my considered opinion that you were too ill to be faced with it.'

'I don't agree with you!'

'Liam, I know how ill you were.' She touched his arm gently. 'And the worry of knowing would have held back your recovery. Please believe me.'

'So when did you plan to tell me?'

'I didn't,' she said honestly, 'I was leaving it to your mother to do that. But I think it's time you understood how much she and Edward care for you. It was a joint decision not to tell you, even when they knew you were here in London. They didn't want any undue pressure put upon you – they were, and are, longing to see you, on your terms, and in your time. You see, in spite of everything, they love you very much.'

It was too much to bear; he turned away, aware of a hard lump in his throat. Because he did not want to accept that, he said brusquely: 'But there they go again – you too – keeping things from me, as though I were still a child! When will you all start being honest? All this secrecy and deceit makes me so angry!'

She said nothing, and he knew she was waiting for him to calm down. Making a supreme effort, he stood up and walked away, leaving Georgina sitting in the shelter of the chapel wall. When he had half-smoked a cigarette, he came back and apologized.

'I suppose Tisha should have kept her mouth shut.'

She smiled, wryly. 'I think perhaps she should. But that's Tisha.'

'Yes, isn't it?' He sat down, feeling cold and shivery; it was a poor day. 'Do you want to go inside?'

'Not unless you do. It's quieter out here.'

After a while, thinking about York, thinking about his sister, he said: 'What's happened to her, Georgina? We never had much in common, but I don't remember her being quite like that.'

'I don't know, she was never easy to understand.'

But a sudden sigh made Liam look into her face.

'Tell me,' he said heavily, 'whatever it is. I don't like to think of you keeping things from me.' It was hurtful, when he wanted so much to be part of her, when he wanted to understand the things that grieved her as well as those that made her happy. 'Tell me.'

But there was little to tell. Small incidents, small cruelties that Georgina had witnessed during her less frequent visits to the cottage after his departure, a moment of revelation for Liam when she admitted feelings of guilt at that time, and the bleak atmosphere which had prevailed at the cottage with both boys gone.

Wanting to question her about the guilt, he let it pass, needing to know, initially, about Tisha. But Georgina's assessment of what ailed the girl was not easy to listen to; most of it only served to increase his own sense of unease, to promote a growing suspicion that perhaps his own actions had much to answer for.

'Something happened to Tisha about the time you left. Don't

ask me what, because I don't know – honestly, I don't. I can only assume that what she heard, what she discovered, was as great a shock to her as it was to you. Except she didn't have your avenue of escape. And I think Edward and Louisa were so shattered by what you did, so absolutely devastated, they ignored her. They didn't realize how much she needed them.

'And Tisha,' Georgina sighed, 'was always the one who wanted to be important, who wanted an audience for every trick. Particularly a male audience. Edward doted on her – but suddenly, he wasn't paying much attention any more. Louisa absorbed most of his time and affection. And she did need it, Liam – she was like...' Breaking off, Georgina shook her head. 'She'd lost you, her eldest son. She didn't know where you were. You might have been dead. The not knowing almost killed her.'

He bowed his head against that. But he had asked, had demanded to know, could not now beg her to stop, unsay the words that spoke the truth.

'Once Robin had heard from you – once you'd written to Edward – all that changed, of course. Louisa was much better, more able to take notice of what was going on around her. But it was too late. At least where Tisha was concerned. In a way, I think they were both quite relieved when she left to come to London. And since then, she's been more or less as you describe her. I don't think she cares for anyone very much. Edwin, perhaps, but he's gone away too. I don't think she expected that.'

Liam shook his head at the folly of it all, scarcely able to believe the extent of destruction caused by one man's hasty words. He supposed he should have been feeling pity for his sister, but all he could think of was that afternoon when he returned from work, that moment when the truth assaulted him.

'If you only knew...' Fumbling for his cigarettes, lighting one, he was aware that his hands were trembling, but the pain, curiously enough, was less than it had ever been. In the face of his mother's suffering it seemed somehow pathetic, even selfish to have nursed it so long. Three years! For God's sake, in war that was a lifetime!

'I never meant...' he began again, then stopped, feeling guilty and inadequate. Georgina's hand on his arm made him turn to look at her. She seemed so stricken by his anguish that he wanted to draw her close, enfold her in his arms and tell her nothing mattered. But it did matter, and he could not hold her, and there was very little comfort elsewhere.

'What is it? Can't you tell me?'

Her voice was gentle, persuasive, but in spite of his need to respond, the words were still locked behind a barrier of remembered pain. Pathetic though it was, he knew it would hurt even more to break that seal, to let the torrent of bitterness go. Amongst it lay the jewel of his love for her.

'I can't,' he said miserably, 'not now.'

'That's all right,' she whispered, 'I understand.'

'Do you?'

Pressing her hand, he rose to his feet; with the ringing of the bell they went inside.

Throughout most of September he had spent mornings in bed, rising for the main meal of the day, staying up until six or seven in the evening, when he was glad to return. By the end of the month, feeling stronger, he was often up and about from breakfast till supper, filling his days in library or grounds, and occasionally performing small tasks in the ward kitchen. When six of the men left for one of the convalescent homes, Liam found himself helping on a fairly regular basis. He rather liked it, enjoying the informality of the kitchen, the young nurses' company and the way they good-naturedly teased and bullied him. The work gave him something to do and stopped him brooding.

Nevertheless, Tisha's visit and that conversation with Georgina had brought to mind an awareness that kept returning. During all the time he had been away from home, beyond the contentment of Australia and the blind intensity of the war, beyond the seclusion of hospital life, time had not stood still. Although in his mind it had been frozen at the point where he left, he was faced now with reports of change, truths it was difficult to avoid. Like having an uncorrected map of no-man's-land, he thought, and with an order to go over the top, suddenly being told of fresh saps and gun-pits and an acre of barbed-wire.

Although he had wanted to hurt them, intended it and obviously succeeded, from this distance it seemed a childish, petty thing. Since that promise to Robin he had imagined going home, his mother begging his forgiveness and he, reluctantly, granting it, like some medieval pontiff; but it seemed to him now that he should be the supplicant, his mother the one dispensing grace.

It was not a comfortable awareness, and one he tried to ignore, pushing it to the back of his mind against the day when he would have to act on it. What he could not ignore were his feelings towards Georgina.

In the beginning it had not been a problem; his relief at being safe, having the joy of her company at regular intervals, amounted almost to euphoria. For long enough that sense of heightened well-being carried him along; and while ever they met within the rarefied atmosphere of hospital and grounds, it was sustained. But they had begun to go out; once or twice up to town for the afternoon, seeing the sights of London from the open-topped deck of a bus. Amidst the bustling, workaday world he was aware of wanting to behave like any other young man with his sweetheart, drawing her arm through his, kissing her cheek as they said goodbye. Or, like the soldier and his girl spied in a shadow of trees at twilight, indulging in a long, passionate embrace.

It was becoming a struggle to remember his obligations, a constant battle to quell the physical desire which seemed to be increasing in direct proportion to his good health.

His twenty-second birthday fell at the end of the first week in October. Georgina had endeavoured to organize her three days' leave to coincide with it; and also to borrow her father's motor car, a dark green, open-topped Ford. Despite his reservations about that, as the weather promised to be good, Liam knew it would have been churlish to refuse. Once he had recovered from the unease of sitting in Robert Duncannon's car, he began to enjoy the sensation of speed and freedom; and to admire the way Georgina handled such a complicated piece of machinery.

Pink spots of colour enlivened her cheeks, the chiffon scarf which anchored her hat blowing back, gaily, in the breeze. A light dust-coat covered her clothes but her skirt beneath it was a shade of old rose, echoed and deepened in the colours of her swathed velvet hat. He thought she looked not just beautiful – she was always that – but extraordinarily pretty. The impression was reinforced when they reached their destination.

Removing the dust-coat and scarf, she left both in the car and turned, a little flirtatiously, he thought, to ask what he thought of her new outfit. The plum velvet jacket, with its deep revers and high waist, was flattering, while the skirt ended several inches above a pair of very pretty ankles. He thought she looked wonderful and said so, but he had to swallow hard first.

In the golden shades of early autumn, Hampton Court was a delight, old stone and brick lending a mellow grandeur to the day, a sense of timelessness, as though nothing in life could be too tragic, when something so lovely had withstood it all. They wandered through the grounds and talked about Cardinal Wolsey, the man who had built this great palace and been forced to give it up to a jealous king; and they took a boat on the river, and talked about Bishopthorpe, Wolsey's other palace outside York. While Liam rowed, Georgina was full of reminiscences, asking did he remember this and that; and particularly the afternoon he had taken her across the river to the fair on St George's Field. He did remember, he remembered everything exceedingly well; but even as he smiled and nodded, his heart was breaking for the loss of innocence. He had loved her then with a boy's romantic adoration; he adored her still, but he wanted her too, and that was hard to bear.

At Bishopthorpe, looking up at that great palace from the river, he had discovered that Georgina was to be forever denied him; at Bishopthorpe, on that lovely late summer afternoon, he had come face to face with the truth.

Those memories coloured everything, lent the afternoon a sad, ironic air and spoiled his enjoyment. He was glad to leave, to get back in the car and be driven on. They went on to Richmond and walked in the park, and the sun was still shining through a faint autumn haze. Liam knew that he should have been happy, but everything that afternoon was tinged with a sense of loss.

Aware of his sadness, although not, he was sure, understanding it, Georgina strolled beside him, remarking softly on the sights and sounds and smells of autumn. He was conscious of her perfume, roses, overlaying the scent of dying leaves, and he listened to the sounds their feet made, rustling through golden carpets beneath the trees. She looked soft and warm in her velvet, in those dusky, muted colours that somehow blended with the falling afternoon. He wanted so much to touch that softness, to draw her close and taste the sweetness of her lips, that he dared not even brush her hand.

Back at the car he held the door for her but did not offer to help her in. Drawing the dust-coat round her knees, she glanced up, enquiring tentatively whether anything was wrong, whether she had said something to upset him. Liam shook his head, wretchedly unable to explain.

'I'm just a bit tired,' was all he could say.

The afternoon was deepening to dusk as they drove back, and there was no time to stop elsewhere. Outside the hospital gates, while he sat for a moment unspeaking, reluctant to leave her, she reached into her bag, drawing out a small slim package.

'I intended to give you this over tea,' she said in that soft, low voice of hers, 'but we ran out of time. It's nothing really – just a small gift to mark your birthday. I wish you could have had it last year, for your twenty-first.'

Mystified, saying with a little laugh that it was the first present he had been given in years, Liam opened the wrapping to find a beautifully chased silver cigarette case. Inside it was inscribed with his initials and the date. For a minute he could not even look at her. Turning it over and over in his hands, he felt crass for having spoiled a potentially perfect day; and with the date engraved he knew he would never forget it. And for what? All for the want of something he could not have. He felt selfish and ashamed.

'I'm so sorry,' he managed at last, 'for the stupid mood I've been in today. You've given me so much, and I...' He broke off, shaking his head. 'Can you forgive me?'

'For what?' she asked lightly, smiling into his eyes. 'It's been a lovely day.'

'Yes,' he said quietly, 'it has. Thank you.'

She was half-turned towards him, her mouth slightly parted in expectancy or puzzlement, he was not sure which. Wanting to express his feelings, wanting to make up for all those silent, brooding moments, he searched for words and found none. With his heart pounding crazily, he leaned across and kissed her very gently on the lips. There was a soft, momentary response, one that made it hard to draw away; with his blood on fire, he forced himself not to kiss her again.

It seemed to take an eternity to move. He would have liked to step out of the car, to utter a casual farewell, but he was trembling quite badly and his breath seemed to be stuck somewhere deep in his chest. Watching her face, her eyes, he thought he saw surprise mingled with both pleasure and confusion before she turned away. With her hands on the steering wheel and colour heightening her cheeks, she murmured something, breathlessly, about it being rather late.

Taking his cue from her, Liam said yes, it was, and he really must go. A voice he hardly recognized as his own, added that he hoped to see her again soon, and that he would drop her a line tomorrow.

The next morning, still enthralled by an inner vision of lustrous eyes and lips, Liam began a letter to Georgina which was full of warm recollections. With gentle self-parody he described pausing on the drive before going in, and the fact that his hands were so unsteady it had taken three matches to light one cigarette.

Musing for a moment, picturing himself, Liam smiled, and as one of the young nurses passed by with a pile of linen, she grinned at him. It was the one who had scrubbed his back that first day, and it was she who had seen him come in last evening, hissing in an undertone that he should wipe the silly smile off his face before Sister wondered what he had been up to.

She knew, or had a good idea, what had taken place; but oh, God, he thought in the next second, if she really knew, she wouldn't smile.

Sobered, he turned back to his letter, and all the silly, romantic, lover-like things he had said and still wanted to say, about the softness of her lips and not sleeping a wink, were suddenly inappropriate. Aware of his own foolishness, he tore the page into shreds and stared, moodily, from the window. That kiss must never be mentioned, not even in apology. If he wished it to remain the casual, friendly, brotherly gesture it might have seemed, then it must be allowed to pass unremarked. He knew full well, however, that brotherly or not, it could never be repeated.

In a fresh beginning after lunch, Liam confined himself to safer topics, to repeated thanks for a lovely day out, and most especially for a gift he would always treasure. His words were sincere but dreadfully bland. Her reply, when it came by return of post, was almost equally so.

Part of him – the sensible, practical part – was considerably relieved by that, but the lover in him was frustrated. Over the next few days, longing to be with her again, he was plagued by subtle torments. What did she think of that kiss? How did she feel? How would he feel when next he saw her, tantalized by closeness, by her perfume and the temptation of her smile? How could he look at her, yet refrain from touching the perfection of her cheek, the softness of her smooth blonde hair? Turbulent emotion gripped him whenever he recalled that parting kiss and the way that she had looked at him afterwards. His dreams were full of unsatisfied desire.

It was more than two weeks before he saw her again. One visit had to be postponed owing to pressure of work, and anyway he was laid low by a couple of anti-dysentery injections and would not have seen her even if he could. On her next afternoon off, the day that he was looking forward to taking her up to town, all passes were cancelled. The entire hospital seethed with resentment, and Liam was furious.

Meeting her at the gates, amongst an indignant, vociferous crowd, there was little opportunity for awkwardness. To clear a path it was necessary to keep her close to his side: but in holding her he also wanted to caress her, and that made him angrier still. Curtly, in answer to her query, Liam related the reason for the ban: two men had gone out for an afternoon and neglected to return for three days. To his further annoyance, the tale seemed to amuse her.

'Where did they go?'

'Oh, nowhere in particular – just on a bender in town. Got so roaring drunk they couldn't remember where they were – or even who they were!'

With a mischievous smile, she said: 'They'll be for it!'

'We all are,' he responded grimly, 'confined to barracks for the rest of the week. As if that will deter anybody! The ones that are ready to go convalescent can't wait to get out of here.' He paused to light a cigarette. 'I'm starting to feel like that myself. In fact I asked about home leave the other day, but it doesn't seem likely until I'm clear. It's ridiculous, I feel fine.'

'Don't rush things,' she said gently, 'it'll take its course.'

'Yes, but when you start straining at the leash, you know you're getting better.'

Because he was also thinking of other restraints, the words came out sharply, and Georgina's smile froze.

He saw the pain he had caused before she glanced away, and could have bitten his tongue. Instantly contrite, he quickly changed the subject. But Liam knew as well as she did that once declared fit he would be moved away from London. Their time together would be over.

When she had gone Liam was left with a bitter taste of regret. With the matter of home leave still on his mind, he was torn between a desire to spend as long as possible within reach of Georgina, and an increasing anxiety about Edward. Although letters from York continued to be reassuring, he had the feeling that time was running out, that he should make every effort to get to York, if only for a couple of days.

The arrival of a new medical officer prompted him to ask again. There was sympathy when he explained why, but the doctor said that further tests would have to be taken before a decision could be made. Another specimen was sent down to the laboratory, and, two days later, on accosting the Sister, Liam was told dryly that the officer in charge of the lab wanted to know whether the patient was still in bed, as evidence of colitis was still present. Although she made no further comment, her expression said quite clearly that if he wanted to retain his current degree of freedom, he must press no further.

Downcast and frustrated, Liam kept the news to himself. Gloomy weather did nothing to lighten his spirits, and his letters to Georgina reflected this. She wrote to suggest a trip to the theatre on her next day off, but the idea was less appealing than it might have been.

Concert parties came to the hospital frequently, some good, most remarkable only for their enthusiasm; and sometimes organized trips went from Wandsworth to the Palladium at Stockwell, just up the road. Liam thought he had had enough of that brand of hearty cheer, but it seemed churlish to refuse. He arranged to meet Georgina in a teashop they had visited before just off Leicester Square.

It was a miserable afternoon, cold with the rawness of winter. There was a leaden, yellowy cast to the sky, and someone said it might be foggy, later, so be sure to get back early; but Liam had no desire to cut short his afternoon. Waiting with his hat pulled down and the collar of his newly issued sheepskin jacket turned up to meet it, he felt chilled to the bone. Seeing the queue for tables, it seemed more prudent to wait inside. Just as one was being allocated, Georgina arrived, in brimmed hat and belted mackintosh, shivering as she joined him.

He wanted to warm her against his heart; instead he ushered her to a chair and ordered some tea. The hot drink revived them both, and they stayed longer than they intended. The popular revue they meant to see was packed out when they arrived, people still waiting on the pavement. Dismayed, Georgina said she was too tired to walk, she wanted to sit down and relax. Liam glanced down at her then, and the pinched look he had attributed to the weather seemed more pronounced in that grey, unforgiving light.

'Come on,' he said, taking her arm, 'we'll go into the first empty theatre we find, and if you like, you can fall asleep on my shoulder!'

She responded with a smile, but he thought she seemed distracted. He wondered if she was worrying about work, or about her father who was presently in Dublin.

Within a few yards, he said: 'Are you sure you wouldn't prefer to go home? You look to me as though you should be tucked up before a nice warm fire, not trailing about town like this.'

'No,' she said quickly, 'I'm fine, really I am. Just in need of a good night's sleep.'

'Let me call you a cab…'

'No, Liam – really.' She tucked her arm in his and he felt the intimacy of the gesture like a warm glow. On a corner, a few yards down the street, was another little theatre, advertising yet another amusing variety performance. Georgina suggested going in there.

The show had already started, but seats were available. Paying for two in the stalls, Liam sighed as they went in: the place was half-empty, which did not augur well for the quality of the performers.

In a quiet aside, Georgina said her patients were funnier than the comedian; laughing, Liam claimed there were more talented jugglers amongst the nurses. But the audience, comprising mainly soldiers, was becoming restive. After half an hour, disturbed by some of the coarser cat-calls, Liam was about to suggest leaving, when a soubrette came on, rather fetchingly dressed in male attire.

The British Tommy's uniform, with its breast pockets and breeches and neatly-wound puttees, fitted her better, Liam thought, than any man. She was a neat, curvaceous girl with an angelic face, and as soon as she appeared the barracking died down, giving place to a series of whistles and hand-claps. When she started to sing, her voice silenced the house.

It was a sweet, rich soprano, eminently suited to the series of sentimental ballads she had chosen to sing. 'Home, Sweet Home!' was followed by, 'Roses are Blooming in Picardy,' so currently popular that the choruses were taken up by the audience; then, when the applause had died down, she began to sing Liam's favourite, sections of which were so well-known to him that he was almost tempted to sing the words with her.

'Far ahead, where the blue shadows fall,
I shall come to contentment and rest,
And the toil of the day
Will be all charmed away,
In my little grey home in the west.

'There are hands that will welcome me in,
There are lips I am burning to kiss;
There are two eyes that shine
Just because they are mine,
And a thousand things other men miss...'

It seemed to express everything he felt for the woman at his side: that longing for the war to be over, a comforting fantasy that one day she might make a home for him, be there every evening when he returned...

On a warm impulse, he reached for her hand, stealing a sidelong glance at her downcast eyes; she seemed as moved by those words as he was, her fingers clasping his in sudden emotion. His heart leapt in response, and he thought how long it had been, weeks in which he had tried, very hard, not to touch her at all. Except for that fleeting kiss and the warmth of her linked arm this afternoon, he had kept apart from her, and he wondered whether she knew how difficult it had been.

Georgina's hand, imprisoned for a moment, opened to his, palm to his palm, the fingers slowly – oh, so slowly – entwining with his. Wanting to lock her to him and never let go, Liam was suddenly conscious of his own strength, the breadth of hands thickened by constant use, and a fear of hurting her. Very gently, he drew her fingers through his in the most intimate caress, while her light, responding touch sent waves of rapture coursing through him, catching the breath in his throat, fusing love and desire so totally he was only marginally surprised by the sudden heat in his loins. The contact between them was so restrained yet so sensual, it seemed there were but two points in the whole universe, linked by a line of acute and exquisite pleasure; it was almost like making love. Or how he imagined it should be.

Did she feel it too? For a moment he was convinced she must, convinced by the sensuality of her caress, by her closed, fluttering lashes, the soft, partly open mouth, the distinct rise and fall of her breasts. She seemed as deep in thrall as he was himself. And then as desire mounted overwhelmingly, as the fire in his loins became more pain than joy, he thought no, she can't be aware of this, it's impossible. If she did she would stop, withdraw this instant before we fall on each other without a care for who or what surrounds us...

But even as he moved to slip an arm around her shoulders and draw her close to him, on an indrawn breath Georgina pressed her fingers to her mouth and shook her head, like one bemused or waking from a dream.

Paralysed, he watched her rise abruptly and push her way out down an empty row of seats.

The encore came to an end. The soubrette bowed to a storm of applause and stamping of feet. Galvanized into action, Liam grabbed jacket and mackintosh and followed at a run for the side exit. Coming out into the dismal street, he saw her hurrying away, heading not for the main thoroughfare, but into the side-streets of Soho.

'Georgina!'

He ran, his heart pounding, catching at her arm as he came up with her; but she would not stop. He pulled her round, quite roughly, to face him. Trembling still, she kept her eyes averted. At a loss for words, he knew, with heart-stopping certainty, that her emotions, her desires, echoed his. In the dark warmth of the theatre, that thought had been exciting; here, in the cold and foggy daylight, it seemed a huge, terrible knowledge, as though on discovering he could swim, he found himself faced with the sea from the top of a cliff.

Instantly sobered, murmuring inadequate apologies, he slipped the mackintosh around her shoulders. 'Let me take you home.'

TWENTY-FIVE

Although she protested, it was in a vague, half-hearted way. Liam had no difficulty in guiding her towards the main thoroughfare and finding a motor-taxi to take them to Queen's Gate. Leaning back into the corner with her eyes closed, she said nothing all the way there. He held her hand in a comforting fashion, feeling both anxious and chronically guilty every time he looked at her.

His intentions were to drop her at the door and make his way back to Wandsworth, but even as he paid the taxi and prepared to say goodbye, Georgina asked him to come up to the flat. 'I think it's time we talked, don't you? Have you time?'

He looked at his watch. 'A couple of hours.'

She smiled slightly at that, a wan, resigned sort of smile that seemed bleaker than the afternoon. 'Time for a cup of tea, at least.'

While she searched for her key he glanced down the broad, tree-lined avenue to where it disappeared into driving mist, finding its elegance as daunting as the moment. On a deep breath he mounted the steps, following her into a wide, marble-floored hall. The broad staircase was carpeted, but she lifted a finger to her lips as they began to climb the first of several flights to the Duncannons' door. In the small lobby she took his hat and sheepskin jacket and laid them across a chair, and without raising her eyes led the way into a large, comfortably furnished room which obviously answered several different functions.

There was a fine dining table and chairs before the windows, and in one alcove a large mahogany desk; a tall bookcase graced the far side of the chimney breast, while a large leather sofa and chairs faced the fire. It was a room with a masculine air, and a faint smell of cigars; the colours, mainly dark greens and golds, were restful, and the sofa well-used. Nevertheless, Liam sat down gingerly, very much aware in those initial seconds that this was

Robert Duncannon's home.

But it was also Georgina's and she was his first priority. With an effort he forced himself to ignore his surroundings and to concentrate on her. Setting a match to the neatly laid fire, she asked him to tend it while she went into the kitchen to make some tea. He wanted to say that tea was not important, but she seemed to need the bustle and the movement. Nursing the fire into reluctant life, he wondered what it was she wanted to say, and dreaded being told that they must not see each other again.

And yet if she said that – and she would, she was bound to say it – Liam knew he could not disagree. With regard to this afternoon, the most he could say in his own defence was that it was a miracle it had not happened before. Wanting her was hell, nevertheless he knew he would promise anything just to be able to go on seeing her.

He went and stood by the window, staring out at the plane trees, their soot-stained yellow leaves hanging limply from blackened boughs. Below, he could see the dark hood of an old hansom cab waiting by the kerb, and less clearly, across the street, a line of forecourt railings; but the light-coloured buildings were becoming difficult to make out. Twilight was deepening with the encroaching fog, and he was anxious, suddenly, about making his way back to Wandsworth. In mounting desperation, he went through into the kitchen. She was setting a tray. Hesitantly, very much afraid that she would flinch or back away, he laid a gentle hand on her arm.

'Please, Georgina, come and sit down. I can't bear this – I need to talk to you, but I don't know what to say...'

She was silent for a moment, very still. Looking down at her bowed head, he sighed and touched a loose strand of hair, smoothing it back from her face. It was fine and soft between his fingers, like silk; he would have liked to loosen the thick coil, see it fall around her shoulders, but did not dare. He let his hand rest against the warmth of her neck. 'I didn't mean to hurt you...'

With a sudden shiver she turned towards him, bending her head to his chest; hardly daring to breathe, he held her very lightly, his whispered plea for forgiveness barely more than a sigh.

'It wasn't your fault.' The words did not come easily, he could tell that, there was a certain bitterness about them, as though she had conducted battles of her own, and this surrender went against every principle.

'Oh, I think it was,' he said manfully, preparing himself for the worst. 'After all, I…'

'Liam, stop. Listen to me.' She looked up, searching his face with those bleak, hurt eyes. Her arms came up around his neck, and she stroked the soft hair at his nape. 'I love you.' But she frowned as she said it, and he knew the admission pained her, even while it set his own heart aflame with joy. 'I know it's wrong and so do you – but I can't bear it…'

His arms went round her then, fiercely, possessively, and he held her hard because he thought he might weep with relief at not having to pretend any longer. He told her that he loved her too, that he had always loved her; that through all the beauty and tenderness of these last weeks he had been longing to tell her so, and that it was for love and love alone that he tried so hard not to touch her nor to give any cause for regret.

The words came out brokenly, a jumbled mix of past and present that miraculously she seemed to understand. 'I know, I know,' she said over and over while her hands touched his face and caressed his shoulders, and her lips returned those tender, hesitant kisses.

'I missed you so much – all those years I missed you, and longed to hear from you. It was so cruel of you to leave like that, without a word – I thought you hated me.'

'I did, I did,' he whispered against her hair, 'but only for a little while and only because I loved you so much, because you knew and I didn't, and you didn't tell me…'

'I wanted to – oh, my darling, I wanted to tell you, but I couldn't, I…'

'Hush now, it doesn't matter, it really doesn't matter…'

And in the joy of her, the bliss of her slender, pliant body pressed so passionately to his, Liam let go of the past, forgetting all the things that should have been remembered, all the things that until now had kept them so carefully apart. He was lost in the scent of her hair and skin, in the soft pressure of her breasts and the touch of her fingers against his cheek. She moved even as he moved, turning her face, her mouth, to meet his. He tasted salt on her lips, and in those spent tears seemed to rest so much love, more than he ever expected, far more than he deserved. With the warmth and passion of her response, all restraint vanished; she set fire to the hunger in him, and he sensed no reservation, no withholding, but rather an eager taking of every caress, and a need to respond in kind.

In his inexperience, Liam might have hesitated, but she seemed to understand so much, to know his body as well as he did; and when he pressed his lips to her throat, she unfastened his shirt and ran her fingers beneath it, sending shivers of delight with every touch. After that, with his hand welcome at her breast, it seemed the most natural thing in the world to release a few tiny buttons, to push back flimsy straps and know the rapture of her firm and naked breasts against his skin.

With senses reeling they clung together, searching, exploring, gasping at each unexpected discovery, at the escalating riot of need. Wanting to be part of her, to quench his desire in the warmth and softness of her most secret place, he was conscious only of its necessity, of that strange act of fusion which would both release and make them one. Lifting her up, he carried her through into the other room, laying her down before the hearth. With her eyes half-closed she took him to her, making no defence of her virginity. But her virginity was, in part, its own defence: he was too reluctant to force that tender place, and in the end movement brought its own release. Too soon to bring joy, but too soon, mercifully, to cause lasting regret.

In those seconds which followed, before remorse or apology or thought could take hold, the telephone rang, startling them both with its loud, insistent ringing. Tense, horrified, still as statues they held each other, conscious of half-nakedness, the terrible intimacy of what had just occurred. It was as shocking as though someone had walked into the room.

Georgina recovered first, scrambling to her feet, pulling at her open blouse and the crumpled folds of her skirt. Almost staggering as she crossed the room, she left open the door to the lobby, and Liam saw her stand for a moment before picking up the jangling instrument.

Then she looked at him, straight at him as she was speaking, alarm in her eyes, her strained voice struggling for clarity. 'No, Tisha, he's still in Ireland... I'm not very well at the moment, nursing a cold... yes it is a nasty one, you wouldn't want to share it...' Liam cringed. 'In fact I've just woken up, I've been sleeping most of the afternoon... No, Father won't be back for another ten days or so, you must have misunderstood...'

Not knowing whether to laugh or cry, as Georgina answered questions about Robert Duncannon's trip to Ireland, Liam went into the kitchen to rescue his cigarettes. As she finished the call at last, he caught hold of her, supporting her across the room to the sofa.

Holding her close in the crook of his arm, he lit a cigarette and expelled a great cloud of blue smoke, aware that all he wanted to do was find a bed and take her to it, and just go on holding her.

'Did she want to come and see you?'

'Not me particularly – she was simply hoping someone might be at home. I managed to put her off.'

'Thank God for that.'

He held her close and stroked her hair, no longer bound in its neat coil. Releasing the last of the pins, he smoothed it as best he could, kissing her all the time. Gradually, her trembling subsided, but his nerves were still raw from reaction, his mind just beginning to grasp the full implications of what had taken place between them. He did not know whether to apologize for attempting to make love to her, or for failing so abysmally; in the end he confessed to severe fright.

'But I wanted you to,' she admitted in a very small voice.

'I know. That frightens me too.' He hugged her closer, kissing the crown of her head as she pressed her face inside his open shirt.

'I love you, Liam.'

'And I love you,' he whispered, caught again by the torment of their situation. 'What are we going to do?'

It seemed an unanswerable question. They talked for a while and Georgina made some tea. While she went to change her crumpled clothes, Liam coaxed the fire back to life and soon had it blazing merrily. He was sitting cross-legged on the hearthrug when she returned in a blue velvet dressing gown, her hair brushed loosely in soft waves around her shoulders. Watching her in the firelight glow, Liam thought she looked like a princess in a fairy tale, more beautiful than he had ever seen her. With no more pretence between them, she was softer, gentler, so infinitely giving that it seemed his love for her doubled each time they touched, each time his glance met hers.

Nevertheless, that sense of joy was not entirely unfettered. They talked about love and loving each other, about its beginnings and its heartbreaks and uncertainties; and they discussed – albeit with some constraint – that sudden, overwhelming culmination. Georgina said that the wrong of their situation was as nothing compared to what was going on across the Channel, which made Liam realize that she had been thinking about this for some time. His view, however, was more specific and personal. It was also very difficult for him to put into words. Concerned for her vulnerability rather than those abstract and relative concepts, he simply said that it must not happen again: he was prepared to exercise restraint if she was.

His bluntness made her smile. It was a soft, indulgent, admiring smile. 'I don't deserve you,' she said.

The dark afternoon had closed in early with a thickening blanket of fog. Around six, when he should have been thinking of leaving, Liam went to the window to stare out at the murky darkness. Even the plane trees had disappeared. Beside him, echoing his thoughts, Georgina voiced the opinion that neither of them stood much chance of reaching their destinations tonight; trams and buses would be stopped, and it would be far more sensible to stay where they were.

'Well,' he smiled, 'I can't pretend I'm sorry. For a night with you, I'd happily be shot at dawn. But what about your matron? What will she say?'

'What can she say? She can't argue with the weather.' Georgina patted his arm. 'I'll telephone, tell them I'm stuck here. And it might be as well for you to get in touch with Wandsworth, then they won't be worrying about you. Say you're staying with relatives.'

Laughing, Liam blessed the weather.

Georgina woke at about six. For the first time in her life, however, she did not wake alone. In her soft feather bed, she and Liam were curled together like a pair of spoons, the length of his body pressed to her back, his arms, warm and heavy, around her. It was a strange but intensely pleasurable sensation, as though her very skin came alive in the instant of awareness, and as memory flooded back she had to stir, had to recapture the tingling thrill that came with every tiny movement against him. Last night she had been dizzy with it, as though intellect had ceased to exist, her only awareness being of him and with him, where his limbs touched hers, where hands and mouth aroused and explored, driving her to the edge of ecstasy and beyond. He had taken such delight in her, needing to look and touch, a little shy at first, unfamiliar with women, uncertain of what was and was not permitted. Inexperienced herself, Georgina had simply known, deep inside, that she wanted him to touch her in all the ways she longed to caress him.

There was advantage for her in that she knew men's bodies, every basic function, each hidden sensitivity; and years of nursing had blunted neither her wonder nor her sense of respect. There was also an odd, half-realized feeling that in making love to him she was in some way expressing all the tenderness she had felt for other men, men who had passed into and out of her care, men who had recovered, or died, or simply returned to the Front without ever knowing a woman's love. And in remembering them she also recalled the young doctor who had so surprised her with his bitterness, his accusation that she had no heart, no soul.

If only you knew, she thought then; and that thought repeated itself now, making her smile a little. But that man had frightened her with his vehemence, made her half-believe he was right. Afterwards she had thought too much about the curse of nursing, the fear that in seeking protection against suffering, the heart shrivelled, so that in the end all feeling was gone. It happened to some.

Liam had saved her from that, proved to her that love and compassion were still there, that she was capable of happiness as well as pain.

After years in which even the acknowledgement of love had been suppressed, these recent weeks had been fraught with conflicting desires. Watching him recover in health and strength, the need to fuss and touch and bestow a thousand kisses had crept up inside like yeast fermenting in a stoppered jar. She had wanted him so much, and been so afraid of showing it.

If his kiss that evening in the car had loosened the lid, then the touch of his hand yesterday had released raw physical desire in such torrents that she had been appalled, unable to reconcile such intense physical need with the tender, romantic fantasies she had previously entertained. Knowing, bleakly, that their relationship could not go on in that false, frustrating manner, she had been aware of a need for honesty, a desire to put all cards on the table and say, however baldly, this is how I feel about you – what must I do?

Rights and wrongs that had kept her awake at night seemed suddenly immaterial; the one remaining fear was for the consequences. Yet even that – yes, even that, she repeated to her shocked other self – she had been prepared to risk for the joy of knowing his embrace. It was shocking, and in the warmth of his arms, Georgina felt she did not deserve the depth of his love, nor the extent of his consideration.

Turning, stretching out slowly, pressing her lips to the smooth muscle of his upper arm, she luxuriated in his presence, hearing him sigh, feeling him stir against her as he woke from sleep. She had switched off the lamp beside her bed hours ago, but the lobby light was still burning; by its dull glow through the open door she was able to see his face, the beginnings of a sensual smile touching his lips. He had changed, she thought, watching the curve of his mouth, just as their relationship had changed, all hesitancy gone in those hours of intimate exploration, hours in which they had discovered each other.

He had brought her to pleasure with gentleness, but he had done it roughly, too, with a kind of urgent desperation she understood, even while it made her writhe and gasp. That first time, driving his fingers into her, she had arched and cried out, and he had moaned at the sight of blood on his hands, for a moment not understanding that it was virginal blood, her cry the cry of all women invaded for the first time. It had, however, deepened the bond between them, subtly altering some delicate balance in their relationship. Prior to that she had been the one to encourage and reassure; afterwards he was more dominant, and also, oddly, more protective.

'I love you,' he said sleepily, nuzzling her neck, burying his fingers in her tangled hair. He ran a hand over her body, over breasts and belly and thighs, teasing her gently. She turned to him and he kissed her with slow, languorous pleasure, murmuring against her lips, 'I shall probably wake up in a minute, in that bloody hard bed in Wandsworth'.

His words, regrettably, broke the spell. As she shivered, Liam wrapped his arms around her and held her close. 'There'll be other times – we'll find ways of being together, you know we will...'

But with a mass of impossibilities flooding her mind, Georgina could only cling to him in disbelief. Loving him, wanting to keep him close forever, she could see only the perfection of what they had shared, and the future's bleak uncertainty. Her father might be away for another ten days, which presupposed one more meeting here; but after that...

There had to be ways, even if it meant meeting in hotels for a few stolen hours; she had money, more than enough, and was prepared to do anything, anything at all, to be with him.

The fog was still thick, but a sense of duty made it incumbent upon them both to attempt a return to their rightful places. Laying out her spare uniform, Georgina set the iron to heat and gathered up Liam's clothes for pressing. She fetched a razor from the collection in her father's room, together with a brush and a keg of sandalwood shaving soap, laying them down before a small mirror on the wash-stand in her room.

'There we are. But if you want to brush your teeth, my darling, you'll have to borrow mine. I haven't got a spare one.'

'Oh, I think I can bear that,' he responded with a grin.

Bringing a jug of hot water from the kitchen, Georgina left him to it. With a towel wrapped around his waist, Liam washed quickly in the early morning chill, hesitating only briefly before attacking the stubble along his jaw. He had to shave, it was a matter of necessity, and stupid to be so finicky about using Robert Duncannon's things. But he disliked it, performing the task with as much speed and efficiency as he could muster. Satisfied, dabbing his face dry, he went in search of Georgina and his clothes. Shirt, jacket and trousers were all pressed and ready to wear, commensurate with his tale of staying with relatives as an overnight guest.

While she prepared breakfast for them both, he returned to her room to dress, noticing that the other bedroom door was also open. He saw a large bed with a maroon eiderdown, and on the bedside chest, facing him, a collection of photographs.

He glanced away, was on the threshold of Georgina's room when recognition swept over him in a wave of guilt. He turned back to look again.

From a silver frame, his mother's face regarded him. It was a familiar photograph, one taken when she was young, with cropped, curly hair and such a proud tilt to her chin. In his surprise at finding it there, that sense of being caught in something shameful disappeared. He was fascinated by her youthful loveliness, which it seemed he had never before noticed: in his memory she was much older, her face softened by time. But even as he stared at it, the photograph blurred and he had to sit down, almost unmanned by images of childhood, his mother's constant, reliable affection, her care and gentleness. Assailed by sorrow and regret, he asked whether she deserved the cruelty he had meted out, and knew she did not. His behaviour towards her had been unforgivable.

He thought of the war, and the dozens upon dozens he had killed in the heat of battle; but he had pitied German and Turkish prisoners, even sharing food and water and cigarettes when necessary. It struck him then, and very bitterly, that he had been kinder to sworn enemies than he had been, in recent years, to his own mother.

He picked up the polished silver frame and looked at that lovely young face, and for the first time he was able to view her, not as his mother, but as a contemporary, with thoughts and feelings akin to his own. Like Georgina, about her age, full of life and passion, with the same needs, the same yearnings, reaching out, crossing barriers, taking what love had to offer, while ever it was offered.

Like Georgina. Just like Georgina.

And he thought of Robert Duncannon, whose room this was, a young man then, not much older than himself; and he thought of that tragic marriage, doomed to misery and failure.

Robert Duncannon: keeping his mother's photograph, still

beside the bed after all these years. Suddenly Liam understood the love that must have been between them then, that need to grab hold of happiness before it could slip away...

And Liam thought about himself, loving Georgina, knowing it should not be, yet committing the unforgivable. Carried away in the heat of the moment, they had both wanted that consummation, both intended it, despite its incestuous nature and regardless of the consequences. If degrees of wrongdoing were to be considered, Liam knew full well that in the scheme of things, adultery was far less culpable than incest.

It made him shiver. He had blamed his mother and Robert Duncannon for heinous sin, yet it seemed to him now that what they had shared was no more than the folly of loving unwisely. He had imagined that his love for Georgina was greater and purer and more magnificent than any man had ever felt before. But in the light of sudden revelation, he wondered whether all men felt like that. All women, too. And passion itself, once tasted, was self-perpetuating; being with Georgina, seeing and touching the beauty of her nakedness, he wanted more, always more.

He would always love her. Always.

Was that what Robert Duncannon felt? Did he, a man in his fifties, still love Louisa Elliott? Did he still long for her in the lonely hours of the night, still regret that parting?

Liam shivered again. That longing seemed present in the room. It clung to the photograph of his mother, to the other, smaller ones which stood beside it. He looked at them for the first time, and with a terrible lurch of the heart, recognized himself as a child. One was familiar, taken with Robin and Tisha some ten or twelve years before, possibly for Robert Duncannon's benefit, and sent to him in India or South Africa, or wherever he had been stationed at the time.

There was another, one Liam had never seen: three children again, but much younger, and not the same three. A little girl of perhaps seven or eight years old, with long blonde ringlets and a pretty dress, holding a baby, awkwardly, on her lap; and beside them on the chaise longue, a chubby toddler in a sailor suit, stiff and frowning as though told to sit still.

Recognizing himself in the sailor-suit, recognizing Georgina, his

425

throat constricted. It was true, then; it was all true. He remembered the house, the house in his dreams, and knew the little girl as he had always known her in his secret memories. It was Ireland, where his mother had been unhappy and cried a lot; where Father was a big man on a beautiful horse, who had once lifted him up, miles it seemed, to view the world from the height of his saddle.

Lost in that secret world, he never noticed Georgina come to him; became aware of her only as she slipped an arm about his shoulders and pressed her cheek to his. He tried hard to compose himself, but the flashes of memory were disconcerting, unconnected and incomplete. Turning to Georgina, he buried his face in the crook of her shoulder, against the silkiness of her hair. It was impossible to speak, impossible to express the anguish he felt, the riot of emotions to which those sudden revelations gave birth. He was beginning to understand what he had never been able to grasp before, and it was painful, in a deep, wrenching, physical way.

Like a wounded man, he clung to her. 'Hold me,' he whispered, 'don't ever let me go...'

The sister on duty that day was on relief from another part of the hospital. Not knowing her, Liam was able to report with a series of half-truths which seemed convincing enough. Having the previous evening's record book before her, she accepted his explanations with no more than an expression of sympathy at the state of the weather. Another Australian, she loathed these London fogs herself, and dreaded the coming winter.

With a sigh of relief, Liam let his stiff facial muscles relax, going into the kitchen to see if he could beg a hot drink. It had taken him more than two hours to get back, almost an hour since leaving Georgina at Vauxhall Bridge, and he had missed the usual mid-morning break.

One of the young nurses put the kettle on the stove to boil.

'Heavens,' she exclaimed, peering up into his face, 'you look a bit peaky this morning. Did you have a bad time getting back? Wasn't it terrible last night? I got lost, just trying to find the nurses' home! Did you set off from your relatives' house, or not even try?'

'Didn't even try,' he said, clearing his throat. 'We were having tea and talking, and never noticed it getting worse. Then I went to the door, and everybody said it'd be folly to set off, and I'd better stay the night. I'm glad I did, otherwise I don't think I'd have made it.'

'Very wise. Kelly and McLaren didn't get back till half-past ten from Stockwell – they'd been wandering round the back streets for nearly three hours! And the terrible trio spent the night on the floor at Horseferry Road – found their way so far, but couldn't get any further. Awful.'

Liam sipped his tea and listened to a few more horror stories, glad to know that he was not the only one missing from the ward last night. Now they were returning to the fold, the wanderers would relate and embellish their stories with gusto, while his tale of a night spent with relatives would be far too dull to provoke interest. It was a relief: he was exhausted after not much more than three hours' sleep, and the emotional upheaval that followed seemed to have drained his mind completely. He felt incapable of rational thought, and had only one idea in his head: to escape to the library as soon as he had eaten, find a quiet corner and a comfortable chair, and sleep.

Improved by supper time, Liam turned in to bed early, but there was an air of restlessness about the ward, raised voices which had the night-sister out of her office on several occasions, telling them all to remember those less fortunate. But there was nobody really ill; their numbers had been reduced to eighteen, most of them fitter than Liam, and just waiting for their cards to be marked convalescent.

Keen though he had been to elicit some leave, he was now back where he had begun: uncertain as to his feelings and praying for a little time to adjust. It was difficult to sleep. He was beset by too many new impressions, not least of which being that sense of things coming together, which had gripped him so forcibly that morning. Loving Georgina, he had been concerned primarily to avoid unpalatable consequences for her, and while his physical need was great, the very last thing he wanted was to leave her with a child. Had it not been for that consideration, he knew he would have made love to her fully. He loved her, and had it been possible, would have married her; the fact that they were brother and sister had no real meaning for him. That was the trouble: he had never been able to accept it. If he had, Liam reasoned, that innocent, boyish passion would have died years ago.

But it was hard to avoid the parallels between making love to her last night and being brought face to face with other realities this morning. Love and pain, past and present, York and Dublin, had all made themselves felt in a peculiarly harsh way, as though two rusty, long-unused parts of his life had suddenly meshed together with a great grinding of cogs and levers, jerking him forward to a point of new perception.

It was not a comfortable sensation. He had moments of gratitude and others of intense irritation, when he wished it would all go away and leave him in peace. In bed he wanted to think about Georgina, idly to dream about the hours they had spent together; he wanted to savour each precious moment, every new discovery. Yet as soon as he relaxed, it seemed something else came into his mind, like the visits Robert Duncannon had made to York when Liam was very young, or the occasion of his fifth birthday, when his mother and Edward had been married.

Because that memory was so clear, he gave in then, and let his mind settle on that for a while: the party, the surprise at coming home from school to find Aunts Emily and Blanche gathered there, everyone's bubbling happiness. Having always thought that party was for him, Liam had felt betrayed when he found out; yet now it seemed a necessary deception, the only way to explain the celebration to three innocent, talkative young children. People must have assumed, for long enough, that Louisa and Edward were married, just as he had assumed that Edward was his father.

When had that happened? He could not recall when or how or why he had abandoned his memories of Dublin and Robert Duncannon, but in the light of Georgina's recollections, he wondered whether, at two years old, the shock of being wrenched away from things known and loved, had had anything to do with it. That dawn parting on a bleak quayside had marked her very deeply: and although he did not recall clinging to her and being dragged away by her aunt, Liam had suffered with her as she told the story. What he did remember, very vaguely, was arriving in the dark of a winter's night at a strange house, and strange people whose accents he did not understand. He remembered crying with fear and loneliness.

Another incident, much later, stood out very clearly, and it was a memory which had returned that day at the Maddox farm, when Ned bent to examine the horse's legs. Even now Liam could see Robert Duncannon doing the same thing, and as he rose, saying wistfully, 'You don't know what to call me, Liam, do you?'

Standing before that imposing man, the child had been so frightened, so guilty in the knowledge of his own disloyalty, so confused by that sudden and unlooked-for return.

Did I know, then, who he was? Liam wondered. But he could not be certain; only emotion remained, and even that was fading fast with the strange new ability to accept old truths. And he could accept them now only because he had begun to understand.

But truth, as ever, was a two-edged sword. If memory had at last consented to show him the indissoluble link which existed between himself and Robert Duncannon, then it had also revealed the connection between himself and Georgina. There was suddenly less pleasure in recalling that long night of love and mutual exploration, and the arousal it produced was tinged, very definitely, with unease.

When he did sleep, it was not to dream of any of those things, but to experience again, for the first time in weeks, another terrible nightmare about Pozières.

Twenty-six

It was a strange, unsettling week. For three days the fog lingered in a claustrophobic blanket that did nothing to ease his introspection or sense of guilt. When he was not hugging the stove on the ward, Liam was in the library searching for fresh books to read, and when he was not reading, he was busy writing letters, most of which he destroyed.

To whom could he confess; to whom turn for advice? No one, that was the short answer, and yet he had never felt more in need of help. There was no escaping the fact that what he felt for Georgina, what they had already shared, was incestuous; and the matter of incest was taboo, with church and state and society unanimously sweeping the whole subject beneath a dusty carpet of ignorance. He looked back on the hours spent with Georgina in this ward, these grounds, under the eyes of both authority and friends, and knew he could never, ever, confess what was between them. Not to anyone.

It would have helped if he could have seen her, to talk over the things that kept going round in his mind, but the weather resolutely prevented that. He found himself praying, with the fervour of a fanatic, that Sunday would be clear enough for them to make their planned assignation.

Another nightmare about Pozières woke him in the early hours, but in the trembling, sweating aftermath, he heard the steady drumming of heavy rain on roofs and windows. It cleared the sulphurous fog, leaving the morning bright and new-washed, raising everyone's spirits like a breath of spring. There was almost a fight for passes that afternoon, but Liam was lucky, and a little after one he was on his way to meet Georgina at Vauxhall Bridge. Within the hour they were climbing the stairs to her apartment, and despite his creeping feeling of guilt, very shortly after that he was again making love to her.

The bedroom smelled of roses from a bowl of pot-pourri on a chest near the window, and her skin gave off a similar fragrance, as though she liked to wear, and be surrounded by, a constant memory of summer. She reminded him of summer days, of those last glorious weeks he had spent at home before the war; open cornfields beneath a wide blue sky, the warmth of gentle sun and larks singing with blithe unconcern. She was warm and happy and giving, allowing nothing to mar their brief time together, allowing nothing to intrude. Relaxed, breathing gently, she lay along the length of him, her long and beautiful legs entwined with his, face hidden in a curve of his shoulder, hair lying in glinting strands across her back.

He wound the long, silky hair through his fingers, heart-breakingly aware of her beauty and the love they shared. But for him the innocence was gone. He knew the depth of his desire and he knew it should have no place here, felt it like a weight at the core of his being. Yet he could no more stay away, he thought, than sprout angel's wings; and he would go on seeing her, go on loving her like this, for as long as it was permitted.

Sensing that difference in him, Georgina stirred, asked what was wrong. He shook his head, said it was nothing, but she was not convinced. Eventually, with much hesitancy, he did manage to put into words what he had been trying to write, without success, for days. Going back to the moment of awareness, that moment when he had finally been able to accept the truth of who his father was, he tried to explain this sudden sense of guilt; and in the telling of it, it seemed to Liam that they had been shown a glimpse of paradise, only to have it snatched away.

He found himself thinking of that book he had found the other day in the library. Not a child's book, that translation of the *Rubaiyat*, with its references to wine and love and all-powerful destiny; a man's probably, left behind in sudden departure and no doubt much regretted. It was not new to him: he had first come across a copy years ago, at home, and read it with interest but little understanding. Reading those lines again, however, they rushed back like old, familiar music, pulsing with meaning and fresh significance, doing their best to defy the sense of guilt. What they could not defy, indeed what they underlined was the fleeting passage of time, brief moments of beauty lost forever in death and decay.

Was that why he dreamed of the war?

'What is it?' Georgina murmured. 'What else is bothering you?'

Liam shook his head, reluctant to upset her further; but again she pressed him until he quoted the one line that kept repeating itself, over and over in his mind like a haunting refrain.

'*One moment in annihilation's waste, one moment of the well of life to taste...*'

'And it makes me think of you, and a place on the Somme that doesn't even exist any more. It's just a name – Pozières – that's all it is, a name, and a shifting wasteland of grit and ashes. It used to be a village on a hill...' He closed his eyes. 'I dreamed about it again last night...'

She did not speak, but hid her face against his chest, while Liam stroked her hair and the smoothness of her back. 'Annihilation's waste,' he repeated, 'that's what it was. A waste land. Nothing. Pounded to oblivion, with men beneath it. And every time another shell landed...' He shuddered, unable to give voice to that vision of burial and disinterment, the shifting shell-holes and mind-shattering noise, the dust and ashes blowing in the wind.

With suddenly trembling fingers he reached for his cigarettes and lit one, drawing smoke deep into his lungs, releasing it slowly as tension disseminated throughout his body. He continued to stroke her hair, finding consolation in its warmth and softness, and something of healing in her tears.

'But you, my love,' he murmured with bleak simplicity, 'are like that well of life to me. You've given me so much, restored me, made me whole again – and I love you so much, it hurts.'

Back at the hospital that night, Georgina spent a long time staring into the darkness, her cheeks wet with tears, her heart aching for him. His memories and regrets bit deep, and it seemed painfully ironic that he should have come to awareness so suddenly, and through loving her.

What he needed was time to assimilate these things, but time was something they had so little of. That was her one, lingering regret, although unlike Liam she had been aware of it all along. That sense of time running out had pressed her most dreadfully, contributing – she could see it now – to the urgency of physical need. That, she did not regret – it seemed to have been essential to them both – and in thinking about it, Georgina had no sense of guilt, only grief that it could not go on forever.

On the Thursday, which was her day off, Liam telephoned to say that he could not get a pass to come up to town, and without one he would have to report back by half-past four. Although he wanted to break the rules and take the risk for an hour of her company, Georgina felt bound to dissuade him. Anxiety had dogged all day, inexplicable and without apparent foundation, yet very real. It was with some difficulty that she persuaded him to stay where he was, and let her come to him.

Saying little, they went out for a walk, each terribly aware of the other, wanting so much more than the chaste kiss of greeting and the respectably linked arms that propriety demanded. More than ever did Georgina realize that they would have to find a meeting place, somewhere within easy reach of both Lewisham and Wandsworth, sufficiently anonymous for them both. It was the last day of October and they had, perhaps, a few more weeks in which to be together; it seemed very important not to waste them.

It was beautiful across the Common, very cold and still, with a faint blue haze of woodsmoke drifting through the trees. On the way back, they sat for a while by the old windmill, watching an elderly gardener raking up leaves, savouring between them an air of sharp nostalgia, of the last days of autumn, with winter waiting on the threshold. The trees were bare and the sky had a strange, translucent beauty; everything seemed clear and poised and not quite real. Georgina felt it echoed in herself, in a heightened awareness of the falling dusk, her own stillness and Liam's quiet presence. Catching his glance and a slow, intimate smile, her eyes lingered on the lines of his face, the sweep of heavy lashes, the firm chin and well-shaped mouth; and within came a stirring that was at once both deeply sexual and deeply grieving. Knowing his strength, she had a sense, too, of his fragility, and that exquisite, momentary happiness that he had talked about, moving on to realms unknown, horizons unseen.

It hovered on the edge of agony, that blend of spirit and sensuality; and the moment of awareness seemed like a threshold, a pause between day and night, autumn and winter, perfect past and uncertain future. But as the shadows lengthened and uncertainty took hold, a sudden, violent shiver dispelled it. Liam took her hand and caressed it, and he was warm and vital and full of concern.

'You're cold,' he said gently, 'and I think we should go...'

She had to return to the flat for her uniform, and as she came up the stairs she was astonished to see the door standing open and her father's servant coming out with what looked like an empty trunk. Too astonished to speak, she simply nodded and gave a feeble smile as he passed and said her father was inside.

Pausing, she had a frantic moment. Imagining the scene had she been in bed with Liam when her father made his unannounced arrival, her breath caught, then she wondered whether the place was truly tidy, whether Liam had left anything behind to raise awkward questions. Still puzzled by the fact that her father was back today, instead of next Monday, as yesterday's letter had indicated, she stepped across the threshold.

They both uttered their surprise together, but neither laughed. After a brief embrace, Robert commented again on her arrival at such a time, and Georgina was forced to give a somewhat convoluted account of her day, including the fact that she had been to Wandsworth to see Liam.

'And how is he?'

With the uneasy feeling that her father could see right through her, she tried to appear nonchalant. 'Well, he seems quite well, but I suppose the doctor must think otherwise, or he wouldn't still be there.'

'And what about you?' he asked. 'Are you home for the night, or going back to the hospital?'

Because she was rostered for an early duty the following morning, she had intended to return that evening; but something about her father's eyes – something in his whole demeanour – prompted her to say that she could stay if he wanted her to do so.

His glance, as it rested on her, softened into gratitude. 'Yes, Georgie, I'd like you to stay.' He pressed her arm, became suddenly brisk, pouring drinks for the two of them even while she removed her coat and hat and went into her bedroom to check swiftly that all was well. An empty match-box in the waste-paper basket seemed the most damning evidence and she snatched at it, thrusting it deep into her pocket. Nothing else was out of place.

Accepting a glass of sherry, Georgina took a seat beside the freshly lit fire; when Robert's servant had left them, she said: 'And what brings you home so early, Daddy? Your letter said Monday.'

She was part prepared for something unpleasant, but oddly enough, she never thought of Robin. When her father said that he had been injured, it was a great shock.

'How? I mean, how badly is he injured?'

'Leg wound – I don't know any more than that.' Robert sank most of his brandy in one gulp, splashed some more into the glass and came to stand before the fire. 'Some bloody place on the Somme – I forget the name of it. A raid on enemy lines, apparently – company commander bought it, with another officer and a couple of men.'

'Including Robin.' She felt sick, thinking of the mud, already notorious on the battlefields, all that ghastliness infecting an open wound. Much would depend on how rapidly he had received attention, how close they were to a field hospital. Even so, he would be lucky to escape without the complications of gangrene. Too familiar with the results of that, she took a deep breath and released it slowly. 'When did you find out? Where is he?'

'Still in Boulogne, I think, and I gather he'll be there for a while. I imagine they'll send him to one of the Yorkshire hospitals, but I don't know. I'll try to establish what's happening, tomorrow. I got the message yesterday morning, and managed to get a letter off to Louisa straight away – then spent most of the day trying to organize my affairs so that I could come home. However, I'd planned to take Letty down to White Leigh on Friday...' His voice tailed away, his eyes staring, unfocused, on the fire.

'How is she?'

'Oh, you know – arthritis playing her up again, but otherwise all right. William seems set on drinking himself to death, though

– and God knows what's happening to the estate. That's why I wanted to go down. But he's lost interest, Georgie, lost interest completely. And as for Dublin...' On a great sigh of weariness and despair, he lowered himself into the chair facing her.

Looking at him, at his hair which was now almost white, and the deep lines of sadness in his face, she was struck by sudden guilt. Since Liam's return, she had given Ireland barely a passing thought. With a sigh to match his, she said, 'I am sorry – it's all such a terrible mess, isn't it? Everywhere you look. What's happening to the world, I often wonder...'

Robert shook his head. 'I don't know, Georgie, and that's the truth. I can't see any hope at all – that's the tragedy. As you say, Ireland's in a shocking mess and I can't see it getting better – and the world's in a worse state, but what can any of us do? We're just a bunch of old men,' he rumbled grimly, 'trying to rein in a team that's bolted. We're old and feeble, and all the young men – all the ones who might have saved us – they're all dying. Every last, decent one...'

He was bitter and despairing, and it showed in his face. Hurt by her father's pain, unable to offer any consolation, Georgina looked away.

For a while they both stared into the fire, occupied by miseries collective and individual. She was thinking about Robin when her father expressed the dismal hope that the injury might act as a catalyst.

'How do you mean, *catalyst*? I don't understand.'

He sighed. 'I mean that I hope it will act on this ridiculous situation – drag Liam out of his self-imposed exile, put him on better terms with his mother.'

That stabbed to the heart. For a moment Georgina sat very still, torn between two very distinct loyalties. The matter of Liam and his mother had weighed on Robert for years, and Georgina had promised – an age ago, it seemed – to act as conciliator. Although she had done little to persuade Liam, if her father were looking for catalysts, then he need search no more.

'I don't suppose you've got any further with him, have you?'

The choice of phrase, she felt, was unfortunate. While she bit her lip, wondering what to tell him and how to explain it, the heat of guilt grew in her breast and spread to her face.

On a deep breath, struggling for equanimity, she said: 'I think I told you in the beginning that it would be a long process, and that you'd have to be patient – but yes, I think the message has finally gone home.'

Robert stared at her, his blue eyes suddenly bright and full of wondering hope. 'Good God Almighty,' he murmured, 'how on earth did you manage that?'

That too was a phrase that jarred; and tiredness made her sharper than she intended. 'I didn't manage anything,' she retorted. 'I told you he would come to it in his own good time – and that's more or less what happened.'

Irritated by her father's scrutiny, she went to pour them both another drink.

'Well? Aren't you going to expand? I'd like to know what he said!'

'At the time,' she declared crisply, 'he didn't say very much at all.' Needing to think, playing for time, she handed Robert his glass and took hers over to the window. It was dark outside, and for a minute she watched the feeble lights of passing traffic, wondering how much she should tell him, balancing loyalty to Liam against her father's need, which at the moment was great.

'He brought me home one afternoon last week – my last day off. We'd been up to town and I was tired – not feeling very well. So he brought me home in a taxi and came up with me to make sure that I was all right.' She frowned and rubbed her forehead. 'It was as he was leaving – your bedroom door was standing open, and he saw that portrait of Louisa by your bed. He went in to look at it – I didn't try to stop him – and he saw the other photographs, too. He seemed most upset.'

'And?'

'I don't know – it's difficult to explain. It just seemed to bring things home to him, that's all. We didn't talk about it then. Today, when I saw him, I had the impression he was viewing things differently.'

Turning, looking back at her father, Georgina said: 'He had already come round to the idea of seeing his mother again, and was talking about the possibility of getting some leave – although that still seems doubtful. But you see, what he couldn't accept – what he didn't want to accept – was the fact that you were his father. He has accepted that now. I don't know what he thought before, but until he saw that photograph beside your bed, I don't think he ever understood how much you loved Louisa...'

Robert glanced away, cleared his throat, made quite a play of searching for his cigars. A moment later, from behind a fragrant cloud of blue smoke, he said huskily: 'I'd dearly love to see the boy. All these years, Georgie, and we've never had the chance to talk...

'Do you think we might get together?' he asked, his uncertainty catching at her heart. 'Do you think he would agree?'

In that moment, she had a sense of something being over. Those precious weeks, which circumstance had decreed should be theirs alone, would never be repeated. The demands of family, halted until now, were about to press forward over Liam's horizon. If only for Robin's sake, he would allow himself to be drawn back into the family circle, which of late appeared to include her father; and she, Georgina, would have to relinquish him.

Shaking her head, blinking away tears, she said with difficulty: 'I never asked him that. But I'm sure you'll see him sooner or later. It's inevitable, really...'

Twenty-seven

Liam was in the library the next morning, not reading, but gazing absent-mindedly from the window and thinking about Georgina, when a messenger came looking for him.

'For God's sake smarten yourself up,' he hissed, 'you've got a visitor – a full bloody colonel from the War Office. What the hell have you been up to?'

He felt the blood rush hot into his face and then drain slowly, leaving a clammy chill in its wake. For several seconds, while his mind worked overtime, calculating and discarding facts and suppositions, he could not move. His companion from the ward nudged him, none too gently, and thrust a comb into his hand.

'Here – rake that thatch of yours. And do up a few bloody buttons!' He twitched at Liam's jacket, glancing over his shoulder. 'I'm sure he was following me down the stairs...'

An icy calm settled over Liam. The Colonel was supposed to be in Ireland, and whatever had brought him back and prompted this visit, it was hardly likely to be good news. And he had seen Georgina yesterday – thank God, not at the flat, but still...

Feeling like a man awaiting execution, he smoothed his hair, straightened his tie and slowly fastened his jacket. Vaguely aware of other men in the room, browsing along shelves, quietly reading, Liam took comfort in the thought that he could hardly be hauled over the coals in here; if the Colonel wanted to reduce him to the level of a naughty child, he would have to choose a different venue.

The thought was barely formed when the door opened, and for the first time he looked on Robert Duncannon knowing that he was his father.

It was a strange feeling. There was apprehension and a certain amount of dread, an involuntary knotting in the pit of his stomach,

439

residue of the hate with which he had lived for so long; but there was, too, a sense of recognition. The last few days had opened Liam to so much, and he was aware now of things in himself that had their origins with this man and no other. It was fleeting, but it quelled the antagonism, leaving part of his mind free to register other things.

The past three years had left their mark. Robert Duncannon looked very different from the man Liam recalled. Hair that had been iron grey was now turned to silver, and he was noticeably thinner. But if the uniform and that loss of weight made him seem taller, it also struck Liam that he had lost his air of invincibility. Despite the marks of rank, he was a man like any other, not an ogre, not an enemy, but a human being as fallible as himself.

From his position against the window, Liam watched him stand for a moment, scanning every face; then he turned and their eyes met. Almost against himself, Liam came to attention, as did the man at his side; but then a slight smile softened those stern features, and the Colonel approached to extend a hand in friendly greeting.

'Liam – how are you? It's been a long time.'

As they shook hands, from a corner of his eye Liam was aware of a startled glance before his companion ducked away. Robert Duncannon seemed not to notice, but continued to clasp his son's hand for a long moment. Had his life depended on it, Liam could not have spoken, and, like any good soldier, left it to his senior officer to suggest that they sit down and talk.

Even in those first seconds, although there was tension between them, it was apparent that there was no antagonism on his father's side, and with Georgina at the forefront of his mind, Liam released a slow breath of relief. For a while, too, it seemed the visit was no more than a social one, an impulse long delayed by circumstance and pressure of work. It was almost credible. They talked of this and that, the weather, the war, Liam's state of health, nurses in general and Georgina's working hours in particular. As the coiled spring in Liam unwound, and he began to respond more naturally, his father gradually brought the conversation round to family and the real reason for his visit.

The news of Robin's injury was put with tact and restraint;

nevertheless, it was a shock. The lack of detailed information left him imagining too much.

'Come on,' Robert said briskly, 'let's take a walk outside. We can smoke, and that will do us both good, I think.'

It was a relief, anyway, to be moving. Hunched against a cold, easterly wind, the two men paced the gravel paths and smoked Robert's cigars. The situation struck Liam as so unlikely that he wanted to laugh. There were very few men about, but when they came upon a couple of his ward-mates, having a quiet smoke in the shelter of the chapel wall, Liam could contain his amusement no longer.

'I'm sorry, sir,' he laughed, 'but if anyone had told me I would be taking a walk in these grounds with a British army colonel, and smoking his cigars, I'd have thought they were mad.'

To his surprise, Robert laughed, too; and for a moment there was such closeness between them, they were almost like friends.

'Considering our collective reputations,' Robert remarked, 'the situation does have its elements of farce. But I would hazard a guess,' he added dryly, 'that when you return to your friends, you may have to suffer for this meeting...'

'Perhaps so. I shan't mind it.'

'No?'

Shrewd eyes looked him over, and Liam laughed again, ruefully this time. 'I've suffered worse.'

'Yes,' his father softly remarked, 'I'm sure you have.'

They walked for a while in silence, until Robert broke it with a suggestion that Liam might like to visit his brother once he was settled into a British hospital. 'I know you've applied for home leave and been refused – but give it another week and apply again. By that time we should know what's happening with Robin, and you may well be fit to travel, of course.'

'I feel fit enough now.'

'And to me you look it,' Robert agreed. 'But you know how these medical chaps are – like to hold the whip hand. If they still want to be awkward, I shall have to see what I can do – and if it comes to it,' he added with smile, 'I dare say we can always wangle some leave for Georgie, and get her to travel with you...'

Liam's heart leapt, and he could not meet his father's eyes.

He was almost abrupt in his dismissal of the idea, and yet the thought of travelling with her, of spending two or three days in her company, filled him with guilty delight.

'Well, we'll see what transpires. I may even take some time off, too. I haven't had any leave to speak of for the last couple of years...'

There was awkwardness, but it was mysteriously ironed out. Liam was granted 48 hours' home leave, and released into the care of a trained nursing sister – Georgina – and her father, Colonel Duncannon.

Ready and waiting for them just before midday, Liam was subject to the kind of ribbing he had endured at the time of Robert's first visit; and more than a few sneers. 'It's all right for some', seemed to be the general tone of it, issued in varying degrees of envy. Although it set him apart from the others, he could tolerate that; what he could not ignore were the slanders heaped upon Robert Duncannon because of his rank. Liam was astonished at the level of anger they provoked in him; even more so to hear himself defending his father in much the same way as Robin had done some four months previously. Yet it was not that he saw him as being suddenly perfect – he was still aware of the other man's shortcomings and an arbitrary manner that took little account of other people – but Robert Duncannon was his father, and Liam had accepted that, and it made all the difference in the world. He might still criticize the man himself, but he would not have others do so.

Of course, he could not admit to the relationship. As far as anyone else was concerned, they were uncle and nephew, and Georgina was still his cousin; but with her connections revealed, he was no longer teased about her devotion to him.

The journey north was a trial, however. They were alone in a First Class compartment, and with Georgina facing him, Liam was afraid of betraying the intimacy between them. He forced himself to focus on the Colonel. While he was happy to answer questions about Australia, talking about the war was a different matter. As a professional soldier, Robert Duncannon was keen to hear Liam's first-hand accounts, especially of the Somme; only as Georgina pressed his arm did he notice that Liam was becoming distressed and change the subject.

After that, Liam spent much of the journey staring out of the window or pretending to be asleep. He was anxious about Robin and worried about the forthcoming meeting with his mother; but he kept thinking too about his last few hours at home, about reactions which had sent him fleeing to the far side of the world. Now the pain had gone, it all seemed so extreme.

He was surprised not to have been interrogated about that. In a subsequent meeting with his father at Queen's Gate, the past had been referred to, but although Liam had steeled himself, the questions never came. Indeed, it was with uncharacteristic difficulty that Robert Duncannon broached the subject at all. And it seemed he had done so only in order to apologize.

'We must all of us,' Liam remembered him saying, 'seem so inadequate – your mother, Edward and myself. And yet we only did what we thought was best at the time. Other than being totally frank with you all from the beginning – and given the circumstances, Liam, that was very difficult – I can't see what else we might have done. None of it was intentional – and I know your mother well enough to say that she was only trying to protect you. She didn't want you – any of you – to suffer the slur of illegitimacy. And whether it was right or not, Edward and I went along with that.

'But still, I haven't forgiven myself for calling on your mother that afternoon. I'll be honest – I wanted to see her, and for no other reason than the pleasure of her company. But she was not pleased to see me, and ultimately, we argued. And that was the argument you overheard. I'm sorry. Believe me, I am truly sorry for that...'

And with a swift glance at his face, Liam had believed him. It was impossible not to. But in that moment he had dreaded any reference to the subject of that quarrel, and in order to deflect it, broke in with acceptance of that apology, and his own assurances that he understood.

For a moment he had endured a very searching glance, but the only questions that were asked were with regard to his mother. How did he feel about seeing her again, and had he forgiven her?

He had, of course. Having now added the sin of deceit to all his other crimes, Liam was no longer standing in judgment on even the smallest omission. The thing that still hurt was his blood tie with Georgina: without it, he could have loved her without deceit, taken her as his wife and looked forward to some kind of future. With her beside him, nothing else would have mattered. But – and his practical mind always came back to this – had his mother never met Robert Duncannon, he, Liam, might never have been born. And even if he had, his world and Georgina's were so far removed, it was unlikely that they would ever have met. And try as he might, Liam could not regret the joy of her, would not willingly have lived without knowing that.

For much of the journey, his mind was a vortex of conflicting emotions, and the only thing that he was truly glad about was the absence of his other sister. Tisha had gone up to York the week before, but would be staying with Aunt Emily in Leeds while Liam was visiting. That, at least, was a blessing. He did not think he could have withstood her sharp eyes and tactless observations. Robert and Georgina planned to stay in town.

It was dark well before they approached their destination, and after what had seemed an interminable time, Liam was surprised to hear the guard shouting: 'York – this is York – change here for Scarborough, Whitby, Harrogate...'

As those old, familiar names caught him, Liam rubbed at the window. The train slowed to a squeaking halt. Through the grime he could just make out dim lights and bobbing heads along the platform; then Robert lowered the window and hailed a porter, and Liam saw the bold sign on a vacant seat – York.

Home. It affected him more deeply than he would ever have believed. He took in the cast iron railings of the barrier, the wooden station-master's office and the clock by the steps. It was after six, and that slow journey via sidings and wayside halts had taken five and a half hours. Cold, sooty air assailed his nostrils as he stepped down onto the platform; behind her father's back, Georgina pressed his hand and he smiled at her, briefly.

They took a taxi to Harker's Hotel, and, ignoring all protests, Robert paid the driver to take Liam on to Clementhorpe. 'Nonsense,' he declared, 'we're supposed to be looking after you – and if I thought you wanted our company, I'd have insisted on seeing you to the door.'

Liam was grateful. 'I'll see you both tomorrow, then?'

'Yes, half-past ten – that should leave us time enough to get to Leeds and have something to eat before we go on to the hospital.'

They shook hands. For a second, Liam was nonplussed, wondering how to part from Georgina, but she squeezed the hand he held out to her and reached up to kiss his cheek. 'Best of luck,' she murmured, and waved as the taxi left the kerb.

In the gas-lit darkness, York seemed no different from the city he had left, but it disturbed him, nevertheless. Needing to find his emotional bearings, he dismissed the taxi by Skeldergate Bridge, and walked the last few hundred yards along the riverside. The scent of the river was the same, dank and cold, racing along with winter rains, carrying with it the mustiness of flour mills and sawn timber from warehouses on his right. Naked trees reached up into the night, and a chill wind increased the tension within him. Too soon, it seemed, those ancient elms gave way to a line of spear-like railings, railings that he had painted in that summer before the war...

It was too much. Shivering, he stopped to light a cigarette, absorbing the dark mass of the cottage against the night sky, two downstairs windows lit, and the half-perceived forms of shrubs beside the path. It seemed he had lived a lifetime since that summer dawn, changed beyond recognition from the boy he was then. What changes would he find within?

The kitchen curtains were not quite drawn. Caught by a movement, his eyes studied the gap. He moved close, paused by the railings, and, on an impulse, climbed over them, not trusting the gate. Edging carefully between the shrubs, he reached the side of the house and the path that ran round to the kitchen door. As he expected, the rear curtains were not drawn at all, and he could see his mother in profile, bent to the range. She looked anxious for a moment, closed the oven door, set down her cloth and pushed back a strand of hair. It was a gesture he remembered well. Flushed by the firelight glow, her face seemed just the same, the cheekbones a little more noticeable, perhaps, but she had not really changed at all.

A great wave of relief swept through him, releasing the tension, leaving him weak as a child. He leaned for a moment against the wall, eyes closed in silent gratitude; only as he moved did he realize that his lashes were wet. He brushed at them roughly and took a deep breath; like going over the top, this would have to be done quickly, or not at all. Passing close to the window, he tapped lightly on the door and then walked in.

Although he was expected, a look of incredulity swept over her. For a second she clung to the edge of the table, swaying a little; then, as he took a step towards her, she moved. He thought she was going to embrace him, but she stopped short about a yard away, stiffly, just looking at him, every conceivable emotion chasing across her features. Then she burst into tears, hiding her face as those great, heaving sobs racked her body.

'Mother...'

Equally distraught, for a moment he was afraid to touch her, and when he did, she was so stiff in his arms he thought she would never unbend, never forgive him.

'Please – don't – I'm *sorry*...' He kept repeating the words, over and over, while the harsh sobs shook him. She felt so small to him and fragile; he could feel the bones of back and shoulders hunched beneath his hands and it frightened him. He had never known her weep like this. To him she had always been so calm, so strong.

But just as he thought the sobs would never stop, they did. She hugged and kissed him, and hugged him again; her tears wet his face, but she was smiling, her sobs more like little laughs as she struggled for control. Liam hugged her to him then, burying his face against her shoulder, and for a full minute he wept like a child. She soothed and petted him, and he was vaguely aware of a door opening, then quietly closing again.

His mother sat him down in her chair, close to the range, and as he searched his pockets, handed him a handkerchief. 'Here – take this – you always did lose every handkerchief I ever gave you...'

He laughed, weakly. 'No, I have got one, somewhere...' But he took the one she gave him, wiped his eyes and blew his nose, and everything was suddenly right, the kettle was on the hob, tea was being made, and his mother was smiling, telling him that she had made his favourite, a shin beef stew with lots of vegetables; the savoury dumplings were ready to go in...

'Go in and see your Dad,' she said, arranging things on a tray. 'He came in a minute ago, but didn't want to intrude. I'll bring the tea.'

In Edward he did see changes, saw them instantly in pallor and slowness of movement as the older man rose to greet him. He was a year or two over sixty, and for the first time looked that and more. As they embraced, Liam was aware that time, for his adoptive father, was running out, and the awareness stabbed at him.

'It's so good to see you...' There were a couple of betraying tears, brushed hastily away.

'And you, Dad...' For a while they just clasped hands and looked at each other. 'How are you?'

'Oh, not quite as tough as I used to be – but all the better for seeing you!'

Liam glanced round. As he came in he had noticed the single bed, standing at the back of the room where Edward's desk had always been.

'Yes, it's a damned nuisance, but we had to bring Tisha's old bed down here for me to use. I don't seem able to manage the stairs these days...'

That weakness evidently annoyed him, but in the next moment he was praising Louisa's care, saying she should have been a nurse; and that despite the chronic wartime shortages, she worked wonders with fuel and food. 'And she works so hard – out in the garden all weathers, digging and planting, hoeing out weeds. The way she goes at them, you'd think each one was a German with a gun!' He laughed. 'But she seems to thrive on it, I don't know why.'

'She always did love her garden,' Liam said, smiling.

'And you,' Edward said. 'She always loved you... I'm so *glad* you've come home...'

What threatened to be another emotional moment was saved by his mother's arrival. The tea was sweet and strong, its freshness an exquisite pleasure after the stewed and adulterated brews he was used to; and although there were more vegetables than meat in the meal they shared later, it was the best food he had tasted in months.

Afterwards, they sat by the fire, talking, until Edward's eyes began to droop; then Louisa boiled the kettle again and put hot-water bottles in all their beds, while Liam volunteered to do the dishes.

Once Edward was settled, the two of them sat on in the kitchen until well after midnight, discussing his illness and Robin's wounds, and the girl to whom Robin had become quite seriously attached.

Liam remembered Sarah Pemberton well, a pretty girl of about his own age, with striking auburn hair. Before the war, Robin had been a particular friend of her brother, Freddie, but, like so many more, he was dead now, killed on the first day of the Somme. Robin had been writing to Sarah since he joined up – or rather, his mother pointed out dryly, she had been writing to him – but since his leave at Christmas, it had become more than just a casual friendship.

'She's been visiting him, which I'm glad about, because I haven't been able to get to Leeds more than once a week. With your Dad not so well, it's been difficult, but they say they'll be moving Robin over here, to the military hospital, once he's a bit better.'

'And how is he? What do the doctors say about that knee of his?'

'Well, he's made good progress, apparently – he's had a couple of operations already, as you know, but it's healing well. He won't lose the leg,' she added tersely, 'although he may never walk properly again.'

'If you ask me,' Liam remarked, 'that can only be a good thing. If he can't march, Mother, the army won't want him back.'

'But –'

'But nothing – he's done his bit, he's been in it since the very beginning, and after what his lot went through, he's lucky to be alive. But if he could march with the best of them, Mother, they'd drag him back tomorrow.' With anger inside him, Liam shook his head. 'Just be thankful.'

'I am. I am thankful – most particularly to have you here, and in one piece.' She pressed his hand. 'I was so afraid – so *afraid*...' Unable to finish the sentence, she looked away and dabbed hurriedly at her eyes.

'I'm all right,' he said gently, 'I'm the lucky one.' With a confidence he did not feel, he added: 'If I could come through Gallipoli without a scratch, then I can survive anything. The proverbial bad penny...'

His grin provoked a smile. 'You can be as bad as you like – just stay alive!'

But that made him think of Georgina, and his eyes slid away. His mother knew of her occasional visits, and had expressed her gratitude as well as concern. She could imagine just how wearing were the journeys, particularly on top of hard work and other responsibilities. It was a pity, she said, that Tisha could not have stirred herself more often. But then came another surprise: it seemed his sister was expecting a baby, which in his mother's eyes excused much. The news was clearly a pleasure, so the topic of Tisha and her husband and the forthcoming child occupied them for some time.

But just as he was yawning and saying that he really must go to bed, his mother turned to the subject he had been trying to avoid all evening. After a brief enquiry as to the arrangements for next day, she said: 'By the way, I do hope you managed to get over that – well, that fancy you had for her once. You did, didn't you?'

She almost caught him off-guard. Only because he had been expecting something like that, did he manage a light laugh. 'Oh, Mother – that was years ago. I've known a lot of girls since then.'

There was relief and approval in her smile. 'Well, I thought you must have, but I had to ask.' With a teasing twinkle in her eye, she asked: 'Nobody serious, then?'

Liam stood up, taking their cups to the sink. 'If it's marriage you're talking about – no. Time enough for that when the war's over.'

Edward had been to the hospital to visit Robin the week before; the tiresome journey and the fact that several were going made him glad to bow out this time. Or so he said. Had he been able, Liam knew he would have gone to see Robin any day of the week. But it was neither practical nor sensible. Aware that he had so little time in York, Liam promised to spend the evening at home, and found himself focusing upon the leave he would have once he was declared fit.

'It may be no more than a week, I don't know, but I should get something – I haven't had leave as such since I joined up in 1914. Anyway,' he promised, 'whatever I get, I'll spend here, with you.'

Edward tried to be dismissive, but he was grateful, Liam could see that. It reminded him most painfully of years that he had to make up to them both.

At last, his mother was ready. She was wearing a hat and coat that Liam did not recognize, not fashionable by Tisha's standards, but elegant. As she pulled on her gloves and checked the furl of her umbrella, he thought how attractive she looked; his comment produced a little flush of pleasure from her and a smile from Edward.

Before they set off, Edward cupped her face between his hands and kissed her tenderly. 'Give Robin my love. Tell him I'll try to see him soon...'

She hugged him, kissed his cheek. 'I will, dear. Have a rest this afternoon – we were all up too late, last night.'

Touched by their affection for one another, for the first time Liam viewed them from an adult perspective, and never doubted that as a child he had been lucky to have them both as parents. The pain he had nursed for four long years burned in his chest and he had to turn away. It seemed so selfish now.

On the way to the hotel, it struck him that it would be the first time he had seen his mother and Robert Duncannon together since that afternoon before the war. He was the one person she had not talked about last night, and Liam wondered what she felt for him now. It occurred to him that perhaps she was suffering a certain embarrassment, trying to compose herself before meeting her ex-lover under the eyes of her son. Just as he was trying to compose himself before meeting Georgina. The irony of it brought forth a smile as well as a sigh.

If there was any constraint on his mother's part – and Liam was far from sure that there was – then Robert Duncannon was singularly unafraid of showing his affection. He kissed her warmly on the cheek, held her for a moment, and smiled at her as though she were the only woman in the world. When he told her that she was looking wonderful, her response was not a blush but a wry smile; and a refusal to take his arm. Far from being put out, Robert simply laughed.

They seemed to know each other very well, which, given the years between, rather surprised Liam. Robert could not resist trying to tease and charm her, while she, with the benefit of past experience, constantly strove to put him in his place. Something about this exercise amused them both, so that together they seemed so much younger, and more alive.

Liam thought it extraordinary, until he recalled that other occasion, when he had been angry and jealous, rubbed all the wrong way because of a vibrancy between them that he simply did not understand. Now, he saw that it was an involuntary thing, and was no longer embarrassed. He was even a little amused by it himself.

Walking behind, he glanced enquiringly at Georgina, and saw that her thoughts echoed his. 'Have they always been like this?'

She suppressed a smile. 'Not always, no. But when Father is happy, he can charm the birds from the trees...'

'Yes,' Liam murmured dryly, 'I'm beginning to understand that.'

'And when he isn't...' For a moment she left the sentence unfinished, then glanced up at Liam. 'You haven't seen the other side of him. When the mood's on him, he can be impatient, overbearing – quite insufferable.' She shook her head. 'So different from Edward.'

Liam nodded. 'I was just thinking that.' Pondering the strangeness of life, he shook his head. His mother had been happy with Edward, and even though she had shouldered several burdens of late, there was a tenderness between them that spoke of limitless understanding. Looking back he could see the richness of contentment, and knew it was not just a hazy, childhood memory, but truth indeed.

And yet, watching her now, she almost sparkled. It caught at him, and, without wishing to be disloyal, he could not help feeling that something had been lost. 'It's a shame, isn't it?'

'What is?'

He shrugged. 'Well, that they never married.'

But Georgina could not agree. 'Oh, Liam, don't be misled. Father's a bachelor – always has been and always will be. He likes his freedom, and being on the move. He was never happy in one place for long. But Louisa – well, you know her, she loves her home and her garden and being settled.' She shook her head, sadly. 'He never really wanted that...'

As they came to Lendal Bridge, the open vista of the river caught his attention and he paused, musing for a moment. 'Was that it then? What made them part?'

'I think so, yes.'

'So you don't think...?'

She shook her head. 'No, I don't. Not really.'

They moved on, but with a safe distance between themselves and the older couple, Georgina said: 'If Louisa were free – which she isn't – I could see them coming to some sort of arrangement...'

'But not marriage.'

'No, I can't see them marrying. They know themselves and each other too well.' A little later, she said: 'Does that bother you?'

Liam smiled and pressed the hand on his arm. 'No. Nothing like that bothers me anymore.'

Relaxed in the knowledge that his parents were too taken up with each other to spare keen eyes for their offspring, Liam enjoyed the journey and his lunch. Georgina was smiling too, chatting to Louisa as though it were no more than a convivial day out. That changed, however, as they drew near the hospital. His mother became rather taut and brisk, explaining that Robin was still confined to bed, still in a lot of pain, and that they would probably have to go into the ward in twos.

'Perhaps if Liam and I go in first...?'

Robert was in full agreement. 'Of course. We don't want to overwhelm him...'

Wooden, temporary structures had been built adjacent to the main hospital, and Robin was in one of those, a good five or six beds down from Sister's office, which was a good sign.

Or should have been. Lying back against the pillows, with his ruffled hair no more than a charcoal smudge on the surrounding whiteness, he seemed barely there. The little mountain of a protecting frame beneath the blankets dwarfed him. Remembering his last sight of Robin, in the square at Albert, Liam was shocked.

His brother's smile, such a pale imitation of that other smile, was almost more than he could bear. Blinking rapidly, for a little while Liam had to let his mother do the talking.

Robin pressed his hand. 'You look disgustingly fit for a sick man,' he said with an echo of his old spirit. 'How are you?'

Still wearing hospital blues, Liam felt like a malingerer in this surgical ward full of injured men. Forcing a smile, he said shortly: 'As you say – disgustingly well. I just wish I could persuade the MO of that fact. I might get some proper leave, then.'

'Don't rush it,' his brother said, echoing Georgina's sentiments. 'It'll come soon enough.'

Liam knew what he meant, but their mother's presence precluded talk of the war. He wanted to know about Robin's injury, the action that had led to it, but did not like to ask. But he would, later, when he had more than just this one day.

They stayed for about half an hour, then left to allow the others in. With an eloquent glance at Georgina as he strode past her in the lobby, Liam went straight outside. His mother came to stand with him for a while, but it was cold, and he was too upset to speak. She went inside, and a little while later, Georgina came to join him.

'It didn't seem fair to take up so much visiting time – I thought I'd let Louisa go in again.'

Liam lit another cigarette. 'What did you think?'

'I had a word with Sister before we went in – he's doing all right.'

'But you – what did you think?'

She pressed his hand and looked away. 'It was a shock – seeing him like that. Yes, it was a shock. Dear Robin...'

He wanted to hold her, needed her physical comfort. The impossibility of it made him swear under his breath. Abruptly, he turned away, pacing afresh the few yards between hut and railings. Georgina stood quite still, watching him.

'Father's taken some leave,' she said as he returned to her side. 'He wants to stay on in York for a few days.'

His heart leapt at that. 'But I thought we were all going back to London together?'

'Apparently not. We shall have to make do with each other's company...'

453

'Then for heaven's sake,' he murmured huskily, 'let's take an early train.'

The general uncertainty of travelling times made an early start advisable. Next morning they were at the station by seven, but so were many others. Without that private compartment arranged by Robert Duncannon on the way from London, Liam knew his First Class ticket would be questioned.

'We're going to have trouble with me in this uniform,' Liam muttered, spotting several staff officers in the forward section of the train.

'We won't get a seat anywhere else, though,' Georgina pointed out. 'Standing room only, by the look of things.'

In the end, they found a compartment with two elderly clerics and an iron-faced lady whose sweeping glance would have withered a sergeant-major. Georgina's youth and nursing sister's uniform attracted benevolent nods from the gentlemen, but they were clearly not quite sure what to think about Liam. The distinctive hat with its rising sun emblem had, thanks to the British press, become synonymous with bravery; and had he worn officer's insignia, they would have been delighted to welcome him. The corporal's stripes on his sheepskin jacket threw them a little; apparently he was in the wrong section of the train, but they were too polite to say so.

Not so the lady with her feathered toque and fur stole. With her umbrella, she tapped him, none too gently, on the knee. 'Young man – this is First Class.'

Her attitude annoyed him. For her, and people like her, his friends were dying, his brother injured. He considered the polite reply, and then discarded it in favour of colonial innocence. While Georgina smothered a smile, he glanced around at plush seats and linen headrest covers, and nodded approvingly. 'Yes, ma'am, I'd say it is and no mistake. *Fair dinkum*, as we say back home.'

With that he took a seat facing Georgina, maintaining a poker-face.

'You'll know about it, young man, when the guard comes round!'

Liam nodded politely, and stared out of the window. It was

still dark, but as the train jerked and shuddered its way out of the station, he saw the first fingers of a grey dawn above the city walls. A savage amusement killed any regret; besides, he knew he would soon be back for a longer stay.

A few minutes later the guard arrived. For the benefit of the female dragon next to him, Liam went through a mime of alarm while the others had their tickets checked and clipped. He even kept the guard waiting in weary impatience before producing that precious piece of card.

'Jeez, thought I'd lost it. Here we are, mate – clip that!'

With stony indifference, the guard did so, tipping his cap perfunctorily as he moved on to the next compartment.

Abandoning that strong Australian accent, as soon as the door closed, he leaned confidentially towards Georgina, and in a passable imitation of a British officer, said: 'You know, for a minute there, darling, I really thought I'd lost that ticket.'

He had the satisfaction of seeing one clergyman's shoulders shake, and the other hide his smile behind a copy of *The Times*. He did not turn his head to look at the woman next to him, but he could feel her indignation.

Eyes dancing, Georgina said, under her breath: 'You're very wicked.'

It was impossible to conduct an intimate conversation, so they said little, but after the strain of guarding even their eyes, it was a relief to be able to look at one another without concern for other people. Liam wanted her so much he ached with it, and by her eyes she wanted him too. During the whole of the journey they were alone for no more than a few minutes, but it was enough to say what was in both their minds.

When they arrived at King's Cross they headed straight for the nearest hotel. Georgina made the booking, and, with the excuse of a train to catch later that night, paid in advance; Liam went into the bar, sidling up the stairs when the clerk's back was turned. On the third floor she was waiting for him, anxiety and impatience written into every line.

He reached for her even before the door was closed, crushing her into his arms, raining hungry, demanding kisses onto face, hair, mouth, while she struggled to unfasten her cape and his jacket, and close the door behind them. In privacy at last, she gave up, opening her mouth to him, responding to that fierce hunger with a need of her own. He loved kissing her, loved the feel of her teeth and the honeyed sweetness of her tongue; but the soft interior of her mouth made him want her in other ways, and that need was becoming very difficult to control.

As he began to tug at the stiff collar of her dress, she forced herself away from him.

'Liam – we have to arrive looking as though we've just stepped off a train...' She paused, gasping a little, holding a firm hand against his chest. 'Let me take off my own clothes – let me *fold* them, please.'

He laughed, a little shakily, pecked at her lips and began to undress. Folding his own uniform, he watched her do the same, knowing she was teasing him a little now, and loving it. She came to him and he kissed her breasts, running his hands down over hipbones and haunches, to cup the soft flesh beneath. His words, as he pressed himself against her, were explicit, as were hers in reply, but it was becoming part of a ritual, a sort of vicarious satisfaction, and he did not want that. Almost roughly, he pushed her onto the bed, kneeling over her before she could rise. 'I mean it,' he said.

But it seemed his intensity killed something. Her desire seemed to evaporate before his eyes. 'All right then, go ahead...'

Her acquiescence was feigned, he knew that, and he could no more have forced her than slapped her face. With a defeated sigh he collapsed on the bed, cradling her in his arms. 'Darling, I'm sorry...'

She was more upset, kissing him, fondling him, despairing at the lack of time and the need they both shared.

That despair tinged the rest of their lovemaking, bringing them closer in anguish than in joy. Afterwards, holding her, Liam found himself thinking that it would always be like this: stolen moments in anonymous places, longings that turned to ashes, and a love that was set to break both their hearts.

Twenty-eight

Queen's Gate, SW
November 28th.

My Dear,

What a pleasure it was to see you again, and,
despite the circumstances, to know that you
are happier than when last we met. Robin is
improving, and in such good hands will continue
to do so, of that I have no doubt. To see Liam again
was for me a pleasure, so for you – well, I could see
the happiness in your face.

He is a fine young man. You have every reason to
be proud of him, you and Edward, both. I had so
little to do with his upbringing, I claim no praise
at all. As his mother, I dare say you will see changes
in him that I have missed, but I do not think he is
the worse for them. If he has suffered from the war,
then I am sure that it has also matured him, and it
strikes me now that his willingness to understand
is a direct result of that. I know that war altered my
perception, all those years ago in the Sudan – but it
came a little too late, didn't it? I thank God that it
was not too late for Liam.

I was pleased to have Tisha's news. Rest assured
that in the absence of young Fearnley, I shall keep
an eye on her as much as I can. It will be strange
to have a grandchild. Here I am, approaching fifty-

five years old, and yet – at the moment, anyway – feeling no more than half that.

Yes, it was good to see you, and this run of good news and good luck is uplifting after all the gloom and despondency of this year. I hope and pray it continues, and that Robin makes a swift recovery. He will, I am sure, and although his regiment is unlikely to want him back, that strikes me as being the best part of all. I never thought I would live to say such a thing, but I am heartily sick of all this death. We need our young men, but I have my moments of wondering whether Sir Douglas understands that.

I may be talking treason, my dear, so perhaps I had better close. My regards to Edward – he seems much better for seeing Liam, and I'm glad to have been instrumental in that –
Ever yours,
Robert.

It was hardly a love letter, yet its warmth touched Zoe. Since 1900 he had written infrequently, and nothing survived of his correspondence before that date, but what Louisa had kept glowed with affection and regard. Reading those letters had changed Zoe's view of him entirely.

'You really loved her, didn't you?' she said to the photograph on the bookcase. 'All those years – she must have been quite a woman.'

Not for the first time, Zoe regretted the lack of anything in Louisa's hand. It was like being party to half a conversation, and always there was the desire to hear the other voice, share the full exchange. As it was, Louisa Elliott remained a partly-perceived, enigmatic figure, while the only living person to have known her remembered her best in old age, when the temperament and passion of youth had faded.

Sighing, Zoe studied her collection of photographs, copied from those in Stephen's possession. They had become so familiar, sometimes it seemed they were more real than members of her immediate family. That sense of presence worried her occasionally, making her wonder whether the obsession was becoming unhealthy; but the intimacy of those letters, their verve and individual style, made the writers seem alive.

Had she been a contemporary, such glimpses into their private lives would never have come her way; nor would Zoe have desired it. It would have been like reading her father's correspondence, or invading her mother's private life. But whereas she had no desire to know the intimate details of her parents' lives, she did want to know what had driven Robert and Louisa apart in the mid-1890s, and what had really transpired between Liam and Georgina. More and more was she sure, despite the lack of hard evidence, that those two had been lovers.

From Stephen's transcript, she saw that two dates in Liam's diary, at the end of October, were underlined, along with four more in November and December. They contained no more information than the initial G. On previous occasions he had noted that, '*G visited today*' or, '*went up to town with G.*' The lack of detail was significant in a diary that contained references to food, weather, the quality of a concert, and places he had visited. Only during that two-day visit to York was there a similar lack of comment. '*Went to Leeds to see Robin. He seems in a poor way just now,*' was the sum of it. No mention of the reunion with his mother and Edward, nor of the long journey north. It was as though he could not bring himself to write about emotional matters, or that he was, for some reason, afraid to do so; instead there was just an aide-memoire, a brief comment, or a solitary initial.

Had he come here, to see Georgina? Zoe was sure he had.

Why else the dreams?

The same dream, with variations, many times repeated. Always Liam, always in uniform, always here. At first the furniture and old-fashioned decor seemed strange. The long room with its single tall window, off-set, contained a bed, shelves full of books and photographs, and a wash-stand. In dream-time she paused in the doorway, surprised to see Liam stretched out on the bed, fully dressed in uniform and boots. His hat was on the bedside chest, and his attitude was one of immense sadness. He did not speak, simply lay there, gazing at her.

Zoe was herself, in modern clothes, and she knew that this was her own time, seventy years on from his, despite the dark surroundings. Astonishment gave way before a sense of love flowing between them.

His silent presence, that sense of loving, was present in every subsequent dream. What changed was the flat itself, and the change was coincident with the spine-tingling discovery that Georgina and Robert Duncannon had lived here during the First World War. After that, the rooms in the dream became more recognizably her own.

She knew now that the bedroom in the dream was her spacious modern bathroom with its airing cupboard and shower-cubicle. The old fittings had been ripped out before Zoe moved in, and her father had asked her advice on colour and layout. At the time, neither of them had given a thought to what the room had been originally.

When Georgina had shared this flat with her father, that tall, off-set window had sported elegant drapes, with a chest of drawers beneath it, a bed to one side and a wash-stand at the foot. It must have been the room where Georgina slept.

Had Liam slept there too? It was a question which came frequently to mind, and no amount of rationalizing on Polly's part could sway Zoe from the conviction that Liam was trying to tell her something about his relationship with Georgina. She constantly reminded Polly, whenever the subject came up, that she had dreamed of Liam in the flat *before* she discovered Georgina's address. But as her friend pointed out, she had been obsessed with Liam long before that.

Was it wish-fulfilment? Or did the essence of the man live on, enabling him to enter her sleeping mind, flooding it with certain images, leaving clues for her to follow?

If that was so, then Zoe had to admit that the clues were obscure. Dreaming, she had seen him in her kitchen, standing there smoking, and looking vaguely lost; she had seen him by her desk, gazing out of the window into busy Queen's Gate.

Waking that morning at the beginning of August, Zoe retained an image of him sitting on the edge of her bed, staring at a photograph in a large silver frame. He was partly turned towards her, head bent, fair hair falling forward across a furrowed brow; and the image was so clear, his distress so real, she had reached out to touch him even before she opened her eyes.

As ever, he eluded her. The image went, and as she opened her eyes she saw only her room, the large wardrobe, the matching Victorian chest, a couple of Pre-Raphaelite prints on the wall, and her favourite photograph of Stephen, in a wooden frame, on her bedside table.

She had taken it herself, on the city walls near his flat with the Minster in the background. He was smiling at her, as though trying to remind her of happier times spent together in York. But it all seemed so long ago, so unreal; even less substantial than the dream which had just faded from sight.

York. Stephen was no longer there, but the city was. Glancing back at the photograph, just for an instant it seemed to Zoe that Liam was smiling, beckoning her away.

Telephoning Joan Elliott, Zoe hoped that she would suggest Stephen's flat as an overnight abode; but apparently some old-fashioned sense of propriety prevented that. Contacting the hotel on Gillygate, she hoped it would not be fully booked at the height of the tourist season. Luckily, Mrs Bilton had a single room available, the same one Zoe had used before; and after that friendly conversation, she found herself more pleased than sorry. After all, Gillygate had been Louisa's home for some twenty years before she and Edward moved out to Clementhorpe, and knowing so much more about the family gave the small hotel even greater significance.

With her ancient Renault recently serviced and running sweetly for the first time in months, Zoe decided to drive up to York, taking the A1 as far as Stamford, then motoring at a leisurely pace through the sleepy country lanes of Lincolnshire. It was not an idle choice: in a village south of Lincoln, Louisa's mother had been born, and from another village nearby, Louisa had received letters from a cousin, John Elliott. Zoe felt it was a fair assumption that the Elliotts had remained in the county for at least a couple of generations, and she wanted to see the area for herself.

It was the day to do it: good harvest weather, with an arc of blue above and billowing white clouds along the horizon. The fields were gold with wheat and barley, acre after acre rolling away across gentle dips and rises, marked by crumbling walls and ancient hedgerows, the towers and spires of village churches standing clear from dark pockets of trees.

The roads wound tortuous routes round woods and fields, became village streets and returned to leafy lanes; fortunately the traffic was light, and she was able to drive slowly, pulling in whenever another car nudged impatiently from behind. She wanted to absorb it all.

A minor road took her from Sleaford to Metheringham, the place of Mary Elliott's birth, but just before it she had the surprise of Blankney, a model village of quaint, neo-gothic cottages set either side of the main road. From here, John Elliott had written to his cousins in York. It gave her a strange feeling. The church, heavily restored, was still in occasional use, but the Hall, to one side and at the head of a curving drive, was in the process of being demolished. Wondering why, and hating the sight of those broken walls, she turned her back on it, staring out across the road at what must have been a sweep of parkland, and was now the rising slope of a golf course. A patch of woodland on the crest caught her eye, and she stood looking at it for a while, although she could not have said what it was about it that intrigued her.

She glanced at her watch: past one o'clock already, and she had to have lunch and make her way to York. There was no time to go strolling across the golf links, just to explore a belt of trees no different from all the other woody coverts she had passed on the way here. Nevertheless, she had a strong feeling that she must bring Stephen here; then, with a shrug, Zoe went back to her car.

A signpost indicated that the side road would bring her into Metheringham. It became a village street, with the church set back on one side, and a couple of inns punctuating the curve of cottages, shops and small businesses that seemed to form the heart of a spreading community. Although it was quiet here, with a hot, noonday stillness, Zoe sensed the presence of natural, homogeneous life, so different from the sterile precision of Blankney, a mile away. And the small pub facing the church boasted upwards of a dozen customers, most of them with plates as well as glasses before them.

She ordered a smoked mackerel salad which was both generous and good, and a glass of orange topped up with ice and soda. Considerably refreshed, and with a little time to spare, she decided to have a look at the church. It was locked, a sad reflection of the times, and the exterior told her very little. In some disappointment, Zoe walked round it, studying gravestones here and there, looking for the Elliott name but by no means expecting to find it. But then, under the East Window, she found a whole row of Elliotts, dating back to the beginning of the 1800s, their names engraved on crosses and arched stones, '*In Loving Memory*' and '*Sacred to the Name of...*' interspersed with biblical quotations.

Her knowledge of village burials and rituals was virtually nonexistent, yet as she gazed at other stones, it came to her that to be buried so grandly, and in such a prime position, these Elliotts must have been people of some substance. Were they Tisha's family, and Liam's? Were they the grandparents and great-grandparents of Edward and Louisa? Impossible to prove from the monuments, but she had a powerful feeling that they were her people, and Stephen's, and that one day, perhaps when he came home, they must return here together, and search the parish records.

She left them in their undisturbed peace, left them to the sun and the birds and the gentle rustling of the breeze in tall trees. Something of that peace settled with her as she headed out on the Lincoln road.

The city, topped by its magnificent cathedral, climbed the ridge before her, dominating the broad agricultural plain in a far more dramatic way than York; and yet there were similarities enough to catch her eye, to make her think of Roman legions building major defensive strongholds on that ridge, and then again, seventy miles to the north, at the fork of two rivers at Eboracum. Norman overlords had seen the same advantages, as had medieval merchants and the princes of the church; and in the 1850s, something had prompted at least two members of the Elliott family to leave one cathedral city for another.

She arrived in York just before five, amidst the bustle of home-bound workers and a crawl of cars and bikes down Gillygate. There was a long-stay car park beyond the junction with Lord Mayor's Walk, fortunately remembered from her last visit. With a sigh compounded of relief and pleasure, Zoe stepped out onto the tarmac, fished her overnight bag from the Renault's back seat, and gave the little black car a pat for not letting her down. The smile stayed all the way down Gillygate as she joined the hurrying feet, feeling part of the city's life, part of its people, its solid stone pavements, and its air, which was golden with dust. It was, Zoe decided, unbelievably good to be back.

Mrs Bilton greeted her like an old friend, made her a cup of tea and sat with her for a few minutes in the front parlour. When she had gone, Zoe found herself staring at the fireplace, thinking of Edward and Louisa, and Mary Elliott who had left her home in the Lincolnshire countryside to live and eventually die here. She thought of the children too as she climbed the stairs, passing rooms any one of which might have been their nursery; and then there was Robert Duncannon, to whom this house must have been very familiar.

So many coincidences. And in the beginning they had been astonishing, but as time went on they began to seem almost normal, part of a distinctive chain that had forged its original link at her meeting with Stephen Elliott. But was that really so? Zoe asked herself as she went upstairs. It was the first in her life, but the links in the chain seemed to have been forged long before that. Perhaps the first one was made in this house.

It was an idea which seemed to come from nowhere, an idea that took root as she paused on the landing and stood before an open door. She gazed into a spacious bedroom with two long windows and a pretty Victorian fireplace on the far wall. The windows were open and looked out onto Gillygate; she could hear the passing traffic and snatches of conversation from people in the street. This had been Mary Elliott's home, but it had also been an hotel. Had Robert Duncannon stayed here? Was this the place where Louisa met him for the very first time?

It was a warm evening, but Zoe shivered; hairs pricked at the back of her neck and along her arms. Rubbing them, she hurried up to the next floor, dumped her bag and went straight down again, pausing only long enough to note that the door which had been open, was now closed.

Refusing to entertain the thought that it had opened and closed of its own volition, she hurried out into the busy street.

Following the directions Joan Elliott had given her, Zoe headed straight for Walmgate.

Away from the town centre it was quieter, with Fossgate practically deserted. The elegant span of Foss Bridge crossed a narrow river which boasted nothing busier than a flotilla of ducklings; further on, Walmgate sat peacefully behind a facade of respectable shops and offices, now closed for the evening. In one guide book Zoe had read that a total of twenty-six inns and alehouses were doing business during the street's notorious heyday in the last century, when the area was known chiefly for its slums. That disease-ridden, cheek-by-jowl poverty was hard to imagine now, with the slums cleared years ago and many of the shop-fronts renovated to the same bijou standard of Gillygate.

The public houses, she noticed, were now reduced to two, and while memories of the area's unsavoury reputation still lived on, much new building had taken place within the city wall. Joan's new flat was on the first floor of a three-storey block, small but practical, and with a view of the inner face of Walmgate Bar.

She apologized to Joan for the unexpected visit, and explaining why, said they would meet, as planned, for lunch the next day. For the time being, however, she was anxious not to stay very long.

'I don't know if you recall, but in one of those trunks you gave Stephen, there was a large, leather-bound visitors' book. We only glanced at it and put it back with all the other books, but I think it covered several years, and I'd like to have a look at it. Really, I'd like to look at it now, if I may. That is, if you don't mind me having Stephen's keys for an hour or so. Or if you have time, perhaps you'd like to come with me?'

'Oh, I don't think so dear. Not this evening – it's a bit warm for me to want to trail up there. Besides,' she smiled, a little guiltily, 'I like to get my feet up after tea and watch the soaps! No, you take the keys – bring them back tomorrow when you come – I'm sure Stephen won't mind. After all, if he didn't trust you, he wouldn't have given you the letters to sort out, now would he?'

Zoe suppressed a smile at Joan's belated logic, realizing that it had never occurred to her to offer the facility of Stephen's flat for the night. Had she asked, Zoe might have stayed there. But in Stephen's flat, would she have thought to check the old visitors' book? Probably not.

At half-past seven, the warmth radiating from mellow brick walls in Bedern was still considerable; Stephen's flat was hot and airless, and the first thing Zoe did was to open all the windows. For some minutes, however, she stood looking out at the evening light and lengthening shadows, the play of rich colour across stone and brick and tile. She was reminded of that first evening spent with Stephen, how they had talked while sitting here and looking from this very window. They had watched the colours change and the shadows fall, and seen the last of the light reflected in each other's eyes.

Abruptly, she turned away. Moving from room to room, she was aware of how strange the place felt without him; like a time-capsule, she thought, finding one of her earrings on the bedside chest. And suddenly she was reliving that last evening, the harsh words and the tears, and that brief hour of passion before the mad dash to Teesport. Three months ago, and it felt like forever; yet every word, every gesture, was etched indelibly upon her mind. If she never saw him again, Zoe knew that last, long night would remain with her, together with the sight of him waving from the deck of the *Damaris*.

She moved around the bedroom, touching his belongings: a Japanese earthenware bowl holding shells and bits of coral, a carved ebony mask and a framed batik print from Africa, and a small laughing Buddha in jade that had been given as a parting gift by a Chinese crew. With his tremendous rolls of fat and all-embracing grin, the Buddha was symbolic of happiness and good fortune, and even in her presently dejected state, he managed to raise from her a small, wan smile. No wonder Stephen kept him.

In a long wardrobe, a row of suits and shirts and jackets still retained a faint scent of their owner, and Zoe gathered them towards her, laying her face against the fine, soft wool of a black doeskin jacket. Only as she opened her eyes did she notice the row of solid brass buttons, and four gold rings on the sleeve.

She dropped the uniform as though the thing had bitten her, in that moment hating all it represented: his job, the war, the danger in which he stood. Anguish and longing fused into instant rage, and she swept everything back with a curse, hating everything that had taken him away, accusing him, cursing him, demanding of his possessions when, when would he be back?

Giving way before her fury, several things fell off their hangers; she sank down after them, bundled on her knees in the bottom of the cupboard. Rage was pursued by an acute sense of futility, and hot, angry tears flowed for some time. Sniffing noisily between muttered pleas and accusations, Zoe eventually pulled herself together, replaced the clothes in their proper places and went to wash her face. Dragging a comb through tangled hair, she plaited it back and told herself there was work to be done. It might well take all night and she had no idea as yet whether she was chasing an illusion.

Putting Stephen and his room behind her, she made a pot of tea and took it into the spare bedroom. She found what she was looking for straight away, amongst books and albums and bound Victorian journals. The Visitors' Book for the 1890s was large and heavy and had the name of the hotel engraved and gilded on the cover. Probably Edward's work, she thought, remembering the albums and Liam's diary. Somehow that calmed her, as though Edward's personality was imbued in the things he had made.

Deciphering other people's handwriting was a lengthy task, but eventually, working back through the entries, Zoe found something. At the beginning of 1892, a full two and a half years before Liam was born, a Robert Devereux had stayed at the hotel on Gillygate, his address given as Fitzwilliam Square, Dublin. She recognized the address from Letty Duncannon's correspondence, and even the signature looked familiar. But the name confused her. Could he have used his middle name to disguise his real identity?

How very odd, she thought. What was he hiding – and why? Answers eluded her, but she was convinced it was Robert, and probably the date of his first meeting with Louisa. The beginning of an affair that had led to love and children and parting. To the dreadful combination of circumstances which drove Liam and Tisha away, and Liam and Georgina into each other's arms.

The tragedy of it oppressed her. As she packed the items away and straightened the bed on which she had been sitting, Zoe wondered whether she really wanted to know these things. Looking into those trunks had been like opening Pandora's box, with all the joys and miseries of the past released to obsess and engulf the present. If she had been lonely in her ignorance, Zoe felt that present knowledge had not brought happiness. Raised questions yes, but the most alarming impression was that the past seemed set on repeating itself.

Back at the hotel, Zoe went straight to her room, but it was a long time before she slept. Next morning, feeling weary and resentful, she headed out into the sunshine, intending to take a quiet stroll away from the crowds before meeting Joan Elliott for lunch at one.

She made her way through town to the river with no particular aim in mind. She did not want to think about the Elliotts, and wished she could banish Stephen from her mind. Of course she would write to him with this latest item of news, this tiny piece of the jigsaw that comprised the Elliotts' lives. But faced with the reality of the present, it was so trivial. Why should he care? Amidst all the stress of what he was doing now, how could any of this ancient history matter to him?

She wished she hadn't come. It had been a mistake. Had it not been for the appointment with Joan, Zoe knew she would have climbed in the car and driven back to London.

But along the open reach of King's Staith the air was warm, sunlight glistening off the water. Despite herself, Zoe's bleak mood began to lift. With Skeldergate Bridge ahead of her, she followed her feet and crossed to the other bank, turning left along the riverside.

Beyond Victorian houses, wooden hoardings blocked her view of a vast building site. On her last visit she and Stephen had studied old Ordnance Survey maps of this area: beyond a factory and warehouses had been a boat yard and slipway. No longer in evidence, but she knew now where her steps were leading: she was following the path to Louisa's cottage.

For a moment, feeling manipulated, Zoe was cross. Would they please stop nudging her along avenues they wanted her to take? But all at once she was smiling and shaking her head. 'But the cottage is no longer here,' she murmured.

No, but how many times did they walk this stretch of riverside? The words sprang, unbidden. *Open your eyes and look.*

On the far bank was New Walk, with grand Georgian houses rising behind the trees. That view can't have changed, she thought. But on the right, with the building site behind her, she saw the bowling greens and tennis courts of the Rowntree Memorial Park. She came to a grand gateway, and for a while gazed at grounds which had been carved from open fields and allotment gardens, and Louisa's little plot of land.

Hard to envisage what it had been like before.

Beyond the park, the vista opened out. She walked on along the riverbank, thinking of Louisa's garden, so much discussed in her letters – and her children growing up here, with fields and woods so close at hand. The countryside was never Tisha's milieu, but it would seem to have been Liam's. Perhaps that feeling for the land, for farming, had always been in his blood, inherited from his Lincolnshire forebears.

With the river flowing virtually past their front door, she guessed this was where Liam had learned to swim. His diary revealed two prime concerns throughout the war: food and water. Water to drink, water in which to wash, and always the joy when he found a place to swim. He must have known this river well, she thought, enjoying its cool, green depths on hot days like this; she imagined him stripping off, diving in from the bank there, and surfacing, flinging back the wet hair from his forehead, striking out with a long, powerful stroke towards the far bank, or floating downstream with the current.

Strangely, she had a sense of his presence here, and a sense of sadness, too. It must have been hard to leave for a new world, an unknown land, a future apart from family and friends and those he had come to love. And what had it felt like to return? When he came back with Georgina and Robert Duncannon in the November of 1916, and then again to spend Christmas with his family, how had it seemed to him then?

There must have been changes, particularly at home, with Edward ill and the restrictions of wartime. Food and fuel would have been in short supply, and in the December gloom York must have seemed a sad, grey place, a city of mourners, with all those boys of the Yorkshire regiments killed on the Somme...

No, Zoe thought sadly, it would not have been the place he had left, any more than wartime York bore much resemblance to what she saw now.

Joan was pleased to see her, and in the warmth of her welcome, Zoe was suddenly glad that she had made the journey. Objectivity returned, and with it, a sense that she should make the most of her time here. She was sure Joan knew far more about the past than even she suspected. Little things, unimportant by themselves, added up to form – if not a full picture – then a shadow, an outline, on which to base further investigation.

Over lunch she introduced the topic of Louisa and her move from the cottage. Stephen had guessed that in buying up the land in the 1920s, Rowntrees had also bought the freehold of Edward and Louisa's cottage. From that, Zoe had assumed that Rowntrees had forced Louisa to move from her home of some twenty years' standing. To her it had seemed a blot on the Quaker reputation. But later, logging the dates and addresses of Louisa's letters, she had noted that Louisa had moved out of the cottage in the summer of 1918.

Joan was surprised by the date. 'Well, like Stephen said, I always thought she'd moved because of Rowntrees wanting the land. But if you're right – and I'm sure you must be, by the dates of those letters – then she must have left not long after Edward died.

'Perhaps that's why,' Joan went on. 'It was very isolated in those days, and I think they were flooded out more than once when my father was young. Maybe she couldn't face it on her own.'

'From the dates, I imagine she moved about a year later.'

'I suppose so – Edward died in 1917, April I think it was, the date's on the headstone.'

Zoe had a sudden, overwhelming desire to see it. 'Could we go to the cemetery?' she asked. 'I'd like to see his grave.'

'It's her grave, too,' Joan said.

An hour later, on their way to the old cemetery off Fulford Road, Zoe returned to the subject of Louisa and her move from the riverside to Lord Mayor's Walk. Joan said the house had been at the Monkgate end, just behind St Maurice's Church; but both house and church were gone now, demolished in the 1960s.

'Of course, it wasn't more than a few minutes from where we lived, which was quite handy, especially when Dad was ill. Gran often came and helped look after him – sitting up at nights, that sort of thing, so Mother could get some rest. Then, at the beginning of the war, my brother decided he was going to join up, and after he went, so did I. That left Mother on her own, and what with the war and everything it seemed silly the pair of them rattling round in separate houses. So Gran sold her place and moved in with Mother.'

'Louisa sold the house? You mean she owned it, didn't rent the place?'

'No, she owned it.'

'How strange – I mean because they rented the cottage, didn't they? I'm sure I've seen a reference to that. Something about the rent going up, but the landlord doing nothing about repairs.' She pondered for a moment. 'Still, I suppose Edward must have left her quite well-placed?'

'No,' Joan said emphatically, 'he didn't. He sold the business during the First World War – for a song, my father always said – and after that there wasn't much at all.'

'Are you sure? She must have had money from somewhere, if she bought that house...'

There was a long silence. 'Well, I'm sure you're right, but I don't think it can have come from Edward.'

'How on earth did she afford it?' Zoe asked, and in the next instant knew the answer. 'Robert,' she breathed. 'I bet you a pound to a penny, Joan, Robert Duncannon bought it for her!'

'Do you think so?'

'Who else?'

Joan seemed stunned by that. In a small, hesitant voice, she said, 'We owned our house too. And Dad had his own business. It never occurred to me before to wonder who set him up. And somebody must have, because after the First War it was hard for everybody.

Most people didn't have two ha'pennies to rub together. And Dad's business – photography – was a luxury, not a necessity, so he didn't make much either.' She sighed, heavily. 'But he often said we were fortunate, that we should count our blessings. Mother always set her mouth at that, and I often wondered why...'

'Perhaps Sarah didn't approve of Robert Duncannon?'

'Maybe she didn't. She certainly never mentioned him to me.'

In the midst of an affluent society, it was hard to imagine the levels of poverty prevalent then, poverty which continued throughout the Great Depression of the 1920s and '30s. Those returning soldiers – many of them disabled – had found work difficult to find. The more she thought about Robert Duncannon, the more likely it seemed that he would have done his best to provide a home and a means of livelihood for his son, Robin.

'Maybe she resented the generosity,' Joan went on. 'My mother was a proud woman, she didn't like to feel beholden to anybody.'

Remembering the stiff, disapproving old lady she had met, Zoe tried to envisage Sarah Elliott's early life and the world that had made her. It was difficult, and her memory of being disliked for no good reason did not promote sympathy. Yet Stephen had been fond of her...

'Yes, I know she was funny with you, but she was old then, and the past, I suppose, was starting to be more important than the present. But she was a good mother and a good wife – she adored my father, and he felt the same way about her. When he was ill, she nursed him – and his heart was bad, you know, it wasn't just the leg. The doctor said it was the effect of all those bombardments, weakened the heart, wore it out. He was only thirty-six, you know, when he died.'

Aware of her own inadequacy, Zoe murmured something sympathetic, while Joan simply shook her head and said yes, it was tragic, but many fared worse, and at least her father had known happiness with the wife and family he treasured.

'He's buried here, too – with Mother.'

Just inside the cemetery gates, Joan filled a plastic bottle with water for the flowers she and Zoe had brought. It was pleasant in the sun, a slight breeze disturbing long, feathery grasses between graves in the old section, rustling the leaves of massive chestnut trees near the chapel.

By Robin Elliott's grave Zoe recalled the many letters he had written to his mother from France. She felt the desperate loneliness of that young man, the forced cheerfulness of his words masking fear and horror and a million things he could never tell the people at home. But he had found his love in Sarah, and been happy with her; and now, as the inscription said, they were reunited.

Robin had never disturbed her dreams, and Zoe felt he was as truly at peace as the atmosphere around his grave suggested.

She watched his daughter perform a ritual that over the years had obviously been repeated innumerable times. Dead flower stalks were removed from the urn and set to one side; the fresh flowers were shortened and arranged, the waste wrapped up and used to wipe the marble base, leaving all neat and tidy.

Standing back, Joan was quite still for a moment, head bowed. Zoe suspected this was part of the ritual too, no doubt more poignant since Sarah's death.

'Now,' she said huskily, taking Zoe's arm, 'we'll go and find Edward and Louisa.'

It was a short distance away, along grassy paths lined with memorials great and small.

'What was she like?' Zoe asked. 'When you knew her, I mean. Was she very sad?'

'Oh, goodness me, no. Well, I should say, not *generally*. I do remember her being sad, of course – anniversaries and Armistice Day, particularly. When Dad was alive we always went together – Dad with his walking stick and his medals, standing ever so straight with Granny by his side. He wouldn't march with the veterans, but he always went to the service. Mother hated it, she usually stayed at home, to see to the dinner, she said. But I think,' Joan added, 'it was mostly that she refused to be seen crying in public. She lost a brother, you know, at the Somme...'

'Then, after Dad died, Granny took us. She was even sadder then, but though she wept, she said it was our *duty* to go, to remember all those who gave their lives in the war to end all wars.' With a shuddering sigh, Joan shook her head.

'Twenty years – it didn't take long, did it? The second war upset her badly. I think, like so many more, she'd have had peace at any price. She'd been so *content*, you see, with her little house and a couple of friends she'd made who lived nearby. And my brother and I used to call from school, and then from work, two or three times a week. And she came to us on Sundays. We loved her, you see, and she spoiled us – we could always take our friends there.

'But then in 1939, the war came. She couldn't believe it was all starting again, and it's only now, when I look back, that I realize she must have imagined it being just like 1914. When my brother Bill joined up – you know, Stephen's father – it almost broke her heart. I'm convinced she thought she'd never see him again. She did, thank heavens, because he didn't go abroad until 1944. But I remember her saying to me that I mustn't let them send me to France – I must come home immediately if that was so much as suggested!' Joan laughed. 'We didn't go to France, of course, but I can just imagine my officer's face if I'd told her what my Granny said!'

'Stephen told me she was a bit confused towards the end.'

Joan sighed. 'Well, yes, she was, but not until the last few weeks. Of course she worried about everything, and as I say, I'm sure it was the war. Shortages, the blackouts, everybody in uniform. And the air-raids! Those sirens were enough to frighten anybody to death. They had an incendiary bomb down the chimney one night – it didn't go off, thank God – Mother picked it up with the fire-tongs and doused it in a bucket of cold water! It sounds funny now,' she said with a laugh, 'but it can't have been at the time, especially with an old lady who flatly refused to go into an air-raid shelter. In many ways she was tougher than she looked, but the strain of it told in the end.

'I saw a big difference in her that last week. I had some leave not long before D-Day and came home. Granny was in bed most of the time, and obviously failing. Mother said she was always talking to Edward, and the sad thing is, when I arrived, she seemed to think I was her mother. Her voice was different, too, lighter, younger...' She paused. 'It was a bit unnerving.'

'What did she say? Can you remember?'

Joan's kindly face seemed distressed. 'Yes, I can remember. She said – *But I loved him, Mamma, what else could I do?*'

Zoe studied the gravel path. 'No names?'

'No. I didn't know who she was talking about, but she was really upset. Tears were streaming down her face.'

Zoe blinked and swallowed hard. 'Poor Louisa...'

'Thinking about it now, I suppose she must have been talking about Robert. I don't recall her ever mentioning his name, though. What I do remember is that just before I went back – the last day, in fact – she suddenly turned towards the door, and said, with real surprise – *So they let you have some leave, after all. I didn't expect to see both of you here.*

'She seemed so lucid,' Joan went on, 'I honestly thought my brother had walked through the door. I turned round, expecting to see him, but there was nobody there and the door was shut. That did frighten me, because I thought it was Bill she'd seen – and that he'd been killed.'

'How awful for you,' Zoe murmured. 'But he was all right?'

'Yes, right as ninepence as we found out later – he came through without so much as a scratch.' With a deep sigh, she said: 'But my man was killed in Normandy, and although Granny never met him, I did wonder afterwards whether it was him she'd seen.'

'Do you still think that?'

'I don't know, Zoe. I know what you're thinking, though – that it was my father and his brother she saw.'

'Robin and Liam – yes.'

'Well, you may be right. She died sometime that night, while I was on my way back to camp in Dorset. Just slipped away in her sleep. I never got to go to the funeral, and I don't know if Tisha came. I imagine there were just a few neighbours and a friend of Granny's, somebody she used to have tea with once a week.' Joan smiled. 'When she came to us, you'd hear the pair of them in the front room, laughing away like girls.' With a shake of her head, Joan laughed again. 'I don't know what they talked about.'

'The past, probably. When they were young.' It was a thought that made Zoe smile, two old ladies reliving the years of their youth, before the turn of the century, when the world must have seemed a different place.

They came to Edward and Louisa's grave, marked by a modest memorial of an open book set back from the main path. Edward's name and dates were inscribed on one page, and on the other were Louisa's, giving her age as 77 years, and the fact that she had been Edward's widow.

As Zoe arranged her flowers before their names, she offered up thanks for Louisa, that warm, generous woman who had loved her family and friends so much that she could not bear to part with her memories, nor the evidence of their affection. They had loved her, that much was obvious from their letters; and if love survived – which Zoe was beginning to think it did – then why should it not be that her sons returned to comfort her in those last, anxious days?

She was with them now, and at peace, of that Zoe was certain. Only her correspondence remained, revealing insights into a life that had contained more than its fair share of anguish and upheaval.

But despite the grief and the hardships, Louisa had found the strength to carry on. Zoe found that heartening.

She gazed at the headstone, remembering the mass of correspondence relating to Edward's death. Well-known and obviously well-liked, Edward Elliott had come to his last resting-place accompanied by the respect and affection of many people.

However devastated Louisa had been at that time, Zoe hoped she was comforted by that show of affection, and most particularly by the presence of her sons. Amidst the dreadful abnormality of war, fortune had decreed that both of them should be there.

Twenty-nine

They stood either side of her, Robin in hospital blues, resting heavily on a walking-stick, Liam in Australian khaki, tunic pressed, puttees wound tightly above polished brown boots, his hat held respectfully against his chest.

The weight he had gained latterly while convalescent, had, Georgina thought, been refined during the last month's training in Lincolnshire. He looked fit, if pale, the last vestiges of French and Egyptian sun having disappeared long ago. His hair was darker, too, cropped by a succession of barbers and quelled, today, by the rain. She watched a wayward lock of hair fall forward, as it inevitably did when he lowered his head, and almost smiled, expecting him to brush it back. But he seemed unaware of it, his thoughts reflected in strain around his mouth and jaw, and in shadows beneath his eyes.

Sadness touched her own heart, but it was for them, that little group by the open grave rather than for Edward or herself. She had seen so much of tragedy that it was hard to grieve for a man who had died peacefully, by his own fireside. He had known the joy of reunion with Liam, the relief of knowing that Robin's war was over, and he had Tisha's news of another generation about to be born; for Edward there was no sadness, only contentment and peace.

Although she hoped Louisa felt something of that, Georgina suspected not; such comfort would come with time, whereas now she was simply bereft, cast adrift without the husband who had always loved and supported her. The future, for her, must seem bleak indeed.

It was not a prospect Georgina wished to pursue. If she thought about the future at all, she knew she would weep. For the moment it was enough to gaze at Liam, to feast her eyes on the sight of

477

him after five long weeks of separation. A short February leave, spent with him in Bournemouth, had created its own particular hell, but she could not regret it. Now that the worst anxiety was past, she was glad things had happened as they did. If it had to be the last time...

She shivered, and with an apprehensive glance at her father, tried to discipline her thoughts. Desire, as she had so often said to Liam, showed in the eyes, and her own were liable to give her away. But it was so hard not to look at him; knowing she should not devour him so, Georgina blessed the rain, the essential umbrella that shielded her eyes from all those immediately facing. They were behaving correctly, studying the crushed grass and the mud, and no doubt the state of their boots, while a surpliced parson intoned the prayers for the dead.

There had been only the briefest note from Liam the other day, to say that he would be here for the funeral, and that while he had expected this, it was still a great shock. It showed in his face, she thought; in a sort of frozen calm. He would be strong while ever it was required of him, she knew that, but still Georgina longed for the chance to offer comfort, to be somewhere private and alone, where they could talk and hold each other, where the world could not intrude. The sheer impossibility of that was painful.

Someone was holding an umbrella over Louisa, high enough to shelter Liam, bending towards her; and another covered Tisha and Robin. They were all standing close, and as Tisha began to weep, Robin transferred his stick to the other hand, slipping an arm around his sister's shoulders. He looked close to tears himself, and the strain showed so plainly in his expression, Georgina was suddenly anxious. As soon as this trial was over, he would need the wheelchair that had brought him from the chapel.

Louisa seemed composed, and alone of the group held her head up, although her eyes were closed as though in prayer. Someone moved and Georgina caught a glimpse of her hands, locked around Liam's, her arm entwined with his as though she would never let him go.

The crowd began to move, slowly and discreetly, away from the environs of the grave. The parson went to utter a few words of consolation, reaching out an arm to lead the grieving widow away. She seemed reluctant, and beside her, Georgina was aware of her father shifting uncomfortably. He wanted to go to Louisa just as much as she wanted to go to Liam, and it was very hard not to, hard to pretend no claim, no special love, hard to have to walk away.

But as Robert took her arm, Liam looked up, his glance encompassing them both; with an almost imperceptible nod he seemed to be thanking them for their presence, and acknowledging the arrangement to meet later. Someone brought up the wheelchair, and as Robin was settled, his head bent with obvious pain, Louisa leaned down to embrace him. A moment later she embraced her daughter, but Tisha, stiff with her eight-month pregnancy, accepted rather than returned it. Georgina bit her lip, wishing her half-sister would be kinder; but that attitude seemed to be her defence, and not even their father could penetrate it. She found herself praying that Edwin Fearnley would be granted some leave, and soon; Tisha was in need of comfort, and from him it might be acceptable.

Stealing a final, backward glance at the family group, she saw that Robin's fiancée, Sarah, had joined them. Tall, like Louisa, she was a fine-featured girl with striking red hair. Although they had met only once before, Georgina had the feeling that she was regarded with a certain suspicion. It was a shame, because she wanted to like the girl for Robin's sake. He was important to her, and she did not want his future wife to set barriers between them.

But that, Georgina reflected sadly, might have been done already. She was unsure how much had been said about their complex relationships, and if Robin, in love and trust, had revealed the truth of his background, then she suspected Sarah would find it difficult to understand.

The antipathy between Sarah and Tisha was mutual and obvious, but as Liam had been at pains to explain, it was a personal thing and went back a long way. They had known each other as girls, and found nothing in each other to like. Tisha was younger, but articulate and sure of herself; she could play to the crowd and have them all hanging on her every word, while Sarah would stand apart, looking both regal and disdainful, until a barb from

Tisha sent her away.

'And is she disdainful?' Georgina had asked.

'I don't think so,' Liam had replied, laughing. 'In fact, I would say the reverse. As I recall, she was always rather shy. She used to come down to the cottage to buy fruit and vegetables, and sometimes she'd stay a while, talking to Mother. But if Robin arrived, she'd blush scarlet and hurry away. We all knew she had a fancy for him, even then.'

That she loved him now was in no doubt. There was no mistaking the tender solicitude with which she cared for him, and if they married – which they would, eventually, when Robin was discharged from the army – then Georgina was sure that Sarah would protect and support him for the rest of his life. Right now he needed that strength, that sense of security, and probably always would. In that sense, he was lucky; the survivors of this war, however many there were at the end of the day, would need a brave generation of women to take up the load on their behalf, of that, Georgina was convinced.

Watching her walk away, Liam took a deep breath, steadying himself against the urge to call her back. He wanted Georgina beside him; yet for the sake of propriety and his mother's concern for what others might think, Georgina and her father were relegated beyond the pale of family, and must only be seen to pay their last respects amongst a crowd of other acquaintances. Aunts Blanche and Emily, and that crowd of female cousins from Leeds, must come back to the cottage, partake of the funeral tea, murmur their platitudes and be tolerated until boredom finally took them away.

Liam hated it, hated them. Pointed looks from Aunt Blanche told him he must expect a pious lecture on past sins; and even Aunt Emily, whom he had met twice in recent months, would no doubt find reasons to repeat all the unasked-for advice she had given already.

All he wanted was Georgina and a place to be alone with her. So long since her visit to Bournemouth, and since that sybaritic few days of luxury and love, he had suffered three weeks of hell at Wareham, retraining. The machine-gunners' course at Belton Park in Lincolnshire, which he had just joined, was joy by comparison. But it would not be for long. In a couple of weeks, maybe less, he would be on his way back to France.

He dreaded it, and the possibility of further leave was doubtful. After leaving hospital he had been granted eighteen days of home leave over Christmas, but the pleasure of being with his family had been constantly curbed by so many changes.

York, he found, was a city dressed in mourning, its depressing shabbiness accentuated by the pinched look of people in the streets. Middle-aged women, hardly recognizable as the cheerful mothers he had known, would stop to speak, their initial smiles quickly fading as conversation turned to absent sons and husbands. Many of his old acquaintances were dead; and his good fortune was so often remarked upon that Liam began to feel guilty, began to feel that he should not have come home to flaunt himself. Mentioning it to his mother at Christmas, she had said the same: that people seemed resentful that she should have two sons in uniform, and both of them in one piece. Robin's injury hardly seemed to count.

Latterly, even the cottage had depressed him. The dankness of the nearby river, a raw wind and a chill in the house that carefully hoarded fuel could not defeat, all conspired to dull his spirits. After years away from it, he had forgotten how bleak a northern winter could be. Warmth and brightness, which was what he remembered most, had been defeated by the war. He was further depressed by knowing that his time – and Edward's – was slipping away

He and Edward had talked for hours on a multitude of subjects, and Liam was left with the knowledge that his adoptive father had been both kind and shrewd, the possessor of a keen intellect and a generous heart. No businessman, to be sure, but a better father would have been hard to find. It did not take long to conclude that as children they had been fortunate in having Edward to guide them. Liam was thankful that they had been allowed that time together, but his one abiding regret was that their relationship as adults had been far too short.

Another penalty of the war. Everything good had come and gone too quickly, while seeming to possess a concentrated power that lingered in the memory like an afterglow. Happiness, it seemed, must go hand in hand with sorrow and regret. Nothing was unalloyed, but after the slow death of emotion in France, even sorrow was welcome. The words of the funeral service had elicited tears, shed as much for those comrades left behind at Pozières and Gallipoli, as for Edward. With the interment of the coffin, Liam had mentally buried all those friends who would never have a grave.

If those boys had missed the proper obsequies, those who mourned them had also been spared the ghastliness of the funeral tea. In this case, being just after one o'clock, it was more of a luncheon, but it was as bad as Liam had envisaged. Robin was so unwell within the hour that he had to be taken up to bed. Liam's ire was further aroused by the fawning of his aunts upon Tisha; their whispered advice and secret, womanly nods infuriated him, while his sister seemed to preen beneath their attention, like a cat.

Only with the aunts' departure did his mother drop the fixed half-smile she had worn all afternoon; slumped in a chair beside the fading fire, she looked worn and tired. There were no tears, however; only once, last night, had she wept, and that was at Liam's arrival. For several minutes she had clung to him and sobbed, and again it had seemed so strange to be holding and comforting her, instead of his mother comforting him.

Kneeling beside her chair, Liam placed a hand over hers. 'Why don't you go upstairs for an hour? I'll make a cup of tea and bring it to you.'

A faint smile brightened her eyes. 'I'd like the tea,' she said softly, patting his hand, 'but I think I'll stay here.'

In the kitchen he found Sarah washing plates and cups; there was no sign of his sister, who had apparently gone up to bed, not feeling well.

Not wanting to spoil her hands, he thought as he returned to the parlour with the tea. His mother poured, but all the while he was bothered by thoughts of her alone in this isolated cottage, with Robin in hospital and incapacitated for months to come. By comparison, his own illness had been trifling. But at least Robin had his Sarah. Liam knew he envied their future happiness, even while he wondered how they would survive financially. Edward had left so little from the sale of the business, there would not be enough to provide for Robin. And Tisha had her own life now; she could hardly be relied upon to give their mother a second thought.

Liam lit a cigarette and tried to put those anxieties into words. The money he had sent home, which Edward had placed in a separate account, was to be used, he said, in whatever way she thought fit. It was no use to him, he could manage very well without it; he just wanted to be sure that his mother had all she needed.

She frowned at him, and in an attempt to be stern, insisted she was adequately provided for. 'I don't need that money – you do. You will, anyway, once the war is over. You'll need it to set yourself up, buy that bit of land you were talking about. That's what Edward wanted for you. And so do I. I shall be all right – with a bit of careful managing, I'll be fine. You mustn't worry about me.'

Her confidence brought a lump to his throat. He forebore to tell her that he had willed the money to her, anyway, and that his own estimate of his chances for survival were not very high. On a surge of emotion he stood up and went to the window to look out over the garden. Apart from a few dejected daffodils in the orchard, all else had been turned over to vegetable production, and was now a bare expanse of rutted soil. After a long winter, it was in need of attention.

'Will you stay here?'

'Oh, I imagine so.' She paused, wearily. 'But I don't know... it's not something I've thought about. Why do you ask?'

'I think you should move into town, get somewhere smaller, more manageable. All this,' he said, gesturing towards the muddy, rain-drenched expanse, 'will be too much for you.'

'Well, I don't know about that,' Louisa said with some asperity, 'I'm only forty-nine, you know – not quite decrepit!'

He smiled then, cheered by her sharpness. 'I'm sorry, I tend to forget. Dad was so much older, wasn't he?'

'Yes. Yes, he was. But he never seemed so...'

Glancing back, Liam saw her distress, and blamed himself for a clumsy fool. He went to her and she leaned against him, taking comfort from his strength.

'I'm so glad you were able to be here,' she whispered. 'I don't know what I'd have done, otherwise.'

Her words expressed his thoughts. 'I know. That's what worries me. I can't bear to think of you being here, all alone.'

'Oh, I shall manage, I expect. People do, you know. I shall get used to it, eventually... No, what I meant was – today – I was glad you and Robin were here with me today. And Tisha, of course,' she added as an afterthought. 'I wasn't sure whether she'd come, whether she'd be able to travel, I mean.'

Liam knew quite well what she meant. Tisha was not predictable, and even Robin had been surprised to see her. But he did not want to talk about his sister. Returning to his main anxiety, he said: 'What will you do when we've gone?'

'Keep busy,' she said firmly, drawing away from him, 'as I've always done. You mustn't worry about me, Liam – I've never been a clinging vine, and I don't intend to start now. And I won't be entirely alone, you know. There's Robin to think about, and even when he comes home, it'll be a while before he's fit enough to get married. But when he is, I'll let him go. I won't interfere.'

That statement, however, did not reassure him. His mother was a proud woman, and might hold off when she needed her family most. Thinking about his father, he said: 'And there's the Colonel. I'm sure he'll be in York from time to time, to see Robin.'

'I'm sure he will,' she said crisply. And then she smiled. 'Oh, I shouldn't speak of him like that, should I? He's been very kind. He always was, Liam, and very generous – the thing is, I never wanted him to be...'

'Well, I hope you won't spurn his kindness in the future. I'd like to think there's one person you can rely on for help and advice, should you need it.'

'I'll remember that,' she said gently, touching his hand.

Reassured, he dropped a kiss on her cheek. 'I'd better go and see how Robin's faring. And Tisha – Sarah said she wasn't feeling very well.'

But at the foot of the stairs he paused, considering the changes in their relationship. Now that Edward was gone, he was very much aware of shouldering an elder son's responsibility, not only for his mother, but for the rest of the family, too. It worried him that the war prevented him from fulfilling those obligations. Ordinarily, he would have been too proud to ask the Colonel for help; but these were not ordinary times. And after all, the Colonel was family, whatever Aunts Emily and Blanche might think.

He went upstairs. Sarah was sitting with Robin, who was looking much brighter, and in her old room Tisha was reading a fashion magazine, feet propped up on pillows on the bed. She said she was hungry, so Liam knew she must be feeling better.

With a sigh he went down again, wondering what was to be prepared for the evening meal, and whether he should make an attempt at it. He was tired more than hungry, yet a sense of restlessness made it impossible for him to relax. There was so little time, he felt he should be doing things, although precisely what eluded him. Standing in the middle of the kitchen he lit a cigarette and glanced at the clock. Almost five, and Georgina would be here about seven. Two hours. And then what? An hour or so of family company, of guarded eyes and studiously bland exchanges between them. He needed to be alone with her, needed to talk, needed to be able to reach out and touch her. Letters were not enough; and besides, it might be the last chance he would ever have.

The thought of having to pretend a commonplace friendliness drove him to distraction. If only he could think of a way of seeing her alone!

He was still wrestling with the problem when Tisha appeared, and, to his great surprise a moment later, started peeling potatoes. She demanded to know whether Sarah was staying to eat with them, and when he said not, expressed voluble relief.

With a nervous, upward glance, Liam begged her to keep her voice down.

'Let her hear me, I don't care. I tell you what, though – if Robin marries her, he can kiss goodbye to the rest of us. She wants him for *herself*, you mark my words, and when she gets him, she'll smother him.'

'I think you're wrong, but why should that matter to you?' Liam asked equably. 'You haven't bothered much about Mother or Dad since you left York, so why bother about him?'

There was a long silence, followed by a suppressed hiccough which might have been laughter or tears. In some amazement, he realized she was crying. He had thought her incapable of tears. Real ones, anyway. But this grief seemed genuine enough. He moved to comfort her, but she shrugged him off, fighting to control that sudden, wayward emotion.

At last, bitterly, she said: 'Because he's the only one of this bloody selfish family who ever cared about me.'

'How can you say that?'

'It's true. Even Dad – even he didn't give a damn what I did...'

'Oh, Tish, that's not true. He did care – he did. Mother, too.' Distressed for her, weighed down by sudden guilt, Liam tried to take her in his arms, but she was stiff and awkward, and the swell of the baby she carried felt very strange to him. Pressing his cheek to hers, he patted her shoulder while trying to think of something convincing to say. But there was nothing that did not sound hollow. In truth, she had always been the odd one out, hard to understand, impossible to reason with; ultimately, when she kicked, they let her carry on. Perhaps that was a lack of caring.

'It's all my fault,' he murmured wretchedly. 'I didn't understand, then – and when I went, I certainly didn't mean to hurt *you*...'

'It was her, wasn't it?' she sobbed. 'If it hadn't been for her, you wouldn't have gone, would you? It's not fair, it shouldn't have been like that... why did she have to come and spoil things?'

He stiffened, released his hold on her. 'What are you talking about?'

Tisha felt her way to a chair, sat down and cried for a while. When the tears eventually subsided, she managed to say with passable control: 'I know why you went. It was Georgina, wasn't it? I heard Mother and Dad talking about the two of you one night. I didn't understand, then. Not until I saw you together, in London. It was the way you looked at her.' She paused to wipe her nose and eyes. 'Are you lovers?'

Liam sat down. He thought he was going to be sick. It took him a minute to find his voice, and when he did, it sounded foreign to him. 'Not in the sense you mean, no.'

If she was unconvinced by that, she did not say, and he dared not look up. As he fumbled with a packet of cigarettes, she took it from him, lit one and then another, with hands that were steadier than his.

'Shocked you there, didn't I? Oh, don't look so worried, I won't say anything.' She puffed inexpertly at the cigarette, picking pits of tobacco from her lower lip. 'Does Robin know?'

Liam shook his head, trying to gather his scattered wits. 'I don't think so. Anyway, it's over, I shall be going tomorrow. And I'll soon be back in France.'

'Just as well. Sarah might drag it out of him, and she would *never* approve.'

'Don't tell me you do.'

Tisha shrugged. 'I'm not shocked, if that's what you mean. It doesn't matter now. In fact,' she admitted, narrowing her eyes through a haze of blue smoke, 'it makes me like you a little better. You were always so bloody pure and perfect, weren't you? Quite priggish, really. It does me good to know you're no better than me.'

'Did I ever claim to be?'

'Not in so many words. But you always thought you were better, always acted that way.'

'If I did, then I'm sorry,' he said sincerely, responding to her pain and quelling his innate distrust of both words and motives. 'I am sorry, Tisha. I wish you'd believe me.'

'Oh, I do,' came the weary reply, 'but it's a bit late now, isn't it? I mean we've all made such a bloody mess of things, haven't we? And you can't go back. What a family! I don't know about cigarettes, Liam, but I could do with a drink. Still,' she sighed, 'I don't expect Mother keeps strong liquor in the house.'

'There's some sherry...'

'No, thanks.'

A moment later, while Liam was reflecting on their various situations, Tisha said bleakly: 'I hope I never fall in love. It's just a shambles, isn't it? Look at Mother – look at you! God, what a mess. And I can't say those two lovebirds upstairs fill me with confidence, either. If that's what love does to people, fawning all over each other, I don't want it.'

He was shocked. 'But what about Edwin? Don't you love him?'

Again, that eloquent shrug, as though Edwin was of no moment. 'I'm fond of him, yes. Besotted by him, no.'

'But – how? I mean, *why*? Why marry him?'

Her glance was pitying. 'He was the best offer I had. The best I was likely to get, what with everybody going off to the war and getting killed. Quite young, nice-looking, plenty of money... kind, too. And madly in love with me. Trouble was,' she added with devastating candour, 'I never counted on him getting called up. I thought he was safe, secure, and ensconced in the bloody War Office for the duration! He used to joke about it, about volunteering and being promoted every time.' She sighed. 'But they called his bluff. Now I expect he'll end up with some dreadful wound, like Robin, and I shall have to be a nursemaid for the rest of my life...The thing is, I can't see myself being very good at that.'

Words failed him.

'Oh, don't look so grim,' she said with affected lightness. 'What does it matter? What does any of it matter? We all die in the end, don't we?' But her voice broke there. 'Like Dad – just like Dad...'

On a flood of grief, she hurried, as fast as her bulk would allow, for the stairs.

Liam felt as though he had been mangled. Remembering the sherry, he poured a generous measure and downed it in one gulp. Tisha was right: it was a mess, and likely to remain so, but with regard to himself, he wished only that he could trust her. If it suited her ends, she was quite likely to blurt out his secret to whoever would listen. And if she did – oh, God, the people it would hurt!

Then another thought struck him. If she had guessed so accurately, then others might have done the same. But no, surely not. If anyone had guessed, he would know from their attitude towards him. Only Tisha could be as nonchalant as that.

Although the thought of food nauseated him, Liam put together a meal of sorts: potatoes and carrots – which with a box of withered apples were the only things to have survived Louisa's winter storage – to go with what remained of the sliced cold meats prepared for the funeral luncheon. There was some cold apple pie to finish.

It seemed no one had eaten much earlier, so Liam's basic meal was much appreciated, especially by his mother. With the return of a little colour to her cheeks, she announced that she would stay on at the cottage, for this summer at least.

'My garden has provided food for us, and helped out a lot of families besides. So I'll do what I did last year – plant vegetables that can be stored – and it will give me something to do. Edward would have wanted it.'

It seemed the last word on the matter, and although Liam would have preferred to think of her in a less isolated place, his mother's determination was heartening; and perhaps the satisfaction of growing things was a good antidote to grief.

As Sarah left, he helped his brother into the parlour, propping him up with cushions on the sofa. The day's strain and activity had made his pain worse. In a silent gesture of sympathy, Liam reached out and held his hand.

'It's good to see you again, despite the circumstances.'

Robin nodded and pressed his hand. 'I'm so glad you came home and made it up with Mother and Dad.'

Liam smiled. 'So am I.'

It was good to see him up and about again. In hospital Liam had wondered whether his brother would live. He had, and strength would return, he was sure of that. Robin was possessed of will and determination; but he would never again be that carefree boy. None of them would.

He shivered, and Robin looked up to read the bleakness in his eyes; there was a flash of understanding between them, and then his brother's fingers gripped with surprising force.

'You'll be all right,' Robin whispered. 'You haven't come this far to go down now. I always thought you were a lot tougher than me, only I seem to have spent most of my life trying to prove otherwise.' He smiled, wanly. 'Anyway, it doesn't matter now. The point is, you're one of life's survivors – you'll come through, I know you will.'

Grateful for that vote of confidence, Liam smiled. 'Well, if you say so...' he remarked lightly, and the moment dissolved in soft laughter.

With the squeak of the garden gate his heart leapt. Two shadowy figures hesitated for a second before advancing down the path, and as they did so he rose, with deliberate lack of haste, to open the front door.

The Colonel shook his hand, eyes urgently questioning even before the words were on his lips. Liam said that his mother was taking things well, although he suspected she was more upset than she allowed herself to appear.

'I shouldn't think she's taken it in yet,' the older man said softly as Liam took coats and hats and hung them on the hall-stand.

'Probably not.' He frowned, wanting to say more. His father went into the kitchen, and Georgina reached up with a chaste kiss for his cheek. There was a tension about her which was echoed in himself. He ached to hold her, to feel that tight anxiety dissipate in the warmth of her embrace; he must see her alone, he must...

But as he began to frame the words, Tisha joined them, and Georgina turned to greet her with a solicitous enquiry. Still talking, they went through into the parlour.

Liam thought his sister's quick, glancing smile was dangerously conspiratorial, but no one else seemed to notice, and in the sun of Georgina's greeting, Robin beamed, assuring her that he was quite well, and in only slight discomfort. Although it was a patent lie, she did not dispute it, passing on to lighter matters, including Tisha in her conversation. She did it so very well, only Liam knew the effort it cost.

As Robert and Louisa joined them, there was a necessary rearrangement of seats. Liam stood up to offer his chair, but Robert declined it, preferring the end of the sofa to what had traditionally been Edward's place. There was a further exchange of enquiries after everyone's health, and subdued comments on the funeral, all perfectly normal under the circumstances; but Liam, listening, looking, experienced a particular feeling of dislocation. The room was much as it had always been, with pictures and ornaments shining in the soft lamplight. The delft tiles framing the fireplace were the same, and the embroidered velvet mantel-cover; the spoon-backed chairs and the table and heavily-carved sideboard were all as he recalled, only the people were different. He was sitting in Edward's chair, something he had not been allowed to do as a boy; and Edward was no longer here.

His absence left an enormous gap, yet that was only part of it. Another awareness dominated, shuttling thoughts back and forth between this gathering and a similar one in the summer of 1913, when they had all sat down in this selfsame room for tea. Then, hostility and unformed suspicion had been uppermost in Liam's mind: he had noted the resemblance between his brother and Robert Duncannon, and his mother's unusual gaiety, and that lively repartee across the table had seemed somehow improper, especially in the shadow of Edward's quiet watchfulness. He understood it now, but at the time, Robert had seemed to be taking far too many liberties.

He could not be accused of that now, however. His affection for them all was palpable but subdued, and if a corner of his heart was in any way relieved by Edward's death, it was not apparent. Rather, to Liam, it seemed that he grieved for them all in their loss, as any caring father would.

For the first time, Liam thought, they were gathered together as a family, around one fireside, knowing the truth of their situation. Mother, father, children, all together for the first time.

It was odd enough to send a tingling shiver down his spine. He wondered whether the others were aware of it, too, and whether it crossed their minds, as it did his, that this one occasion might be the last. Tisha would soon return to London, to bear her child and greet Edwin on his return, making a family of her own. Sooner or later, Robin would be in a similar position, while Georgina would always be Georgina, full of compassion for others, making her life with them and for them. As for himself, well, with first light he would be away, and once he returned to France, his fate would lie in other hands.

Remembering those few days in Bournemouth, it seemed just as well. The war would roll on, and if he survived, Liam knew he must return to Australia. There could be nothing for him here. To stay in England, with Georgina close enough to reach yet more than ever forbidden, would be impossible. If there had been hopes and fantasies before, then those stolen days together had revealed the impossibilities. Their relationship could go no further, not without the direst of consequences, not without destroying the already fragile threads holding this family together. Liam had done enough damage, and in his struggle to repair it, would not willingly blast them apart again. Nor could he bear to think of Georgina's fears made reality.

If the death of innocence had killed their high ideals, then weeks of separation had finally broken all the curbs. It had not been intentional. In the joy of reunion it had simply happened, almost before either of them realized it; and once joined, there could be no going back. Nor had there been. The physical sense of being part of her was too seductive, and the emotional sense too comprehensive. And with that awareness of impending separation the wanting had been equal, so that they had made love far too often. Oh, he had been very careful, particularly after the first time; and, looking back, he thought how strange it was that he should have been so calm, so absolutely sure of himself and what he was doing. It was as though he were saying to her, as he had longed to do in the beginning, that in this they were one, and could never be divided.

In the heart of the flame, pain did not exist, there was only a sense of calm, of being insulated and protected against all else. They were loving and tender with each other, perfectly content for the first time; they did not discuss what was happening between them, there was no point, no need. It simply was, and in a short time, it would be no more. They both knew that.

They had parted at the station, Georgina to return to London, while Liam had travelled the short distance to the training camp at Wareham.

That was where reality took centre stage, leading torment with burned and blistered hands. Compared to what was going on in his mind, the physical hell of retraining was almost a pleasure. When he finally received the letter to say that all was well, he was light-headed with relief. Georgina made it clear that they must never tempt fate in such a way again, and with that Liam heartily concurred. Only afterwards, with all the ramifications clear to him, did he realize what she was saying. It was over, it had to be; they could never meet like that again.

As things were, it was no longer possible, and for that he had a small measure of gratitude. But it was no match for the pain which overwhelmed him every time he thought about saying goodbye.

She was sitting close to Robin, her hand resting lightly on his shoulder, part of the family circle which in that moment was almost a physical entity. Slightly apart from the rest, Liam was aware that in some strange way the break lay with him, that he was the odd one out, divided by thought and consciousness and the nature of his love for her.

Exhaustion broke into the group, and as Tisha went upstairs, Liam helped his brother to bed. As in the old days, they were sharing a room again; knowing he would see Robin later, Liam went down, wondering how he could contrive to speak to Georgina alone. Hesitating at the foot of the stairs, it came to him that if he offered to make a pot of tea, she would probably come through to the kitchen to help. But as he set the kettle to boil, it was his father who came in, closing the door behind him.

'I wonder would you see Georgina back to the hotel? It's been a long day, and she's tired, but I'd like to stay with your mother for a little while.' For a second he hesitated, then went on: 'It won't take long, but there are a few things we need to discuss.'

Liam prayed that his expression betrayed none of his relief and only a fraction of his willingness to obey. 'Of course, sir,' he murmured, allowing himself a small smile. 'I'll see her safely back.'

Robert seemed unusually tense. 'What time is your train in the morning?'

'Half-past six – that is, if it's not delayed.'

'And a slow journey back to Grantham, I've no doubt. Would you like me to come to the station, see you off?'

Liam's heart lurched. 'No, sir, really, I'd rather be alone. Much rather, but thanks all the same.'

His father's level gaze met his, regarding him somberly. 'Don't worry about your mother. I'll take care of her – in fact I shall insist on doing so,' he added with a small, dry smile, 'whether she wants me to, or not.'

As he tried to express his thanks, Robert cut him off. 'No, it's the very least I can do. In the meantime, take great care of yourself. No foolish heroics, promise me that?'

'I promise. I got these stripes for long service, not heroics!'

'In that case, let's be seeing another next time you're home.'

'I'll do my best, sir.'

There was a silence, and apprehension suddenly struck Liam, he could not say why. His father frowned and looked down for a moment, but although he had his hand on the door, it seemed the interview was not over. 'By the way,' he said at last, and his voice was suddenly sharp with accusation, 'did you know about Georgina's plans? That she's volunteered for service abroad?'

The question caught him completely off-guard, as afterwards he was sure it was meant to do. Liam felt the blood drain from his face, and when he found his voice, he stammered. 'A-abroad? No – no, she – she didn't tell me...' On a vision of casualty clearing stations, often under fire, he closed his eyes.

'I'm sure,' Robert continued heavily, 'that you have a better idea than any of us just what that might mean.' There was a repressed anger in his words that in spite of shock, set every sense on the alert.

'I'm counting on you, Liam, to dissuade her. She's done enough already, for God's sake – I don't want her risking her life out there.' He paused. 'I shouldn't imagine you do, either.'

There was a sharper edge to his voice as he said that, and his glance, steady and penetrating, told Liam that he knew – or suspected – the true state of affairs. It was worse – far worse – than Tisha's confrontation, because no accusations were leveled. There was nothing for Liam to deny. Instead of the dressing-down he might have expected, there was just this terribly restrained civility.

'I've spoken to Georgina, and I realize there is no point in discussing it further. With anyone.' His voice was hushed, deceptively so, because every word had the sharpness of an incision. 'You're going away tomorrow, and you'll soon be back in France. Although it grieves me to say so, Liam, it's just as well. You know the folly of what you've been doing as well as I do. Only because I blame myself more than anyone else do I beg you – *beg you* – to end it.'

'The decision has already been made,' Liam said gruffly, forcing the words through trembling lips. His whole body was shaking; he found himself clinging to the back of a chair, wanting to apologize, wanting to explain to his father just how it had come about. He wanted to be forgiven. But there was no time. 'I'm sorry...' he whispered, and the words were grossly inadequate.

There was a momentary brilliance in his father's eyes. 'So am I,' he breathed, 'so am I.' With a sudden compression of his mouth, he looked away. 'Do something useful, Liam – stop her from committing another folly.'

'She's not – not volunteering *to be close to me*, is she?'

'No, oddly enough. She seems to think that active service will remove her entirely from your sphere of influence. When you come home on leave, she won't be here. It will also make communication difficult.'

The truth of that was like a hammer-blow. He could give no more than a puppet's nod in answer to it.

'But staying away from each other is one thing – getting yourselves killed is quite another. I don't want to lose either of you – and if your mother knew, she'd say the same. It would break her heart, for God's sake.

'Promise me you'll speak to Georgina – persuade her to change her mind?'

'I'll do my best,' Liam said.

Robert glanced at his watch. 'Shall we say an hour?'

'If I had a week,' his son responded bitterly, 'I'm not sure it would be long enough. But I'll try.' He moved towards the door and Robert opened it for him; as he donned his heavy overcoat, he said: 'Tell Georgina I'll be waiting outside.'

The rain had turned to a fine, drenching mist that obscured everything, even the river. The only light was that from the cottage doorway, and, like a blanket, the night absorbed it. Seeking support rather than cover, he stood beneath the first tree beyond the gate and shivered like a man with palsy. April, and it felt like January, and the shocks and miseries of the day gave him no warmth, no comfort.

A couple of minutes later she followed him out, pausing only to raise her umbrella. He called to her and she hurried to his side; she was upon him before his expression could halt her eagerness, reaching out to embrace him as he grasped both arms and shook her, angrily.

'Why didn't you tell me? Jesus Christ, I walked straight into that! Why didn't you tell me he knew?'

He saw the shock on her face, saw, too, the sense of betrayal. She glanced back over her shoulder, then up at Liam, and then she hung her head. 'He said – he promised – that he wouldn't say anything to you. I'm sorry – I didn't – didn't want to tell you... and in a letter, how could I?'

'*When*, for God's sake? How did he find out? What did he say?'

She leaned against him, touching her forehead to his shoulder. Almost against his will, Liam embraced her. 'Tell me,' he whispered urgently, 'I have to know – *all* of it.'

Time was passing but he could not move until he knew. The umbrella provided shelter as he lit a cigarette and listened to her brief, staccato explanation. Those stolen few days in Bournemouth: Georgina had arranged her leave with the hospital, but neglected to tell her father; he had needed to speak to her, telephoned, and been told she was on leave. When she came back, he had, quite naturally, wanted to know where she had been.

'It was a risk, of course, and I'd worried about it for days before I came to you. And the trouble was, I couldn't think of a convincing story to cover the situation...'

'You should have told me – I thought he was in Ireland!'

'I didn't see the point of worrying you, too.' With a sigh, she said, 'Anyway, as soon as I saw his face, I knew that lying would have been a waste of time. He knew, Liam, he knew full well where I'd been. He'd had plenty of time to work it out. He'd even checked with the convalescent home, and been told you were on leave, too. Only the fact that he didn't want to believe the worst made him accept my version of the truth.'

'And what, for God's sake, was that?'

'I said we'd taken separate rooms, that I went down to Bournemouth simply because we wanted to spend some time together before you went away...' Her voice broke on that. 'And that, as God's my witness, is the truth, isn't it?'

'Except I never slept in mine.' He threw the stub of his cigarette in the direction of the river, and took her arm. 'We'd better get moving – I'm supposed to be seeing you back to the hotel, and we haven't got long.'

'I told him we loved each other. God, he was so upset, and so angry – I thought at one point he was going to hit me, and he's never done that in his life.' On a little sob, she went on, 'I had to go right back to the beginning, to that summer before the war, and tell him everything. He knew how I naïve I was, and so he believed me when I said I thought we were just good friends…

'I told him that it was being together – visiting so regularly when you were in hospital. I said it made us both realize that what we felt for each other was more than just friendship. That was what hurt him – because he'd *wanted* me to see you…'

'Why?'

Her voice dropped so much that Liam had to strain to hear her next words. 'He wanted me to explain the past. He wanted you to understand what he did and why he did it. He wanted your forgiveness. And he knew you wouldn't listen, or even agree to see him, so he sent me, instead.'

'Oh, my God.' There was something so ironic in that, Liam was torn between tears and laughter. 'So he blames himself, does he? Well, he needn't. I just pray to God he doesn't say anything to my mother. She won't take it the way he has.'

'He won't. She's had enough grief, he wouldn't do that to her.'

'He promised – you said – not to say anything to me!' But the bitterness waned as Liam went over what had been said to him by Robert Duncannon. Nothing direct, nothing specific; it had all been contained in the eyes, in the tone of voice as he dropped the bombshell of Georgina's plans.

Liam faced her with that as they walked through town, as deserted streets echoed to every footfall, and a driving mist chilled their faces. Few lamps were lit, and most of those were dimmed. They found their way less by sight than familiarity, realizing with some surprise that they were not far from the hotel. The matter, however, was far from over, a long way from being settled to Liam's satisfaction. For a moment he thought of her private room, its warmth and seclusion; but there was too little time, and he had no desire to compromise her further.

They walked on past the Minster, its looming mass shadowed and silent, suggesting an emptiness that made a mockery of existence. Shivering, Liam drew Georgina towards him, seeking the shelter of a little archway off Goodramgate. Mist and smoke and fine, drenching rain made a blanket of the night, cutting them off, in that dry place, from the probing eyes of passers-by. At the sound of muffled footsteps they dropped their voices, huddling against a dry wall, its ancient bricks warm from some interior chimney.

'You might be sent anywhere,' Liam murmured against the softness of her cheek. 'And I don't just mean Boulogne or Flanders or places behind the front lines. There are British nurses in Egypt and Malta, and the seas, my darling, are *crawling* with German submarines. Didn't you see that report in the paper? More than fifty ships went down last week, including a troopship with nurses aboard. Why risk that when you can do so much good here?'

When she did not immediately answer, he drew away. 'Look, you're being silly about this. You know how impossible it was for me to get leave before – and after six months off, God knows when I'll get leave again.' With an exasperated sigh, he added: 'Do you want me to make that promise again? I won't try to see you – and if you don't want to hear from me, I won't even write.'

'What use are promises?' she whispered brokenly. 'It wouldn't be any use. If I knew you were home on leave, I'd want to see you, and if I thought we could keep in touch easily, I'd always be looking for your letters. Or writing to you.'

'Georgina,' he got out bitterly, 'you're making this so difficult...'

'But don't you see why I want to go away? Can't you see that if I stay, where you and I were together and happy, I'll never forget? London – the places we went, even the buses we took, everything reminds me of *you*. At home in the apartment I see your face wherever I look – in the kitchen, the drawing room, by the window, in my bed. God, in my bed. I never sleep. I doze, and I dream of you beside me. I wake and search for you. I even run my hands over my body and pretend they are your hands.' She clung to him, sobbing. 'I can't bear it, Liam. I cannot bear it. All this time, and it doesn't get any easier. I want you more, not less. I have to go away – I have to.'

He held her, and he thought his heart was breaking.

'But I just want you to be safe. Don't torture me with that kind of worry. I have to go – you don't. Stay, please, where I can think of you in safety...'

'I don't want safety,' she said harshly, pulling back from him. 'I want a place where the work and the danger, and the sheer hell of existence, takes my mind off the worse hell of living without you!'

'You're being childish. You haven't the faintest idea what it's like.'

She turned on him then, and even in the darkness he saw the flash of fury in her eyes. 'Don't, please, accuse me of that – I nurse the casualties! Have you any idea what it's like living in a place of safety, and worrying – day in, day out, week in, week out – about the people you love, in constant danger? You don't know what's happening, you haven't the remotest idea whether they are alive or dead, and you live for the letters while you dread the telegrams. And the newspapers tell of glorious victories while every other page is full of casualty lists. I nurse those casualties, Liam – I know about the lies!'

'I don't want you to go,' he said quietly. 'There's killing enough, and your life's too precious.'

'And so is yours, to me! But I can't beg you to stay, and you couldn't if I did!'

In great agitation she paced their little square of shelter, and through the darkness he watched her, bent against the pain, her face a pale oval of anguish. Aware of the trembling in his limbs, he leaned back against the wall. The truth of everything she said was undeniable. It hurt more because they were arguing, because these might be the last minutes they would ever have together. That much had been agreed already: that when he left England this time he would never try to see her again.

He might have said, in answer to her harrowed distress, that the future seemed just as meaningless to him, that without her, he did not even want to live. There was nothing left for him, and he had nothing more to give; all that he had, had been given, already, to her. It was unbearable to think of it being thrown away like this, on such an empty gesture.

But he said none of those things. Instead he took her arms, calming her resistance, soothing her towards the bitter release of tears. She clung to his strength, touching his face and hair and neck with passionate, feverish hands, as though needing to impress the feel of him forever.

That almost destroyed him, and when he found his voice, it was low and husky with grief. It hurt to tell her that pain was a thing to be borne, that there was no escaping it in flight.

He kissed her then, a deep, tender, loving kiss, and against the silkiness of her hair he murmured that it was time to go, they had to go, it was already late.

Together they moved out from beneath the archway and into Minster Yard, heads down against the swirling mist. The blank windows of the old College watched them pass, and the great sweep of the Minster's east end looked down as they paused in the triangle of space before it. They embraced again, and there was passion and desperation in the way their lips met, a feverish longing in the clinging of hands at the parting.

He took a step or two towards her but she stayed him with a gesture, backing away, hurrying, turning, running, her skirts caught up, cape flying into the darkness.

'Pray for me...' he whispered, but she could not possibly have heard.

He stood there for some time, sheltered by the night and the mist, and the air was like a cold, wet shroud against his face. Then, blinded by grief, he stumbled forward to cling to the support of a great buttress in the wall. He raged then, and cried out, beating his head against the stone, demanding in the name of all that was holy, why this agony should have to be.

There was no answer, no consolation.

Eventually the storm of anguish passed, and he was able to move on leaden feet towards home. He followed a meandering route which took him nowhere near the hotel.

It was well past the hour he had been allowed when he reached the cottage. Robert Duncannon had already left, and a note on the kitchen table said his mother was tired and had gone to bed. Liam set his overcoat to dry in front of the range and went upstairs.

THIRTY

It seemed, at first, that he could not go on without her. The animus was gone, and all that remained was unfeeling flesh.

He stumbled through the days, earned a dozen reprimands and suffered the ensuing bitter weather without complaint. The shooting ranges at Grantham were under several inches of snow, fuel was scarcer than ever, and the activity of German submarines on British shipping meant that rations were very short. For ten days he was cold and wet and hungry, yet it seemed no more than a fitting match for the chill in his soul.

The news of another big push near Arras touched him in only one way: he prayed that his return to France would come soon, and that death might erase this terrible emptiness.

The former prayer was answered quickly enough. By the third week in April he was on his way to join a large batch of reinforcements heading for the south coast port of Folkestone. The journey to King's Cross was cramped and cold, but he was pleased to be moving, pleased to be on his way to that other life he hated but knew so well, the life that had nothing whatever to do with Georgina. As he left the huge, echoing station behind, and set forth with a score of others to cross London, his bitter pleasure withered before an agony he had failed to predict. He knew then what Georgina meant, knew exactly the level of torture she must suffer in her journeys back and forth across the city.

Oxford Street, where they had wandered in and out of little shops and massive stores; Hyde Park, bleak beneath a grey shroud of snow; Buckingham Palace, where they had stood and watched the changing of the guard one sunny day last October...

The wait at Victoria was interminable. On a walk round the station precincts he found a public telephone and was tempted to use it. Forcing himself away, he went to the bar and sank two pints of beer in quick succession, but instead of numbing the pain, the alcohol only blunted the fine edge of his decision, and within the hour he was back, demanding the hospital number from the operator. Georgina, however, was not on duty, and the ward-sister was too new to be able to tell him anything. There was no reply from Queen's Gate.

They spent five hours in Folkestone before boarding the transport for Boulogne, but that was all right: Georgina had never been to Folkestone. Huddled in overcoat and sheepskin, Liam took the chance of rest in a corner of the great cargo shed where hundreds were waiting. Some were playing cards, others writing letters, while a few were singing to the plaintive strains of a harmonica. It reminded him of the night before Gallipoli, except it was a damn sight colder and he did not wish to be part of it. He dozed for a while, to be woken by an anxious group of youngsters as soon as there was a rumour of boarding. They were excited and jumpy, eager to stay close to him with his veteran's experience of war. Like the boys who had accompanied him to France from Egypt a year ago, they regarded him as some kind of oracle, pouncing upon every utterance and repeating it in hushed whispers amongst themselves. That he said little seemed only to make each word more profound.

His shrug of unconcern regarding submarines was observed with awe; and his words, '*Well, you take your chance, don't you?*' went down the line with the speed of an express train. Their involuntary straightening gave him a certain bitter amusement. He wondered whether they would have been so keen to worship had they realized he genuinely did not care, one way or the other, whether a German torpedo sent him to the watery depths, or an explosion from hell scattered him across the mud of France.

Any wild acts of heroism or aggression he might have been tempted to perform, were foiled, initially, by further training near Armentières, which was so familiar it seemed he had never been away. Exactly a year, and little had changed, even the weather was the same. Bitter winter clinging on, then suddenly giving way before a wild outbreak of sun and green leaves. In a week, blossoms were everywhere, and the old Flemish faces in shops and bars were starting to smile again. But they were thinner and greyer and more wearied, and in his walks along the Lys, he saw that the cemeteries were fuller, and new ones created.

He found himself thinking often about those stolen few days in Bournemouth, the scent of the pines in a narrow ravine close by the hotel, and the salty tang of the sea. With a pale sun glistening across the waves, it had seemed, in those few days, that even winter was being kind. They had strolled along the beach beneath the cliffs, dodging incoming waves and skimming pebbles out to sea, and happiness had been theirs – not a wild excitement, but a calm, sure awareness of contentment and each other. He had never been so relaxed, so absolutely himself, as in those days with Georgina. And for her it had been the same. Perfection, but perfection is such a fragile thing: they were aware of that, too. That last evening, returning at twilight along the promenade, the frosty air had been disturbed by a low, continuous rumbling, like thunder in the distance. Georgina, bemused, had asked what it could be; while Liam, knowing, had shivered in recognition.

The beginnings of another massive bombardment across the Channel had seemed to herald the end of things, not just that brief escape from reality, but the end of everything.

Here, the rumblings, if not particularly intense, were more or less permanent, and he had learned not to wince with every explosion, learned to school his expression into blank acceptance while his heart pounded and stomach turned to water at the memories each one invoked.

There was no word from Georgina, despite resurrected hope. What did arrive was a short, sad letter from his father, saying that she had been accepted for service in Egypt, and had left London within a couple of weeks of his departure for France. Later, came a further missive, confirming her safe arrival. Unless Liam requested specific news of her, his father wrote, he would leave the situation at that.

No address, and Cairo had several hospitals. It was a relief, however, to know she was safe, not in France where her presence might tempt him to go looking for her, nor in danger of being blown to pieces by stray shells or a sudden German advance. In Liam's opinion, Egypt was not a pleasant place to be, but the officer status of nursing sisters would no doubt ensure a better standard of food and accommodation than he had ever enjoyed.

He even felt the ancient history of the place would appeal to her; she had been fascinated by his descriptions of the tombs and monuments and museums. But even as he remembered those conversations, Liam was struck by a certain irony: if London had been unbearable because they had enjoyed it together, how would she feel about Egypt, where he had spent more than eight months of the war? Would she watch the moon rise over the Pyramids and see his shadow in the sand? While she wandered through the gardens and the palaces, would she feel his presence beside her?

He would imagine her there, see the flaming desert sunsets again through her eyes, smell the orange blossom in the courtyards of Heliopolis and watch the fountains playing in their marble pools. All the hospitals were grand hotels or former palaces; he had convalesced at the summer home of the German Crown Prince, and that particular irony had given him a vast amount of pleasure at the time.

That memory made him think of the last time he had seen Mary Maddox, and by association her brother Lewis. According to the last letter Liam had received from him, Lew was still in Egypt with the Light Horse, full of verve and confidence now that he had been promoted to captain. That he had continued to keep in touch was warming, a testimony to the reality of those months immediately preceding the war, and to the odd friendship which had sprung up between them.

Liam might have let it lapse, particularly during the worst periods of the war, when Australia had seemed no more than a passing dream, but Lewis had kept on writing. Liam wondered now whether it was something other than friendship that prompted him. It seemed there was a need for reassurance, a need to know that he was not the only one left of those boys from Dandenong, that someone other than himself was still surviving. Perhaps he felt guilty, or slightly freakish in his ability to dodge death. Liam had known moments like that himself.

He was saved from guilt, however, by a strong streak of fatalism; and by an inner conviction that for every man there is a time to die. It had not been his destiny to catch a burst of shrapnel on Gallipoli, nor to breathe his last with pneumonia at Heliopolis, and that strange dream of Ned had as much as told him so.

In London he had mostly been too happy to think about it; but the subject had arisen once with Georgina, and she, surprisingly, had not disputed it. Nor had she entirely agreed with him: for her, the sense of appalling, unjustified waste was too strong. But she had seen the calm that came over dying men, as though old friends beckoned them away from pain and into peace. She did not think it was hallucination, and did not doubt the veracity of his experience.

But she had no explanation for it, either.

Since then, there had been too many other matters, more pressing, for him to dwell on it. Now, looking back on his friendship with Ned and at the love he still bore for Georgina, he had to wonder why such things came about, and why they had to end. In the midst of what he recognized as the pain of bereavement, it all seemed so pointless; and a small part of him wondered whether it might have been better to know none of it. Without love, could that sense of loss exist? But with Georgina there had been such happiness, such ecstasy; a sense of being one, with the same thoughts and feelings, desires and despairs. Through her, he had come to understand so much, and he was aware that in giving up her love he had lost far more than could ever have been imagined four years ago.

Knowing she suffered too, made everything worse.

That deep, constant ache, and the bouts of misery which continued to sweep over him, made communication with his family difficult. He had to force himself to write, force himself to express what he hoped was a natural level of concern, when in effect he was experiencing both envy and resentment towards them all. Robin had Sarah, and now Tisha had her baby, a little girl. Although he was pleased for her, he loathed her cynical attitude, which took such precious things as marriage and children for granted. Even his mother, about whom he had been so worried before leaving, seemed more blessed than himself. She had known twenty years of happiness with Edward, and five before that with Robert Duncannon. Even now, whether she wanted to accept it or not, Liam knew she need do no more than say yes, to have her former lover permanently by her side. It seemed grossly unfair.

Communication with Georgina, however much he might wish it, was not only forbidden, but impossible. Against a setting of Egypt, she was constantly in his thoughts, and in the end, coming across that three-month-old missive from Lewis, Liam wrote to him. Towards the close of a letter which briefly recounted the least personal of recent events, he mentioned Georgina – '*a close relative of mine*' – and made a casual request that Lewis look out for her, should he be in Cairo.

It was not quite the long-shot it might have seemed. Officers managed a fair amount of leave, and the military community in Cairo was a close one. Georgina might be reluctant to make herself known to him, but on a specific request, Lewis would most certainly enquire after her. Knowing someone, even at one remove, might just ease things; and Lewis was a decent bloke. If he did come across Georgina, he would write and say so.

The simple act of writing and posting the letter eased his mind, and the news that he was to rejoin his old company provided a further lift to his spirits. There had been some savage fighting at Bullecourt – twice in recent weeks – and in many ways he was sorry to have missed it. Although he was looking forward to seeing familiar faces again, travelling down by train to Amiens brought mixed feelings.

Amongst his companions were reinforcements for the 1st Division, some still raw, others, like himself, lately recovered from wounds or sickness. The word was that three Australian divisions – the 1st, 2nd and 5th – were to be pulled out of the line for a long and much-needed rest. Everyone else latched onto this news with enthusiasm, but Liam knew that behind the lines, rest was a comparative term. What it meant was weeks of training to grind the new boys into the machine. It was boring and soul-destroying and left too much time to ponder the pointlessness of things.

Nevertheless, for his old comrades-in-arms, he was relieved. Since July the previous year, the Australians had been involved in almost continuous fighting, on the Somme and at Ypres, followed by another return to the Somme for the winter. Sent in pursuit of the sudden German withdrawal, men who had slogged so hard to break the German line on the Bapaume Road in August, were at last allowed to take Bapaume itself in March.

In Liam's book that was excellent news, but he knew success had come at a price. It had been a savage winter on the Somme, in which sleet and snow and glutinous mud were far worse enemies than good old Fritz. In hospital in London, he had read the newspapers and shivered. Recalling November on Gallipoli, when men had died of frostbite and exposure, he could hardly imagine how they had survived the depths of a continental winter. But survive they had. They deserved their rest.

The old Somme battlefield was oddly silent, a barren, windswept heath that at night seemed to moan with the souls of the dead. A blasted heath indeed, a fitting stage for tragedy beneath a climbing moon, although the worst of it had come and gone. Only memory was left, and even those days and weeks at Pozières paled beside more recent tragedy.

By day, as a riotous spring settled into glorious summer, the first green shoots of growth appeared, and all along that barren line the poppies bloomed, bright pools of scarlet amongst the gauzy white of mayweed. *Blood and Bandages*, he thought, like the shoulder-patch of the 8th, his old battalion.

Within a few miles of the old front line, in little, sheltered valleys, crops started to appear, tended only by women and children and very old men, but for Liam they were a sign of hope, a sign of life. And meanwhile, the decimated battalions began to replenish themselves, absorbing new men, new equipment, new strategies. Gradually the greyness disappeared, and the sun made them brown again, and laughter was heard in the camps at night. They drank and gambled, and drank and brawled, and some of them looked up old girlfriends while others found new ones. The bars and brothels of Amiens did excellent trade with the Australians that summer, and Liam obtained enough twenty-four hour passes to roister with the best. But his vow to make the most of wine, women and song was only partially successful. The songs and the wine he could enjoy, it was the women he had no taste for. It was not that they were unattractive; but what they offered was a poorly degraded currency, worthless after the gold he had possessed.

He would look at that old photograph of Georgina and

507

compare it with another he treasured, taken of the two of them in a studio off Oxford Street. There was sweetness in her smile, but the serenity had gone; her eyes were sad and full of knowledge, shadowed by the hours she worked and the suffering she had seen. It was a woman's face, not a girl's, and every time he looked at it his heart bled for her.

His father wrote to say that she was well, working fewer hours and enjoying something of the social life in Egypt. Liam hoped that was true. There was still nothing from Lewis.

His old friend Matt went on Blighty leave for three weeks, and came back full of himself, having painted the town red, seen every show worthy of the name, and cut a swathe through all the girls. Liam smiled and took it with a pinch of salt. Promoted to lance-corporal, his friend was now with a different team, and Carl had gone, too, after being gassed at Ypres. Not badly, but he was still in hospital. Somebody said Liam must have just missed him at Wandsworth, and wasn't that a shame? But the shame was that so many old mates had gone, to be replaced by unfamiliar faces. Even his sergeant, Keenan, had recently lost an arm at Bullecourt. Liam could scarcely believe how much he missed seeing that repulsive gooseberry glare.

Their new sergeant, however, was younger, fitter, and more able, and Liam both liked and respected him. He was a veteran of Gallipoli too, but had recently been transferred from one of the infantry battalions; and although he had done the requisite courses, he seemed glad of Liam's experience with the Vickers guns.

In June, the 3rd and 4th Divisions had a great success at Messines, although the casualties were horrifying. Just as at Bullecourt in April, and Pozières the previous year, the British commanders failed to follow up that success. The bitterness amongst the Australian troops was wholehearted and universal, the only consolation being that they, as soldiers, had not betrayed themselves.

Haig's plan for another great push in Flanders struck dismay into every heart. The artillery was moved up in July, the infantry and their supports, in September.

If August had been a month of storms, September came in like an Indian summer, hot and fine and dry, as though determined to set the scene for their success. Infantry and artillery that had been bogged down, found the quagmire to the east of Ypres drained by the heat, and by the time the Australians were ready to take their part in the second stage of the Third Battle of Ypres, that shallow depression in the landscape resembled a cracked and rutted bowl.

The planning was detailed and thorough, and secrecy, for once, was paramount. The care with which every man was prepared for the coming battle largely dispersed their initial dismay, and after four months' training on the Somme, the men were fit and raring to go, ready to pull the British army out of the mire and crack the German defences once and for all. It was generally felt and often said, that with all these new strategies and any luck at all, Sir Douglas might actually remember to follow-through this time.

Physically, Liam was feeling particularly good, conscious of professional pride and satisfaction, and delighted that the battle-plan, with maps and models, had been the subject of detailed lectures for days. Every man was aware of the aims and objectives and how these were to be achieved; and for the first time not one Australian division but two were to be fighting side by side, as the central spearhead of a push to take the ridge from Gheluvelt to Passchendaele.

The first major objective was Polygon Wood with its huge butte, the long, high mound of the shooting range once used by the Belgian army; but before that were two more woods, Glencorse and Nonne Bosschen, and dozens of concrete pillboxes, from which the worst danger would come during the advance. There was, however, to be no hours-long bombardment, rather a creeping barrage behind which the attacking troops would hide. The danger there, of course, lay in the inevitable short-falling shells. In that situation there was always a chance that a man might be despatched by his own side, although the majority of them had a touching faith in the accuracy of their own artillery.

They moved up from the Somme on 12th September, and settled in small villages south-west of Ypres, with orders to keep out of sight. On the 18th, the battalions moved in attacking order to within easy reach of the front line. They were due to march to their jumping-off positions at midnight on the 19th.

Ypres, Liam decided, was no more beautiful than it had been a year ago, but at least the sun was shining on its shapeless brickwork and battered, crumbling towers. The medieval streets were no more than tracks between piles of rubble and gaping shell-holes, littered with charred oak beams and faceless, broken statues of saints and kings and merchants. They lay like the dead beside the shattered wheels of limbers and the gleaming metal of modern artillery, and they made him think of York with its churches and its carvings and its people. But there were no people here, only soldiers, and this medieval town was dead.

Military police with clipboards stood at every intersection, directing the streams of human traffic; the atmosphere was taut, voices sharp with pre-battle nerves, everybody keyed up and anxious to be off. The machine-gun companies were attached in supporting positions to their respective battalions, and on that sunny afternoon there was little to do, once they were in position, but to check the guns and wait. And waiting was the hellish part, when doubts attacked in force and fear screwed the gut.

Trying to relax, Liam climbed the crumbling mound of the old ramparts, settling himself beneath the stump of a tree to look out along the Menin Road. It was no more than a rutted, pock-marked track in an ochre wilderness, striped with barbed wire and dotted with the detritus of war. In the heat-haze, the slight rise of the ridge seemed an impossible distance away, with little puffs of smoke appearing here and there, followed by the inevitable series of dull thuds. On the still air, the chatter of gunfire occasionally intruded upon the buzz of voices from below.

Beneath him, either side of that gap in the fortifications known as the Menin Gate, men were packed like sardines along the battered inner face of the wall. There was an overplayed joke about this place that sprang to mind as he watched: 'Would the last man through please shut the Gate?' But there was no gate to shut, and the streams of men were endless.

Many went out and few returned. Would he? It was hardly a new thought, but eternity had lost its attraction, and as in every other battle, Liam simply wanted to survive. With Georgina very much on his mind, he wondered whether he should write to her.

A year ago, with death a constant companion, the idea of penning a final word would have seemed faintly ridiculous, but this coming confrontation would be the first for him since last September, and death had become a stranger whose face he might not recognize.

Even so, he hesitated. From a crumpled packet, he took out a cigarette and lit it, and then he found the silver case in which he kept, not cigarettes, but those two precious photographs and a single letter of hers. A short note, loving but less erotic than the ones he had felt bound to destroy. If he should die, if his things were sent back home, he did not want that degree of intimacy revealed to others. It would have been unendurable for Georgina and hurtful to his family. Reading that well-thumbed note again, he supposed he should destroy that, too; but he could not bear to have nothing of her; he needed just this one reminder that she loved him, and that their love had been true.

The past few months had brought acceptance of a kind, but it had been hard-won. Since April he had scraped the barrel of despair before anger reached out to save him, a petty, illogical fury that was directed mainly at himself. Since then emotion had settled to a more tolerable level in which the craving was occasional rather than constant. Looking back on the pain he had already endured, Liam had no wish to open those wounds afresh, and he knew it must be the same for her; but still he ached for news. In the past few months he had torn up innumerable letters to his father, begging for her address, and he imagined her doing much the same.

But still, if she knew what was facing him tomorrow...

As shadows began to lengthen, he could stand it no longer. With indelible pencil on a scrap of paper torn from his notebook, he wrote: *I haven't forgotten, and I know I never will. I love you and I'm always thinking of you. I wish it could have been different. Yours, always and forever, Liam.*

He penned a note to his mother, too, and with a covering few lines to Robert Duncannon, instructed him to use his discretion about forwarding both; then, glad of a need for action, he hurried to find an orderly who might take the letter to a battalion post office. He was one of many with last-minute missives, and there was much grumbling and passing of cigarettes as bribes. It was more than his life was worth, the orderly said, to leave the massing-point; but he went in the end.

By early evening the sky was clouding over, and after dark it began to drizzle with rain. Spirits sank; it seemed the fates were determined to make life hard. By midnight, although the rain had ceased, the cross-country tracks leading off the Menin Road were slippery with surface mud.

As they set off the going was slow indeed. Flanked on both sides by British troops, almost thirty-thousand Australians moved up to their markers in silence. Intermittent shell-fire from a nervous enemy lit their way as dawn's first fingers touched the sky, but the rain proved to have been a friend, creating a low-lying mist to shroud the advancing armies from view.

On the left, by Glencorse Wood, battalions of the 3rd Brigade were caught by a sudden barrage of fire. The feeling of vulnerability increased. Then the 8th, one of the last battalions to find their places on the far right, ran into another barrage. Moving up on the right flank, the youngsters in Liam's company were suddenly nervous. For a moment, catching sight of their officer's anxious face, Liam knew what he was thinking: that the plan was blown. But it seemed no more than a random strike, and as the shelling stopped he found himself craving a forbidden cigarette.

In that final ten minutes, sighs and muffled coughs could be heard, and the sounds of men furtively relieving themselves. Liam set the range on the gun and counted the seconds. Suddenly, at 05:40 all hell broke loose, the heavens rent by the flash and crack and ear-splitting thuds of heavy artillery. Firing the Vickers, Liam hardly noticed it. One man fed belts through the gun, another lit two cigarettes and placed one between his lips. He drew deeply as the belt was changed but did not take his hands from the mechanism, smoking and firing with savage pleasure as the barrage held its curtain 150 yards away. Four minutes later, as it began, quite visibly, to move beyond that point, the signal came to stop firing.

The German bombardment came even as they were dismantling the Vickers. Their sergeant was shouting at them all to get a bloody move on, their officer urging them forward, out of the line of fire.

Liam hoisted the heavy tripod, his Number Two slung the barrel across his shoulder while the others grabbed boxes of ammunition, running with the surge of men following the curtain of their own barrage. They were horrifyingly close, obscured by smoke, lit up as shells burst in front, deafened by explosions, punched by the blasts; it was a taste of hell on earth but they were beneath the arc of the counter-bombardment and heading for the first objective.

As German pillboxes came to light through that dense cloud of dust and smoke, they were bombed and captured; Glencorse Wood was taken, and Nonne Bosschen on the left, and on the right the Victorian Battalions also took 'Fitzclarence Farm', capturing an officer and forty men. Moving forward, fighting as they went, the Australians reached that first line, almost 600 yards from the off, within half an hour. All was in precise accordance with the timetable.

Possessed by a wild sense of elation as they dug into a shell-hole, Liam could scarcely credit the success, the timing. Stunned by that barrage and the speed of the attacking force, the Germans were giving up without much of a fight: it was unbelievable.

There was to be a halt of three-quarters of an hour, to allow for assessment and reorganization. It had seemed excessive beforehand, but in practice proved essential. Men from the different battalions had been mixed up in that surge to escape the German shelling, and now they were sorted out and dug in to await the next stage of the advance. The barrage continued to provide cover, and to the minute it began to move forward. Again the Vickers was dismantled and hoisted, the men shouldering forward over rutted, slippery ground to reach the next objective.

If there had been little resistance to the first attack, there was less with the second. The next 300 yards were covered according to plan, and the second line was reached by 07:45.

On the right flank, struggling to keep ahead of the battalion, and gasping a little from the weight he carried, Liam led his men from shell-hole to shell-hole, keeping an eye on the officer in front. From the rim of one old crater, he directed Matt's team to another, and Liam's to a third where they dug in and set up the gun. What little rain had fallen the previous evening was mainly absorbed into cracks in the clay, but there was old mud in the bottom and the surface was greasy. With a wait of two hours ahead of them, it was worth digging a decent firing-step and ledges to hold the ammunition.

Months of practice made short work of the job; and while the barrage moved up to strike the further German lines, the team lit cigarettes and took turns with the binoculars, eager to know the state of play.

It was full daylight but misty with dust and smoke. The far left of the line was perhaps 500 yards away, almost touching the southern tip of Polygon Wood. A mass of stumps rather than trees, it looked like a skeleton army standing in a sunlit haze, with the massive hump of the butte like a shadow behind.

Much closer was the point known as 'Black Watch Corner': there, a blockhouse was still in frantic action, bursts of fire playing havoc with the 5th Battalion. Nearer still, at 'Lone House', stood another pillbox; and most worrying of all to Liam, a line of six to the right, stretching away above the Reutelbeek. He was instructed to cover that sector by the sergeant, while Matt, some twenty yards away on the next gun, would work in conjunction with him, providing covering fire for the attacking infantry. He hoped they would get going; the occupying Germans might be stunned for a while, but they would soon recover...

Excited chatter from the rest of the team told him that an attack was being made on 'Black Watch Corner' by a company of the 5th. Trying to concentrate, he told them to shut up, but they were too wound-up, too concerned with what was going on. An officer was shot; his men were going mad, slaughtering the Germans who were trying to surrender; other officers were intervening... it was stopped, prisoners were being taken... the 5th were digging in...

'They can take care of their bloody selves,' Liam muttered, his concern closer to home. A platoon of the 8th was moving out towards the nearest pillbox when a sudden blaze of fire revealed a German machine-gun team still very much on the alert. Rattling off a burst of bullets, he swore viciously as two men went down.

He heard the echo of Matt's supporting fire, then the eager demand of a young voice on his left. A head popped up beside him, binoculars raised. He yelled at the boy to get down, out of the way; dragged hard at his collar...

For a split second he heard and felt the violence of a massive explosion, and for that split second the heat and noise and pain were unendurable. The violence erupted into a great, deafening display of rockets and shells and bursting flares, lighting the black sky... it seemed to go on and on for ever...

As the mist cleared, he looked about to see who was hurt. For a moment he thought he was alone, but a man beside him murmured his name. Liam turned and saw the face of his friend. His uniform was torn and bloody in places, but it was Ned, all right, it was definitely Ned...

The bullet that killed Liam also injured the boy he had saved. Hit in the hand, all he could do was stare at the inert body beside him, at the bloody mass that had been the side of his corporal's face. Matt saw it all, and at a break in the firing, came dashing across to give assistance. Seeing his old mate was dead, he simply unfastened the useless steel helmet and held him for a moment, not caring about the blood.

'He was one of the originals, you know,' Matt said softly, to anyone who cared to listen. 'He was there at Anzac...'

When their officer came, crouching in the mud at the crater's foot, the Number Two gave a whispered report on what had happened. The boy with his injured hand lay back, tears streaming down his white face. Matt emptied the pockets. A crumpled pack of cigarettes, a silver case, matches, notebook, a stub of pencil, letters in dog-eared envelopes, and a diary...

'Were you his friend? Then you'd better hang on to them,' the officer said. He sighed, glancing anxiously at his watch, then peered over the crater's rim. 'Bury him. Mark the grave as best you can. We can't take him back.'

Beneath that superficial covering of mud, the ground was hard. Digging enough of it to bury a man was far from easy, but they managed it. Matt, who was not religious, could think of nothing more than to bid farewell to a brave man and a good mate. He concluded those few words with a prayer that he might rest in peace, although at that moment, and even to him, the words had a hollow ring.

They fashioned a rough cross from pieces of an ammunition

box and gouged his name and number with a bayonet in the hope that the grave would later be found, the body reinterred in a proper place.

But the ground they won that day was swamped by autumn rains. Polygon Wood was taken, and later – much later – the combined forces also took Passchendaele. That winter their Russian allies made a separate peace, and the following spring the German armies recaptured the Ypres Salient and almost forty miles of Allied territory. Along with so many more, Liam Elliott's grave was lost.

THIRTY-ONE

Opening an unusually thick envelope, Stephen rapidly scanned the single page of Zoe's letter and was disappointed by its brevity. In a futile search for more, he flicked through the accompanying wad of photocopied army forms and headed letters, to be caught by a typewritten sheet with Liam's name and serial number and *2nd M. G. Coy. A.I.F.* listed at the top.

Almost in spite of himself, he let his eyes run down the page.

'... *on Sep 20th, 1917, Cpl. Elliott was... advancing with the infantry... made a halt and took cover in shell-holes to the left of Northampton Farm... waiting for our barrage to lift... lot of German snipers... while Cpl Elliott had his head exposed... a bullet struck him in the right side of the head... He died instantly, he suffered no pain, before he had time to realize the first shock he was dead... bullet that killed him also wounded another...*'

As though to staunch a sudden wound, Stephen pressed those pages back together and held them, tight, within his hands. It was several seconds before he drew a cautious breath, and when he did the pain flooded in, on a hot, unwelcome wave. The news might have been recent, intensely personal, the death of a close and much-loved friend; the sense of grief and compassion was overwhelming.

With bowed head he sat quite still, unaware of his surroundings, contemplating that death, its suddenness, the years snatched away by one stray bullet.

Footsteps, a tap at the door. Stephen averted his head, stood up, peering from the office window as though something vital had caught his attention. He addressed the man without looking at him, and only when he had himself under control did he turn and apologize.

The problem was soon solved. A moment later he was alone

again, the papers still in his hand, rolled now like a baton. With great care he returned them to their envelope, all the time wondering at the power of those words. He had known, Stephen kept telling himself, all the time he had known that Liam was dead, and that date, 20th September 1917, was not news to him. Knowing should have lessened the impact, but it didn't. Having come to know Liam Elliott more intimately than his closest friend, Stephen felt bereaved.

Mingled with sorrow was a sense of needless waste; anger, too, that the world seemed so unchanged. Suddenly vulnerable, he wished that Zoe might have kept hold of that information rather than sending it on. It made him all too aware of the transient nature of human life, and remembering the dreams, he began to wonder whether sudden death was his destiny, too.

He thrust the idea away. That was depression working, and tiredness, and the knowledge that he was sick to the heart of this endless stress.

Karachi was no improvement. After forty-eight hours, Stephen was more than usually glad to be leaving. The inevitable barrage of port officials had descended at unpredictable times to deliver their various assaults upon his patience and ingenuity, and had departed, weighed down with cigarettes and paperwork and duty-free whisky, leaving nothing but the memory of their gleeful smiles.

As he jammed on his hat and adjusted the chin-strap, the pilot wished him a pleasant voyage, but there was a glint in his eye as he turned to leave. The south-west monsoons were blowing, and he knew as well as Stephen that the next couple of days and nights would be far from pleasant.

Lurching in the swell in the lee of the *Damaris*, the pilot-boat hovered, its engines growling over the noise of the wind. Stephen leaned over the starboard bridge-wing, watched the pilot down the ship's side and his nifty leap onto the boat; with a full-throated roar, it surged away, bouncing as it caught buffeting wind and waves beyond the ship. Envy clutched Stephen's heart as it disappeared into the evening murk: he wished he was on it and going home, not facing his tenth trip through the jaws of Hormuz, with no specific date for relief. Both 2nd Mate and 2nd Engineer had been relieved last time round in Kuwait, and watching them go had been hellish. Until then, he had not realized just how much he wanted to be off. Ah, well, he was getting to know the new men, and they seemed decent.

He watched the Bosun and a seaman hoist the pilot-ladder inboard, and with a bitter sigh, turned and closed the bridge door behind him. It was cooler inside.

With the anchorage astern of them and a Force 8 gale on the port bow, Stephen ordered the speed kept down to 10 knots. With no cargo the ship was light and high in the water, yet tanks had to be cleaned and freed from flammable gases; in spite of the weather that meant men on deck, working throughout the night. The Mate, who had been up for most of their forty-eight hours in Karachi, supervising the discharge of cargo, had grabbed a couple of hours' sleep and something to eat, and was about to go on deck to start washing the dregs of petrol from Numbers 1 and 2 tanks, up by the fo'c'sle. It was not an arduous task, but the pumping of inert gas into all the cargo tanks was long and tedious, with valves and pressures to be constantly monitored. Altogether, it would take approximately 24 hours, and with this weather to contend with, Stephen did not envy the job.

Still, he had done it often, himself, and without an understanding Master to split those hours on deck. The utter exhaustion of discharging a cargo, then getting to sea and having to tank-clean without chance to sleep at all, was a memory that could still make him wince. He had once worked a straight forty hours without sleep, a nightmare that he was determined never to impose upon anyone else.

His standard arrangements required no more than the briefest acknowledgement. With the arrival of the 3rd Mate, Stephen handed the watch over to him, and told him to speak to the Mate on deck – via the walkie-talkie radio – if he needed advice. Meeting Johnny in oilskins and hard-hat a few minutes later, Stephen said he would be relieved on deck at midnight.

He checked his watch: twenty-five minutes to seven and it was time to have his dinner and go to bed. At midnight he would take over the bridge-watch for six hours, while the Second Mate took over the tank-cleaning. They would each work six on, six off, until the job was finished. Nor could the engineers go to bed and rest: after working round the clock in port, they must continue to man the engine control room until the job was done. Not an easy time for anybody, and Mac's men were as tired as his own.

Stephen ate with Mac in the saloon, mostly in silence. They were both too weary for small-talk, too used to the harassment of Karachi even to comment on it. As though by mutual consent they made short work of the meal and rose from the table together. The ship was rolling heavily, and the climb up several flights of stairs was an effort. By the time Stephen reached his cabin he had the beginnings of a headache.

He lifted the heavy typewriter from his office desk and set it on the floor, siding paperwork away, and locking drawers and cupboards for safety; in his dayroom, he retrieved a handful of music-tapes that had already found their way to the deck. Having made sure nothing else could wake him with bangs and crashes, he switched on some music, dimmed the lights, poured himself a large measure of whisky, and raised the blind on the forward window. It was too dark to see much, but he could just make out white-tipped spray, rising in sheets from the port bow, and a glimmer of torches on the starboard side. With a sigh he lowered the blind, dragged off his damp shirt and sat down to read his mail.

Joan's letter was full of Zoe's visit to York, and the fact that there had been a reply, at long last, from the Australian War Memorial. Months ago, Stephen had persuaded her to write to Canberra regarding Liam's war record, and the reply, apparently, had been well worth the wait. Very sad, Joan's letter said, and she had shed a few tears over it, but Zoe thought he would be pleased by the detail, and was sending on copies.

Pleased was the wrong word, he thought, but he turned again to Zoe's letter, as disappointed now as he had been earlier. The account of her trip to York was much briefer than Joan's, expanding only to mention the hunch which had led her to check the old visitors' book at his flat.

'*But I didn't stay long, the place felt very empty and strange without you...*'

For some reason that disturbed him. It seemed to stress his

current sense of unreality, and made him even more aware that his life was lived in separate boxes, that each journey between the two required him to assume another identity. Inevitably, there was an awkwardness about that, particularly going home, a feeling of dissociation until he found again the requisite colour and character to blend in with his surroundings. From here, in this situation, he could scarcely recall the man who lived in York, the man who, for a few short weeks, had been so absolutely happy in the company of a young woman called Zoe Clifford. And he had been happy; she had made him feel light-hearted and young, as though the world still had something to offer, something worth striving for. Looking back, it seemed so strange, he began to wonder whether he had imagined it; worse, that this other half of him had sunk without trace.

He read the letter through again and sighed over it, over the change in tone, the change in her. At first she had written in an easy, conversational style that evoked voice, humour, enthusiasm; and yes, her affection, too, which came through the lines to warm him in a silent embrace. Of late, however, her letters had become rather stilted, very much confined to the research she was doing. The rest of her life was barely mentioned. He wondered why. Perhaps she thought he was no longer interested; perhaps there was someone else. Zoe had closed a door somewhere, and the view was now restricted.

But perhaps, Stephen reasoned, the fault was not all hers. He suspected he was equally to blame, that in his dogged determination to stick to his own rules, he had managed to alienate her affection. And anyway, he asked himself, what did he write about these days? Not his own emotions, that was for sure; they were shackled to a wall in some remote dungeon of his soul, and would not be released until he was home and free. The lacerating stress of these weekly voyages between Kuwait and Karachi was another topic he avoided, which left his correspondence as unadorned as extracts from the log-book.

Even his response to the research was lacking in vitality, and yet he would read her letters, logging opinions and assumptions along with every new discovery, and feel a tingle of excitement. When it came to setting it down on paper, however, his enthusiasm seemed to wane. It was a new and unwelcome phenomenon to one who had always enjoyed writing as a form of communication, and the weary thought, 'I'll tell her when I see her...' had become a habit.

He felt as dry and barren as the desert, and across the harsh landscape of his inner vision, Zoe appeared with no more substance than a mirage.

Glancing at the first page of those photocopied sheets, he saw the heading Australian War Memorial, and knew a deep reluctance to read further. His eyes were dry with fatigue, head aching with the increasingly violent motion of the ship. He should get to bed, get some sleep. And yet...

The letter stated that there were five eye-witness reports to Corporal Elliott's death in the Red Cross files, which made Stephen think that someone must have queried the facts, either because his body was never found, or someone did not believe the manner of his death. Perhaps Robin, to whom that tale of a bullet through the head must have sounded exceedingly suspect; yet despite being a convenient fiction for the poor souls who were literally blown to bits, some men had to die like that, cleanly, with all their limbs intact. But his body was never found: ergo, the Red Cross enquiry.

What a hell of a job, Stephen thought, mind unable to grasp the extent of such a task, if all the thousands upon thousands of missing were investigated to that extent. Tracing five eye witnesses for one man's death... and from the dates of those statements, taken up to eighteen months later, from Grantham in Lincolnshire to the State of Victoria, the size and scope of the investigation was almost incredible.

After that, he had to read the statements, just to see how well they tallied with that first account, given by a sergeant at Grantham in March 1918. Apart from one, who seemed to be out with regard to location, they tallied very well, too well to be making things up for the benefit of anybody's sensibilities. But even though he had steeled himself to read those accounts, Stephen found himself unbearably moved by the personal detail.

'He was a tall man, well-built, fair, about 25 years of age...'

'He was known as Bill...'

'I knew him – I saw him killed... I have already written to his people *about it...'*

'I was 20 yards away at the time – I saw his body a few minutes later...'

'He was buried on the battlefield...'

It was enough; he did not want to read more. The rest could wait for another time. Bracing himself against the motion of the ship, he poured himself another drink, knowing it must be the last, he really had to get some sleep. He sipped the measure of twelve-year-old malt slowly, savouring its smoothness, letting his mind drift on the question of Liam's death and the enigma of his relationship with Georgina. What must she have felt? In the next moment he was thinking about Zoe, trying to imagine what her reaction would be, if...

But that made him shiver. There were too many similarities for comfort, too many coincidences that would never be explained, and he did not want to make one more. Please God, let there be no stray bullets for him!

He sank the rest of the whisky in one gulp, tucked the empty glass against a protecting cushion, and lurched across to his bedroom, not even slightly drunk. From a cupboard he rescued his bright orange lifejacket, and lifting the mattress of his double-bunk, stuffed it underneath, making a well between the raised edge and the wall.

His bunk ran fore and aft, a bad design fault, but wedged into that small valley, Stephen was prevented from rolling side-to-side; it did not prevent the other motion, that tipping from head-to-toe, like some fairground swing-boat. The ship pitched and lifted with every wave, an unpleasant corkscrew motion made worse by the lack of cargo. With weight in those massive tanks, the *Damaris* was not a bad old girl; but light, she could perform somersaults on a wet facecloth, of that Stephen was convinced. He tensed, listening as the bow plunged into those heavy seas and the stern lifted beneath him, right out of the water. The noise rose to a scream as the propeller raced; then came the unearthly groan and shudder as the stern slammed down and the prop bit deep. Everything quaked and trembled, steel decks and bulkheads, interior walls, cupboards, fittings, and in the darkness the noise and vibration seemed worse, as though the ship were being physically wrenched apart.

The ship surged across to port, forcing his back against the wall, pitched forward with a rising shriek, rolled again to starboard and slammed back with a particularly violent shuddering groan... a bad one, that.

Searching for the rhythm, trying to relax with it, Stephen found himself thinking of Ruth. Storms had always unnerved her, and the typhoon they had met off Japan that time had seen her in a state of terror, convinced with every pounding wave that death was no more than minutes away. When the corrugated awnings were torn off the aft accommodation, she had dissolved into helpless, hysterical tears, and the sight of the foredeck bending under the strain of wind and sea finished her completely. It availed nothing to explain that the ship was *designed* to bend, that if it did not, it would break in two... Ruth had been huddled in a lifejacket, deaf to all reason.

Stephen had been ashamed of her. He could admit that now. He had been Mate at the time, Ruth the only wife aboard. He would never forget the pitying glances of the other officers. They had tried to be kind, but he knew what they were thinking, and the Master had rapidly lost all patience, ordering her off his bridge where she was starting to unnerve him. It had been a humiliating experience, made worse by a genuinely worrying situation. With the unpredictability of typhoons, that one had turned and caught them in its new path, just as they were running away from it. And it had been particularly violent, Force 12 and more.

And then he thought of another such incident, a few years later when he was Master. The Mate's daughter, on holiday from school, had been giggling with glee as enormous green seas broke over the foredeck, swamping the fully-loaded ship. Laughing with her, he had remarked on her bravery.

'I used to be scared at night,' she admitted airily to Stephen, 'thinking we were sinking and we were all going to die any minute. But you know you can't escape, so you just have to accept it. I'm not scared of dying any more...'

How old had she been? Thirteen, fourteen? No more than that. *Out of the mouths of babes*, he thought, recalling her guts and her wisdom, and knowing she was right. Living with the thought of dying made the idea lose all its terrors, inducing a certain fatalism, a readiness to accept the worst.

Had Liam felt like that?

Or had he felt, like Stephen, that it was not the idea of death that was frightening, but the endurance required to survive?

Called at midnight, he finished his watch at six in the morning. Over the sea, the pitch-black murk became grey, then pink and orange, and finally a sickly yellow, like thick industrial pollution. The dust was so fine it was almost like talcum, collected by winds blowing with the force of hurricanes across North Africa and the Arabian Desert. It found its way through every crack and crevice, leaving its evidence across charts and instruments, blearing the windows with muck and salt, so that it was necessary to peer through spinning, clear-view screens and consult the radar every few minutes.

The *Damaris* was still punching those seas, sending up great walls of water over the port bow; as she rose, they came tumbling back over the foredeck, to swirl against the accommodation. Standing on the central cat-walk, Johnny and the 2nd Mate were soaked by spray. Stephen watched them shouting against the wind, bright yellow oilskins glistening as they turned and parted. Clinging to the rails, the Mate made his way forward, while young Paul, after six hours on deck, staggered inside to breakfast and his bunk.

Stephen went down to his office, timing his descent of the steps with the roll of the ship. He spent an uncomfortable hour at his desk in an attempt to make some impression upon the paperwork, then went down for breakfast in the saloon. After that he retired to his bunk, sleeping solidly for four hours before returning to the bridge at twelve. The gas-freeing was completed by eight that evening, but the weather was still too bad to increase speed. By the time they reached the vicinity of Fujairah, an hour before dawn of the third day, it was too late to reach Hormuz with any degree of safety.

As though gunboats and helicopters were not enough to contend with, Stephen had received warning of mines in the approaches to the Kuwaiti terminals. Only a few days before, on the BBC World Service, had come reports of an American supertanker, the *Texaco Caribbean*, hitting a mine in the Gulf of Oman, eight miles off Fujairah. It was thought to be a stray, drifting down from the Straits, but no one could be sure.

It was a daunting prospect, but as Stephen had said to his senior officers at the time, a tanker is a very difficult vessel to sink. With buoyancy retained by all those sealed compartments, providing the vessel was hit in the bows – the most obvious place under way – then little damage would be sustained. A hefty claim on the insurance, into Dubai for repairs, and with any luck at all, the company would fly most of them home.

Brave words, cheerfully said. But in the teeth of that still-howling gale, with visibility down to a couple of hundred yards, Stephen's nerves were twitching. Never yet had he damaged a ship, and he did not intend to start now. Damage was damage, however slight, and there was always the unnerving possibility of someone being in the wrong place at the wrong time. He could do without that on his conscience.

In the pre-dawn darkness he was glad they were late, glad of some necessary hours at the deep-water anchorage off Fujairah. It meant a much-needed rest. As they came slowly within the shelter afforded by the land, the wind lessened appreciably. In the wheelhouse, studying the charts, it was suddenly possible to stand without clinging on, and to move about with some degree of ease.

The broad sweep of the radar revealed dozens of ships at anchor and the protecting ridge of land to the west. With their speed reduced to a half, he found a suitable area, checked it against the radar, and plotted a position where it was possible to swing with ease. Marking the place on the chart he gave directions to the 3rd Mate and the helmsman at the wheel. As he checked the depth of water – 45 fathoms – against the echo-sounder, the crackle of his walkie-talkie radio told him the Mate was out on deck with the anchor-party.

Responding, Stephen picked up the telephone to ask the duty engineer for Dead Slow Ahead. As the revs and the ship's speed came right down, he spoke on the radio.

'She's down to 3 knots, walk the anchor back to 1 shackle...'

He could see the flash of torches on the fo'c'sle, hear the creaks and groans of the port anchor being slowly lowered by winch, the dull clunks of that massive chain going out over the side. In this depth of water, just to let go would be to burn out the windlass. Slowly, slowly, was the trick...

A couple of minutes, and the Mate's voice came back: 'One shackle and holding...'

'Hold till we're in position.' He glanced at the helmsman on the wheel, and the 3rd Mate moving between chart and radar. On the Mate's signal, Stephen took the telegraph, rang down to Stop, and then to Slow Astern. He dashed out to the bridge-wing to watch the action of the propeller-wash against the ship's side. When it was just coming back and passing him, he knew the ship was stopped in the water.

'OK she's stopped,' he said into the radio. 'Just walk the anchor out, and let me know how she's leading.'

He listened to the Mate's voice, counting each shackle off as it descended those 45 fathoms to the sea-bed below. After three shackles, Johnny said, 'Cable starting to lead astern...'

'OK.' The anchor was down, the cable starting to lay along the sea-bed.

'Four shackles, cable leading astern...'

Stephen turned and shouted to the 3rd Mate. 'Stop Engines.'

'Five shackles, cable up and down...'

He waited, hearing creaks and groans from the windlass. It might be time to give that cable a bit of assistance, rather than let it fall in a heap round the anchor.

'Six shackles, cable beginning to lead ahead...'

'OK, we'll pull her back a bit.' He shouted to the 3rd Mate, 'Ring down for Slow Astern.'

'Slow Astern it is, Captain.'

He leaned over the port side, watching those flickering torches on the fo'c'sle. The weather was clearing, ahead and to port he could see the misted lights of other ships. He glanced at his watch: almost half-past five, not long to daybreak.

With the familiar crackle that preceded the Mate's regular report, there was suddenly an almighty flash from somewhere below and astern, and a simultaneous explosion that knocked Stephen sideways.

Stunned, deafened, his ears ringing from the blast, for a second or two he lay on the deck wondering why the night should be glowing like November 5th, and what the hell had gone wrong in the engine-room.

He tried to get up, pushing with his right hand against the step of the compass – and cried out as pain shot like red-hot steel through his shoulder to chest and spine and wrist. For a moment, he almost passed out. Fending off the 3rd Mate's assistance, he took a painful breath and demanded to know what had happened.

'I don't know, sir!' His voice was high, panicky. 'I think something's blown in the engine-room... the alarms went, then stopped...'

'Well, then, press the manual alarms, for God's sake – and pass me that bloody radio!'

'Are you all right, Captain?'

'No, but I can manage,' Stephen insisted, hauling himself to his feet and shouting above the ringing in his head. 'Alarms, Marcus – now!'

As the young man ran to obey, Stephen pressed the transmit button to answer the faint, crackling voice of the Mate. 'No, Johnny, I don't know for sure – might be the engine, more likely a fucking mine. Start the fire-pump for'ard, and get yourself back here, sharp as you can. Out.'

He leaned for a moment on the bridge-front, dragging air into his lungs, fighting to conquer the nausea coming in waves. His right arm hurt like hell, and he did not seem able to move it. With his arm hanging useless, he forced himself back to the wheelhouse, ordering the 3rd Mate to his emergency station.

As he clattered away down an outer ladder, the inner door opened to admit the Chief and the Radio Officer, and a blast of ringing from the alarms. Sparks was only half-dressed, his boots and boiler suit trailing. As he dragged on his gear, Mac fastened a lifejacket and listened to Stephen's very brief report. His red beard bristled as he set his jaw.

'So both of them were down there? Second and Third? I'd better get down and investigate.'

'Keep me advised, Chief.'

Armed with torch and radio, Mac went back the way he had

come. Watching him descend into darkness, for the first time Stephen realized that all the lights were out, even those that should have been powered by the emergency generator. Familiar with the unlit bridge, he had not noticed before. It must be bad down there, whatever the cause. He switched off the manual alarms, and in the ensuing silence could hear the rattling of feet on steps and steel ladders, and the excited, slightly panicky chatter of the crew rising from the stairwell. Everything was echoing round the accommodation, and it was a weird, unnatural sound, accentuating the deadness of the ship, its lack of a heartbeat.

For a second, it almost unnerved him. He thought about the anchor and thanked God the cable was out, enough to hold, at least. His radio crackled, and Mac's voice reported that he had met the Electrician on the stairs – Lecky had tried to get to his emergency station in the engine-room, but all he could see were flames...

'Second and Third Engineers? Have they turned up?' The reply was negative and Stephen's heart sank. 'OK – get to Emergency HQ right away. I'll be in touch.'

He turned to Sparks, hovering by the VHF. Thank God that thing worked off its own batteries, everything else was down, radar, computers, direction-finder. 'Put out a Mayday, all frequencies, with present position – on fire, request immediate assistance.'

The 2nd and 3rd Mates reported in. With the exception of the anchor party, all crew were present and correct at boat stations. Stephen bit back a curse.

'Well get them to their *emergency* stations – and tell them to stop panicking. We're in no danger of sinking, but the engine-room's on fire, and two engineers are missing. The Chief and Mate are on their way to you now...'

Where was the Mate? 'Did you hear that, Johnny?'

'I heard you, Captain – I'm on my way – coming round the accommodation now.' He left his radio on, and Stephen could hear his breathing, slightly ragged, as though he were running. It was a long way from the fo'c'sle... 'I tell you what, it's bloody hot out here...'

Stephen glanced at his watch. Twenty-three minutes to six, just seven minutes since he had glanced at it, seconds before the blast. It seemed an eternity. He steeled himself for what he had to say next.

'Chief, when the Mate gets to you, I want him and Lecky geared up – flame suits, breathing apparatus – to search the engine-room for the missing men.'

'Captain, I'm all geared up already – let me go down.'

It was as he expected. 'No, Chief. Absolutely not. I know how you feel, but you're the only engineer I've got just now, and I need you.'

'It's my engine-room!'

'And it's my ship. Stay out, Mac – and that's an order.' Stephen took a deep breath, and winced at the ensuing pain. 'You'd better go round and trip the fuel shut-downs.'

'I've done that.' He sounded furious.

'Good. Stay where you are and keep me informed.'

He glanced again at the time, urging a response from Fujairah. He thought about the missing men, realizing medical aid would be essential, if only to treat victims of shock and smoke. Please God, nothing worse. As he turned to Sparks, a loud, heavily accented voice startled them both. A port control officer from Fujairah announced that fire-fighting tugs would be with them in thirty minutes; Sparks responded, requesting the assistance of a doctor. Moments later, there was another call, this time from a salvage-tug from Hormuz, offering to come and stand by; the offer was followed by several more.

'The vultures are gathering,' Stephen murmured bitterly, aware that an abandoned ship was a rich prize for the salvage companies. Well, they could gather; he had no intention of abandoning anything, least of all his ship.

'How's that arm, Captain?'

He shook his head. 'It'll do for the time being.' He was more concerned for those men in the engine-room, envisaging the different levels from propeller-shaft up to control-room, and trying to relate that mental map to the blast. The control-room was on the port side, and the loss of power could be attributable to a wipe-out in that area. At least one of those men must have been there when the explosion occurred.

He felt for his cigarettes and realized they were missing. Sparks passed one of his own across, and left the packet within reach.

Stephen inhaled on a shuddering breath and went out to peer over the port bridge-wing. A dull glow lit up the surrounding area and was reflected by the dancing waves. In the east, a pale band of lighter cloud streaked the horizon. The sun was coming up, and would soon add to the heat travelling up through steel decks and bulkheads.

Wondering what was happening down there, praying for a miracle, he found himself questioning, illogically, the safety of the cargo-tanks. How thoroughly had they been inerted? And to what point of destruction did theory apply? If those tugs didn't get here soon, they might all be blown to kingdom come.

His walkie-talkie sparked into life. 'Emergency HQ to bridge.'

'Go ahead, Chief.'

'Lecky and the Mate have found the Second. He's got a gash on the head and he's not too good – only half-conscious. But he's out, he's alive. No sign yet of the Third...'

Oh, thank God. One of them alive at least... But what of the other man? 'Let me speak to the Mate.'

Johnny's voice was hoarse, his report staccato. 'Tried the port entrance – full of smoke and flame. We just shut the door on it. Starboard side – smoke, but no flame.' He paused for breath, and Stephen could hear it rasping in his throat. 'Went in, down ladder – couldn't see a damn thing. Stuck together. Halfway down on starboard side – found the Second crawling along the plates towards us. Practically unconscious. Dragged him out. He's got a bad gash on his head, but I think he'll live...'

'Well done, Johnny. Pass that on to Lecky, too.' For a second Stephen paused, thinking about the missing man, recollecting his whiskery grin, and a cheery greeting as they passed on the stairs. When was that? Yesterday? He tried to keep his voice steady. 'Do you feel able to go back? To search again?'

There was another pause, as though the men at the other end were consulting. Then the Mate's voice again. 'Affirmative, Captain. We're going down now.'

'Be careful, Johnny – no heroics. From either of you.'

Something like a laugh came back at him. 'Heroics? Us? We're more like Laurel and bloody Hardy.'

Stephen smiled at the image: the tall, lanky Mate and the

Electrician who was short and round... He pulled himself up short and asked for Mac. 'Detach the 2nd Mate, Chief, and get your man to the hospital.'

Back in the wheelhouse, Sparks lit him another cigarette; a few minutes later, Mac was calling with the news that they had managed to get some sense out of the injured man. He had answered a generator alarm, and as he left the control-room to check it out, the explosion occurred. The Third Engineer was still in there.

'Not good.'

'No. He's almost sure that something hit the ship from outside, just by the control-room.'

'A mine.'

'Sounds like it.'

'The *bastards*...'

It struck him again how fortunate they were to have got the anchor laid out before the blast; otherwise the ship would have been drifting, helpless and on fire, a danger to half the ships in the anchorage. And there were plenty. All tankers.

In the unnatural silence he could hear the wind buffeting the funnel, flapping the radio aerials and stays; the sea was making a shushing noise to windward, as it did when they were under way...

Stephen suddenly became aware that the deck beneath him had a tilt to it; water was rushing into the engine-room, pulling the ship down by the stern.

The Mate's voice intruded upon that consideration. 'It's no go, Captain. Everything's on fire down there. We managed to get pretty close, though – spotted a clear space round the hole, water flooding in just there –' He broke off, sniffed audibly, and seemed to be having difficulty getting the next words out. 'The body was in bits. I've told the Chief – no chance of getting near it.'

Hearing those words, Stephen knew that while he had not consciously framed the thought, he had expected it. Nevertheless, an image sprang to mind of Jim Stubbs, Third Engineer, short, thick-set, with wild grey hair and always a couple of days' stubble on his chin. An unkempt, scruffy Liverpudlian, unmarried, uncertificated, and wedded to the job. His humour was abrasive, and he was a bit too fond of the booze, but he was reliable, and a bloody good engineer.

What a way to die.

And for what?

Sorrow and pity washed over him, together with the vaguely consolatory thought that it must have been instantaneous. That was the only decent thing about it.

With an effort he found his voice and forced it to remain calm. 'I understand. You've done all you could. Thanks for that. Is Lecky OK?'

'He's wheezing like hell, but he'll be all right.'

'Good.' Now, back to business. 'Right, Johnny, in your considered opinion, is it now time to batten everything down and flood with CO2?'

'It certainly is, Captain.'

'Right, Johnny – put me on to the Chief.'

He ordered Mac to close all openings and ventilators and to release the carbon dioxide gas; then he called the 3rd Mate to see to the boundary cooling.

'Get those firehoses through the accommodation, leave them running, and *get out*. Make sure the crew are away from the area. Get them up for'ard and onto the fo'c'sle – and give the Bosun a radio, we'll need to keep in touch. Then come to the bridge.'

Over the starboard bow he could see the tugs approaching, bright orange hulls standing out in the soupy daylight; behind them, coming up fast, was a pilot-boat. Stephen spoke to the 2nd Mate, in the ship's hospital with the injured man. 'Get your party up for'ard, Paul, with the crew. The pilot-boat's on its way with a doctor.'

From the bridge-wing he watched the crew, bobbing about in twos and threes as they hurried along the main deck, followed at a more sedate pace by the stretcher-party. The injured man's face was dappled, white patches against the black where the Second Mate had cleaned his cuts and dressed them. Still, a couple of days in a proper hospital, and he should be all right. Be up and chasing the nurses in no time...

The Mate and Lecky, both haggard and dishevelled, joined him, Lecky collapsing onto the compass-step as though his chubby legs would not hold out another instant. He looked in poor shape, trembling visibly as Sparks lit him a cigarette. Johnny was grey with strain but bearing up.

'Well, here we are, smoking on deck...' He gave a weak little laugh, but suddenly his mouth was working. He turned away to watch the activity on deck, while Stephen studied his back and decided to be brisk.

'I think you should go with them, see a doctor. Both of you,' he added, turning back to the other man. He really did look bad. Aware of what he had put them through, Stephen felt guilty.

Lecky nodded his agreement; it was clear he wanted to be off the ship, and who could blame him? Johnny, however, shook his head. He was staying, he said, and would be fine once he had rested and had something to drink.

'Any chance of liberating a few cans of coke? I've got a mouth like the bottom of a birdcage.'

Stephen's cabin was nearest, with a recently stocked fridge of soft drinks and a cupboard full of spirits for entertaining. Sparks volunteered to go, while Stephen manned the VHF.

Calls were still coming in from other ships and tugs eager to offer assistance, and on the port quarter, the fire-fighters were busily hosing sea-water over the after-deck and into that gaping hole below.

Mac came up to join them, his steps dragging like an old man's. His face was ashen. As he propped himself up against the pilot-chair, he seemed incapable of speech. He glanced at Stephen and away, and simply shook his head.

'Mac, I'm sorry...' For everything, he might have added – that shocking death, the ruin below decks, and most of all for having to forbid his friend the opportunity to search his own engine-room for his own men. It felt like a betrayal; and yet Stephen's first duty was to the ship.

'No, you did what you had to...' He lit a cigarette and smoked in silence for a while. Then, noticing Stephen's useless arm, asked what had happened.

'The blast knocked me over – I fell against that bloody thing,' he said, indicating the compass-repeater on the bridge-wing, 'and must have hit the deck awkwardly. I think it's dislocated.'

'Could be broken – you'd better get the doctor up here, let

him have a look at it.'

But Stephen for the first time was indecisive, torn between the pain he was suffering and the need to stay aboard. While he debated what to do, Mac took his radio and called up the 2nd Mate, asking him to escort the doctor up to the bridge once the injured man was safely off the ship.

Twenty minutes later he was with them, a small, dapper Arab in a smart linen suit, only slightly soiled by his climb up the pilot ladder to the fo'c'sle. His command of their language spoke of several years training in an English hospital.

Slender fingers examined the injured arm, and a pair of dark, unsmiling eyes studied Stephen's face as he tried to answer questions and avoid too many grunts of pain. Behind and to one side of the doctor, the 2nd Mate, as ship's medical officer, hovered uncomfortably. Grimy and sweat-stained, wearing a ragged boilersuit open to the navel, and with his hair plastered to his head, he was not the average nurse. Meeting his anxious gaze, Stephen managed a lop-sided grin.

The doctor said, 'I think no break or fracture, but a dislocation of the shoulder. I can manipulate it back into position now, but it will be very painful. You should come to hospital. There we can give anaesthetic. And also X-ray for possible small fractures in the wrist.'

'I'm not leaving the ship.'

There was an eloquent shrug. 'You wish me to perform the operation now?'

Stephen glanced at his medical officer. 'Get Sparks. Tell him to bring the whisky.'

A slight curl of the lip expressed the doctor's disapproval. 'Alcohol is not good for shock.'

'I know that. But it's bloody good for pain.'

He reached for the bottle, removed the cap and took a hefty slug from the neck. Then he took another. It caught his breath for a moment and made his eyes water, but he still held the little doctor's gaze. It felt like a battle of wills, one that Stephen was not at all sure he would win. Never mind, he would go down trying. And he would not leave the ship.

'Lie down, please. On the floor, on your side.'

He felt the knee in his back, one hand against his shoulder, the other at his wrist. There was a sudden wrench and agonizing pain, and a grinding crack that seemed to explode in his skull...

The reek of ammonia brought him round. Wafting the sal volatile beneath Stephen's nose, the 2nd Mate looked as though he were the one about to faint. The doctor was checking the contents of his bag.

'You should rest,' that cool voice advised. 'Go to bed.'

'Don't be bloody silly...'

Standing over him, with surprising gentleness the doctor eased him forward; between them, he and the 2nd Mate got Stephen to his feet and through the open door of the sea cabin. Sparks had folded the sheets back and stood beside the bunk like a hotel manager.

As though instructing a child, the doctor said: 'Here is a bed – rest in it.' To the 2nd Mate, he added: 'He will need the arm supported by a sling. There will be much bruising, much pain. You should give him something to relieve it.'

Stephen sat on the edge of the bunk, nursing his arm; he felt sick and shaky, and took several deep breaths to control it. As the doctor glided out towards the bridge-wing, he glanced at Sparks, who rolled his eyes and sagged with sudden relief. Sweat dripped off his unshaven chin.

'What's he doing now?'

'Giving the Mate and Lecky a once-over. The Chief asked him to.'

'Right. As soon as he's gone we'll have to try and raise the office.' His watch said it was ten minutes to seven. In London, his ship-manager would be in bed and asleep. 'Four in the morning – Jack Porteous'll love that.'

'Five,' Sparks reminded him, 'it's Summer Time.'

Fatigue dragged at him, and pain throbbed through ribs and shoulder right down to the wrist. But the thought of all those office wallahs being dragged out of their beds was strangely satisfying.

With the 2nd Mate in tow, the doctor returned, giving Stephen to understand that in his opinion all the officers were suffering from some degree of shock and exhaustion, and should by rights be taken off the ship. Only one, however, had agreed to go.

'Well,' Stephen explained, 'as we don't have any electricity to speak of, we can manage without our electrician... which he is well aware of. Everybody else is essential.'

'I see.' He glanced round like a prince finding himself in the unfortunate surroundings of a labour camp. Then he smiled. 'Well, Captain, I must go. I wish you good luck.'

'Thank you.'

As soon as he was away, Stephen went outside, fighting dizziness and nausea on his way to the bridge-wing. The pilot boat was still alongside, the crew hanging hopefully over the fo'c'sle. One of the fire-fighting tugs had stopped its hoses and was coming in. The VHF crackled, the tug master asking permission to put a crew aboard. Stephen acknowledged and agreed, passed on instructions to the 3rd Mate, and watched the half-dozen men scramble up the ship's side.

Within half an hour the fire was reported to be under control; with that news Stephen felt able to breathe easier, able to give a constructive report to his ship-manager in London. He raised Fujairah and requested a call to be put through; it took some time, but eventually he had Jack Porteous's sleepy voice over the static on the line.

'Jack, it's Stephen Elliott – on the *Damaris*. Sorry to wake you, but we're in an emergency situation...' From sleepy, Jack Porteous was businesslike at once. Reassured, Stephen went on to report events in brief.

'I'm getting good reports from the fire-fighting team, so once it's out I'll need a tow to a repair yard. I think Dubai – that's nearest. Also I'll need to appoint agents in Fujairah to deal with the injured and the crew...'

'OK – go ahead. I'll do the necessary at this end – I'll get in touch with next-of-kin myself, and get your engineer superintendent on the first available flight. Do you need any reliefs at this stage?'

'No, we'll get her to the repair yard ourselves – we can talk about reliefs later.'

'What about you, Steve? Are you all right?'

'I'm OK now, but I've got things to attend to, Jack. I'll call you back as soon as I can.'

'Or I'll call you. The media are bound to get onto this... can you cope?'

'As long as they don't want to come aboard.'

'If they get too pressing, just refer them to us.'

'OK, will do.'

It was not until a representative of ITN news called him up that Stephen gave a thought to his own next-of-kin. While he demanded assurances that names and ranks of casualties would not be used without contacting the shipping company first, he suddenly remembered his sister Pamela, and prayed she would have the sense to phone Joan before the news hit television and radio broadcasts. And that Joan would be able to contact Zoe...

Thirty-two

For some time, Zoe had not been sleeping well, but she woke that night with the impression that someone or something had disturbed her. Instantly alert, for a moment her eyes scanned the darkness while she listened for unaccustomed sounds. Nothing, not even a disturbance of the air, and yet her heart was hammering against her breast, every muscle tensed as though for flight.

She glanced at the clock, its small, illuminated hands pointing to half-past three. Not even light yet. Swallowing hard, she slipped out of bed, dragged on a light cotton housecoat and tiptoed through the tiny lobby to her sitting room. The blinds were up and she saw at once that nothing had been disturbed. The kitchen was empty. More confident now, but still anxious, she opened the door to the staircase and crept out onto the landing. Listening, looking up the stairs and down, she waited a couple of minutes until a sudden shiver drove her back inside. With her door locked again and bolted, Zoe went back into the kitchen to make some coffee.

The hot drink restored her nerve, yet anxiety lurked, indefinably, at the edge of her mind. Eventually, she came to the conclusion that she must have been dreaming; something disturbing but elusive, disappearing from consciousness at the moment of waking. The trouble was that she was now too alert to sleep. She picked up a novel, but it was too bland to hold her attention; in the end it seemed a better idea to utilize the time by working. If nothing else, work could always absorb her concentration.

With no more than a quick wash, she dragged a brush through her hair, fastened it back, and pulled on an old pair of jeans and a paint-stained khaki shirt. She switched on the angle-poise lamps above her work-table and studied the piece of work in progress. From a large sheet of fine paper colours glowed, rich dark reds and blues, muted greys and greens in a stylized pattern of leaves and branches against the carved stone of an ancient monument. Tendrils of ivy curled round the page and into the picture, while the climbing stem of a velvety, blood-red rose wound sinuously over the stone, its petals littering the grass. In the distance, between the leaves, was a glimpse of open meadow bisected by a path.

The illustration had been inspired, in part, by that visit to the old cemetery in York. It was one reason why she had chosen that particular verse as one of the six she was commissioned to paint. The other was that the lines reminded her so strongly of Liam and those sleepy villages in Picardy that he had described so evocatively in his letters: roses running wild over ruined walls, and a long white ribbon of Roman road...

> I sometimes think that never blows so red
> The Rose as where some buried Caesar bled.

Did Liam know those lines from Edward Fitzgerald? Remembering that Victorian edition in the trunk of books at Stephen's flat, Zoe thought he must have done. And therein lay another coincidence, that out of this new, illustrated series of major Victorian poets, Zoe should have been commissioned to work on the *Rubaiyat*.

When first approached by the publishers, she had remembered that slender volume and been tempted to suggest that they produce, instead, a facsimile edition. Economics sealed her tongue, however; that and a burning desire to work on such a sumptuous project. But although she had seen that old book only once, Zoe had coveted it, impressing the illustrations on her mind.

They were hard to forget, so she used the memory as inspiration, deliberately choosing different verses to illustrate. And anyway, it was difficult to be truly original; the brief was that it should look Victorian, which meant following the symbolism so beloved of the age.

Eminently quotable though it was, the *Rubaiyat* must have seemed anarchic to those brought up on duty and the principle of suffering being good for the soul. Zoe could find no merit in that idea, nor imagine anyone relishing agony against the promise of a place in heaven. Although by that yardstick, she felt the last three or four months should have earned some worthy spiritual reward.

Even so, acceptance was not her strong point, and the worst part of those months had not been the loneliness, which she had thought she was used to, but the suspense of not knowing about Stephen. Not knowing from one minute to the next if he was safe; and not knowing what he felt about her.

'If I thought you loved me...' she often murmured aloud to his photograph, but there was no reply, not even from his letters, which had become as barren as the desert he described. Only the research kept her going, and the thought of Liam. Enthralled by his diary and letters, and even by the bureaucratic comments that comprised his army record, she sometimes felt his presence behind her, as though he were drawn by what she was reading. But she was no longer alarmed by that. Sometimes she even spoke to him, as though to a friend determined to play hide-and-seek; but he kept silence and never showed himself. She wondered whether her obsessions were getting out of hand.

With this most recent commission it seemed that the tangled emotions of love and doubt and longing were at last finding a means of outlet. With feverish inspiration she had rapidly outlined ideas and sketches for a dozen illustrations. If death was present, there was life too, in vines and luscious grapes, in the brilliant reflection of sun from carved Moorish arches, and in the shadowed figures seated beneath exotic, floral bowers.

The hard work came in translating those rough colour sketches to the formal, intricate patterns demanded by the style of the period, which in itself was allied to medieval forms. Zoe was attempting to inject these forms with a suggestion of Byzantine opulence. She thought of Istanbul and wished she could have visited with Stephen; instead she had to make do with books from the London Library.

While freshness lasted and her hands were steady, Zoe applied colour in small sections to the first of her chosen pieces. It was detailed, painstaking work that required absolute concentration. The most she could do was a couple of hours; after that, fatigue set in and the hand started to wander. Usually she took a break then, continuing for a while with trial pieces, working out patterns to be used later, or experimenting with colours. This morning, however, after two hours Zoe had had enough.

Tired, shaky from tension and too little sleep, she made some coffee and tried to relax. For a while she considered going back to bed, but the sun was up and it promised to be a beautiful day.

Suddenly, Wandsworth sprang to mind. For some time Zoe had been trying to arrange a suitable day to go there with Polly, but her friend had been inundated with work and was now on holiday. Although it had been vaguely agreed that they would go when she got back, today was as good a day as any, and there was no reason why she should not go alone.

The decision cheered her considerably. A hot shower banished the gloom and a hearty breakfast put strength into her sense of purpose. With her hair freshly washed and wearing her favourite summer dress, she set off to join the morning rush-hour crowds.

After making enquiries about the former hospital at Wandsworth, Zoe had been eager to see the place where Liam had spent almost four months of the war. Thinking about the damage done during the London Blitz, it seemed incredible that the place had survived. Not just undamaged, but recently renovated after years of dereliction.

Desirable flats and craft studios had been created from the old orphanage and school, together with a bistro restaurant. For weeks she had been promising herself lunch there, finding it astonishing that after decades in which the place must have been forbidden territory, the presence of a restaurant now gave any member of the public legitimate entry. If that was coincidence again, then it was fortunate indeed; and if it should be more than mere coincidence, she thought, then somebody's sense of timing was impeccable.

Just beyond the station she left the bus to walk down Windmill Road. Here, everything opened out, with pretty Victorian houses facing the tree-lined Common, and the black tower of an ancient windmill over to the left. Children were playing on the grass, women pushing prams and walking dogs; an old gentleman out enjoying the sun raised his panama hat as she passed by, and Zoe was aware of a sense of timelessness, as though in outward terms at least, nothing here had changed very much. That, she acknowledged, was an odd feeling in London, where things seemed to be changing all the time.

Her first sight of the building was partially obscured by trees; needing a clearer view, she walked across the grass to a point where she could see it properly, a huge place standing in solitary grandeur, like a castle, overlooking the Common. Honey-coloured stone and brick, raised in a mid-Victorian gothic so restrained it might have been genuinely medieval, with turrets and towers, pointed arches, ornate windows, all perfectly balanced and restored.

Photographs seen at the library portrayed a huge black building, stark and grim. Seeing it now, looking as it must have looked when first built, Zoe sent up a silent message of thanks for whichever council or entrepreneur had paid for the restoration. May you thrive and prosper, she thought, making her way back to the road.

The sight of two hideous 1960s accommodation blocks, just inside the gate, halted her for a moment. Glaring at them as though they had absolutely no right to be there, she wished upon them concrete fatigue and a rapid, crumbling death.

But one step beyond, all such considerations fled. A tingling thrill from scalp to fingertips, possessed her, banishing thought, defying logic, filling her with unexpected and unlooked-for joy. It took her so completely by surprise that she wanted to laugh, to say, hang on a minute, let me get my bearings, but her unseen companion was laughing, impatient, bearing her up as he swept her along.

It was like arriving at a party and being swept immediately into the dance by an exuberant admirer; and she knew him this time, she was no longer afraid.

And he was aware of that, drawing her with him as though he simply could not wait to show her this place. For a moment he allowed her to pause before the main entrance, but even while her eyes took in a wealth of architectural detail, that external sense of delight remained.

In a niche above the doorway was a carving of St George and the dragon, no doubt as black as the building when Liam was here. 'Especially with the railway so close,' she murmured, 'and all the soot and smoke. It must have been forbidding then, especially in the last quarter of the year...'

But it was impossible to feel that now. She thought of all the orphans who had passed through those portals; she pictured the sick and wounded who had been Liam's companions here, but there was no sense of sadness. She felt light and happy, full of astonishment and wonder as she toured the precincts, remarking softly on the chapel which stood at the far side, knowing from the diary that Liam had sometimes worshipped there. For a little while she stood in a sheltered alcove, every instinct telling her that there had once been a seat here, where Liam had regularly spent part of the afternoon.

All the while he was touching her face and hands with that gentle, tingling caress, invading her heart and mind with joy; and then he led her on, through a rear courtyard and a low doorway. Zoe saw directions to a craft studio, but she ignored them, following her guide down a stone-flagged passage and into a half-glazed walkway bordering a quadrangle. A vaulted ceiling and cast-iron pillars gave it the look of a cloister; at the corner, hesitating for the first time, she had the feeling he was about to leave her.

She wanted to say, *don't go*, but even as the words formed, she saw him quite distinctly, in uniform, his hat tipped at a rakish angle, striding towards her with a smile of love and triumph, as though he was saying: *Look, just see what I can do when I really try...*

She gasped in astonishment. He looked so real, so physically solid, so full of warm vitality that her heart leapt with the urge to run to him, to be swept up in his embrace. Rooted to the spot, all she could do was gaze at that happy, purposeful approach.

He was almost within reach when he disappeared. Staring at the empty corridor, for a second Zoe was stunned; then her spine was tingling, the fine hairs on her arms and at the nape of her neck stirring as at a physical caress. She wanted, desperately, to reach out and hold him; half-turned, arms raised, before realizing its futility. He was with her and he was touching her, but he was no longer flesh and blood; she could not clasp him to her breast the way she longed to do, and he could show love only by bringing with him this sense of joy.

Suddenly, her eyes were wet. It was too much. So brief, so elusive, as fleeting as a dream and just as insubstantial.

Breathing deeply, she leaned against an open window, looking out on the courtyard and trying to contain her emotion.

Why me? What was this about? Had she lived before as Georgina Duncannon? But a firm, no, came into her mind at that, and Zoe was left with the impression that she was loved for herself. She tried framing other questions, but no answers came. She felt the waning of Liam's presence then, as though the power he had summoned to be with her was now beyond his control to retain. She sensed regret, and a final, lingering touch on her cheek; and then he was gone, taking with him every anxiety, every petty frustration. A feeling of well-being remained, of calm and peace and absolute contentment. He was alive. What else mattered?

A fine lunch was set before her in the bistro, but even after a second stroll in the grounds – this time alone – Zoe's appetite was lacking.

As the other diners left, she spent some time chatting to the owner, whose passion for the old building led him to air his knowledge of its history. While he cleared away, he suggested she might like to wander round the mezzanine restaurant, where he displayed his collection of prints and photographs of the hospital era. Zoe found it strange, viewing those pictures of coy nurses and grinning soldiers, knowing that Liam had been here then, and that she had just seen him walking towards her in the corridor.

Half-tempted to ask whether the place was haunted, she desisted, knowing that it was unimportant to her. Liam was not a ghost imprisoned by place or a moment in time; he had simply chosen that moment to show himself, to share with her the joy he felt at her visit. At least, that was how it had seemed. Instinct said that he had been happy there, away from the war, and with thoughts of Georgina to counter his bleakest days.

And if Georgina had given him solace when it was most needed, then Liam in his turn had brought ease and comfort to Zoe at a time when misery and chill depression had threatened to swamp her completely. She was immensely grateful for that.

It seemed to her that even if Stephen had ceased to care, Liam had not. Perhaps he had always been there, on the edge of her awareness. She began to think that he had wanted her to find him again, and that the interest in the Elliott family had been in some way instigated by Liam, not Tisha, as first appeared.

But why? There seemed no rhyme or reason to it. It was extraordinary, and she knew her experience of him that morning was something she would never forget. That sense of peace, afterwards, was still with her. It was as though he were trying to tell her that everything would be all right...

The telephone was ringing as she struggled to unlock her door, but just as she dashed across the room to answer it, it stopped. Trying to think who her caller might have been, she looked at her watch. Almost five-thirty. She stood for a moment wondering, then shrugged and went to make herself some coffee, returning to the sitting room for the early evening news.

The ITN headlines were being announced as she sat down. '... from Northern Ireland, and in the Gulf, a Liberian tanker hits a mine, killing one British officer and injuring another. More about that later, and now to...'

Oh, God. With a sickly feeling of apprehension, Zoe sat down, her heart lurching with every change of topic, willing the newsreader to hurry up, ignore the rest of the world's tragedies and just get to the Gulf. The suspense was agonizing.

'Oh, bloody get on with it!' she muttered ferociously as the Prime Minister was pontificating on a new atmosphere of co-operation between London and Dublin. At any other time she might have been interested, but right now...

'And now, to the Gulf of Oman, where Jeremy Brown reports on the latest casualty in the Gulf War...'

Squinting against the glare, a sunburned young man faced the camera, while behind him stretched a dazzling sea, dotted with ships. 'Behind me you see the Fujairah deep-water anchorage, favourite stopping-place for tankers on their way into and out of the Gulf. Here, just before dawn today, a Liberian-registered oil tanker, manned by British officers, struck a mine during the anchoring procedure...'

The young man's face on screen was replaced by an anonymous aerial photograph of a large ship, while his professionally flat, unemotional voice went on: 'The tanker – the *Damaris* – was hit in the stern, causing an explosion in the engine-room where a British engineering officer was killed, and another injured. The ship's Master was also slightly hurt by the blast, but he was able to speak to us over the ship's radio...'

Icy with shock, Zoe heard Stephen's voice, terse and distorted by the VHF, giving a brief account of events, including the fact that the fire had been rapidly brought under control, and the ship was now under tow to Dubai. Only towards the close of the report did the reporter interject with a question.

'But I understand that you too were hurt by the blast, Captain?'

'Very slightly. A dislocated shoulder which has been attended to.'

'Are you anxious about returning through the Straits of Hormuz?'

'Not at all. The damage has been done, another tanker is incapacitated and that's what it's all about. The fact that one of my officers is dead and another injured, is purely incidental to the people who direct and carry out these attacks on international shipping.'

He sounded so bitter.

The recording ended, the picture faded, and with the usual cryptic question about what this new turn of events might mean, ITN's man in Fujairah signed off and returned the picture to the studio.

Zoe stared blankly at the screen, taking in nothing of the following summary of who was doing what in the Gulf, and to whom. Eventually, the jolly jingle of the local news magazine penetrated her consciousness and she rose to switch the television off. Her body felt like lead, her brain paralyzed. She stood, poised, by the telephone, knowing she had to speak to someone, had to find out what was going on...

Who?

She thought of Irene, then recoiled from the idea. What if Mac was the one who was killed? She had to find out before she spoke to her.

'Joan...' Reaching for her address book, she dropped it, had great difficulty retrieving it, fumbling as she searched for the right page. Dialling the York number, first her hands, and then her body, started to tremble. She sat down, but by the time Joan answered on the third or fourth ring, Zoe was almost incapable of speech.

'Oh, Zoe – I've been trying to get you *all day*, since just after nine this morning. You've been out, obviously – did you see the news?'

'Yes – just now.'

'Yes, on ITV – wasn't it dreadful? It was on at lunchtime, too. Now listen, Zoe, you are not to worry. He's all right. Somebody from the London office telephoned Pamela this morning. It's a terrible thing that's happened, I know, but Stephen is all right, and that's the main thing.'

'But he was *hurt* – and Mac, what about Mac?'

'He's all right,' Joan assured her firmly, adding on a softer note, 'it was the Third Engineer, poor man. I don't know if he had any family, but he wasn't married, which I suppose is a blessing...'

'Oh, God... And poor Stephen, having to cope with all that...'

'He's very capable, love – very capable. And he won't die of a dislocated shoulder. I telephoned the ship-manager myself this morning, just to make sure Pamela had everything straight – she was dashing off to work when they got in touch with her, and she's a born worrier, you know, panics at the slightest thing, just like his wife. Sorry, just like Ruth...'

Zoe closed her eyes as the words washed over her. Finally, Joan caught herself and returned to the matter in hand.

'Anyway, it seems they're going to do their best to get everybody home from... oh, Lord, where is it now? Abu Dhabi? No, *Dubai*, that's it. As soon as they get to Dubai, the company will get things sorted out and fly him home. Shouldn't be more than a few days, a week at the most – he was most insistent about that. And Stephen is *fine*, Zoe. If he wasn't, he wouldn't still be aboard, now would he?'

Although Joan sounded very convincing, Zoe was not at all sure about that. A man with Stephen's determination would probably need to be taken off in a stretcher...

With a repeat of all those assurances, Joan advised her to make a good strong cup of tea with plenty of sugar in it, and to call in a friend to stay with her.

Zoe found it hard to think of anyone she wanted to be with. Polly would have been ideal, but Polly was at the moment sunning herself in Marbella with a man friend.

'Well, why don't you call your mother?'

There were dozens of reasons why Zoe preferred not to call either of her parents, not least of which being the time it would take them to get here. Finally, however, she said that she would.

Joan repeated her instructions about that cup of tea, and said she would call Zoe back in an hour. But before she could say goodbye, Zoe interrupted.

'Joan – I saw Liam today.'

There was a short silence. 'Sorry dear – what did you say?'

'I went down to Wandsworth, to the old hospital – remember I told you about it? That's why I was out all day. Anyway, Liam was there. I saw him, clear as day, coming down a corridor towards me... Strange, isn't it? And now this...'

She was not at all sure Joan believed her. She thought she did, but it was hard to tell over the phone. Anyway, what did it matter? The point was that she had seen him and had felt his presence beside her for some considerable time; she would defy anyone to tell her it was an illusion.

What she could not understand was why. None of it made sense, particularly today of all days, when this terrible thing had happened to Stephen. It was beyond her.

Trying to follow Joan's advice, Zoe opted for coffee instead of tea, and two chocolate wafer bars in place of sugar. Chilled to the bone, she changed her dress for trousers and a warm sweater, and gradually the trembling abated. Her thoughts remained a jumble, anxiety for Stephen vying with confusion over Liam, and a pressing need to find out more about the situation aboard the *Damaris*.

Longing to speak to Stephen, or to someone who had spoken to him, she cursed the impulse that had led her to Wandsworth today. If only she had been at home, it would have been possible to telephone the shipping company, speak to the manager Joan had mentioned.

She picked up her address book. Irene, Mac's wife, might know more...

But even as she reached for the telephone, it rang.

The clicks and sighs of a distant connection met her ears; then a man's voice, foreign, asking her to stand by for a call from a ship.

For a moment she did not fully understand what was said. Hardly daring to breathe, she gripped the receiver like a lifeline, and then suddenly Stephen's voice, faint but unmistakable, was speaking her name.

Incredulous, thankful, overjoyed to the verge of tears, she could do no more than utter his name in response, while in her heart she thanked God for this minor miracle.

'Zoe, darling, are you all right? I'm so sorry I wasn't able to call you earlier – it really has been chaotic here, so much to organize, you wouldn't believe it...'

'Oh, Stephen, I'm fine, it's just so good to hear your voice – but how are *you*?'

'A bit tired, but otherwise all right. We seem to have got most of the problems ironed out, and there's not much more I can do now until we get to Dubai. I should be able to get my head down for a few hours. Anyway, what about you? It must have been a bit of a shock – did Joan or Irene manage to get in touch?'

'No, I was out all day. I didn't get back until just before the news came on – and that was a shock, believe me.' Zoe paused and swallowed hard. 'Anyway, I phoned Joan, and she said she'd been trying to get hold of me since first thing this morning – and I was just about to phone Irene when you called.'

'Oh, love, I'm sorry about that – sorry you had to hear it on the bloody news – that wasn't the idea at all. I'm just glad I managed to get through to you now – we've had one or two problems during the day with calls. Anyway, not to worry. The thing is, we're all OK, and we should be in Dubai sometime tomorrow. I expect it'll be a dry-dock job, and it's bound to be lengthy – the engine-room's virtually destroyed.

'Mac's really sick,' he added with a short laugh, 'we always used to joke about it being so clean down there. His little ice-cream parlour, we used to call it... Well, we won't be saying that any more, I'm afraid...'

Zoe was faintly shocked. How could he joke at a time like this? And anyway, a man was killed... 'Stephen, what happened? I didn't really take in what you were saying in that interview.'

There was a silence before he answered her; and when he did, the strain in his voice was clear. 'We hit a mine, love. Backed into it while we were laying out the anchor. It blew a bloody great hole in the port quarter, and wiped out the control-room. Including one of the engineers.' He paused for a moment. 'The irony is, Jim joined us in Kuwait, after the original Third demanded off. He volunteered for the job. Sick, isn't it?'

Wincing, Zoe could think of no words of consolation. 'What about the other man – is he all right? And you – you haven't told me about yourself...'

'Well, the Second's in hospital now. He got a bash on the head, but I think he'll be all right, and we put Lecky ashore as well. I was daft enough to be hanging over the bridge-wing at the time, so I took a bit of a knock as well – dislocated my shoulder, but it's been put back.'

'Was that terribly painful?' she asked tentatively.

She heard him laugh. 'Yes, you might say that... but not to worry, I keep taking the tablets! Actually,' he confessed. 'I was bloody lucky not to do worse. I had a look afterwards, to see where I'd fallen, and how the hell I missed cracking my head open on the compass-repeater, I do not know. There's a metal ridge and locking nuts on either side, so I'm really thankful I didn't hit that on the way down. The damage might've been permanent...'

Zoe winced. 'But you're all right?'

'Fine, honestly. It's been a hellish situation, but I'm still here... hard to believe, but true...'

As his voice tailed away, she said brokenly: 'I've missed you, Stephen – missed you dreadfully... and I've been so *worried*...' Her voice choked on that, and she struggled against tears. Eventually, she said: 'Do you think they might send you home?'

The lengthy pause that followed made her wish that she had not given voice to those sentiments.

When it came, his reply was suddenly softer and deeper, as though for some reason he had stopped shouting into the telephone. She had to struggle to make out his words, something to the effect that he was not alone on the bridge, and that he would try to contact her again from Dubai, which would make conversation easier.

'I'll know more when I've had chance to talk to the Super – the trouble-shooter from the office. But it may be quite a while before we get home, Zoe – Masters and Chief Engineers usually stay with their ships in dry-dock. I'm sorry, love, but that's the way it is.'

His brusqueness hurt her, silencing further questions. The line was crackling, and anyway, she thought, that promise to get everybody home was probably no more than a placebo to keep the relatives quiet. Acute disappointment silenced her.

'I'll phone you from Dubai – give me a couple of days, all right?'

'Yes – yes, of course. I'll be waiting...'

'Must go, love – take care.'

'Yes – you too... Stephen?'

But he was gone. The empty line hummed, stressing the distance between them; very slowly she replaced the receiver, while tears streamed down her cheeks. She was unsure whether it was anxiety, disappointment, relief, or just the release of tension, but she let them run, mopping them with paper tissues as they dripped off her chin. One way or another, she decided, it really had been one hell of a day. Eventually the tears ceased of their own accord and she poured herself a brandy, which restored both heart and reason.

He was all right. He had telephoned. He had called her *darling,* which took Zoe back to the passionate days of their first acquaintance; but he mostly called her *love,* which she had long ago come to realize might mean all or nothing. The Yorkshire endearment was akin to the Cockney *ducks* and West Country *m'dear,* apparently applicable to anyone short of the totally obnoxious.

And to think that only a massive lump in her throat had stopped her from blurting out that she loved him, wanted him, couldn't bear to go on like this a moment longer...

She felt a fool, a weak-kneed, love-sick, adolescent *idiot.*

On the other hand, she thought with the second tot of brandy, while it had taken him a moment to respond to the emotion in her voice, there had been something approaching emotion in his... Perhaps when he called again from Dubai, on a more private line, perhaps then he would sound less impersonal.

She picked up the telephone and dialled Irene's number in Northumberland.

Thirty-three

For the next two days, Zoe did not stir from the flat. There was no call from Dubai, but on the morning of the third day, Jack Porteous telephoned with flight details.

'But I thought... I mean, Stephen said he would have to stay for the dry-dock,' she said foolishly, torn between disbelief and a desire to kiss the man on the other end of the line.

There was a short bark of laughter. 'Well, that's Steve for you. Talk about having to lever him free!' He laughed again. 'Don't worry, Zoe, a relieving Master is on his way out there at the moment. They'll hand over as soon as he arrives, and Steve will be on his way home in the morning, along with the others. He wanted me to let you know, as he thought you might like to meet him at Heathrow.'

'Oh, yes! Yes, of course I'll be there...'

'There's only one slight problem. With Steve and the Chief Engineer, Mr Petersen, living so far from London, we'd like them to come into the office immediately for a first-hand report on the accident. It saves them going home and then having to travel back later in the week – I hope you understand?'

'Of course – that sounds sensible to me.'

'Good. So there'll be someone from the office at Heathrow tomorrow – a Mr Goodall. He knows them and they know him, so there shouldn't be any problems about meeting up. He'll have transport arranged into the city... I hope a journey to the office and back won't disrupt your day too much?'

'Oh, no, not at all...'

'Good. Well, Zoe, I look forward to meeting you tomorrow – until then, try not to worry. Steve's fine.'

'Thank you – yes, I'm sure he is...'

Her sense of relief was so vast, Zoe hardly knew whether to

laugh or cry. With Polly home at last, she now had someone to celebrate with; in a dizzy whirl of delight she dashed up the stairs and almost fell through her friend's door. They hugged each other and did a little dance round the kitchen, then Polly grabbed a bottle of Spanish bubbly from the fridge and they toasted Stephen and each other, Jack Porteous, Polly's man friend and the glories of Marbella. Then they toasted Stephen again.

Half an hour later, silly with champagne and relief and sheer, unbridled joy, Zoe remembered her obligations and left to make a series of telephone calls. She shared her joy with her mother and Joan, and very briefly with her father's secretary – as usual, James Clifford was in a meeting and could not be disturbed – and then she contacted Irene, making arrangements to meet up at Heathrow the following day.

'It's going to be quite a party,' Irene said, 'I wonder if the company will treat us all to lunch?'

They were both nervous waiting by the barrier at Heathrow, trying to distract themselves by guessing possible identities amongst the crowd. The man from the office could have been one of several, and there were so many women about it was impossible to know who might be connected to the men from the *Damaris*.

The flight had landed some time ago, and Zoe's eyes were torn between the clock and the exit from the Customs area. To begin with a thin trail of passengers carrying hand-luggage came through, followed in ones and twos by those with trolleys and babies. Eventually a whole bunch emerged together.

She and Irene spotted Mac's red hair and beard in the same instant, and Irene was gripping Zoe with one hand, and waving madly with the other. Mac grinned and edged round the trolleys, dropping his suitcase and scooping up his wife in a bear-like hug. Behind them, Stephen was hidden for a moment, then another man, laughing, was telling Mac and Irene to clear a path there, other people wanted to get through. He pushed past them, to be grabbed by a glamorous blonde who brushed Zoe out of the way in order to get to him; that he was astonished to see her was obvious.

Zoe turned her head to see Stephen edging towards her, still blocked by the crush of passengers in that narrow space. His hair was long and surprisingly curly; like his deeply tanned skin, it seemed at variance, somehow, with the grey suit and tie. His face looked thinner, etched with lines of exasperation; then he glanced up and saw her, and for a moment his eyes held hers with such longing, Zoe's heart swelled with love.

Then he was free, and smiling. As she moved forward, shyness seemed to catch them both. A second's hesitation and then he opened his arms, embracing her as though he would never let go. Breathless, on tiptoe, she clung to him while he buried his face against her hair; and then he found her mouth and kissed her hard.

'It's so good to see you,' he said huskily, 'you've no idea...' And then he laughed to cover his emotion, hugged her and kissed her again.

A moment later, he said ruefully, 'I'm afraid there's a man we have to see – and some business to attend to...'

'Yes, I know.'

Glancing round, Stephen spotted the man from the office, already talking to Sparks and the 3rd Mate.

'Well, we'd better get it over with. I must introduce you to Johnny – and the others, too, they've been a great bunch of lads, I don't know what I'd have done without them.'

They were surprisingly shy, Zoe found. Only the Mate seemed at ease, and he kissed her cheek as though he had known her for years. But in a strange way, Zoe understood – she'd heard so much about him from Stephen's letters, it was like meeting an old acquaintance.

Johnny's girlfriend, she noted, was determined not to let him go, clinging to his arm even while he was talking to the man from the office. Keen not to do likewise, Zoe stood with Irene while the men talked and laughed, and finally organized themselves for the next moves in their separate journeys.

She had been under the impression that all the officers were needed for the de-briefing, but Irene told her that it would only be Mac and Stephen. Watching as they all shook hands and said their goodbyes, Zoe did not miss the respect and affection with which they parted. Only the Mate addressed Stephen by his Christian name, and that seemed to be a mark of personal friendship. The others gave him his title along with their thanks, and that depth of sincerity touched Zoe deeply. Almost bursting with love and pride, she could not have spoken had her life depended on it. How Stephen managed to voice his farewells, she had no idea.

Mr Goodall saved the day, moving in at just the right moment to whisk his group away to a waiting taxi. He sat with Stephen, while Mac squeezed between Zoe and Irene, tucking both their hands in his, and saying he had by far the best of the bargain.

It was a journey full of jokes and hilarity, the repartee between Mac and Stephen flying back and forth with unremitting mirth. Zoe felt she had never laughed so much, her sides aching by the time they arrived at the office on Leadenhall Street. She knew this part of the city well; her father's business premises were just around the corner on St Mary Axe.

Although she kept that to herself, Stephen remembered. As they stepped out of the taxi, he asked about him.

She blushed and nodded. 'We spoke the other evening – he said if you were staying a few days, he'd like to take us both out to lunch. But you don't have to,' she added quickly. 'I didn't say for sure that we would.'

'No,' Stephen said, 'I'd like to meet him. In fact I'm looking forward to it...'

That pleased her, buoying her up through what seemed an interminable wait while the men were being interviewed. A receptionist brought them coffee, and Zoe and Irene gazed uncomprehendingly at shipping journals while catching up on each other's news. Having had an early start, Irene was ravenous and longing for something to eat. Eventually, just after one o'clock, Mac and Stephen reappeared with Jack Porteous and another man to whom they were introduced. Only afterwards did they discover that he was one of the company directors.

They dined in a nearby restaurant, but the interview seemed to have quelled their good humour. Jack Porteous kept the conversation away from the Gulf, and behaved with gallantry towards the ladies; but the other two were showing signs of strain, Zoe thought, both of them drinking more than they ate during that hour at the table. At last politeness was satisfied and Jack said he had to get back to the office, while Irene confessed she was anxious not to miss the four o'clock train from King's Cross.

They collected their baggage, and on a promise to meet again soon, Stephen waved Mac and Irene away in one cab and handed Zoe into the next. Joining Zoe on the rear seat, he slipped an arm around her shoulders and pulled her close.

Closing his eyes, he released a long breath. 'I am *exhausted*.'

'Do you want to go straight to bed?' Zoe asked as soon as they arrived. 'To sleep, I mean.'

He grinned. 'No, I'll be fine. I just want to sit and talk to you.'

So they sat and talked and drank coffee and tried to pretend that there was not a wall of diffidence between them. Zoe told herself that four months was a long time, and so much had happened in the interim. To Stephen, particularly. That he did not immediately want to sweep her off to bed was a disappointment; and although she was not sure she could have coped, it did seem to her the best cure for an awkwardness which seemed to be growing rather than receding.

It was not that he was silent; indeed, he talked a great deal, about Kuwait and Karachi, the red tape at one end and the corruption at the other, but when she asked direct questions about those journeys through the Gulf, he side-stepped every one, returning to the idiosyncrasies encountered at either end.

Noticing – as she had since meeting him that morning – that he was using his left hand most of the time, she asked about his shoulder, but he was dismissive about that, saying it was badly bruised, but otherwise fine. Clearly, he did not want to talk about the explosion or the accident, or even the subsequent journey to Dubai. He asked what Zoe had been doing, about the research and her latest commission, but she was equally reluctant to explain those esoteric connections. It did not seem the right moment to be talking about Liam.

And then the flow of conversation suddenly dried up. She went to pour some wine, and when she returned, Stephen was slumped into a corner of the sofa, jacket off, staring blankly at the empty fireplace. He looked so exhausted that her heart went out to him, overriding awkwardness and the awful suspicion that they were strangers with nothing at all in common. Leaning across the sofa back, she kissed his cheek and stroked his hair.

'I think you're very tired,' she said as he loosened his tie and unbuttoned his shirt. 'I know it's only six o'clock, but why don't you go to bed for a couple of hours? I'll make a chicken casserole and put it in the oven, and it won't matter whether we eat it or not. But if you have some sleep, Stephen, you might feel better.'

For a moment she thought he was about to protest, but he gave in, pausing only to collect his shaving things from the suitcase in the lobby. A few minutes later, going through to the bedroom to turn down the sheets for him, Zoe heard the shower running; when he came out, wrapped in a towel, she saw the bruising around his shoulder. It was black and blue and alarmingly extensive. With an involuntary gasp she reached out to touch him, but he drew her into his arms, kissing her tenderly before she could speak. He smelled damp and sweet and his mouth tasted of toothpaste, and that combination was suddenly the most erotic thing she could imagine. When he kissed her again there was an urgency about it, and in that mounting passion it seemed that all the strangeness fell away. They were together, and everything was going to be all right.

'Come with me and lie down,' he whispered, 'I don't want to sleep alone.'

She ran her fingers over his shoulder, touched the bruised flesh lightly with her lips; as though he felt her unspoken question, he said: 'It looks worse than it is. Although,' he added with a grin, 'I don't think it would stand up to twenty press-ups just now. Still, never mind, perhaps I should just lie back and think of England... what do you say?'

She laughed. 'Well, if you will make these offers I can't refuse...' She kissed him, lingeringly, and smoothed the damp hair from his brow. 'But if you want to eat later, just let me pop that casserole into the oven – two ticks, I promise!'

It was almost ready for the oven, prepared while Stephen had been soaking away his exhaustion in the shower. She added mushrooms to the chicken breasts and covered them with a creamy sauce, slipped the dish into the oven and shut the door. There, that was that. The salad and new potatoes could wait.

But a tremor of nerves caught her as she crossed the sitting room, making her pause and wonder why she felt so much like the mythical bride on her wedding night. She had never felt like this before... But there again, she had never been in this situation before.

She opened the bedroom door. The westering sun flooded the room, and Stephen was lying back against the pillows, an arm across his eyes. He seemed to be asleep, yet that was strangely more of a relief than a disappointment. With a sigh she undressed quickly, her back to him. Only as she slipped between the sheets did she realize her mistake: he was not asleep, and had been watching her.

'You're so lovely,' he whispered, folding his warm limbs around her, and she melted to him willingly, giving herself up to hands and lips and gentleness. She wanted him so much, could hardly wait to be joined with him; she needed to banish this sense of separateness and relegate the last four months to the nature of a distressing dream.

But she sensed, very quickly, that something was wrong, and was suddenly threatened by panic. Irrational fears, prompted by more than one similar experience with Philip, left her incapable of thought or action. With a plummeting heart she tried to pretend that nothing was amiss, but the last few months rose mockingly before her, the bleak letters, the lack of any genuine endearment. All had been wonderful before, with the excitement of novelty and that instantaneous attraction; but that was then, and the attraction had waned, it was just that he did not know how to tell her...

For a moment or two she wanted to cry; with an effort she summoned rational thought and told herself that he was tired, that he had suffered an incredible amount of stress, and just because he could not make love to her right now, did not mean that he had stopped wanting her.

But with Philip in mind she was not entirely convinced, and the fact that Stephen drew away from her did nothing for her self-esteem. Had she possessed sufficient courage to look into his face, she might have seen that he was equally distressed, but Zoe was too concerned with hiding her own emotions, her face buried in the crook of his good shoulder, while she prayed he would not notice how deeply she was hurt.

For a long time, neither of them spoke. She lay with her face against his chest, while his hand rested slackly against her neck. At last, in a soft, flat voice, Stephen said that he was sorry, that he was very tired, and that she mustn't think that it was anything to do with her; and with a similar lack of joy she said that she understood, of course he was tired, and it was silly to imagine otherwise...

He held her gently and stroked her hair, and after a while the tension in him relaxed. When she dared to lift her head, Zoe saw that he was asleep.

Very gently, she eased herself away from him, and when she was sure that he would not stir, crept out of the bedroom with her clothes. It was a ridiculous situation. She had the strongest urge to walk out; and yet this was her flat, and Stephen Elliott was asleep in her bed. And if she wanted to get any rest tonight, she would have to creep in again beside him, and try to sleep.

When the casserole was cooked, she turned it off and made a sandwich. She poured some more wine and watched an old film on television. When that was over she read until her eyes would no longer focus, and only then crept back to bed. Stephen stirred slightly, murmuring something about fuel lines, but did not wake.

Zoe slept badly and rose early. Eager to avoid a repeat of the previous evening, she found her jeans and a cotton shirt and escaped to the bathroom. By the time Stephen was stirring she had already been working for an hour. Not wanting to discuss that commission, however, she quickly covered it and, in a breezy imitation of normality, offered to make him some breakfast.

Whatever else was amiss, she decided, there was nothing wrong with his appetite. He consumed eggs and sausages and bacon, several slices of toast and marmalade, and two cups of coffee; and said that it was the best meal he had eaten in months. Gratified, she allowed herself to unbend a little, but when he reached for her afterwards, she stiffened. With a faintly hurt expression, he let her go and lit a cigarette. As she clattered about, clearing the kitchen table, he managed to startle her by saying that he felt he should return to York.

Turning sharply, she caught his gaze, illumined by full sunlight, and in those astonishing blue eyes was something accusatory.

'You don't have to go... surely?'

'Oh, yes,' he said quietly, stubbing out his cigarette, 'I think I do.'

Chilled, for a moment she could think of nothing to say. Then, foolishly, she remarked: 'But I thought you were planning to stay for a few days?'

'There are things I should attend to,' he said, rising from the table, 'and people I ought to see. And I really do think I need some time to sort myself out...'

Instantly, she felt guilty, as though she had let him down; but although she said she did not want him to go, and almost begged him to stay, Stephen pointed out that he had three months' leave due. He was going to take all of it, he said, come hell or high water. There would be plenty of time to see each other later.

He was outwardly pleasant, but there was something so implacable about him, it froze every argument, every persuasion. Short of flinging herself at his feet, there seemed no way of denting his decision. Watching him zip up his suitcase, she felt weak and ineffectual, a fair match for that ex-wife of his. But if she had this sort of thing to contend with, Zoe thought, then I feel sorry for her.

In the end, all she could do was insist upon taking him to the station, overriding all his objections. She drove atrociously, swearing at every driver to cross her path, but apart from a few sharply indrawn breaths, he made no comment.

At King's Cross there was nowhere to park. He leaned across, kissed her briefly, and said he would be in touch. 'And if you need me, you know where I am.'

But I need you now, she almost wailed, watching him drag his luggage, left-handedly, from the Renault's back seat. Taxis were pipping their horns: she had to move the car. Helplessly, she glanced up at him, but he simply smiled and waved. It was a taut smile, and the salute was abrupt.

Blinking away tears, Zoe gritted her teeth and swung out into the traffic.

If Zoe was miserable, then so was Stephen. The difference was that he was more angry with himself than with her, and too far beyond rational thought to be able to react other than instinctively. And his instincts were to escape and lick his wounds in private. Which was what he should have done in the first place, he told himself, cursing the fantasy that had led him to think he could bury four months of hell in the peace of her arms.

The trouble was, he had wanted her so much – too much, he supposed – expecting everything to happen brilliantly, just like the first time. Initially, there had been a moment's promise, and then – nothing. And how to explain that while the spirit was willing, the flesh was flatly refusing to respond? He had been too appalled to explain anything; too bitterly aware of disappointment on both sides, and too demoralized to utter more than a word of apology. Vaguely, as he drifted unwillingly into oblivion, he had thought that things might be better in the morning; but she had deliberately avoided being there when he awoke, and that was what hurt most of all.

The journey north passed in a blur, the sight of golden fields ready for harvest making no more impression than a flat expanse of ocean. As a rule he took great delight in his first view of England after months at sea, but this time nothing could lift his spirits. Even his first sight of the city walls failed to stir more than a bleak glance, and it was with no pleasure at all that Stephen returned to his flat in Bedern.

He opened windows, turned on water and electricity, and made a cup of black coffee. There was no milk, no food laid in for his return. Joan, obviously, was not expecting him for several days. The thought of having to contact her, to answer questions about his speedy return from London, was too much. He unpacked, phoned the garage about his car, then went to the pub for several pints and a sandwich. In the afternoon he slept. His car was delivered just before six, and immediately afterwards he went to Sainsbury's to do some shopping. That evening he ate out.

At a loss the following day he took the car out for a drive through Helmsley and Farndale and over the North York Moors, returning in a wide arc via the market towns of Thirsk and Ripon. There was pleasure in pushing the Jaguar round snaking bends, feeling the surge of power with which it conquered every hill. With Harrogate in sight and feeling slightly better, Stephen thought he would drop in to see his sister and brother-in-law.

Pamela was just back from school and alone, but within half an hour he knew that the visit had been a mistake, that he should have waited until his mental faculties were better prepared for Pamela's particular style of interrogation. She was pleased to see him so soon, but piqued by the idea that he had stopped off in London to see his girlfriend, rather than coming straight home to his family. Especially after what had happened.

'I stayed there one night,' he said, 'and that was largely because I had to go into the office. I got back to York yesterday lunchtime.'

'Joan never said.'

'I haven't spoken to Joan yet.'

'Why not?'

He answered vaguely, while Pamela's eyes seemed to rake his face for the truth. She changed tack then, wanting to know about this girlfriend of his, the one he had said so little about.

'Oh, for God's sake, she's more of a cousin than girlfriend – didn't Joan tell you? She's involved with family history – I was helping her for a while, that's all.'

'Yes, I can imagine,' she remarked sardonically, pouring boiling water onto instant coffee. 'Poor Ruth was so upset, you know. When that piece came on the news about your ship, she had to come over here straight away. She was in tears – it brought it all back to her...'

'Brought what back?'

'Oh, you know – that awful trip she did with you, the storm and everything.'

'Don't be ridiculous – that must be all of ten years ago.'

'So? People don't forget things like that.' Her voice dropped, and she glanced up at him over her coffee-cup. 'Ruth still cares about you.'

For a moment he held his sister's gaze. 'I'm impressed. If I recall, she had a lovely way of showing it.'

Pamela glanced away, chewed her lip for a moment. 'I don't think it's working out with Dave...'

'Tough.'

'God, you're so bloody hard, Stephen – doesn't anything touch you? She was your wife, for heaven's sake – doesn't that mean anything?'

'*Was* my wife, Pam. Isn't any more. Hasn't been for six years. And even when she was my wife, it didn't seem to mean a lot. She met somebody else, somebody she preferred to me – and if it ain't working out, sis, well pardon me for saying so, but that's *her* problem. Not yours, and certainly not mine.'

He drained his coffee and stood up. 'I'm going to tell you something now, something I should have said a hell of a long time ago. I don't know why I didn't, except for the fact that you're my sister, and I didn't want to cause a breach between us.

'But I'm sick to death of hearing about Ruth – I'm not interested any more. She was neurotic, and she made a big bloody mess of my life – and it doesn't sound as though she's changed very much. It's time she grew up – and it's time you stopped sympathizing with her. Next time she comes here, crying her eyes out, kick her backside for her and tell her to sort her own bloody problems.'

Had he slapped her, his sister could not have looked more stunned.

Stephen turned by the door. 'You know, I used to think it was my fault – that I made her unhappy. I've laboured under that delusion for years – and you, Pam, managed to keep the guilt alive. Well, you've just wiped it out. I'm glad it's not working out with *Dave* – that makes me feel one hell of a lot better. Maybe it wasn't all my fault after all.'

He drove too fast back to York, and when he slammed the door of the flat behind him, Stephen found he was sweating. He lit a cigarette and poured a drink and then he realized that he had better call Joan before his sister managed to upset her too.

She was pleasantly surprised to hear from him, and if something in his voice alerted her to trouble, she made no comment. She did, however, invite him round for something to eat.

'What, now?'

'Yes, why not? I think there's enough for two, and I've baked today...'

It was a much more comfortable reunion. With Joan Elliott,

Stephen could be himself, and he managed to relieve some of his frustrations by telling her about Pam and the fact that he had finally said what he thought on the subject of his ex-wife.

'Well, that's Pamela for you – she could never leave a thing alone, even when she was little. She would never be told, somehow, at least not until you'd got really cross with her.' Joan sighed over the vagaries of human nature. 'Still, there's one blessing, love – it's made you realize about Ruth. I never much cared for her, myself – too much the clinging vine, particularly for you.'

He was surprised at that. 'You never said.'

She laughed. 'You weren't after my opinion in those days!'

'And I wouldn't have believed you,' he admitted. 'But you know, Pam scared the life out of me when she said things weren't going too well for Ruth, and that she still cared for me – God! The last thing I want is to get involved again with her.'

Joan gave him a sidelong look. 'I shouldn't worry about that. It'll have been the high drama of what happened – especially with it being all over the news – and then Pam making mountains out of molehills as usual. Anyway,' she said briskly, 'you've got bigger fish to fry, unless I'm very much mistaken.'

'Have I?' He was puzzled. 'What do you mean?'

'Zoe.'

Avoiding his aunt's penetrating gaze, Stephen made no comment.

'I'm not going to ask for details, love, but if there's something wrong between you and her, I suggest you try and get things sorted out. She thinks a lot about you, and she's a good girl – too good to lose for the sake of a petty argument.'

'We didn't have an argument.'

'Well, then – it might have been better if you had.'

That raised a dry smile. Before he left, she said something else that made him think on the way home. It was to the effect that bottling things up never did anyone much good; if he could face up to what happened in the Gulf, and talk about it, then he would recover more quickly from its effects.

'Is it that obvious?'

She nodded. 'You're not yourself, just now.'

'Mmm. Well, you might be right, at that...'

When he got home, Stephen poured himself a large whisky and spent a long time just looking at the telephone. Part of him was desperate for the sound of Zoe's voice, but the rest of him was very reluctant to be exposed to more pain. And he was tired. Perhaps he would call her tomorrow.

He switched on the television for the late news, but there was something on about the Gulf, so he switched it off again and went to bed. Unlike the previous evening, he fell asleep straight away, but about two he woke again, shaking and sweating, having had a horrifying dream about the *Damaris*. There was an explosion, and there was fire, spreading rapidly throughout the accommodation. The anchor was unsecured, the ship drifting closer and closer to another tanker full of petroleum spirit...

It was so real, so vivid, every time he closed his eyes the images came back. In the end he forced himself out of bed and went to make a pot of tea. Two cups and several cigarettes later, he had managed to come to terms with his fear and to clear his mind of it. How odd, he thought, that he had never been particularly afraid of drowning, yet the thought of being burned alive terrified him. He had once been on a fire-fighting course and never forgotten it...

The worst thing he had ever had to do was send the Mate and Lecky down into the engine-room, seeing all too clearly what they would have to face.

And poor old Jim...

Stephen had written to his next-of-kin, a brother in Wallasey with whom he stayed when on leave. It had been a terrible task, made only slightly easier by the fact that Mac had also offered to write. But however well-phrased those letters, nothing could alleviate the shocking manner of his death, its pointlessness, and the terrible irony that Jim had volunteered for the job. The company would pay a considerable sum in compensation – that much at least had been established during that visit to the office – but what was money in exchange for a life?

The more he thought about it, the more convinced Stephen became that he was lucky to be alive. They all were. If things had gone wrong – if that fire had taken hold in the accommodation, it would have swept through in no time...

Enough. Don't think about it, Stephen told himself: go back

to bed.

Passing the half-open door of the spare room, Stephen's eye caught sight of the old trunk full of books. Zoe's recent commission came to mind, the one she had been strangely reluctant to talk about. Out of curiosity he thought he would take a look at that old edition of the *Rubaiyat*.

She had enthused about it months ago, but at the time his mind had been concerned with other things. Now its beauty struck him more forcefully, and he could see why she was so taken with it. He had intended to give her the book as a sort of farewell present, a good intention forgotten in the unexpected haste of his departure for Teesport.

Well, he could still give it to her. She was, he decided, as entitled to own it as anyone else in the family. More so, because of her ability to appreciate its value as a work of art.

Glancing through, he found the illustrations more intriguing than he had realized. As he studied them, he began to read the verses alongside; and then other verses seemed to leap out at him.

> Ah, make the most of what we yet may spend,
> Before we too into the Dust descend;
> Dust into Dust, and under dust to lie,
> Sans wine, sans Song, sans Singer, and – sans End!

> There was a Door to which I found no Key:
> There was a Veil past which I could not see:
> Some little Talk awhile of Me and Thee
> There seemed – and then no more of Thee and Me.

> One Moment in Annihilation's Waste,
> One Moment of the Well of Life to taste --
> The Stars are setting and the Caravan
> Starts for the Dawn of Nothing – Oh, make haste!

The images were dazzling, the message unmistakable; that last verse particularly sent chills down his spine. He stared at it for some time before gently setting the book down. His eyes were drawn to the smaller trunk, empty now of its letters, with just the treasured items in the tray at the top...

He lifted out the little shoes, opening an old envelope containing locks of hair in tissue paper. There was a small leather box containing two gold rings, and another with a diamond and sapphire brooch. Stephen held it up, seeing lights winking through the dust, wondering what its story was, knowing he must give it to Joan. He put it back, bemused for a moment, knowing these things were not what he was looking for; and yet he could not have said what it was.

With the trunk empty, he turned to its base, carefully feeling along the corners, wondering whether it contained a false bottom. The soft leather lining was torn in a couple of places, bulging a little where it was loose. Running his fingers down the sides, he felt the ridge of something hard. Very gently, trying to raise it without tearing that fragile lining, he finally extracted a slim cigarette case. The silver was tarnished, and it had been closed so long the catch was stiff, but even before he opened it, Stephen knew that this was what he was looking for.

Running the edge of a thumbnail down the join, he managed to ease it open, and out fell a couple of photographs and a square of folded paper. Engraved within the case were Liam's initials and the date of his twenty-second birthday. Remembering an entry in the diary, Stephen guessed that this had been the '*Birthday present from G.*'

There was no mistaking her, Stephen thought as he retrieved the photographs: Georgina Duncannon, smooth fair hair swept back from classic features. She really was very lovely, he thought, feeling a strong pull of sympathy as he glanced from one to the other, recognizing the possessive pride in Liam's eyes.

It was a little while before he noticed the worn piece of paper, but as he opened it, Stephen was aware that his heart was beating faster. More than any of the others, this letter both touched and awed him. It was a direct communication from Georgina to Liam: probably the only one still in existence. And her neat italic script reminded him, sharply, of Zoe's.

'My Dearest,

'How I miss you! From here, Barton-on-
Sea seems a whole world away, despite your
wonderful, loving, precious letters. How
good you are, writing to me every day,
keeping up my flagging spirit, giving me
such an amusing picture of your fellow-
convalescents in that little seaside hotel! I do
so wish that I had time just now to send you
more than these few lines.

'I refuse to make excuses about the ward and
work – but my darling, you know how and
why it is, none better. Remember always
that I love you, that my spirit loves you even
when my hands and mind are occupied, and
that I think of you in my quiet times, and
especially during the lonely nights.

'Soon, my dearest, soon. We will be together,
come what may, and then these lonely weeks
will be forgotten.
'My love, my heart,
'G.'

The words became a blur. Overwhelmed for a moment, Stephen
bowed his head, heart and eyes aching at the sadness and the
waste.

The note shivered in his fingers, sending a tingling shock right
through him; the air was suddenly charged with urgency, and
he looked up, startled, half-expecting to see Liam standing there
before him, arms raised in supplication, the way he had seen him
in so many dreams.

For perhaps a minute he could do nothing; and then, as the
urgency faded, he slowly nodded in understanding and acceptance.
'All right,' he said softly, 'I'm not entirely stupid, I know what you're
trying to say. I'd just about worked it out for myself, anyway.'

He refolded that fragile paper, placing it with the photographs inside the cigarette case where they belonged. While he dressed and pushed a change of clothes into an overnight bag, he laid it on the bed, hardly taking his eyes from it. When he was ready to leave, he slipped it into the breast pocket of his shirt, picked up a warm sweater and went down to the garage.

Thirty-four

He stopped once on the motorway for petrol, and was approaching the outskirts of London as the sun came up. It had been a fine, dry night with little traffic, and he could not recall when he had enjoyed a drive so much. The Jaguar performed on the open road as it was meant to do, he saw two police cars before they saw him, slowed to an acceptable speed, then returned to a steady ninety-five as soon as they were gone. And everything, but everything, was crystal clear in his mind.

The only doubt at all was whether Zoe would still be there. As he drove through London, wending a tortuous route through already thickening traffic, he prayed that either from anger or misery she had not abandoned the flat in favour of her mother's cottage in Sussex, or worse, gone to friends elsewhere.

The anxiety grew stronger with every passing mile, and he cursed the indecision that had prevented him from calling her last night. Then he began to worry about where he might leave the car, but as he came down Queen's Gate from the Park, he saw one of the residents pulling away from the kerb, and pulled neatly in before the space could be taken by anyone else. No doubt he would be in trouble with somebody for leaving it there, but in that moment it was the least of his worries. Climbing out of the car, he stretched and flexed his long legs, took a long look at Zoe's window, and on a deep breath crossed the road. On the steps, just for a moment he was daunted; then he thought of Liam and pressed the bell.

It rang in Zoe's flat as a sort of crackling buzz, and that buzzing continued, on and off, for more than a minute before she became aware that the noise was real and not part of a dream. In a sleeveless nightshirt that skimmed her knees, she staggered to the intercom in the lobby, wondering why the postman always rang her bell when he needed to leave a parcel.

'Yes?'

'Zoe? It's me, Stephen.'

Stephen? What time was it? What was he doing here?

'Zoe? Look, I'm sorry I was such an idiot the other day... won't you let me in so we can talk?'

'Oh. Yes. Push the door.' She pressed the button, gave him a second or two to enter, then shook her head as though to clear it. Panic set in.

She flew to the bathroom, grabbed a toothbrush, scrubbing furiously at her teeth while she surveyed the mess in the mirror. Yesterday's mascara smudged beneath her eyes, her hair looking like an untrimmed hedge...

Her face was washed, hairbrush dragging at the last of the tangles as he knocked at her door. Startled grey eyes set in a somewhat shiny face stared back at her from the mirror. The well-scrubbed look with a vengeance, she thought, but it would have to do.

The cool, nonchalant image that she had cherished, on and off, for the last forty-eight hours, would have been satisfying had she been able to carry it off; but Zoe's heart was beating a wild tattoo, and besides, she was too thankful to pretend. As soon as she saw him, tall and tanned and slightly crumpled from the journey, all the heartbreak disappeared. She wanted to hate him, but the only thing in her heart was love.

His eyes, so brightly blue, were softened by a discernible amount of shame and a lot of love. 'Forgive me?' he murmured.

Zoe was too overcome to speak. She wanted to say she was sorry, too, but all she could do was nod and let him in. The door swung to of its own accord.

Between sighs and kisses and little sobs of laughter, she managed to say that she had tried to telephone him yesterday, several times; and between her eyes and mouth and throat he managed to tell her where he had been.

'But then I woke about two, and I couldn't sleep for thinking of you, and...' He found her mouth again. 'I knew I had to see you, couldn't tell you how much I love you over the telephone...

I tried twice before, and each time…'

For a second, Zoe was still. With a quizzical smile she looked up at him. 'What did you say?'

He was very serious. 'I love you, Zoe. Will you marry me?'

Bubbles of happiness seemed to explode; her smile broadened into a grin, and seemed to go on forever. Laughing, she said: 'Stephen Elliott, you are incredible. After all you've put me through, and you turn up, at seven in the morning, when I'm not even awake, and ask me to marry you. I ought to turn you down and throw you out!'

'Please don't.'

She shook her head. 'I love you.' For a long moment she looked at him, the desire to kiss him battling with an urge to return some of the pain she had suffered, particularly in the last two days. The kiss won, by a narrow margin. It was fierce and hard and very passionate.

'Enough to marry me?'

'Oh, more than enough,' she whispered, as the anger evaporated. 'It's been more than enough for a long, long time.'

She looked up, at his eyes and his mouth, and was caught for a second by an uncanny resemblance to Liam. Remembering his touch, she felt it again; and at her sudden shiver Stephen hesitated, as though he sensed something too. His eyes searched her face, then, very tenderly, he traced the outline of her mouth. 'I've loved you,' he said softly, 'almost from the moment I first saw you. I just wish that I could have believed it…'

Little shocks ran through her.

'It was meant, wasn't it? Our meeting – everything since…'

'Yes,' she whispered, wanting him, needing him, a little afraid of what else was happening. He touched his mouth to hers with a tenderness that quickly flared to passion. It seemed an array of shooting stars exploded across a midnight sky, and she clung as he lifted her up and carried her back to that rumpled bed.

In a daze she watched him undress, her own fingers fumbling until she was naked too, reaching out to hold him as he came towards her. She pressed her face against his body, kissing him, hearing him gasp at every touch. He was trembling and so was she, the shocks between them so exquisite they were almost unbearable.

With the lightest touch he pushed her back, and slowly, as though performing part of a ritual, entered her with such gentleness it seemed no more than an extension of a light caress.

One flesh, joined but barely moving, the centre of awareness not deep in the flesh but spreading from the mind, encompassing them both. Slowly, he began to move, with steadily mounting urgency driving sighs and moans of pleasure from her lips, while she felt her soul expanding, drifting somewhere on a sea of rapture, tied to bodily sensation, but only just. She heard her own voice, and his, through the pulsing of a heartbeat, a beat that rushed and swelled like the booming of the sea, taking her with it in huge waves that curled and broke against an unfamiliar shore. Her soul was the sea and the cry of a bird, and his was the unrelenting force that drove her on; the night and the stars were Liam's.

She was borne up, lifted, broken in a vast cascade of shimmering light; and from somewhere came a long drawn-out cry that could not have been hers, but it was, it was, and so far away...

The aftermath lingered like the wash of the tide when the storm is over, and they clung together like half-drowned castaways, speechless, blinded, deafened, aware of nothing but each other and the fact of being alive. Inert, locked as one, it seemed that time and place had ceased to be; everything was shimmering and echoing, the smallest movement such torture that even breathing brought its pain. It was like being bathed in a burning light, and the silence and the stillness were alive with tremendous power.

Slowly, very slowly, the intensity waned, and as it finally left them, tears seeped unbidden from Zoe's eyes, silent at first, and then in great, heaving sobs that were impossible to control. Stephen moved then, cradling her like a child, murmuring soft words of comfort against her hair.

'I know, I know... darling, I know.' He kissed her wet cheeks and her lips, tasting the saltiness of her tears, and he knew what it was that racked her, because he had felt it too.

Neither of them wanted to talk about it, particularly at first. Words seemed a desecration, but the awareness was in their eyes, in every touch. Stephen referred to it only once, and that was later, after he had made love to her again. 'That was beautiful,' he said softly, a smile lighting his eyes, 'but it didn't blow my mind. And I think that's how I prefer it.'

Exaltation was one thing, but in that coming together they had not been alone, he would swear to it; never, in the whole of his life, not even in the most abandoned of lovemaking, had he experienced anything like that. And that lovemaking had been far from abandoned. It was controlled, but not by him, and certainly not by Zoe. From that moment in the doorway, Liam had been with them. Everything seemed to have been orchestrated, like a symphony played many times before.

Stephen did not pretend to understand it. It was not something that worried him, exactly, but it stayed in his mind and he thought of it often; and so, he suspected, did Zoe.

Over the next few days, memories, facts, discoveries occupied them, moving constantly back and forth between Zoe's research in London to the Elliotts in York, and from there to Stephen's experiences in the Gulf.

Once that subject had been broached, he found it easier than he had imagined. Somehow, discussing his own experience in relation to Liam's during the First World War, helped to set much of it in perspective. He found Zoe's attitude practical as well as sympathetic, and the fact that she was interested in his job rather than resentful of it, not only eased the stress, but reinforced his confidence in her. Sensitive she might be; but she was stronger than he had previously given her credit for, and Stephen was happy to acknowledge his mistake. If, in the future, he had to leave her, he knew full well that she would not buckle at the first crisis. The Gulf, for her as much as himself, had been a baptism of fire; if she could withstand that, he reasoned, then she would probably weather most things.

She was honest enough not to spare him the worst of her anguish during those dreadful weeks, just as he was honest enough to admit that he had been wrong in keeping silent; but with love and trust between them, there was no longer any room for foolish pride.

'Either yours or mine,' he gently reminded her.

They were in Kensington Gardens when he mentioned, casually, the idea of Zoe travelling with him. It was a beautiful afternoon, the manicured expanse of London's parkland as far from the barren expanse of oceans and deserts as it was possible to be; but the contrast forced Stephen to think of what would, eventually, have to be faced again. Not the Gulf: he had played his part for the company, and had told them he was not going back there; but life at sea was something different. He hoped Zoe understood that.

Her eyes were shining as she glanced up at him. 'Do you mean it? Could I really come with you?'

Stephen laughed. 'All the time, if you wanted to.'

'But I thought – didn't you say, before, that you were thinking of giving it up?'

On a deep breath, he said: 'If you wanted me to, I would...'

With a sudden, fierce hug, she shook her head. 'I don't need that kind of sacrifice. It's you I want, and your work is part of you, just as what I do is part of me – and we'll make it succeed together.'

'I suppose your work's portable?'

'I'll make it so,' she said fervently.

It was not until they returned to Queen's Gate that afternoon that Stephen remembered the things he had brought from York. He gave her, first of all, that illustrated copy of the *Rubaiyat*, and watching her face as she opened it, full of wonder and delight, knew he could not have given her anything better. All at once she started to talk about her commission, to show him the work already done, explaining the symbolism and the ideas which had inspired every illustration. Stephen was enthralled; he knew almost nothing about art, and less about the history of design, but her enthusiasm was catching and the subject held them even while she was preparing dinner.

Settling down afterwards, with lamps lit against a falling dusk, Stephen refreshed their glasses and lit himself a cigarette; then he reached into his pocket and brought out the little silver case. It was strange to realize, as he handed it to Zoe, that Georgina's gift was no stranger to this flat.

'I haven't cleaned it, and it's difficult to open, but I'd rather you tried it for yourself...'

She was intrigued, and while she felt for a way to spring the catch, he told her where he had found it, and about the inner certainty that had led to the search. 'Somebody had obviously hidden it. Probably Louisa.'

As Zoe agreed, the cigarette case suddenly opened, its contents falling into her lap. She looked first at the photographs, and as she saw the one of Liam and Georgina together, her frown softened into a sad, compassionate smile. 'Together,' she whispered. 'I'm not at all surprised, are you?'

He shook his head, unable to speak, tenderly pushing back a lock of hair from her face. She stared at that photograph for a long time before opening the little square of cheap paper on which Georgina had penned those few lines to Liam all those years ago. For a long time she said nothing.

Seeing the tears in her eyes, Stephen drew her close. 'You know, I might have written those words,' he whispered, 'while I was away. I wish I had, because that's exactly how I felt.'

For a while they clung together, and Zoe wept a little. When she was calmer, she said: 'But we were right, weren't we? They were a lot more to each other than brother and sister. No wonder Louisa hid the evidence.'

'It's a wonder she didn't destroy it,' he murmured, trying to envisage the depth of shock.

'Perhaps she'd always known, deep-down. Maybe she felt guilty...'

'Maybe she did. We'll never know.'

They were lost for a while in contemplation: there had been neither time nor place for Liam and Georgina, and never a chance of happiness. Whatever it was they shared, that affair could never have been resolved, no matter how long Liam lived. As lovers, they were doomed from the beginning.

'By an accident of birth,' Zoe said softly. Suddenly, she thought of Tisha, and could have wept. 'And Tisha just didn't understand, did she? She had that independent streak, and it saved her – but not knowing, not understanding... She must have been so hurt by what happened. No wonder she was as she was...'

Stephen held her close. 'It all goes back to Robert and Louisa, doesn't it? If he hadn't been married, or if they'd never met...'

'Well,' she sighed, 'if they hadn't met, we wouldn't be here, would we?'

That gave Stephen a strange feeling, akin to his old suspicion that somehow his life was linked to that of Robert Duncannon, as much as to his son, Liam; that somewhere old accounts had been rendered and were now being settled through himself and Zoe.

It struck him then that Robert and Louisa had never married, and he wondered why, when both of them were free. Had Liam and Georgina's affair rebounded on them, made it impossible?

Zoe voiced his thoughts, and for a while they discussed the many different facets of that life-long relationship, and certain parallels began, rather chillingly, to emerge.

'You say he didn't die until 1923, six years after Edward's death. Well, even granting the fact that they were both in late middle-age by then, they could have married. Why didn't they?' Stephen tapped Georgina's letter. 'Imagine it – and if you think of where we stand today, it shouldn't be too difficult to put ourselves in their shoes.

'I'm unhappily married, but I can't get a divorce. We meet, fall in love, and at some stage or another, I persuade you to become my mistress. For a while, life's wonderful, but I'm away a lot with my job, and after a few years it all starts to fall apart at the seams. We eventually go our separate ways. You, as Louisa, marry the cousin who's always loved you, and to make life simpler, our three children are brought up as his. Then, years later, our eldest son and my grown-up daughter meet, and fall in love...'

Stephen paused to let that sink in, and as it did so, he saw the mounting aversion in Zoe's eyes.

'Yes,' he said. 'It's a horrifying thought. We'd blame ourselves, wouldn't we? We'd be saying we should never have met, never given in to that overwhelming passion, and certainly never had children. Even if they weren't hung up on sin, Zoe, the guilt must have been like a lead weight, no matter what else they felt for each other.'

As her gaze slid away from his, he touched her cheek. 'I don't wonder the rest of the family kept quiet about the Duncannons.'

He woke, early the next morning, thinking about Robert, and about the years in which this flat had been a base for him and a refuge for Georgina. In the dim light, Zoe's period furniture and elaborate cornices fostered the illusion that little had changed. When Stephen considered world upheavals and the bitter continuation of struggle in Ireland, it seemed to him that progress was no more than superficial gloss, a coat of paint on the rusty old tub of human nature, making its journey between the same old ports. Tolerance tried very hard to cure it, but religion and politics were as corrosive as ever, and while the crew battled on, the brokers sat on a sunny quay, totting up the profits.

Robert Duncannon must have seen plenty of that, Stephen reflected, particularly during the last ten years of his life, when he was approaching his sixtieth year and treading a fine line between government expediency and his own sense of what was just. Judging by his letters of that date, the Easter Rising and its bitter aftermath had broken Robert's faith in a peaceful settlement. With the advent of the Black and Tans he had resigned his post, given up this War Office flat and become something of a nomad, dividing his time between Dublin, Waterford and York. Stephen wondered briefly whether he had become involved in any anti-British activity then, but it seemed unlikely, except perhaps to turn a blind eye from time to time, or withhold information from those arrogant thugs, the Black and Tans. Robert's attitude, it seemed, had been one of contempt.

It seemed, too, that as a professional soldier he had resented being kept from the war in Europe. For a man who had been decorated twice for bravery, in the Sudan and South Africa, Stephen could understand the depth of Robert's frustration caused by his enforced involvement with the holding operation in Ireland. It was false diplomacy, a papering over of the cracks, until a burst of madness that Easter of 1916 tore everything apart.

Reading again, last night, Robert's description of the devastation, Stephen mentally substituted York for Dublin, and understood exactly how he must have felt. He could understand, too, why Georgina had never wanted to go back.

The war in Europe, conducted over a strip of land extending from the North Sea to the Swiss border, had destroyed a generation, taking with its Robert's eldest son, his two nephews and Tisha's husband, Edwin Fearnley. Ultimately, it had killed Robin too.

A generation, a way of life, was gone forever, and the face of Europe was irrevocably altered. Bitterness and grief, Stephen reckoned, must have been standard baggage in every family, from the steppes of Russia to the Isle of Ushant in the far west. For a man who had been prevented from doing what he was trained and qualified to do, there must also have been a large measure of self-recrimination.

In the summer of 1921 Robert Duncannon had gone abroad for two months, on a motoring tour of the battlefields, sending Louisa letters and postcards from all the places mentioned by his sons in their correspondence. Clearly, that journey had been something of a catharsis for him, a means of coming to terms with the unalterable truth of Liam's death.

And towards the end of the following year, he had followed Georgina, via Egypt, to Australia.

Thinking about her, Stephen's eyes were drawn to Zoe as she slept. He gazed at her for a long time, aware of an inexpressible tenderness, a love for her that went far deeper than the physical desire which had initially drawn them together. Looking back, it struck him that even then there had been something else, a mutual sympathy and understanding, a sense of recognition, somehow, that he could only think was inspired by shared blood and a common inheritance. It had acted like an emotional short-cut, obviating the need to discover things like background and social interests, and going straight to the heart of the matter.

The full extent of that other relationship between Liam and Georgina could only be guessed at. Nevertheless, he was convinced the emotions were shared to every last nuance; and just as he wanted more than anything that Zoe should be safe, and cared for, and happy, so he knew that Liam would have wanted the same for the woman he loved so completely.

Stephen had only heard about those final letters of hers, never seen them, for they had been pushed down amongst earlier bundles, as though Louisa wanted nothing to leap out and remind her of that illicit affair.

After breakfast, Zoe set aside the letters from Robert that had occupied their attention the evening before, handing to Stephen those written by Georgina. There was a note of sympathy, posted from Cairo almost a month after Liam's death, and in its terse, wrung-out phrases, it was almost possible to hear the heartbreak.

Knowing what both of them now knew, it required little imagination to transport themselves back to that date in October, 1917, and envisage a young woman's agony at the death of her lover. The worst nightmare realized, dread made fact, and the added anguish of being so far from home, without the comfort of being able to grieve with others who had loved him. Zoe thought it must have near-killed Georgina to write that note, to sympathize without being able to beg for sympathy.

Stephen felt her isolation.

Remembering the deaths of his parents, he knew how emotionally crippling distance could be, how hard it was to believe that they were gone, how lengthy the period of grief. He had not fully understood his own sense of loss until his wife's betrayal released it, and then the bereavement pain had been almost unendurable.

He understood the course of Georgina's pain, could follow it so easily in those widely-spaced letters to Louisa.

In earlier missives, written before Liam's death, Georgina had described the strangeness of Egypt while confessing a liking for it. After the bleak, unremitting years in London, Cairo was exciting and the bazaars compulsive, constantly tempting her to buy things for which she had no use; and there was a sybaritic splendour in the shady halls of those great, converted palaces in which she spent her days. As long as there was shade to cling to, Georgina wrote, she found she rather liked the heat; that off-duty, relaxing, it made her feel like a cat, content with absolutely nothing to do, which was a luxury she could not ever recall enjoying before.

Even if she was telling Louisa only the best part of her experience in Egypt, it was possible to read a lot of truth in those lines, to understand that for many years Georgina's life must have been a long, exhausting round of activity. Compared to London, and York and Dublin before that, Cairo was obviously a relief; and after the additional stress of her affair with Liam, and an agony of parting that Zoe and Stephen could only guess at, it seemed those first few months in Egypt were like balm to her soul.

But there was more. Her remarks on the loneliness of the desert, and the eeriness of the Pyramids at sunset, seemed, even after all these years, to be alive with thoughts of Liam. For her, his memory was there, even if he was not.

In one postscript, she mentioned that a friend of Liam's, Lewis Maddox from Dandenong, had very recently surprised her by introducing himself.

'...I thought it an odd coincidence, until he said that he had had a letter from his old friend Bill – as he calls Liam – asking him to look out for me here. It was kind of him to do so, and we spent a pleasant hour talking about Dandenong and our mutual friend...'

That was in August 1917, and after October's letter of condolence there was nothing more for several years. But in June 1922, she pressed Louisa to join her father in coming out to Australia for a holiday:

'... I would dearly love to see you again, Louisa, if only to talk as we used to do so long ago. Surely the time has come for us all to put the past behind us – the saddest things, anyway – and work towards a better future. That is what I have spent the last few years trying to do. Liam has not been forgotten, and here amongst his old friends in Dandenong, you would be touched and surprised, I think, by the reverence accorded to his memory. It's not a morbid thing, but a deep sense of respect for all those who made Australia's name in the world, particularly at Gallipoli.

'I have found it a deep and lasting comfort, and am so glad that I came here. There was nothing for me in either England or Ireland, and the impulse to come here, to see what it was that had so inspired Liam, was more deeply-felt than I can ever describe. It was as though I had to come, and I have not regretted it.

'Lewis sets great store by the fact that Liam virtually introduced us, and he has used that fact unashamedly in all his attempts to persuade me to marry him. He asked me first a long time ago – before he left Egypt, in fact. But I could not answer him then. I am sure you understand why.

'Fortunately, Lewis also understood that it had nothing to do with the injuries he sustained at Beersheba; and after all, what are they to me, after all these years of nursing? But a strong will and great determination has made his recovery far better than anyone expected, and I think we know each other well enough by now to be assured of a happy future together. There will be no children, of course, but that is a relief to me rather than a sadness, and anyway, there are children enough about the farm, a multitude of nephews and nieces, all delightful enough to satisfy us both.

'His elder brother served with the 5th Battalion in France, and returned some time after Lewis, reasonably sound in wind and limb, but less well-disposed to company. He and his family live out at Warragul, but the children stay often with their grandparents, so I am getting to know them well. Lewis's widowed sister lives here too, with her three children, so it is quite a little commune, or will be when we settle in to the new bungalow being built near the old homestead.

'Mary – do you remember Liam writing about her? – has married and is living now in Sydney. We became quite friendly when I was working with her in Melbourne, but she rarely spoke about Ned. Lewis still talks about him, and Liam of course. We talk about Liam a lot.

'I think you would like Lewis, he is very frank and open, and cares so passionately about growing things. Too much, probably, to be a very successful farmer, but he listens to his father these days, which he apparently did not, before! His family are good, honest people, and they have accepted me very well. I know my father is looking forward to meeting them, if only because they were so good to Liam before the war, and have been good to me, since.

'I wish you would come with him, Louisa. Just being here would be so good for you, and the journey out and back would be a wonderful experience.

'If it should be entirely out of the question, I do hope that the reason is not because you still blame me – or yourself – for what happened. I think we have all punished ourselves enough, and all the tears in the world won't bring him back, or undo the circumstances in which we found ourselves.

'Write to me, please, and tell me you understand. That is all the blessing I need before my marriage to Lewis.

'My love to you, as always – Georgina.'

It was a letter that could not have failed to strike some chord in a woman whose life had contained more than its fair share of tragedy. And it seemed the letter had provoked a sympathetic response, because Georgina had written again, thanking Louisa for her generosity and expressing regret only at her inability to accept the invitation to Dandenong.

Louisa had apparently used Robin's uncertain health as her excuse, but Zoe was of the opinion that embarrassment lay behind her refusal. Louisa was not, after all, married to Robert Duncannon, and it seemed she would not wish to advertise their unconventional relationship. Nor subject herself to questions about the connection between her son and Robert's daughter.

So, Robert had set off alone. It was clear from his letters to Louisa that he planned to be away for up to six months. The wedding was set for the beginning of January 1923, and his last missive was full of that homely little ceremony in Dandenong, descriptions of the family, and his admiration for his new son-in-law. The fact that Lewis had always been a horseman, and had served with the mounted Australian forces in Egypt and Palestine, had given the two men much to talk about. The impression of that last letter was of a man cheered considerably by his daughter's happiness, and full of hope for the future.

He died, three weeks later, of a sudden seizure, while out riding with Lewis.

THIRTY-FIVE

There was a letter from Lewis Maddox, written in a strong, upright hand, but nothing, apparently, from Georgina for several months. She had, it seemed, been devastated by her father's death.

With personal experience to draw on, Stephen could imagine only too well the effects of that second blow, releasing all the shock and grief she had probably been unable to express after Liam's death.

Zoe's understanding was more detached, but even so she could imagine Georgina's situation.

'Nursing, in the midst of war, surrounded by the dying – grieving would be impossible, wouldn't it? It was the era of the stiff upper lip,' she remarked sardonically, 'when they all pretended they were just fine, and carried on regardless.' On an exasperated sigh she shook her head, then said: 'But yes, I can see she would go to pieces when Robert died. She thought the world of him, didn't she? I think, too, that it would be like letting go of all the other deaths, all that stress and anguish she'd suffered – not to mention losing Liam.'

'Poor girl,' Stephen murmured, drawing Zoe close into the crook of his arm.

'Yes. Thank God she wasn't alone. He sounds to have been a pretty decent sort, that guy she married.'

'And a decent family, from all accounts.' Turning over the Australian correspondence, Stephen recalled something his aunt had said, months ago, about Louisa receiving letters from Australia. 'Do you remember? Joan said something about her keeping in touch with the people Liam had worked for, before the war. It never struck me before.'

'No, because we didn't know about Georgina!' Zoe interjected. 'But then she said – '

'That Sarah hadn't bothered after Louisa died, because she was never much of a letter-writer!'

Zoe laughed. 'Sarah wouldn't have known Georgina. I mean, if she met her once or twice, it wouldn't have been more than that, would it?'

'And I doubt whether Sarah would have known about the relationship between Georgina and Liam – Louisa wouldn't have advertised that, would she?'

'No.' After a moment's thought, Zoe said: 'Whatever Robin felt, I don't think Sarah wanted to know about the Duncannons. I can imagine Robert's death must have been, for her, anyway, the end of an embarrassment. No wonder she kept quiet about that half of the family!'

'And it wouldn't be the sort of complication that Louisa could explain to my father and Joan,' Stephen added. 'Not when they were young, anyway.'

They were both struck by the roundabout route they had pursued to reach that conclusion, and by the years which had elapsed between those final letters from Georgina, written mostly before 1939, and interrupted by the war.

It was hardly likely that she was still alive, but Zoe felt that Georgina Duncannon would still be remembered by someone in Australia.

'Strange, isn't it? She lived here for no more than a couple of years, and yet for me she left a lasting impression. She welcomed me when I first came here, I know she did.'

At her dreamy, slightly speculating expression, Stephen could not restrain a smile. 'You've got something on your mind. What is it?'

'Oh, nothing, really,' she said vaguely; but a moment later, watching him return those letters to their envelopes, she said: 'You know, I think I might try writing to them...'

'Who?'

'The Maddox family. There sounds to have been enough of them, and I bet somebody's still running that farm...'

He was unconvinced. 'Listen, the last time I was in Melbourne was twenty years ago, and it was growing fast. Whoever owned the Maddox farm probably sold out and made a fortune.'

'Oh, don't be so defeatist – Dandenong's miles from Melbourne. And anyway,' she continued, silencing him with a kiss, 'nothing ventured, nothing gained. Look what I got when I wrote to all fifty-two Elliotts in the York phone book...' She kissed him again, passionately.

'In that case,' Stephen murmured, minutes later, 'I think I should forbid you even to try. Lord knows what you might come up with next time.'

'A handsome hunk of an Australian?' she enquired wickedly.

'Guzzling Fosters and grunting *G'day,*' he retorted, laughing.

For a while the teasing continued, but a couple of days later, determined to prove a point to Stephen, Zoe put together a letter, enquiring about Georgina Maddox, nee Duncannon. Feeling positive, she posted it to that old address. Even the longest shots, in her opinion, were worth attempting. As she remarked to Stephen, there had been so many beneficial results already, perhaps the letter would produce one more.

With that he could not disagree.

They were invited by Zoe's father to a lunch which lasted most of the afternoon, and on another evening to dinner with Zoe's mother at her cottage in Sussex. Although the former meeting had initially caused him much apprehension, Stephen found James Clifford much as Zoe had described him. As affable as he was sharp-witted, his smiles and good humour helped to disguise, along with much conversational padding, the most pertinent questions. Although Stephen was familiar with interview techniques, he had to admire Zoe's father for his expertise, while being thankful that he had nothing to hide. Afterwards, he was able to smile because he knew he had passed the test: James Clifford had given them both his blessing before they left.

'Not that it would have mattered a jot,' Zoe assured him. 'I'd have married you, my darling, whether my father approved or not. But still,' she grinned, 'it's nice that he likes you.'

'I like him,' Stephen said frankly. 'And yes, it is a relief to know he thinks me capable of taking care of you.' And flattering, he thought but did not say, to think he had the older man's respect.

His reaction to Zoe's mother, however, was less clear-cut.

Marian was an elegant woman whose looks belied her age. Stephen found it disconcerting to realize that just as he was ten years older than Zoe, her mother was a mere ten years older than him. He remembered then that he and Marian were second cousins, and technically of the same generation; to quell the feeling that he was cradle-snatching, he had to remind himself that at twenty-seven, Zoe was no child.

Everything about Zoe's mother had the high gloss of perfection. The thatched cottage was picture-perfect, its interior such a showplace of antique furniture and *objets d'art*, he was almost afraid to sit down.

While her mother poured sherry from a crystal decanter, Zoe went in search of an ashtray, pushing it ostentatiously towards him as she flopped down on luxurious cushions.

'Stephen smokes, Mummy. You don't mind, do you?'

The challenge with which this was said would have credited a far braver man than Stephen; but by the answering glance he knew that Mummy would mind, and very much. Despite her gracious acquiescence and several nudges from Zoe, he managed to hold out until after dinner, when his nerve had relaxed sufficiently to persuade him that just one might be forgiven. Even so, he took his cigarette outside.

On the drive home, he chain-smoked while Zoe giggled.

'After we're married,' he said heavily, 'I shall do my best not to offend her – but if she visits us in our own home, I'm afraid she'll have to put up with my obnoxious habits.'

'Have you noticed something? People keep asking us when we're going to get married, and where we're going to live – and giving us some very odd looks when we say we haven't discussed it yet!'

'Well, they're two very good questions,' he replied. 'When and where?'

He glanced at her while she was considering that, not exactly dreading her reply, but hoping that she would want to marry soon. Marian's references to bridesmaids and guest lists had given him a sinking feeling. Big weddings took time to arrange, as he knew from past experience, and in his job, dates were practically impossible to guarantee. And there was, of course, the major problem of his divorce: not a point that could be overlooked by the average man of the cloth.

The maturity of her reply took him by surprise.

'Well, my darling, I would have liked to be married in church – but I don't think it's going to be possible, is it? At least not without an unseemly touting round for somebody willing to perform the ceremony. Anyway, as far as I'm concerned, it's the rest of our lives that matter, not just the place and the number of bridesmaids, and a guest list as long as your arm. Which is what Mummy's envisaging.' The sigh that followed, was, he realized, inspired by thoughts of Marian. 'She'll hate it, of course. Me being an only daughter, and all that. But quite honestly, I can't think of more than half a dozen people I'd like to be there, so what does it matter?'

Stephen said nothing, but gently squeezed her knee.

'It's you and me that matter, isn't it? Our promises to each other? I'm sure God will hear us, whether it's in church, in the middle of a field, or in the local registry office...'

'I'm sure He will,' Stephen said quietly, thinking of nights far out at sea, the vastness of the ocean and the endless stars. Amidst all that mystical beauty, it was possible to feel closer to God than in the most fanciful or familiar church. One day, he wanted Zoe to experience that, to understand that naked sense of solitude and humility, in which the slender division between flesh and the spirit seemed so very fragile.

But, perhaps, he thought, she understood something of that already.

Thirty-six

The question of place and date was easily disposed of. Zoe said she could not envisage anywhere but York, and as they were both keen to set the seal of legality on their relationship, the date was set for a Thursday in the middle of September.

It left little time for the final detail of other arrangements, and Zoe's mother was both furious and panic-stricken. September was always a busy time, and how could she possibly leave the business at such short notice? There would be clothes to buy, a wedding dress to arrange, and other essentials such as flowers and a reception. 'Although how on earth you expect me to organize that, from here,' she had wailed to her daughter, 'I really do not know!'

Stephen sent a bouquet of flowers to his future mother-in-law by way of apology and reassurance. *Leave everything to me,* said the enclosed card; which she might not like, he thought, but at least she could absolve herself should the arrangements be less than she expected. Zoe's father, however, had been far more amenable. 'Use your discretion,' he had said when they met at his home by the Thames at Sunbury, 'and just send me the bills.'

While Zoe did her best to organize her work and a certain amount of shopping in London, Stephen returned to York to enlist Joan's help. Delight at his news was not spoiled by thoughts of Marian's celestial standards. 'Well,' she said firmly, 'we'll just have to make sure we don't let the side down, won't we?' And with that she set about making enquiries as to a suitable venue for the reception.

She had a surprising number of friends and acquaintances. Stephen had not realized the extent of her connections until she announced that an old friend from her ATS days, who lived in a glorious Georgian mansion just outside the city, would be willing to place her home at their disposal. 'She does it regularly, for charitable functions,' Joan explained, 'and always uses the same firm of caterers. And I can vouch for their excellence. I don't think we could do better.'

'You're a wonder,' he declared, kissing his aunt roundly. 'It sounds just right.'

And it was. Meeting Joan's friend and viewing the house the week before, he was able to assure Zoe that even her mother would be impressed. 'It's a beautiful old place with a long drive and fabulous windows. You'll love it. And the trees in the park are just beginning to turn – we should get some great photographs.'

Leaving his flat for the use of Zoe and Polly, Stephen moved out the afternoon before, to stay with Mac and Irene at the old family hotel on Gillygate. Mrs Bilton, it seemed, could not have been more thrilled; feeling a certain proprietorial interest in this forthcoming marriage, she insisted upon giving Stephen the best room, the large double that fronted Gillygate, with its own private bathroom. Across the corridor, Mac and Irene had an excellent view of the ramparts. The next morning, serving breakfast, she was quite fluttery with excitement, fussing over Stephen like a mother as he tried, without much success, to eat.

While Mac tucked into an old-fashioned English breakfast, and Irene's brown eyes sparkled with laughter, Stephen picked at scrambled eggs. In honour of the occasion, Mac had trimmed his beard, which transformed him from rampaging Viking to distinguished Rear-Admiral, especially once he had changed into his best uniform.

In Stephen's room he complained long and loudly, however, about the necessity for it. 'If I'd known square-rig was the order of the day, you bloody con-merchant, I'd never have agreed to be best man!'

'Oh, do be quiet, Mac,' his wife ordered as she reached up to brush his jacket. 'I've not seen you looking so smart in *years.*'

She turned to Stephen, who was struggling with the top button of a new white shirt, and managed to fasten it for him, watching through the mirror as he anxiously adjusted his black tie. 'For goodness' sake, relax. Zoe's not going to bite you!'

'No, but her mother might,' he declared pessimistically as Irene held out his jacket.

She laughed. 'You're not marrying her mother.'

'I'm pleased to know that.'

He stood still while Irene brushed away a few clinging specks of dust, fastened his jacket and glanced in the long mirror. Hair neat, no shaving cuts, tie in a perfect Windsor knot, and the old uniform looking as good as ever. Brass buttons gleamed, gold braid shone against the near-black doeskin, and after almost eight years, it still fitted perfectly. Just as well, he reflected, since there would have been no time to have another made, and the uniform had been a specific request from Zoe.

Irene handed him his cap with its starched white cover, and as he brushed at the gold oak leaves on the brim, he stared for a moment at the anchor of the Merchant Navy badge. Remembering that other anchor, the one that held when it was so vital, Stephen felt his tension miraculously lift. He was here and very much alive, and today, he realized with heartfelt gratitude, was the first day of the rest of his life.

Glancing up, meeting Mac's eyes, there was a sudden flash of understanding between them. On an impulse, they embraced, brief emotion finding release in laughter as Irene hugged them both and, with a long, happy sigh, stood back to look at Stephen.

'Oh, Robert Redford, eat your heart out! You look so good, I could marry you myself!'

'That's the best offer I've had all day,' he grinned, kissing her warm cheek. 'And I must say, you look pretty tempting...'

'Now just a minute,' Mac interrupted, taking his wife's arm, 'I'm supposed to be the best man here!'

They went out, laughing. About to close the door of his room, Stephen turned, on the impression that someone had called his name. It was so clear, he even went to look in the adjoining bathroom; but no one was there. A shiver touched his spine as he remembered Robert Duncannon and his Elliott forebears, and he was aware, as he had been on his first visit to this house, of links stretching back into the past. Then he glanced round, noticed that the long windows were slightly open, and he told himself that what he had heard was no more than a man's voice, rising from the street. But it had sounded so close...

He shrugged and went downstairs. Mrs Bilton was waiting in

the hall. She kissed his cheek and wished him luck, and said that she would follow them in a few minutes: she wanted to see Zoe and congratulate them both as soon as the ceremony was over.

They went on foot to the Registrar's on Bootham, causing several female heads to turn during that short walk. Mac's mutterings of discontent were echoed, as soon as they arrived, by Johnny, who was waiting for them on the steps.

'Jesus, thank God you're here – I've only been waiting five minutes, and already three people have stopped to ask me the time of the next bus!'

'You're a lying hound, Walker – and you look smarter than I've ever seen you, so stop complaining!'

'Let's get inside,' Mac muttered, 'we look like the three bloody musketeers, standing here.'

'You're enjoying it,' Irene declared, linking arms with Johnny, 'and I'm having the time of my life.'

During the next ten minutes, the other guests assembled, Stephen effecting a few introductions while they all waited for the bride. Pamela arrived with her husband and Joan, and a moment later Zoe's mother came in with a tall, distinguished man in a dark suit. She seemed unusually tense and flustered, and Stephen had a panic-stricken moment wondering what could have gone wrong; but hard on her heels came Polly, all smiles and vibrant colour. She shot him a beaming smile and a discreet thumbs-up sign, which enabled him to breathe again, and immediately made a bee-line for Johnny. They seemed quite taken with each other, he thought, remembering the laughter of the evening before...

Moments later, alerted by a sudden hush, all such considerations vanished.

Holding her father's arm, Zoe seemed to drift towards him, layers of silk and chiffon stirring as she crossed the room. The dress was of a style and material reminiscent of the early twenties, but looking at her, Stephen was reminded of one of her own illustrations, Titania, perhaps, or the Spirit of the Rose. Her hair was as fine and flyaway as the chiffon bandeau she wore, sunlight catching a skein of tiny flowers nestling amongst the curls. He had always known she was beautiful, but in that moment she was breathtakingly so; had his life depended on it, he could not have spoken.

With an effort, he tore his eyes away, placed his cap on the Registrar's desk, and took hold of Zoe's hand. She was trembling, and that surprised him. He glanced down at her and met a tentative smile that immediately restored his confidence. Squeezing her fingers, he felt a responding pressure as the Registrar cleared his throat to begin.

The ceremony was short; within minutes it seemed all the formalities were complete and two single people had been joined as one. They stared at each other in happy amazement until a nudge from Mac reminded him that he was supposed to kiss the bride. Almost hesitantly, he bent his head, but Zoe flung her arms around his neck and hugged him, and in the joy of that embrace, Stephen swept her off her feet and swung her round, his kiss raising cheers from the gathered company.

'We couldn't have done that in church!' she said with a giggle as he set her down.

'Start off as you mean to go on,' he replied, and kissed her again.

The reception was a great success, the guests few enough to limit the need for constant circulation; before long, the wedding breakfast had become a party.

Afterwards, Zoe's mother was almost effusive in her praise, raising a dry smile from Stephen only as she intimated that she had not thought him capable of organizing things so well. But James Clifford's compliments were unalloyed by any such qualification. And he said, succinctly, that he liked Stephen's friends. It was tantamount to a seal of approval.

Zoe nudged Stephen later, pointing out Marian and Joan deep in conversation, and said that his sister Pamela had seemed both friendly and sincere when they had spoken earlier.

'Don't let this go to your head,' Stephen told her, 'but Pam actually confessed that she likes you...'

'So she might accept me, yet?'

'She might indeed,' he said warmly, squeezing her waist. He glanced at his watch. 'I hate to break up the party when they're all getting on so well, but it's time we were shedding all this finery and getting on the road.'

Zoe ran her fingers beneath the soft doeskin lapels of his jacket. 'That's a shame,' she said, 'because I must confess to rather liking you in that uniform. I think it's incredibly sexy...'

He chuckled. 'Go on – get up those stairs.'

They emerged, some twenty minutes later, in clothes that were considerably more suited to travelling, to find that their presence had scarcely been missed. For a moment they were both tempted simply to creep away, but Mac drew everyone's attention, demanding to know, unless it was a state secret, where they were going for their honeymoon.

'We're going to France,' Zoe said brightly, glancing up at Stephen.

'To look at a few vineyards and chateaux, and sample the food,' he added with a disarming smile.

For some reason, no one seemed inclined to believe them. He had to produce the ferry tickets, Hull to Zeebrugge, before anyone was remotely satisfied, yet even then an air of suspicion lingered.

'I know,' Johnny declared, 'you're going for a dirty weekend in Amsterdam – Canal Street and naughty things by candle-light!'

'No, we'd have taken the Rotterdam ferry for that,' Stephen said, keeping his face straight.

Zoe's father erupted into laughter, while his ex-wife looked faintly shocked.

A few minutes later, Marian said wistfully to Stephen, 'I thought you might have taken Zoe to the Caribbean?'

'Oh, not at *this* time of year – the weather's appalling. Hurricanes, you know. No, Zoe and I have a taste for something a little closer to home. France will suit us fine.'

'They didn't believe a word of it,' she said happily as the Jaguar took them out of sight and hearing.

Grinning, Stephen changed gear and let the car pick up a little speed. 'Well, they wouldn't have believed the truth, that's for sure. Anyway, we didn't tell any lies.'

Her smile broadened and broke into laughter; glancing at her, Stephen was caught again by her beauty and high spirits. She looked so lovely when she laughed, all he wanted to do was kiss her. Laughing at himself, he turned his eyes back to the road. 'Can you imagine...' He shook his head, unable to finish the sentence.

'They'd have thought us so eccentric!'

The idea continued to amuse them all the way to Hull.

The cabin was small but beautifully fitted out, and with its own tiny bathroom; the only drawback, as far as they were concerned, being the single, tiered bunks.

'Ah, well, never mind,' Stephen muttered, inspecting everything with an expert's eye, 'where there's a will, there's a way...'

'You've got a one-track mind,' Zoe observed as he reached for her.

'Are you complaining? Or even surprised?'

She laughed. 'No.'

'Good. Because,' he informed her between kisses, 'this is our wedding night, and despite the... somewhat... *cramped* conditions... I've always had this erotic fantasy about...'

But he never did manage to tell her; banged heads and elbows and snatches of conversation from cabins either side, reduced them both to near-hysterical laughter. In the end they gave up in favour of drinks and dinner.

The wine was good, the food forgivable, and the lounge bar had a resident pianist. He was charming, and played requests. Stephen and Zoe decided that perhaps 'The First Time Ever I Saw Your Face,' ought to be their song; it was that kind of evening, with a calm sea shushing past and stars appearing in the twilight. They even took the requisite stroll along the boat deck.

But it was chilly and they told each other that it had been a long day.

Ensconced in that narrow lower bunk, holding each other close after making love with more urgency than finesse, it seemed to strike them both, very suddenly, that they were married.

Raising her left hand to his lips, Stephen kissed the palm and the base of her third finger with its pair of slender rings. 'So tell me, Miss Clifford – how does it feel to be Mrs Stephen Elliott?'

Pushing back the short, damp curls from his forehead, Zoe's

pretty mouth curved into a smile. 'I think the word, Captain Elliott, is loved – and amazingly secure…'

'I'm glad,' he whispered, 'because I do love you, so very, very much.'

'I know. And I love you. I always will.'

That word, *always*, seemed neither strange nor impossible on her lips. It seemed to him that love in the Elliott family was like that.

Zeebrugge at eight in the morning was a gloom of rain drizzling from a leaden sky, and streams of cars with glaring headlights, their drivers fighting through to factories and offices for a day on the treadmill.

'God, I couldn't do this every day,' Stephen swore as he dodged traffic, searched for the right lane, and struggled with the initial strangeness of driving on the other side of the road.

'Never mind, you don't have to,' Zoe observed equably, a map on her knee. 'Just think, most of these people couldn't bear to do what you do, either.'

'Look, spare me the philosophy just now, darling, and tell me what road we should be on.'

'Keep following the signs for Ostend.'

It was simple enough, dual carriageway to the seaside town of Ostend, with the Jaguar nicely eating up the miles, then south on a minor road to Dixmude, towards Ypres and Armentières. Their plans were flexible, the main idea being to follow Liam's footsteps from Flanders down to the Somme, and back to Flanders again for 20th September.

The 70th anniversary of Liam's death was also the 70th anniversary of the Battle of the Menin Road. They had been warned that the town would be busy that weekend, so had booked their hotel in advance; but for the rest they were easy enough, content to take choice and chance as it came. They had Michelin guides with maps, a book of battlefield tours, and even an ancient guide, complete with photographs, that Stephen had found amongst the books in the trunk. Published in 1920, it had Robert Duncannon's signature scrawled across the flyleaf.

Zoe had invested in a waxed jacket and green wellies in case of mud and bad weather, while Stephen had boots and sea-boot socks, and said his old Burberry would have to do. They were both rather looking forward to tramping through woods and across ploughed fields in the rain.

As they turned inland the weather improved, the sun struggling through a hazy autumn mist over countryside that, to their joint surprise, appeared not unlike the Vale of York.

Bypassing Ypres, the first town they came to was Poperinghe. Parking the car off a cobbled market square, after lunch they found themselves wandering round, rather as Liam once did, and being drawn towards Talbot House. The tall, white town house, where a British chaplain called Tubby Clayton had set up a home-from-home for weary and distressed troops, was now a place of pilgrimage for battlefield travellers.

When Stephen and Zoe called, the door was open to visitors and a friendly young man with perfect English invited them in. He explained how the Everyman's Club had come about, and what a refuge it had been in the darkest days of the war. The garden was still there, and the chapel beneath the rafters, its chairs and the little altar ready for the next service. Below it was the study, with its instruction to '*Abandon rank all ye who enter here.*'

There was a sense of peace and solace in that room, and, affected by the knowledge that Liam had been there, at what was probably the lowest point of his war, neither of them wanted to leave. But it was late afternoon, and both Stephen and Zoe were aware of sudden fatigue, a need for baths and rest and a quiet meal before turning in for the night. They found a comfortable hotel just off the square which provided all their requirements.

Pouring the last of the wine as they finished their meal, Stephen said: 'You would say, wouldn't you, if you didn't want to go on?'

'Of course I would. Why, don't you?'

'Oh, I want to go on, no doubt about that. It's just...' He broke off, drank some more wine, and finally shook his head. 'This afternoon – you were on the verge of tears a couple of times, and so was I. It made me think that – well, there's going to be a lot more of it, and we are going to be sad, maybe even very upset at times. Is this a good idea for a honeymoon? I know it's what we said we'd do, but there's no shame in changing our minds – we could motor on down to the Côte d'Azur, if you'd prefer...'

'And come back another time?'

Stephen nodded, toying with his glass. He saw her eyes darken before she glanced away, watching diners at other tables, waiters passing.

'I know what you're saying,' she said at last, 'but no, I don't think so. We talked about this, didn't we, before we finally decided. And if you recall, we both had it in mind that this was what we needed to do, honeymoon or not.' A sudden smile dispelled the shadows. 'We just decided to get married first.'

Relieved, he clasped her hand across the table. 'So you want to carry on?'

'Yes, I do. I think we have to.'

'I've just remembered,' Zoe said as they reached their room, 'I had a letter before I left London. Can't think how I forgot to tell you,' she added, glancing up at him with an ironic grin, 'unless it was that wedding we attended the other day...' She fished in her capacious shoulder-bag and produced, with a flourish, an airmail envelope bearing the Southern Cross emblem of Australia.

'The farm's gone – most of it, anyway. But the old house and the bungalows are still there, in a few acres of land, and guess what? The family still own it.'

'You're kidding.' He took the envelope and opened it, scanning the contents quickly before settling down to read properly. The writer was a Mrs Laura Maddox, widow of David, son of Lewis Maddox's elder brother. She was sixty-seven years old, and remembered Uncle Lew and Aunt Gina very well. In fact, since her husband's death some six years previously, she had moved into their old bungalow, leaving the farmhouse to her son and his wife.

Although she was not sure exactly what it was Miss Clifford wanted to know about the old lady, Mrs Maddox felt she could say without fear of contradiction that Aunt Gina had been one of the kindest people it had ever been her pleasure to know, and much missed after her death in 1973.

'... Lord knows how old she was. In her eighties, I'm sure, but she always kept her age a secret. Bright as a button, though, right up to that last week or so. Then she suddenly failed, like old people do, and got a bit muddled. She took a chill that turned to pneumonia, and died at the end of September. Uncle Lew went in 1949. Nice old bloke he was, frail when I knew him, but always had a joke for you, in spite of being a sick man. She was a nurse, though, looked after him and did a lot of good for the folks round here, especially between the wars. Delivered I don't know how many babies, people always sent for her before the doctor. Uncle Lew said if it hadn't been for her, he would have given up years ago.

'Lew and her brother were best friends in the war, and I seem to think he worked here before that. She had a lovely picture of him on the mantelpiece, a nice portrait photo taken in uniform. I still have it, couldn't bear to throw it away, but I don't think it would interest anybody else. If you would like it, I could send it on, you being related to the other brother...'

Stephen looked up at Zoe, who was standing over him, and his happy smile gave way to appreciative laughter. Her luck was phenomenal, and he would have been hard pressed to say which touched him most: the fact that yet another of her shots in the dark had reached its mark, or the contents of that letter from Mrs Maddox.

On balance, he thought, drawing Zoe close against his shoulder, it was the latter. Knowing that Georgina's marriage had been a happy one, that she had gone on to enjoy a long and apparently fulfilled life, eased much of the tragedy attached to her affair with Liam. Louisa and Robert, he felt – and Edward, too – should have been able to rest in peace, knowing that.

But what of Liam? The more Zoe told him, and the more he thought about it, the less Stephen understood. Having come to accept Liam Elliott's presence in their lives, and his inescapable influence, it was increasingly apparent that in his case, the term, *at rest*, was simply not applicable. Zoe's experience that day at the hospital served only to underline it; yet belief and understanding were still miles apart. It was one thing to acknowledge Liam's power, to look back and realize that all his efforts so far had been to the good; but it was quite another to chart a definite pattern and to see what it meant.

Part of it, they were both convinced, was to do with themselves, in the love they shared, and the resolving of problems which had remained outstanding for more than seventy years. That sense of things coming right was almost overwhelming. And yet somehow, questions still remained.

Whatever else Liam was trying to say, the only way to understand it was to be open to him, to subdue logic and reason, and give him access to instinct. As far as either of them could tell, that was the way in which he worked best. So however hard reason might argue against subjecting themselves to the sadness of this journey, instinct said to carry on.

Next morning they were on the road shortly after nine, heading directly south for Bailleul and the area which had been the training ground for most of the troops arriving in France. Driving between hedges along narrow country lanes, it was possible to ignore the broad new swathe of *autoroute* over to the left, and to imagine Liam seeing this rich farmland for the very first time.

The villages had a sleepy, timeless atmosphere, as though nothing much had changed in the years between, and it was easy to pretend that nothing had. Within just a few miles, however, they had a rude awakening to reality. The string of hamlets and small towns that followed the meandering River Lys towards Armentières started to blend into one, with industry crowding out what farms and fields remained.

Stephen had no desire to be embroiled in the maze of a busy city centre. On a sharp decision he turned away from the river and the factories, along a less busy but much narrower road that seemed to serve a string of farms and hamlets. Here, at last, in a flat land divided by hedge and fence, was it possible to visualize the lines of waterlogged trenches, barbed-wire entanglements and the sandbagged ruins of barns and houses. Somewhere along here had been the front line; in the region of this road Liam had spent a couple of months with his company of machine-gunners, learning to cope with the mud and the rats and the terrifying moments, learning to live with the deadly business of war.

They followed the road back to Estaires, and thence in a meandering curve away from the industrial areas of Bethune and Lens and Arras. Liam's route south had been via St Pol and Doullens, and that was the way Stephen intended to go. It was an unexpectedly beautiful drive, past shorn wheatfields and woods ablaze with the first tints of autumn. Having lunched early, they stopped again at a wayside cafe just after four, and then continued south into Picardy.

On the Michelin map, Zoe had marked all the villages mentioned by Liam in his diary; they stretched in a broad, horizontal sweep either side of the main road between Doullens and Amiens, from the wide valley of the Somme near Abbeville in the west, to Albert and the valley of the Ancre in the east.

The distance was perhaps some thirty miles, which was, Zoe thought, a lot of marching, particularly after the stress and exhaustion of battle. Much easier by car, she decided, even while they debated which route to take; but Stephen said it had been a long day, even in the comfort of the Jaguar. He thought it advisable to head directly for Amiens and a bed for the night.

The following day, after a morning spent motoring through a wealth of tiny villages, Stephen and Zoe arrived in Albert at lunch-time. The basilica with its massive red and white brick tower was visible for miles, the sun glinting from the gilded Virgin and Child which crowned it. It was easy to see what a gift that had been as a marker for enemy artillery; so easy to cringe at the thought of shells landing with such accuracy in the square below.

There was a cafe in the square; sitting at a pavement table in the warm September sun, Stephen wondered whether it was the same *estaminet* where Liam and Robin had met in the summer of 1916. In a sentimental gesture, he ordered two beers, and while they were waiting for the *omelettes et frites*, he gazed up at that massive edifice across the way, comparing it to the postcard reproduction of a 1916 photograph. The battered church with its famous statue poised like a diver had been completely restored; so well that it was hard to believe that it had not always looked so solid. The town held no pretensions to grandeur, but they walked its streets before driving out to Fricourt, where Robin Elliott had survived the carnage of July 1st.

Nestling in a dip of those rolling chalk downs beyond Albert, the village was a pretty enough place in an attractive setting. But viewing the field of combat from the Green Howards' memorial was horrifying. Beyond the wall of the cemetery lay a small field, bounded by a dense copse of trees to the left and a low ridge which curved from the right. At most, the ridge, which now bore a line of modern bungalows, was no more than a hundred yards away, a twelve-second sprint to a fit young athlete keen to gain his objective. In that field the young men of the 7th Battalion had been mown down by the score as they attempted to take the German guns.

Zoe shivered in the sun, knowing that what had happened here had, that very same day, been repeated along a front that extended for eighteen miles.

Stephen left a small wooden cross, bearing a scarlet poppy and his grandfather's name, by the granite memorial. Robin Elliott, as much as the men who died here, had been a victim, too. Thinking about all those ordinary men, the clerks and the labourers, artists, miners and scholars, it seemed no more than an echo of his thoughts to find that someone else had written in the visitor's book: *'There are no politicians buried here…'*

A short distance away was the German cemetery, as neatly kept but bleaker, somehow, lacking the gentling effect of flowers. Simple black crosses, set amongst trees, looked out from higher ground over the battlefield. Here and there an arched stone, bearing a Star of David, marked the last resting place of a Jewish soldier. In the light of that other war, a mere twenty years later, there was a dreadful irony about that.

Through a drift of fallen leaves they made their way back to the car. With a deep sigh, Stephen picked up the maps and guides, and made quite a show of studying the various routes to Pozières. Zoe looked out over the battlefield and said nothing at all.

He turned the car, going back the way they had come, through the village and right towards Bécourt. By that deserted roadside lay another cemetery, row upon row of white headstones against a stubble field, with woods, gold and green, crowning the rise beyond. Within a few hundred yards, where the road curved into the next village, a large white crucifix stood at the junction of two cart tracks, one leading into the wood, the other skirting it, leading to open fields above.

'This must be Bécourt Wood,' Stephen said, looking again at

the enlarged map from the battlefield guide, 'and that track, if I'm not mistaken, must lead to "Sausage Valley" – or "Gully" as the Aussies called it.' He glanced at Zoe and she smiled. 'Do you want to walk?'

'Better get the welly boots,' she replied, stepping out of the car. 'I've a feeling that chalk uplands, after rain, will be greasy and muddy.'

She was right; and Stephen knew that it would take more than these few days of fine, sunny weather to dry out the ploughed fields that rose gently to either side. In scarves, sweaters and jeans they walked hand in hand along 'Sausage Gully'. Hugging a raised hedge part of the way, the track swept up the centre of that shallow bowl before curving away to the left, towards a crown of trees and shrubs that Stephen thought might be close to the village of La Boisselle. Straight ahead of them, a slender stand of trees indicated the village of Contalmaison, while beyond that, according to the map, lay Pozières.

Distances were deceptive, and the stiff climb to La Boisselle took longer than they thought. They were both breathing heavily by the time they reached the crest. What struck each of them with equal force was the time it had taken to climb one side of that shallow valley, and the absolute exposure. There were no hedges to conceal them from watchers on that horseshoe ridge, and it seemed fair to assume that any hedges pre-1914 had been grubbed up or blasted out of existence long before the Australians arrived. There had been trenches, of course, but still, to traverse that place in journeys to and from the forward line seemed hazardous in the extreme.

Looking back the way they had come, in the midst of those recently ploughed acres, it was possible to see white lines meandering across the earth, and large white patches, roughly circular, that marked the position of old craters and shell-holes. After seventy years, there was something faintly chilling about it, as though the earth itself was determined to keep its own memorial to those bitter days. More chilling still was the little pile of rusty, unexploded shells propped against a stone where the track became a road.

'Seventy years,' Stephen murmured, 'and they're still digging them up.' He looked down, and amongst the bits of chalk spotted a shrapnel ball, a heavy lead pellet the size of a child's marble, just one of the hundreds packed into every shrapnel shell, designed to burst in mid-air like deadly rain. Weighing it in his palm, he imagined it biting through tender flesh, breaking bones with the force of its impact...

He slipped the small thing into his pocket, joining Zoe as she rounded the shrouding line of shrubs at the crest. There before them stood a wooden cross, right on the lip of a massive crater, the size and depth of which took Stephen's breath away.

So this was the crater of La Boisselle, blown by mines before the Australians arrived, part of the British attempt to dislodge the German forces from their position on the ridge. Once, there had been trenches here, and deep dugouts; the rest had gone, but the crater remained, a deep well in the chalk, some sixty feet deep.

Stephen gazed into it and fingered the tiny lead ball in his pocket: from the large to the small, the opposing forces had tried everything to annihilate each other. Little had been achieved, barring the waste of a generation; and the land continued to tell the story.

A car with British plates drew up before the cross, the occupants two middle-aged men in overcoats. They smiled and nodded, looked up at the memorial, and down into the crater, and proceeded to walk the rim. Watching them for a moment, with a blustery wind sharpening the air, Stephen and Zoe debated what to do. The village of La Boisselle was a couple of fields away down the asphalt road, with the arrow of the Bapaume Road immediately beyond it. Pozières was perhaps another two miles. In the end, neither of them wanted to walk that distance along a main road, and as the afternoon was drawing on, it was decided to return for the car.

Zoe's research into the action at Pozières made clear that nowadays there was little to see beyond a single main street, the Australian Memorial, and the base of the old windmill beyond the village. With a glance at his watch, Stephen decided that there was still enough daylight to do that before returning to their hotel in Amiens for a well-deserved dinner. So, a look at the rebuilt village, a visit to the Memorial, and back to Amiens for the night.

Old photographs reprinted in a modern account of the battle, revealed that Pozières had been a singularly plain French village of mainly single-storied houses, hugging the Roman road to Bapuame. Its gardens and orchards, according to the old maps, were all to the rear.

Nothing seemed to have changed. Driving up the hill from the direction of Albert, the village appeared as a short stretch of unpretentious dwellings, the kind of place to drive through, at speed, on the way to somewhere infinitely more interesting. Talking to Zoe, Stephen did just that before realizing where they were. As luck would have it, he slowed and stopped by the old windmill. Again, it was so modest as to be hardly noticeable. Along a strip of mown grass, a white path led to a flat memorial stone and the rough mound where the windmill had once stood; the old concrete fortifications were now sunk into the ground.

How many lives had it cost to take this place? Stephen did not know, could not even guess; but with its commanding view of the countryside to the north and east, he could understand why the Australians wanted it. From there it must have been possible to see the German guns.

At the other end of the village, by 'Fort Gibraltar' – a bramble-covered mass this time – stood the obelisk erected to the memory of those men of the 1st Australian Division who had fought so doggedly and endured so bravely throughout three long years of war in France. There was a plaque naming the legendary places of those engagements, from Pozières to Passchendaele, and a dozen more between Bullecourt and the Hindenburg Line. Above it, bronze against granite, rose the rising sun emblem with its imperial crown and curl of motto beneath, striking and instantly memorable.

Zoe called it a brilliant piece of design, but there were tears in her eyes as she said it, and Stephen knew she was thinking of Liam in this place, and trying not to weep.

In the west the sun was setting in a hazy, azure sky; to the north, a lilac mist wreathed the woods of Thiepval and its huge memorial, while night clouds gathered over Pozières. All around were the gentle slopes of cultivated land, a sense of peace accentuated by the twitter of birds settling down for the night, the murmur of a passing car and a distant buzz from a home-going tractor. It was hard to believe that this place had been obliterated, reduced to a naked, barren, ash-strewn heath; that earth and sky had been riven, night and day, by the constant thunder of the guns. Hard to believe, until the eye caught the glimmer of light on tall crosses between the trees, until the number of cemeteries were counted.

Thirty-seven

The lights of a small cafe caught Stephen's attention as they returned to the car, and thoughts of hot coffee were suddenly more pressing than anything else. They were both chilled, so he ordered cognac too, Zoe responding in careful French to *Madame's* warm and friendly welcome.

She was a plump, middle-aged, cheerful woman, the personification of her cosy and old-fashioned establishment. Delft racks and huge, dark dressers lined the walls, filled with an assortment of meat-plates and jugs and the myriad examples of wartime memorabilia. There were regimental insignia, photographs and flags, caps and helmets, polished brass shell-cases from the enormous to the minute, nose-cones, water bottles and bayonets. It was a collector's dream and a place of endless fascination for anyone even remotely interested in the battlefields.

Glass in hand, Zoe wandered around, peering at everything, while *Madame* bustled in and out of the kitchen with plates of food for a group of travellers in the corner. The aroma was tantalizing, the presentation enough to capture a gourmet. Catching Zoe's eye, Stephen shot her an enquiring look, and instantly she smiled and nodded. Why trail back to their hotel, when there were feasts to be had right here?

The pâté was rich, the chicken delicately flavoured, and the cheese excellent. They drank a recommended wine and exclaimed over it, and finished with a colourless liqueur, on the house. With her other visitors gone, *Madame* was pleased to talk, about Pozières, her little cafe and its museum, and the people who regularly stopped to eat, drink and say *bonjour*. On 1st July the previous year, which had been the 70th anniversary of the Battle of the Somme, she said she had served hundreds of meals, to Australians, Canadians, Irish, Scots and English: a memorable day for her family and the people of Pozières.

Some might have said, cynically, that the old war was good for business, and yet despite the difficulties of language, it was easy to understand that business was secondary to the fact that Pozières was not forgotten. The young men who died here might have been foreigners, but *Madame's* forebears had suffered, too; to the north and the south they had died under arms, and in the village itself, their lives had been wrecked by the destruction of their village and the land itself. The Gallic shrug said: *well, that's how it was, you have to accept it*, yet this woman cared too much for the living not to be affected by that senseless waste. Zoe did not think she was unusual.

What struck her particularly – and Stephen, too, as they discussed it on the drive back to Amiens – was the tenacity of these people, their brave determination to come back and start again. Not only to return, but to rebuild their village *as it had been before*.

It must have taken years to clear their lands of the detritus of war, to reclaim those fields from the dead, but they had done just that, and done it with courage and respect. Here, it was impossible to forget the past; the young men who had given up their lives in one of the bloodiest wars the world had ever known, were part of these people's present. They could never be forgotten, not here, not in Albert, nor in the hundreds of towns and villages that had formed the battlegrounds of seventy years ago.

That thought, having taken root, continued to grow as they eventually made their way north, back to Flanders and the medieval town of Ypres. Its wealth, accrued in the thirteenth and fourteenth centuries from the wool trade, had given birth to a series of fine gothic buildings, most notably the massive Cloth Hall, whose tower dominated a grand market place.

Parking the car in that cobbled square, Stephen and Zoe stepped out in noonday sun to be faced by a dazzling array of medieval architecture, steep roofs and stepped gables, tall, narrow houses, tiny shops and cafes, and the glowing sandstone of the Cloth Hall itself. Here, the best of the past had been recreated to shine for the future; everywhere, date-stones from the 1920s proclaimed a new beginning after the holocaust. The whole town was a monument to endurance and determination.

Crossing the road to their hotel, Stephen and Zoe were, without realizing it, in line with the Menin Road. Glancing each way for traffic, they suddenly saw the Memorial, massive, white, bridging the narrow street before it like a classical version of one of York's ancient gates. They both paused, a car slowed, but neither of them noticed. Mesmerized they wandered to the far pavement, and then along the street, unable to focus on anything else.

'I don't know why, but I always imagined it standing on its own, like the Arc de Triomphe, but out in the countryside.'

'Yes, me too,' Stephen murmured, thinking of the memorial at Thiepval, grim and isolated amongst its woods and fields and cemeteries. This was just as imposing, but more pleasing, integral with the town's old defences, and overlooking a peaceful moat. There were trees on the ramparts, shedding golden leaves into the water below, and traffic passing back and forth beneath the enormous tunnel of the archway itself.

Like the city of York, Ypres formed the hub of several main roads, and the one to Menin was as busy now as it had ever been. There was something reassuring about that, a sense of life and continuation in a place that had seen so much of death. It seemed singularly appropriate that Liam's name should be here amongst the living, in a place that had so much in common with his childhood home.

Almost every regiment and unit of the Empire had seen service here, passing along a via dolorosa of Ypres' ruins to front lines that straddled the Menin Road. Those who passed through and did not come back, those who fell and were denied the privilege of a marked grave, were remembered here. 55,000 names: Australians, Canadians, South Africans, Indians and West Indians, with more than forty thousand British soldiers amongst them.

Stephen and Zoe stood beneath the great vault of the central arch, gazing up at those high walls, smooth blocks of white stone, each bearing so many names, so many regiments. Above them, sunlight streamed through open roundels, while to either side twin arches faced each other across the road, with steps leading up to more walls, more names.

They found the Australians at last, and among the Machine Gun Corps, Liam's surname and initials at eye-level, carved into the stone. Familiar, yet strange, and as Stephen reached out to trace those fading letters, he was possessed by a sharp sense of his own mortality.

Embracing Zoe with sudden need, he realized more sharply than ever how fortunate he was to be alive, to have her love, and, just as importantly, her understanding. And what they shared, which seemed so much a part of Liam's gift to them both, was a living, growing thing which had its roots embedded firmly in the past. But its branches were now reaching out towards the future.

For Robert and Louisa, who began all this, time and fate had decreed something other than natural fulfillment, while the legacy bequeathed to Liam and Georgina had cast a blight on happiness, ended by Liam's untimely death. For Stephen and Zoe, however, sharing the same blood, the same inheritance, there were no such tragedies, no such impediments.

With arms around each other, they went back to the hotel. A couple of hours later, as a beam of sun glinted through her hair on the pillow, he said softly: 'I feel so much at peace, as though everything, at last, is right. Not just you and me, but everything to do with us. Even those odd coincidences seem to have slipped into place. He wanted us together, didn't he? And he wanted us to come here.'

'Yes, of course he did.'

Kissing the fingers she raised to his lips, he smiled into her eyes. Dark lashes cast shadows against her cheek, and it seemed to him that she knew so much, understood with greater depth the things he was just beginning to see. Yet she did not try to tell him, did not attempt to push him down roads with which she was already familiar; she was content, instead, to let him discover things for himself. Wondering whether she was fey, or simply very wise, he smiled again, remembering his first impression of her, that she was like a misty Irish morning, soft, gentle, and slightly mysterious. And when the sun shone through, she sparkled, as her eyes were sparkling now, full of light and love and an uncanny knowledge of what was in his mind.

'And do you know what I want?'

She tried to suppress a smile, but her eyes gave her away. 'No, tell me.'

'I want us to have children.'

That was something Stephen had never said before, because as a man who lived very much in the present, he had never wanted to look that far ahead, or in that particular direction; but here, with Zoe, he was beginning to see the importance of the future. Their future, his and hers, with a family of their own.

'But not this very minute,' he said laughingly a few minutes later. 'I'm selfish enough to want you to come to sea with me, a couple of times at least.'

'And I want to enjoy living in your flat…'

'Our flat,' he reminded her.

'I want to enjoy that glorious view for a little while, before we have to think in terms of a house and garden, and domestic bliss!'

'You're sure you won't miss London?' It was a question he had asked several times, and when he asked it, he did not really mean London, but her flat on Queen's Gate, the one that had belonged to Robert and Georgina.

'I won't miss London at all, I've told you that, and as for Queen's Gate – well, yes, I will miss it, but it's not something I want to cling to at the expense of my life with you. It's part of the past,' she said softly, 'like Robert and Georgina. But I won't ever forget it, just as I won't forget them.' With a sudden smile, she said: 'Anyway, it doesn't belong to me, it was only ever on loan, so to speak…'

'At the right time,' he murmured.

'Oh, yes – like everything else, it was at the right time…'

They enjoyed a satisfying meal that evening in a tiny restaurant across the square, a place that, like their hotel, seemed full of English visitors here for the following day's anniversary. At the next table they spotted the same two middle-aged men seen previously at La Boisselle. Recognition and warmer greetings led to a fruitful conversation. The two men were battlefield pilgrims of some twenty years' standing, one an ex-soldier whose grandfather had died leading his men on the first day of the Somme, while the other's great-uncle had been killed at Passchendaele. Their knowledge of both areas was comprehensive.

Zoe asked what it was that drew them back, time after time, and for a moment both seemed surprised by the question. Between them they provided several reasons, from a pair of understanding wives to the beauty of the countryside and the welcome of local people. Ultimately, however, they both agreed that what really brought them back, year after year, was the very special atmosphere.

'There's something about the place – both here and on the Somme. I don't know whether you've noticed it yet, but you probably will, in time. It's not the sadness you'd expect – far from it. It's a sense of tremendous peace.Very healing, somehow,' the ex-soldier said unexpectedly, and without a trace of embarrassment. 'I often come here feeling as though I've got the weight of the world on me, but I go away again quite restored.'

The other man nodded, while Stephen and Zoe glanced at each other. 'Yes,' she said, 'we have noticed it.'

As Stephen squeezed her fingers, she knew what he was thinking, that after the shocks and stress of several months in the Gulf, he had not truly recovered himself until the last few days. He was more relaxed and at peace now than she had ever known him. So was she; and in her heart she knew that it was not simply because they were happy with each other. It went far deeper than that. It was both curious and reassuring to realize that other people felt it too.

Stephen mentioned their particular interest in the initial stages of the Australians' advance, and in return received clear instructions on how to approach the area. The ex-soldier, with his appreciation of aims and strategy, was able to clarify the separate objectives and achievements, and to indicate roughly the place where Liam must have met his end.

Next morning, after an early cup of coffee, Zoe stuffed their pockets with chocolate and biscuits before setting off at first light to drive out towards Polygon Wood.

Against a brightening sky streaked with pink in the east, the great, dense stand of oaks and conifers loomed dark and brooding across a landscape wreathed in low-lying mist. It was eerie and beautiful, and also faintly chilling to realize that on a morning such as this the battalions had formed for their advance. To their left, mist clung in tattered shrouds to the shivering green and gold of Glencorse Wood, while isolated farmhouses appeared like ghostly mirages across the fields. They parked the car and walked along a narrow country lane towards what had been marked on their map as the second objective. The line came down at an angle, just beyond another lane which joined this one between Nonne Bosschen and Polygon Wood, and led back towards the Menin Road.

The junction of the two lanes formed the apex of a triangle, and as they came to the corner the sun came up in all its glory, flooding sky and mist with light. Polygon Wood seemed to float before them, a dark island on a milky sea, while they waded waist deep through the clinging, shifting fog. They passed an isolated dwelling, and further on, a group of houses with barns and outbuildings, some new, others that might have been built on or near the fortified remains of old farms.

From the information they had, it was hard to be sure of even an approximate place, but somewhere close to this lane, a sniper's bullet had caught Liam as he raised his head. Somewhere near here he had been buried.

It doesn't matter. The words came into Zoe's mind even as she dwelt on the tragedy, even as the pair of them looked round at fields and farms and back at the looming darkness of Polygon Wood. *None of this matters.* It came again, so clear that she looked up at Stephen, almost convinced that he had spoken. For a moment his blue eyes, catching the sun, were brilliant; and then he smiled and shook his head and slipped an arm around her shoulders.

'No,' he said huskily, 'I don't suppose it does matter. Not now. Not to him, anyway.'

She knew what he meant. Seventy years ago today, as the sun rose over these autumn woods and misty fields, Liam had met his death; but for him it had been the beginning of a life that ranged far beyond these Flanders fields. That, she felt sure, was by far the greater part of what he had always been trying to tell them: that life was important, but death was by no means the end. And if love in all its forms was the most essential part of life itself, then love was eternal, all-powerful, and it was with love that he had come to them.

His power was unmistakable, although whether it was exceptional was a question neither could answer. Whether their love and remembrance of him increased that power, or through them he was fulfilling a destiny denied to him in life, was another imponderable. The only surety was that he was with them now, communicating in his own inimitable fashion.

A sense of lightness, akin to that Zoe had experienced at the Wandsworth hospital, possessed them both: calmer, less heady, but equally unmistakable. Although they were conscious that he had left them before they reached the car, there was, as before, that lingering sense of clarity and peace.

Returning to the Menin Gate, they stood quietly for a while, watching a pair of swans amongst the drifting leaves, conscious of past and present and the changes seventy years had wrought. Above them were the old brick and earth walls of the ramparts, and, dominating the Menin Road, that great triumphal arch. And it was triumphal, despite the names of the dead – or even, perhaps, because of them. A triumph of the spirit was invested here, as dazzling as the morning sun, as glowing as the love and hope and blessedness in their hearts.

Together they placed their wreath of remembrance poppies on the steps beneath Liam's name, and with hands locked, felt his presence encompass them like a loving embrace.

After a moment or two they climbed those broad steps to the ramparts above, and from there the world seemed a blessed place, full of light and love and perfect clarity. A great surge of spiritual joy came then, and a tingling of the blood; and in each other's eyes and faces was a radiance that owed much to what had so long been denied, and what could now be fulfilled. Stephen looked at Zoe and saw for a moment Louisa's smile and Georgina's serenity, and in her, he knew, was combined the legacy of the past and all his future promise.

And Liam knew that too. Liam had always known it.

Awareness flooded through him then, like a great tidal wave, so clear and absolute that Stephen could only wonder, afterwards, at the completeness of that vision. It was all there, in the lives of Robert and Louisa and Edward, in that diary which was written like a series of notes for the book Liam intended to write when the war was over. It was tied in with his life, and Zoe's, and the shared experience of this past, astonishing year. Stephen knew what Liam wanted, he wanted it written down for the living to read. It shook him so much that all he could do was reach for Zoe and hold her, very close, against his heart.

'I'll do my best,' he whispered as he raised his face to the light. 'I'll do my very best.'

'A magnificent novel… a portrait of an extraordinary
woman of her time – for all time.'

Catherine Gaskin, author of *Sara Dane* and *The Lynmara Legacy*

What do you do if you fall in love with the wrong man? And if you
follow your heart, how do you deal with the consequences?

Based on a true story, this classic 19th century romance is the sweeping
chronicle of the life and loves of a remarkable woman – Louisa Elliott.
Proud and determined, she battles to overcome the stigmas of the past:
a past shared by her cousin Edward Elliott, Loving her, Edward must
stand by while she falls passionately in love with another man.

Robert Duncannon, an Irish officer with the Royal Dragoons, is
everything steadfast, loyal Edward can never be. But Robert has secrets
of his own…

Loving them both, Louisa must choose between the respectability she
craves and the uncertainty of life with a man she may never marry.

A great, rich novel, peopled with characters you come to know
intimately and care about deeply, *Louisa Elliott* will linger with you long
after the final page has been turned.

'Compelling and thought-provoking reading, right to the
very last page' *Chicago Sun-Times*

'Ann Victoria Roberts is an unusually gifted author' *Daily Mail*

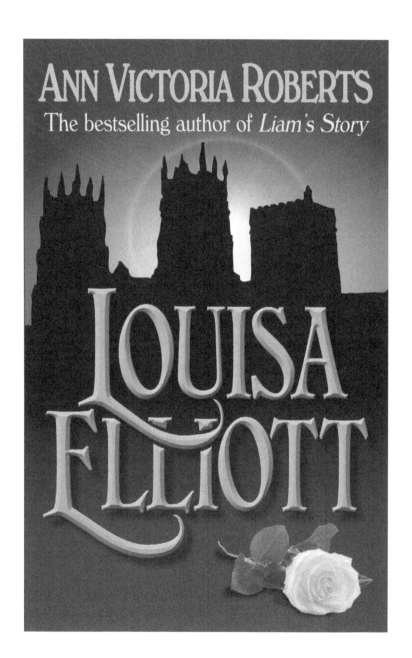

ANN VICTORIA ROBERTS

The bestselling author of *Liam's Story*

LOUISA ELLIOTT

THE MASTER'S TALE

A NOVEL OF THE TITANIC

Haunted by his final voyage, shackled to a place beyond time, only the truth can set Titanic's master free.

Captain Smith's spirit relives his past: the ships he sailed, the women he loved, his rise from obscurity to one of the world's finest mariners.

Until bad luck and coincidence turn against him:

Fire rages below decks, a Jonah among his passengers predicts doom, and a mysterious young woman evokes the love he had to leave behind.

Burdened by guilt, he makes the voyage again, seeking his fatal mistake. As the past fuses into his eternal present the truth is, at last, revealed.

Uncovering dramatic and little known events,
Ann Victoria Roberts explores themes of time and coincidence in her haunting new novel based on the life of Captain Edward Smith.

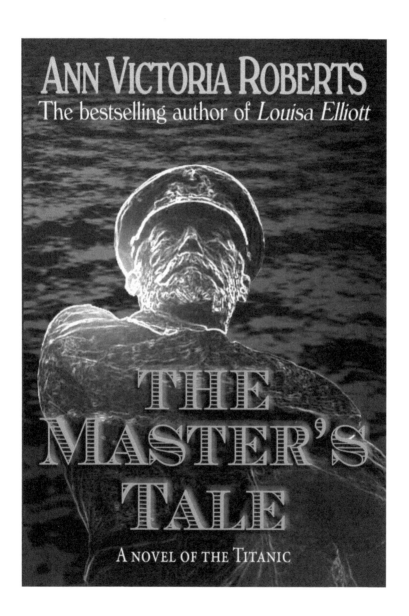

ANN VICTORIA ROBERTS
The bestselling author of *Louisa Elliott*

THE
MASTER'S
TALE

A NOVEL OF THE TITANIC